PENGUIN

THE HEART OF MID-LOTHIAN

SIR WALTER SCOTT was born in Edinburgh in 1771, educated at the High School and University there, and admitted to the Scottish Bar in 1792. From 1799 until his death he was Sheriff of Selkirkshire, and from 1806 to 1830 he held a well-paid office as a principal clerk to the Court of Session in Edinburgh, the supreme Scottish civil court. From 1805, too, Scott was secretly an investor in, and increasingly controller of, the printing and publishing businesses of his associates, the Ballantyne brothers.

Crippling polio in infancy, conflict with his Calvinist lawyer father in adolescence, rejection by the woman he loved in his twenties and financial ruin in his fifties seem scarcely to have checked Scott's productive energy and personal warmth. His first literary efforts, in the late 1790s, were translations of German poems and plays, romantic and historical. In 1805 Scott's first considerable original work, *The Lay of the Last Minstrel*, launched a series of narrative poems that romanticized key incidents and settings of early Scottish history and brought him fame and fortune.

In 1813, however, Scott declined the poet laureateship, recommending Southey instead, and turned towards fiction, devising a new form that was to dominate the early nineteenth-century novel. *Waverley* (1814) and its successors draw on the social and cultural contrasts and the religious and political conflicts of recent Scottish history to examine the nature and the cost of political and cultural change and the relation between historical process and individual human beings. Many of the novels after *Ivanhoe* (1819) extend their range to the England and Europe of the Middle Ages and the Renaissance.

Scott was created baronet in 1820. During the financial crisis of 1825 Ballantyne, Scott and their London partner Constable became insolvent, though Scott managed to avoid formal bankruptcy. Acknowledging his authorship at last in 1827, he worked at a heroic pace despite failing health, writing new novels, revising and annotating a new edition of the earlier ones, and setting down his private thoughts in a revealing and moving *Journal*. Scott died in September 1832; the creditors were finally paid in full by the sale of his copyrights.

TONY INGLIS was born in Edinburgh in 1935 and (as did Scott) attended the High School there. He now teaches literature at the University of Sussex. He has edited D. H. Lawrence's *A Selection from Phoenix* for Penguin and has published essays on Scott, Henry James and Virginia Woolf.

SIR WALTER SCOTT

THE HEART OF MID-LOTHIAN

EDITED
WITH AN INTRODUCTION AND NOTES BY
TONY INGLIS

PENGUIN BOOKS

PENGUIN BOOKS

Published by the Penguin Group
Penguin Books Ltd, 27 Wrights Lane, London w8 5tz, England
Penguin Books USA Inc., 375 Hudson Street, New York, New York 10014, USA
Penguin Books Australia Ltd, Ringwood, Victoria, Australia
Penguin Books Canada Ltd, 10 Alcorn Avenue, Toronto, Ontario, Canada m4v 3b2
Penguin Books (NZ) Ltd, 182–190 Wairau Road, Auckland 10, New Zealand

Penguin Books Ltd, Registered Offices: Harmondsworth, Middlesex, England

This edition published in Penguin Books 1994

1 3 5 7 9 10 8 6 4 2

Introduction and Notes copyright © Tony Inglis, 1994
All rights reserved

The moral right of the editor has been asserted

Filmset by Datix International Limited, Bungay, Suffolk
Printed in England by Clays Ltd, St Ives plc
Filmset in Monophoto Ehrhardt

CONTENTS

ACKNOWLEDGEMENTS

MATERIAL from the manuscript and from the 'Magnum Opus' inter-leaved volumes that underlie the New Edition of 1830 appears by permission of the Trustees of the National Library of Scotland. Aberdeen University Library kindly provided the copy of the first edition of 1818 from which the working photocopy was made.

Thanks are due to the staffs of the National Library of Scotland (both Manuscripts and Printed Books), the London Library, and both the Library and the Media Services Unit of the University of Sussex.

David Daiches and James Cochrane originally encouraged me to undertake this work. Its completion depended on a number of terms of research leave generously granted by the University of Sussex. Individuals who have helped practically and intellectually at various stages of the project, perhaps more than they realized, include the late Arthur Pollard, the late George Spater, Alistair Wood, Alan Bell, Judith Woolf, Angus Ross, Peter and Siân France and Elizabeth Inglis. An annotator of course does his own rummaging, but he inevitably incurs general debts to earlier editors, in this case Andrew Lang (1893) and Harold Boardman (1907). A few particular debts to contemporaries (specifically, Claire Lamont's 1982 edition of the novel, James Anderson's various writings on Scottish history in Scott, and Caroline Jackson-Houlston's generous sharing of her remarkable know-ledge of English and Scottish folksong) are acknowledged in the Notes as they occur, by name or initials.

                                                                    T.I.

PREFACE

THE Heart of Mid-Lothian is distinctive among Scott's novels, and is
– debatably – his masterpiece. This Penguin Classics edition presents
a purified text based on the first edition of 1818, incorporating
selected corrections from the manuscript, from corrected printings in
Scott's lifetime, and from the interleaved set that Scott prepared for
the New Edition of 1830. It is the first time that such an editorial task
has been undertaken in respect of this novel – full particulars can be
found in the headnote to the Textual Notes, pp. 679–81. There are
no large-scale surprises, but the sharpness and richness of Scott's
writing is revealed afresh in many details that had been obscured in
transcription and printing in the earliest editions and by excessive
standardization in later ones.

The Editor's Introduction seeks to contextualize and rehistoricize
discussion of this contested *chef d'œuvre* and its genesis and production,
to look in some detail at Scott's writing and its implications, and to
take account of the kinds of discussion the novel has evoked.

Scott's own Introduction and the Notes he added in 1830,
originally interspersed between chapters, are grouped together after the
main text of the novel; then follow the present Editor's Notes, which
seek both to move the modern reader towards the position of an ideal
'original' one (where cultural change has eroded access to meaning)
and to document some of the webs and patterns of textuality and
allusion that play through Scott's writing, hidden or visible according
to a reader's observation and knowledge. Sources for the two dozen
apparent quotations still noted as 'untraced' will be welcomed by the
editor, but note should be taken of Scott's remarks quoted in the note
to the epigraph to Chapter 19.

The Editor's Notes offer to supplement and decode aspects of
Scott's writing, but modern readers are likely also to need help with
Scott's vast and diverse vocabulary of Scots, French, Latin, Gaelic
and English dialect. A Glossary, placed late in the volume, offers
access of this kind, and also clarifies obsolete and semantically changed
words, real and invented place-names and significant names of fictitious characters in the novel.

Tony Inglis
University of Sussex, 6 January 1992

NOTE ON THE TEXT

THE text of this edition is based on a photocopy of a copy (x82373 1.6) of the first edition of 1818 in Aberdeen University Library. Corrections have been incorporated selectively from Scott's manuscript of the novel (National Library of Scotland MS 1548), from editions published with his approval or apparent approval in his lifetime, and from his own manuscript set of intended corrections (National Library of Scotland MS 23009–10), by no means all of which reached the authorized revised edition of 1830. This is the first time that *The Heart of Mid-Lothian* has been edited with use of all three types of textual evidence. Although few dramatic changes have come to light in the textual detail, many errors have been corrected and linguistic detail has been restored. The changes are fully documented in the Textual Notes on pp. 677–722, and some are discussed in the Editor's Notes.

SCOTT'S NOTES AND FOOTNOTES

In the first edition of 1818 Scott provided a few footnotes of translation and explanation, mostly brief; these are all printed as footnotes in this edition. In the New Edition of 1830 he added several similar footnotes, as well as footnote references to longer discursive notes and reprinted documents that were placed between chapters. All 1830 footnotes, of both kinds, are here printed as footnotes, in square brackets. The longer notes to which they refer have been grouped at the end of the novel, after Scott's 1830 Introduction and its Postscript. Footnote symbols and page numbers of references have been silently standardized to maintain coherence.

INTRODUCTION

I

SCOTLAND, which occupies the northern third of the land surface of
Great Britain, has on the whole a harsher climate than the lands to the
south. In the period under consideration it had fewer perceived
natural resources and a much smaller population than England and
Wales: about one million against their five at the time of the earliest
events represented in *The Heart of Mid-Lothian*, and by 1818 when
the novel was written the even smaller ratio of one and a half million
against their fourteen. Firmly established as an independent state at
least from 1314, when the Battle of Bannockburn decided the Wars of
Independence in which the laird's son Wallace and the aristocrat
Bruce successively led national resistance to the feudal claims of
Edward I and his Plantagenet successors, the smaller and weaker
country regularly suffered, over the three following centuries, through
the geopolitical logic that drew it into diplomatic and military alliance
with England's continental enemies. In the late Middle Ages and early
Renaissance, most notably in the reign of James IV (1488–1513),
Scotland attained a high level of artistic and intellectual culture, only
to emerge from a turbulent Reformation of religion with a newly
prominent Calvinist and theocratic emphasis that led to successive
unstable compromises between episcopal and presbyterian forms of
Church government. Both the early state and the Reformation had
their north-western boundary of influence at the Highland line, which
demarcated a relatively autonomous region with a distinctive social
structure, Gaelic language, and much in common with Irish society
rather than with Lowland Scotland—differences that, if anything,
increased during the upheavals of the seventeenth century.

In 1603 James VI of Scotland inherited the English crown as James
I and took the Scottish court to London with him, removing from
Scotland potential cultural and economic stimuli such as foreign
embassies, royal patronage of technology and the arts, and conspicuous
expenditure by courtiers. In the mid-seventeenth century struggle
with Stuart absolutism, the Scots in 1638 engaged *en masse* in an anti-

papal religious oath (the National Covenant) and took the field against Charles I, precipitating events leading to the Civil War in England. After a further sworn bond in 1643 (the Solemn League and Covenant) had apparently pledged England too to Presbyterianism, the divided Scots played an equivocal part in the war, sheltering Charles I and negotiating with him after the defeat of royal armies at Naseby and Philiphaugh but handing him over to the English Parliament and intervening ineffectually in the course of intrigues that led to his trial and execution in 1649. Next, the Scots supported Charles II's claim to the throne at the cost of military defeat at Dunbar and Worcester (1650, 1651) and eight years of incorporating union with England as a conquered province under Cromwell's Protectorate. The old religious conflicts resumed in full force after the Restoration in 1660 of both Charles II and the Scottish Parliament (the Estates), when the increasingly absolutist and covertly Romanizing Stuart regime determinedly imposed episcopal organization and ritual against widespread though localized 'Covenanter' resistance. The polarized fanaticism and repression continued to bedevil all aspects of the country's life until and even after the Revolution of 1688–90, which put relatively moderate Presbyterians back in power in Scotland—without, however, their implementing the Covenants. Colonization schemes launched in the 1690s were hampered by the lack of independent diplomatic relations, while customs barriers and navigation laws, restricting direct trade even with England and her colonies, caused friction and held back development.

In 1707 the vote for a new incorporating Union of England and Scotland was pushed through the Estates, partly by bribery in the manner of the age, by upper-class groups who expected to profit by new flows of trade and patronage and who in their turn oriented themselves on London. In the early days of the Union various pieces of Westminster legislation offended Scottish opinion: modernization of the taxes to meet the cost of eighteenth-century wars; the 'abjuration oath', which both asserted state power over the Church and restricted succession to the throne to members of the Church of England; the imposition of royal or seigneurial 'patronage' of Church appointments over the established mode of selection by the middling landowners of a parish in conjunction with the Kirk-session of minister and elders. Meanwhile the religious and political tension between the Protestant/ Presbyterian/Whig/Hanoverian interest and the Catholic/Episcopalian/ Tory/Stuart one remained more acute in Scotland than elsewhere, especially in the North, and fuelled successive Jacobite insurrections, notably those of 1715 and 1745—the latter being put down with genocidal brutality. As the century wore on, low-keyed indirect government through a 'manager' and the economic benefits of the First British Empire to Scottish trade and industry, notably through the American tobacco trade in the Glasgow area, made the Union a less sensitive question; agricultural 'improvement' and city-building typical of Enlightenment Europe both brought about and reflected stages of economic, social and intellectual modernization. In the absence of a legislature, a framework of national institutions was provided by the bodies preserved by the Act of Union: the legal system, the Church (which controlled the relatively advanced educational provision) and the universities. The Church became 'Moderate'—tolerant, enlightened, somewhat secularized and conformist—while traditionalist fractions left it in successive schisms. The Edinburgh of David Hume and the Glasgow of Adam Smith participated strikingly in the European culture of their day, while at the other end of the country dispossessed victims of the change from the clan system to cash landlordism were living on mussels in the open as they waited for the recruiting sergeant or the emigrant ship. Similar contrasts could be found in France or Russia.

After 1789 the French Revolution and the Napoleonic wars led to domestic political deadlock in Britain, with an acute right/left polarization based on entrenched and increasingly reactionary patriotism, economic and military mobilization on an unprecedented scale, the indefinite postponement of social and constitutional reform, and in Scotland show-trials and the deportation of would-be reformers. In Scotland and England alike, there set in forty years of political and intellectual ferment and repression, to be partly and temporarily stilled only by the 1832 Reform Act. The early textile-and-water-power-led stage of the Industrial Revolution greatly expanded the relatively well-off, leisured and literate middle class and added to their comforts, while a materially deprived but politically conscious working class began to form in the towns and cities. In parallel and complex relation to these events and to each other, the family of European romanticisms, with their new ideology valorizing the natural, the particular and the organic, began to supersede the universalist intellectualism of the eighteenth century. Increased leisure, changes in taste, improved transport and the closure of the Continent by war began the process that has been called 'the discovery of Britain'. The elite culture began its self-aware *rapprochement* with and interest in the people's culture that had for a while seemed too backward to bother with; now that too was modernizing and coming of age, and—not always in authentic forms or for disinterested motives—the primitive, the popular and the distinctively national claimed attention.[1]

Scott participated fully in the social and economic currents of his age. Born in 1771 in the mixed society of the still virtually medieval Old Town of Edinburgh, one of six children to survive out of his parents' twelve, he lived for most of his adult life in the middle-class Enlightenment 'New Town' built across the valley from 1767. His grandfather on one side was a professor of medicine at Edinburgh University; the other grandparents were Border farmers who, Scott remembered, wrapped him in a freshly flayed raw lambskin as an intended cure for the childhood polio that left him lame for life. An early career step in his father's Edinburgh law practice entailed riding into the Highlands with a sergeant and a file of soldiers to enforce a warrant, an episode turned to account more than once in the fiction; many years later he noted in his journal (15 December 1827) that his legal offices as Sheriff of Selkirkshire and a principal clerk to the Court of Session in Edinburgh kept him 'in the carreer and stream of actual life... a great advantage to a literary man'. Born into the presbyterian Church of Scotland, and serving as an elder in one of its Edinburgh parishes, Scott nevertheless preferred and adopted episcopalian ritual. Assisting the Whig *Edinburgh Review* in its early days and always remaining on good personal terms with its editors, Scott helped launch the *Quarterly*, its London Tory rival, a few years later.

Scott's first independent literary venture of importance was the enthusiastic ballad-collecting that led to *Minstrelsy of the Scottish Border* (1802). For some years he purveyed romantic narrative poems to the Regency public, until outstripped in popularity by Byron's sexier pose and more exotic subject-matter; other ventures included editions of Dryden and Swift, as well as much Scottish historical and antiquarian writing and publishing. From 1811 he bought land in the Borders, built a Gothic country house and called it Abbotsford (a picturesque invented name, rural, medieval, ecclesiastical—it may be salutary to remember that its Gothic, Regency rather than Victorian, surprised Nathaniel Hawthorne in 1853 by being so unexpectedly modest and unbaronial).

Scott invested the considerable proceeds of his literary successes only partly in land: much went back into the printing and publishing trade (compare Balzac's similar involvement). In an age of heroic finance, Scott virtually owned the printing-house that produced his novels, and eventually risk-taking, mismanagement and perhaps greed were to lead to insolvency during the general financial crisis of 1825 that also decisively checked the expansion of the New Town. But meanwhile, with *Waverley* (1814), *Guy Mannering* (1815), *The Antiquary* (1816) and *Rob Roy* (1817), all novels with Scottish settings in the recent past from 1715 to the end of the eighteenth century, the formally anonymous 'Author of Waverley' outstripped all previous levels of sale and price for his fiction. His hand was also detected in *Tales of My Landlord* (1816), especially in *Old Mortality*, the principal Tale, whose account of the Covenanters of the 1670s challenged certain established, albeit partisan, interpretations of the history of the period.[2]

II

Early in 1817 Scott received from an anonymous correspondent a brief account of Helen Walker, the obscure Dumfries-shire woman who, eighty years before, after declining to lie under oath to save her sister's life, had walked to London to beg a reprieve for her. As Scott pondered the letter, Helen's story came to promise a subject for 'the best volumes which have appeared', on which 'I pique myself', 'far superior. . . in point of interest' to *Rob Roy*, his novel currently in hand. Over the summer he bought, for the country house he was still extending at Abbotsford, assorted stones and fittings from the 'heart of Lothian', the ancient Edinburgh Tolbooth, or city jail, then being demolished. By November Scott had the title of his new novel and an agreement with his preferred publisher, Constable, under which he would receive £5,000 for Constable's right to sell 10,000 copies of the four-volume *Tales of My Landlord Second Series*, comprising *The Heart of Mid-Lothian* and a second shorter tale. By mid-January 1818 he was 'in great glee', asking Constable's man for 'all the tracts, pamphlets etc., that we can get him about Captain Porteous' mob', the Edinburgh riot of 1736, which culminated in the lynching of the Captain of the City Guard; and the new *Tales* were reported to be at press at the end of that month. At Abbotsford, Scott wrote in the early mornings to escape the bustling life of his household and his builders; in Edinburgh, in the evenings after his legal duties during the daytime sittings of the Court of Session—this novel, indeed, was apparently the occasion for his son-in-law Lockhart's improving account of the young rake reformed by the industrious moving hand glimpsed perpetually at work in the neighbouring house.[3] Scott found the single Tale growing to drive out the intended companion story (abandoned apparently in early May), to 'fill more pages than I opined' and to miss the promised publication date of the king's birthday, 4 June.

The Heart of Mid-Lothian came out in the last days of July 1818,[4] and on 1 August the *Scotsman* (then a new Edinburgh radical newspaper, politically opposed to Scott's Toryism) declared it 'at once the best and the worst of the author's numerous productions', 'abounding with flatness', 'certainly too long by a volume'—but 'unquestionably his masterpiece' for vivid and distinct pictures of 'whatever was eccentric or uncommon in national or individual character' and even more for the combined powers of painter and moralist displayed in the rendering of Jeanie Deans, the fictional counterpart of Helen Walker. 'This surprising and fascinating writer' would be 'read and admired in spite of all that can be said against him; nay, in spite of all that can be felt against him.'

The key issues raised in that early review by no means exhaust the interest of the novel elaborated from Mrs Goldie's letter (here reprinted in Scott's 1830 Introduction on pp. 537-9). As well as reworking that straightforward tale of heroic integrity and heroic action, *The Heart of Mid-Lothian* is the first British novel to present an urban riot, and perhaps only the third (after *Moll Flanders* and *Pamela*) to take as its principal character a lower-class woman. Articulating some of the historic and recurrent discontent of the people of Scotland over the Union of 1707, it also takes up the relations among classes and among regional cultures and ways of life within Scotland; in its rendering of rural society—noblemen, bonnet-lairds and tenants—and the urban culture of merchants, craftsmen and advocates, it embraces all the typical social groups enumerated by modern historians. A thoughtful work of the late Enlightenment, of the twilight of aristocratic Europe as Beaumarchais gave way to *Biedermeier*, it exposes, probes and satirizes fissures and contradictions in contemporary ideologies of truth, justice and legality, and it expands its static analysis of spirit versus letter in law and religion to explore dynamically changes in civic consciousness and religious sensibility under the pressures of economic and cultural modernization. These very processes produced and embodied the crisis of Scottish national identity during which the novel was written in 1818, the shifts in power and cultural relationships among gentry, professionals and the newly forged working class that span Scott's lifetime, and the international literary market extending from Philadelphia to St Petersburg in which *The Heart of Mid-Lothian* became an early bestseller. In its retrieval and deployment of folktale, ballad and proverb, the novel takes part in the Romantic generations' rediscovery of the culture of the common people. It draws points of reference consciously from the high culture of the past, and two or three of its intense dramatic confrontations are unmatched earlier except in Shakespeare.[5]

Scott's novels have, however, been read and valued in changing ways since they began to appear in 1814. Initially, the 'Waverley' manner and content captivated an important part of the reading public in Britain and throughout the western world, first raising the price of fiction but later broadening its audience and transforming both career prospects and artistic possibilities for writers of fiction (and arguably for writers of history as well) in Scotland, England, Europe and the USA for the rest of the nineteenth century. The ten or so 'Scottish novels' were always more commonly read in Britain, and especially in Scotland, whereas in nineteenth-century Europe and America the medieval romances from the *Ivanhoe* stable proved more popular. Each kind found its imitators—Hawthorne and Stevenson in one case, Bulwer-Lytton, Ainsworth and Dumas in the other. In the relatively cheap collected edition revised by the ailing Scott and published monthly from 1829 to 1833 in unprecedented print-runs of over 30,000, the novels continued to dominate early Victorian culture, though not without challenge. Scott's countryman Carlyle, the method and focus of whose historical writing arguably owe much to Scott, mordantly characterized him as 'writing impromptu novels to buy farms with', and Mark Twain held Scott 'in great measure responsible for' the American Civil War. From the 1850s the frankness, strenuousness and economy of the Realist movement in fiction made Scott's work seem both prudish and self-indulgent, and after about 1870 'the system of literature gradually moved Scott to its periphery', relegating the novels to children's reading with the peculiar position of great cultural influence but low critical esteem which that implies. In the twentieth century the Modernist antipathy to 'Romantic' values and to narrative and history (according to Joyce's Stephen Dedalus, 'a nightmare from which I am trying to awake') left Scott's work on the shelf. Despite subtly appreciative discussion by Henry James, despite

Virginia Woolf's oblique use of Scott's fiction ('fetched up from oblivion') as a crucial test for human value in *To the Lighthouse*, Modernist aesthetics left Scott marginalized, through much of the twentieth century, as local cult or private enthusiasm.[6] Within Scotland, continuing endorsement by an Anglo-Scottish establishment only sharpened rejection by radical thinkers, who since the 1930s have vigorously debated whether Scott saved Scottish national consciousness by complicating, enriching and defining it at a moment when extinction seemed possible, or (as they more commonly argue) gravely damaged Scottish identity either by 'fixing' its false image as a tartan idyll or by some more insidious failure of stance in relation to social and national questions.[7]

Developments in the history of ideas and the reading of fiction—some specific to Scott and some general—have combined over the last forty years to restore access to Scott's novels and release again their pleasure and interest. First, one common dismissive view of Scott as a naïve romantic antiquarian was fruitfully complicated by recognition of his context in the intellectual world of late eighteenth-century Scotland, a small yet heterogeneous country in which, as already indicated, 'Scottish Enlightenment' critical and speculative thought about the nature of civilization and history marched in parallel with practical innovation in the early stages of the agricultural and industrial revolutions. Second, Lukacs's Marxist study of the historical novel as an instrument for the articulation and analysis of economic and cultural change, and of Scott's role as the deviser of its classic form, reopened questions about the whole nature of Scott's work, displacing attention from ostensible plot to underlying process. Third, as late Modernist criticism, retreating from the extreme attitudes of the movement's early polemics against Romanticism, came to realize the extent of its own stake in the problematics of the Romantic sensibility, Realism and Symbolism could no longer appear to exhaust, between them, the whole range of artistic possibilities; indeed, arguments have recently been put for recognizing as distinct the phase of fiction, between the respective realisms of the eighteenth century and the high Victorians, into which Scott's work falls.[8] Work on fictional rhetoric (the construction and manipulation of the figures of 'author', 'narrator' and 'reader'), on the relation of overt fictions to other forms of narrative, to cultural ideology and to reality, on the covertly encoded concerns that frame, establish and on occasion contradict the ostensible main thrust of a novel, and on the polyphonic interrelation of borrowed and mimicked languages in the total effect of the text—all have helped to make Scott's fiction accessible again. Renewed awareness of the shagginess and indeterminacy of textual relations, of the role of fantasy and storytelling in both literary creation and in the pleasure of reading, of the intricacy of the connections between high and popular cultures—all have restored possibilities in novel-reading that were overshadowed by the unduly hierarchic and exclusive critical habits of mid-century. The late Northrop Frye's relation to Scott sums up the process: Frye read the Waverley Novels enthusiastically but almost as a matter of course in childhood, rejected them utterly as an intellectually conscious young man, and returned to them with appreciation and understanding later in life.[9]

The Heart of Mid-Lothian, seventh of the Scottish novels and the only one to take its name from a building rather than a character, has, however, been at a special, paradoxical disadvantage with commentators, and doubtless with readers—if not with writers, for it was taken up and more or less directly imitated by Pushkin, Manzoni, Balzac, Hugo, Hawthorne, Dickens and George Eliot.[10] Always the obvious 'classic' among Scott's works, it has been admired almost exclusively for the simplest embodiment of its claim to that status, the gravity and intensity which it shares with Mrs Goldie's core anecdote and concentrates in its treatment of that narrative and its cultural setting. Conversely, as the obvious classic, *The Heart of Mid-Lothian* has attracted over-severe, even patronizing, comment from readers eager to sift and explode excessive claims. However one historicizes it, the over-arching providentialism must now seem naïve, and the novel's advance towards, retreat from, and final hasty and incomplete acceptance of a tragic denouement may well irritate. If it is a classic that corresponds to notions of epic simplicity in its authority and swiftness of production, its play of song and proverb, and its closeness to the bone of a particular national experience, it often banteringly departs from epic gravity while also flouting the standards of realism and tight symbolic coherence set by later developments in the art of the novel. Accordingly, it has been found unsatisfactorily episodic and incoherent, sacrificing its central interests to melodramatic plotting and various kinds of stock characterization. An early accusation that the novel was padded out for financial reasons, though obviously suspect from its apparent origin in the pique of a disappointed rival publisher, has not been convincingly refuted. Assumptions about both sexual and ethical norms have changed; as long ago as the 1890s Bernard Shaw objected to the way in which the central ethical dilemma is put and resolved, and modern readers are disconcerted by a novel that addresses questions of imprisonment and capital punishment not with the mordant irony of Fielding or the passionate analysis of Dickens but with a matter-of-fact acceptance more like Defoe's. *The Heart of Mid-Lothian* departs from Scott's 'neutral-hero' pattern, and neither Lukacs, the exponent of historical process, nor Frye, the advocate of fictional romance, gives the novel prominence in his account (though Lukacs discusses the heroine as a socially representative figure). Favourable critics, in short, usually show an enthusiasm that is muted by the need to explain things away or to reject substantial parts of the novel. Two mid-century comments are typical: characterizing Scott as an 'inspired folk-lorist . . . not having the creative writer's interest in literature . . . [who] made no serious attempt to work out his own form', F.R. Leavis denied greatness to *The Heart of Mid-Lothian* because 'too many allowances and deductions have to be made', and Mary Lascelles, an alert expositor of Scott's art as a short-story writer, thought that Scott the novelist, 'fatally committed to expansion', had produced something 'radically unworthy of the original' anecdote.[11] Scott, however, in his 1830 Introduction, places the interest of the novel precisely in his *development* of Helen Walker's story, and invites the reader 'to judge how far the author has improved on, or fallen short of, the pleasing and interesting sketch of high principle and steady affection' provided by the prototype.

III

By Lukacs's account, Scott's novels repeatedly present a necessarily weak and neutral hero. This socially or geographically displaced young gentleman, a trespasser on the margin of great historical events, tentatively rebellious and with a head turned by too much reading, passes literally from the modern, metropolitan side of a cultural boundary or historical conflict to the primitive side, the Other. There he may touch the hem of the garment of a major historical figure or encounter more closely a fictitious or fictionalized historical type; often he witnesses a climactic conflict, an actual battle such as Prestonpans in *Waverley* or Bothwell Bridge in *Old Mortality*, or some equivalent such as the tournament in *Ivanhoe* or the dispersal of the conspirators in *Redgauntlet*. Having learned the cost, in human suffering and dislocation, of historical change (seen none the less as inevitable and ultimately beneficial), he returns to his true social place a sadder and wiser man, usually with a bride embodying the correct historical choice that has been thrust upon him.

The Heart of Mid-Lothian inverts many of these elements, without producing a neatly symmetrical reversal of the entire pattern. The historical event, the Porteous Mob, comes early in the novel, seemingly in an enigmatic relation of indicative counterpoint to the personal plot. The central character, Jeanie Deans, is a plain country dairymaid in her late twenties—in age, sex, class, style and culture certainly no 'Waverley hero'. (Weakened and transposed aspects of that figure may be detected here and there in the contrasted yet surprisingly parallel temperaments and careers of Reuben Butler and George Robertson, the lovers of Jeanie and her sister Effie.) With the Waverley hero disappears his comic retainer derived from Cervantes's Sancho Panza—a departure that leaves space for bold yet intricate patterns of doubling and parallelism among Butler and Robertson, Jeanie and Effie, Madge Wildfire and various lesser characters. In *The Heart of Mid-Lothian* the journey is undertaken *towards* the metropolis, from the residual culture to the dominant one, and it has proved hard to establish a sense in which either the journey or the events of the last quarter of the novel lead towards any specific and recognizable new threshold in history. Such discrepancies have led critics to declare *The Heart of Mid-Lothian* 'a great but disunified novel', or 'a medley of disparate genres', and to stress the 'episodic' aspect of Scott's method.[12]

It may, however, be helpful to perceive *The Heart of Mid-Lothian* as neither episodic nor a medley but as a fairly systematic progress through, and exploration of, narrative modes. After the introductory chapter that vividly demonstrates both the refracted nature of narration and the mediating roles of chance and social institutions in the choice of subject, the novel proper begins with historical narrative—an unsolved historical mystery just passing beyond the horizon of living memory, a specific train of public events which, in their brutality, intractability and inscrutability, call in question notions of authority, legality and justice. The novel next adopts a fictional realist method, displaying the formative pressures of economic circumstance, political events and religious ideology on individuals in private life, with a field of action that broadens from the farm to the city and its underworld and to the documentary presentation of the system of justice in Effie's trial for infanticide. At the end of the trial the dilemma, heading towards tragedy, can be avoided only by modulation of genre into folktale; Scott, licensed both by his source anecdote and by the already established analogy with *Measure for Measure*, makes the shift not by a Shakespearean trick of beds and identities, but with the fully-fledged folktale hero's journey, complete with donors, talismans, tests, deceitful waylayings, assault, physical wounding, guidance, helpers, achievement of the object by a trick, and pursuit on the journey home. In folktale, the success of the hero's mission leads to a royal marriage and enthronement of the hero; Jeanie's success leads only to marriage within her own rank and to a further shift of genre to the pastoral comedy of the 'highland Arcadia' in the final section of the novel, where Death, proverbially present in Arcadias, intrudes under the forms of archetypal myth. Under the lively and urbane mosaic surface of Scott's writing there lies like a paradigm this deep programme of narrative modes: history, fictional realism, folktale, pastoral, myth.[13]

Before the reader reaches the history, the opening Prolegomen 'by' Jedediah Cleishbotham and the Introductory Chapter 'by' Peter Pattieson interpose one further literary mystification, in the context of the open yet carefully guarded secret of Scott's authorship. Scott's fourth and fifth prose fictions had appeared together in 1816, ostensibly dissociated from the *Waverley* series by title, format and publisher (*Tales of My Landlord*, four volumes instead of the usual three, Blackwood instead of Constable) and supposedly 'Collected and re-ported' by Cleishbotham, whose Introduction reveals him as parochial, pedantic, out of date and self-serving in his appropriation of the writing of his late assistant Pattieson. Each Tale has its preliminary chapter by Pattieson, and the second and longer, *Old Mortality*, concluded, after dialogue between Pattieson and the importunate reader Miss Buskbody, with Jedediah's 'Peroration' promising a continuation. Small wonder that the editor of the Penguin *Old Mortality* advises his readers to 'vault over' the introductory matter, or that others have likened it to 'vicious undergrowth' and 'a bore who has got us into a corner'.[14]

The Second Series, now again published by Constable, uses the convention more economically and effectively to frame a single Tale. Readers are alerted to a narrative supposedly refracted from many narrators and documents through first the hard-headed lawyers, then the young schoolteacher (sensitive but doomed, touching yet slightly ridiculous, a figure out of the sentimental tradition of Sterne and

Mackenzie) and finally through Jedediah, this time the vehicle, at once aggressive and evasive, for thinly disguised gloating over Scott's recent financial and territorial successes and for a half-serious placement of the new novel in relation to the controversy stirred up by *Old Mortality*. Questions of the status of the text and of the authority for the narrative are thus light-heartedly brought into play for the reader. At the same time the opening chapter broaches matters of substance, great and small, to be taken up again in the main part of the novel— the modernization of Scotland, the detail of legal and political processes, contrasting moral and intellectual perspectives, prison as human life in metaphor.

It has to be admitted that Scott, having established this elaborate refracting apparatus, does not make much direct use of it. The wielder of the novel's narrative voices later emerges as well travelled and very well read, educated at the High School of Edinburgh and legally learned, a friend of the painters Wilkie and Allan and of the writers Crabbe, Wordsworth, Southey and Joanna Baillie—in short someone extremely like Scott. But the introductory device sufficiently serves its purpose, prompting and stimulating the reader, keeping up the nominal mystery and distancing the text from its author's personal position.

IV

The range of apparent sources and apparent voices in *The Heart of Mid-Lothian* is matched by the novel's variety of linguistic and stylistic surfaces, the most distinctive being Lowland Scots, which originally some London reviewers thought vulgar and which may still give rise to anxiety among non-Scottish readers.[15] The Lowland Scots language was once the vehicle of a full and complex culture at all social and most intellectual levels, until, marginalized after 1603 by the developing political union with England and by the dominant Authorized Version of the Bible, it failed to modernize during the seventeenth and eighteenth centuries and became more and more excluded from educated Scottish discourse and from the speech of Scots who had become assimilated to the rich and confident culture to the south. By the early nineteenth century a first stage of patriotic literary reaction against that process had reached its peak with the career of Robert Burns (1759–96) and with Scott's own collection of *Minstrelsy of the Scottish Border* (1802–3, partly fieldwork, partly pastiche). The

narrative poetry with which Scott first established a reputation outside
Scotland was all in English, though with Scottish content and settings
of a kind acceptable to Regency readers. In his prose fiction, which
projected a more everyday, socially and historically aware version of
Scotland, the question of language was at first approached through
comic retainers such as David Gellatly in *Waverley* and Andrew
Fairservice in *Rob Roy*, but Scott's range swiftly widened to include
the rendering of internal Scottish differences of class and culture. In
The Heart of Mid-Lothian Scott prudently withheld dense Scots until
the street-dialogue in the fourth chapter, later concentrating it (very
effectively) in Ratcliffe and the other low-life characters, and in the
touching rhetoric of the Deans sisters. Elsewhere, however, the apparently 'English' speech and thought-processes of the Scots characters
are significantly tinged with Scots rhythms and idioms; references to
distinctive history, institutions and practices abound, and the epigraphs
and quotations from Fergusson and the ballads stake the claim of
Scots in the discourse as well as in the dialogue. Later the novel
diversifies in language: some characters speak demotic East Lowland
Scots; others, such as Deans, a Bible-influenced 'standard' Scots;
and others conventionalized 'Highland English'. Although the staple
discourse of the novel remains apparently in English, its vocabulary,
idiom, frequent close involvement with the fully Scots passages and
the not infrequent paraphrasing of speech and thoughts all give
grounds for Scotticizing the apparent English with the inner ear—
'Scott's language is not a phonetic transcription; it is a rhetorical
mode that points the differences in the speech of the social classes'.[16]

In interplay within scenes and in the course of their development,
the speech of particular characters can modulate into or out of Scots,
often a sign of changing relationships to modernity, authority or
power. Argyle uses Scots to signal his solidarity to Jeanie; Baillie
Middleburgh speaks Scots in Chapter 16 when he is being confidential
with the procurator fiscal and in Chapter 18 in asserting his authority
over Meg Murdockson, but keeps to English in his attempt at influen-
cing David Deans; in the trial scene Jeanie speaks only English, Effie
only Scots. The speech of the Highlanders is a particularly awkward
area; the conventions for representing it in print derive from Lowland
traditions of jeering mimicry of an out-group, well documented in the
eighteenth century and traceable back to the late Middle Ages, so that
the rank-and-file Highlanders tend to sound foolish. The supposed
'court-Scotish' of the older gentry is also a matter of contention,

perhaps a genteel fiction—though, given its role in Argyle's self-deception over Effie, Scott may have been well aware of that.

While bringing out the suppleness and originality of Scott's Scots dialogue, and dealing quite subtly with the question of anachronism (i.e. to what purpose would a writer in 1818 offer his readers exact reproduction of the idiom of the 1730s or any other specific period, even if he were capable of reproducing it?), recent writers on language tend to deplore Scott's English narrative basis and his restriction of Scots to dialogue and low-life characters, on the grounds that 'by limiting Scots to dialogue, Scott restricted its range'. That emphasis surely underestimates the originality and the actual achievement, in Jeanie's and Effie's eloquence, in the sardonic pithiness of the scenes from the police and street cultures, in the use of cultural registers of song and proverb beyond the mere fact of the language employed. Even Scott's most sustained passage of prose in Scots, 'Wandering Willie's Tale' in *Redgauntlet*, purports to be oral narrative. To under-value that actual achievement in comparison with an imaginably wider-ranging, but unactualized, mode of Scots writing is worse than mere wishful-thinking—it virtually reinscribes in the field of subject-matter the very marginalization of the nature and significance of 'Scots' experience that it seeks to correct in the field of language. And the apparently acceptable English surface of Scott's prose was a condition of the access to a world-wide audience on which his success, cultural and financial, depended.

Over the play of languages lies that of distinct stylistic registers, usually associated with particular characters—Jedediah's introductory 'love to be precise in matters of importance' (a parody of a parody, Scott acknowledged, relating the 'quaint style' to Gay's *Pastorals*[17]), Robertson's drama-saturated letters and harangues, Deans's Patrick Walker-derived mixture of biblical English and the distinctive phraseo-logy of the Saints of the Covenant, Effie's teasing songs in her youth and convent-trained hauteur in her later role. Proverbs, or fresh epigrams with proverbial force, spring to the lips of some characters under stress, especially Effie; for others, especially the jailer Ratcliffe and the madwoman Madge, proverbs sustain their day-to-day transac-tions. The authorial discourse too can pointedly modulate into a 'sublime' account of a landscape or a figure, a sententious or aphoristic generalization, or a revelation of personal taste or reminiscence. Scott's prose is sometimes accused of an inert Latinism of syntax and vocabu-lary; that too, when properly attended to, often turns out to be functional, and seems less intrusive under the leaner punctuation of the first edition and the barely existent punctuation of the manuscript.

One regular effect of mastery of an idiom, however, is imperviousness to messages coming from outside it and to the values they encode; Jedediah, Saddletree, Robertson, Deans, Effie and others all habitually talk people down, imposing their will and in the end suffering through doing so. At the end of Chapter 4 Butler and Saddletree are parties to a dialogue of the deaf in which they discourse 'the one on the laws of Scotland, the other on those of Syntax, and neither listening to a word which his companion uttered'. Saddletree is the most remarkable case; he still contrives to use the idiom of the law to extend his own authority among his peers, while being excluded from access to its discourse of power by his lack of training and of Latin. Saddletree's legalism, like the introduction of the stanzas of Fergusson, also shows Scott's tact in exposition; ridiculous though Saddletree appears, his legal comments are wrong only when ludicrously so; when correct, or corrected, he neatly conveys necessary information. Deans, on the other hand, has apparent mastery of a religious idiom, but he is never shown with a co-religionist or as a member of a congregation or in any other way wielding it effectively. Each character, sidelined by history or life, displaces his desire for power on to his family.

If language can armour a character, it can also betray through its instability—sometimes to ludicrous effect, as in the shooting of 'deuks and fules' or the confusion of Latin and Gaelic surrounding Donald Gorm, sometimes more gravely as in Jeanie's unawareness of the range of meanings of 'minister'. In the interview with Queen Caroline, Jeanie's repeated and unimpeachable moral generalizations seem to threaten her mission with their 'chance hits', and have to be corrected by Argyle's silent gesture before Jeanie can release the Scots eloquence that persuades the queen.

Several instances of the treacherous relation between language and reality combine to form the matrix of the novel. The child-murder law of 1690 itself creates a presumptive crime where none may exist— something for which, Mrs Saddletree thinks, the legal system itself should be hanged, a parallel absurdity. The smuggler Wilson defines the proceeds of his illegal trade as his true property in such a way as to justify to his circle his robbery of the Collector. The lynch mob is eager to do all its business in due form. Deans's wish to repress the very word 'dance' interrupts the conversation in which Effie may open her heart to Jeanie, and his understanding of urban dangers as theological in nature is only the first of the series of unaddressed issues that contribute to his daughters' ordeal. Deans, Staunton and Saddle-tree have isolated themselves behind the language-barriers of covenant, stage and half-understood law. Deans eventually 'reconciles his specu-lative principles to existing circumstances', and Effie, in Chapter 50, declares herself 'a Lie of fifteen years' standing'. Conversely, refusal to utter falsely despite the pressures on her is the essence of Jeanie's position, and its consequences can be redeemed only by hazardous physical action and a feat of eloquence at Richmond suffi-cient to transcend and cancel her earlier non-performance before judge and jury.

V

One major aspect of Scott's writing remains to be discussed—the feature indicated but not exhausted by Tulloch's observation that 'Scott quotes more often probably than any English novelist of equal stature'. Scott's practice extends the range of feigned voices and supposed documents already mentioned to include a mosaic of stanzas from songs and ballads, aphorisms from the libertine yet genteel traditions of Chesterfield and Rochefoucauld, phrases from the Bible, the Latin classics, Shakespeare, Milton and other English poets and dramatists, the Covenanting preachers and controversialists, the wisdom or folly of jurists' maxims, and the varied oral culture of folktale, proverb and children's story. (There is, however, almost nothing from the sixteenth-century Scots Makars and nothing expli-citly from the intellectuals of the Scottish or any other Enlightenment.) Some elements stand as epigraphs to chapters, flashing an advance signal (often enigmatic, sometimes paradoxical) to the reader; of these, some stand alone, cryptic or anonymous, others virtually bring their texts and contexts with them. Others still are used in dialogue, by characters who define themselves or claim authority through them; others are marked in the text, by typography or by allusion; yet others lie unidentified, stirring with alien life as the reader's eye passes over them, as at the opening of Chapter 35. The point is not that the reader should contextualize or even recognize every source (indeed some, such as Deans's own pamphlet, Meg Murdockson's Last Dying Words and the parish register of Knocktarlitie, are themselves fictitious), but that the composite texture of the writing, the infinite regression of the

borrowed and recirculated aspects of literary language, should be felt
and acknowledged. The Introductory Chapter explicitly discusses the
circumstances of the novel's own production—the current craze for
fiction, the mock anxiety surrounding reading practices, the physical
form of the 'half-bound and slip-shod volumes' from the circulating
library, precisely the form in which all but the most privileged of
readers were likely to be consuming the Tale. One of the lawyers
recasts his client's plight as a witty paragraph and offers to compile a
book; even the Tolbooth itself might tell its story as a ghost-written
broadsheet. In an extreme instance of reflexivity in Chapter 38, Argyle
hums part of the ludicrous ballad written about (and supposedly but
doubtfully *by*) himself.

Below this play with textuality and the knitting-in of texts at the
verbal level lies a layer of intertextuality of meaning—certain main
parallels that Scott draws chiefly from English poetry, though he
counterpoints them with stanzas from the Scottish ballads. The seduced women in the novel are approached through the verse tales of
Crabbe and Wordsworth—poets who had preceded Scott in writing
revealingly and sympathetically about women of the lower classes. In
formulating Jeanie's dilemma, and in the consideration of law, justice
and social control in city life, the parallels to Shakespeare's profound
and disconcerting comedy *Measure for Measure* are made prominent
(even the involvement of a duke may take its cue from there, and in
the manuscript Scott for a time intended to double his magistrates, as
Shakespeare does, though Bailie Culbertson did not survive into the
printed version). *Comus*, Milton's masque of female chastity and
resolution, is invoked in connection with Jeanie's journey and *The
Pilgrim's Progress* (in 1818, very far from being an accepted literary
text) is perhaps too directly used to give to Madge Wildfire on her
deathbed the coherence that she is denied in life. (One wholly unac-
knowledged intertextuality, a series of features large and small in
parallel with Smollett's *Humphry Clinker*, played an obscure and
unexpected part in the later stages of composition, but here can be
mentioned only in passing.[18]) There are unexpected and improbable
links with actuality: Scott already owned the door, doorway and key of
the Edinburgh Tolbooth when he wrote the novel; in choosing Staunton as the 'real' name of the character introduced as Robertson, he
identified the village, squire and mansion whose location near
Grantham he apparently had in mind (something which the *Monthly
Review* of December 1818 condemned as an error of taste); in Dumfries

the novel generated local journalistic interest in Helen Walker, which
involved Scott in manoeuvres to safeguard his anonymity, and almost
his last significant act before his death in 1832 was to provide both
the funds and the inscription for Helen's tombstone in Irongray
churchyard.

Some of the quotation may be virtually unconscious, on the analogy
of Scott's curious habit of repeating the same word in different senses
within a few lines, a chief object of textual amendments in proof and
in the 1830 corrections. Much, it is clear, came welling up from
memory as Scott wrote swiftly across his page in his lawyer's hand—
only the most elaborate passages are pasted into the manuscript in the
hand of a copyist, or the subject of a cross-reference to a book or a
'printed paper apart'. It typifies the hazardous brilliance of Scott's
working method, in which, he recalled, 'the pen passed over the
whole as fast as it could move and the eye never again saw them
excepting in proof. . . the action of composition always dilated some
passages and abridged or omitted others and personages were rendered
important or insignificant not according to their agency in the original
conception of the plan but according to the success or otherwise with
which I was able to bring them out' (*Journal*, 12 February 1826).
Scott's intertextuality arises in an art, if not of actual improvisation,
then of rapid execution, of kaleidoscopically swift movement across a
mental landscape of remembered physical reality, imagined characters
and events and literary texts, quotations and narrative figures both
actual and postulated. His writing practice runs counter to his being
included in unproblematic narratives of bourgeois fiction-making,
Flaubert's search for the *mot juste* or Trollope's average ten thousand
words per week, but it is at the same time too brilliantly literary to be
describable exclusively in formulaic terms of *folk* techniques, sources
and values. The outcome is a rich and flexible prose medium with
many available registers, capable of moving between the grotesque and
the intense and profound, and with urbanely ludic elements in which
lies much of the appeal of the writing.

VI

After the talk in the inn at Gandercleugh the novel's next and crucial
move, without which Helen Walker's story would remain material
only for a lyrical ballad, is directly into the changing mores, uncertain

values and daily turbulence of the national capital. Chapter 2, after a swift allusion to justice as practised in Paris and London, settles on Edinburgh and recounts the series of crimes, loosely linked to the Walker story by issues of law and evidence, justice and mercy, that culminate in the Porteous Mob. If the presence of this raw historical incident in the novel can be thus broadly justified, not everyone has thought that Scott carried it off; no less a reviewer than Francis Jeffrey in the *Edinburgh* in 1820 found it 'rather heavily described', modern critics have found the writing unduly Latinate and unspecific, and the apparent ringleader Robertson's later role in the plot has been thought to trivialize the episode.[19]

It is, surely, a very well-organized and effective piece of writing. Each chapter (except Chapter 5, which negotiates a transition of viewpoint) builds towards a climactic event—the escape of Robertson, the execution of Wilson and the firing by the City Guard, the announcement of Porteous's reprieve, the breaking of the prison—and the whole set culminates in the lynching. Each chapter indeed opens in a flat understated prose of description, exposition and generalization, but the grey orotundity is swiftly dispelled by the recollection of the frightened schoolboys in Chapter 2, the introduction of Fergusson and of *King Lear* in Chapter 3, the tigerish roar of indignation and disappointed revenge in Chapter 4. The novel's old/new axis comes ironically into play—the gallows, with its machinery and officers, has been brought up to date in the 1780s, just as the coaches of the previous chapter have been. Far from being rigid, the point of view is marked by a play of positions and paradoxes. The neutral 'omniscient' expository prose undercuts its own rationalizing modernity through disconcerting effects such as the impersonal sequence ('it was the custom. . .', 'it was supposed. . .', 'it was thought. . .', 'the practice has been discontinued. . .', 'we are about to detail. . .'), and it carefully analyses the vocabulary of social distinction as an increasingly refined phrasing traverses 'groups', 'the populace' and 'the multitude', 'the vulgar and their betters', 'the peasantry. . . farmers and inferior gentry' who all, it turns out, unite as '*the people*' to approve of smuggling. There is no convenient moment at which the reader can draw back from these smooth expositions, which become increasingly uncomfortable as the bland guide proceeds. Chapter 3 shifts from social hierarchy in the abstract to the movements of rank and function that accompany actual events—the details of Porteous going about his business, framed by the pleas to, and denunciations of, the City Guard in the passages of Fergusson, lead inwards to his 'internal emotions of jealousy and rage' and his 'truly diabolical' treatment of Wilson. The adverse criticism underestimates the power of the sustained, cool, analytic writing in these chapters, so pointedly in contrast to the lively conversational overture that precedes and interrupts them. To another objection, that the members of the mob are not sufficiently individualized, one might reply that they are individual enough for members of a mob—their functional anonymity, their category as members rather than as individuals, is precisely the point, and the anonymity that was successfully maintained in fact is built into the fiction. At the same time, the street dialogues of Chapters 4 and 5 do provide a rich inventory of sharply focused examples of individual character and idiom to offset the emphasis on the collective. The introduction of Butler (who develops rapidly on the page, or between pages, from his first appearance in the manuscript as Mr Whackbairn, a double of Jedediah) provides a further, more highly individualized point of view on the events of the night. After laying a misleading trail about 'reasons much deeper than those dictated by mere humanity' for Butler's interest in Effie, the writing takes the reader through a town 'stark-mad' to a 'Gothic entrance', to Macbeth's castle and to hell-gate; locked out of the prison and under threat of being locked into the city, Butler is conscripted by the Mob to 'discharge the duty', and his perception and responses to the final events of the night remain available to the narrative voice until the schoolmaster flees the scene in horror. Neither the passing presence of Robertson as a rioter nor the varied responses of the prisoners to the chance of release distracts the reader from the unfolding events, and the much later revelation that for purposes of plot Robertson was the hidden hand organizing the Mob does not, in this reader's experience, reach back through the novel to spoil the deep initial impression, which revives in subsequent readings.

Full of admiration for the repeated touches of sombre acuteness in Scott's writing about the Mob, I remain disconcerted by the conclusion the novel seems to derive from its fictionalized history. The lynching of Porteous is a revenge taken by virtually a living creature, the collectivity of Edinburgh citizens, who, in carnival disguise and with midsummer ritual fire-leaping, go about their work righteously, claiming authority from Heaven. Porteous is doomed almost metaphysically, and condemned in the writing—he is Agag, he is Haman, he is old Hamlet with sins full-blown, and the 'hardy insurgents' who kill him are credited with Roman virtue as 'Conspirators'. Butler is horrified, and we are apparently not spared details, but the narrative voice of the novel, on some level, *approves*, in a way strangely at odds with Scott's personal humanity, his public position and his known political attitudes. We have seen Scott calling for source-material about the riot: does the way in which he adapted it throw any light on the paradox?

Scott makes three kinds of change to the eyewitness accounts that he read in court transcripts and official correspondence. Not wishing to provide a revolutionist's handbook, he omits the detail that the Mob, having seized the Guard's muskets, also broke open a gunsmith's for powder and shot. For narrative convenience and various kinds of effect, he adapts incidents and condenses time. Robertson escapes from the Tolbooth Church not before but after his own funeral sermon (which we therefore hear, in summary). Scott invents the crowd on the morning of 7 September and its sudden frustration, and he invents Porteous's drunken dinner-party that evening. These changes heighten the tension of the narrative, yet the latter helps to demonize Porteous and the former, with its implication of spontaneous popular action with little time for planning on either side, deepens the mystery while muddying the waters over matters of premeditation and official connivance. The shorter the notice, after all, the less the likelihood of either; the longer the reprieve has been known, the more time for planning and the exchange of nods and winks, the greater the possibility and the probability of both. News of Porteous's 'respite' came from London on 2 September and became the talk of the city. By 4 September the provost had been warned of an intended attack, but he refused to order any preventive action. The zeal, and perhaps the wholeheartedness, of the city authorities thus come into question, in ways that the novel evades. Moreover the novel positively suggests that the magistrates tried to contact the Castle (they didn't), that the rioters had only one door to burn through (there were two, the keys of the inner one apparently being yielded through bribery, connivance or stupidity), and that the rioters provided a clergyman (far from doing so, they told Porteous they wanted him damned before he had time to pray). Scott also smooths down the horrors of the death and the handling of the victim, which (with broken bones, attempted mutilation, repeated hoistings-and-lowerings and the like) were much more violent and unpleasant than the novel acknowledges—indeed it was only in the 1829 revision that Scott added the culminating clause in which Butler sees 'men striking. . . with their Lochaber-axes and partisans' at the suspended figure. In consequence the novel on the one hand occludes, without actually denying, the theories of official negligence tantamount to connivance that concerned the Westminster authorities at the time and that in retrospect seem only too probable, while on the other hand it blurs the horrors of the actual lynch-mob in order to elevate its action into a people's justice, ancient, traditional, solemn, quasi-religious. This effect is maintained by Argyle's supposed 'patriotic' riposte to the queen at the close of the chapter (actually worked up from a quite different episode in traditional history), which also serves as a transition to the novel's principal narrative.[20]

VII

After the Mob's intensity tapers off in anecdote, the novel quite slowly develops its main realist section—and, most readers have thought, its chief glory—the historically precise and psychologically shrewd account of the Deans family up to Effie's trial half-way through the novel.[21] While Butler meditates on events and observes from Arthur's Seat a distant view of Edinburgh, romantic in the dawn light in direct contrast to the preceding macabre torch-lit scene, the hidden linkages of the fiction unfold in three chapters of laconic exposition that recall the swift wit of Hardie in Chapter 1. The political, agrarian and religious history, shrewdly summarized through representative careers and incidents, is interrupted by David Deans's exchanges with Judith Butler and by the death-of-the-auld-laird genre-piece—the first sustained passage of Scots in the novel, for the speech of the Mob is (surprisingly) set down in apparent English, and the chorus of citizens utters only short sentences. Deans, at this stage a tenant subsistence farmer rather than the 'rural capitalist' it has been claimed that he eventually becomes, begins to emerge through his language, shrewd and conceited, a master of the manner of the Presbyterian saints that serves him alike to browbeat Judith Butler and poignantly to mourn his second wife. These lives are treated with gravity and respect—the perspective is not uncritical, angularities in temperament and limitations in experience are acknowledged, but such matters are faced squarely as the substance of the characters' being: among earlier writers, Smollett would have brought out the grotesque aspects and Mackenzie the pathetic, while even Maria Edgeworth writes about her peasants only *de haut en bas*, with caricaturing effect. The booby-laird

Dumbiedikes family rather than the peasant Deanses serve as butts for the humour, yet at the same time the novel's critical attitude towards Deans avoids the sentimental idealization of the cotter way of life into which even the frequently tough-minded Burns sometimes falls.

The 'Arthur's Seat' ballad stanza in its epigraph sheds a resonance of lost love over Chapter 8, something that the quotations from Crabbe first reinforce, then redirect towards Jeanie's 'deferred' union with her preferred suitor and her 'sedative' frown towards Dumbiedikes. In the dense Chapter 10 earlier hints develop with shocking speed; its opening pages show unexpected resources in Scott's narrative manner, the more interestingly in that they do not include any of the moments of 'operatic' eloquence for which the novel is famous. After another 'decoy' epigraph from Crabbe, with no hint of trouble to come (unless for the most cynically alert reader!), and the facetious discourse of sexual enchantment involving Dumbiedikes, come the elaborately genteel hints that Jeanie is approaching (at all of twenty-six) 'the middle age, which is impolitely held to begin a few years earlier with their more fragile sex than with men', and that the Laird may transfer his affections to her sister (Butler too? Even the innocent reader must wonder). Effie, however tenderly described as attracting the gaze of the weary traveller, the village lads and the rigid Presbyterians, is equally subject to the conventional generalization and the cruel reality behind it—her 'juvenile profusion' will run to fat ('too robust, the frequent objection to Scottish beauty') as well as coming, before the chapter is over, to be looked on 'with malicious curiosity or degrading pity' as 'once beautiful and still interesting' in her scarcely concealed state of pregnancy.[22] Two analytic paragraphs try a little too hard to account sociologically for Effie's blend of 'guileless purity of thought, speech and action' with her 'little fund of self-conceit and obstinacy', and find their illustration in 'a cottage evening scene' that, so declared, again both feeds on and undercuts the idiom of sentimental pastoral. On being detected with her lover, Effie sings nonchalantly, 'to hide surprise and confusion', a ballad stanza of much beauty and apparent innocence, saturated though it is with allusions to sexuality, incest and murder. Jeanie challenges Effie in down-to-earth Scots prose, and the sisters fence in word-play and proverbs, until Effie taunts Jeanie with another song that sounds like acceptable teasing so far as it goes but whose very next line, if uttered, would change the effect to cruelly coarse sexual insult. (Some of the original readers must have taken this point, though doubtless many missed it.)

The whole exchange has an intimate and probing quality unprecedented in Scots prose—not for nothing had Scott lately reviewed *Emma*, one feels—and Effie's use of song and proverb also sets up her link to Madge Wildfire, later found to be her parallel in other ways. Reconciled after reaching that brink of the unforgivable, the sisters recover towards frankness and affection—until their father, catching one unacceptable word of their conversation, represses the moment of confidence with his page-long tirade against dancing, and the chapter proceeds, with less manifest brilliance in its treatment of family dynamics but still with rich shifts of idiom and sly manipulations of viewpoint through direct and indirect speech, to the moment of Effie's arrest and David's fierce despairing rejection of Dumbie's offer of money—and indeed of all hope, as he equates retributive justice with 'the law of God, and the law of man'.

Varied textual resources of similar quality are employed, not always in so concentrated a way, throughout this part of the novel, but it is less urgent to trace them in detail than to consider (however sketchily) the issues at stake and what has been made of the contradictory aspects they present. A minimal account might offer Jeanie as a representative heroine of integrity and truthfulness—a transposed Antigone who chooses truth over family affection and loyalty as unhesitatingly as the Theban princess places duty to her dead brother higher than the command of Creon. For the Scottish Antigone, however, the case is resolved not tragically in a living tomb but part heroically in the self-sacrificial walk through England and part comically in the edgy exchanges in the royal garden at Richmond, and the novel's manifest hesitation between a lofty appeal to tragic absolutes and a secular resolution through comedy has opened space for critical speculation. Deans, it has been argued, is a satirical presentation of a sanctimonious hypocrite; Jeanie herself tells rather too many white lies to be acceptable as an apostle of truth, even, like Jacob, obtaining a paternal blessing by deception; her intransigence towards Effie may even be motivated by sexual envy; at the very least, she should have adopted a more pragmatic ethic in the first place, like Bernard Shaw's apocryphal stage Ratcliffe who 'wad hae sworn a hole through an iron pot' before seeing a sister condemned; at best, the absence of enacted mental anguish over the choice implies, on Jeanie's part, a lack of inner life that, along with her apparent asexuality, reduces her to a 'lay-figure' compared to the complexity of character appropriate to novel-writing.[23] Such interventions, eager to nail issues down, usually push too far against the anti-judgemental spirit of most of the novel, which works by elision and compromise of differences. It is true and not irrelevant that Deans mellows by stages under the pressure of experience, that Jeanie equivocates readily enough in tactical matters, that there is more than a hint of sexual (and, later, social) tension between the sisters, that the pragmatic argument is forcefully urged by Ratcliffe and that though Jeanie feels distress she never wavers from the view that she 'daured na swear to an untruth'—but these points neither need nor bear all the adversarial weight that has sometimes been placed on them.

A less condemnatory kind of analysis seeks to explain Jeanie's clarity of decision in terms of 'Calvinism' or 'Puritanism', a doctrine or an analogous frame of mind and character at some particular stage of decline or at least modification between the older and the younger Deanses.[24] The ethical issues are surely less specialized than this; being a Puritan entails more than a refusal to perjure oneself, and Calvinism is not among the issues raised by Scott's presentation of Deans, for whom religion has become almost entirely congealed into particular outdated (though *not*, it is important to note, utterly extreme) rigorisms towards Church–state relations and Church government, at the expense of personal spiritual life and of intellectual alertness on theological matters. Here as elsewhere Scott, whose 1818 review of Kirkton's *The Secret and True History of the Church of Scotland from the Restoration to 1678* took the line that there were 'no doctrinal, and scarcely any ceremonial points in controversy' between the Church parties in the seventeenth century,[25] is clearly not interested in the theology of Calvinism at all; he leaves questions of spiritual depravity and despair and the paradoxes surrounding election and damnation for James Hogg to explore in *The Private Memoirs and Confessions of a Justified Sinner*. The only distinctively Calvinist position in *The Heart of Mid-Lothian* is taken up by Robertson (of all people) in Chapter 15, manifestly in the form of a melodramatic vulgar error when he declares himself 'a wretch predestined to evil'. The celebrated misunderstanding between father and daughter in Chapter 19, as to the bearing of Deans's advice to 'follow your conscience' in court, shows in effect how little her father and his beliefs have to contribute on the *substance* of the question Jeanie faces. Where Deans saw God's law and man's law aligned against Effie, Jeanie puts it that 'we are cruelly stad between' the two, and her sense of a tragic disjunction, of the horns of a dilemma between which she has to pass, prompting her accordingly to effort and action, is more fruitful than her father's passive assimilation of the two codes. It is a typically concrete response, for Jeanie thinks in images (Ingleborough, the sun-blink on a stormy sea, coins combed from the haffet locks) and in quick-witted argumentative replies which (unlike her sister's) do not tend towards epigram or aphorism. The novel does not attribute to Jeanie the sort of inner life that engages in speculative or discursive thought—she is no Maggie Tulliver. Yet the terms chosen for her rejection of possible sophistry around the commandment against bearing false witness (pp. 206–7) do endow Jeanie with a basis for intellectual life which, not being one that can easily be reduced to description, accordingly baffles discursive accounts of character and growth. Working with an art of tones, hints and indirectness, Scott to a large extent takes Jeanie as given, as a specimen from Scotland's 'dingles and cliffs', a natural phenomenon to be observed rather than explained, and not certainly to be chuckled over as some readers do. As H.E. Shaw puts it, Scott 'makes no attempt to depict her mental state directly', exercising 'an ultimate modesty in [his] treatment of the minds of men and women separated from him in time'.[26] Jeanie's being inscrutable to this extent makes it easier to accept that Effie, too, does not come equipped with a reliable explanation—which is fortunate, for in her case the novel proposes two, over-indulgence and repression, that are seemingly incompatible.

In looking towards recent discussion of the construction and assessment of the Deanses, this account of the main movement of the novel has left aside its denouement in the trial (the first fully-fledged 'courtroom drama' in prose fiction, competently if perhaps a little too deliberately worked out) and in the sisters' remarkable interviews before and afterwards (Chapters 20 and 25), where Ratcliffe's bracingly rough yet shrewd and precise advice counterpoints their flow of intense emotion—emotion both stated and pointedly unstated, as when, in the earlier prison interview in Chapter 20, with Jeanie manifestly on the point of giving in, Effie does *not* reiterate her plea (p. 215). Similarly omitted has been the neat plotting of Butler's own arrest, which brings the reader into contact with the alarming Murdocksons while keeping them well away from Jeanie and which introduces, with hints from *Measure for Measure*, the novel's virtuoso construction of the whole mirror-image Ratcliffe-and-Sharpitlaw world. There, in the first police-office in literature, the pragmatic municipal concern with how to run a city includes the knack of getting information out of a maniac, but apparently takes no more account of the values of jurisprudence than it does of those of religion and ethics.

Within a dozen lines of Effie's response to her sentence 'God is mair mercifu' to us than we are to each other', Saddletree and the Edinburgh close-head chorus from Chapters 4 and 5 have joined with the judge in dismissing her chance of pardon. Jeanie, 'pale as ashes', almost accepts the absence of hope, but another pragmatic character, Mrs Saddletree—not her husband, not Butler, and not any of the lawyers with whom the recent chapters have been so thickly strewn—enumerates to Jeanie the recent cases of royal pardon that indicate the path she must now follow.

VIII

Now comes the break in narrative mode. From the relative realism of the first half of the novel Jeanie enters a folktale world in which events typically occur threefold on the lines of pre-established formulae. Already the narrative has embodied folktale elements: rival half-siblings living in rural innocence, a prohibition and its breach, a departure from home, the appearance of the villain and verbal confrontation with the hero, and a remarkable or mysterious birth. Now comes what Propp calls the conjunctive moment, when the hero is dispatched with the aid of an intermediary and bearing threats, promises and equipment, obtained during visits to and conversation with a series of donors and helpers.[27] With Mrs Saddletree's information and advice and her father's deceitfully obtained blessing—another folktale motif—Jeanie proceeds, in successive chapters, to the prison and Ratcliffe (who gives her the 'jark'), to Dumbiedikes, where she is challenged by Mrs Balchristie and locked into the laird's strong-room before being released with money, and to Butler's sickroom, where, having evaded Saddletree, she leaves with 'the paper for MacCallummore'. The first part of her journey into England (marked by the reappearance of the earlier discourse of improvement in communications) is naturalistically presented, but with a brevity that is surprising if the actual walk is to count as the ordeal of heroic self-assertion for which readers have been prepared. It takes Jeanie through the socio-cultural paradoxes of the north of England (*less* courteous than Scotland because less unfrequented) and the silencing effect of the 'far worse patois than her own' as far as York, where, in the first of the three inns at which she stays, Mrs Bickerton ('the lady of the Seven Stars') gives her advice—and yet another talisman.

Chapters 29 to 34 develop an aspect of the novel that will be discussed later, but the events there again fall within Propp's folktale formulae: a second appearance of the villain, with his retinue, his peculiarities of external appearance (whether bedizened, as Madge, or 'turban'd with bandages', as Staunton), his dialogue with the hero and even the marking of the person of the hero during a struggle, as Madge dishevels Jeanie and pulls out tufts of her hair in Willingham churchyard. At the same time, new intertextualities appear. Some, presumably, the reader is not meant to notice—the night-scene in the robbers' hut is a reprise of *Guy Mannering*, Chapters 27–8, itself partly taken over from Smollett's *The Adventures of Ferdinand Count Fathom*, Chapters 20–21. Others are avowed, even emphasized—quotations from the Milton of *Comus*, the Bunyan of *The Pilgrim's Progress* (both also Proppian folktales in structure) and the Wordsworth of the *Lyrical Ballads* supersede the reference-points in Crabbe and Shakespeare adopted earlier in the novel. Yet 'our British Juvenal', Crabbe, is quoted again at the end of the section when Jeanie and the reader, discharged at last from the mills of narrative exposition in which both have been embroiled, complete in a few lines the journey to the London dwelling of the new and most decisive Helper for the heroine, John, second Duke of Argyle and Greenwich.

Already mentioned half a dozen times by Saddletree, Jeanie and the narrator (and in the 1830 edition also the subject of a note to Chapter 24), Argyle is fully established at the beginning of Chapter 35 by an account stretching to seven paragraphs, unusually rich in quotation and cross-reference. Pope's praise of the duke, and the popular ballad concerning him, are quoted, along with his own words in Parliament; suppressed quotations dissociate him from the ambitious behaviour of Macbeth and (less obviously—see p. 360 and n. 5) from that of his old commanding officer Marlborough. In pursuing 'those measures which were at once just and lenient' after the Fifteen, Argyle has a record of combining justice with mercy as neither the Porteous Mob nor the High Court of Justiciary has done—and although Scott does not make the point explicitly, Argyle's loss of court favour and government offices in 1716 may be seen as arising from his unacceptable desire, as commander-in-chief the preceding year, to compromise with the defeated Jacobites rather than pursue them to destruction. Scott's summary of Argyle's position as an intermediary and protector of

Scottish interests in the difficult early days of the Union is broadly
borne out by modern historians, who add that the duke was a 'great
and difficult man', 'so evidently designed for a brilliant part, yet
eternally at odds with the script, with his fellow players and with
himself'. In 1818 the printed references to Argyle (coming from the
archives of the Walpole circle, whose memoirs and biographies had
been emerging over the preceding thirty years) were thoroughly unflat-
tering, stressing his difficulty, unreliability and pride. Scott's friend
and correspondent Lady Louisa Stuart, a channel for first-hand traditions from the middle of the eighteenth century and probably the main
source for Scott's alternative account, wrote to praise the light in
which *The Heart of Mid-Lothian* had placed the duke, 'whom Mr
Coxe so ran down to please Lord Orford'. Part of Scott's thrust here,
therefore, is a corrective to reigning views and reputations, a historical
revision—in favour, incidentally, of a great *Whig* leader—based on his
perception of the Scottish past and of current needs; Scott's Scotland
too (and indeed his Britain) was 'divided into intestine factions, which
hated each other bitterly' (Tory, Whig and—the new factor—Radical),
and there was no unifying or mediating figure corresponding to Argyle.
Admittedly, the contemporary point is not made explicit in any way.
Equally, the novel makes nothing of Argyle's side of the well-known
contrast with his brother, colleague and successor Archibald, Earl of
Ilay, who—'cool, shrewd, penetrating, argumentative' according to
Lady Louisa—might with the duke have formed a diptych of political,
moral and intellectual types corresponding to the contrast between
duke and deputy in *Measure for Measure*. But by now the parallel with
Shakespeare's play has clearly been exhausted; some attributes of
Duke Archibald are actually applied to Duke John (see p. 646, n. 13
and p. 651, n. 13), and the later duke is mentioned merely in passing,
at the beginning of Chapter 49. One remembers Scott's remark about
developing only the parts of his writing that went well.[28]

If these wider issues are raised but not pursued in any sustained
way through the later chapters, the duke's immediate functions are
carried out to the full—both as a fresh, seemingly objective and wisely
reliable point of view on Jeanie to confirm and enrich the reader's
perception of her, as the source of advice and guidance for her during
the chapters culminating in the remaining high point of the novel, the
interview at Richmond, and as an embodiment of an ideal view of
relations between social ranks. Rather as Ratcliffe acted as jailer,
catalyst, buffer and commentator in the prison interviews between

Jeanie and Effie, Argyle first makes possible, then 'produces' and observes Jeanie's petition to the queen, acting literally as Scott's ideal instance of the good meaning of 'condescension' in relationships in a rank-stratified society, and secondarily as vehicle for oblique authorial comment on the scene. Argyle's combination of formality with mediating teasing humour ('And about five miles more') sustains Jeanie as she is duly guided among the shoals and rocks of the conversation, being lucky with the questions put to her, and finding suitably equivocal answers when necessary. Finally she brings out the *personal* appeal that unlocks the wards of royal mercy, not only with her mention of the hour of death (in 1737, not far away for the historical Queen Caroline) and the earthy image of hanging 'the haill Porteous mob at the tail of ae tow', but with the particular argument about the relation between personal suffering and the capacity for sympathy, couched unexpectedly in echoes of her father's idiom but taking an outward-looking ethical direction specific to Jeanie herself.

IX

After the interview at Richmond, Argyle as 'benevolent enchanter' and as living challenge to David Deans's view of Church government continues to dominate Jeanie for a time, through their attractive exchanges about cattle-breeding and the annual cheese (this last a detail transposed from Helen Walker's story) and through his role in the scenes at Rosneath, the final dozen chapters. Despite their generous offering of pastoral, *folklorique* and picturesque charm, these have seemed to many readers a betrayal of the earlier part of the novel. The *Scotsman*'s judgement, 'too long by a volume', was put more tendentiously by the *British Review* in November 1818—had the author, 'compelled by his mercantile engagement to spin out the thread of his story, with or without materials' to a prearranged length, therefore filled up with 'trash'?[29] Any compulsion on Scott's part must have been of a different nature, for in fact he had in mind for the later volumes a second tale about the concealment of the Scottish regalia during the Commonwealth, a project mentioned enthusiastically in letters to intimates and collaborators from January 1818 until as late as 30 April.[30] The existence of the abandoned project might not in itself decisively acquit Scott of padding, but the final volume reads more like a case of extravagant, abundant, perhaps indeed compulsive

writing than as an instance of eking-out. Crammed with incidents that
are individually under- rather than over-written, it runs to 375 pages
in the 1818 edition against the 333, 322 and 328 respectively of the
earlier volumes, and even that length was achieved only by moving an
entire chapter of 32 pages back from its original position in Volume 4
into Volume 3 at a late stage of production. In over-running so
copiously Scott was clearly not behaving like a penny-a-liner with a
rational eye on the main chance.

Can some better account of the last volume be offered? To find the
later part weaker than the rest of the novel is not necessarily to dismiss
it as worthless, and general but qualified approval remains possible.
The *Quarterly* critic of 1821 found that he could relish Knockdunder,
the transformation of Effie into Lady Staunton, and the 'delightful. . .
new and most entertaining light' on Deans as he revised his speculative
principles and acquiesced in Butler's preferment, but thought none
the less that when characters who had hitherto 'harrowed the reader's
mind. . . have nothing to do but to show foibles and enjoy prosperity'
it 'lowers sadly their poetical dignity' and 'has the effect of a farce
after a tragedy'.[31] Readerly expectations of narrative closure do
require some account of events after Effie's pardon, if only to solve the
mystery of the missing child—Helen Walker's aesthetically pleasing
return to real-life obscurity is not detachable, after all, from the ugliest
fact in her sister's case, the dead baby in the River Cluden.[32] The
ambiguous comedy of Deans's mellowing brings full circle his development in response to historical change since his youth in the moss-hags
and the Canongate pillory. Jeanie's modest and culturally plausible
success in life allows her social and historical interest to develop
beyond the single heroic act into an optimistic blueprint for the
nineteenth century as an age of prosperity and ideologically iconic
status for the peasant in Scotland and other small countries of Europe.
The critical comedy surrounding Effie's acquired aristocratic ways and
Argyle's gullibility concerning her past certainly touched unexpectedly
varied nerves in the original reviewers, offending the decorum of some
who claimed that it was of course impossible for such a social climber
to 'pass', and gratifying others for whom the point was precisely that
Effie emerged in the end as an '*unamiable* fine lady'.[33]

In recent years one more specific kind of defence has been prominent. Based on historians' evidence which goes some way to confirm
that Argyle indeed engaged in 'improvement' of the management of
his estates after 1737, it draws the novel further into discourses of

modernization by way of benevolent aristocratic landlordism. This is, however, a treacherous line of argument to pursue, not so much because of the questions that it reopens about the relation between literature and history as because of the slipperiness of historical 'fact' and interpretation themselves. Duke John's procedures seem not in fact to have been very successful, and after 1743 his policies were apparently repudiated in detail, along with his whole style and spiritual legacy, by his successor Archibald; Scott himself thought very poorly of the condition of the Argyle territories that he visited in 1810.[34] Defence of the Knocktarlitie chapters on grounds of historical plausibility, or of concomitance with the conclusions of modern investigation, thus starts too many hares to be comfortable and can be conducted only on a very general level. If Scott was indeed offering 'history' here it is much inferior, in detail, penetration, atmosphere, to his writing elsewhere. Moreover, the vigorous writing in these chapters lies not in the detail of modernized cottages or the routines of farm improvement, but in the genre-scenes—the last creagh, the ordination feast and the cultural misunderstandings there, the comic clashes between Effie and Knockdunder, the 'anthropological' meeting with Donacha's band of contemporary and ignoble savages who recognize silver but know not gold.

Neither the general nor the special defences of the half dozen Knocktarlitie chapters really account for the character of the fourth volume. Can the preceding chapters that conclude the story of Madge Wildfire, or the three final ones of denouement when Effie and her husband and their son reappear, contribute to a clearer account of the novel's structural puzzles?

X

To understand the later part of the novel and the terms in which the whole work coheres—including the relation of the Porteous Mob to the main action, still only loosely accounted for—it is now necessary to turn back to the material excluded by following the route 'Jeanie—Argyle—Knocktarlitie' so far through the novel: that is, to the dark and 'Gothic' aspects embodied in Staunton and his meetings in the King's Park with Butler and Jeanie, and in Madge Wildfire and her mother, who preside over the striking interruptions of Jeanie's southward and northward journeys. This disturbing material fits into neither the realistic nor the folktale strands of the fiction. Mid-century criticism tended to keep it at arm's length by stressing in a dismissive way its inauthentically 'literary' origins—the less unacceptable 'Shakespearean Madwoman' in Madge's case, the contemptible Gothic novel in Staunton's. A range of work over the last thirty years (historians' research into the psychopathology of the witch-persecutions, literary critics' appropriation of psychoanalytic accounts of the 'Uncanny', and the application of symptomatic cultural reading to the 'Gothic' movement[35]) compel us to take such material more seriously, as evidence that the art which embodies or contains it is indeed grappling with troubling and unassimilated emotional content at the level of the individual and/or the culture. What sicknesses are being shed, what anxieties addressed, by these parts of *The Heart of Mid-Lothian*, and how do they relate to the ostensible plot that places family loyalty and affection in conflict with the demands of truth and public justice?

Madge, the more traditional figure, yields her secret fairly readily. Scott introduces Madge with a passing reference to the comic gaucherie of Audrey in *As You Like It*, but after a few pages of writing her out in this role he reclassifies her as a 'madwoman'—like Ophelia, yet unlike her in being provoking rather than affecting. In 1830 he somewhat confuses that distinction by printing the long rambling note provided by the 'persevering kindness' of Mr Train (pp. 575–8), which none the less may serve to bring out the issues. Train's Feckless Fannie, like Sterne's Maria and the 'affecting' Regency Ophelia, was a sentimental madwoman; Madge, 'tall', 'strapping', with 'coarse and masculine features' and a 'commanding profile', 'provoking' and ready for aggression with her tongue or her fists, is no polite distributor of flowers and verses. As Owen Dudley Edwards puts it, Scott's account of Madge is 'an astonishing achievement in the modern realism of its medical portrayal but also a cool use of insanity's obsessions with the past as mirrored in its experience. . . the consciousness of whence and why Meg knows her folklore is as strong as it is weak in the sheltered Ophelia's command of indecent ballads'. Madge falls not within the Sentimental discourse of madness but within the Romantic one.[36] Ostensibly embodying the threat and anger of a betrayed and deprived woman of the eighteenth century, she signifies in a nineteenth-century way, pointing towards Bertha Mason, Gwendolen Harleth and Tess Durbeyfield. Scott's next comparable character, after all, this time right at the centre of her novel, fully expressed in her violence and bound for a central place in the nineteenth-century operatic repertoire, is Lucy Ashton in *The Bride of Lammermoor*.

Not only does this third powerful figure of protest exist among the female characters in *The Heart of Mid-Lothian*, speaking with the glancing, piercing insight of the half-mad, but she is constructed in allusive parallel and contiguity to each of the Deans sisters—most obviously to Effie, who like Madge is seduced by Staunton and bears and loses his child. It is, however, Jeanie whom Madge really haunts—in the past on Arthur's Seat, again on the Great North Road, claiming spiritual kinship, revealing unasked her most intimate secrets, attacking Jeanie physically yet rescuing her from real danger by guiding her to the 'Interpreter's House', finally appealing in vain for rescue at Haribee and dying with Jeanie at her side, singing as her swan-song the most haunting of Romantic poems on sexuality and death. In the series of parallelisms and condensations that make up the novel's unconscious, Madge is a transposed version of Effie, darker, violent, inexpugnable, and virtually embedded in Jeanie's psyche. Moreover in the perspective of doubling and parallelism, the resemblances and differences between Jeanie and Effie, Butler and Staunton, multiply headily. Jeanie and Effie, children of different mothers, are and are not sisters; the novel hesitates between their both being fair, and their being respectively fair and dark. Their names resemble each other in being two-syllabled Scots diminutives; Effie's becomes unmentionable during the novel so that her niece, still christened Euphemia after her missing aunt, is known as Femie (something that Effie explicitly challenges in Chapter 50). The husbands too are formally brothers and not brothers; each suffers from disabling illnesses, including in Butler's case a lameness that makes clear the relation to their lame creator. Staunton too loses his name for a time, and (like Effie, and like Porteous) is the black sheep of a family. Both Staunton and Porteous commit crimes, while purporting to act justly; both Effie and Porteous are convicted for acts only doubtfully criminal; both Butler and Porteous behave badly, in different ways, when challenged by a mob—Porteous by firing in excess of his orders, Butler (like the Edinburgh magistrates) by yielding without resistance. Surprisingly, these aspects of the novel, dynamically written up, have the power to overwhelm and occlude, for chapters at a time, the ostensible project of the middle part of the book, Jeanie's heroic and, until Gunnerby Hill, alertly observed walk from Edinburgh to London. In the 'melodramatic' ending of the novel, the re-enactment of the myth of

Telegonus under the shadow of solemn debate on natural law and the working of providence, they reassert themselves with full force.

Some such processes of splitting, identification and condensation of characters, attributes and narrative figures must, it seems, also underlie Scott's initial combination of the Mob with Jeanie's family story. No single piece of information is likely to serve as key to a work so intricate, suggestive and multiple in its interests as *The Heart of Mid-Lothian*, and there is always a risk of saying too much or too little when bringing to bear on a particular text biographical information or psychological speculation about its author. Scott, moreover, has usually seemed rather beyond such approaches both because of his magnetic, powerful and integrated personality and because of the effective covering of tracks in Lockhart's copious yet reticent biography; even Lockhart's would-be 'corrector' Grierson asserts that this novel 'has no intimate link with Scott's own life'. Nevertheless there *is* just such a rabbit in the hat: Daniel Scott (1776–1806), Scott's much loved but ultimately rejected youngest brother, the black sheep of *his* family. Daniel, a disappointment in respect of money, drink and women, was shipped out to the West Indies for a time, with the very fact of their brotherhood suppressed by Scott, who acknowledged him merely as a young relation. There he fell further: 'ordered to subdue a revolt among a band of rebellious Negroes he showed the white feather and was dismissed in disgrace. . . returned to Scotland a dishonoured man. . . died. . . Scott refused to attend his brother's funeral and wore no mourning.' As late as 1828 Scott expressed what Lockhart calls 'a deep feeling of contrition' over the episode and declared, apropos of the character Conchobar in his recent novel, *The Fair Maid of Perth*, 'my secret motive was to perform a sort of expiation'.[37] It seems probable that ten years earlier the tension between brotherly affection and exaggeratedly rigid censure of Daniel, ambivalent emotions complicated by guilt, account also for the assembly of such disparate elements and attitudes in *The Heart of Mid-Lothian*, for the enthusiasm and sense of fitness with which Scott embarked on a main plot that so attractively reconciled family affection with moral integrity, for the commitment with which he carried his myth of reparation through to the end of the fourth volume, and for its sudden resolution by the apparent fierce and contradictory resurgence of retributive feeling in the final chapter.

There, after a muted reprise of the earlier events—the aged Saddletrees, the promoted Ratcliffe, Porteous's silent widow, all in a comparative atmosphere of modernity, success, prosperity and up-to-date Moderate intellectualism with the exchanging of classical tags, the benefice offered and declined, the urbane philosophical debate over providentialism and the pathetic fallacy—the repressed returns by means of archetypal parricidal myth, the fatal scuffle on the shore with the child begotten in former life, first articulated in the *Telegonia*'s account of the death of Odysseus. Staunton falls by an unspecified weapon in the hands of his son, Duncan runs through his own black namesake, Staunton's hair shirt and (later) Effie's inward wound come to light, and Jeanie enables her nephew to escape Duncan's gallows by fleeing to the American woods where Daniel Scott's reputation had been finally lost. Undeniably melodramatic (though no more so than the denouements of *The Mill on the Floss* and *Tess of the Durbervilles*), this intricate and disruptive closure simultaneously reveals, records and fulfils the psychic imperatives that gave *The Heart of Mid-Lothian* its distinctive form.

NOTES

1. Michael Lynch, *Scotland: A New History* (1991) gives an up-to-date overall account in one volume. For readers of Scott, his own *Tales of a Grandfather* (1827–9) is illuminating for the period down to 1745 if used with due caution. For more detailed treatments, see W. Ferguson, *Scotland: 1689 to the Present* (1968); T.C. Smout, *A History of the Scottish People 1560–1830* (1969); Rosalind Mitchison, *Lordship to Patronage: Scotland 1603–1745* (1983); Bruce Lenman, *Integration, Enlightenment and Industrialization: Scotland 1746–1832* (1981). Hugh Kearney, *The British Isles: A History of Four Nations* (1989) gives a comparative perspective. For the 'rediscovery' of the culture of the people, see Peter Burke, *Popular Culture in Early Modern Europe* (1978), Chapter 9 and Appendix 1.

2. Best known of the many biographies is the *Life* of 1837 by John Gibson Lockhart, Scott's son-in-law. The fullest modern one is Edgar Johnson, *Sir Walter Scott: The Great Unknown* (1970).

3. Scott's remarks, *The Letters of Sir Walter Scott*, H.J.C. Grierson and others, eds. (1932–7), 14 September 1817, 10 November 1817, 14 January 1818; 'heart of Lothian' used by the supplier of the stones, *Letters*, 30 July 1817, but recorded by 1713, (*Scottish National Dictionary* 10, 498); Constable's man, *Archibald Constable and His Literary Correspondents* (1873), 3, 107; the anecdote, Johnson, 619–20 (and n. 82 for his revision of Lockhart's date).

4. Not 4 June as originally announced and still sometimes asserted. The copies for London were shipped from Leith on 17 July (Johnson, 622); the

advertisement in *The Times* of 23 July still has the *Tales* 'in the press and shortly to be published', and the *Scotsman* review appeared on 1 August.

5. 'Modern historians', specifically C. Larner, *Enemies of God* (1981), 45; 'shifts in power. . .', K. Sutherland, 'Fictional Economies: Adam Smith, Walter Scott and the Nineteenth-century Novel', *ELH*, 54 (1987), 97–128.

6. Print-runs, Jane Millgate, *Scott's Last Edition* (1987), 125; Carlyle, reviewing Lockhart in *London and Westminster Review*, 28 (January 1838), 341; Twain, *Life on the Mississippi* (1883), Chapter 46; 'system of literature', Martin Green, *Dreams of Adventure, Dreams of Empire* (1979), 109, 170; James, 1864 notice of Nassau Senior's reviews collected as *Essays on Fiction* (James, *Literary Criticism: Essays on Literature*, Leon Edel, ed., 1984, 1, 196–1, 204); Woolf, *To the Lighthouse* (1927), 183–6, 215.

7. Edwin Muir, *Scott and Scotland* (1936); Hugh MacDiarmid, *Lucky Poet* (1943), Chapter 4; David Craig, *Scottish Literature and the Scottish People 1680–1830* (1961); P.H. Scott, *Walter Scott and Scotland* (1981); Andrew Noble, 'Highland History and Narrative Form in Scott and Stevenson' in Noble, ed., *Robert Louis Stevenson* (1983); Christopher Harvie, 'Scott and the Image of Scotland' in Alan Bold, ed., *Sir Walter Scott: The Long-forgotten Melody* (1983).

8. Scottish Enlightenment context, first argued by Duncan Forbes, 'The Rationalism of Sir Walter Scott', *Cambridge Journal*, 7 (1953), 20–35, and recently developed in P.H. Scott, *Walter Scott and Scotland* (1981), Chapters 5 and 6; Georg Lukács, *The Historical Novel* (1937, translated 1962), Chapter 1; 'distinct phase of fiction', Daniel Cottom, *The Civilized Imagination* (1985), and Gary Kelly, *English Fiction of the Romantic Period* (1989), Chapter 1.

9. Respectively, Wayne Booth, *The Rhetoric of Fiction* (1961); Gillian Beer, *Darwin's Plots* (1983); Roland Barthes, *S/Z* (1970); M.M. Bakhtin, 'Discourse in the Novel' in *The Dialogic Imagination* (1981); Northrop Frye, *The Secular Scripture: A Study of the Structure of Romance* (1976), 5.

10. In, respectively, *The Captain's Daughter*, *The Betrothed*, *Les Chouans*, *Notre-Dame de Paris*, *The Scarlet Letter* and 'My Kinsman Major Molyneux', *Barnaby Rudge* and *Adam Bede*.

11. G.B. Shaw, 'The Quintessence of Ibsenism' (1891), *Major Critical Essays* (1932), 117–18; F.R. Leavis, *The Great Tradition* (1948), 5, n. 2 (one quip among many in Leavis's notorious and brilliant slash-and-burn clearance of the pre-Victorian novel to make way for the psychological-realist 'tradition'); Mary Lascelles, *The Storyteller Retrieves the Past* (1980), 98–9.

12. 'no Waverley hero': Millgate notes that Jeanie is also innocent of reading in romances and indeed of any literature, and has no taste for the picturesque (*Walter Scott: The Making of the Novelist*, 1984, 153); 'disunified', Harry E. Shaw, *The Forms of Historical Fiction* (1983), 245; 'medley', James Kerr, 'Scott's Fable of Regeneration: *The Heart of Mid-Lothian*', *ELH*, 53 (1986), 801; 'episodic', Lascelles, 34.

13. For V. Propp's inventory of folktale elements, see *Morphology of the Folktale* (1928, translated 1968). The design becomes clearer in Scott's first intentions for the division of volumes, as they appear in the MS. Volume 2 was to begin with Jeanie's excursion at Chapter 14 and to remain focused on her until immediately after Effie's trial and the interview with Dumbiedikes at the end of Chapter 26. Volume 3 had Jeanie 'pursuing her solitary journey' from Chapter 27 to the gate of the royal garden. Volume 4 opened with her interview with Queen Caroline (Chapter 37). In the event, insertion or expansion of the present Introductory Chapter displaced each of the earlier divisions to one chapter further on than had been intended, and later still Scott's apparent difficulty in bringing the novel to a conclusion pushed the royal interview back from Volume 4 to Volume 3. Compare n. 30 below.

14. 'Vault over', Angus Calder, *Old Mortality* (Penguin edition, 1975), p. 9; 'undergrowth' (source lost); 'bore', A.N. Wilson, *The Laird of Abbotsford* (1980), 120. Scott used the framework twice more, but the extra layer of mystery was given up when in 1819 all his prose fiction to date was issued by Constable in one uniform series of volumes. In recent years the narrative frames have been taken seriously and defended by e.g. Owen Dudley Edwards in Alan Bold, 74–6, who finds that the formula conveys 'an attitude transcending class on the part of the narrator' and that each of the imaginary schoolmasters resembles Scott in significant ways; by David Hewitt in Douglas Gifford, ed., *The History of Scottish Literature: Volume 3* (1988), 79–81, who finds in Pattieson a substantial and developing literary persona; and by Marilyn Orr in *Scottish Literary Journal* (November 1989), who treats them as a device for 'disrupting the form of the novel' in order to enhance the reality of the narrative. Scott stands as a prime example in *Seuils*, G. Genette's 1987 study of 'paratexts'.

15. Readers unfamiliar with Scots or suspicious of travesties they have encountered may wish to consult the historical and linguistic notes prefixed to *The Concise Scots Dictionary*, M. Robinson, ed. (1985) or a fuller account either academic, e.g. A.J. Aitken and A.T. McArthur, eds., *Languages of Scotland* (1979), or popular, e.g. B. Kay, *Scots: The Mither Tongue* (1986).

16. 'not a transcription', Hewitt, 74. The lexicographer David Murison also stresses that 'Scott's Scots is actually thicker than it looks' in his short essay 'The Two Languages in Scott' (A.N. Jeffares, ed., *Scott's Mind and Art*, 1969, 220). The fullest account of Scott's language is Graham Tulloch, *The Language of Sir Walter Scott* (1980) where 'Highland English' is discussed at 255–6, 'court-Scots' at 173–4 and Scott's general effect at 180–81. Scott's Scots is placed in a wider context in Emma Letley, *From Galt to Douglas Brown: Nineteenth-century Fiction and Scots Language* (1988). Both writers consider *The Heart of Mid-Lothian* in some detail; Letley, like Judith Wilt in *Secret Leaves* (1985), regards the use of Scots as a significant performative act in itself.

17. *The Miscellaneous Prose Works of Sir Walter Scott* (1834–6), 19, 22.

18. For detail, see Tony Inglis, '"And an Intertextual Heart. . .": Rewriting Origins in *The Heart of Mid-Lothian*' in J.H. Alexander and David Hewitt, eds., *Scott in Carnival* (1993), 216–31.

19. Francis Jeffrey, *Edinburgh Review*, 33, 3; the other objections are raised by Donald Davie, *The Heyday of Sir Walter Scott* (1961), Chapter 2; David Craig, in Alan Bell, ed., *Scott Bicentenary Essays* (1973), 106–8, and Lascelles, 13.

20. The fullest account of the Mob, with narrative, analysis and many documents, is W. Roughead, *Trial of Captain Porteous* (1909). Sir Tresham Lever ('Sir Walter Scott and the Murder of Porteous', *Blackwood's Magazine*, 310, 1971, 212–24) follows Roughead on the facts but shares the present writer's poor impression of the provost and council and dismay at Scott's apparent whitewashing of the killers. The most recent historical study, by H.T. Dickinson and K. Logue in the *Scottish Labour History Society Journal*, 10 (June 1976, expanded from *History Today*, April 1972) concludes that the riot was organized and carried out by Edinburgh workmen (not rabble) with moral support from their middle-class employers and some tacit connivance from town officials; the outcome was 'a complete victory over the forces of law and order in Britain' showing 'the power of an urban populace when united in a common aim'. Logue's *Popular Disturbances in Scotland 1780–1815* (1979) gives relevant context in the Scotland of Scott's time.

21. In the original arrangement of the MS, the summary of the family histories and Butler's adventures with the mysterious stranger, Sharpitlaw and Ratcliffe were included in Volume 1, with Volume 2 focusing entirely on Jeanie from her midnight excursion until after the post-trial interview in prison.

22. One would like to be sure that Scott does ironically dissociate himself from this knowing and dubious vocabulary of female appraisal, which can mediate class and gender stereotypes in a distanced way without actually disowning them—cf. 'that affected liveliness of manner which, in her rank and sometimes in those above it, females occasionally assume to hide surprise or confusion', p. 100.

23. Deans as hypocrite, O.D. Edwards in Alan Bold, 73, and J.M. D'Arcy, 'David Deans and Bothwell Bridge: A Re-evaluation' in *Scottish Literary Journal*, 12, 2 (1985); Jeanie attacked, J.O. Hayden, 'Jeanie Deans: The Big Lie (and a Few Small Ones)', *Scottish Literary Journal*, 6, 1 (1979), and defended, Thomas Dale, 'The Jurists, the Dominie and Jeanie Deans', *Scottish Literary Journal*, 11, 1 (1984); her motives, Avrom Fleishman, *The English Historical Novel* (1971), 87, who attributes the charge to another critic (Van Ghent, below) in whose discussion the present writer cannot discern it; Bernard Shaw, as n. 11 above; Jeanie as a 'lay-figure', D.F. Hannigan, *Westminster Review*, 144 (July 1895), 17, and as not achieving entry to 'the realm of moral interest', Dorothy Van Ghent, *The English Novel: Form and Function* (1953), 120.

24. Winifred Lynskey, 'The Drama of the Elect and the Reprobate in Scott's *Heart of Mid-Lothian*', *Boston University Studies in English*, 4 (1960), 39–48; Susan Manning, *The Puritan-provincial Vision* (1990), 171–81.

25. *The Miscellaneous Prose Works of Sir Walter Scott*, 19, 243–4.

26. Harry E. Shaw, 146–7. Martin Green relates this externality to more impersonal cultural change: 'The characterization of Jeanie translates the Puritanism of her forebears into the kind of virtue suitable to the Victorian novel—as the figure of Clarissa did for the eighteenth-century novel. The theology, the piety, the religious practices dissolve into this decent, quiet, tidy, little figure, strong feeling but anti-passionate, anti-hedonist, anti-erotic' (*Dreams of Adventure, Dreams of Empire*, 1979, 367).

27. V. Propp, 37.

28. On Argyle and his brother: 'great and difficult', A. Murdoch, *The People Above* (1980), 30; 'brilliant... at odds...', J.M. Simpson, 'Who Steered the Gravy Train, 1707–66?' in N.T. Phillipson and Rosalind Mitchison, eds, *Scotland in the Age of Improvement* (1970), 58; 'Walpole circle', notably W. Coxe's life of Sir Robert Walpole (1798), 1, 610–15 with its charge of 'political versatility'; Lady Louisa, in John Gibson Lockhart, Chapter 42, and in her contrast between the Argyle brothers in her *Selections* (1899), 13: 'The one was, properly speaking, a hero; the other, altogether a man of this world.' It is a further piquant fact that the historical duke, through his daughter the frequently mentioned Lady Caroline Campbell, was grandfather and great-grandfather to the successive Dukes of Buccleuch, who were Scott's 'clan chiefs', friends and patrons; a substantial loan to Scott for which the fourth Duke of Buccleuch had stood guarantor was actually repaid from the proceeds of the novel that also sought to vindicate his ancestor.

29. *British Review*, 12, 396–406. The charge was casually revived by Sir Herbert Grierson (*Sir Walter Scott Bart.: A New Life Supplementary to and Corrective of Lockhart's Biography*, 1938, 164–5), whose citations, however, show that the *British Review* was sharpening a comment in *Blackwood's Magazine*, organ of the presumably disappointed rival publisher; it continues to pass current in the standard edition of Scott's *Journal*, W.E.K. Anderson, ed. (1972), 32, n. 4. Francis R. Hart has commented usefully on the 'riot of intentional fallacies and psychological irrelevance' surrounding the issue (*Scott's Novels: The Plotting of Historic Survival*, 1966, 130–31) and Jane Millgate notices the intended 'regalia tale' (*Walter Scott: The Making of the Novelist*, 1984, 157–8 and notes).

30. The decision in early May to make *The Heart of Mid-Lothian* the whole of the new *Tales* entailed changes, at once drastic and ingeniously minimal, in what had already been written. The Prolegomen and the Introductory Chapter were apparently written and inserted at this stage, not only disturbing the previous pagination of the MS but also leading to the transfer of one chapter (already set in type) from Volume 1 to Volume 2

and of another from Volume 2 to Volume 3. The new end-point for Volume 2 was settled while the printer and confidant Ballantyne was still reacting to Chapter 23, among the trial scenes (undated note in *Letters*, 5, 67). From this stage onwards, too, Scott leant on or drew from Smollett's *Humphry Clinker* as a starting-block or source of second wind for the new phase of the novel. Alistair M. Duckworth (*Scottish Literary Journal*, 7, 1, 1980) has already demonstrated the link between Smollett's novel and the topographical writing later in *The Heart of Mid-Lothian*, but there are many other parallels of significant detail: for example the coach upset in Scott's Introductory Chapter corresponds in viewpoint, incidents and phraseology with one in *Humphry Clinker*. For details, follow n. 18 above.

31. Nassau Senior in *Quarterly Review* (October 1821), 26, 109–48, in particular 117–18.

32. The sparse surviving court records of Isobel Walker's case are printed in W.S. Crockett, *The Sir Walter Scott Originals* (1912), Appendix. From their silences Miss Lascelles (95–6) infers that Helen and Isobel Walker did not in fact meet in court, so that Scott's development of the 'pleasing and interesting sketch' must have included the whole trial, as well as the Deanses' family background and the sub-plot.

33. *Literary Journal* (15 August 1818), 327.

34. 'historians' evidence', Eric Cregeen, 'The Changing Role of the House of Argyll in the Scottish Highlands' in N. Phillipson and Rosalind Mitchison, *Scotland in the Age of Improvement* (1970), 5–23, which led Thomas Crawford to revise the 1982 edition of his excellent short study of Scott; 'repudiated', Lady Louisa Stuart's account and I.G. Lindsay and M. Cosh, *Inveraray and the Dukes of Argyll* (1973), Chapter 1; Scott's view, *Letters*, 30 September 1810. One further recent line of defence of Knocktarlitie, offered very persuasively by Graham McMaster ('Realism and Romance in *The Heart of Mid-Lothian*', *Cambridge Quarterly*, 10, 3, 1982, 202–18) recasts the novel's realism/folktale dyad as cyclical alternation of 'birth and rebirth. . . reform and renewal, an embodiment of grace'.

35. Norman Cohn, *Europe's Inner Demons* (1975); Christine Brooke-Rose, *A Rhetoric of the Unreal* (1981); David Punter, *The Literature of Terror* (1980).

36. Owen Dudley Edwards, 'Scott as a Contemporary Historian' in Alan Bold, 72. For the Sentimental/Romantic distinction, see P.W. Martin, *Mad Women in Romantic Writing* (1987).

37. Sir Herbert Grierson, 165; Edgar Johnson, 257; John Gibson Lockhart, Chapter 75.

SELECTED READING

PLACE of publication is London unless stated otherwise. An asterisk indicates that a book contains a substantial discussion of *The Heart of Mid-Lothian*.

SCOTT

BIBLIOGRAPHIES
James C. Corson, *A Bibliography of Sir Walter Scott... 1797–1940* (Edinburgh, 1943)
Jill Rubinstein, *Sir Walter Scott: A Reference Guide* (Boston, 1978). Lists books and articles 1932–77

BIOGRAPHY
John Gibson Lockhart, *Memoirs of the Life of Sir Walter Scott, Bart.*, 7 vols. (Edinburgh, 1837–8)
John Buchan, *Sir Walter Scott* (1932)
Sir Herbert Grierson, *Sir Walter Scott, Bart.: A New Life Supplementary to and Corrective of Lockhart's Biography* (1938)
*Edgar Johnson, *Sir Walter Scott: The Great Unknown*, 2 vols. (1970)

Scott on Himself, David Hewitt, ed. (Edinburgh, 1981) re-edits the unfinished autobiographical memoir of Scott's first twenty years with which Lockhart's life opens, and assembles other personal writings.
Arthur Melville Clark, *Sir Walter Scott: The Formative Years* (1969) and Paul H. Scott, *Walter Scott and Scotland* (Edinburgh, 1981) also concentrate on early experience and cultural context.

The Journal of Sir Walter Scott (1825–32) was most recently edited by W.E.K. Anderson (1972).

LETTERS

Sir Herbert Grierson and others, eds., 12 vols. (1932–7), with *Notes and Index* by James C. Corson (1979)

Correspondence is excerpted in Wilfred Partington, ed., *The Private Letter-books of Sir Walter Scott* (1930) and *Sir Walter's Postbag* (1932)

GENERAL STUDIES

*Thomas Crawford, *Scott* (1965, revised Edinburgh, 1982)

*John Lauber, *Sir Walter Scott* (New York, 1966, revised 1989)

*Robin Mayhead, *Walter Scott* (1973)

*A.N. Wilson, *The Laird of Abbotsford* (1980)

David Daiches, *Sir Walter Scott and His World* (1971) is generously illustrated

COLLECTIONS OF ESSAYS

A.N. Jeffares, ed., *Scott's Mind and Art* (Edinburgh, 1969)

Alan Bell, ed., *Scott Bicentenary Essays* (1973)

J.H. Alexander and David Hewitt, eds., *Scott and His Influence* (Aberdeen, 1983)

Alan Bold, ed., *Sir Walter Scott: The Long-forgotten Melody* (1983)

J.H. Alexander and David Hewitt, eds., *Scott in Carnival* (Aberdeen, 1993)

The Scott Newsletter has been published semi-annually since 1982 by the Department of English, University of Aberdeen

THE WAVERLEY NOVELS

Philip Bradley, *An Index to the Waverley Novels* (Metuchen, NJ, 1975)

QUESTIONS OF COMPOSITION AND PRODUCTION

Gillian Dyson, 'The Manuscripts and Proof Sheets of Scott's Waverley Novels', *Edinburgh Bibliographical Society Transactions*, 14 (1960), 15–42

G.A.M. Wood, 'The Great Reviser; or the Unknown Scott', *Ariel*, 2, 3, (1971), 27–45

Peter Garside, 'Rob's Last Raid: Scott and the Publication of the Waverley Novels' in R. Myers and M. Harris, eds., *Author/Publisher*

Relations during the Eighteenth and Nineteenth Centuries (Oxford, 1983), 88–118

David Hewitt, 'Scott, Hogg and Galt Unimproved' in *Studies in Scottish Fiction: Nineteenth Century*, H.W. Drescher and J. Schwend, eds., (Frankfurt, Berne and New York, 1985)

Jane Millgate, *Scott's Last Edition* (Edinburgh, 1987)

Iain Gordon Brown, ed., *Scott's Interleaved Waverley Novels* (Aberdeen, 1987)

STUDIES OF OTHER SPECIFIC ASPECTS

*W.S. Crockett, *The Sir Walter Scott Originals* (1912)

David Marshall, *Sir Walter Scott and Scots Law* (1932)

*Coleman O. Parsons, *Witchcraft and Demonology in Scott's Fiction* (1964)

Jerome K. Mitchell, *The Walter Scott Operas* (University, Alabama, 1977)

Richard Ford, *Dramatizations of Scott's Novels: A Catalogue*, Oxford Bibliographical Society Occasional Publication 12 (1979)

*Graham Tulloch, *The Language of Sir Walter Scott* (1980)

*James Anderson, *Sir Walter Scott and History* (Edinburgh, 1981)

Older criticism is surveyed in *James T. Hillhouse, *The Waverley Novels and Their Critics* (Ann Arbor, Michigan, 1936) and collected selectively, down to 1883, in John O. Hayden, ed., *Scott: The Critical Heritage* (1970)

MODERN DISCUSSIONS

*Georg Lukács, *The Historical Novel* (1937, trans. H. and S. Mitchell, 1962)

David Daiches, 'Scott's Achievement as a Novelist', *Literary Essays* (Edinburgh, 1956)

*Alexander Welsh, *The Hero of the Waverley Novels* (1963)

*Francis R. Hart, *Scott's Novels: The Plotting of Historic Survival* (Charlottesville, Virginia, 1966)

D.D. Devlin, *The Author of Waverley* (1966)

*A.O.J. Cockshut, *The Achievement of Sir Walter Scott* (1969)

*Robert C. Gordon, *Under Which King?* (1969)

*Lars Hartveit, *Dream within a Dream* (Bergen and New York, 1974)

*David Brown, *Walter Scott and the Historical Imagination* (1979)

Graham McMaster, *Scott and Society* (1981)

*Harry E. Shaw, *The Forms of Historical Fiction* (1983)
*Jane Millgate, *Walter Scott: The Making of the Novelist* (1984)
*Judith Wilt, *Secret Leaves* (Chicago, 1985)
*James Kerr, *Fiction against History: Scott as Storyteller* (1989)

COLLECTIONS OF ESSAYS

D.D. Devlin, ed., *Walter Scott: Modern Judgements* (1968)
A.N. Jeffares, ed., *Scott's Mind and Art*, (Edinburgh, 1969)

RECENT ARTICLES THAT EXPLORE QUESTIONS OF
APPROACH AND READING

Richard L. Stein, 'Historical Fiction and the Implied Reader: Scott and Iser', *Novel*, 14 (1981), 213–31

Elaine Jordan, 'The Management of Scott's Novels' in F. Barker and others, eds., *Europe and Its Others: Essex Conference on the Sociology of Literature 1984* (Colchester, 1985), 2, 146–61

Ina Ferris, 'Storytelling and the Subversion of Literary Form in Walter Scott's Fiction', *Genre*, 18 (Spring 1985), 23–35

Kathryn Sutherland, 'Fictional Economies: Adam Smith, Walter Scott and the Nineteenth-century Novel', *ELH*, 54 (1987), 97–128

Ina Ferris, 'The Historical Novel and the Problem of Beginning: The Example of Scott', *Journal of Narrative Technique*, 18 (1988), 73–82

Marilyn Orr, 'Voice and Text: Scott the Storyteller, Scott the Novelist', *Scottish Literary Journal*, 16, 2 (November 1989), 41–59

THE HEART OF MID-LOTHIAN

BIBLIOGRAPHICAL

Philip Gaskell, *From Writer to Reader: Studies in Editorial Method* (Oxford, 1978), example 5, 101–17

Arnold Kettle, *An Introduction to the English Novel* (1951)
Dorothy Van Ghent, *The English Novel: Form and Function* (New York, 1953)
E.M.W. Tillyard, *The Epic Strain in the English Novel* (1958)
David Craig, *Scottish Literature and the Scottish People* (1961)
Donald Davie, *The Heyday of Sir Walter Scott* (1961)
Avrom Fleishman, *The English Historical Novel* (1971)
Mary Lascelles, *The Story-teller Retrieves the Past* (Oxford, 1980)

George Levine, *The Realistic Imagination* (1981)

Daniel Cottom, *The Civilized Imagination* (1985)

Douglas Gifford, ed., *The History of Scottish Literature: Volume 3*, (Aberdeen, 1988)

Gary Kelly, *English Fiction of the Romantic Period 1789–1830* (1989)

John MacQueen, *The Enlightenment and Scottish Literature. Volume 2: The Rise of the Historical Novel* (Edinburgh, 1989)

Susan Manning, *The Puritan-provincial Vision* (1990)

ARTICLES IN PERIODICALS

P.F. Fisher, 'Providence, Fate and the Historical Imagination in Scott's *Heart of Mid-Lothian*', *Nineteenth-century Fiction*, 10 (1955), 99–114

Robin Mayhead, '*The Heart of Mid-Lothian*: Scott as Artist', *Essays in Criticism*, 6 (1956), 266–77 (with rejoinders by Joan Pittock, 7, 1957, 477–9, and David Craig, 8, 1958, 217–25)

Winifred Lynskey, 'The Drama of the Elect and the Reprobate in Scott's *Heart of Mid-Lothian*', *Boston University Studies in English*, 4 (1960), 39–48

D. Biggins, '*Measure for Measure* and *The Heart of Mid-Lothian*', *Études Anglaises*, 14 (1961), 193–205

William H. Marshall, 'Point of View and Structure in *The Heart of Mid-Lothian*', *Nineteenth-century Fiction*, 16 (1961), 257–62

James Anderson, 'Sir Walter Scott as Historical Novelist', *Studies in Scottish Literature*, 4 (1966–7), 173–8

David Burt, '*The Heart of Mid-Lothian*: Madge Wildfire's Rational Irrationality', *Studies in Scottish Literature*, 8 (1971), 86–92

Frances M. Clements, '"Queens Love Revenge as Well as Their Subjects": Thematic Unity in *The Heart of Mid-Lothian*', *Studies in Scottish Literature*, 10 (1972), 10–17

William J. Hyde, 'Jeanie Deans and the Queen: Appearance and Reality', *Nineteenth-century Fiction*, 28 (1973), 86–92

Claire Lamont, 'The Poetry of the Early Waverley Novels', *Proceedings of the British Academy*, 51 (1975), 315–36 (on 'Proud Maisie')

John O. Hayden, 'Jeanie Deans: The Big Lie (and a Few Small Ones)', *Scottish Literary Journal*, 6, 1 (May 1979), 34–44

Alistair M. Duckworth, 'Scott's Fiction and the Migration of Settings', *Scottish Literary Journal*, 7, 1 (May 1980), 97–112 (part of a longer essay printed in full in *Landscape in the Gardens and the Literature of Eighteenth-century England*, Los Angeles, 1981)

Nicole Ward, 'The Prison-house of Language: *The Heart of Mid-Lothian* and *La Chartreuse de Parme*', *Comparative Criticism*, 2 (1980), 93–107

Rick A. Davies, 'The Demon Lover Motif in *The Heart of Mid-Lothian*', *Studies in Scottish Literature*, 16 (1981), 91–6

Graham McMaster, 'Realism and Romance in *The Heart of Mid-Lothian*,' *Cambridge Quarterly*, 10 (1982), 202–18

Susan Morgan, 'Old Heroes and a New Heroine in the Waverley Novels', *ELH*, 50 (1983), 559–85

Margaret M. Criscuola, 'The Porteous Mob: Fact and Truth in *The Heart of Mid-Lothian*', *English Language Notes*, 22, 1 (1984), 43–50

Thomas Dale, 'The Jurists, the Dominie and Jeanie Deans', *Scottish Literary Journal*, 11, 1 (May 1984), 36–44

Julian M. D'Arcy, 'Davie Deans and Bothwell Bridge: A Re-evaluation', *Scottish Literary Journal*, 12, 2 (November 1985), 23–34

Robert Mayer, 'The Internal Machinery Displayed: *The Heart of Mid-Lothian* and Scott's Apparatus for the Waverley Novels', *Clio*, 17 (1987), 1–20

Jon Thompson, 'Sir Walter Scott and Madge Wildfire: Strategies of Containment in *The Heart of Mid-Lothian*', *Literature and History*, 13, 2 (Autumn 1987), 188–99

Jana Davis, 'Walter Scott, *The Heart of Mid-Lothian* and Scottish Commonsense Morality', *Mosaic*, 21 (1988), 55–63

Alistair D. Walker, 'The Tentative Romantic – An Aspect of *The Heart of Mid-Lothian*', *English Studies*, 69 (1988), 146–57

M.A. Schofield, '*The "Heart" of Mid-Lothian*: Jeanie Deans as Narrator', *Studies in Eighteenth-century Culture*, 19 (1989), 153–64

Harry E. Shaw, 'Scott's "Daemon" and the Voices of Historical Narrative', *Journal of English and Germanic Philology*, 88 (1989), 21–33

Critiques of Scott from specifically Scottish viewpoints are listed in n. 7 to the Introduction, and accounts of the Porteous Mob in n. 20.

THE HEART OF MID-LOTHIAN

The first edition of *The Heart of Mid-Lothian*
appeared anonymously without any dedication.
In the New Edition of 1829–33 the entire series
of Waverley novels was dedicated to

KING GEORGE IV

(Scott's wording can be found on p. 571 of Andrew Hook's
edition of *Waverley* in the Penguin Classics)

The editorial work on the present edition
is dedicated to the memory of
two Scottish teachers of language and literature:

Hector MacIver (1910–1966)
Ian Hunter (1937–1969)

This day were published,

IN ONE VOLUME,

CRIMINAL TRIALS,

ILLUSTRATIVE OF THE TALE ENTITLED " THE HEART
OF MID-LOTHIAN."

—————

————— " A thousand heads,
A thousand hands, ten thousand tongues and voices
Employ'd at once in several acts of malice !
Old men not staid with age, virgins with shame,
Late wives with loss of husbands, mothers of children,
Losing all grief in joy of his sad fall,
Run quite transported with their cruelty !"

BEN JONSON.

—————

Printed by James Ballantyne and Co.

TALES OF MY LANDLORD,

Second Series,

COLLECTED AND ARRANGED

BY

JEDEDIAH CLEISHBOTHAM,

SCHOOLMASTER AND PARISH-CLERK OF GANDERCLEUGH.

Hear, Land o' Cakes and brither Scots,
Frae Maidenkirk to Jonny Groats',
If there's a hole in a' your coats,
    I rede ye tent it,
A chiel's amang you takin' notes,
            An' faith he'll prent it.
                                    BURNS

IN FOUR VOLUMES.

VOL. I.

EDINBURGH:

PRINTED FOR ARCHIBALD CONSTABLE AND COMPANY.

1818.

*Title-page of the first edition of 1818, with an
advertisement on the facing page.*

Ahora bien, dixo el Cura, traedme, senor huésped, aquesos libros, que los quiero ver. Que me place, respondió el, y entrando, en su aposento, sacó dél una maletilla vieja cerrada con una cadenilla, y abriéndola, halló en ella tres libros grandes y unos papeles de muy buena letra escritos de mano.—Don Quixote, Part I. Capitulo 32.

It is mighty well, said the priest; pray, landlord, bring me those books, for I have a mind to see them. With all my heart, answered the host; and, going to his chamber, he brought out a little old cloke-bag, with a padlock and chain to it, and opening it, he took out three large volumes, and some manuscript papers written in a fine character.— Jarvis's *Translation*.

TO THE BEST OF PATRONS,

A PLEASED AND INDULGENT READER,

JEDEDIAH CLEISHBOTHAM

WISHES HEALTH, AND INCREASE, AND CONTENTMENT.

COURTEOUS READER,

IF ingratitude comprehendeth every vice, surely so foul a stain worst of all beseemeth him whose life has been devoted to instructing youth in virtue and in humane letters. Therefore have I chosen, in this prolegomen, to unload my burden of thanks at thy feet, for the favour with which thou hast kindly entertained the Tales of my Landlord. Certes, if thou hast chuckled over their facetious and festivous descriptions, or hast had thy mind fulfilled with pleasure at the strange and pleasant turns of fortune which they record, verily, I have also simpered when I beheld a second story with atticks,[1] that has arisen on the basis of my small domicile at Gandercleugh, the walls having been aforehand pronounced by Deacon Barrow to be capable of enduring such an elevation. Nor has it been without delectation, that I have endued a new coat, (snuff-brown, and with metal buttons), having all nether garments corresponding thereto. We do therefore lie, in respect of each other, under a reciprocation of benefits, whereof those received by me being the most solid, (in respect that a new house and a new coat are better than a new tale and an old song,[2]) it is meet that my gratitude should be expressed with the louder voice and more preponderating vehemence. And how should it be so expressed?—Certainly not in words only, but in act and deed. It is with this sole purpose, and disclaiming all intention of purchasing that

pendicle or pofle of land[3] called the Carlinescroft, lying adjacent to my
garden, and measuring seven acres, three roods, and four perches, that
I have committed to the eyes of those who thought well of the former
tomes, these four additional volumes of the Tales of my Landlord.
Not the less, if Peter Prayfort be minded to sell the said pofle, it is at
his own choice to say so; and, peradventure, he may meet with a
purchaser: unless (gentle reader) the pleasing pourtraictures of Peter
Pattieson, now given unto thee in particular, and unto the public in
general, shall have lost their favour in thine eyes, whereof I am no way
distrustful. And so much confidence do I repose in thy continued
favour, that should thy lawful occasions call thee to the town of
Gandercleugh, a place frequented by most at one time or other in their
lives, I will enrich thine eyes with a sight of those precious manuscripts
whence thou hast derived so much delectation, thy nose with a snuff
from my mull, and thy palate with a dram from my bottle of strong
waters, called by the learned of Gandercleugh, the Dominie's dribble
of drink.

It is there, O highly esteemed and beloved reader, thou wilt be able
to bear testimony, through the medium of thine own senses, against
the children of vanity, who have sought to identify thy friend and
servant with I know not what inditer of vain fables;[4] who hath
cumbered the world with his devices, but shrunken from the responsibility thereof. Truly, this hath been well termed a generation hard of
faith; since what can a man do to assert his property in a printed tome,
saving to put his name in the title-page thereof, with his description,
or designation as the lawyers term it, and place of abode? Of a surety,
I would have such sceptics consider how they themselves would brook
to have their works ascribed to others, their names and professions
imputed as forgeries, and their very existence brought into question;
even although, peradventure, it may be it is of little consequence to
any but themselves, not only whether they are living or dead, but even
whether they ever lived or no. Yet have my maligners carried their
uncharitable censures still farther.

These cavillers have not only doubted mine identity, although thus
plainly proved, but they have impeached my veracity and the authenticity[5] of my historical narratives! Verily, I can only say in answer,
that I have been cautelous in quoting mine authorities. It is true,
indeed, that if I had hearkened with only one ear, I might have
rehearsed my tale with more acceptation from those who love to hear
but half the truth. It is, it may hap, not altogether to the discredit of

our kindly nation of Scotland, that we are apt to take an interest, warm, yea partial, in the deeds and sentiments of our forefathers. The descendants of one, whom his adversaries describe as a perjured prelatist, are desirous that their predecessor should be held moderate in his power, and just in his execution of its privileges, when, truly, the unimpassioned peruser of the Annals of those times shall deem him sanguinary, violent, and tyrannical. Again, the representatives of the suffering non-conformists desire that their ancestors, the Cameronians, shall be represented not simply as honest enthusiasts, oppressed for conscience-sake, but persons of fine breeding and valiant heroes. Truly, the historian cannot gratify these predilections. He must needs describe the cavaliers as proud and high spirited, cruel, remorseless, and vindictive; the suffering party as honourably tenacious of their opinions under persecution; their own tempers being, however, sullen, fierce, and rude; their opinions absurd and extravagant, and their whole course of conduct that of persons whom hellebore would better have suited than prosecutions unto death for high-treason. Natheless, while such and so preposterous were the opinions on either side, there were, it cannot be doubted, men of virtue and worth on both, to entitle either party to claim merit from its martyrs. It has been demanded of me, Jedediah Cleishbotham, by what right I am entitled to constitute myself an impartial judge of these discrepancies of opinion, seeing (as it is stated) that I must necessarily have descended from one or other of the contending parties, and be, of course, wedded for better or for worse, according to the reasonable practice of Scotland, to its dogmata or opinions, and bound, as it were, by the tie matrimonial, or, to speak without metaphor, *ex jure sanguinis*, to maintain them in preference to all others.

But, nothing denying the rationality of the rule, which calls on all now living to rule their political and religious opinions by those of their great-grandfathers, and inevitable as seems the one or the other horn of the dilemma betwixt which my adversaries conceive they have pinned me to the wall, I yet spy some means of refuge, and claim a privilege to write and speak of both parties with impartiality. For, O ye powers of logic! when the prelatists and presbyterians of old times went together by the ears in this unlucky country, my ancestor (venerated be his memory!) was one of the people called Quakers, and suffered severe handling from either side, even to the extenuation of his purse and the incarceration of his person.[6]

Craving thy pardon, gentle Reader, for these few words concerning

me and mine, I rest, as above expressed, thy sure and obligated
friend,[*]

J.C.
GANDERCLEUGH,
this 1st of April, 1818.[7]

[*See p. 543 for the note on Scott's Quaker ancestors printed here in 1830.]

CHAPTER 1
Being Introductory

So down thy hill, romantic Ashbourn, glides
The Derby dilly, carrying six insides.

FRERE

THE times have changed in nothing more (we follow as we are wont the manuscript of Peter Pattieson,[1]) than in the rapid conveyance of intelligence and communication betwixt one part of Scotland and another. It is not above twenty or thirty years,[2] according to the evidence of many credible witnesses now alive, since a little miserable horse-cart, performing with difficulty a journey of thirty miles *per diem*, carried our mails from the capital of Scotland to its extremity. Nor was Scotland much more deficient in these accommodations, than our richer sister had been about eighty years before. Fielding, in his Tom Jones,[3] and Farquhar, in a little farce called the Stage-Coach,[4] have ridiculed the slowness of these vehicles of public accommodation. According to the latter authority, the highest bribe could only induce the coachman to promise to anticipate by half an hour the usual time of his arrival at the Bull and Mouth.[5]

But in both countries these ancient, slow, and sure modes of conveyance are now alike unknown; mail-coach races against mail-coach, and high-flyer against high-flyer, through the most remote districts of Britain. And in our village alone, three post-coaches, and four coaches with men armed, and in scarlet cassocks, thunder through the streets each day, and rival in brilliancy and noise the invention of the celebrated tyrant,

Demens, qui nimbos et non imitabile fulmen,
Ære et cornipedum pulsu, simulat, equorum.[6]

Now and then, to complete the resemblance, and to correct the presumption of the venturous charioteers, it does happen that the career of these dashing rivals of Salmoneus meets with as undesirable and violent a termination as that of their prototype. It is on such occasions that the Insides and Outsides, to use the appropriate vehicular phrases, have reason to rue the exchange of the slow and safe motion of the ancient Fly-coaches, which, compared with the chariots of Mr Palmer,[7] so ill deserve the name. The ancient vehicle used to settle quietly down, like a ship scuttled and left to sink by the gradual influx of the waters, while the modern is smashed to pieces with the velocity of the same vessel hurled against breakers, or rather with the fury of a bomb bursting at the conclusion of its career through the air. The late ingenious Mr Pennant,[8] whose humour it was to set his face in stern opposition to these speedy conveyances, had collected, I have heard, a formidable list of such casualties, which, joined to the imposition of innkeepers, whose charges the passenger has no time to dispute, the sauciness of the coachman, and the uncontrouled and despotic authority of the tyrant called the Guard, held forth a picture of horror, to which murder, theft, fraud, and peculation lent all their dark colouring. But that which gratifies the impatience of the human disposition will be practised in the teeth of danger, and in defiance of admonition; and, in despite of the Cambrian Antiquary, Mail-coaches not only roll their thunders round the base of Penmen-Maur and Cader-Edris, but

> Frighted Skiddaw hears afar
> The rattling of the unscythed car.[9]

And perhaps the echoes of Ben-Nevis may soon be awakened by the bugle, not of a warlike chieftain, but of the guard of a mail-coach.

It was a fine summer day, and our little school had obtained a half holiday by the intercession of a good-humoured visitor.* I expected by the coach a new number of an interesting periodical publication, and walked forward on the highway to meet it, with the impatience which Cowper has described as actuating the resident in the country when longing for intelligence from the mart of news:

> ————————The grand debate,
> The popular harangue,—the tart reply,—
> The logic, and the wisdom, and the wit,
> And the loud laugh,—I long to know them all;—
> I burn to set the imprison'd wranglers free,
> And give them voice and utterance again.[10]

It was with such feelings that I eyed the approach of the new coach,

---

* His Honour Gilbert Goslinn of Gandercleugh; for I love to be precise in matters of importance.—J.C.

lately established on our road, and known by the name of the Somerset, which, to say truth, possesses some interest for me, even when it conveys no such important information. The distant tremulous sound of its wheels was heard just as I gained the summit of the gentle ascent, called the Goslin-brae, from which you command an extensive view down the valley of the river Gander. The public road, which comes up the side of that stream, and crosses it at a bridge about a quarter of a mile from the place where I was standing, runs partly through enclosures and plantations, and partly through open pasture land. It is a childish amusement perhaps,—but my life has been spent with children, and why should not my pleasures be like theirs?—childish as it is then, I must own I have had great pleasure in watching the approach of the carriage, where the openings of the road permit it to be seen. The gay glancing of the equipage, its diminished and toy-like appearance at a distance, contrasted with the rapidity of its motion, its appearance and disappearance at intervals, and the progressively increasing sounds that announce its nearer approach, have all to the idle and listless spectator, who has nothing more important to attend to, something of awakening interest. The ridicule may attach to me, which is flung upon many an honest citizen, who watches from the window of his villa the passage of the stage-coach; but it is a very natural source of amusement notwithstanding, and many of those who join in the laugh are perhaps not unused to resort to it in secret.

On the present occasion, however, fate had decreed that I should not enjoy the consummation of the amusement, by seeing the coach rattle past me as I sat on the turf, and hearing the hoarse grating voice of the guard as he skimmed forth for my grasp the expected packet, without the carriage checking its course for an instant. I had seen the vehicle thunder down the hill that leads to the bridge with more than its usual impetuosity, glittering all the while by flashes from a cloudy tabernacle[11] of the dust which it had raised, and leaving a train behind it on the road resembling a wreath of summer mist. But it did not appear on the top of the nearer bank within the usual space of three minutes, which frequent observation had enabled me to ascertain was the medium time for crossing the bridge and mounting the ascent. When double that space had elapsed, I became alarmed, and walked hastily forward. As I came in sight of the bridge, the cause of delay was too manifest, for the Somerset had made a summerset in good earnest, and overturned so completely, that it was literally resting upon the ground, with the roof undermost, and the four wheels in the air. The "exertions of the guard and coachman," both of whom were gratefully commemorated in the newspapers, having succeeded in disentangling the horses by cutting the harness, were now proceeding to extricate the *insides* by a sort of summary and Cæsarean process of delivery, forcing the hinges from one of the doors which they could not open otherwise. In this manner were two disconsolate damsels set at liberty from the womb of the leathern conveniency. As they immediately began to settle their clothes, which were a little deranged, as may be presumed, I concluded they had received no injury, and did not venture to obtrude my services at their toilette, for which, I understand, I have since been reflected upon by the fair sufferers. The *outsides*, who must have been discharged from their elevated situation by a shock resembling the springing of a mine, escaped, nevertheless, with the usual allowance of scratches and bruises, excepting three, who, having been pitched into the river Gander, were dimly seen contending with the tide,[12] like the reliques of Æneas's shipwreck,—

Rari apparent nantes in gurgite vasto.[13]

I applied my poor exertions where they seemed to be most needed, and, with the assistance of one or two of the company who had escaped unhurt, easily succeeded in fishing out two of the unfortunate passengers, who were stout active young fellows; and but for the preposterous length of their great-coats, and the equally fashionable latitude and longitude of their Wellington trowsers, would have required little assistance from any one. The third was sickly and elderly, and might have perished but for the efforts used to preserve him.

When the two great-coated gentlemen had extricated themselves from the river, and shaken their ears like huge water-dogs, a violent altercation ensued betwixt them and the coachman and guard, concerning the cause of their overthrow. In the course of the squabble, I observed that both my new acquaintances belonged to the law, and that their professional sharpness was like to prove an overmatch for the surly and official tone of the guardians of the vehicle. The dispute ended in the guard assuring the passengers that they should have seats in a heavy coach which would pass that spot in less than half an hour, providing it was not full. Chance seemed to favour this arrangement, for when the expected vehicle arrived there were only two places occupied in a carriage which professed to carry six. The two ladies who had been disinterred out of the fallen vehicle were readily admitted, but positive objections were stated by those previously in possession to the admittance of the two lawyers, whose wetted garments being much of the nature of well-soaked spunges, there was every reason to believe they would refund a considerable part of the water they had collected, to the manifest inconvenience of their fellow-passengers. On the other hand, the lawyers rejected a seat on the roof, alleging that they had only taken that station for pleasure for one stage, but were entitled in all respects to free egress and regress from the interior, to which their contract positively referred. After some altercation, in which something was said upon the edict *Nautæ caupones stabularii*,[14] the coach went off, leaving the learned gentlemen to abide by their action of damages.

They immediately applied to me to guide them to the next village and the best inn; and from the account I gave them of the Wallace-head,[15] declared they were much better pleased to stop there than to go forward upon the terms of that impudent scoundrel the guard of the Somerset. All that they now wanted was a lad to carry their travelling bags, who was easily procured from an adjoining cottage; and they prepared to walk forward, when they found there was another passenger in the same deserted situation with themselves. This was the elderly and sickly-looking person, who had been precipitated into the river along with the two young lawyers. He, it seems, had been too modest to push his own plea against the coachman when he saw that of his betters rejected, and now remained behind with a look of timid anxiety, plainly intimating that he was deficient in those means of recommendation which are necessary passports to the hospitality of an inn.

I ventured to call the attention of the two dashing young blades, for such they seemed, to the desolate condition of their fellow-traveller. They took the hint with ready good-nature.

"O true, Mr Dunover," said one of the youngsters, "you must not remain on the pavé here; you must go and have some dinner with us— Halkit and I must have a post-chaise to go on, at all events, and we will set you down wherever suits you best."

The poor man, for such his dress, as well as his diffidence, bespoke him, made the sort of acknowledging bow by which a Scotsman says, "It's too much honour for the like o' me;" and followed humbly behind his gay patrons, all three besprinkling the dusty road as they walked along with the moisture of their drenched garments, and exhibiting the singular and somewhat ridiculous appearance of three persons suffering from the opposite extreme of humidity, while the summer sun was at its height, and every thing else around them had the expression of heat and drought. The ridicule did not escape the young gentlemen themselves, and they had made what might be received as one or two tolerable jests on the subject before they had advanced far on their peregrination.

"We cannot complain, like Cowley," said one of them, "that Gideon's fleece[16] remains dry, while all around is moist; this is the reverse of the miracle."

"We ought to be received with gratitude in this good town; we bring a supply of what they seem to need most," said Halkit.

"And distribute it with unparalleled generosity," replied his companion; "performing the part of three water-carts for the benefit of their dusty roads."

"We come before them too," said Halkit, "in full professional force—counsel and agent"—

"And client too," said the young advocate, looking behind him, and then added, lowering his voice, "that looks as if he had kept such dangerous company too long."

It was, indeed, too true, that the humble follower of the gay young men had the thread-bare appearance of a worn-out litigant, and I could not but smile at the conceit, though anxious to conceal my mirth from the object of it.

When we arrived at the Wallace Inn, the elder of the Edinburgh gentlemen, and whom I understood to be a barrister, insisted that I should remain and take part of their dinner; and their enquiries and demands speedily put my Landlord and his whole family in motion to produce the best cheer which the larder and cellar afforded, and proceed to cook it to the best advantage, a science in which our entertainers seemed to be admirably skilled. In other respects, they were lively young men in the hey-day of youth and good spirits, playing the part which is common to the higher classes of the law at Edinburgh, and which nearly resembles that of the young Templars in the days of Steele and Addison.[17] An air of giddy gaiety mingled with the good sense, taste, and information which their conversation exhibited; and it seemed to be their object to unite the character of men of fashion and lovers of the polite arts. A fine gentleman, bred up in the thorough idleness and inanity of pursuit, which I understand is absolutely necessary to the character in perfection, might in all probability have traced a tinge of professional pedantry which marked the barrister in spite of his efforts, and something of active bustle in his companion, and would certainly have detected more than a fashionable mixture of information and animated interest in the language of both. But to me, who had no pretensions to be so critical, my companions seemed to form a very happy mixture of good breeding and liberal information, with a disposition to lively rattle, pun, and jest, amusing to a grave man, because it is what he himself can least easily command.

The thin pale-faced man, whom their good nature had brought into their society, looked out of place, as well as out of spirits; sate on the edge of his seat, and kept the chair at two feet distance from the table; thus incommoding himself considerably in conveying the victuals to his mouth, as if by way of penance for partaking of them in the company of his superiors. A short time after dinner, declining all entreaty to take any share of the wine, which circulated freely round, he informed himself of the hour when the chaise had been ordered to attend; and saying, he would be in readiness, modestly withdrew from the apartment.

"Jack," said the barrister to his companion, "I remember that poor fellow's face; you spoke more truly than you were aware of; he really is one of my clients, poor man."

"Poor man!" echoed Halkit—"I suppose you mean he is your one and only client."

"That's not my fault, Jack," replied the other, whose name I discovered was Hardie. "You are to give me all your business, you know; and if you have none, the learned gentleman here knows nothing can come of nothing."[18]

"You seem to have brought something to nothing though, in the case of that honest man," said the agent; "he looks as if he were just about to honour with his residence the HEART OF MID-LOTHIAN."

"You are mistaken—he is just delivered from it—our friend here looks for an explanation. Pray, Mr Pattieson, have you ever been in Edinburgh?"

I answered in the affirmative.

"Then you must have passed, occasionally at least, though probably not so frequently and faithfully as I am doomed to do, through a narrow intricate passage, leading out of the north-west corner of the Parliament Square, and passing by a high and antique building, with turrets and iron grates,

Making good the saying odd,
Near the church and far from God"—[19]

Mr Halkit broke in upon his learned counsel, to contribute his moiety to the riddle—"Having at the door the sign of the Red Man"——[20]

"And being on the whole," resumed the counsellor, interrupting his friend in his turn, "a sort of place where misfortune is happily confounded with guilt, where all who are in wish to get out"——

"And where none who have the good luck to be out wish to get in," added his companion.

"I conceive you, gentlemen," replied I; "you mean the prison."

"The prison," added the young lawyer—"You have hit it—the very reverend Tolbooth itself; and let me tell you, you are obliged to us for describing it with so much modesty and brevity; for with whatever amplifications we might have chosen to decorate the subject, you lay entirely at our mercy, since the Fathers Conscript of our city have decreed, that the venerable edifice itself shall not remain[21] in existence to confirm or to confute us."

"Then the Tolbooth of Edinburgh is called the Heart of Mid-Lothian?" said I.

"So termed and reputed, I assure you."

"I think," said I, with the bashful diffidence with which a man lets slip a pun in presence of his superiors, "the metropolitan county may, in that case, be said to have a sad heart."

"Right as my glove,[22] Mr Pattieson," added Mr Hardie; "and a close heart, and a hard heart—Keep it up, Jack."

"And a wicked heart, and a poor heart," answered Halkit, doing his best.

"And yet it may be called in some sort a strong heart, and a high heart," rejoined the advocate. "You see I can put you both out of heart."

"I have played all my hearts," said the younger gentleman.

"Then we'll have another lead,"[23] answered his companion.—"And as to the old and condemned Tolbooth, what pity the same honour cannot be done to it as has been done to many of its inmates. Why should not the Tolbooth have its 'Last Speech, Confession, and Dying Words?'[24] The old stones would be just as conscious of the honour, as many a poor devil who has dangled like a tassel at the west end[25] of it, while the hawkers were shouting a confession the culprit had never heard of."

"I am afraid," said I, "if I might presume to give my opinion, it would be a tale of unvaried sorrow and guilt."

"Not entirely, my friend," said Hardie; "a prison is a world within itself, and has its own business, griefs, and joys peculiar to its circle. Its inmates are sometimes short-lived, but so are soldiers on service; they are poor relatively to the world without, but there are degrees of wealth and poverty among them, and so some are relatively rich also. They cannot stir abroad, but neither can the garrison of a besieged fort, or the crew of a ship at sea; and they are not under a dispensation quite so desperate as either, for they may have as much food as they have money to buy, and are not obliged to work whether they have food or not."[26]

"But what variety of incident," said I, (not without a secret view to my present task), "could possibly be derived from such a work as you are pleased to talk of?"

"Infinite," replied the young advocate. "Whatever of guilt, crime, imposture, folly, unheard of misfortune, and unlooked-for change of fortune, can be found to chequer life, my Last Speech of the Tolbooth should illustrate with examples sufficient to gorge even the public's all-devouring appetite for the wonderful and horrible. The inventor of fictitious narratives has to rack his brains for means to diversify his tale, and after all can hardly hit upon characters or incidents which have not been used again and again, until they are familiar to the eye of the reader, so that the elopement, the *enlevement*, the desperate wound of which the hero never dies, the burning fever from which the heroine is sure to recover, become a mere matter of course. I join with my honest friend Crabbe,[27] and have such an unlucky propensity to hope when hope is lost, and to rely upon the cork-jacket, which carries the heroes of romance safe through all the billows of affliction." He then declaimed the following passage, rather with too much than too little emphasis:

> "Much have I fear'd, but am no more afraid,
> When some chaste beauty, by some wretch betray'd,
> Is drawn away with such distracted speed,
> That she anticipates a dreadful deed.
> Not so do I—Let solid walls impound
> The captive fair, and dig a moat around;
> Let there be brazen locks and bars of steel,
> And keepers cruel, such as never feel;
> With not a single note the purse supply,

And when she begs, let men and maids deny;
Be windows those from which she dares not fall,
And help so distant, 'tis in vain to call;
Still means of freedom will some Power devise,
And from the baffled ruffian snatch his prize.[28]

"The end of uncertainty," he concluded, "is the death of interest, and hence it happens that no one now reads novels."

"Hear him, ye gods!" returned his companion. "I assure you, Mr Pattieson, you will hardly visit this learned gentleman, but you are likely to find the new novel most in repute lying on his table, snugly intrenched, however, beneath Stair's Institutes,[29] or an open volume of Morrison's Decisions."[30]

"Do I deny it?" said the hopeful jurisconsult, "or wherefore should I, since it is well known these Dalilahs seduce my wisers and my betters? May they not be found lurking amidst the multiplied memorials of our most distinguished counsel, and even peeping from under the cushion of a judge's arm-chair? Our seniors at the bar, within the bar,[31] and even on the bench read novels, and, if not belied, some of them have written novels into the bargain. I only say, that I read from habit and from indolence, not from real interest; that, like Ancient Pistol[32] devouring his leek, I read and swear till I get to the end of the narrative. But not so in the real records of human vagaries—not so in the State Trials, or in the Books of Adjournal, where every now and then you read new pages of the human heart, and turns of fortune far beyond what the boldest novelist ever attempted to produce from the coinage of his brain."[33]

"And for such narratives," I asked, "you suppose the History of the Prison of Edinburgh might afford appropriate materials?"

"In a degree unusually ample, my dear sir," said Hardie—"fill your glass, however, in the meanwhile. Was it not for many years[34] the place in which the Scottish parliament met? Was it not Jamie's place of refuge, when the mob,[35] inflamed by a seditious preacher, broke forth on him with the cries of 'The sword of the Lord and of Gideon[36]—bring forth the wicked Haman?'[37] Since that time how many hearts have throbbed within these walls, as the tolling of the neighbouring bell announced to them how fast the sands of their life were ebbing; how many must have sunk at the sound—how many were supported by stubborn pride and dogged resolution—how many by the consolations of religion? Have there not been some, who, looking back on the motives of their crimes, were scarce able to understand how they should have had such temptation as to seduce them from virtue? and have there not, perhaps, been others, who, sensible of their innocence, were divided between indignation at the undeserved doom which they were to undergo, consciousness that they had not deserved it, and racking anxiety to discover some way in which they might yet vindicate themselves? Do you suppose any of these deep, powerful, and agitating feelings can be recorded and perused without exciting a corresponding depth of deep, powerful, and agitating interest?—O! do but wait till I publish the *Causes Celebres* of Caledonia,[38] and you will find no want of a novel or a tragedy for some time to come. The true thing will triumph over the brightest inventions of the most ardent imagination. *Magna est veritas et prævalebit.*"[39]

"I have understood," said I, encouraged by the affability of my rattling entertainer, "that less of this interest must attach to Scottish jurisprudence than to that of any other country. The general morality of our people, their sober and prudent habits"—

"Secure them," said the barrister, "against any great increase of professional thieves and depredators, but not against wild and wayward starts of fancy and passion, producing crimes of an extraordinary description, which are precisely those to the detail of which we listen with thrilling interest. England has been much longer a highly civilized country; her subjects have been very long strictly amenable to laws administered without fear or favour, a complete division of labour[40] has taken place among her subjects, and the very thieves and robbers form a distinct class in society, subdivided among themselves according to the subject of their depredations, and the mode in which they carry them on, acting upon regular habits and principles, which can be calculated and anticipated at Bow Street, Hatton Garden, or the Old Bailey.[41] Our sister kingdom is like a cultivated field,—the farmer expects that, in spite of all his care, a certain number of weeds will rise with the corn, and can tell you before hand their names and appearance. But Scotland is like one of her own Highland glens, and the moralist who reads the records of her criminal jurisprudence, will find as many curious and anomalous facts in the history of mind, as the botanist will detect rare specimens among her dingles and cliffs."

"And that's all the good you have obtained from three perusals of the Commentaries[42] on Scottish Criminal Jurisprudence?" said his companion. "I suppose the learned author very little thinks that the facts which his erudition and acuteness have accumulated for the illustration of legal doctrines, might be so arranged as to form a sort of appendix to the half-bound and slip-shod[43] volumes of the circulating library."[44]

"I'll bet you a pint of claret,"[45] said the elder lawyer, "that he will not feel sore at the comparison. But as we say at the bar, 'I beg I may not be interrupted;' I have much more to say upon my Scottish collection of *Causes Celebres*. You will please recollect the scope and motive given for the contrivance and execution of many extraordinary and daring crimes, by the long civil dissentions of Scotland—by the hereditary jurisdictions,[46] which, until 1748, rested the investigation of crimes in judges, ignorant, partial, or interested—by the habits of the gentry, shut up in their distant and solitary mansion-houses, nursing their revengeful passions just to keep their blood from stagnating—not to mention that amiable national qualification, called the *perfervidum ingenium Scotorum*,[47] which our lawyers join in alleging as a reason for the severity of some of our enactments. When I come to treat of matters so mysterious, deep, and dangerous, as these circumstances have given rise to, the blood of each reader shall be curdled, and his epidermis crisped into goose skin.—But 'st—here comes the landlord, with tidings, I suppose, that the chaise is ready."

It was no such thing—the tidings bore, that no chaise could be had that evening, for Sir Peter Plyem had carried forward my landlord's two pair of horses that morning to the ancient royal borough of Bubbleburgh, to look after his interest there. But as Bubbleburgh is only one of a set of five boroughs which club their shares for a member of parliament, Sir Peter's adversary had judiciously watched his departure, in order to commence a canvass in the no less royal borough of Bitem, which, as all the world knows, lies at the very termination of Sir Peter's avenue, and has been held in leading strings by him and his ancestors for time immemorial. Now Sir Peter was thus placed in the situation of an ambitious monarch, who, after having commenced a daring inroad into his enemies' territories, is suddenly recalled by an invasion of his own hereditary dominions. He was obliged in consequence to return from the half-won borough of Bubbleburgh, to look after the half-lost borough of Bitem, and the two pair of horses which had carried him that morning to Bubbleburgh, were now forcibly detained to transport him, his agent, his valet, his jester, and his hard-drinker, across the country to Bitem. The cause of this detention, which to me was of as little consequence as it may be to the reader, was important enough to my companions to reconcile them to the delay. Like eagles, they smelled the battle afar off,[48] ordered a magnum of claret and beds at the Wallace, and entered at full career into the Bubbleburgh and Bitem politics, with all the probable "petitions and complaints" to which they were likely to give rise.

In the midst of an anxious, animated, and, to me, most unintelligible discussion concerning provosts, baillies, deacons, sets of boroughs, leets, town-clerks, burgesses resident and non-resident, all of a sudden the lawyer recollected himself. "Poor Dunover, we must not forget him;" and the landlord was dispatched in quest of the *pauvre honteux*, with an earnestly civil invitation to him for the rest of the evening. I could not help asking the young gentlemen if they knew the history of this poor man, and the counsellor applied himself to his pocket to recover the memorial or brief from which he had stated his cause.

"He has been a candidate for our *remedium miserabile*," said Mr Hardie, "commonly called a *cessio bonorum*. As there are divines who have doubted the eternity of future punishments, so the Scottish lawyers seem to have thought that the crime of poverty might be atoned for by something short of perpetual imprisonment. After a month's confinement, you must know, a prisoner for debt is entitled, on a sufficient statement to our Supreme Court, setting forth the amount of his funds, and the nature of his misfortunes, and surrendering all his effects to his creditors, to claim to be discharged from prison."

"I had heard," I replied, "of such a humane regulation."

"Yes," said Halkit, "and the beauty of it is, as the foreign fellow said, you may get the *cessio* when the *bonorums* are all spent—But what, are you puzzling in your pockets to seek your only memorial among old play-bills, letters requesting a meeting of the Faculty, rules of the Speculative Society, syllabus' of lectures—all the miscellaneous contents of a young advocate's pocket, which contains every thing but brieves and bank-notes? Can you not state a case of *cessio* without your memorial? Why it is done every Saturday. The events follow each other as regularly as clock-work, and one form of condescendence might suit every one of them."

"This is very unlike the variety of distress which this gentleman stated to fall under the consideration of your judges," said I.

"True," replied Halkit; "but Hardie spoke of criminal jurisprudence, and this business is purely civil. I could plead a *cessio* myself without the inspiring honours of a gown and three-tailed periwig—

Listen.—My client was bred a journeyman weaver—made some little money—took a farm—(for conducting a farm, like driving a gig, comes by nature)—late severe times—induced to sign bills with a friend, for which he received no value—landlord sequestrates—creditors accept a composition—pursuer sets up a public-house—fails a second time—is incarcerated for a debt of ten pounds, seven shillings and sixpence—his debts amount to blank—his losses to blank—his funds to blank—leaving a balance of blank in his favour. There is no opposition; your lordships will please grant commission to take his oath."

Hardie now renounced his ineffectual search for the brief, in which there was perhaps a little affectation, and told us the tale of poor Dunover's distresses, with a tone in which a degree of feeling, which he seemed ashamed of as unprofessional, mingled with his attempts at wit, and did him more honour. It was one of those tales which seem to argue a sort of ill luck or fatality attached to the hero. A well informed, industrious, and blameless, but poor and bashful man, had in vain essayed all the usual means by which others acquire independence, yet had never succeeded beyond the attainment of bare subsistence. During a brief gleam of hope, rather than of actual prosperity, he had added a wife and family to his cares, but the dawn was speedily overcast. Every thing retrograded with him towards the verge of the miry Slough of Despond,[49] which yawns for insolvent debtors: and after catching at each twig, and experiencing the protracted agony of feeling them one by one elude his grasp, he actually sunk into the miry pit whence he had been extricated by the professional exertions of Hardie.

"And, I suppose, now you have dragged this poor devil ashore, you will leave him half naked on the beach to provide for himself?" said Halkit. "Hark ye,"—and he whispered something in his ear, of which the penetrating and insinuating words, "Interest with my Lord," alone reached mine.

"It is *pessimi exempli*," said Hardie, laughing, "to provide for a ruined client; but I was thinking of what you mention, providing it can be managed—But hush! here he comes."

The recent relation of the poor man's misfortunes had given him, I was pleased to observe, a claim to the attention and respect of the young men, who treated him with great civility, and gradually engaged him in a conversation, which, much to my satisfaction, again turned upon the *Causes Celebres* of Scotland. Emboldened by the kindness with which he was treated, Mr Dunover began to contribute his share to the amusement of the evening. Jails, like other places, have their ancient traditions, known only to the inhabitants, and handed down from one set of the melancholy lodgers to the next who occupy their cells. Some of these, which Dunover mentioned, were interesting, and served to illustrate the narratives of remarkable trials, which Hardie had at his finger-ends, and which his companion was also well skilled in. This sort of conversation passed away the evening till the early hour when Mr Dunover chose to retire to rest, and I also retreated to take down memorandums of what I had learned, in order to add another narrative to those which it has been my chief amusement to collect, and to write out in detail. The two young men ordered a broiled bone, Madeira negus, and a pack of cards, and commenced a game at picquet.

Next morning the travellers left Gandercleugh. I afterwards learned from the papers that both have been since engaged in the great political cause of Bubbleburgh and Bitem, a summary case, and entitled to particular dispatch; but which, it is thought, nevertheless, may outlast the duration of the parliament to which the contest refers. Mr Halkit, as the newspapers informed me, acts as agent or solicitor; and Mr Hardie opened for Sir Peter Plyem with singular ability, and to such good purpose, that I understand he has since had fewer play-bills and more briefs in his pocket. And both the young gentlemen deserve their good fortune; for I learned from Dunover, who called on me some weeks afterwards, and communicated the intelligence with tears in his eyes, that their interest had availed to obtain him a small office for the decent maintenance of his family; and that, after a train of constant and uninterrupted misfortune, he could trace a dawn of prosperity to his having the good fortune to be flung from the top of a mail-coach into the river Gander, in company with an advocate and a writer to the signet. The reader will not perhaps deem himself equally obliged to the accident, since it brings upon him the following narrative, founded upon the conversation of the evening.

CHAPTER 2

Whoe'er's been at Paris must needs know the Grêve,
The fatal retreat of the unfortunate brave,
Where honour and justice most oddly contribute,
To ease heroes' pains by an halter and gibbet.

There death breaks the shackles which force had put on,
And the hangman completes what the judge but began;
There the squire of the pad, and the knight of the post,
Find their pains no more baulk'd, and their hopes no more cross'd.

PRIOR

IN former times, England had her Tyburn,[1] to which the devoted victims of justice were conducted in solemn procession, up what is now called Oxford-Road. In Edinburgh, a large open street, or rather oblong square, surrounded by high houses, called the Grassmarket,[2] was used for the same melancholy purpose. It was not ill chosen for such a scene, being of considerable extent, and therefore fit to accommodate a great number of spectators, such as are usually assembled by this melancholy spectacle. On the other hand, few of the houses which surround it were, even in early times, inhabited by persons of fashion; so that those likely to be offended or over deeply affected by such unpleasant exhibitions, were not in the way of having their quiet disturbed by them. The houses in the Grassmarket are, generally speaking, of a mean description; yet the place is not without some features of grandeur, being overhung by the southern side of the huge rock on which the castle stands, and by the moss-grown battlements and turreted walls of that ancient fortress.

It was the custom, until within these five-and-twenty years,[3] or thereabouts, to use this esplanade for the scene of public executions. The fatal day was announced to the public, by the appearance of a huge black gallows-tree towards the eastern end of the Grassmarket. This ill-omened apparition was of great height, with a scaffold surrounding it, and a double ladder placed against it, for the ascent of the unhappy criminal and the executioner. As this apparatus was always arranged before dawn, it seemed as if the gallows had grown out of the earth in the course of one night, like the production of some foul demon; and I well remember the fright with which the schoolboys, when I was one of their number,[4] used to regard these ominous signs of deadly preparation. On the night after the execution the gallows again disappeared, and was conveyed in silence and darkness to the place where it was usually deposited, which was one of the vaults under the Parliament House, or courts of justice.[5] This mode of execution is now exchanged for one similar to that in front of Newgate,[6]—with what beneficial effect is uncertain. The mental sufferings of the convict are indeed shortened. He no longer stalks between the attendant clergymen, dressed in his graves-clothes, through a considerable part of the city, looking like a moving and walking corpse, while yet an inhabitant of this world; but, as the ultimate purpose of punishment has in view the prevention of crimes, it may at least be doubted, whether, in abridging the melancholy ceremonial, we have not in part diminished that appalling effect upon the spectators which is the useful end of all such inflictions, and in consideration of which alone, unless in very particular cases, capital sentences can be altogether justified.

On the 7th day of September, 1736,[7] these ominous preparations for execution were descried in the place we have described, and at an early hour the space around began to be occupied by several groupes, who gazed on the scaffold and gibbet with a stern and vindictive shew of satisfaction very seldom testified by the populace, whose good-nature, in most cases, forgets the crime of the condemned person, and dwells only on his misery. But the act of which the expected culprit had been convicted was of a description calculated nearly and closely to awaken and irritate the resentful feelings of the multitude. The tale is well known; yet it is necessary to recapitulate its leading circumstances, for the better understanding what is to follow; and the narrative may prove long, but I trust not uninteresting, even to those who have heard its general issue. At any rate, some detail is necessary, in order to render intelligible the subsequent events of our narrative.

Contraband trade, though it strikes at the root of legitimate government, by encroaching on its revenues,—though it injures the fair trader, and debauches the minds of those engaged in it,—is not usually looked upon, either by the vulgar or by their betters, in a very heinous point of view. On the contrary, in those counties where it prevails, the cleverest, boldest, and most intelligent of the peasantry, are uniformly engaged in illicit transactions, and very often with the sanction of the farmers and inferior gentry. Smuggling was almost

universal in Scotland in the reigns of George I. and II.;[8] for the
people, unaccustomed to imposts,[9] and regarding them as an unjust
aggression upon their ancient liberties, made no scruple to elude them
whenever it was possible to do so.

The county of Fife, bounded by two firths on the south and north,
and by the sea on the east, and having a number of small sea-ports,
was long famed for maintaining successfully a contraband trade; and,
as there were many seafaring men residing there, who had been pirates
and buccaneers in their youth, there were not wanting a sufficient
number of daring men to carry it on. Among these, a fellow, called
Andrew Wilson,[10] originally a baker in the village of Pathhead, was
particularly obnoxious to the revenue officers. He was possessed of
great personal strength, courage, and cunning,—was perfectly acquainted with the coast, and capable of conducting the most desperate
enterprizes. On several occasions he succeeded in baffling the
pursuit and researches of the king's officers; but he became so much
the object of their suspicious and watchful attention, that at length he
was totally ruined by repeated seizures. The man became desperate.
He considered himself as robbed and plundered; and took it into his
head, that he had a right to make reprisals, as he could find opportunity. Where the heart is prepared for evil, opportunity is seldom long
wanting. This Wilson learned, that the Collector of the Customs at
Kirkcaldy had come to Pittenweem, in the course of his official round
of duty, with a considerable sum of public money in his custody. As
the amount was greatly within the value of the goods which had been
seized from him, Wilson felt no scruple of conscience in resolving to
reimburse himself for his losses, at the expence of the Collector and
the revenue. He associated with himself one Robertson, and other two
idle young men, whom, having been concerned in the same illicit
trade, he persuaded to view the transaction in the same justifiable light
in which he himself considered it. They watched the motions of the
Collector; they broke forcibly into the house where he lodged,—
Wilson, with two of his associates, entering the Collector's apartment,
while Robertson, the fourth, kept watch at the door with a drawn
cutlass in his hand. The officer of the customs, conceiving his life in
danger, escaped out of his bed-room window, and fled in his shirt, so
that the plunderers, with much ease, possessed themselves of about
two hundred pounds of public money. This robbery was committed in
a very audacious manner, for several persons were passing in the street
at the time. But Robertson, representing the noise they heard as a

dispute or fray betwixt the Collector and the people of the house, the worthy citizens of Pittenweem felt themselves no way called on to interfere in behalf of the obnoxious revenue officer; so, satisfying themselves with this very superficial account of the matter, like the Levite in the parable,[11] they passed on the opposite side of the way. An alarm was at length given, military were called in, the depredators were pursued, the booty recovered, and Wilson and Robertson tried and condemned to death, chiefly on the evidence of an accomplice.

Many thought, that in consideration of the men's erroneous opinion of the nature of the action they had committed, justice might have been satisfied with a less forfeiture than that of two lives. On the other hand, from the audacity of the fact, a severe example was judged necessary, and such was the opinion of the government. When it became apparent that the sentence of death was to be executed, files and other implements necessary for their escape, were transmitted secretly to the culprits by a friend from without. By these means they sawed a bar out of one of the prison-windows, and might have made their escape, but for the obstinacy of Wilson, who, as he was daringly resolute, was doggedly pertinacious of his opinion. His comrade, Robertson, a young and slender man, proposed to make the experiment of passing the foremost through the gap they had made, and enlarging it from the outside, if necessary, to allow Wilson free passage. Wilson, however, insisted on making the first experiment, and being a robust and lusty man, he not only found it impossible to get through betwixt the bars, but, by his struggles, he jammed himself so fast, that he was unable to draw his body back again. In these circumstances discovery became unavoidable, and sufficient precautions were taken by the jailer to prevent any repetition of the same attempt. Robertson uttered not a word of reflection on his companion for the consequences of his obstinacy; but it appeared from the sequel, that Wilson's mind was deeply impressed with the recollection, that, but for him, his comrade, over whose mind he exercised considerable influence, would not have engaged in the criminal enterprise which had terminated thus fatally; and that now he had become his destroyer a second time, since, but for his obstinacy, Robertson might have effected his escape. Minds like Wilson's, even when exercised in evil practices, sometimes retain the power of thinking and resolving with enthusiastic generosity. His whole thoughts were now bent on the possibility of saving Robertson's life, without the least respect to his own. The resolution which he adopted, and the manner in which he carried it into effect, were striking and unusual.

Adjacent to the Tolbooth or city jail of Edinburgh, is one of the three churches into which the Cathedral of St Giles is now divided,[12] called, from its vicinity, the Tolbooth Church. It was the custom, that criminals under sentence of death were brought to this church, with a sufficient guard, to hear and join in public worship on the Sabbath before execution. It was supposed that the hearts of these unfortunate persons, however hardened before against feelings of devotion, could not but be accessible to them upon uniting their thoughts and voices, for the last time, along with their fellow-mortals, in addressing their Creator. And to the rest of the congregation, it was thought it could not but be impressive and affecting, to find their devotions mingling with those, who, sent by the doom of an earthly tribunal to appear where the whole earth is judged, might be considered as beings trembling on the verge of eternity. The practice, however edifying, has been discontinued in consequence of the incident we are about to detail.

The clergyman, whose duty it was to officiate in the Tolbooth Church, had concluded an affecting discourse, part of which was particularly directed to the unfortunate men, Wilson and Robertson, who were in the pew set apart for the persons in their unhappy situation, each secured betwixt two soldiers of the city guard. The clergyman had reminded them, that the next congregation they must join would be that of the just, or of the unjust: that the psalms they now heard must be exchanged, in the space of two brief days, for eternal hallelujahs, or eternal lamentations; and that this fearful alternative must depend upon the state to which they might be able to bring their minds before the moment of awful preparation: that they should not despair on account of the suddenness of the summons, but rather feel this comfort in their misery, that, though all who now lifted the voice, or bent the knee in conjunction with them, lay under the same sentence of certain death, they only had the advantage of knowing the precise moment at which it should be executed upon them. "Therefore," urged the good man, his voice trembling with emotion, "redeem the time, my unhappy brethren, which is yet left, and remember, that, with the grace of Him to whom space and time are but as nothing, salvation may yet be assured, even in the pittance of delay which the laws of your country afford you."

Robertson was observed to weep at these words; but Wilson seemed as one whose brain had not entirely received their meaning, or whose thoughts were deeply impressed with some different subject;—an expression so natural to a person in his situation, that it excited neither suspicion nor surprise.

The benediction was pronounced as usual, and the congregation was dismissed, many lingering to indulge their curiosity with a more fixed look at the two criminals, who now, as well as their guards, rose up, as if to depart when the crowd should permit them. A murmur of compassion was heard to pervade the spectators, the more general, perhaps, on account of the alleviating circumstances of the case; when all at once, Wilson, who, as we have already noticed, was a very strong man, seized two of the soldiers, one with each hand, and calling at the same time to his companion, "Run, Geordie, run!" threw himself on a third, and fastened his teeth on the collar of his coat. Robertson stood for a second as if thunderstruck, and unable to avail himself of the opportunity of escape; but the cry of "Run, run," being echoed from many around, whose feelings surprised them into a very natural interest in his behalf, he shook off the grasp of the remaining soldier, threw himself over the pew, mixed with the dispersing congregation, none of whom felt inclined to stop a poor wretch taking this last chance for his life, gained the door of the church, and was lost to all pursuit.

The generous intrepidity which Wilson had displayed on this occasion augmented the feeling of compassion which attended his fate. The public, where their own prejudices are not concerned, are easily engaged on the side of disinterestedness and humanity, admired Wilson's behaviour, and rejoiced in Robertson's escape. This general feeling was so great, that it excited a vague report that Wilson would be rescued at the place of execution, either by the mob or by some of his old associates, or by some second extraordinary and unexpected exertion of strength and courage on his own part. The magistrates thought it their duty to provide against the possibility of disturbance. They ordered out, for protection of the execution of the sentence, the greater part of their own City Guard, under the command of Captain Porteous, a man whose name became too memorable from the melancholy circumstances of the day and subsequent events. It may be necessary to say a word about this person, and the corps which he commanded. But the subject is of importance sufficient to deserve another chapter.

CHAPTER 3

And thou, great god of aqua-vitæ!
Wha sways the empire of this city,
(When fou we're sometimes capernoity,)
Be thou prepared,
To save us frae that black banditti,
The City-Guard!
FERGUSSON'S *Daft Days*

CAPTAIN John Porteous,[1] a name memorable in the traditions of Edinburgh, as well as in the records of criminal jurisprudence, was the son of a citizen of Edinburgh, who endeavoured to breed him up to his own mechanical trade of a tailor. The youth, however, had a wild and irreclaimable propensity to dissipation, which finally sent him to serve in the corps long maintained in the service of the States of Holland, and called the Scotch-Dutch. Here he learned military discipline; and, returning afterwards, in the course of an idle and wandering life, to his native city, his services were required by the magistrates of Edinburgh in the disturbed year 1715,[2] for disciplining their City Guard, in which he shortly afterwards received a captain's commission. It was only by his military skill, and an alert and resolute character as an officer of police, that he merited this promotion, for he is said to have been a man of profligate habits, an unnatural son, and a brutal husband. He was, however, useful in his station, and his harsh and fierce manners rendered him formidable to rioters or other disturbers of the public peace.

The corps[3] in which he held his command is, or perhaps we should rather say *was*, a body of about one hundred and twenty soldiers, divided into three companies, and regularly armed, clothed, and embodied. They were chiefly veterans who enlisted in this corps, having the benefit of working at their trades when they were off duty. These men had the charge of preserving public order, repressing riots and street robberies, acting, in short, as an armed police, and attending on all public occasions where confusion or popular disturbance might be expected.[*] Poor Fergusson,[5] whose irregularities sometimes led

[* The Lord Provost was ex-officio commander and colonel of the corps, which might be increased to three hundred men when the times required it. No other drum but theirs

him into unpleasant rencontres with these military conservators of public order, and who mentions them so often that he may be termed their poet laureate, thus admonishes his readers, warned doubtless by his own experience:

> Gude folk, as ye come frae the fair,
> Bide yont frae this black squad;
> There's nae sic savages elsewhere
> Allow'd to wear cockad.[6]

In fact, the soldiers of the City Guard, being, as we have said, in general discharged veterans, who had strength enough remaining for this municipal duty, and being, moreover, for the greater part Highlanders, were neither by birth, or education and former habits, trained to endure with much patience the insults of the rabble, or the provoking petulance of truant schoolboys, and idle debauchees of all descriptions, with whom their occupation brought them into contact. On the contrary, the tempers of the poor old fellows were soured by the indignities with which the mob distinguished them on many occasions, and frequently might have required the soothing strains of the poet we have just quoted—

> O soldiers! for your ain dear sakes,
> For Scotland's love, the Land o' Cakes,
> Gie not her bairns sic deadly paiks,
>> Nor be sae rude,
> Wi' firelock or Lochaber axe,
>> As spill their bluid![7]

On all occasions when a holiday licensed some riot and irregularity, a skirmish with these veterans was a favourite recreation with the rabble of Edinburgh. These pages may perhaps see the light when many have in fresh recollection such onsets as we allude to. But the venerable corps, with whom the contention was held, may now be considered as totally extinct. Of late the gradual diminution of these civic soldiers reminds one of the abatement of King Lear's hundred knights. The edicts of each succeeding set of magistrates have, like those of Goneril and Regan, diminished this venerable band with the similar question,[8] "What need we five-and-twenty?—ten?—or five?" And it is now nearly come to, "What need one?" A spectre may indeed here and there still be seen of an old grey-headed and grey-

---

was allowed to sound on the High Street between the Luckenbooths and the Netherbow.[4]]

bearded Highlander, with war-worn features, but bent double by age; dressed in an old-fashioned cocked-hat,[9] bound with white tape instead of silver lace; and in coat waistcoat and breeches of a muddy-coloured red, bearing in his withered hand an ancient weapon, called a Lochaber-axe, a long pole namely, with an axe at the extremity and a hook at the back of the hatchet.[*] Such a phantom of former days still creeps, I have been informed, round the statue of Charles the Second,[10] in the Parliament Square, as if the image of a Stuart were the last refuge for any memorial of our ancient manners; and one or two others are supposed to glide around the door of the guard-house assigned to them in the Luckenbooths, when their ancient refuge[11] in the High Street was laid low.[†] But the fate of manuscripts bequeathed to friends and executors[14] is so uncertain, that the narrative containing these frail memorials of the old Town Guard of Edinburgh, who, with their grim and valiant corporal, John Dhu,[15] (the fiercest looking fellow I ever saw,) were, in my boyhood, the alternate terror and derision of the petulant brood of the High School, may perhaps only come to light when all memory of the institution has faded away, and then serve as an illustration of Kay's caricatures, who has preserved the features of some of their heroes. In the preceding generation, when there was a perpetual alarm for the plots and activity of the Jacobites, some pains was taken by the magistrates of Edinburgh to keep this corps, though composed always of such materials as we have noticed, in a more effective state than was afterwards judged necessary, when their most dangerous service was to skirmish with the rabble on the king's birth-day.[16] They were, therefore, more the object of hatred, and less that of scorn, than they were afterwards accounted.

To Captain John Porteous, the honour of his command and of his corps seems to have been a matter of high interest and importance. He was exceedingly incensed against Wilson for the affront which he construed him to have put upon his soldiers, in the effort he made for

[* This hook was to enable the bearer of the Lochaber-axe to scale a gateway, by grappling the top of the door, and swinging himself up by the staff of his weapon.]

[† This ancient corps is now entirely disbanded.[12] Their last march to do duty at Hallow-fair, had something in it affecting. Their drums and fifes had been wont on better days to play, on this joyous occasion, the lively tune of

"Jockey to the fair;"[13]

but on this final occasion the afflicted veterans moved slowly to the dirge of

"The last time I came ower the muir."]

the liberation of his companion, and expressed himself most ardently on the topic. He was no less indignant at the report, that there was an intention to rescue Wilson himself from the gallows, and uttered many threats and imprecations upon that subject, which were afterwards remembered to his disadvantage. In fact, if a good deal of determination and promptitude rendered Porteous, in one respect, fit to command guards designed to suppress popular commotion, he seems, on the other, to have been disqualified for a charge so delicate, by a hot and surly temper, always too ready to come to blows and violence; a character void of principle; and a disposition to regard the rabble, who seldom failed to regale him and his soldiers with some marks of their displeasure, as declared enemies, upon whom it was natural and justifiable that he should seek opportunities of vengeance. Being, however, the most active and trust-worthy among the captains of the City Guard, he was the person to whom the magistrates confided the command of the soldiers appointed to keep the peace at the time of Wilson's execution. He was ordered to guard the gallows and scaffold, with about eighty men, all the disposable force that could be spared for that duty.

But the magistrates took farther precautions, which affected Porteous's pride very deeply. They requested the assistance of part of a regular infantry regiment, not to attend upon the execution, but to remain drawn up on the principal street of the city, during the time that it went forward, in order to intimidate the multitude, in case they should be disposed to be unruly, with a display of force which could not be resisted without desperation. It may sound ridiculous in our ears, considering the fallen state of this ancient civic corps, that its officer should have felt punctiliously jealous of its honour. Yet so it was. Captain Porteous resented, as an indignity, the introducing the Welsh Fusileers within the city, and drawing them up in the street where no drums but his own were allowed to be sounded, without the special command or permission of the magistrates. As he could not show his ill humour to his patrons the magistrates, it increased his indignation and his desire to be revenged on the unfortunate criminal Wilson, and all who favoured him. These internal emotions of jealousy and rage wrought a change on the man's mien and bearing, visible to all who saw him on the fatal morning when Wilson was appointed to suffer. Porteous's ordinary appearance was rather favourable. He was about the middle size, stout, and well made, having a military air, and yet rather a gentle and mild countenance. His complexion was brown, his face somewhat fretted with the scars of the small-pox, his eyes rather languid than keen or fierce. On the present occasion, however, it seemed to those who saw him as if he were agitated by some evil demon. His step was irregular, his voice hollow and broken, his countenance pale, his eyes staring and wild, his speech imperfect and confused, and his whole appearance so disordered, that many remarked he seemed to be *fey*, a Scottish expression, meaning the state of those who are driven on to their impending fate by the strong impulse of some irresistible necessity.

One part of his conduct was truly diabolical, if, indeed, it has not been exaggerated by the general prejudice entertained against his memory. When Wilson, the unhappy criminal, was delivered to him by the keeper of the prison, in order that he might be conducted to the place of execution, Porteous, not satisfied with the usual precautions to prevent escape, ordered him to be manacled. This might be justifiable from the character and bodily strength of the malefactor, as well as from the apprehensions so generally entertained of an expected rescue. But the handcuffs which were produced being found too small for the wrists of a man so big-boned as Wilson, Porteous proceeded with his own hands, and by great exertion of strength, to force them till they clasped together, to the exquisite torture of the unhappy criminal. Wilson remonstrated against such barbarous usage, declaring that the pain distracted his thoughts from the subjects of meditation proper to his unhappy condition.

"It signifies little," replied Captain Porteous; "your pain will be soon at an end."

"Your cruelty is great," answered the sufferer. "You know not how soon you yourself may have occasion to ask the mercy, which you are now refusing to a fellow-creature. May God forgive you."[17]

These words, long afterwards quoted and remembered, were all that passed between Porteous and his prisoner; but as they took air, and became known to the people, they greatly increased the popular compassion for Wilson, and excited a proportionate degree of indignation against Porteous; against whom, as strict, and even violent in the discharge of his unpopular office, the common people had some real, and many imaginary causes of complaint.

When the painful procession was completed, and Wilson, with the escort, had arrived at the scaffold in the Grassmarket, there appeared no signs of that attempt to rescue him which had occasioned such precautions. The multitude, in general, looked on with deeper interest than at ordinary executions; and there might be seen, on the countenances of many, a stern and indignant expression, like that with which the ancient Cameronians might be supposed to witness the execution of their brethren, who glorified the covenant[18] on occasions something similar,[19] and at the same spot. But there was no attempt at violence. Wilson himself seemed disposed to hasten over the space that divided time from eternity. The devotions proper and usual on such occasions were no sooner finished than he submitted to his fate, and the sentence of the law was fulfilled.

He had been suspended on the gibbet so long as to be totally deprived of life, when at once, as if occasioned by some newly-received impulse, there arose a tumult among the multitude. Many stones were thrown at Porteous and his guards; some mischief was done; and the mob continued to press forward with whoops, shrieks, howls, and exclamations. A young fellow, with a sailor's cap slouched over his face, sprung on the scaffold, and cut the rope by which the criminal was suspended. Others approached to carry off the body, either to secure it for a decent grave,[20] or to try, perhaps, some means of resuscitation. Captain Porteous was wrought by this appearance of insurrection against his authority into a rage so headlong as made him forget, that, the sentence having been fully executed, it was his duty not to engage in hostilities with the misguided multitude, but to draw off his men as fast as possible. He sprung from the scaffold, snatched a musket from one of his soldiers, commanded the party to give fire, and, as several eye-witnesses concurred in swearing, set them the example by discharging his piece, and shooting a man dead on the spot. Several soldiers obeyed his command or followed his example; six or seven[21] persons were slain, and a great many more hurt and wounded.

After this act of violence, the Captain proceeded to withdraw his men towards their guard-house in the High Street. The mob were not so much intimidated as incensed by what had been done. They pursued the soldiers with execrations, accompanied by vollies of stones. As they pressed on them, the rear-most soldiers turned, and again fired with fatal aim and execution. It is not accurately known whether Porteous commanded this second act of violence; but of course the odium of the whole transactions of the fatal day attached to him, and to him alone. He arrived at his guard-house, dismissed his soldiers, and went to make his report to the magistrates concerning the unfortunate events of the day.

Apparently by this time Captain Porteous had begun to doubt the propriety of his own conduct, and the reception he met with from the magistrates was such as to make him still more anxious to gloss it over. He denied that he had given orders to fire; he denied he had fired with his own hand; he even produced the fusee which he carried as an officer for examination; it was found still loaded. Of three cartridges which he was seen to put in his pouch that morning, two were still there; a white handkerchief was thrust into the muzzle of the piece, and returned unsoiled or blackened. To the defence founded on these circumstances it was answered, that Porteous had not used his own piece, but had been seen to take one from a soldier. Among the many who had been killed and wounded by the unhappy fire, there were several of better rank; for even the humanity of such soldiers as fired over the heads of the mere rabble around the scaffold, proved in some instances fatal to persons of better condition who were stationed in windows, or observed the melancholy scene from a distance. The voice of public indignation was loud and general; and, ere men's temper had time to cool,[22] the trial of Captain Porteous took place before the High Court of Justiciary. After a long and patient hearing, the jury had the difficult duty of balancing the positive evidence of many persons, and those of respectability, who deposed absolutely to the prisoner's commanding his soldiers to fire, and himself firing his piece, of which some swore that they saw the smoke and flash, and beheld a man drop at whom it was pointed, with the negative testimony of others, who, though well stationed for seeing what had passed, neither heard Porteous give orders to fire, nor saw him fire himself; but, on the contrary, averred that the first shot was fired by a soldier who stood close by him. A great part of his defence was also founded on the turbulence of the mob, which witnesses, according to their feelings, their predilections, and their opportunities of observation, represented differently; some describing as a formidable riot, what others represented as a trifling disturbance, such as always used to take place on the like occasions, when the executioner of the law, and the men commissioned to protect him in his task, were generally exposed to some indignities. The verdict of the jury sufficiently shews how the evidence preponderated in their minds. It declared that John Porteous fired a gun among the people assembled at the execution; that he gave orders to his soldiers to fire, by which many persons were killed and wounded; but, at the same time, that the prisoner and his guard had been wounded and beaten, by stones thrown at them by the multitude. Upon this verdict,[23] the Lords of Justiciary passed sentence of death against Captain John Porteous, adjudging him, in the common form, to be hanged on a gibbet at the common place of execution, on Wednesday, 8th September, 1736,[24] and all his moveable property to be forfeited to the king's use, according to the Scottish law in cases of wilful murder.

CHAPTER 4

"The hour's come, but not the man."[*]
Kelpie

ON the day when the unhappy Porteous was expected to suffer the sentence of the law, the place of execution, extensive as it is, was crowded almost to suffocation. There was not a window in all the lofty tenements around it, or in the steep and crooked street called the Bow, by which the fatal procession was to descend from the High Street, that was not absolutely filled with spectators. The uncommon height and antique appearance of these houses, some of which were formerly the property of the Knights Templars, and the Knights of St John, and still exhibit on their fronts and gables the iron cross[1] of these orders, gave additional effect to a scene in itself so striking. The area of the Grassmarket resembled a huge dark lake or sea of human heads, in the centre of which arose the fatal tree, tall, black, and ominous, from which dangled the deadly halter. Every object takes interest from its uses and associations, and the erect beam and empty noose, things so simple in themselves, became, on such an occasion, objects of terror and of solemn interest.

Amid so numerous an assembly there was scarce a word spoken, save in whispers. The thirst of vengeance was in some degree allayed by its supposed certainty; and even the populace, with deeper feeling than they are wont to entertain, suppressed all clamorous exultation, and prepared to enjoy the scene of retaliation in triumph, silent and decent, though stern and relentless. It seemed as if the depth of their hatred to the unfortunate criminal scorned to display itself in any thing resembling the more noisy current of their ordinary feelings. Had a stranger consulted only the evidence of his ears, he might have supposed that so vast a multitude were assembled for some purpose

[* There is a tradition, that while a little stream was swollen into a torrent by recent showers, the discontented voice of the Water Spirit was heard to pronounce these words. At the same moment a man, urged on by his fate, or, in Scottish language, *fey*, arrived at a gallop, and prepared to cross the water. No remonstrance from the bystanders was of power to stop him—he plunged into the stream, and perished.]

which affected them with the deepest sorrow, and stilled those noises which, on all ordinary occasions, arise from such a concourse; but if he gazed upon their faces, he would have been instantly undeceived. The compressed lip, the bent brow, the stern and flashing eye of almost every one on whom he looked, conveyed the expression of men come to glut their sight with triumphant revenge. It is probable that the appearance of the criminal might have somewhat changed the temper of the populace in his favour, and that they might in the moment of death have forgiven the man against whom their resentment had been so fiercely heated. It had, however, been destined, that the mutability of their sentiments was not to be exposed to this trial.

The usual hour for producing the criminal had been past for many minutes, yet the spectators observed no symptom of his appearance. "Would they venture to defraud public-justice?" was the question which men began anxiously to ask at each other. The first answer in every case was bold and positive,—"They dare not." But when the point was farther canvassed, other opinions were entertained, and various causes of doubt were suggested. Porteous had been a favourite officer of the magistracy of the city, a numerous and fluctuating body, that requires for its support a degree of energy in its functionaries, which the individuals who compose it cannot at all times alike be supposed to possess in their own persons. It was remembered, that in the Information for Porteous, (the paper, namely, in which his case was stated to the judges of the criminal court), he had been described by his counsel as the person on whom the magistrates chiefly relied in all emergencies of uncommon difficulty. It was argued too, that his conduct on the unhappy occasion of Wilson's execution, was capable of being attributed to an imprudent excess of zeal in the execution of his duty, a motive for which those under whose authority he acted might be supposed to have great sympathy. And as these considerations might move the magistrates to make a favourable representation of Porteous's case, there were not wanting others in the higher departments of government, which would make such suggestions favourably listened to.

The mob of Edinburgh, when thoroughly excited, had been at all times one of the fiercest which could be found in Europe; and of late years they had risen repeatedly[2] against the government, and sometimes not without temporary success. They were conscious, therefore, that they were no favourites with the rulers of the period, and that if Captain Porteous's violence was not altogether regarded as good service, it might certainly be thought, that to visit it with a capital punishment would render it both delicate and dangerous for future officers, in the same circumstances, to act with effect in repressing tumults. There is also a natural feeling, on the part of all members of government, for the general maintenance of authority; and it seemed not unlikely, that what to the relatives of the sufferers appeared a wanton and unprovoked massacre, should be otherwise viewed in the cabinet of St James's. It might be there supposed, that, upon the whole matter, Captain Porteous was in the exercise of a trust delegated to him by the lawful civil authority; that he had been assaulted by the populace, and several of his men hurt; and that, in finally repelling force by force, his conduct could be fairly imputed to no other motive than self-defence in the discharge of his duty.

These considerations, of themselves very powerful, induced the spectators to apprehend the possibility of a reprieve; and to the various causes which might interest the rulers in his favour, the lower part of the rabble added one which was peculiarly well adapted to their comprehension. It was averred, in order to increase the odium against Porteous, that while he repressed with the utmost severity the slightest excesses of the poor, he not only overlooked the licence of the young nobles and gentry, but was very willing to lend them the countenance of his official authority, in execution of such loose pranks as it was chiefly his duty to have restrained. This suspicion, which was perhaps much exaggerated, made a deep impression on the minds of the populace; and when several of the higher rank joined in a petition, recommending Porteous to the mercy of the crown, it was generally supposed he owed their favour not to any conviction of the hardship of his case, but to the fear of losing a convenient accomplice in their debaucheries. It is scarce necessary to say how much this suspicion augmented the people's detestation of this obnoxious criminal, as well as their fear of his escaping the sentence pronounced against him.

While these arguments were stated and replied to, and canvassed and supported, the hitherto silent expectation of the people became changed into that deep and agitating murmur, which is sent forth by the ocean before the tempest begins to howl. The crowded populace, as if their motions had corresponded with the unsettled state of their minds, fluctuated to and fro without any visible cause of impulse, like the agitation of the waters, called by sailors the ground-swell. The news, which the magistrates had almost hesitated to communicate to them, were at length announced, and spread among the spectators with a rapidity like lightning. A reprieve[3] from the Secretary of State's office, under the hand of his Grace the Duke of Newcastle,[4] had arrived, intimating the pleasure of Queen Caroline,[5] (regent of the kingdom during the absence of George II.[6] on the continent,) that the execution of the sentence of death pronounced against John Porteous, late Captain-lieutenant of the City Guard of Edinburgh, present prisoner in the tolbooth of that city, be respited for six weeks from the time appointed for his execution.

The assembled spectators, of almost all degrees, whose minds had been wound up to the pitch which we have described, uttered a groan, or rather a roar of indignation and disappointed revenge, similar to that of a tiger from whom his meal has been rent by his keeper when he was just about to devour it. This fierce exclamation seemed to forebode some immediate explosion of popular resentment, and, in fact, such had been expected by the magistrates, and the necessary measures had been taken to repress it. But the shout was not repeated; nor did any sudden tumult ensue, such as it seemed to announce. The populace appeared to be ashamed of having expressed their disappointment in a vain clamour, and the sound changed, not into the silence which had preceded the arrival of these stunning news, but into stifled mutterings, which each groupe maintained among themselves, and which were blended into one deep and hoarse murmur which floated above the assembly.

Yet still, though all expectation of the execution was over, the mob remained assembled, stationary, as it were, through very resentment, gazing on the preparations for death, which had now been made in vain, and stimulating their feelings, by recalling the various claims which Wilson might have had on royal mercy, from the mistaken motives on which he acted, as well as from the generosity he had displayed towards his accomplice. "This man," they said,—"the brave, the resolute, the generous, was executed to death without mercy for stealing a purse of gold, an act which in some sense he might consider as a fair reprisal; while the profligate satellite, who took advantage of a trifling tumult, inseparable from such occasion, to shed the blood of twenty of his fellow-citizens, is deemed a fitting object for the exercise of the royal prerogative of mercy. Is this to be borne?—would our fathers have borne it? Are not we, like them, Scotsmen and burghers of Edinburgh?"

The officers of justice began now to remove the scaffold, and other preparations which had been made for the execution, in hopes, by doing so, to accelerate the dispersion of the multitude. The measure had the desired effect; for no sooner had the fatal tree been unfixed from the large stone pedestal or socket in which it was secured, and sunk slowly down upon the wain intended to remove it to the place where it was usually deposited, than the populace, after giving vent to their feelings in a second shout of rage and mortification, began slowly to disperse to their usual abodes and occupations.

The windows were in like manner gradually deserted, and groupes of the more decent class of citizens formed themselves, as if waiting to return homewards when the streets should be cleared of the rabble. Contrary to what is frequently the case, this description of persons agreed in general with the sentiments of their inferiors, and considered the cause as common to all ranks. Indeed, as we have already noticed, it was by no means amongst the lowest class of the spectators, or those most likely to be engaged in the riot at Wilson's execution, that the fatal fire of Porteous's soldiers had taken effect. Several persons were killed who were looking out at windows at the scene, who could not of course belong to the rioters, and were persons of decent rank and condition. The burghers, therefore, resenting the loss which had fallen on their own body, and proud and tenacious of their rights, as the citizens of Edinburgh have at all times been, were greatly exasperated at the unexpected respite of Captain Porteous.

It was noticed at the time, and afterwards more particularly remembered, that, while the mob were in the act of dispersing, several individuals were seen busily passing from one place and one groupe of people to another, remaining long with none, but whispering for a little time with those who appeared to be declaiming most violently against the conduct of government. These active agents had the appearance of men from the country, and were generally supposed to be old friends and confederates of Wilson, whose minds were of course highly excited against Porteous.

If, however, it was the intention of these men to stir the multitude to any sudden act of mutiny, it seemed for the time to be fruitless. The rabble, as well as the more decent part of the assembly, dispersed, and went home peaceably; and it was only by observing the moody discontent on their brows, or catching the tenor of the conversation they held with each other, that a stranger could estimate the state of their minds. We will give the reader this advantage, by associating ourselves with one of the numerous groupes who were painfully ascending the steep declivity of the West Bow to return to their dwellings in the Lawnmarket.

"An unco thing this, Mrs Howden," said old Peter Plumdamas to his neighbour the rouping-wife, or saleswoman, as he offered her his arm to assist her in the toilsome ascent, "to see the grit folk at Lunnon set their face against law and gospel, and let loose sic a reprobate as Porteous upon a peaceable town."

"And to think o' the weary walk they hae gien us," answered Mrs Howden, with a groan; "and sic a comfortable window as I had gotten, too, just within a penny-stane-cast of the scaffold—I could hae heard every word the minister said—and to pay twal pennies for my stand, and a' for naething!"

"I am judging," said Mr Plumdamas, "that this reprieve wad na stand gude in the auld Scots law,[7] when the Kingdom *was* a Kingdom."

"I dinna ken muckle about the law," answered Mrs Howden; "but I ken, when we had a king, and a chancellor, and parliament-men o' our ain, we could aye peeble them wi' stanes when they were na gude bairns—But naebody's nails can reach the length o' Lunnon."

"Weary on Lunnon, and a' that e'er came out o't!" said Miss Grizell Damahoy, an ancient seamstress; "they hae taen awa our parliament, and they hae oppressed our trade.[8] Our gentles will hardly allow that a Scots needle can sew ruffles on a sark, or lace on an owerlay."

"Ye may say that, Miss Damahoy, and I ken o' them that hae gotten raisins frae Lunnon by forpits at ance," responded Plumdamas; "and then sic an host of idle English gaugers and excisemen as hae come down to vex and torment us, that an honest man canna fetch sae muckle as a bit anker o' brandy frae Leith to the Lawnmarket, but he's like to be rubbit o' the very gudes he's bought and paid for.— Weel, I winna justify Andrew Wilson for pitting hand on what was na his; but if he took nae mair than his ain, there's an awfu' difference between that and the fact that this man stands for."

"If ye speak about the law," said Mrs Howden, "here comes Mr Saddletree, that can settle it as weel as ony on the bench."

The party she mentioned, a grave elderly person, with a superb periwig, dressed in a decent suit of sad-coloured clothes, came up as she spoke, and courteously gave his arm to Miss Grizell Damahoy.

It may be necessary to mention, that Mr Bartoline Saddletree kept an excellent and highly-esteemed shop for harness, saddles, &c. &c. at the sign of the Golden Nag, at the head of Bess-Wynd. His genius, however, (as he himself and most of his neighbours conceived,) lay towards the weightier matters of the law, and he failed not to give frequent attendance upon the pleadings and arguments of the lawyers and judges in the neighbouring square, where, to say the truth, he was oftener to be found than would have consisted with his own emolument; but that his wife, an active pains-taking person, could, in his absence, make an admirable shift to please the customers and scold the journeymen. This good lady was in the habit of letting her husband take his way, and go on improving his stock of legal knowledge without interruption, but, as if in requital, she insisted upon having her own will in the domestic and commercial departments which he abandoned to her. Now, as Bartoline Saddletree had a considerable gift of words, which he mistook for eloquence, and conferred more liberally upon the society in which he lived than was at all times gracious and acceptable, there went forth a saying, with which wags used sometimes to interrupt his rhetoric, that, as he had a golden nag at his door, so he had a grey mare[9] in his shop. This reproach induced Mr Saddletree, on all occasions, to assume rather a haughty and stately tone towards his good woman, a circumstance by which she seemed very little affected, unless he attempted to exercise any real authority, when she never failed to fly into open rebellion. But such extremes Bartoline seldom provoked; for, like the gentle King Jamie, he was fonder of talking of authority than really exercising it.[10] This turn of mind was, on the whole, lucky for him; since his substance was increased without any trouble on his part, or any interruption of his favourite studies.

This word in explanation has been thrown in to the reader, while Saddletree was laying down, with great precision, the law upon Porteous's case, by which he arrived at this conclusion, that, if Porteous had fired five minutes sooner, before Wilson was cut down, he would have been *versans in licito*, engaged, that is, in a lawful act, and only liable to be punished *propter excessum*, or for lack of discretion, which might have mitigated the punishment to *pœna ordinaria*.

"Discretion!" echoed Mrs Howden, on whom it may well be supposed the fineness of this distinction was entirely thrown away,— "whan had Jock Porteous either grace, discretion, or gude manners?—I mind when his father"——

"But, Mrs Howden," said Saddletree——

"And I," said Miss Damahoy, "mind when his mother"——

"Miss Damahoy," entreated the interrupted orator——

"And I," said Plumdamas, "mind when his wife"——

"Mr Plumdamas—Mrs Howden—Miss Damahoy," again implored the orator,—"mind the distinction, as Counsellor Crossmyloof says—

'I,' says he, 'take a distinction.' Now, the body of the criminal being cut down, and the execution ended, Porteous was no longer official; the act which he came to protect and guard being done and ended, he was no better than *cuivis ex populo*."

"*Quivis—quivis*, Mr Saddletree, craving your pardon," said (with a prolonged emphasis on the first syllable) Mr Butler,[11] the deputy schoolmaster of a parish[12] near Edinburgh, who at that moment came up behind them as the false Latin was uttered.

"What signifies interrupting me, Mr Butler?—but I am glad to see ye notwithstanding—I speak after Counsellor Crossmyloof, and he said *cuivis*."

"If Counsellor Crossmyloof used the dative for the nominative, I would have crossed *his* loof with a tight leathern strap, Mr Saddletree; there is not a boy on the booby form but should have been scourged for such a solecism in grammar."

"I speak Latin like a lawyer, Mr Butler, and not like a schoolmaster," retorted Saddletree.

"Scarce like a school-boy, I think," rejoined Butler.

"It matters little," said Bartoline; "all I mean to say is, that Porteous has become liable to the *pœna extra ordinem*, or capital punishment—which is to say, in plain Scotch, the gallows—simply because he did not fire when he was in office, but waited till the body was cut down, the execution whilk he had in charge to guard implemented, and he himself exonered of the public trust imposed on him."

"But, Mr Saddletree," said Plumdamas, "do ye really think John Porteous's case wad hae been better if he had begun firing before ony stanes were flung at a'?"

"Indeed do I, neighbour Plumdamas," replied Bartoline, confidently, "he being then in point of trust and in point of power, the execution being but inchoat, or, at least, not implemented, or finally ended; but after Wilson was cut down it was a' ower—he was clean exauctorate, and had nae mair ado but to get awa wi' his guard up this West Bow as fast as if there had been a caption after him—And this is law, for I heard it laid down by Lord Vincovincentem."

"Vincovincentem?—Is he a lord of state or a lord of seat?" enquired Mrs Howden.[*]

[* A nobleman was called a Lord of State. The Senators of the College of Justice were termed Lords of Seat, or of the Session.]

"A lord of seat—a lord of the Session.—I fash mysell little wi' lords o' state; they vex me wi' a wheen idle questions about their saddles, and curpels, and holsters, and horse-furniture, and what they'll cost, and whan they'll be ready—a wheen galloping geese—my wife may serve the like o' them."

"And so might she, in her day, hae served the best lord in the land, for as little as ye think o' her, Mr Saddletree," said Mrs Howden, somewhat indignant at the contemptuous way in which her gossip was mentioned; "when she and I were twa gilpies, we little thought to hae sitten doun wi' the like o' my auld Davie Howden, or you either, Mr Saddletree."

While Saddletree, who was not bright at a reply, was cudgelling his brains for an answer to this home-thrust, Miss Damahoy broke in on him.

"And as for the lords of state," said Miss Damahoy, "ye suld mind the riding o' the parliament, Mr Saddletree, in the gude auld time before the Union,—a year's rent o' mony a gude estate gaed for horse-graith and harnessing, forbye broidered robes and foot-mantles, that wad hae stude by their lane wi' gold and brocade, and that were muckle in my ain line."

"Ay, and then the lusty banquetting, with sweet-meats and comfits wet and dry, and dried fruits of divers sorts," said Plumdamas. "But Scotland was Scotland in these days."

"I'll tell ye what it is, neighbours," said Mrs Howden, "I'll ne'er believe Scotland is Scotland ony mair, if our kindly Scots sit doun with the affront they hae gien us this day. It's not only the blude that *is* shed, but the blude that might hae been shed, that's required at our hands; there was my daughter's wean, little Eppie Daidle—my oe, ye ken, Miss Grizell—had plaid the truant frae the school, as bairns will do, ye ken, Mr Butler"——

"And for which," interjected Mr Butler, "they should be soundly scourged by their well-wishers."

"And had just cruppen to the gallows' foot to see the hanging, as was natural for a wean; and what for might na she hae been shot as weel as the rest o' them, and where wad we a' hae been then? I wonder how Queen Carline (if her name be Carline), wad hae liked to hae had ane o' her ain bairns in sic a venture?"

"Report says," answered Butler, "that such a circumstance would not have distressed her majesty[13] beyond endurance."

"Aweel," said Mrs Howden, "the sum o' the matter is, that, were I a man, I wad hae amends o' Jock Porteous, be the upshot what like o't,[14] if a' the carles and carlines in England had sworn to the nay-say."

"I would claw down the tolbooth door wi' my nails," said Mrs Grizell, "but I wad be at him."

"Ye may be very right, ladies," said Butler, "but I would not advise you to speak so loud."

"Speak!" exclaimed both the ladies together, "there will be naething else spoken about frae the Weigh-house to the Water-gate,[15] till this is either ended or mended."[16]

The females now departed to their respective places of abode. Plumdamas joined the other two gentlemen in drinking their *meridian* (a bumper-dram of brandy), as they passed the well-known low-browed shop in the Lawnmarket, where they were wont to take that refreshment. Mr Plumdamas then departed towards his shop, and Mr Butler, who happened to have some particular occasion for the rein of an old bridle, (the truants of that busy day could have anticipated its application,) walked down the Lawnmarket with Mr Saddletree, each talking as he could get a word thrust in, the one on the laws of Scotland, the other on those of Syntax, and neither listening to a word which his companion uttered.

CHAPTER 5

Elswhair he colde right weel lay down the law,
But in his house was meke as is a daw.

DAVIE LINDSAY

"THERE has been Jock Driver the carrier here, speering about his new graith," said Mrs Saddletree to her husband, as he crossed his threshold, not with the purpose by any means of consulting him upon his own affairs, but merely to intimate, by a gentle recapitulation, how much duty she had gone through in his absence.

"Weel," replied Bartoline, and deigned not a word more.

"And the Laird of Girdingburst has had his running footman here, and ca'd himsell (he's a civil pleasant young gentleman), to see when the broidered saddle-cloth for his sorrel horse will be ready, for he wants it agane the Kelso races."

"Weel, aweel," replied Bartoline, as laconically as before.

"And his lordship, the Earl of Blazonbury, Lord Flash and Flame, is like to be clean daft, that the harness for the six Flanders mears, wi' the crests, coronets, housings, and mountings conform, are no sent hame according to promise gien."

"Weel, weel-weel, weel-weel, gude-wife," said Saddletree, "if he gangs daft, we'll hae him cognosced—it's a' very weel."

"It's weel that ye think sae, Mr Saddletree," answered his helpmate, rather nettled at the indifference with which her report was received; "there's many ane wad hae thought themselves affronted, if sae many customers had caad and naebody to answer them but women-folk, for a' the lads were aff sae sune as your back was turned to see Porteous hanged, that might be counted upon; and sae, you no being at hame"——

"Houts, Mrs Saddletree," said Bartoline, with an air of consequence, "dinna deave me wi' your nonsense; I was under the necessity of being elsewhere—*non omnia*—as Mr Crossmyloof said, when he was called by two macers at ance, *non omnia possumus—pessimus—possimis*—[1] I ken our law-latin offends Mr Butler's ears, but it means naebody, an it were the Lord President himsell, can do twa turns at ance."

"Very right, Mr Saddletree," answered his careful helpmate, with a sarcastic smile, "and nae doubt it's a decent thing to leave your wife to look after young gentlemen's saddles and bridles, when ye gang to see a man, that never did ye nae ill, raxing a halter."

"Woman," said Saddletree, assuming an elevated tone, to which the *meridian* had somewhat contributed, "desist—I say—forbear from intromitting with affairs thou canst not understand. D'ye think I was born to sit here broggin an elshin through bend leather, when sic men as Duncan Forbes,[2] and that other Arniston[3] chield there, without muckle greater parts, if the close-head speak true, than mysell, maun be Presidents and King's Advocates nae doubt, and wha but they? Whereas, were favour equally distribute, as in the days of the Wight Wallace"——

"I ken naething we wad hae gotten by the Wight Wallace," said Mrs Saddletree, "unless, as I hae heard the auld folk tell, they fought in thae days wi' bend-leather guns,[4] and then it's a chance but what if he had bought them he might have forgot to pay for them. And as for the greatness of your parts, Bartley, the folk in the close-head maun ken mair about them than I do, if they make sic a report of them."

"I tell ye, woman," said Saddletree, in high dudgeon, "that ye ken naething about these matters. In Sir William Wallace's days, there was nae man pinned down to sic a slavish wark as a saddler's, for they got ony leather graith that they had use for ready made out o' Holland."[5]

"Well," said Butler, who was, like many of his profession, something of an humourist and a dry joker, "if that be the case, Mr Saddletree, I think we have changed for the better; since we make our own harness, and only import our lawyers from Holland."[6]

"It's ower true, Mr Butler," answered Bartoline with a sigh; "if I had had the luck—or rather, if my father had had the sense to send me to Leyden and Utrecht to learn the Substitutes and Pandex"——[7]

"You mean the Institutes—Justinian's Institutes, Mr Saddletree," said Butler.

"Institutes and substitutes are synonymous words, Mr Butler, and used indifferently as such in deeds of tailzie, as you may see in Balfour's Practiques,[8] or Dallas of St Martin's Stiles.[9] I understand these things pretty weel, I thank God; but I own I should have studied in Holland."

"To comfort you, you might not have been farther forward than you now are, Mr Saddletree," replied Mr Butler; "for our Scottish advocates are an aristocratic race—Their brass is of the right Corinthian[10] quality, and *Non cuivis contigit adire Corinthum*[11]—aha, Mr Saddletree?"

"And aha, Mr Butler," rejoined Bartoline, upon whom, as may well be supposed, the jest was lost, and all but the sound of the words, "ye said a gliff syne it was *quivis*, and now I heard ye say *cuivis* with my ain ears, as plain as ever I heard a word at the fore-bar."

"Give me your patience, Mr Saddletree, and I'll explain the discrepancy in three words," said Butler, as pedantic in his own department, though with infinitely more judgment and learning, as Bartoline was in his self-assumed profession of the law—"Give me your patience for a moment—You'll grant that the nominative case is that by which a person or thing is nominated or designed, and which may be called the primary case, all others being formed from it by alterations of the termination in the learned languages, and by prepositions in our modern Babylonian jargons—You'll grant me that, I suppose, Mr Saddletree?"

"I dinna ken whether I will or no—*ad avisandum*, ye ken—naebody should be in a hurry to make admissions, either in point of law or in point of fact," said Saddletree, looking, or endeavouring to look, as if he understood what was said.

"And the dative case," continued Butler——

"I ken what a tutor dative is brawly," said Saddletree readily enough.

"The dative case," resumed the grammarian, "is that in which any thing is given or assigned property as belonging to a person, or thing—You cannot deny that, I am sure."

"I am sure I'll no grant it though," said Saddletree.

"Then, what the *deevil* d'ye take the nominative and the dative cases to be?" said Butler, hastily, and surprised at once out of his decency of expression and accuracy of pronounciation.

"I'll tell you that at leisure, Mr Butler," said Saddletree, with a very knowing look; "I'll take a day to see and answer every article of your condescendence, and then I'll hold you to confess or deny as accords."

"Come, come, Mr Saddletree," said his wife, "we'll hae nae confessions and condescendences here; let them deal in thae sort o' wares that are paid for them—they suit the like o' us as ill as a demipique saddle would set a draught ox."

"Aha!" said Mr Butler, "*Optat ephippia bos piger*,[12] nothing new under the sun—But it was a fair hit of Mrs Saddletree, however."

"And it wad far better become ye, Mr Saddletree," continued his helpmate, "since ye say ye hae skeel o' the law, to try if ye can do ony thing for Effie Deans, puir thing, that's lying up in the tolbooth yonder, cauld and hungry and comfortless—a servant lass of ours, Mr Butler, and as innocent a lass to my thinking, and as usefu' in the chop—When Mr Saddletree gangs out,——and ye're aware he's seldom at hame when there's ony o' the plea-houses open,——puir Effie used to help me to tumble the bundles o' barkened leather up and doun, and range out the gudes, and suit a'body's humours—And troth, she could aye please the customers wi' her answers, for she was aye civil, and a bonnier lass was na in Auld Reekie. And when folk were hasty and unreasonable, she could serve them better than me, that am no sae young as I hae been, Mr Butler, and a wee bit short in the temper into the bargain. For when there's ower mony folks crying on me at anes, and nane but ae tongue to answer them, folk maun speak hastily or they'll ne'er get through wark—Sae I miss Effie daily"—

"*De die in diem*," added Saddletree.

"I think," said Butler, after a good deal of hesitation, "I have seen the girl in the shop—a modest-looking, fair-haired girl?"[13]

"Ay, ay, that's just puir Effie," said her mistress. "How she was abandoned to hersell, or whether she was sackless o' the sinfu' deed, God in Heaven kens; but if she's been guilty, she's been sair tempted, and I wad amaist take my bible-aith she has na been hersell at the time."

Butler had by this time become much agitated; he fidgetted up and down the shop, and shewed the greatest agitation that a person of such strict decorum could be supposed to give way to. "Was not this girl," he said, "the daughter of David Deans, that had the parks at St Leonard's taken? and has she not a sister?"

"In troth has she—puir Jeanie Deans, ten years aulder than hersell; she was here greeting a wee while syne about her tittie. And what could I say to her, but that she behoved to come and speak to Mr Saddletree when he was at hame? It was na that I thought Mr Saddletree could do her or ony other body muckle good or ill, but it wad aye serve to keep the puir thing's heart up for a wee while; and let sorrow come when sorrow maun."[14]

"Ye're mistaen though, gudewife," said Saddletree scornfully, "for I could hae gien her great satisfaction; I could hae proved to her that her sister was indicted upon the Statute[15] Saxteen hundred and ninety, chapter twenty-ane, For the mair ready prevention of child-murder—for concealing her pregnancy, and giving no account of the child which she had borne."

"I hope," said Butler,—"I trust in a gracious God, that she can clear herself."

"And sae do I, Mr Butler," replied Mrs Saddletree. "I am sure I wad hae answered for her as my ain daughter; but, waes my heart, I had been tender a' the simmer, and scarce ower the door o' my room for twal weeks. And as for Mr Saddletree, he might live a week in a lying-in hospital, and ne'er find out what the women cam there for. Sae I could see little or naething o' her, or I wad hae had the truth o' her situation out o' her, I'se warrant ye—But we a' think her sister maun be able to speak something to clear her."

"The haill Parliament House," said Saddletree, "was speaking o' naething else, till this job o' Porteous's put it out o' head—It's a beautiful point of presumptive murder, and there's been nane like it in the Justiciar Court since the case of Luckie Smith[16] the howdie, that suffered in the year saxteen hundred and seventy-nine."

"But what's the matter wi' you, Mr Butler?" said the good woman; "ye are looking as white as a sheet; will ye take a dram?"

"By no means," said Butler, compelling himself to speak. "I walked in from Dumfries yesterday,[17] and this is a warm day."

"Sit down," said Mrs Saddletree, laying hands on him kindly, "and rest ye—ye'll kill yoursell, man, at that rate.—And are we to wish you joy o' getting the scule, Mr Butler?"

"Yes—no—I do not know," answered the young man vaguely. But Mrs Saddletree kept him to the point, partly out of real interest, partly from curiosity.

"Ye dinna ken whether ye are to get the free scule o' Dumfries or no, after hinging on and teaching it a' the simmer?"

"No, Mrs Saddletree—I am not to have it," replied Butler, more collectedly. "The Laird of Black-at-the-bane had a natural son bred to the Kirk[18] that the presbytery could not be prevailed on to license;[19] and so"——

"Ay, ye need say nae mair about it; if there was a laird that had a puir kinsman or a bastard that it wad suit, there's eneugh said.—And ye're e'en come back to Libberton to wait for dead men's shoon?— and, for as frail as Mr Whackbairn is, he may live as lang as you, that are his assistant and successor."

"Very like," replied Butler with a sigh; "I do not know if I should wish it otherwise."

"Nae doubt it's a very vexing thing," continued the good lady, "to be in that dependent station; and you that hae right and title to sae muckle better, I wonder how ye bear these crosses."

"*Quos diligit castigat*,"[20] answered Butler; "even the pagan Seneca[21] could see an advantage in affliction. The Heathens had their philosophy, and the Jews their revelation, Mrs Saddletree, and they endured their distresses in their day. Christians have a better dispensation than either—but doubtless"——

He stopped and sighed.

"I ken what ye mean," said Mrs Saddletree, looking toward her husband; "there's whiles we lose patience in spite of baith book and Bible—But ye are no gaun awa, and looking sae poorly—ye'll stay and take some kail wi' us?"

Mr Saddletree laid aside Balfour's Practiques, (his favourite study, and much good may it do him,) to join in his wife's hospitable importunity. But the teacher declined all entreaty, and took his leave upon the spot.

"There's something in a' this," said Mrs Saddletree, looking after him as he walked up the street; "I wonder what makes Mr Butler sae distressed about Effie's misfortune—there was nae acquaintance atween them that ever I saw or heard of; but they were neighbours when David Deans was on the Laird o' Dumbiedikes' land. Mr Butler wad ken her father, or some o' her folk.—Get up, Mr Saddletree—ye have set yoursell down on the very brecham that wants stitching— And here's little Willie, the prentice.—Ye little rin-there-out deil that ye are that I should say sae, what takes you raking through the gutters to see folk hangit?—how wad ye like when it cums to be your ain chance, as I winna ensure ye, if ye dinna mend your manners?— And what are ye maundering and greeting for, as if a word were breaking your banes? gang in bye, and be a better bairn another time, and tell Peggy to gie ye a bicker o' broth, for ye'll be as gleg as a gled, I'se warrant ye.—It's a fatherless bairn, Mr Saddletree, and motherless, whilk in some cases may be waur, and ane wad take care o' him, if they could—it's a Christian duty."

"Very true, gudewife," said Saddletree in reply, "we are *in loco parentis* to him during his years of pupillarity, and I hae had thoughts of applying to the Court for a commission as factor *loco tutoris*, seeing there is nae tutor nominate, and the tutor-at-law declines to act; but only I fear the expence of the procedure wad not be *in rem versam*, for I am not aware that Willie has ony effects whereof to assume the administration."

He concluded this sentence with a self-important cough, as one who has laid down the law in an indisputable manner.

"Effects!" said Mrs Saddletree, "what effects has the puir wean?—he was in rags when his mother died; and the blue polonie that Effie made for him out of an auld mantle of my ain, was the first decent dress the bairn ever had on. Puir Effie! can ye tell me na really, wi' a' your law, will her life be in danger, Mr Saddletree, when they are na able to prove that ever there was a bairn born ava?"

"Whoy," said Mr Saddletree, delighted at having for once in his life seen his wife's attention arrested by a topic of legal discussion—"Whoy, there are two sorts of *murdrum* or *murdragium*, or what you *populariter et vulgariter* call murther. I mean there are many sorts; for there's your *murthrum per vigilias et insidias*, and your *murthrum* under trust."

"I am sure," replied his moiety, "that murther by trust is the way the gentry murther us merchants, and whiles makes us shut the booth up—but that has naething to do wi' Effie's misfortune."

"The case of Effie (or Euphemia) Deans," resumed Saddletree, "is one of those cases of murder presumptive, that is, a murder of the law's inferring or construction, being derived from certain *indicia* or grounds of suspicion."

"So that," said the good woman, "unless puir Effie has communicated her situation, she'll be hanged by the neck, if the bairn was still-born, or if it be alive at this moment?"

"Assuredly," said Saddletree, "it being a statute made by our sovereign Lord and Lady, to prevent the horrid delict of bringing forth children in secret—the crime is rather a favourite of the law, this species of murther being one of its ain creation."[22]

"Then, if the law makes murders," said Mrs Saddletree, "the law should be hanged for them; or if they wad hang a lawyer instead, the country wad find nae faut."

A summons to their frugal dinner interrupted the further progress of the conversation, which was otherwise like to take a turn much less favourable to the science of jurisprudence and its professors, than Mr Bartoline Saddletree, the fond admirer of both, had at its opening anticipated.

CHAPTER 6

But up then raise all Edinburgh,
They all rose up by thousands three.
Johnnie Armstrang's Goodnight

BUTLER, on his departure from the sign of the Golden Nag, went in quest of a friend of his connected with the law, at whom he wished to make particular enquiries concerning the circumstances in which the unfortunate young woman mentioned in the last chapter was placed, having, as the reader has probably already conjectured, reasons much deeper than those dictated by mere humanity, for interesting himself in her fate. He found the person he sought absent from home, and was equally unfortunate in one or two other calls which he made upon acquaintances whom he hoped to interest in her story. But every body was, for the moment, stark-mad on the subject of Porteous, and engaged busily in attacking or defending the measures of government in reprieving him; and the ardour of dispute had excited such universal thirst, that half the young lawyers and writers, together with their very clerks, the class whom Butler was looking after, had adjourned the debate to some favourite tavern. It was computed by an experienced arithmetician, that there was as much twopenny ale consumed on the discussion as would have floated a first-rate man-of-war.

Butler wandered about until it was dusk, resolving to take that opportunity of visiting the unfortunate young woman, when his doing so might be least observed; for he had his own reasons for avoiding the remarks of Mrs Saddletree, whose shop-door opened at no great distance from that of the jail, though on the opposite or south side of the street, and a little higher up. He passed, therefore, through the narrow and partly covered passage leading from the north-west end of the Parliament Square.

He stood now before the Gothic entrance of the ancient prison,[1] which, as is well known to all men, rears its ancient front in the very middle of the High Street, forming, as it were, the termination to a huge pile of buildings called the Luckenbooths, which, for some inconceivable reason, our ancestors had jammed into the midst of the principal street of the town, leaving for passage a narrow street on the north, and on the south, into which the prison opens, a narrow crooked lane, winding betwixt the high and sombre walls of the Tolbooth and the adjacent houses on the one side, and the buttresses and projections of the old Cathedral upon the other. To give some gaiety to this sombre passage, (well known by the name of the Krames,) a number of little booths, or shops, after the fashion of coblers' stalls, are plaistered, as it were, against the Gothic projections and abutments, so that it seemed as if the traders had occupied with nests, bearing the same proportion to the building, every buttress and coign of vantage,[2] as the martlett did in Macbeth's Castle. Of later years these booths have degenerated into mere toy-shops, where the little loiterers chiefly interested in such wares are tempted to linger, enchanted by the rich display of hobby-horses, babies, and Dutch toys, arranged in artful and gay confusion; yet half-scared by the cross looks of the withered pantaloon, or spectacled old lady, by whom these tempting stores are watched and superintended. But, in the times we write of, the hosiers, the glovers, the hatters, the mercers, the milliners, and all who dealt in the miscellaneous wares now termed haberdasher's goods, were to be found in this narrow alley.

To return from our digression. Butler found the outer turnkey, a tall thin old man, with long silver hair, in the act of locking the outward door of the jail. He addressed himself to this person, and asked admittance to Effie Deans, confined upon accusation of child-murder. The turnkey looked at him earnestly, and, civilly touching his hat out of respect to Butler's black coat and clerical appearance, replied, "It was impossible any one could be admitted at present."

"You shut up earlier than usual, probably on account of Captain Porteous's affair?" said Butler.

The turnkey, with the true mystery of a person in office, gave two grave nods, and withdrawing from the wards a ponderous key[3] of about two feet in length, he proceeded to shut a strong plate of steel, which folded down above the key-hole, and was secured by a steel spring and catch. Butler stood still instinctively while the door was made fast, and then looking at his watch, walked briskly up the street, muttering to himself almost unconsciously—

"Porta adversa, ingens, solidoque adamante columnæ;
Vis ut nulla virûm, non ipsi exscindere ferro
Cœlicolæ valeant—Stat ferrea turris ad auras"—&c.*[4]

Having wasted half an hour more in a second fruitless attempt to
find his legal friend and adviser, he thought it time to leave the city
and return to his place of residence, in a small village, about two miles
and a half to the southward of Edinburgh. The metropolis was at this
time surrounded by a high wall, with battlements and flanking projections at intervals, and the access was through gates, called in the
Scottish language *ports*, which were regularly shut at night. A small
fee to the keepers would indeed procure egress and ingress at any
time, through a wicket left for that purpose in the large gate, but it
was of some importance to a man so poor as Butler, to avoid even this
slight pecuniary mulct; and fearing the hour of shutting the gates
might be near, he made for that to which he found himself nearest,
although, by doing so, he somewhat lengthened his walk homewards.
Bristo Port was that by which his direct road lay, but the West Port,
which leads out of the Grassmarket, was the nearest of the city gates
to the place where he found himself, and to that, therefore, he directed
his course. He reached the port in ample time to pass the circuit of the
walls, and enter a suburb called Portsburgh, chiefly inhabited by the
lower order of citizens and mechanics. Here he was unexpectedly interrupted.

He had not gone far from the gate before he heard the sound of a drum,
and, to his great surprise, met a number of persons, sufficient to occupy
the whole front of the street, and form a considerable mass behind,
moving with great speed towards the gate he had just come from, and
having in front of them a drum beating to arms. While he considered
how he should escape a party, assembled, as it might be presumed, for
no lawful purpose, they came full on him and stopped him.

"Are you a clergyman?" one questioned him.[5]

Butler replied that "he was in orders, but was not a placed minister."

"It's Mr Butler from Libberton," said a voice from behind; "he'll
discharge the duty as weel as ony man."

*Wide is the fronting gate, and raised on high
With adamantine columns threats the sky;
Vain is the force of man, and Heaven's as vain,
To crush the pillars which the pile sustain;
Sublime on these a tower of steel is rear'd.
                    DRYDEN's *Virgil*, Book vi.

"You must turn back with us, sir," said the first speaker, in a tone civil but peremptory.

"For what purpose, gentlemen?" said Mr Butler. "I live at some distance from town—the roads are unsafe by night—you will do me a serious injury by stopping me."

"You shall be sent safely home—no man shall touch a hair of your head[6]—but you must, and shall come along with us."

"But to what purpose or end, gentlemen?" said Butler. "I hope you will be so civil as to explain that to me?"

"You shall know that in good time. Come along—for come you must, by force or fair means; and I warn you to look neither to the right hand nor the left,[7] and to take no notice of any man's face, but consider all that is passing before you as a dream."[8]

"I would it were a dream I could awaken from," said Butler to himself; but, having no means to oppose the violence with which he was threatened, he was compelled to turn round and march in front of the rioters, two men partly supporting and partly holding him. During this parley the insurgents had made themselves masters of the West Port, rushing upon the Waiters (so the people were called who had the charge of the gates), and possessing themselves of the keys. They bolted and barred the folding doors, and commanded the person, whose duty it usually was, to secure the wicket, of which they did not understand the fastenings. The man, terrified at an incident so totally unexpected, was unable to perform his usual office, and gave the matter up, after several attempts. The rioters, who seemed to have come prepared for every emergency, called for torches, by the light of which they nailed up the wicket with long nails, which, it appeared probable, they had provided on purpose.

While this was going on, Butler could not, even if he had been willing, avoid making remarks on the individuals who seemed to lead this singular mob. The torch-light, while it fell on their forms and left him in the shade, gave him an opportunity to do so without their observing him. Several of those who appeared most active were dressed in sailors' jackets, trowsers, and sea-caps; others in large loose-bodied great-coats, and slouched hats; and there were several, who, judging from their dress, should have been called women,[9] whose rough deep voices, uncommon size, and masculine deportment and mode of walking, forbade their being so interpreted. They moved as if by some well-concerted plan of arrangement. They had signals by which they knew, and nick-names by which they distinguished each other. Butler remarked, that the name of Wildfire was used among them, to which one stout Amazon seemed to reply.

The rioters left a small party to observe the West Port, and directed the Waiters, as they valued their lives, to remain within their lodge, and make no attempt for that night to repossess themselves of the gate. They then moved with rapidity along the low street called the Cowgate, the mob of the city every where rising at the sound of their drum, and joining them. When the multitude arrived at the Cowgate Port, they secured it with as little opposition as the former, made it fast, and left a small party to observe it. It was afterwards remarked, as a striking instance of prudence and precaution, singularly combined with audacity, that the parties left to guard those gates did not remain stationary on their posts, but flitted to and fro, keeping so near the gates as to see that no efforts were made to open them, yet not remaining so long as to have their persons closely observed. The mob, at first only about one hundred strong, now amounted to thousands,[10] and were increasing every moment. They divided themselves so as to ascend with more speed the various narrow lanes which lead up from the Cowgate to the High Street; and still beating to arms as they went, and calling on all true Scotsmen to join them, they now filled the principal street of the city.

The Netherbow Port might be called the Temple-bar of Edinburgh, as, intersecting the High Street at its termination, it divided Edinburgh, properly so called, from the suburb named the Canongate, as Temple-bar separates London from Westminster. It was of the utmost importance to the rioters to possess themselves of this pass, because there was quartered in the Canongate at that time a regiment of infantry, commanded by Colonel Moyle, which might have occupied the city by advancing through this gate, and would possess the power of totally defeating their purpose. The leaders therefore hastened to the Netherbow Port, which they secured in the same manner, and with as little trouble, as the other gates, leaving a party to watch it, strong in proportion to the importance of the post.

The next object of these hardy insurgents was at once to disarm the City Guard, and to procure arms for themselves; for scarce any weapons but staves and bludgeons had been yet seen among them. The Guard-house was a long, low, ugly building, (removed in 1787,) which to a fanciful imagination might have suggested the idea of a long black snail crawling up the middle of the High Street and deforming its beautiful esplanade.[11] This formidable insurrection had been so unexpected, that there were no more than the ordinary serjeant's guard[12] of the city-corps upon duty; even these were without any supply of powder and ball; and sensible enough what had raised the storm, and which way it was rolling, could hardly be supposed very desirous to draw on themselves by a valiant defence the animosity of so numerous and desperate a mob, to whom they were on the present occasion much more than usually obnoxious.

There was a sentinel upon guard, who (that one town-guard soldier might do his duty on that eventful evening,) presented his piece, and desired the foremost of the rioters to stand off. The young amazon, whom Butler had observed particularly active, sprung upon the soldier, seized his musket, and after a struggle succeeded in wrenching it from him, and throwing him down on the causeway. One or two soldiers who endeavoured to turn out to the support of their sentinel, were in the same manner seized and disarmed, and the mob without difficulty possessed themselves of the Guard-house, disarming and turning out of doors the rest of the men on duty. It was remarked, that notwithstanding the city soldiers had been the instruments of the slaughter which this riot was designed to revenge, no ill usage or even insult was offered to them. It seemed as if the vengeance of the people disdained to stoop at any head meaner than that which they considered as the source and origin of their injuries.

On possessing themselves of the guard, the first act of the multitude was to destroy the drums by which they supposed an alarm might be conveyed to the garrison in the castle; for the same reason they now silenced their own, which was beaten by a young fellow, son to the drummer of Portsburgh, whom they had forced upon that service. Their next business was to distribute among the boldest of the rioters the guns, bayonets, partizans, halberds, and battle or Lochaber axes. Until this period the principal rioters had preserved silence on the ultimate object of their rising, as being that which all knew, but none expressed. Now, however, having accomplished all the preliminary parts of their design, they raised a tremendous shout of "Porteous! Porteous! To the Tolbooth! To the Tolbooth!"

They proceeded with the same prudence when the object seemed to be nearly in their grasp, as they had done hitherto when success was more dubious. A strong party of the rioters, drawn up in front of the Luckenbooths, and facing down the street, prevented all access from the eastward, and the west end of the defile formed by the Luckenbooths was secured in the same manner; so that the Tolbooth was completely surrounded, and those who undertook the task of breaking it open effectually secured against the risk of interruption.

The magistrates, in the mean while, had taken the alarm, and assembled in a tavern, with the purpose of raising some strength to subdue the rioters. The Deacons, or presidents of the trades, were applied to, but declared there was little chance of their authority being respected by the craftsmen, where it was the object to save a man so obnoxious. Mr Lindsay,[13] member of parliament for the city, volunteered the perilous task of carrying a verbal message from the Lord Provost to Colonel Moyle, the commander of the regiment lying in the Canongate, requesting him to force the Netherbow Port, and enter the city to put down the tumult. But Mr Lindsay declined to charge himself with any written order, which, if found on his person by an enraged mob, might have cost him his life; and the issue of the application was, that Colonel Moyle, having no written requisition from the civil authorities, and having the fate of Porteous before his eyes as an example of the severe construction put by a jury on the proceedings of military men acting on their own responsibility, declined to encounter the risk to which the Provost's verbal communication invited him.

More than one messenger was dispatched by different ways to the Castle, to require the commanding officer to march down his troops, to fire a few cannon-shot, or even to throw a shell among the mob, for the purpose of clearing the streets. But so strict and watchful were the various patroles whom the rioters had established in different parts of the street, that none of the emissaries of the magistrates could reach the gate of the Castle. They were, however, turned back without either injury or insult, and with nothing more of menace than was necessary to deter them from again attempting to accomplish their errand.

The same vigilance was used to prevent every body of the higher, and those which, in this case, might be deemed the more suspicious orders of society, from appearing in the street, and observing the movements, or distinguishing the persons, of the rioters. Every person in the garb of a gentleman was stopped by small parties of two or three of the mob, who partly exhorted, partly required of them, that they should return to the place from whence they came. Many a quadrille table was spoiled that memorable evening; for the sedan-chairs of ladies, even of the highest rank, were interrupted in their passage from one point to another, in despite of the laced footmen and blazing flambeaux. This was uniformly done with a deference and attention to the feelings of the terrified females, which could hardly have been expected from the videttes of a mob so desperate. Those who stopped the chair usually made the excuse, that there was much disturbance on the street, and that it was absolutely necessary for the lady's safety that the chair should turn back. They offered themselves to escort the vehicles which they had thus interrupted in their progress, from the apprehension, probably, that some of those who had casually united themselves to the riot might disgrace their systematic and determined plan of vengeance, by those acts of general insult and licence which are common on similar occasions.

Persons are yet living[14] who remember to have heard from the mouths of ladies interrupted on their journey in the manner we have described, that they were escorted to their lodgings by the young men who stopped them, and even handed out of their chairs, with a polite attention far beyond what was consistent with their dress, which was apparently that of journeymen mechanics.[*] It seemed as if the conspirators, like those who assassinated the Cardinal Beatoun[16] in former days, had entertained the opinion, that the work about which they went was a judgment of Heaven, which, though unsanctioned by the usual authorities, ought to be proceeded in with order and gravity.

While their outposts continued thus vigilant, and suffered themselves neither from fear nor curiosity to neglect that part of the duty assigned to them, and while the main guards to the east and west secured them against interruption, a select body of the rioters thundered at the door of the jail, and demanded instant admission. No one answered, for the outer keeper had prudently made his escape with the keys at the commencement of the riot, and was nowhere to be found. The door was instantly assailed with sledge-hammers, iron crows, and the coulters of ploughs, ready provided for the purpose, with which they prized, heaved, and battered for some time with little effect, the door being of double oak planks, clenched both end-long and athwart with iron, studded besides with broad-headed nails, and so hung and secured as to yield to no means of forcing, by any degree of violence, without the expenditure of much time. The rioters, however, appeared determined to gain admittance. Gang after gang relieved each other at

[*A near relation[15] of the author's used to tell of having been stopped by the rioters, and escorted home in the manner described. On reaching her own home, one of her attendants, in appearance a *baxter*, *i.e.* a baker's lad, handed her out of her chair, and took leave with a bow, which, in the lady's opinion, argued breeding that could hardly be learned beside the oven.]

the exercise, for, of course, only a few could work at a time; but gang after gang retired, exhausted with their violent exertions, without making much progress in forcing the prison-door. Butler had been led up near to this the principal scene of action; so near, indeed, that he was almost deafened by the unceasing clang of the heavy forehammers against the iron-bound portals of the prison. He began to entertain hopes, as the task seemed protracted, that the populace might give it over in despair, or that some rescue might arrive to disperse them. There was a moment at which the latter seemed probable.

The magistrates, having assembled their officers, and some of the citizens who were willing to hazard themselves for the public tranquillity, now sallied forth from the tavern where they held their sitting, and approached the point of danger. Their officers went before them with links and torches, with a herald to read the riot-act,[17] if necessary. They easily drove before them the outposts and videttes of the rioters; but when they approached the line of guard which the mob, or rather, we should say, the conspirators, had drawn across the street in the front of the Luckenbooths, they were received with an unintermitted volley of stones, and, on their nearer approach, the pikes, bayonets, and Lochaber-axes, of which the populace had possessed themselves, were presented against them. One of their ordinary officers, a strong resolute fellow, went forward, seized a rioter, and took from him a musket; but, being unsupported, he was instantly thrown on his back in the street, and disarmed in his turn. The officer was too happy to be permitted to rise and run away without receiving any farther injury; which afforded another remarkable instance of the mode in which these men had united a sort of moderation towards all others, with the most inflexible inveteracy against the object of their resentment. The magistrates, after vain attempts to make themselves heard and obeyed, possessing no means of enforcing their authority, were constrained to abandon the field to the rioters, and retreat in all speed from the showers of missiles that whistled around their ears.

The passive resistance of the Tolbooth door promised to do more to baffle the purpose of the mob than the active interference of the magistrates. The heavy sledge-hammers continued to din against it without intermission, and with a noise which, echoed from the lofty buildings around the spot, seemed enough to have alarmed the garrison in the Castle. It was circulated among the rioters, that the troops would march down to disperse them, unless they could execute their purpose without loss of time; or that, even without quitting the fortress, the garrison might attain the same end by throwing a bomb or two upon the street.

Urged by such motives for apprehension, they eagerly relieved each other at the labour of assailing the Tolbooth door; yet such was its strength, that it still defied their efforts. At length, a voice was heard to pronounce the words, "Try it with fire." The rioters, with an unanimous shout, called for combustibles, and as all their wishes seemed to be instantly supplied, they were soon in possession of two or three empty tar-barrels. A huge red glaring bonfire speedily arose close to the door of the prison, sending up a tall column of smoke and flame against its antique turrets and strongly grated windows, and illuminating the ferocious faces and wild gestures of the rioters who surrounded the place, as well as the pale and anxious countenances of those who, from windows in the vicinage, watched the progress of this alarming scene. The mob fed the fire with whatever they could find fit for the purpose. The flames roared and crackled among the heaps of nourishment piled on the fire, and a terrible shout soon announced that the door had kindled, and was in the act of being destroyed. The fire was suffered to decay, but, long ere it was quite extinguished, the most forward of the rioters rushed, in their impatience, one after another, over its yet smouldering remains. Thick showers of sparkles rose high in the air, as man after man bounded over the glowing embers and disturbed them in their passage. It was now obvious to Butler, and all others who were present, that the rioters would be instantly in possession of their victim, and have it in their power to work their pleasure upon him, whatever that might be.[*]

[* See p. 547 for the note, "The Old Tolbooth".]

CHAPTER 7

The evil you teach us, we will execute; and it shall go hard but we will better
the instruction.

Merchant of Venice

THE unhappy object of this remarkable disturbance had been that day
delivered from the apprehension of a public execution, and his joy was
the greater, as he had some reason to question whether government
would have run the risk of unpopularity by interfering in his favour,
after he had been legally convicted by the verdict of a jury, of a crime
so very obnoxious. Relieved from this doubtful state of mind, his heart
was merry within him,[1] and he thought, in the emphatic words of
Scripture on a similar occasion, that surely the bitterness of death was
past.[2] Some of his friends, however, who had watched the manner and
behaviour of the crowd when they were made acquainted with the
reprieve, were of a different opinion. They augured, from the unusual
sternness and silence with which they bore their disappointment, that
the populace nourished some scheme of sudden and desperate vengeance, and they advised Porteous to lose no time in petitioning the
proper authorities, that he might be conveyed to the Castle under a
sufficient guard, to remain there in security until his ultimate fate
should be determined. Habituated, however, by his office, to overawe
the rabble of the city, Porteous could not suspect them of an attempt
so audacious as to storm a strong and defensible prison; and, despising
the advice by which he might have been saved, he spent the afternoon
of the eventful day in giving an entertainment to some friends who
visited him in jail, several of whom, by the indulgence of the Captain
of the Tolbooth, with whom he had an old intimacy, arising from their
official connection, were even permitted to remain to supper with
him,[3] though contrary to the rules of the jail.

It was, therefore, in the hour of unalloyed mirth, when this unfortunate wretch was "full of bread," hot with wine, and high in mistimed
and ill-grounded confidence, and alas! with all his sins full blown,[4]
when the first distant shouts of the rioters mingled with the song of
merriment and intemperance. The hurried call of the jailor to the

guests, requiring them instantly to depart, and his yet more hasty intimation that a dreadful and determined mob had possessed themselves of the city gates and guard-house, were the first explanation of these fearful clamours.

Porteous might, however, have eluded the fury from which the force of authority could not protect him, had he thought of slipping on some disguise, and leaving the prison along with his guests. It is probable that the jailor might have connived at his escape, or even that in the hurry of this alarming contingency he might not have observed it. But Porteous and his friends alike wanted presence of mind[5] to suggest or execute such a plan of escape. The latter hastily fled from a place where their own safety seemed compromised, and the former, in a state resembling stupefaction, awaited in his apartment the termination of the enterprize of the rioters. The cessation of the clang of the instruments with which they had at first attempted to force the door, gave him momentary relief. The flattering hopes, that the military had marched into the city, either from the Castle or from the suburbs, and that the rioters were intimidated and dispersing, were soon destroyed by the broad and glaring light of the flames, which, illuminating through the grated window every corner of his apartment, plainly showed that the mob, determined on their fatal purpose, had adopted a means of forcing entrance equally desperate and certain.

The sudden glare of light suggested to the stupified and astonished object of popular hatred the possibility of concealment or escape. To rush to the chimney,[6] to ascend it at the risk of suffocation, were the only means which seem to have occurred to him; but his progress was speedily stopped by one of those iron gratings, which are, for the sake of security, usually placed across the vents of buildings designed for imprisonment. The bars, however, which impeded his farther progress, served to support him in the situation which he had gained, and he seized them with the tenacious grasp of one who esteemed himself clinging to his last hope of existence. The lurid light, which had filled the apartment, lowered and died away; the sound of shouts was heard within the walls, and on the narrow and winding stair, which, cased within one of the turrets, gave access to the upper apartments of the prison. The huzza of the rioters was answered by a shout wild and desperate as their own, the cry, namely, of the imprisoned felons, who, expecting to be liberated in the general confusion, welcomed the mob as their deliverers. By some of these the apartment of Porteous was pointed out to his enemies. The obstacle of the lock and bolts was soon overcome, and from his hiding-place the unfortunate man heard his enemies search every corner of the apartment, with oaths and maledictions which would but shock the reader if we recorded them, but which served to prove, could it have admitted of doubt, the settled purpose of soul with which they sought his destruction.

A place of concealment so obvious to suspicion and scrutiny as that which Porteous had chosen, could not long screen him from detection. He was dragged from his lurking-place, with a violence which seemed to argue an intention to put him to death on the spot. More than one weapon was directed towards him, when one of the rioters, the same whose female disguise[7] had been particularly noticed by Butler, interfered in an authoritative tone. "Are ye mad?" he said, "or would ye execute an act of justice as if it were a crime and a cruelty? This sacrifice will lose half its savour if we do not offer it at the very horns of the altar.[8] We will have him die where a murderer should die, on the common gibbet—We will have him die where he spilled the blood of so many innocents!"

A loud shout of applause followed the proposal, and the cry, "To the gallows with the murderer!—To the Grassmarket with him!" echoed on all hands.

"Let no man hurt him," continued the speaker; "let him make his peace with God, if he can; we will not kill both his soul and body."

"What time did he gie better folk for preparing their account?" answered several voices. "Let us mete to him[9] with the same measure he measured to them."

But the opinion of the spokesman better suited the temper of those he addressed, a temper rather stubborn than impetuous, sedate though ferocious, and desirous of colouring their cruel and revengeful action with a shew of justice and moderation.

For an instant this man quitted the prisoner, whom he consigned to a selected guard, with instructions to permit him to give his money and property to whomsoever he pleased. A person confined in the jail for debt received this last deposit from the trembling hand of the victim, who was at the same time permitted to make some other brief arrangements to meet his approaching fate. The felons, and all others who wished to leave the jail, were now at full liberty to do so; not that their liberation made any part of the settled purpose of the rioters, but it followed as almost a necessary consequence of forcing the jail doors. With wild cries of jubilee they joined the mob, or disappeared among the narrow lanes to seek out the hidden receptacles of vice and infamy, where they were accustomed to lurk and conceal themselves from justice.

Two persons, a man about fifty years old, and a girl about eighteen, were all who continued within the fatal walls, excepting two or three debtors, who probably saw no advantage in attempting their escape. The persons we have mentioned remained in the strong-room of the prison, now deserted by all others. One of their late companions in misfortune called out to the man to make his escape, in the tone of an acquaintance. "Rin for it, Ratcliffe—the road's clear."

"It may be sae, Willie," answered Ratcliffe, composedly, "but I have taen a fancy to leave aff trade, and set up for an honest man."

"Stay then and be hanged for a donnard auld deevil,"[10] said the other, and ran down the prison-stair.

The person in female attire whom we have distinguished as one of the most active rioters, was about the same time at the ear of the young woman.[11] "Flee, Effie, flee," was all he had time to whisper. She turned towards him an eye of mingled fear, affection, and upbraiding, all contending with a sort of stupified surprise. He again repeated, "Flee, Effie, flee, for the sake of all that's good and dear to you."[12] Again she gazed on him, but was unable to answer. A loud noise was now heard, and the name of Madge Wildfire was repeatedly called from the bottom of the stair-case.

"I am coming,—I am coming," said the person who answered to that appellative; and then reiterating hastily, "For God's sake—for your own sake—for my sake, flee, or they'll take your life!" he left the strong-room.

The girl gazed after him for a moment, and then, faintly muttering, "Better tyne life, since tint is gude fame,"[13] she sunk her head upon her hand, and remained, seemingly, unconscious as a statue of the noise and tumult which passed around her.

That tumult was now transferred from the inside to the outside of the Tolbooth. The mob had brought their destined victim forth, and were about to conduct him to the common place of execution, which they had fixed as the scene of his death. The leader, whom they distinguished by the name of Madge Wildfire, had been summoned to assist at the procession by the impatient shouts of his confederates.

"I will ensure you five hundred pounds," said the unhappy man, grasping Wildfire's hand—"five hundred pounds for to save my life."

The other answered in the same under-tone, and returning his grasp with one equally convulsive, "Five hundred-weight of coined gold should not save you—Remember Wilson."

A deep pause of a minute ensued, when Wildfire added, in a more composed tone, "Make your peace with Heaven—Where is the clergyman?"

Butler, who, in great terror and anxiety, had been detained within a few yards of the Tolbooth door, to wait the event of the search after Porteous, was now brought forward, and commanded to walk by the prisoner's side, and to prepare him for immediate death. His answer was a supplication that the rioters would consider what they did. "You are neither judges nor jury," said he. "You cannot have, by the laws of God or man, power to take away the life of a human creature, however deserving he may be of death. If it is murder even in a lawful magistrate to execute an offender otherwise than in the place, time, and manner which the judges' sentence prescribes, what must it be in you, who have no warrant for interference but your own wills? In the name of Him who is all Mercy! shew mercy to this unhappy man, and do not dip your hands in his blood, nor rush into the very crime which you are desirous of avenging."

"Cut your sermon short—you are not in your pulpit," answered one of the rioters.

"If we hear more of your clavers," said another, "we are like to hang you up beside him."

"Peace—hush!" said Wildfire. "Do the good man no harm[14]—he discharges his conscience, and I like him the better."

He then addressed Butler. "Now, sir, we have patiently heard you, and we just wish you to understand, in the way of answer, that you may as well argue to the ashler-work and iron-staunchels of the Tolbooth as think to change our purpose—Blood must have blood.[15] We have sworn to each other by the deepest oaths ever were pledged, that Porteous shall die the death he deserves so richly; therefore, speak no more to us, but prepare him for death as well as the briefness of his change will permit."

They had suffered the unfortunate Porteous to put on his night-gown and slippers, as he had thrown off his coat and shoes, in order to facilitate his attempted escape up the chimney. In this garb he was now mounted on the hands of two of the rioters, clasped together, so as to form what is called in Scotland, "The King's Cushion." Butler was placed close to his side, and repeatedly urged to perform a duty always the most painful which can be imposed on a clergyman deserving of the name, and now rendered more so by the peculiar and horrid circumstances of the criminal's case. Porteous at first uttered some supplications for mercy, but when he found that there was no chance that these would be attended to, his military education, and the natural stubbornness of his disposition, combined to support his spirits.

"Are you prepared for this dreadful end?" said Butler, in a faultering voice. "O turn to Him, in whose eyes time and space have no existence, and to whom a few minutes are as a life-time, and a life-time as a minute."

"I believe I know what you would say—," answered Porteous, sullenly. "I was bred a soldier; if they will murder me without time for repentance, let my sins as well as my blood lie at their door."

"Who was it," said the stern voice of Wildfire, "that said to Wilson at this very spot, when he could not pray, owing to the galling agony of his fetters, that his pains would soon be over?—I say to you to take your own tale home; and if you cannot profit by the good man's lessons, blame not them that are still more merciful to you than you were to others."

The procession now moved forward with a slow and determined pace. It was enlightened by many blazing links and torches; for the actors of this work, far from affecting any secrecy on the occasion, seemed even to court observation. Their principal leaders kept close to the person of the prisoner, whose pallid yet stubborn features were seen distinctly by the torch-light, as his person was raised considerably above the concourse which thronged around him. Those who bore swords, muskets, and battle-axes, marched on each side, as if forming a regular guard to the procession. The windows, as they went along, were filled with the inhabitants, whose slumbers had been broken by this unusual disturbance. Some of the spectators muttered accents of encouragement, but in general they were so much appalled by a sight so strange and audacious, that they looked on with a sort of stupified astonishment. No one offered, by act or word, the slightest interruption.

The rioters, on their part, continued to act with the same air of deliberate confidence and security which had marked all their proceedings. When the object of their resentment dropped one of his slippers, they stopped, sought for it, and replaced it upon his foot with great deliberation.[*] As they descended the Bow towards the fatal spot

[* This little incident, characteristic of the extreme composure of this extraordinary mob, was witnessed by a lady, who, disturbed, like others, from her slumbers, had gone to the window. It was told to the author by the lady's daughter.]

where they designed to complete their purpose, it was suggested that there should be a rope got in readiness. For this purpose the booth of a man who dealt in cordage was forced open, a coil of rope fit for their object was selected to serve as a halter, and the dealer next morning found that a guinea had been left on his counter in exchange; so anxious were the perpetrators of this daring action to shew that they meditated not the slightest wrong or infraction of law, excepting so far as Porteous was himself concerned.

Leading, or carrying along with them, in this determined and regular manner, the object of their vengeance, they at length reached the place of common execution, the scene of his crime, and destined spot of his sufferings. Several of the rioters (if they should not rather be described as conspirators) endeavoured to remove the stone which filled up the socket in which the end of the fatal tree was sunk when it was erected for its fatal purpose; others sought for the means of constructing a temporary gibbet, the place in which the gallows itself was deposited being reported too secure to be forced, without much loss of time. Butler endeavoured to avail himself of the delay afforded by these circumstances, to turn the people from their desperate design. "For God's sake," he exclaimed, "remember it is the image of your Creator which you are about to deface in the person of this unfortunate man! Wretched as he is, and wicked as he may be, he has a share in every promise of Scripture, and you cannot destroy him in impenitence without blotting his name from the Book of Life—Do not destroy soul and body; give him time for preparation."

"What time had they," returned a stern voice, "whom he murdered on this very spot?—The laws both of God and man call for his death."

"But what, my friends," insisted Butler, with a generous disregard to his own safety—"what hath constituted you his judges?"

"We are not his judges," replied the same person; "he has been already judged and condemned by lawful authority. We are those whom Heaven, and our righteous anger, have stirred up to execute judgment, when a corrupt government would have protected a murderer."

"I am none," said the unfortunate Porteous; "that which you charge upon me fell out in self-defence, in the lawful exercise of my duty."

"Away with him—away with him!"[16] was the general cry. "Why do you trifle away time in making a gallows?—that dyester's pole is good enough for the homicide."

The unhappy man was forced to his fate with remorseless rapidity.

Butler, separated from him by the press, escaped the last horrors of his struggles.[17] Unnoticed by those who had hitherto detained him as a prisoner, he fled from the fatal spot, without much caring in what direction his course lay. A loud shout proclaimed the stern delight with which the agents of this deed regarded its completion. Butler then, at the opening into the low street called the Cowgate, cast back a terrified glance, and, by the red and dusky light of the torches, he could discern a figure wavering and struggling as it hung suspended above the heads of the multitude, and could even observe men striking at it with their Lochaber-axes and partisans. The sight was of a nature to double his horror, and to add wings to his flight.

The street down which the fugitive ran opens to one of the eastern ports or gates of the city. Butler did not stop till he reached it, but found it still shut. He waited nearly an hour, walking up and down in inexpressible perturbation of mind. At length he ventured to call out, and rouse the attention of the terrified keepers of the gate, who now found themselves at liberty to resume their office without interruption. Butler requested them to open the gate. They hesitated. He told them his name and occupation.

"He is a preacher," said one; "I have heard him preach in Haddo's-hole."[18]

"A fine preaching has he been at the night," said another; "but maybe least said is sunest mended."

Opening then the wicket in the main-gate, the keepers suffered Butler to depart, who hastened to carry his horror and fear beyond the walls of Edinburgh. His first purpose was, instantly to take the road homeward; but other fears and cares, connected with the news he had learned in that remarkable day, induced him to linger in the neighbourhood of Edinburgh until daybreak. More than one groupe of persons passed him as he was whiling away the hours of darkness that yet remained, whom, from the stifled tones of their discourse, the unwonted hour when they travelled, and the hasty pace at which they walked, he conjectured to have been engaged in the late fatal transaction.

Certain it was, that the sudden and total dispersion of the rioters, when their vindictive purpose was accomplished, seemed not the least remarkable feature of this singular affair. In general, whatever may be the impelling motive by which a mob is at first raised, the attainment of their object has usually been only found to lead the way to farther excesses. But not so in the present case. They seemed completely satiated with the vengeance they had prosecuted with such staunch and sagacious activity. When they were fully satisfied that life had abandoned their victim, they dispersed in every direction, throwing down the weapons which they had only assumed to enable them to carry through their purpose. At daybreak there remained not the least token of the events of the night, excepting the corpse of Porteous, which still hung suspended in the place where he had suffered, and the arms of various kinds which the rioters had taken from the city guard-house, which were found scattered about the streets as they had thrown them from their hands, when the purpose for which they had seized them was accomplished.

The ordinary magistrates of the city resumed their power, not without trembling at the late experience of the fragility of its tenure. To march troops into the city, and commence a severe enquiry into the transactions of the preceding night, were the first marks of returning energy which they displayed. But these events had been conducted on so secure and well-calculated a plan of safety and secrecy, that there was little or nothing learned to throw light upon the authors or principal actors in a scheme so audacious. An express was dispatched to London with the tidings, where they excited great indignation and surprise in the council of regency, and particularly in the bosom of Queen Caroline, who considered her own authority as exposed to contempt by the success of this singular conspiracy. Nothing was spoke of for some time save the measure of vengeance which should be taken, not only on the actors of this tragedy, so soon as they should be discovered, but upon the magistrates who had suffered it to take place, and upon the city which had been the scene where it was exhibited.　　On this occasion, it is still recorded in popular tradition, that her Majesty, in the height of her displeasure, told the celebrated John, Duke of Argyle,[19] that, sooner than submit to such an insult, she would make Scotland a hunting-field. "In that case, Madam," answered that high-spirited nobleman, with a profound bow, "I will take leave of your Majesty, and go down to my own country to get my hounds ready."

The import of the reply had more than met the ear; and as most of the Scottish nobility and gentry seemed actuated by the same national spirit, the royal displeasure was necessarily checked in mid-volley, and milder courses were recommended and adopted, to some of which we may hereafter have occasion to advert.[*]

[* See p. 548 for the note to Chapter 7, printed at this point in 1830.]

CHAPTER 8

Arthur's Seat shall be my bed,
    The sheets shall ne'er be press'd by me;
St Anton's well shall be my drink,
    Sin' my true love's forsaken me.

Old Song

IF I were to chuse a spot from which the rising or setting sun could be seen to the greatest possible advantage, it would be that wild path winding around the foot of the high belt of semi-circular rocks, called Salisbury Crags,[1] and marking the verge of the steep descent which slopes down into the glen on the south-eastern side of the city of Edinburgh. The prospect, in its general outline, commands now a close-built high-piled city, stretching itself out beneath in a form, which, to a romantic imagination, may be supposed to represent that of a dragon; now, a noble arm of the sea, with its rocks, islets, distant shores, and boundary of mountains; and now a fair and fertile champaign country, varied with hill, dale, and rock, and skirted by the picturesque ridge of the Pentland Mountains. But as the path gently circles around the base of the cliffs, the prospect, composed as it is of these enchanting and sublime objects, changes at every step, and presents them blended with or divided from each other, in every possible variety which can gratify the eye and the imagination. When a piece of scenery so beautiful, yet so varied,—so exciting by its intricacy, and yet so sublime,—is lighted up by the tints of morning or of evening, and displays all that variety of shadowy depth, exchanged with partial brilliancy, which gives character even to the tamest of landscapes, the effect approaches near to enchantment. This path used to be my favourite evening and morning resort, when engaged with a favourite author, or new subject of study. It is, I am informed, now become totally impassable; a circumstance which, if true, reflects little credit on the taste of the Good Town or its leaders.[*]

[* A beautiful and solid pathway has, within a few years, been formed around these romantic rocks; and the author has the pleasure to think, that the passage in the text gave rise to the undertaking.]

It was from this fascinating path,—the scene to me of so much delicious musing, when life was young and promised to be happy, that I have been unable to pass it over without an episodical description— it was, I say, from this romantic path that Butler saw the morning arise the day after the murder of Porteous. It was possible for him with ease to have found a much shorter road to the house to which he was directing his course, and, in fact, that which he chose was extremely circuitous. But to compose his own spirits, as well as to while away the time, until a proper hour for visiting the family without surprise or disturbance, he was induced to extend his circuit by the foot of the rocks, and to linger upon his way until the morning should be considerably advanced. While, now standing with his arms across, and waiting the slow progress of the sun above the horizon, now sitting upon one of the numerous fragments which storms had detached from the rocks above him, he is meditating, alternately, upon the horrible catastrophe which he had witnessed, and upon the melancholy, and to him most interesting, news which he had learned at Saddletree's, we will give the reader to understand who Butler was, and how his fate was connected with that of Effie Deans, the unfortunate hand-maiden of the careful Mrs Saddletree.

Reuben Butler was of English extraction, though born in Scotland. His grandfather was a trooper in Monk's army,[2] and one of the party of dismounted dragoons which formed the forlorn hope at the storm of Dundee in 1651. Stephen Butler (called, from his talents in reading and expounding, Scripture Stephen and Bible Butler,) was a staunch independent, and received in its fullest comprehension the promise that the saints should inherit the earth. As hard knocks were what had chiefly fallen to his share hitherto in the division of this common property, he lost not the opportunity which the storm and plunder of a commercial place afforded him, to appropriate as large a share of the better things of this world as he could possibly compass. It would seem that he had succeeded indifferently well, for his exterior circumstances appeared, in consequence of this event, to have been much mended.

The troop to which he belonged was quartered at the village of Dalkeith,[3] as forming the body guard of Monk, who, in the capacity of general for the Commonwealth, resided in the neighbouring castle. When, on the eve of the Restoration, the general commenced his march from Scotland, a measure pregnant with such important consequences, he new-modelled his troops, and more especially those

immediately about his person, in order that they might consist entirely
of individuals devoted to himself. On this occasion Scripture Stephen
was weighed in the balance, and found wanting.⁴ It was supposed he
felt no call to any expedition which might endanger the reign of the
military sainthood, and that he did not consider himself as free in
conscience to join with any party which might be likely ultimately to
acknowledge the interest of Charles Stuart, the son of "the last man,"
as Charles I. was familiarly and unreverently termed by them in their
common discourse, as well as in their more elaborate predications and
harangues. As the time did not admit of cashiering such dissidents,
Stephen Butler was only advised in a friendly way to give up his horse
and accoutrements to one of Middleton's⁵ old troopers, who possessed
an accommodating conscience of a military stamp, and which squared
itself chiefly upon those of the colonel and pay-master. As this hint
came recommended by a certain sum of arrears presently payable,
Stephen had carnal wisdom enough to embrace the proposal, and with
great indifference saw his old corps depart for Coldstream, on their
route for the south, to establish the tottering government of England
on a new basis.

The *zone* of the ex-trooper, to use Horace's phrase,⁶ was weighty
enough to purchase a cottage and two or three fields (still known by
the name of Beersheba,⁷) within about a Scottish mile of Dalkeith; and
there did Stephen establish himself with a youthful helpmate, chosen
out of the said village, whose disposition to a comfortable settlement
on this side of the grave reconciled her to the gruff manners, serious
temper, and weather-beaten features of the martial enthusiast. Stephen
did not long survive the falling on "evil days and evil tongues,"⁸ of
which Milton, in the same predicament,⁹ so mournfully complains. At
his death his consort remained an early widow, with a male child of
three years old, which, in the sobriety wherewith it demeaned itself, in
the old-fashioned and even grim cast of its features, and in its
sententious mode of expressing itself, would sufficiently have vindicated the honour of the widow of Beersheba, had any one thought
proper to challenge the babe's descent from Bible Butler.

Butler's principles had not descended to his family, or extended
themselves among his neighbours. The air of Scotland was alien to the
growth of independency, however favourable to fanaticism under
other colours. But, nevertheless, they were not forgotten; and a certain
neighbouring Laird, who piqued himself upon the loyalty of his
principles "in the worst of times," (though I never heard they exposed

him to more peril than that of a broken head, or a night's lodging in the main guard, when wine and cavalierism predominated in his upper story,) had found it a convenient thing to rake up all matter of accusation against the deceased Stephen. In this enumeration his religious principles made no small figure, as, indeed, they must have seemed of the most exaggerated enormity to one whose own were so slight and so faintly traced, as to be well nigh imperceptible. In these circumstances, poor widow Butler was supplied with her full proportion of fines for non-conformity,[10] and all the other oppressions of the time, until Beersheba was fairly wrenched out of her hands, and became the property of the Laird who had so wantonly, as it had hitherto appeared, persecuted this poor forlorn woman. When his purpose was fairly achieved, he shewed some remorse or moderation, or whatever the reader may please to term it, in permitting her to occupy her husband's cottage, and cultivate, on no very heavy terms, a croft of land adjacent. Her son, Benjamin, in the meanwhile, grew up to man's estate, and, moved by that impulse which makes men seek marriage, even when its end can only be the perpetuation of misery, he wedded and brought a wife, and, eventually, a son, Reuben, to share the poverty of Beersheba.

The Laird of Dumbiedikes[*] had hitherto been moderate in his exactions, perhaps because he was ashamed to tax too highly the miserable means of support which remained to the widow Butler. But when a stout active young fellow appeared as the labourer of the croft in question, Dumbiedikes began to think so broad a pair of shoulders might bear an additional burthen. He regulated, indeed, his management of his dependents (who fortunately were but few in number,) much upon the principle of the carters whom he observed loading their carts at a neighbouring coal hill, and who never failed to clap an additional brace of hundred-weights on their burthen, so soon as by any means they had compassed a new horse of somewhat superior strength to that which had broken down the day before. However reasonable this practice appeared to the Laird of Dumbiedikes, he ought to have observed, that it may be overdone, and that it infers, as a matter of course, the destruction and loss of both horse, cart, and loading. Even so it befell when the additional "prestations" came to be

---

[* Dumbiedikes, selected as descriptive of the taciturn character of the imaginary owner, is really the name of a house bordering on the King's Park, so called because the late Mr Braidwood, an instructor of the deaf and dumb, resided there with his pupils. The situation of the real house is different from that assigned to the ideal mansion.]

demanded of Benjamin Butler. A man of few words, and few ideas, but attached to Beersheba with a feeling like that which a vegetable[11] may be supposed to entertain to the spot in which it chances to be planted, he neither remonstrated with the Laird, nor endeavoured to escape from him, but toiling night and day to accomplish the terms of his task-master,[12] fell into a burning fever and died. His wife did not long survive him, and, as if it had been the fate of this family to be left orphans, our Reuben Butler was, about the year 1704-5, left in the same circumstances in which his father had been placed, and under the same guardianship, being that of his grandmother, the widow of Monk's old trooper.

The same prospect of misery hung over the head of another tenant of this hard-hearted lord of the soil. This was a tough true-blue presbyterian, called Deans, who, though most obnoxious to the Laird on account of principles in church and state, contrived to maintain his ground upon the estate by regular payment of mail duties, kain, arriage, carriage, dry multure, lock, gowpen, and knaveship, and all the various exactions now commuted for money, and summed up in the emphatic word RENT. But the years 1700 and 1701,[13] long remembered in Scotland for dearth and general distress, subdued the stout heart of the agricultural whig. Citations by the ground-officer, decreets of the Baron Court, sequestrations, poindings of outsight and insight plenishing, flew about his ears as fast as ever the tory bullets whistled around those of the Covenanters at Pentland, Bothwell Brigg, or Airdsmoss.[14] Struggle as he might, and he struggled gallantly, "douce David Deans" was routed horse and foot, and lay at the mercy of his grasping landlord just at the time that Benjamin Butler died. The fate of each family was anticipated, but they who prophesied their expulsion to beggary and ruin, were disappointed by an accidental circumstance.

On the very term-day when their ejection should have taken place, when all their neighbours were prepared to pity, and not one to assist them, the minister of the parish, as well as a doctor from Edinburgh, received a hasty summons to attend the Laird of Dumbiedikes.[15] Both were surprised, for his contempt for both faculties had been pretty commonly his theme over an extra bottle, that is to say, at least once every day. The leech for the soul and he for the body alighted in the court of the little old manor-house at almost the same time, and when they had gazed a moment at each other with some surprise, they in the same breath expressed their conviction that Dumbiedikes must needs be very ill indeed, since he summoned them both to his presence at once. Ere the servant could usher them to his apartment the party was augmented by a man of law, Nichil Novit,[16] writing himself procurator before the Sheriff Court, for in those days there were no solicitors.[17] This latter personage was first summoned to the apartment of the Laird, where, after some short space, the soul-curer and the body-curer were invited to join him.

Dumbiedikes had been by this time transported into the best bed-room, used only upon occasions of death and marriage, and called, from the former of these occupations, the Dead-Room. There were in this apartment, besides the sick person himself and Mr Novit, the son and heir of the patient, a tall gawky silly-looking boy of fourteen or fifteen, and a housekeeper, a good buxom figure of a woman, betwixt forty and fifty, who had kept the keys and managed matters at Dumbiedikes since the lady's death. It was to these attendants that Dumbiedikes addressed himself pretty nearly in the following words; temporal and spiritual matters, the care of his health and his affairs, being strangely jumbled in a head which was never one of the clearest.

"These are sair times wi' me, gentlemen and neibours! amaist as ill as at the aughty-nine, when I was rabbled by the collegeaners.[*]— They mistook me muckle—they ca'd me a papist, but there was never a papist bit about me, minister.—Jock, ye'll take warning it's a debt we maun a' pay, and there stands Nichil Novit that will tell you I was never gude at paying debts in my life.—Master Novit, ye'll no forget to draw the annual rent that's due on the yerl's band—if I pay debt to other folk, I think they suld pay it to me—that's but equals aquals.— Jock, when ye hae naething else to do, ye may be aye sticking in a tree; it will be growing, Jock, when ye're sleeping.[†] My father tauld me sae forty years sin', but I ne'er fand time to mind him—Jock, ne'er drink brandy in the morning, it files the stamach sair; gin ye take a morning's draught, let it be aqua mirabilis; Jenny there makes it weel.—Doctor, my breath is growing as scant as a broken-winded

[* Immediately previous to the Revolution, the students at the Edinburgh College were violent anti-catholics. They were strongly suspected of burning the house of Priestfield, belonging to the Lord Provost; and certainly were guilty of creating considerable riots in 1688–9.]

[† The author has been flattered by the assurance, that this *naïve* mode of recommending arboriculture (which was actually delivered in these very words by a Highland laird, while on his death-bed, to his son) had so much weight with a Scottish earl,[18] as to lead to his planting a large tract of country.]

piper's, when he has played for four-and-twenty hours at a penny-wedding—Jenny, pit the cod aneath my head—but it's a' needless!—Mass John, could ye think o' rattling ower some bit short prayer, it wad do me gude maybe, and keep some queer thoughts out o' my head.—Say something, man."

"I cannot use a prayer like a rat-rhyme," answered the honest clergy-man; "and if you would have your soul redeemed like a prey from the fowler,[19] Laird, you must needs shew me your state of mind."

"And shouldna ye ken that without my telling you?" answered the patient. "What have I been paying stipend and teind parsonage and vicarage for, ever sin' the aughty-nine, an I canna get a spell of a prayer for't, the only time I ever asked for ane in my life?—Gang awa wi' your whiggery, if that's a' ye can do; auld Curate Kiltstoup wad hae read half the Prayer-Book[20] to me by this time—Awa w'ye!—Doctor, let's see if ye can do ony thing better for me."

The Doctor, who had obtained some information in the meanwhile from the housekeeper on the state of his complaints, assured him the medical art could not prolong his life many hours.

"Then damn Mass John and you baith!" cried the furious and intractable patient. "Did ye come here for naething but to tell me that ye canna help me at the pinch? Out wi' them, Jenny—out o' the house! and, Jock, my curse, and the curse of Cromwell[21] go wi' ye, if ye gie them either fee or bountith, or sae muckle as a black pair o' cheverons."[*]

The clergyman and doctor made a speedy retreat out of the apart-ment, while Dumbiedikes fell into one of those transports of violent and profane language, which had procured him the surname of Damn-me-dikes—"Bring me the brandy bottle, Jenny, ye b——,"[22] he cried, with a voice in which passion contended with pain. "I can die as I have lived, without fashing ony o' them. But there's ae thing," he said, sinking his voice—"there's ae fearful thing hings about my heart, and an anker of brandy winna wash it away—The Deans at Woodend!—I sequestrated them in the dear years, and now they are to flitt they'll starve—and that Beersheba, and that auld trooper's wife and his oe, they'll starve—they'll starve!—Look out, Jock; what kind o' night is't?"

"On-ding o' snaw, father," answered Jock, after having opened the window, and looked out with great composure.

[* *Cheverons*—gloves.]

"They'll perish in the drift," said the expiring sinner—"they'll perish wi' cauld!—but I'll be het eneugh, gin a' tales be true."

This last observation was made under breath, and in a tone which made the very attorney shudder. He tried his hand at ghostly advice, probably for the first time in his life, and recommended, as an opiate for the agonized conscience of the laird, reparation of the injuries he had done to these distressed families, which, he observed by the way, the civil law called *restitutio in integrum*. But Mammon was struggling with Remorse for retaining his place in a bosom he had so long possessed; and he partly succeeded, as an old tyrant proves often too strong for his insurgent rebels.

"I canna do't," he answered, with a voice of despair. "It would kill me to do't—how can ye bid me pay back siller, when ye ken how I want it? or dispone Beersheba, when it lies sae weel into my ain plaid-nuik? Nature made Dumbiedikes and Beersheba to be ae man's land—She did by ——. Nichil, it wad kill me to part them."

"But ye maun die whether or no, Laird," said Mr Novit; "and maybe ye wad die easier—it's but trying. I'll scroll the disposition in nae time."

"Dinna speak o't, sir," replied Dumbiedikes, "or I'll fling the stoup at your head.—But, Jock, lad, ye see how the warld warstles wi' me on my death-bed—Be kind to the puir creatures the Deanses and the Butlers—be kind to them, Jock. Dinna let the warld get a grip o' ye, Jock—but keep the gear thegither! and whate'er ye do, dispone Beersheba at no rate. Let the creatures stay at a moderate mailing, and hae bite and soup; it will maybe be the better wi' your father whare he's gaun, lad."

After these contradictory instructions, the Laird felt his mind so much at ease that he drank three bumpers of brandy continuously, and "soughed awa," as Jenny expressed it, in an attempt to sing "Deil stick the minister."[23]

His death made a revolution in favour of the distressed families. John Dumbie, now of Dumbiedikes in his own right, seemed to be close and selfish enough, but wanted the grasping spirit and active mind of his father; and his guardian happened to agree with him in opinion, that his father's dying recommendation should be attended to. The tenants, therefore, were not actually turned out of doors among the snow wreaths, and were allowed wherewith to procure butter-milk and pease bannocks, which they eat under the full force of the original malediction.[24] The cottage of Deans, called Woodend, was not very distant from that at Beersheba. Formerly there had been little intercourse between the families. Deans was a sturdy Scotchman, with all sort of prejudices against the Southron, and the spawn of the Southron. Moreover, Deans was, as we have said, a staunch presbyterian, of the most rigid and unbending adherence to what he conceived to be the only possible straight line, as he was wont to express himself, between right-hand heats and extremes, and left-hand defections;[25] and, therefore, he held in high dread and horror all independents, and whomsoever he supposed allied to them.

But, notwithstanding these national prejudices and religious prepossessions, Deans and the widow Butler were placed in such a situation, as naturally and at length created some intimacy between the families. They had shared a common danger and a mutual deliverance. They needed each other's assistance, like a company, who, crossing a mountain stream, are compelled to cling close together, lest the current should be too powerful for any who are not thus supported.

On nearer acquaintance, too, Deans abated some of his prejudices. He found old Mrs Butler, though not thoroughly grounded in the extent and bearing of the real testimony against the defections of the times, had no opinions in favour of the independent party; neither was she an Englishwoman. Therefore, it was to be hoped, that, though she was the widow of an enthusiastic corporal of Cromwell's dragoons, her grandson might be neither schismatic nor anti-national, two qualities concerning which Goodman Deans had as wholesome a terror as against papists and malignants. Above all, (for Douce Davie Deans had his weak side,) he perceived that widow Butler looked up to him with reverence, listened to his advice, and compounded for an occasional fling at the doctrines of her deceased husband, to which, as we have seen, she was by no means warmly attached, in consideration of the valuable counsels which the presbyterian afforded her for the management of her little farm. These usually concluded with, "they may do otherwise in England, neighbour Butler, for aught I ken;" or, "it may be different in foreign parts;" or, "they wha think differently on the great foundation of our covenanted reformation,[26] overturning and mishguggling the government and discipline of the kirk, and breaking down the carved work[27] of our Zion, might be for sawing the craft wi' aits; but I say pease, pease."[28] And as his advice was shrewd and sensible, though conceitedly given, it was received with gratitude, and followed with respect.

The intercourse which took place betwixt the families at Beersheba and Woodend became strict and intimate, at a very early period, betwixt Reuben Butler, with whom the reader is already in some degree acquainted, and Jeanie Deans, the only child of Douce Davie Deans by his first wife, "that singular Christian woman,"[29] as he was wont to express himself, "whose name was savoury to all that knew her for a desirable professor,[30] Christian Menzies in Hochmagirdle."[31] The manner of which intimacy, and the consequences thereof, we now proceed to relate.

CHAPTER 9

Reuben and Rachel, though as fond as doves,
Were yet discreet and cautious in their loves,
Nor would attend to Cupid's wild commands,
Till cool reflection bade them join their hands.
When both were poor, they thought it argued ill
Of hasty love to make them poorer still.

CRABBE'S *Parish Register*

WHILE widow Butler and widower Deans struggled with poverty, and the hard and sterile soil of those "parts and portions"[1] of the lands of Dumbiedikes which it was their lot to occupy, it became gradually apparent that Deans was to gain the strife, and his ally in the conflict was to lose it. The former was a man, and not much past the prime of life—Mrs Butler a woman, and declined into the vale of years. This, indeed, ought in time to have been balanced by the circumstance, that Reuben was growing up to assist his grandmother's labours, and that Jeanie Deans, as a girl, could be only supposed to add to her father's burthens. But Douce Davie Deans knew better things, and so schooled and trained the young minion, as he called her, that from the time she could walk, upwards, she was daily employed in some task or other suitable to her age and capacity, a circumstance which, added to her father's daily instructions and lectures, tended to give her mind, even when a child, a grave, serious, firm, and reflecting cast. An uncommonly strong and healthy temperament, free from all nervous affection and every other irregularity, which, attacking the body in its more noble functions, so often influences the mind, tended greatly to establish this fortitude, simplicity, and decision of character.

On the other hand, Reuben was weak in constitution, and, though not timid in temper, might be safely pronounced anxious, doubtful, and apprehensive. He partook of the temperament of his mother, who had died of a consumption in early age. He was a pale, thin, feeble, sickly boy, and somewhat lame, from an accident in early youth. He was, besides, the child of a doting grandmother, whose too solicitous attention to him soon taught him a sort of diffidence in himself, with a disposition to over-rate his own importance, which is one of the very worst consequences that children deduce from over-indulgence.

Still, however, the two children clung to each other's society, not more from habit than from taste. They herded together the handful of sheep, with the two or three cows, which their parents turned out rather to seek food than actually to feed upon the uninclosed common of Dumbiedikes. It was there that the two urchins might be seen seated beneath a blooming bush of whin, their little faces laid close together under the shadow of the same plaid drawn over both their heads, while the landscape around was embrowned by an overshadowing cloud, big with the shower which had driven the children to shelter. Upon other occasions they went together to school, the boy receiving that encouragement and example from his companion, in crossing the little brooks which intersected their path, and encountering cattle, dogs, and other perils, upon their journey, which the male sex in such cases usually consider it as their prerogative to extend to the weaker. But when, seated on the benches of the school-house, they began to con their lesson together, Reuben, who was as much superior to Jeanie Deans in acuteness of intellect, as inferior to her in firmness of constitution, and in that insensibility to fatigue and danger which depends on the conformation of the nerves, was able fully to requite the kindness and countenance with which, in other circumstances, she used to regard him. He was decidedly the best scholar at the little parish school, and so gentle was his temper and disposition, that he was rather admired than envied by the little mob who occupied the noisy mansion, although he was the declared favourite of the master. Several girls, in particular, (for in Scotland they are taught with the boys) longed to be kind to, and comfort the sickly lad, who was so much cleverer than his companions. The character of Reuben Butler was so calculated as to offer scope both for their sympathy and their admiration, the feelings, perhaps, through which the female sex (the more deserving part of them at least) is more easily attached.

But Reuben, naturally reserved and distant, improved none of these advantages; and only became more attached to Jeanie Deans, as the enthusiastic approbation of his master assured him of fair prospects in future life, and awakened his ambition. In the mean time, every advance that Reuben made in learning (and, considering his opportunities, they were uncommonly great) rendered him less capable of attending to the domestic duties of his grandmother's farm. While studying the *pons asinorum* in Euclid, he suffered every *cuddie* upon the common to trespass upon a large field of pease belonging to the Laird, and nothing but the active exertions of Jeanie Deans, with her little dog Dustiefoot, could have saved great loss and consequent punishment. Similar miscarriages marked his progress in his classical studies. He read Virgil's Georgics[2] till he did not know bear from barley; and had nearly destroyed the crofts of Beersheba, while attempting to cultivate them according to the practice of Columella and Cato the Censor.[3]

These blunders occasioned grief to his grand-dame, and disconcerted the good opinion which her neighbour, Davie Deans, had for some time entertained of Reuben.

"I see naething ye can make of that silly callant, neighbour Butler," said he to the old lady, "unless ye train him to the wark o' the ministry. And ne'er was there mair need of poorfu' preachers than e'en now in these cauld Gallio[4] days, when men's hearts are hardened like the nether mill-stone,[5] till they come to regard none of these things. It's evident this puir callant of yours will never be able to do an usefu' day's wark, unless it be as an ambassador from our Master; and I will make it my business to procure a licence when he is fit for the same, trusting he will be a shaft cleanly polished,[6] and meet to be used in the body of the kirk;[7] and that he shall not turn again, like the sow, to wallow in the mire[8] of heretical extremes and defections,[9] but shall have the wings of a dove, though he hath lain among the pots."[10]

The poor widow gulped down the affront to her husband's principles, implied in this caution, and hastened to take Butler from the High School,[11] and encourage him in the pursuit of mathematics and divinity, the only physics and ethics that chanced to be in fashion at the time.

Jeanie Deans was now compelled to part from the companion of her labour, her study, and her pastime, and it was with more than childish feeling that both children regarded the separation. But they were young, and hope was high, and they separated like those who hope to meet again at a more auspicious hour.

While Reuben Butler was acquiring at the University of St Andrews[12] the knowledge necessary for a clergyman, and macerating his body with the privations which were necessary in seeking food for his mind, his grandame became daily less able to struggle with her little farm, and was at length obliged to throw it up to the new Laird of Dumbiedikes. That great personage was no absolute Jew, and did not cheat her in making the bargain more than was tolerable. He even gave her permission to tenant the house in which she had lived with her husband, as long as it should be "tenantable," only he protested against paying for a farthing of repairs, any benevolence which he possessed being of the passive, but by no means of the active mood.

In the meanwhile, from superior shrewdness, skill, and other circumstances, some of them purely accidental, Davie Deans gained a footing in the world, the possession of some wealth, the reputation of more, and a growing disposition to preserve and increase his store; for which, when he thought upon it seriously, he was inclined to blame himself. From his knowledge in agriculture, as it was then practised, he became a sort of favourite with the Laird, who had no pleasure either in active sports or in society, and was wont to end his daily saunter by calling at the cottage of Woodend.

Being himself a man of slow ideas and confused utterance, Dumbiedikes used to sit or stand for half an hour with an old laced hat of his father's upon his head, and an empty tobacco-pipe in his mouth, with his eyes following Jeanie Deans, or "the lassie," as he called her, through the course of her daily domestic labour, while her father, after exhausting the subject of bestial, of ploughs, and of harrows, often took an opportunity of going full sail into controversial subjects, to which discussions the dignitary listened with much seeming patience, but without making any reply, or, indeed, as most people thought, without understanding a single word of what the orator was saying. Deans, indeed, denied this stoutly, as an insult at once to his own talents for expounding hidden truths, of which he was a little vain, and to the Laird's capacity of understanding them. He said, "Dumbiedikes was nane of these flashy gentles, wi' lace on their skirts and swords at their tails, that were rather for riding on horseback to hell than ganging bare-footed to Heaven.[13] He was na like his father—he was nae profane company-keeper[14]—nae swearer—nae drinker—nae frequenter of play-house, or music-house, or dancing-house[15]—nae Sabbath-breaker—nae imposer of aiths, or bonds,[16] or denyer of liberty to the flock.—He clave to the warld, and the warld's gear, a wee ower muckle, but then there was some breathing of a gale upon his spirit," &c. &c.[17] All this honest Davie said and believed.

It is not to be supposed, that, by a father and a man of sense and observation, the constant direction of the Laird's eyes towards Jeanie was altogether unnoticed. This circumstance, however, made a much greater impression upon another member of his family, a second helpmate, to wit, whom he had chosen to take to his bosom ten years after the death of his first. Some people were of opinion, that Douce Davie had been rather surprised into this step, for in general he was no friend to marriages or giving in marriage, and seemed rather to regard that state of society as a necessary evil,—a thing lawful, and to be tolerated in the imperfect state of our nature, but which clipped the wings with which we ought to soar upwards, and tethered the soul to its mansion of clay,[18] and the creature-comforts[19] of wife and bairns. His own practice, however, had in this material point varied from his principles, since, as we have seen, he twice knitted for himself this dangerous and ensnaring entanglement.

Rebecca, his spouse, had by no means the same horror of matrimony, and as she made marriages in imagination for every neighbour round, she failed not to indicate a match betwixt Dumbiedikes and her step-daughter Jeanie. The goodman used regularly to frown and pshaw whenever this topic was touched upon, but usually ended by taking his bonnet and walking out of the house to conceal a certain gleam of satisfaction, which, at such a suggestion, involuntarily diffused itself over his austere features.

The more youthful part of my readers may naturally ask, whether Jeanie Deans was deserving of this mute attention of the Laird of Dumbiedikes; and the historian, with due regard to veracity, is compelled to answer, that her personal attractions were of no uncommon description. She was short, and rather too stoutly made for her size, had grey eyes, light-coloured hair, a round good-humoured face, much tanned with the sun, and her only peculiar charm was an air of inexpressible serenity, which a good conscience, kind feelings, contented temper, and the regular discharge of all her duties, spread over her features. There was nothing, it may be supposed, very appalling in the form or manners of this rustic heroine; yet, whether from sheepish bashfulness, or from want of decision and imperfect knowledge of his own mind on the subject, the Laird of Dumbiedikes, with his old laced hat and empty tobacco-pipe, came and enjoyed the beatific vision[20] of Jeanie Deans day after day, week after week, year after year, without proposing to accomplish any of the prophecies of the step-mother.

This good lady began to grow doubly impatient on the subject, when, after having been some years married, she herself presented Douce Davie with another daughter, who was named Euphemia, by corruption, Effie. It was then that Rebecca began to turn impatient with the slow pace at which the Laird's wooing proceeded, judiciously arguing, that, as Lady Dumbiedikes would have but little occasion for tocher, the principal part of her gudeman's substance would naturally descend to the child by the second marriage. Other step-dames have tried less laudable means for clearing the way to the succession of their own children; but Rebecca, to do her justice, only sought little Effie's advantage through the promotion, or which must have generally been accounted such, of her elder sister. She therefore tried every female art within the compass of her simple skill to bring the Laird to a point; but had the mortification to perceive that her efforts, like those of an unskilful angler, only scared the trout she meant to catch. Upon one occasion, in particular, when she joked with the Laird on the propriety of giving a mistress to the house of Dumbiedikes, he was so effectually startled, that neither laced hat, tobacco-pipe, nor the intelligent proprietor of these moveables, visited Woodend for a fortnight. Rebecca was therefore compelled to leave the Laird to proceed at his own snail's pace, convinced, by experience, of the grave-digger's aphorism,[21] that your dull ass will not mend his pace for beating.

Reuben, in the meantime, pursued his studies at the university, supplying his wants by teaching the younger lads the knowledge he himself acquired, and thus at once gaining the means of maintaining himself at the seat of learning, and fixing in his mind the elements of what he had already obtained. In this manner, as is usual among the poorer students of divinity at Scottish universities, he contrived, not only to maintain himself according to his simple wants, but even to send considerable assistance to his sole remaining parent,[22] a sacred duty, of which the Scotch are seldom negligent. His progress in knowledge of a general kind, as well as in the studies proper to his profession, was very considerable, but was little remarked, owing to the retired modesty of his disposition, which in no respect qualified him to set off his learning to the best advantage. And thus, had Butler been a man given to make complaints, he had his tale to tell, like others, of unjust preferences, bad luck, and hard usage. On these subjects, however, he was habitually silent, perhaps from modesty, perhaps from a touch of pride, or perhaps from a conjunction of both.

He obtained his licence as a preacher of the gospel, with some compliments from the presbytery by whom it was bestowed; but this did not lead to any preferment, and he found it necessary to make the cottage at Beersheba his residence for some months, with no other income than was afforded by the precarious occupation of teaching in one or other of the neighbouring families. After having greeted his aged grandmother, his first visit was to Woodend, where he was received by Jeanie with warm cordiality, arising from recollections which had never been dismissed from her mind, by Rebecca with good-humoured hospitality, and by old Deans in a mode peculiar to himself.

Highly as Douce Davie honoured the clergy, it was not upon each individual of the cloth that he bestowed his approbation; and, a little jealous, perhaps, at seeing his youthful acquaintance erected into the dignity of a teacher and preacher, he instantly attacked him upon various points of controversy, in order to discover whether he might not have fallen into some of the snares, defections, and desertions of the time. Butler was not only a man of staunch presbyterian principles, but was also willing to avoid giving pain to his old friend by disputing upon points of little importance; and therefore he might have hoped to have come like refined gold[23] out of the furnace of Davie's interrogatories. But the result on the mind of that strict investigator was not altogether so favourable as might have been hoped and anticipated. Old Judith Butler, who had hobbled that evening as far as Woodend, in order to enjoy the congratulations of her neighbours upon Reuben's return, and upon his high attainments, of which she was herself not a little proud, was somewhat mortified to find that her old friend Deans did not enter into the subject with the warmth she expected. At first, indeed, he seemed rather silent than dissatisfied; and it was not till Judith had essayed the subject more than once that it led to the following dialogue.

"Aweel, neibor Deans, I thought ye wad hae been glad to see Reuben amang us again, puir fallow."

"I *am* glad, Mrs Butler," was the neighbour's concise answer.

"Since he has lost his grandfather and his father, (praised be Him that giveth and taketh!) I ken nae friend he has in the world that's been sae like a father to him as the sell o' ye, neibor Deans."

"God is the only father of the fatherless,"[24] said Deans, touching his bonnet and looking upwards. "Give honour where it is due,[25] gudewife, and not to an unworthy instrument."

"Aweel, that's your way o' turning it, and nae doubt ye ken best; but I hae kend ye, Davie, send a forpit o' meal to Beersheba when there was na a bow left in the meal-ark at Woodend; ay, and I hae kend ye"——

"Gudewife," said Davie, interrupting her, "these are but idle tales to tell me; fit for naething but to puff up our inward man wi' our ain vain acts. I stude beside blessed Alexander Peden,[26] when I heard him call the death and testimony of our happy martyrs but draps of blude and scarts of ink[27] in respect of fitting discharge of our duty; and what suld I think of ony thing the like of me can do?"

"Weel, neibor Deans, ye ken best; but I maun say that, I am sure you are glad to see my bairn again—the halt's gane now,[28] unless he has to walk ower mony miles at a stretch; and he has a wee bit colour in his cheek, that glads my auld een to see it; and he has as decent a black coat as the minister, and"——

"I am very heartily glad he is weel and thriving," said Mr Deans, with a gravity that seemed intended to cut short the subject; but a woman who is bent upon a point is not easily pushed aside from it.

"And," continued Mrs Butler, "he can wag his head in a pulpit now, neibor Deans, think but of that—my ain oe—and a'body maun sit still and listen to him, as if he were the Paip o' Rome."

"The what?—the who?—woman?" said Deans, with a sternness far beyond his usual gravity, as soon as these offensive words had struck upon the tympanum of his ear.

"Eh, guide us!" said the poor woman; "I had forgot what an ill will ye had aye at the Paip, and sae had my puir gudeman, Stephen Butler. Mony an afternoon he wad sit and take up his testimony again the Paip, and again baptizing of bairns,[29] and the like."

"Woman!" reiterated Deans, "either speak about what ye ken something o', or be silent; I say that independency is a foul heresy, and anabaptism a damnable and deceiving error, whilk suld be rooted out of the land wi' the fire o' the spiritual, and the sword o' the civil magistrate."

"Weel, weel, neibor, I'll no say that ye mayna be right," answered the submissive Judith. "I am sure ye are right about the sawing and the mawing, the sheering and the leading, and what for suld ye no be right about kirk-wark, too?—But concerning my oe, Reuben Butler"——

"Reuben Butler, gudewife," said David with solemnity, "is a lad I wish heartily weel to, even as if he were mine ain son—but I doubt there will be outs and ins in the tract of his walk.[30] I muckle fear his gifts will get the heels of his grace. He has ower muckle human wit and learning, and thinks as muckle about the form of the bicker as he does about the healsomeness of the food[31]—he maun broider the marriage-garment with lace and passments,[32] or its no gude eneugh for him. And its like he's something proud o' his human gifts and learning, whilk enable him to dress up his doctrine in that fine airy dress. But," added he, moved at seeing the old woman's uneasiness at his discourse, "affliction may gie him a jagg,[33] and let the wind out o' him as out o' a cow that's eaten wet clover, and the lad may do weel, and be a burning and a shining light;[34] and I trust it will be yours to see, and his to feel it, and that soon."

Widow Butler was obliged to retire, unable to make any thing more of her neighbour, whose discourse, though she did not comprehend it, filled her with undefined apprehensions on her grandson's account, and greatly depressed the joy with which she had welcomed him on his return. And it must not be concealed, in justice to Mr Deans's discernment, that Butler, in their conference, had made a greater display of his learning than the occasion called for, or than was like to be acceptable to the old man, who, accustomed to consider himself as a person pre-eminently entitled to dictate upon theological subjects of controversy, felt rather humbled and mortified when learned authorities were placed in array against him. In fact, Butler had not escaped the tinge of pedantry which naturally flowed from his education, and was apt, on many occasions, to make parade of his knowledge, when there was no need of such vanity.

Jeanie Deans, however, found no fault with this display of learning, but, on the contrary, admired it; perhaps on the same score that her sex are said to admire men of courage, on account of their own deficiency in that qualification. The circumstances of their families threw the young people constantly together; their old intimacy was renewed, though upon a footing better adapted to their age; and it became at length understood betwixt them, that their union should be deferred no longer than until Butler should obtain some steady means of support, however humble. This, however, was not a matter speedily to be accomplished. Plan after plan was formed, and plan after plan failed. The good-humoured cheek of Jeanie lost the first flush of juvenile freshness; Reuben's brow assumed the gravity of manhood, yet the means of attaining a settlement seemed remote as ever. Fortunately for the lovers, their passion was of no ardent or enthusiastic cast, and a sense of duty on both sides induced them to bear, with patient fortitude, the protracted interval which divided them from each other.

In the meanwhile, time did not roll on without effecting his usual changes. The widow of Stephen Butler, so long the prop of the family of Beersheba, was gathered to her fathers; and Rebecca, the careful spouse of our friend Davie Deans, was also summoned from her plans of matrimonial and domestic economy. The morning after her death, Reuben Butler went to offer his mite of consolation to his old friend and benefactor. He witnessed, on this occasion, a remarkable struggle betwixt the force of natural affection, and the religious stoicism, which the sufferer thought it was incumbent upon him to maintain under each earthly dispensation, whether of weal or woe.

On his arrival at the cottage, Jeanie, with her eyes overflowing with tears, pointed to the little orchard, "in which," she whispered with broken accents, "my poor father has been since his misfortune." Somewhat alarmed at this account, Butler entered the orchard, and advanced slowly towards his old friend, who, seated in a small rude arbour, appeared to be sunk in the extremity of his affliction. He lifted his eyes somewhat sternly as Butler approached, as if offended at the interruption; but as the young man hesitated whether he ought to retreat or advance, he arose, and came forward to meet him, with a self-possessed, and even dignified air.

"Young man," said the sufferer, "lay it not to heart, though the righteous perish and the merciful are removed, seeing it may well be that they are taken away from the evils to come. Woe to me, were I to shed a tear for the wife of my bosom, when I might weep rivers of water for this afflicted Church, cursed as it is with carnal seekers, and with the dead of heart."[35]

"I am happy," said Butler, "that you can forget your private affliction in your regard for public duty."

"Forget, Reuben?" said poor Deans, putting his handkerchief to his eyes,—"She's not to be forgotten on this side of time; but He that gives the wound can send the ointment. I declare there have been times during this night when my meditation has been so rapt, that I knew not of my heavy loss. It has been with me as with the worthy John Semple,[36] called Carspharn John,[*] upon a like trial,—I have been this night on the banks of Ulai,[37] plucking an apple here and there."

Notwithstanding the assumed fortitude of Deans, which he conceived to be the discharge of a great Christian duty, he had too good a heart not to suffer deeply under this heavy loss. Woodend became altogether distasteful to him; and as he had obtained both substance and experience by his management of that little farm, he resolved to employ them as a dairy farmer,[38] or cow-feeder, as they are called in

[* See p. 558 for the note, "Carspharn John".]

Scotland. The situation he chose for his new settlement was at a place called Saint Leonard's Crags, lying betwixt Edinburgh and the mountain called Arthur's Seat, and adjoining to the extensive sheep pasture still named the King's Park, from its having been formerly dedicated to the preservation of the royal game. Here he rented a small lonely house, then nearly half a mile distant from the nearest point of the city, but the site of which, with all the adjacent ground, is now occupied by the buildings which form the south-eastern suburb. An extensive pasture-ground adjoining, which Deans rented from the Keeper of the Royal Park, enabled him to feed his milk-cows; and the unceasing industry and activity of Jeanie, his eldest daughter, was exerted in making the most of their produce.

She had now less frequent opportunities of seeing Reuben, who had been obliged, after various disappointments, to accept the subordinate situation of assistant in a parochial school of some eminence, at three or four miles' distance from the city. Here he distinguished himself, and became acquainted with several respectable burgesses, who, on account of health, or other reasons, chose that their children should commence their education in this little village. His prospects were thus gradually brightening, and upon each visit which he paid at Saint Leonard's he had an opportunity of gliding a hint to this purpose into Jeanie's ear. These visits were necessarily very rare, on account of the demands which the duties of the school made upon Butler's time. Nor did he dare to make them even altogether so frequent as these avocations would permit. Deans received him with civility indeed, and even with kindness; but Reuben, as is usual in such cases, imagined that he read his purpose in his eyes, and was afraid too premature an explanation on the subject would draw down his positive disapproval. Upon the whole, therefore, he judged it prudent to call at Saint Leonard's just so frequently as old acquaintance and neighbourhood seemed to authorise, and no oftener. There was another person who was more regular in his visits.

When Davie Deans intimated to the Laird of Dumbiedikes his purpose of "quitting wi' the land and house at Woodend," the Laird stared and said nothing. He made his usual visits at the usual hour without remark, until the day before the term, when, observing the bustle of moving furniture already commenced, the great east-country *awmrie* dragged out of its nook, and standing with its shoulder to the company, like an awkward booby about to leave a room, the Laird again stared mightily, and was heard to ejaculate, "Hegh, sirs!" Even after the day of departure was past and gone, the Laird of Dumbiedikes, at his usual hour, which was that at which David Deans was wont to "loose the pleugh," presented himself before the closed door of the cottage at Woodend, and seemed as much astonished at finding it shut against his approach as if it was not exactly what he had to expect. On this occasion he was heard to ejaculate, "Gude guide us!" which, by those who knew him, was considered as a very unusual mark of emotion. From that moment forward, Dumbiedikes became an altered man, and the regularity of his movements, hitherto so exemplary, was as totally disconcerted as those of a boy's watch when he has broken the main-spring. Like the index of the said watch, did Dumbiedikes spin round the whole bounds of his little property, which may be likened unto the dial of the time-piece, with unwonted velocity. There was not a cottage into which he did not enter, nor scarce a maiden on whom he did not stare. But so it was, that although there were better farm-houses on the land than Woodend, and certainly much prettier girls than Jeanie Deans, yet it did somehow befall that the blank in the Laird's time was not so pleasantly filled up as it had been. There was no seat accommodated him so well as the "bunker" at Woodend, and no face he loved so much to gaze on as Jeanie Deans's. So, after spinning round and round his little orbit, and then remaining stationary for a week, it seems to have occurred to him, that he was not pinned down to circulate on a pivot, like the hands of the watch, but possessed the power of shifting his central point, and extending his circle if he thought proper. To realize which privilege of change of place, he bought a pony from a Highland drover, and with its assistance and company stepped, or rather stumbled, as far as Saint Leonard's Crags.

Jeanie Deans, though so much accustomed to the Laird's staring that she was sometimes scarce conscious of his presence, had nevertheless some occasional fears lest he should call in the organ of speech to back those expressions of admiration which he bestowed on her through his eyes. Should this happen, farewell, she thought, to all chance of an union with Butler. For her father, however stout-hearted and independent in civil and religious principle, was not without that respect for the laird of the land so deeply imprinted on the Scottish tenantry of the period. Moreover, if he did not positively dislike Butler, yet his fund of carnal learning was often the object of sarcasms on David's part, which were perhaps founded in jealousy, and which certainly indicated no partiality for the party against whom they were launched. And, lastly, the match with Dumbiedikes would have presented irresistible charms to one who used to complain that he felt himself apt to take "ower grit an armfu' o' the warld." So that, upon the whole, the Laird's diurnal visits were disagreeable to Jeanie from apprehension of future consequences, and it served much to console her, upon removing from the spot where she was bred and born, that she had seen the last of Dumbiedikes, his laced hat, and tobacco-pipe. The poor girl no more expected he could muster courage to follow her to Saint Leonard's Crags, than that any of her apple-trees or cabbages which she had left rooted in the "yard" at Woodend, would spontaneously, and unaided, have undertaken the same journey. It was, therefore, with much more surprise than pleasure that, on the sixth day[39] after their removal to Saint Leonard's, she beheld Dumbiedikes arrive, laced hat, tobacco-pipe, and all, and, with the self same greeting of "how's a' wi' ye, Jeanie?—Whare's the gudeman?" assume as nearly as he could the same position in the cottage at Saint Leonard's which he had so long and so regularly occupied at Woodend. He was no sooner, however, seated, than with an unusual exertion of his powers of conversation, he added, "Jeanie—I say, Jeanie woman"—here he extended his hand towards her shoulder with all the fingers spread out as if to clutch it, but in so bashful and awkward a manner, that when she whisked herself beyond its reach, the paw remained suspended in the air with the palm open, like the claw of a heraldic griffin— "Jeanie," continued the swain, in this moment of inspiration,—"I say, Jeanie, it's a braw day out bye, and the roads are no that ill for boot-hose."

"The deil's in the daidling body," muttered Jeanie between her teeth; "wha wad hae thought o' his daikering out this length?" And she afterwards confessed that she threw a little of this ungracious sentiment into her accent and manner, for her father being abroad, and the "body," as she irreverently termed the landed proprietor, "looking unco gleg and canty, she didna ken what he might be coming out wi' next."

Her frowns, however, acted as a complete sedative, and the Laird relapsed from that day into his former taciturn habits, visiting the cow-feeder's cottage three or four times every week, when the weather permitted, with apparently no other purpose than to stare at Jeanie Deans, while Douce Davie poured forth his eloquence upon the controversies and testimonies of the day.

CHAPTER 10

Her air, her manners, all who saw admired,
Courteous, though coy, and gentle, though retired;
The joy of youth and health her eyes display'd,
And ease of heart her every look convey'd.

CRABBE

THE visits of the Laird thus again sunk into matters of ordinary course, from which nothing was to be expected or apprehended. If a lover could have gained a fair one as a snake is said to fascinate a bird, by pertinaciously gazing on her with great stupid greenish eyes, which began now to be occasionally aided by spectacles, unquestionably Dumbiedikes would have been the person to perform the feat. But the art of fascination[1] seems among the *artes perditæ*,[2] and I cannot learn that this most pertinacious of starers produced any effect by his attentions beyond an occasional yawn.

In the meanwhile, the object of his gaze was gradually attaining the verge of youth, and approaching to what is called in females the middle age,[3] which is impolitely held to begin a few years earlier with their more fragile sex than with men. Many people would have been of opinion, that the Laird would have done better to have transferred his glances to an object possessed of far superior charms to Jeanie's, even when Jeanie's were in their bloom, who began now to be distinguished by all who visited the cottage at St Leonard's Crags.

Effie Deans, under the tender and affectionate care of her sister, had now shot up into a beautiful and blooming girl. Her Grecian-shaped head[4] was profusely rich in waving ringlets of brown hair, which, confined by a blue snood of silk, and shading a laughing Hebe countenance, seemed the picture of health, pleasure, and contentment. Her brown russet short-gown set off a shape, which time, perhaps, might be expected to render too robust, the frequent objection to Scottish beauty, but which, in her present early age, was slender and taper, with that graceful and easy sweep of outline, which at once indicates health and beautiful proportion of parts.

These growing charms, in all their juvenile profusion, had no power to shake the stedfast mind,[5] or divert the fixed gaze, of the constant Laird of Dumbiedikes. But there was scarce another eye that could behold this living picture of health and beauty, without pausing on it with pleasure. The traveller stopped his weary horse on the eve of entering the city which was the end of his journey, to gaze at the sylph-like form that tripped by him, with her milk-pail poised on her head, bearing herself so erect, and stepping so light and free under her burthen, that it seemed rather an ornament than an encumbrance. The lads of the neighbouring suburb, who held their evening rendezvous for putting the stone, casting the hammer, playing at long bowls, and other athletic exercises, watched the motions of Effie Deans, and contended with each other which should have the good fortune to attract her attention. Even the rigid presbyterians of her father's persuasion, who held each indulgence of the eye and sense to be a snare at least, if not a crime, were surprised into a moment's delight while gazing on a creature so exquisite,—instantly checked by a sigh, reproaching at once their own weakness, and mourning that a creature so fair should share in the common and hereditary guilt and imperfection[6] of our nature. She was currently entitled the Lily of Saint Leonard's, a name which she deserved as much by her guileless purity of thought, speech, and action, as by her uncommon loveliness of face and person.

Yet there were points in Effie's character, which gave rise not only to strange doubt and anxiety on the part of Douce David Deans, whose ideas were rigid, as may easily be supposed, upon the subject of youthful amusements, but even of serious apprehension to her more indulgent sister. The children of the Scotch of the inferior classes are usually spoiled by the early indulgence of their parents; how, wherefore, and to what degree, the lively and instructive narrative of the amiable and accomplished authoress of "Glenburnie"*[7] has saved me and all future scribblers the trouble of recording. Effie had had a double share of this inconsiderate and misjudged kindness. Even the strictness of her father's principles could not condemn the sports of infancy and childhood; and to the good old man, his younger daughter, the child of his old age, seemed a child for some years after she attained the years of womanhood, was still called the "bit lassie" and "little Effie," and was permitted to run up and down uncontrolled, unless upon the Sabbath, or at the times of family worship.[8] Her

* Mrs Elizabeth Hamilton, now no more.—*Editor.*

sister, with all the love and care of a mother, could not be supposed to possess the same authoritative influence, and that which she had hitherto exercised became gradually limited and diminished as Effie's advancing years entitled her, in her own conceit at least,[9] to the right of independence and free agency. With all the innocence and goodness of disposition, therefore, which we have described, the Lily of St Leonard's possessed a little fund of self-conceit and obstinacy, and some warmth and irritability of temper, partly natural perhaps, but certainly much increased by the unrestrained freedom of her childhood. Her character will be best illustrated by a cottage evening scene.[10]

The careful father was absent in his well-stocked byre, foddering those useful and patient animals on whose produce his living depended, and the summer evening was beginning to close in, when Jeanie Deans began to be very anxious for the appearance of her sister, and to fear that she would not reach home before their father returned from the labour of the evening, when it was his custom to have "family exercise," and when she knew that Effie's absence would give him the most serious displeasure. These apprehensions hung heavier upon her mind, because, for several preceding evenings, Effie had disappeared about the same time, and her stay, at first so brief as scarce to be noticed, had been gradually protracted to half an hour, and an hour, and on the present occasion had considerably exceeded even this last limit. And now, Jeanie stood at the door, with her hand before her eyes to avoid the rays of the level sun, and looked alternately along the various tracks which led towards their dwelling, to see if she could descry the nymph-like form of her sister. There was a wall and a stile which separated the royal domain, or King's Park, as it is called, from the public road; to this pass she frequently directed her attention, when she saw two persons appear there somewhat suddenly, as if they had walked close by the side of the wall to screen themselves from observation. One of them, a man, drew back hastily; the other, a female crossed the stile, and advanced towards her—it was Effie. She met her sister with that affected liveliness of manner, which, in her rank, and sometimes in those above it, females occasionally assume to hide surprise or confusion; and she carolled as she came—

> "The elfin knight sate on the brae,
>   The broom grows bonnie, the broom grows fair;
> And by there came lilting a lady so gay,
>   And we daurna gang down to the broom nae mair."[11]

"Whisht, Effie," said her sister; "our father's coming out o' the byre."—The damsel stinted in her song.—"Whare hae ye been sae late at e'en?"

"It's no late, lass," answered Effie.

"It's chappit eight on every clock o' the town, and the sun's gaun down ahint the Corstorphine hills—Whare can ye hae been sae late?"

"Nae gate," answered Effie.

"And wha was that parted wi' you at the stile?"

"Nae body," replied Effie once more.

"Nae gate?—Nae body?—I wish it may be a right gate, and a right body, that keeps folk out sae late at e'en, Effie."

"What needs ye be aye speering then at folk?" retorted Effie. "I'm sure, if ye'll ask nae questions, I'll tell ye nae lees.[12] I never ask what brings the Laird of Dumbiedikes glowering here like a wull-cat, (only his een's greener, and no sae gleg,) day after day, till we are a' like to gaunt our chafts aff."

"Because ye ken very weel he comes to see our father," said Jeanie, in answer to this pert remark.

"And Dominie Butler—Does he come to see our father, that's sae taen wi' his Latin words?" said Effie, delighted to find that, by carrying the war into the enemy's country, she could divert the threatened attack upon herself, and with the petulance of youth she pursued her triumph over her prudent elder sister. She looked at her with a sly air, in which there was something like irony, as she chaunted, in a low but marked tone, a scrap of an old Scotch song—[13]

> "Through the kirk-yard
> I met wi' the Laird,
> The silly puir body he said me nae harm;
> But just ere 'twas dark
> I met wi' the clerk"——

Here the songstress stopped,[14] looked full at her sister, and, observing the tear gather in her eyes, she suddenly flung her arms round her neck, and kissed them away. Jeanie, though hurt and displeased, was unable to resist the caresses of this untaught child of nature,[15] whose good and evil seemed to flow rather from impulse than from reflection. But as she returned the sisterly kiss, in token of perfect reconciliation, she could not suppress the gentle reproof—"Effie, if ye will learn fule-sangs, ye might make a kinder use of them."

"And so I might, Jeanie," continued the girl, clinging to her sister's neck; "and I wish I had never learned ane o' them—and I wish we had never come here—and I wish my tongue had been blistered or I had vexed ye."

"Never mind that, Effie," replied her affectionate sister; "I canna be muckle vexed wi' ony thing ye say to me—but O dinna vex our father!"

"I will not—I will not," replied Effie; "and if there were as mony dances the morn's night as there are merry dancers in the north firmament on a frosty e'en, I winna budge an inch to gang near ane o' them."

"Dance?"[16] echoed Jeanie Deans in astonishment. "O, Effie, lassie, what could tak ye to a dance?"

It is very possible, that, in the communicative mood into which the Lily of St Leonard's was now surprised, she might have given her sister her unreserved confidence, and saved me the pain of telling a melancholy tale; but at the moment the word dance was uttered, it reached the ear of old David Deans, who had turned the corner of the house, and came upon his daughters ere they were aware of his presence. The word *prelate*, or even the word *pope*, could hardly have produced so appalling an effect upon David's ear; for, of all exercises, that of dancing, which he termed a voluntary and regular fit of distraction,[17] he deemed most destructive of serious thoughts, and the readiest inlet to all sort of licentiousness; and he accounted the encouraging, and even permitting, assemblies or meetings, whether among those of high or low degree, for this fantastic and absurd purpose, or for that of dramatic representations, as one of the most flagrant proofs of defection and causes of wrath. The pronouncing of the word *dance* by his own daughters, and at his own door, now drove him beyond the verge of patience. "Dance!" he exclaimed. "Dance?— dance, said ye? I daur ye, limmers that ye are, to name sic a word at my door-cheek! It's a dissolute profane pastime, practised by the Israelites only at their base and brutish worship of the Golden Calf at Bethel, and by the unhappy lass wha danced aff the head of John the Baptist, upon whilk chapter I will exercise this night for your farther instruction, since ye need it sae muckle, nothing doubting that she has cause to rue the day, lang or this time, that ere she suld hae shook a limb on sic an errand. Better for her to hae been born a cripple,[18] and carried frae door to door, like auld Bessie Bowie, begging bawbees, than to be a king's daughter, fiddling and flinging the gate she did. I hae often wondered that ony ane that ever bent a knee for the right purpose, should ever daur to crook a hough to fyke and fling at piper's wind and fiddler's squealing. And I bless God, (with that singular worthy, Peter Walker the packman[19] at Bristo Port,[*]) that ordered my lot in my dancing days, so that fear of my head and throat, dread of bloody rope and swift bullet, and trenchant swords and pain of boots and thumkins, cauld and hunger, wetness and weariness, stopped the lightness of my head, and the wantonness of my feet. And now, if I hear ye, quean lassies, sae muckle as name dancing, or think there's sic a thing in this warld as flinging to fiddler's sounds and piper's springs, as sure as my father's spirit is with the just, ye shall be no more either charge or concern of mine! Gang in, then—gang in, then, hinnies," he added, in a softer tone, for the tears of both daughters, but especially those of Effie, began to flow very fast,—"Gang in, dears, and we'll seek grace to preserve us frae all manner of profane folly, whilk causeth to sin, and promoteth the kingdom of darkness, warring with the kingdom of light."[20]

The objurgation of David Deans, however well meant, was unhappily timed. It created a diversion of feelings in Effie's bosom, and deterred her from her intended confidence in her sister. "She wad haud me nae better than the dirt below her feet," said Effie to herself, "were I to confess I hae danced wi' him four times on the green down bye, and ance at Maggie Macqueen's; and she'll maybe hing it ower my head that she'll tell my father, and then she wad be mistress and mair. But I'll no gang back there again. I'm resolved I'll no gang back. I'll lay in a leaf of my Bible,[†] and that's very near as if I had made an aith, that I winna gang back." And she kept her vow for a week, during which she was unusually cross and fretful, blemishes which had never before been observed in her temper, except during a moment of contradiction.

There was something in all this so mysterious as considerably to alarm the prudent and affectionate Jeanie, the more so as she judged it unkind to her sister to mention to their father grounds of anxiety which might arise from her own imagination. Besides, her respect for the good old man did not prevent her from being aware that he was both hot-tempered and positive, and she sometimes suspected that he carried his dislike to youthful amusements beyond the verge that

[* See p. 559 for the note, "Peter Walker".]

[† This custom, of making a mark by folding a leaf in the party's Bible when a solemn resolution is formed, is still held to be, in some sense, an appeal to Heaven for his or her sincerity.]

religion and reason demanded. Jeanie had sense enough to see that a sudden and severe curb upon her sister's hitherto unrestrained freedom might be rather productive of harm than good, and that Effie, in the headstrong wilfulness of youth, was likely to make what might be overstrained in her father's precepts an excuse to herself for neglecting them altogether. In the higher classes, a damsel, however giddy, is still under the dominion of etiquette, and subject to the surveillance of mammas and chaperones; but the country girl, who snatches her moment of gaiety during the intervals of labour, is under no such guardianship or restraint, and her amusement becomes so much the more hazardous. Jeanie saw all this with much distress of mind, when a circumstance occurred which appeared calculated to relieve her anxiety.

Mrs Saddletree, with whom our readers have already been made acquainted, chanced to be a distant relation of Douce David Deans, and as she was a woman orderly in her life and conversation, and, moreover, of good substance, a sort of acquaintance was formally kept up between the families. Now, this careful dame, about a year and a half before our story commences, chanced to need in the line of her profession a better sort of servant, or rather shop-woman. "Mr Saddletree," she said, "was never in the shop when he could get his nose within the Parliament House, and it was an awkward thing for a woman-body to be standing among bundles o' barkened leather her lane, selling saddles and bridles; and she had cast her eyes upon her far-awa cousin Effie Deans, as just the very sort of lassie she would want to keep her in countenance on such occasions."

In this proposal there was much that pleased old David,—there was bed, board, and bountith—it was a decent situation—the lassie would be under Mrs Saddletree's eye, who had an upright walk,[21] and lived close by the Tolbooth Kirk,[22] in which might still be heard the comforting doctrines of one of those few ministers of the Kirk of Scotland who had not bent the knee unto Baal,[23] according to David's expression, or become accessary to the course of national defections,—union, toleration, patronages, and a bundle of prelatical Erastian oaths[24] which had been imposed on the church since the Revolution, and particularly in the reign of "the late woman," (as he called Queen Anne), the last of that unhappy race of Stuarts. In the good man's security concerning the soundness of the theological doctrine which his daughter was to hear, he was nothing disturbed on account of the snares of a different kind, to which a creature so beautiful, young, and wilful, might be exposed in the centre of a populous and corrupted city. The fact is, that he thought with so much horror on all approaches to irregularities of the nature most to be dreaded in such cases, that he would as soon have suspected and guarded against Effie's being induced to become guilty of the crime of murder. He only regretted that she should live under the same roof with such a worldly-wise man as Bartoline Saddletree, whom David never suspected of being an ass as he was, but considered as one really endowed with all the legal knowledge to which he made pretension, and only liked him the worse for possessing it. The lawyers, especially those amongst them who sate as ruling elders in the General Assembly of the Kirk, had been forward in promoting the measures of patronage, of the abjuration oath, and others, which, in the opinion of David Deans, were a breaking down of the carved work[25] of the sanctuary, and an intrusion upon the liberties of the kirk. Upon the dangers of listening to the doctrines of a legalized formalist,[26] such as Saddletree, David gave his daughter many lectures; so much so, that he had time to touch but slightly on the dangers of chambering, company-keeping, and promiscuous dancing, to which, at her time of life, most people would have thought Effie more exposed, than to the risk of theoretical error in her religious faith.

Jeanie parted from her sister, with a mixed feeling of regret, and apprehension, and hope. She could not be so confident concerning Effie's prudence as her father, for she had observed her more narrowly, had more sympathy with her feelings, and could better estimate the temptations to which she was exposed. On the other hand, Mrs Saddletree was an observing, shrewd, notable woman, entitled to exercise over Effie the full authority of a mistress, and likely to do so strictly, yet with kindness. Her departure to Saddletree's, it was most probable, would also serve to break off some idle acquaintances, which Jeanie suspected her sister to have formed in the neighbouring suburb. Upon the whole, then, she viewed her removal from Saint Leonard's with pleasure, and it was not until the very moment of their parting for the first time in their lives, that she felt the full force of sisterly sorrow. While they repeatedly kissed each other's cheeks, and wrung each other's hands, Jeanie took that moment of affectionate sympathy, to press upon her sister the necessity of the utmost caution in her conduct while residing in Edinburgh. Effie listened, without once raising her large dark eye-lashes, from which the drops fell so fast as almost to resemble a fountain. At the conclusion she sobbed again, kissed her sister, and promised to recollect all the good counsel she had given her, and they parted.

During the first few weeks, Effie was all that her kinswoman expected, and even more. But with time there came a relaxation of that early zeal which she manifested in Mrs Saddletree's service. To borrow once again from the poet, who so correctly and beautifully describes living manners,—

> Something there was, what, none presumed to say,—
> Clouds lightly passing on a summer's day;
> Whispers and hints, which went from ear to ear,
> And mixed reports no judge on earth could clear.[27]

During this interval, Mrs Saddletree was sometimes displeased by Effie's lingering, when she was sent upon errands about the shop business, and sometimes by a little degree of impatience which she manifested at being rebuked on such occasions. But she good-naturedly allowed, that the first was very natural to a girl to whom every thing in Edinburgh was new, and the other was only the petulance of a spoiled child, when subjected to the yoke of domestic discipline for the first time. Attention and submission could not be learned at once—Holy-Rood was not built in a day—use would make perfect.[28]

It seemed as if the considerate old lady had presaged truly. Ere many months had passed, Effie became almost wedded to her duties, though she no longer discharged them with the laughing cheek and light step, which at first had attracted every customer. Her mistress sometimes observed her in tears, but they were signs of secret sorrow, which she concealed as often as she saw them attract notice. Time wore on, her cheek grew pale, and her step heavy. The cause of these changes could not have escaped the matronly eye of Mrs Saddletree, but she was chiefly confined by indisposition to her bed-room for a considerable time during the latter part of Effie's service. This interval was marked by symptoms of anguish almost amounting to despair. The utmost efforts of the poor girl to command her fits of hysterical agony were often totally unavailing, and the mistakes which she made in the shop the while were so numerous and so provoking, that Bartoline Saddletree, who, during his wife's illness, was obliged to take closer charge of the business than consisted with his study of the weightier matters of the law, lost all patience with the girl, who, in his law Latin, and without much respect to gender, he declared ought to be cognosced by inquest of a jury, as *fatuus, furiosus,* and *naturaliter idiota*. Neighbours, also, and fellow-servants, remarked, with malicious curiosity or degrading pity, the disfigured shape, loose dress, and pale cheeks of the once beautiful and still interesting girl. But to no one would she grant her confidence, answering all taunts with bitter sarcasm, and all serious expostulation with sullen denial, or with floods of tears.

At length, when Mrs Saddletree's recovery was likely to permit her wonted attention to the regulation of her household, Effie Deans, as if unwilling to face an investigation made by the authority of her mistress, asked permission of Bartoline to go home for a week or two, assigning indisposition, and the wish of trying the benefit of repose and the change of air, as the motives of her request. Sharp-eyed as a lynx (or conceiving himself to be so) in the nice sharp quillets[29] of legal discussion, Bartoline was as dull at drawing inferences from the occurrences of common life as any Dutch professor of mathematics. He suffered Effie to depart without much suspicion, and without any enquiry.

It was afterwards found that a period of a week intervened betwixt her leaving her master's house and arriving at Saint Leonard's. She made her appearance before her sister in a state rather resembling the spectre than the living substance of the gay and beautiful girl, who had left her father's cottage for the first time scarce seventeen months before. The lingering illness of her mistress had, for the last few months, given her a plea for confining herself entirely to the dusky precincts of the shop in the Lawnmarket, and Jeanie was so much occupied, during the same period, with the concerns of her father's household, that she had rarely found leisure for a walk into the city, and a brief and hurried visit to her sister. The young women, therefore, had scarcely seen each other for several months, nor had a single scandalous surmise reached the ears of the secluded inhabitants of the cottage at St Leonard's. Jeanie, therefore, terrified to death at her sister's appearance, at first overwhelmed her with enquiries, to which the unfortunate young woman returned for a time incoherent and rambling answers, and finally fell into a hysterical fit. Rendered too certain of her sister's misfortune, Jeanie had now the dreadful alternative of communicating her ruin to her father, or of endeavouring to conceal it from him. To all questions concerning the name or rank of her seducer, and the fate of the being to whom her fall had given birth, Effie remained mute as the grave, to which she seemed hastening; and indeed the least allusion to either seemed to drive her to distraction. Her sister, in distress and in despair, was about to repair to Mrs Saddletree to consult her experience, and at the same time to obtain what lights she could upon this most unhappy affair, when she was saved that pains by a new stroke of fate, which seemed to carry misfortune to the uttermost.

David Deans had been alarmed at the state of health in which his daughter returned to her paternal residence; but Jeanie had contrived to divert him from particular and specific enquiry. It was, therefore, like a clap of thunder to the poor old man, when, just as the hour of noon had brought the visit of the Laird of Dumbiedikes as usual, other and sterner, as well as most unexpected guests, arrived at the cottage of St Leonard's. These were the officers of justice, with a warrant of justiciary to search for and apprehend Euphemia, or Effie, Deans, accused of the crime of child-murther. The stunning weight of a blow so totally unexpected bore down the old man, who had in his early youth resisted the brow of military and civil tyranny, though backed with swords and guns, tortures and gibbets. He fell extended and senseless upon his own hearth; and the men, happy to escape from the scene of his awakening, raised, with rude humanity, the object of their warrant from her bed, and placed her in a coach, which they had brought with them. The hasty remedies which Jeanie had applied to bring back her father's senses were scarce begun to operate, when the noise of the wheels in motion recalled her attention to her miserable sister. To run shrieking after the carriage was the first vain effort of her distraction, but she was stopped by one or two female neighbours, assembled, by the extraordinary appearance of a coach in that sequestered place, who almost forced her back to her father's house. The deep and sympathetic affliction of these poor people, by whom the little family at Saint Leonard's were held in high regard, filled the house with lamentation. Even Dumbiedikes was moved from his wonted apathy, and, groping for his purse as he spoke, ejaculated, "Jeanie woman—Jeanie woman! dinna greet—it's sad wark but siller will help it;"[30] and he drew out his purse as he spoke.

The old man had now raised himself from the ground, and, looking about him as if he missed something, seemed gradually to recover the sense of his wretchedness. "Where," he said, with a voice that made the roof ring, "where is the vile harlot, that has disgraced the blood of an honest man?—Where is she, that has no place among us, but has come foul with her sins, like the Evil One, among the children of God?—Where is she, Jeanie?—Bring her before me, that I may kill her with a word and a look."

All hastened around him with their appropriate sources of consolation—the Laird with his purse, Jeanie with burnt feathers and strong waters, and the women with their exhortations. "O neighbour—O, Mr Deans, it's a sair trial, doubtless—but think of the Rock of Ages,[31] neighbour—think of the promise!"[32]

"And I do think of it, neighbours—and I bless God that I can think of it, even in the wrack and ruin of a' that's nearest and dearest to me—But to be the father of a cast-away—a profligate—a bloody Zipporah[33]—a mere murderess!—O, how will the wicked exult in the high places of their wickedness!—the prelatists, and the latitudinarians, and the hand-waled murderers,[34] whose hands are hard as horn wi' hauding the slaughter-weapons—they will push out the lip,[35] and say that we are even such as themselves. Sair, sair I am grieved, neighbours, for the poor cast-away—for the child of mine old age—but sairer for the stumbling-block and scandal[36] it will be to all tender and honest souls!"

"Davie—winna siller do't?" insinuated the Laird, still proffering his green purse, which was full of guineas.

"I tell ye, Dumbiedikes," said Deans, "that if telling down my haill substance could hae saved her frae this black snare, I wad hae walked out wi' naething but my bonnet and my staff to beg an awmous for God's sake, and ca'd mysell an happy man—But if a dollar, or a plack, or the nineteenth part of a boddle, wad save her open guilt and open shame frae open punishment, that purchase wad David Deans never make!—Na, na—an eye for an eye,[37] a tooth for a tooth, life for life, blood for blood—it's the law of God and it's the law of man[38].—Leave me, sirs—leave me—I maun warstle wi' this trial in privacy and on my knees."

Jeanie, now in some degree restored to the power of thought, joined in the same request. The next day found the father and daughter still in the depth of affliction, but the father sternly supporting his load of ill through a proud sense of religious duty, and the daughter anxiously suppressing her own feelings to avoid again awakening his. Thus was it with the afflicted family until the morning after Porteous's death, a period at which we are now arrived.

CHAPTER 11

Is all the counsel that we two have shared,
The sisters' vows, the hours that we have spent
When we have chid the hasty-footed time
For parting us—Oh! and is all forgot?

Midsummer Night's Dream

WE have been a long while in conducting Butler to the door of the cottage at Saint Leonard's; yet the space which we have occupied in the preceding narrative does not exceed in length that which he actually spent on Salisbury Crags on the morning which succeeded the execution done upon Porteous by the rioters. For this delay he had his own motives. He wished to collect his thoughts, strangely agitated as they were, first by the melancholy news of Effie Deans's situation, and afterwards by the frightful scene which he had witnessed. In the situation also in which he stood with respect to Jeanie and her father, some ceremony, at least some choice of fitting time and season, was necessary to wait upon them. Eight in the morning was then the ordinary hour for breakfast, and he resolved that it should arrive before he made his appearance in their cottage.

Never did hours pass so heavily. Butler shifted his place, and enlarged his circle to while away the time, and heard the huge bell of St Giles's toll each successive hour in swelling tones, which were instantly attested by those of the other steeples in succession. He had heard seven struck in this manner, when he began to think he might venture to approach nearer to St Leonard's, from which he was still a mile distant. Accordingly he descended from his lofty station as low as the bottom of the valley which divides Salisbury Crags from those small rocks which take their name from Saint Leonard. It is, as many of my readers may know, a deep, wild, grassy valley, scattered with huge rocks and fragments which have descended from the cliffs and steep ascent to the east.

This sequestered dell, as well as other places of the open pasturage of the King's Park, was, about this time, often the resort of the gallants of the time who had affairs of honour to discuss with the sword. Duels were then very common in Scotland, for the gentry were at once idle, haughty, fierce, divided by faction and addicted to intemperance, so that there lacked neither provocation, nor inclination to resent it when given; and the sword, which was part of every gentleman's dress, was the only weapon used for the decision of such differences. When, therefore, Butler observed a young man, skulking, apparently to avoid observation, among the scattered rocks at some distance from the footpath, he was naturally led to suppose that he had sought this lonely spot upon that evil errand. He was so strongly impressed with this, that, notwithstanding his own distress of mind, he could not, according to his sense of duty as a clergyman, pass this person without speaking to him. There are times, thought he to himself, when the slightest interference may avert a great calamity—when a word spoken in season may do more for prevention than the eloquence of Tully could do for remedying evil—And for my own griefs, be they as they may, I shall feel them the lighter, if they divert me not from the prosecution of my duty.

Thus thinking and feeling, he quitted the ordinary path, and advanced nearer the object he had noticed. The man at first directed his course towards the hill, in order, as it appeared, to avoid him; but when he saw that Butler seemed disposed to follow him, he adjusted his hat fiercely, turned round, and came forward, as if to meet and defy scrutiny.

Butler had an opportunity of accurately studying his features as they advanced slowly to meet each other. The stranger seemed about twenty-five years old. His dress was of a kind which could hardly be said to indicate his rank with certainty, for it was such as young gentlemen sometimes wore while on active exercise in the morning, and which, therefore, was imitated by those of the inferior ranks, as young clerks and tradesmen, because its cheapness rendered it attainable, while it approached more nearly to the apparel of youths of fashion than any other which the manners of the times permitted them to wear. If his air and manner could be trusted, however, this person seemed rather to be dressed under than above his rank; for his carriage was bold and somewhat supercilious, his step easy and free, his manner daring and unconstrained. His stature was of the middle size, or rather above it, his limbs well-proportioned and strong, yet not so strong as to infer the reproach of clumsiness. His features were uncommonly handsome, and all about him would have been interesting and prepossessing, but for that indescribable expression which habitual dissipation gives to the countenance, joined with a certain audacity in look and manner, of that kind which is often assumed as a mask for confusion and apprehension.

Butler and the stranger met—surveyed each other—when, as the latter, slightly touching his hat, was about to pass by him, Butler, while he returned the salutation, observed, "A fine morning, sir—You are on the hill early."

"Sir, I have business here," said the young man, in a tone meant to repress further enquiry.

"I do not doubt it, sir," said Butler. "I trust you will forgive my hoping that it is of a lawful kind?"

"Sir," said the other, with marked surprise, "I never forgive impertinence, nor can I conceive what title you have to hope any thing about what no way concerns you."

"I am a soldier, sir,"[1] said Butler, "and have a charge to arrest evil-doers in the name of my Master."

"A soldier?" said the young man, stepping back, and fiercely laying his hand on his sword—"A soldier, and arrest me? Did you reckon what your life was worth before you took the commission upon you?"

"You mistake me, sir," said Butler gravely; "neither my warfare nor my warrant is of this world—I am a preacher of the gospel, and have power, in my Master's name, to command the peace upon earth[2] and good will towards men, which was proclaimed with the gospel."

"A minister!" said the stranger, carelessly, and with an expression approaching to scorn. "I know the gentlemen of your cloth in Scotland claim a strange right of intermeddling[3] with men's private affairs. But I have been abroad, and know better than to be priest-ridden."

"Sir, if it be true that any of my cloth, or, it might be more decently said, of my calling, interfere with men's private affairs, for the gratification either of idle curiosity, or for worse motives, you cannot have learned a better lesson abroad than to contemn such practices. But, in my Master's work, I am called to be busy in season and out of season,[4] and, conscious as I am of a pure motive, it were better for me to incur your contempt for speaking, than the correction of my own conscience for being silent."

"In the name of the devil," said the young man impatiently, "say what you have to say, then; though whom you take me for, or what earthly concern you can have with me, a stranger to you, or with my actions and motives, of which you can know nothing, I cannot conjecture for an instant."

"You are about," said Butler, "to violate one of your country's wisest laws—you are about, which is much more dreadful, to violate a law, which God himself has implanted within our nature, and written, as it were, in the table of our hearts, to which every thrill of our nerves is responsive."

"And what is the law you speak of?" said the stranger, in a hollow and somewhat disturbed accent.

"Thou shalt do no MURDER,"[5] said Butler, with a deep and solemn voice.

The young man visibly started, and looked considerably appalled. Butler perceived he had made a favourable impression, and resolved to follow it up. "Think," he said, "young man," laying his hand kindly upon the stranger's shoulder, "what an awful alternative you voluntarily chuse for yourself, to kill or be killed. Think what it is, to rush uncalled into the presence of an offended Deity, your heart fermenting with evil passions, your hand hot from the steel you had been urging, with your best skill and malice, against the breast of a fellow-creature. Or, suppose yourself the scarce less wretched survivor, with the guilt of Cain,[6] the first murderer, in your heart, with his stamp upon your brow—that stamp, which struck all who gazed on him with unutterable horror, and by which the murderer is made manifest to all who look upon him. Think——"[7]

The stranger gradually withdrew himself from under the hand of his monitor; and, pulling his hat over his brows, thus interrupted him. "Your meaning, sir, I dare say, is excellent, but you are throwing your advice away. I am not in this place with violent intentions against any one. I may be bad enough—you priests say all men are so—but I am here for the purpose of saving life, not of taking it away. If you wish to spend your time rather in doing a good action than in talking about you know not what, I will give you an opportunity. Do you see yonder crag to the right, over which appears the chimney of a lone house? Go thither, enquire for one Jeanie Deans, the daughter of the goodman; let her know that he she wots of remained here from day-break till this hour, expecting to see her, and that he can abide no longer. Tell her, she *must* meet me at the Hunter's Bog to-night, as the moon rises behind St Anthony's Hill, or that she will make a desperate man of me."

"Who, or what are you," replied Butler, exceedingly and most unpleasantly surprised, "who charge me with such an errand?"

"I am the devil!"——answered the young man hastily.

Butler stepped instinctively back, and commended himself internally to Heaven; for, though a wise and strong-minded man, he was neither wiser nor more strong-minded than those of his age and plan of education, with whom, to disbelieve witchcraft or spectral appearances, was held an undeniable proof of atheism.[8]

The stranger went on without observing his emotion. "Yes, call me Apollyon, Abaddon, whatever name you shall chuse, as a clergyman acquainted with the upper and lower circles of spiritual denomination, to call me by, you shall not find an appellation more odious to him that bears it, than is mine own."

This sentence was spoken with the bitterness of self-upbraiding, and a contortion of visage absolutely demoniacal. Butler, though a man brave by principle, if not by constitution, was overawed; for intensity of mental distress has in it a sort of sublimity which repels and overawes all men, but especially those of kind and sympathetic dispositions. The stranger turned abruptly from Butler as he spoke, but instantly returned, and, coming up to him closely and boldly, said, in a fierce determined tone, "I have told you who and what I am— who, and what are you? What is your name?"

"Butler," answered the person to whom this abrupt question was addressed, surprised into answering it by the sudden and fierce manner of the querist—"Reuben Butler, a preacher of the gospel."

At this answer the stranger again plucked more deep over his brows the hat which he had thrown back in his former agitation. "Butler!" he repeated,—"the assistant of the schoolmaster at Libberton?"

"The same," answered Butler composedly.

The stranger covered his face with his hand, as if on sudden reflection, and then turned away, but stopped when he had walked a few paces; and seeing Butler follow him with his eyes, called out in a stern yet suppressed tone, just as if he had exactly calculated that his accents should not be heard a yard beyond the spot on which Butler stood. "Go your way, and do mine errand. Do not look after me. I will neither descend through the bowels of these rocks, nor vanish in a flash of fire; and yet the eye that seeks to trace my motions shall have reason to curse it was ever shrouded by eye-lid or eye-lash. Begone, and look not behind you. Tell Jeanie Deans, that when the moon rises I shall expect to meet her at Nicol Muschat's Cairn,[9] beneath Saint Anthony's Chapel."

As he uttered these words, he turned and took the road against the hill, with a haste that seemed as peremptory as his tone of authority.

Dreading he knew not what of additional misery to a lot which seemed little capable of receiving augmentation, and desperate at the idea that any living man should dare to send so extraordinary a request, couched in terms so imperious, to the half-betrothed object of his early and only affection, Butler strode hastily towards the cottage, in order to ascertain how far this daring and rude gallant was actually entitled to press on Jeanie Deans a request which no prudent, and scarce any modest young woman was likely to comply with.

Butler was by nature neither jealous nor superstitious; yet the feelings which lead to those moods of the mind were rooted in his heart, as a portion derived from the common stock of humanity. It was maddening to think that a profligate gallant, such as the manner and tone of the stranger evinced him to be, should have it in his power to command forth his future bride and plighted true love, at a place so improper, and an hour so unseasonable. Yet the tone in which the stranger spoke had nothing of the soft half-breathed voice proper to the seducer who solicits an assignation; it was bold, fierce, and imperative, and had less of love in it than of menace and intimidation.

The suggestions of superstition seemed more plausible, had Butler's mind been very accessible to them. Was this indeed the Roaring Lion,[10] who goeth about seeking whom he may devour? This was a question which pressed itself on Butler's mind with an earnestness that cannot be conceived by those who live in the present day.[11] The fiery eye, the abrupt demeanour, the occasionally harsh, yet studiously subdued tone of voice,—the features, handsome, but now clouded with pride, now disturbed by suspicion, now inflamed with passion— those dark hazel eyes which he sometimes shaded with his cap, as if he were averse to have them seen while they were occupied with keenly observing the motions and bearing of others—those eyes that were now turbid with melancholy, now gleaming with scorn, and now sparkling with fury—was it the passions of a mere mortal they expressed, or the emotions of a fiend, who seeks, and seeks in vain, to conceal his fiendish designs under the borrowed mask of manly beauty? The whole partook of the mien, language, and port of the ruined archangel;[12] and, imperfectly as we have been able to describe it, the effect of the interview upon Butler's nerves, shaken as they were at the time by the horrors of the preceding night, was greater than his understanding warranted, or his pride cared to submit to. The very place where he had met this singular person was desecrated, as it were, and unhallowed, owing to many violent deaths, both in duels and by suicide, which had in former times taken place there; and the spot which he had named as a rendezvous at so late an hour, was held in general to be accursed, from a frightful and cruel murder which had been there committed by the wretch from whom the place took its name, upon the person of his own wife.[*] It was in such places, according to the belief of that period, (when the laws against witchcraft were still in fresh observance, and had even lately been acted upon[13]), that evil spirits had power to make themselves visible to human eyes, and to practise upon the feelings and senses of mankind. Suspicions, founded on such circumstances, rushed on Butler's mind, unprepared as it was, by any previous course of reasoning, to deny that which all of his time, country, and profession, believed; but common sense[14] rejected these vain ideas as inconsistent, if not with possibility, at least with the general rules by which the universe is governed,—a deviation from which, as Butler well argued with himself, ought not to be admitted as probable upon any but the plainest and most incontrovertible evidence. An earthly lover, however, or a young man, who, from whatever cause, had the right of exercising such summary and unceremonious authority over the object of his long-settled, and apparently sincerely returned affection, was an object scarce less appalling to his mind, than those which superstition suggested.

His limbs exhausted with fatigue, his mind harassed with anxiety, and with painful doubts and recollections, Butler dragged himself up the ascent from the valley to Saint Leonard's Crags, and presented himself at the door of Deans's habitation, with feelings much akin to the miserable reflections and fears of its inhabitants.

[* See p. 561 for the note, "Muschat's Cairn".]

CHAPTER 12

Then she stretched out her lily hand,
 And for to do her best;
"Hae back thy faith and troth, Willie,
 God gie thy soul good rest."
Old Ballad

"COME in," answered the low and sweet-toned voice he loved best to hear, as Butler tapped at the door of the cottage. He lifted the latch, and found himself under the roof of affliction. Jeanie was unable to trust herself with more than one glance towards her lover, whom she now met under circumstances so agonizing to her feelings, and at the same time so humbling to her honest pride. It is well known, that much, both of what is good and bad in the Scottish national character, arises out of the intimacy of their family connections. "To be come of honest folk," that is, of people who have borne a fair and unstained reputation, is an advantage as highly prized amongst the lower Scotch, as the emphatic counterpart, "to be of a good family," is valued among their gentry. The worth and respectability of one member of a peasant's family is always accounted by themselves and others, not only a matter of honest pride, but a guarantee for the good conduct of the whole. On the contrary, such a melancholy stain as was now flung on one of the children of Deans, extended its disgrace to all connected with him, and Jeanie felt herself lowered at once in her own eyes and in those of her lover. It was in vain that she repressed this feeling, as far subordinate and too selfish to be mingled with her sorrow for her sister's calamity. Nature prevailed; and while she shed tears for her sister's distress and danger, there mingled with them bitter drops of grief for her own degradation.

As Butler entered, the old man was seated by the fire with his well-worn pocket Bible in his hands, the companion of the wanderings and dangers of his youth, and bequeathed to him on the scaffold by one of those, who, in the year 1686, sealed their enthusiastic principles with their blood. The sun sent its rays through a small window at the old man's back, and, "shining motty through the reek," to use the expression of a bard of that time and country,[1] illumined the grey hairs of the sufferer, and the sacred page which he studied. His features, far from handsome, and rather harsh and severe, had yet, from their expression of habitual gravity and contempt for earthly things, an expression of stoical dignity amidst their sternness. He boasted, in no small degree, the attributes which Southey[2] ascribes to the ancient Scandinavians, whom he terms "firm to inflict, and stubborn to endure." The whole formed a picture, of which the lights might have been given by Rembrandt, but the outline would have required the force and vigour of Michael Angelo.[3]

Deans lifted his eye as Butler entered, and instantly withdrew it, as from an object which gave him at once surprise and sudden pain. He had assumed such high ground with this carnal-witted scholar, as he had in his pride termed Butler, that to meet him of all men, under feelings of humiliation, aggravated his misfortune, and was a consummation like that of the dying chief in the old ballad[4]—"Earl Percy sees my fall."

Deans raised the Bible with his left hand, so as partly to screen his face, and putting back his right as far as he could, held it towards Butler in that position, at the same time turning his body from him, as if to prevent his seeing the working of his countenance. Butler clasped the extended hand which had supported his orphan infancy, wept over it, and in vain endeavoured to say more than the words,—"God comfort you—God comfort you!"

"He will—he doth, my friend," said Deans, assuming firmness as he discovered the agitation of his guest; "he doth now, and he will yet more, in his own gude time. I have been ower proud of my sufferings in a gude cause, Reuben, and now I am to be tried with those whilk will turn my pride and glory into a reproach and a hissing.[5] How muckle better I hae thought mysell than them that lay saft, fed sweet, and drank deep,[6] when I was in the moss-haggs and moors, wi' precious Donald Cameron,[7] and worthy Mr Blackadder,[8] called Guess-again; and how proud I was o' being made a spectacle to men and angels, having stood on their pillory at the Canongate afore I was fifteen years old, for the cause of a deserted covenant. To think, Reuben, that I, wha hae been sae honoured and exalted in my youth, nay, when I was but a hafflins callant, and that hae borne testimony again the defections o' the times yearly, monthly, daily, hourly, minutely, striving and testifying with uplifted hand and voice, crying aloud, and sparing not,[9] against all great national snares, as the nation-wasting and church-sinking abomination of union, toleration, and patronage, imposed by the last woman of that unhappy race of Stuarts;[10] also against the infringements and invasions of the just powers of eldership, whereanent I uttered my paper, called 'A Cry of an Howl in the Desart,'[11] printed at the Bow-head, and sold by all flying stationers[12] in town and country—and *now*"——

Here he paused. It may well be supposed that Butler, though not absolutely coinciding in all the good old man's ideas about church government, had too much consideration and humanity to interrupt him, while he reckoned up with conscious pride his sufferings, and the constancy of his testimony. On the contrary, when he paused under the influence of the bitter recollections of the moment, Butler instantly threw in his mite of encouragement.

"You have been well known, my old and reverend friend, a true and tried follower of the Cross; one who, as Saint Jerome[13] hath it, '*per infamiam et bonam famam grassari ad immortalitatem,*' which may be freely rendered, 'who rusheth on to immortal life, through bad report and good report.' You have been one of those to whom the tender and fearful souls cry during the midnight solitude,—'Watchman, what of the night?—Watchman, what of the night?'[14]—And, assuredly, this heavy dispensation, as it comes not without Divine permission, so it comes not without its special commission and use."

"I do receive it as such," said poor Deans, returning the grasp of Butler's hand, "and, if I have not been taught to read the Scripture in any other tongue but my native Scottish, (even in his distress Butler's Latin quotation had not escaped his notice,) I have, nevertheless, so learned them, that I trust to bear even this crook in my lot[15] with submission. But O, Reuben Butler, the kirk, of whilk, though unworthy, I have yet been thought a polished shaft,[16] and meet to be a pillar,[17] holding, from my youth upward, the place of ruling elder—what will the lightsome and profane think of the guide that cannot keep his own family from stumbling? How will they take up their song and their reproach, when they see that the children of professors are liable to as foul back-sliding as the offspring of Belial! But I will bear my cross with the comfort, that whatever shewed like goodness in me or mine, was but like the light that shines frae creeping insects, on the brae-side, in a dark night—it kythes bright to the ee, because all is dark around it; but when the morn comes on the mountains, it is but a puir crawling kail-worm[18] after a'. And sae it shows, wi' ony rag of human righteousness,[19] or formal law-work, that we may pit round us to cover our shame."

As he pronounced these words, the door again opened, and Mr Bartoline Saddletree entered, his three-pointed hat set far back on his head, with a silk handkerchief beneath it, to keep it in that cool position, his gold-headed cane in his hand, and his whole deportment that of a wealthy burgher, who might one day look to have a share in the magistracy, if not actually to hold the curule chair itself.

Rochefoucault,[20] who has torn the veil from so many foul gangrenes of the human heart, says, we find something not altogether unpleasant to us in the misfortunes of our best friends. Mr Saddletree would have been very angry had any one told him that he felt pleasure in the disaster of poor Effie Deans, and the disgrace of her family; and yet there is great question whether the gratification of playing the person of importance, inquiring, investigating, and laying down the law on the whole affair, did not offer, to say the least, full consolation for the pain which pure sympathy gave him on account of his wife's kinswoman. He had now got a piece of real judicial business by the end, instead of being obliged, as was his common case, to intrude his opinion where it was neither wished nor wanted; and felt as happy in the exchange as a boy when he gets his first new watch, which actually goes when wound up, and has real hands and a true dial-plate. But besides this subject for legal disquisition, Bartoline's brains were also overloaded with the affair of Porteous, his violent death, and all its probable consequences to the city and community. It was what the French call *l'embarras des richesses*, the confusion arising from too much mental wealth. He walked in with a consciousness of double importance, full fraught with the superiority of one who possesses more information than the company into which he enters, and who feels a right to discharge his learning on them without mercy. "Good morning, Mr Deans,—good-morrow to you, Mr Butler,—I was not aware that you were acquainted with Mr Deans."

Butler made some slight answer; his reasons may be readily imagined for not making his connection with the family, which, in his eyes, had something of tender mystery, a frequent subject of conversation with indifferent persons, such as Saddletree.

The worthy burgher, in the plenitude of self-importance, now sate down upon a chair, wiped his brow, collected his breath, and made the first experiment of the restored pith of his lungs, in a deep and dignified sigh, resembling a groan in sound and intonation—"Awfu' times these, neighbour Deans, awfu' times."

"Sinfu', shamefu', heaven-daring[21] times," answered Deans, in a lower and more subdued tone.

"For my part," continued Saddletree, swelling with importance, "what between the distress of my friends, and my puir auld country, ony wit that ever I had may be said to have abandoned me, sae that I sometimes think mysell as ignorant as if I were *inter rusticos*. Here when I arise in the morning, wi' my mind just arranged touching what's to be done in puir Effie's misfortune, and hae gotten the hale statute at my finger-ends, the mob maun get up and string Jock Porteous to a dyester's beam, and ding a' thing out of my head again."

Deeply as he was distressed with his own domestic calamity, Deans could not help expressing some interest in the news. Saddletree immediately entered on details of the insurrection and its consequences, while Butler took the occasion to seek some private conversation with Jeanie Deans. She gave him the opportunity he sought, by leaving the room, as if in prosecution of some part of her morning labour. Butler followed her in a few minutes, leaving Deans so closely engaged by his busy visitor, that there was little chance of his observing their absence.

The scene of their interview was an outer apartment, where Jeanie was used to busy herself in arranging the productions of her dairy. When Butler found an opportunity of stealing after her into this place, he found her silent, dejected, and ready to burst into tears. Instead of the active industry with which she had been accustomed, even while in the act of speaking, to employ her hands in some useful branch of household business, she was seated listless in a corner, sinking apparently under the weight of her own thoughts. Yet the instant he entered, she dried her eyes, and, with the simplicity and openness of her character, immediately entered on conversation.

"I am glad you have come in, Mr Butler," said she, "for—for—for I wished to tell ye, that all maun be ended between you and me—it's best for baith our sakes."

"Ended!" said Butler, in surprise; "and for what should it be ended?—I grant this is a heavy dispensation, but it lies neither at your door nor mine—it's an evil of God's sending, and it must be borne; but it cannot break plighted troth, Jeanie, while they that plighted their word wish to keep it."

"But, Reuben," said the young woman, looking at him affectionately, "I ken weel that ye think mair of me than yourself; and, Reuben, I can only in requital think mair of your weal than of my ain. Ye are a man of spotless name, bred to God's ministry, and a' men say that ye will some day rise high in the kirk, though poverty keep ye doun e'en now. Poverty is a bad back-friend, Reuben, and that ye ken ower weel; but ill fame is a waur ane, and that is a truth ye sall never learn through my means."

"What do you mean?" said Butler, eagerly and impatiently; "or how do you connect your sister's guilt, if guilt there be, which, I trust in God, may yet be disproved, with our engagement?—how can that affect you or me?"

"How can you ask me that, Mr Butler? Will this stain, d'ye think, ever be forgotten as lang as our heads are abune the grund? Will it not stick to us, and to our bairns, and to their very bairns' bairns? To hae been the child of an honest man, might hae been saying something for me and mine; but to be the sister of a —— O, my God!"—With this exclamation her resolution failed, and she burst into a passionate fit of tears.

The lover used every effort to induce her to compose herself, and at length succeeded; but she only resumed her composure to express herself with the same positiveness as before. "No, Reuben, I'll bring disgrace hame to nae man's hearth; my ain distresses I can bear, and I maun bear, but there is nae occasion for buckling them on other folks' shouthers. I will bear my load alone—the back is made for the burthen."[22]

A lover is by charter wayward and suspicious; and Jeanie's readiness to renounce their engagement, under pretence of zeal for his peace of mind and respectability of character, seemed to poor Butler to form a portentous combination with the commission of the stranger he had met with that morning. His voice faultered as he asked, "Whether nothing but a sense of her sister's present distress occasioned her to talk in that manner?"

"And what else can do sae?" she replied with simplicity. "Is it not ten long years since we spoke together in this way?"

"Ten years?" said Butler. "It is a long time—sufficient perhaps for a woman to weary"——

"To weary of her auld gown," said Jeanie, "and to wish for a new ane, if she likes to go brave, but not long enough to weary of a friend—The eye may wish change, but the heart never."

"Never?" said Reuben,—"that is a bold promise."

"But not more bauld than true," said Jeanie, with the same quiet simplicity which attended her manner in joy and grief, in ordinary affairs, and in those which most interested her feelings.

Butler paused, and, looking at her fixedly—"I am charged," he said, "with a message to you, Jeanie."

"Indeed! From whom? Or what can ony ane have to say to me?"

"It is from a stranger," said Butler, affecting to speak with an indifference which his voice belied—"A young man whom I met this morning in the Park."

"My God!" said Jeanie eagerly; "and what did he say?"

"That he did not see you at the hour he proposed, but required you should meet him alone at Muschat's Cairn this next night, so soon as the moon rises."

"Tell him," said Jeanie hastily, "I shall certainly come."

"May I ask," said Butler, his suspicions increasing at the ready alacrity of the answer, "who this man is to whom you are so willing to give the meeting at a place and hour so uncommon?"

"Folk maun do muckle they have little will to do, in this world," replied Jeanie.

"Granted," said her lover; "but what compels you to this?—who is this person? What I saw of him was not very favourable—who, or what is he?"

"I do not know," replied Jeanie composedly.

"You do not know?" said Butler, stepping impatiently through the apartment—"You propose to meet a young man whom you do not know, at such a time, and in a place so lonely—you say you are compelled to do this—and yet you say you do not know the person who exercises such an influence over you!—Jeanie, what am I to think of this?"

"Think only, Reuben, that I speak truth, as if I were to answer at the last day.—I do not ken this man—I do not even ken that I ever saw him, and yet I must give him the meeting he asks—there's life and death upon it."

"Will you not tell your father, or take him with you?" said Butler.

"I cannot," said Jeanie; "I have no permission."

"Will you let *me* go with you? I will wait in the Park till nightfall, and join you when you set out."

"It is impossible," said Jeanie; "there maunna be mortal creature within hearing of our conference."

"Have you considered well the nature of what you are going to do?—the time—the place—an unknown and suspicious character?— Why, if he had asked to see you in this house, your father sitting in the next room, and within call, at such an hour, you should have refused to see him."

"My weird maun be fulfilled, Mr Butler; my life and my safety are in God's hands, but I'll not spare to risk either of them on the errand I am gaun to do."

"Then, Jeanie," said Butler, much displeased, "we must indeed break short off, and bid farewell. When there can be no confidence betwixt a man and his plighted wife on such a momentous topic, it is a sign that she has no longer the regard for him that makes their engagement safe and suitable."

Jeanie looked at him and sighed. "I thought," she said, "that I had brought myself to bear this parting—but—but—I did not ken that we were to part in unkindness. But I am a woman and you are a man—it may be different wi' you—if your mind is made easier by thinking sae hardly of me, I would not ask you to think otherwise."

"You are," said Butler, "what you have always been—wiser, better, and less selfish in your native feelings, than I can be, with all the helps philosophy can give to a Christian.—But why—why will you persevere in an undertaking so desperate? Why will you not let me be your assistant—your protector, or at least your adviser?"

"Just because I cannot, and I dare not," answered Jeanie.—"But hark, what's that? Surely my father is no weel?"

In fact, the voices in the next room became obstreperously loud of a sudden, the cause of which vociferation it is necessary to explain before we go farther.

When Jeanie and Butler retired, Mr Saddletree entered upon the business which chiefly interested the family. In the commencement of their conversation he found old Deans, who, in his usual state of mind, was no granter of propositions,[23] so much subdued by a deep sense of his daughter's danger and disgrace, that he heard without replying to, or perhaps without understanding, one or two learned disquisitions on the nature of the crime imputed to her charge, and on the steps which ought to be taken in consequence. His only answer at each pause was, "I am no misdoubting that ye wuss us weel—your wife's our far-awa' cousin."

Encouraged by these symptoms of acquiescence, Saddletree, who, as an amateur of the law, had a supreme deference for all constituted authorities, again recurred to his other topic of interest, the murder, namely, of Porteous, and pronounced a severe censure on the parties concerned.

"These are kittle times—kittle times, Mr Deans, when the people take the power of life and death out of the hands of the rightful magistrate into their ain rough grip. I am of opinion, and so I believe will Mr Crossmyloof and the Privy-Council,[24] that this rising in effeir of war, to take away the life of a reprieved man, will prove little better than perduellion."

"If I hadna that on my mind whilk is ill to bear, Mr Saddletree," said Deans, "I wad make bold to dispute that point wi' you."

"How could ye dispute what's plain law, man?" said Saddletree, somewhat contemptuously; "there's no a callant that e'er carried a pock wi' a process in't, but will tell you that perduellion is the warst and maist virulent kind of treason, being an open convocating of the king's lieges against his authority, (mair especially in arms, and by touk of drum, to baith whilk accessories my een and lugs bore witness,) and muckle warse than lese-majesty, or the concealment of a treasonable purpose—It winna bear a dispute, neighbour."

"But it will though," retorted douce Davie Deans; "I tell ye it will bear a dispute—I never like your cauld, legal, formal doctrines, neighbour Saddletree. I haud unco little by the Parliament House, since the awfu' downfall of the hopes of honest folk that followed the Revolution."

"But what wad ye hae had, Mr Deans?" said Saddletree impatiently; "did na ye get baith liberty and conscience made fast, and settled by tailzie on you and your heirs for ever?"

"Mr Saddletree," retorted Deans, "I ken ye are one of those that are wise after the manner of this world,[25] and that ye haud your part, and cast in your portion wi' the lang heads and lang gowns, and keep with the smart witty-pated lawyers of this our land—Weary on the dark and dolefu' cast that they hae gien this unhappy kingdom, when their black hand of defection was clasped in the red hand of our sworn murtherers:[26] when those who had numbered the towers of our Zion, and marked the bulwarks[27] of our reformation, saw their hope turn into a snare, and their rejoicing into weeping."

"I canna understand this, neighbour," answered Saddletree. "I am an honest presbyterian of the Kirk of Scotland, and stand by her and the General Assembly, and the due administration of justice by the fifteen Lords o' Session and the five Lords o' Justiciary."

"Out upon ye, Mr Saddletree!" exclaimed David, who, in an opportunity of giving his testimony on the offences and backslidings of the land, forgot for a moment his own domestic calamity—"out upon your General Assembly, and the back of my hand to your Court o' Session!—What is the tane but a waefu' bunch o' cauldrife professors and ministers, that sate bien and warm when the persecuted remnant

were warstling wi' hunger, and cauld, and fear of death, and danger of
fire and sword, upon wet brae-sides, peat-haggs, and flow-mosses, and
that now creep out of their holes, like blue-bottle flees in a blink of
sunshine, to take the pu'pits and places of better folk—of them that
witnessed, and testified, and fought, and endured pit, prison-house,
and transportation beyond seas?—A bonny bike[28] there's o' them!—
And for your Court o' Session"——

"Ye may say what ye will o' the General Assembly," said Saddletree,
interrupting him, "and let them clear them that kens them; but as for
the Lords o' Session, forbye that they are my next door neighbours, I
would have ye ken, for your ain regulation, that to raise scandal anent
them, whilk is termed, to *murmur* again them, is a crime *sui generis*—
sui generis, Mr Deans—ken ye what that amounts to?"

"I ken little o' the language of Antichrist,"[29] said Deans; "and I
care less than little what carnal courts may call the speeches of honest
men. And as to murmur again them, it's what a' the folk that losses
their pleas, and nine-tenths o' them that win them, will be gay sure to
be guilty in. Sae I wad hae ye ken that I haud a' your gleg-tongued
advocates, that sell their knowledge for pieces of silver,[30] and your
worldly-wise judges, that will gie three days of hearing in presence to a
debate about the peeling of an ingan, and no ae half-hour to the gospel
testimony, as legalists and formalists, countenancing, by sentences,
and quirks, and cunning turns of law, the late begun courses of
national defections—union, toleration, patronages, and Yerastian prelatic oaths.[31] As for the soul and body-killing Court o' Justiciary"——

The habit of considering his life as dedicated to bear testimony in
behalf of what he deemed the suffering and deserted cause of true
religion, had swept honest David along with it thus far; but with the
mention of the criminal court, the recollection of the disastrous
condition of his daughter rushed at once on his mind; he stopped short
in the midst of his triumphant declamation, pressed his hands against
his forehead, and remained silent.

Saddletree was somewhat moved, but apparently not so much so as
to induce him to relinquish the privilege of prosing in his turn,
afforded him by David's sudden silence. "Nae doubt, neighbour," he
said, "it's a sair thing to hae to do wi' courts of law, unless it be to
improve ane's knowledge and practique, by waiting on as a hearer; and
touching this unhappy affair of Effie—ye'll hae seen the dittay doubtless?" He dragged out of his pocket a bundle of papers,[32] and began to
turn them over. "This is no it—this is the information of Mungo

Marsport, of that ilk, against Captain Lackland, for coming on his lands of Marsport with hawks, hounds, lying-dogs, nets, guns, bows, cross-bows, hagbuts of found, or other engines more or less for destruction of game, sic as red-deer, fallow-deer, capper-cailzies, grey-fowl, moor-fowl, paitricks, herons, and sic like; he the said defender not being ane qualified person in terms of the statute sixteen hundred and twenty-ane; that is, not having ane plough-gate of land. Now the defences proponed say, that *non constat* at this present what is a plough-gate of land, whilk uncertainty[33] is sufficient to elide the conclusions of the libel. But then the answers to the defences, (they are signed by Mr Crossmyloof, but Mr Younglad drew them,) they propone, that it signifies naething, *in hoc statu*, what or how muckle a plough-gate of land may be, in respect the defender has nae lands whatsoe'er, less or mair. 'Sae grant a plough-gate'" (here Saddletree read from the paper in his hand,) "'to be less than the nineteenth part of a guse's grass'[34] (I trow Mr Crossmyloof put in that—I ken his style,)—'of a guse's grass, what the better will the defender be, seeing he hasna a divot-cast of land in Scotland?—*Advocatus* for Lackland duplies, that *nihil interest de possessione*, the pursuer must put his case under the statute'—(now, this is worth your notice, neighbour,)—'and must show, *formaliter et specialiter*, as well as *generaliter*, what is the qualification that defender Lackland does *not* possess—let him tell me what a plough-gate of land is, and I'll tell him if I have one or no. Surely the pursuer is bound to understand his own libel, and his own statute that he founds upon. *Titius* pursues *Mævius*[35] for recovery of ane *black* horse lent to Mævius—surely he shall have judgment; but if Titius pursue Mævius for ane *scarlet* or *crimson* horse, doubtless he shall be bound to show that there is sic ane animal *in rerum natura*. No man can be bound to plead to nonsense—that is to say, to a charge which cannot be explained or understood'—(he's wrang there—the better the pleadings the fewer understand them,)—'and so the reference unto this undefined and unintelligible measure of land is, as if a penalty was inflicted by statute for any man who suld hunt or hawk, or use lying-dogs, without having and wearing about him ane sky-blue scarlet pair of breeches——' But I am wearying you, Mr Deans, we'll pass to your ain business,—though this case of Marsport against Lackland has made an unco din in the Outer-house—Weel, here's the dittay against puir Effie: 'Whereas it is humbly meant and shown to us,' &c. (they are words of mere style,) 'that whereas, by the laws of this and every other well-regulated realm, the murder of any one, more especially of an infant child, is a crime of ane high nature, and severely punishable: And whereas, without prejudice to the foresaid generality, it was, by ane act[36] made in the second session of the First Parliament of our most High and Dread Soverains William and Mary, especially enacted, that ane woman who shall have concealed her condition, and shall not be able to show that she hath called for help at the birth, in case that the child shall be found dead or amissing, shall be deemed and held guilty of the murder thereof; and the said facts of concealment and pregnancy being found proven or confessed, shall sustain the pains of law accordingly; yet, nevertheless, you Effie, or Euphemia Deans' "——

"Read no farther," said Deans, raising his head up; "I would rather ye thrust a sword into my heart than read a word farther."

"Weel, neighbour," said Saddletree, "I thought it wad hae comforted ye to ken just the best and the warst o't. But the question is, what's to be dune?"

"Nothing," answered Deans firmly, "but to abide the dispensation that the Lord sees meet to send us. O if it had been His will to take the grey-head to rest before this awful visitation on my house and name! But His will be done.[37] I can say that yet, though I can say little mair."

"But, neighbour," said Saddletree, "ye'll retain advocates for the puir lassie? it's a thing maun needs be thought of."

"If there was ae man of them," answered Deans, "that had held fast his integrity—but I ken them weel, they are a' carnal, crafty, and warld-hunting self-seekers, Yerastians, and Arminians, every ane o' them."

"Hout tout, neighbour, ye maunna take the warld at its word," said Saddletree; "the very deil is no sae ill as he's ca'd;[38] and I ken mair than ae advocate that may be said to hae some integrity as weel as their neighbours; that is, after a sort o' fashion o' their ain."

"It is indeed but a fashion of integrity that ye will find amang them," replied David Deans, "and a fashion of wisdom, and a fashion of carnal learning—gazing, glancing-glasses[39] they are, fit only to fling the glaiks in folk's een, wi' their pawky policy, and earthly ingine, their flights and refinements and periods of eloquence, frae heathen emperors and popish canons.[40] They canna, in that daft trash ye were reading to me, sae muckle as ca' men that are sae ill-starred as to be amang their hands, by ony name o' the dispensation o' grace, but maun new baptize them by the names of the accursed Titus,[41] wha

was made the instrument of burning the holy Temple, and other sic
like heathens."

"It's Tishius," interrupted Saddletree, "and no Titus. Mr Crossmyloof cares as little about Titus or the Latin learning as ye do.—But it's
a case of necessity—she maun hae counsel. Now I could speak to Mr
Crossmyloof—he's weel kenned for a round-spun presbyterian,[42] and
a ruling-elder to boot."

"He's a rank Yerastian," replied Deans; "one of the public and
polititious[43] warldly-wise men that stude up to prevent ane general
owning of the cause in the day of power."

"What say ye to the auld Laird of Cuffabout?" said Saddletree;
"he whiles thumps the dust out of a case gay and weel."

"He? the fause loon!" answered Deans—"he was in his bandaliers
to hae joined the ungracious Highlanders in 1715,[44] an they had ever
had the luck to cross the Firth."

"Weel, Arniston? there's a clever chield for ye," said Bartoline, triumphantly.

"Ay, to bring popish medals in till their very library from that
schismatic woman in the north, the Duchess of Gordon."[45]

"Weel, weel, but somebody ye maun hae—What think ye o' Kit-
tlepunt?"

"He's an Arminian."

"Woodsetter?"

"He's, I doubt, a Cocceian."

"Auld Whulliewhaw?"

"He's ony thing ye like."

"Young Næmmo?"

"He's naething at a'."

"Ye're ill to please, neighbour," said Saddletree; "I hae run ower
the pick o' them for you, ye maun e'en choose for yoursell; but
bethink ye that in the multitude of counsellors there's safety.[46]—What
say ye to try young Mackenyie?[47] he has a' his uncle's practiques[48] at
the tongue's end."

"What, sir, wad ye speak to me," exclaimed the sturdy presbyterian
in excessive wrath, "about a man that has the blood of the saints at his
fingers' end? Didna his eme die and gang to his place wi' the name of
the Bluidy Mackenyie? and winna he be kenned by that name sae lang
as there's a Scots tongue to speak the word? If the life of the dear
bairn that's under a suffering dispensation, and Jeanie's, and my ain,
and a' mankind's, depended on my asking sic a slave o' Satan to speak

sae muckle as a word for me or them, they should a' gae down the water[49] thegither for Davie Deans."

It was the exalted tone in which he spoke this last sentence that broke up the conversation between Butler and Jeanie, and brought them both "ben the house," to use the language of the country. Here they found the poor old man half frantic, between grief, and zealous ire against Saddletree's proposed measures, his cheek inflamed, his hand clenched, and his voice raised, while the tear in his eye, and the occasional quiver of his accents, shewed that his utmost efforts were inadequate to shaking off the consciousness of his misery. Butler, apprehensive of the consequences of his agitation to an aged and feeble frame, ventured to utter to him a recommendation to patience.

"I *am* patient," returned the old man, sternly—,"more patient than any one who is alive to the woeful backslidings of a miserable time can be patient; and in so much, that I need neither sectarians, nor sons nor grandsons of sectarians,[50] to instruct my grey hairs how to bear my cross."

"But, sir," continued Butler, taking no offence at the slur cast on his grandfather's faith, "we must use human means. When you call in a physician, you would not, I suppose, question him on the nature of his religious principles?"

"Wad I *no?*" answered David—"But I wad though; and if he didna satisfy me that he had a right sense of the right-hand and left-hand defections of the day, not a goutte of his physic should gang through my father's son."

It is a dangerous thing to trust to an illustration. Butler had done so and miscarried; but, like a gallant soldier when his musket misses fire, he stood his ground, and charged with the bayonet.[51]—"This is too rigid an interpretation of your duty, sir. The sun shines, and the rain descends on the just and unjust,[52] and they are placed together in life in circumstances which frequently render intercourse between them indispensible, perhaps that the evil may have an opportunity of being converted by the good, and perhaps, also, that the righteous might, among other trials, be subjected to that of occasional converse with the profane."

"Ye're a silly callant, Reuben," answered Deans, "with your bits of argument. Can a man touch pitch and not be defiled?[53] Or what think ye of the brave and worthy champions of the Covenant, that wadna sae muckle as hear a minister speak, be his gifts and graces as they would, that hadna witnessed against the enormities of the day? Nae lawyer shall ever speak for me and mine that hasna concurred in the testimony of the scattered, yet lovely remnant,[54] which abode in the clifts of the rocks."[55]

So saying, and as if fatigued, both with the arguments and presence of his guests, the old man arose, and seeming to bid them adieu with a motion of his head and hand, went to shut himself up in his sleeping apartment.

"It's thrawing his daughter's life awa," said Saddletree to Butler, "to hear him speak in that daft gate. Where will he ever get a Cameronian advocate? Or wha ever heard of a lawyer's suffering either for ae religion or another? The lassie's life is clean flung awa."

During the latter part of this debate, Dumbiedikes had arrived at the door, dismounted, hung the pony's bridle on the usual hook, and sunk down on his ordinary settle. His eyes, with more than their usual animation, followed first one speaker, then another, till he caught the melancholy sense of the whole from Saddletree's last words. He rose from his seat, stumped slowly across the room, and, coming close up to Saddletree's ear, said, in a tremulous anxious voice, "Will—will siller do naething for them, Mr Saddletree?"

"Umph!" said Saddletree, looking grave,—"siller will certainly do it in the Parliament House, if ony thing *can* do it; but whare's the siller to come frae? Mr Deans, ye see, will do naething; and though Mrs Saddletree's their far-awa friend, and right gude weel-wisher, and is weel disposed to assist, yet she wadna like to stand to be bound *singuli in solidum* to such an expensive wark. An ilka friend wad bear a share o' the burthen, something might be dune—ilka ane to be liable for their ain input—I wadna like to see the case fa' through without being pled—it wadna be creditable, for a' that daft whig body says."

"I'll—I will—yes," (assuming fortitude,) "I will be answerable," said Dumbiedikes, "for a score of punds sterling,"—and he was silent, staring in astonishment at finding himself capable of such unwonted resolution and excessive generosity.

"God Almighty bless ye, Laird!" said Jeanie in a transport of gratitude.

"Ye may ca' the twenty punds thretty," said Dumbiedikes, looking bashfully away from her and towards Saddletree.

"That will do bravely," said Saddletree, rubbing his hands; "and ye sall hae a' my skill and knowledge to gar the siller gang far—I'll tape it out weel—I ken how to gar the birkies tak short fees, and be glad o' them too—it's only garring them trow ye hae twa or three cases of importance coming on, and they'll work cheap to get custom. Let me alane for whillywhaing an advocate;—it's nae sin to get as muckle frae them for our siller as we can—after a', it's but the wind o' their mouth—it costs them naething; whereas, in my wretched occupation of a saddler, horse-milliner, and harness-maker, we are out unconscionable sums just for barkened hides and leather."

"Can I be of no use?" said Butler. "My means, alas! are only worth the black coat I wear; but I am young—I owe much to the family— Can I do nothing?"

"Ye can help to collect evidence, sir," said Saddletree; "if we could but find ony ane to say she had gien the least hint o' her condition, she wad be brought aff wi' a wat finger[56]—Mr Crossmyloof tell'd me sae. The crown, says he, canna be craved to prove a positive—was't a positive or a negative they couldna be ca'd to prove?[57]—it was the tane or the tither o' them, I am sure, and it maksna muckle matter whilk. Wherefore, says he, the libel maun be redargued by the pannel proving her defences. And it canna be done otherwise."

"But the fact, sir," argued Butler, "the fact that this poor girl has borne a child; surely the crown lawyers must prove that?" said Butler.

Saddletree paused a moment, while the visage of Dumbiedikes, which traversed, as if it had been placed on a pivot, from the one spokesman to the other, assumed a more blithe expression.

"Ye—ye—ye—es," said Saddletree, after some grave hesitation; "unquestionably that is a thing to be proved, as the Court will more fully declare by an interlocutor of relevancy in common form; but I fancy that job's done already, for she has confessed her guilt."

"Confessed the murder?" exclaimed Jeanie, with a scream that made them all start.

"No, I didna say that," replied Bartoline. "But she confessed bearing the babe."

"And what became of it then?" said Jeanie; "for not a word could I get from her but bitter sighs and tears."

"She says it was taken away from her by the woman in whose house it was born, and who assisted her at the time."

"And who was that woman?" said Butler. "Surely by her means the truth might be discovered.—Who was she? I will fly to her directly."

"I wish," said Dumbiedikes, "I were as young and as supple as you, and had the gift of the gab as weel."

"Who is she?" again reiterated Butler impatiently.—"Who could that woman be?"

"Ay, wha kens that but hersell," said Saddletree; "she deponed further, and declined to answer that interrogatory."

"Then to herself will I instantly go," said Butler; "farewell, Jeanie;" then coming close up to her.—"Take no *rash steps* till you hear from me. Farewell," and he immediately left the cottage.

"I wad gang too," said the landed proprietor, in an anxious, jealous, and repining tone, "but my powney winna for the life o' me gang ony other road than just frae Dumbiedikes to this house-end, and sae straight back again."

"Ye'll do better for them," said Saddletree, as they left the house together, "by sending me the thretty punds."

"Thretty punds?" hesitated Dumbiedikes, who was now out of the reach of those eyes which had inflamed his generosity; "I only said *twenty* punds."

"Ay; but," said Saddletree, "that was under protestation to add and eik; and so ye craved leave to amend your libel,[58] and made it thretty."

"Did I? I dinna mind that I did," answered Dumbiedikes. "But whatever I said I'll stand to." Then bestriding his steed with some difficulty, he added, "Dinna ye think poor Jeanie's een wi' the tears in them glanced like lamour beads, Mr Saddletree?"

"I kenna muckle about women's een, laird," replied the insensible Bartoline; "and I care just as little. I wuss I were as weel free o' their tongues; though few wives," he added, recollecting the necessity of keeping up his character for domestic rule, "are under better command than mine, Laird. I allow neither perduellion nor læse-majesty against my sovereign authority."

The Laird saw nothing so important in this observation as to call for a rejoinder, and when they had exchanged a mute salutation, they parted in peace upon their different errands.

CHAPTER 13

I'll warrant that fellow from drowning, were the ship no stronger than a nut-shell.

The Tempest

BUTLER felt neither fatigue nor want of refreshment, although from the mode in which he had spent the night he might well have been overcome with either. But in the earnestness with which he hastened to the assistance of the sister of Jeanie Deans, he forgot both.

In his first progress he walked with so rapid a pace as almost approached to running, when he was surprised to hear behind him a call upon his name, contending with an asthmatic cough, and half-drowned amid the resounding trot of an Highland pony. He looked behind, and saw the Laird of Dumbiedikes making after him with what speed he might, for it happened fortunately for the Laird's purpose of conversing with Butler, that his own road homeward was for about two hundred yards the same with that which led by the nearest way to the city. Butler stopped when he heard himself thus summoned, internally wishing no good to the panting equestrian who thus retarded his journey.

"Uh! uh! uh!" ejaculated Dumbiedikes, as he checked the hobbling pace of the pony by our friend Butler. "Uh! uh! it's a hard-set willyard beast this o' mine." He had in fact just overtaken the object of his chase at the very point beyond which it would have been absolutely impossible for him to have continued the pursuit, since there Butler's road parted from that leading to Dumbiedikes, and no means of influence or compulsion which the rider could possibly have used towards his Bucephalus could have induced the Celtic obstinacy of Rory Bean (such was the pony's name) to have diverged a yard from the path that conducted him to his own paddock.

Even when he had recovered from the shortness of breath occasioned by a trot much more rapid than Rory or he was accustomed to, the high purpose of Dumbiedikes seemed to stick as it were in his throat and impede his utterance, so that Butler stood for nearly three minutes ere he could utter a syllable, and when he did find voice, it was only to say, after one or two efforts, "Uh! uh! uhu! I say, Mr—Mr Butler, it's a braw day for the ha'rst."

"Fine day, indeed," said Butler. "I wish you good morning, sir."

"Stay—stay a bit," rejoined Dumbiedikes; "that was no what I had gotten to say."

"Then pray be quick, and let me have your commands," rejoined Butler; "I crave your pardon, but I am in haste, and *Tempus nemini*— you know the proverb."

Dumbiedikes did not know the proverb, nor did he even take the trouble to endeavour to look as if he did, as others in his place might have done. He was concentrating all his intellects for one grand proposition, and could not afford any detachment to defend outposts.

"I say, Mr Butler," said he, "ken ye if Mr Saddletree's a great lawyer?"

"I have no person's word for it but his own," answered Butler drily; "but undoubtedly he best understands his own qualities."

"Umph!" replied the taciturn Dumbiedikes, in a tone which seemed to say, "Mr Butler, I take your meaning." "In that case," he pursued, "I'll employ my ain man o' business, Nichil Novit[1] (auld Nichil's son, and amaist as gleg as his father), to agent Effie's plea."

And having thus displayed more sagacity than Butler expected from him, he courteously touched his gold-laced cocked hat, and by a punch on the ribs, conveyed to Rory Bean, it was his rider's pleasure that he should forthwith proceed homewards; a hint which the quadru-ped obeyed with that degree of alacrity, with which men and animals interpret and obey suggestions that entirely correspond with their own inclinations.

Butler resumed his pace, not without a momentary revival of that jealousy, which the honest Laird's attention to the family of Deans, had at different times excited in his bosom. But he was too generous long to nurse any feeling, which was allied to selfishness. "He is," said Butler to himself, "rich in what I want; why should I feel vexed that he has the heart to dedicate some of his pelf to render them services, which I can only form the empty wish of executing? In God's name, let us each do what we can. May she be but happy!—saved from the misery and disgrace that seems impending—Let me but find the means of preventing the fearful experiment of this evening, and farewell to other thoughts, though my heart-strings break in parting with them."

He redoubled his pace, and soon stood before the door of the

Tolbooth, or rather before the entrance where the door had formerly been placed. His interview with the mysterious stranger, the message to Jeanie, his agitating conversation with her on the subject of breaking off their mutual engagements, and the interesting scene with old Deans, had so entirely occupied his mind as to drown recollection even of the tragical event which he had witnessed the preceding evening. His attention was not recalled to it by the groupes who stood scattered on the street in conversation, which they hushed when strangers approached, or by the bustling search of the agents of the city police, supported by small parties of the military, or by the appearance of the Guard-House, before which were treble sentinels, or, finally, by the subdued and intimidated looks of the lower orders of society, who, conscious that they were liable to suspicion, if they were not guilty of accession to a riot likely to be strictly enquired into, glided about with an humble and dismayed aspect, like men whose spirits being exhausted in the revel and the dangers of a desperate debauch over night, are nerve-shaken, timorous, and unenterprizing on the succeeding day.

None of these symptoms of alarm and trepidation struck Butler, whose mind was occupied with a different, and to him still more interesting subject, until he stood before the entrance to the prison, and saw it defended by a double file of grenadiers, instead of bolts and bars. Their "Stand, stand," the blackened appearance of the door-less gate-way, and the winding stair-case and apartments of the Tolbooth, now open to the public eye, recalled the whole proceeding of the eventful night. Upon his requesting to speak with Effie Deans, the same tall, thin, silver-haired turnkey, whom he had seen on the preceding evening, made his appearance.

"I think," he replied to Butler's request of admission, with true Scottish indirectness, "ye will be the same lad that was for in to see her yestreen?"

Butler admitted he was the same person.

"And I am thinking," pursued the turnkey, "that ye speered at me when we locked up, and if we locked up earlier on account of Porteous?"

"Very likely I might make some such observation," said Butler; "but the question now is, can I see Effie Deans?"

"I dinna ken—gang in bye, and up the turnpike stair, and turn till the ward on the left hand."

The old man followed close behind him, with his keys in his hand, not forgetting even that huge one which had once opened and shut the outward gate of his dominions, though at present it was but an idle and useless burthen. No sooner had Butler entered the room to which he was directed, than the experienced hand of the warder selected the proper key and locked it on the outside. At first Butler conceived this manœuvre was only an effect of the man's habitual and official caution and jealousy. But when he heard the hoarse command, "Turn out the guard," and immediately afterwards heard the clash of a sentinel's arms, as he was posted at the door of his apartment, he again called out to the turnkey, "My good friend, I have business of some consequence with Effie Deans, and I beg to see her as soon as possible." No answer was returned. "If it be against your rules to admit me," repeated Butler, in a still louder tone, "to see the prisoner, I beg you will tell me so, and let me go about my business.—*Fugit irrevocabile tempus!*"² muttered he to himself.

"If ye had business to do, you suld hae dune it before ye cam here," replied the man of keys from the outside; "ye'll find it's easier wunnin in than wunnin out here—there's sma' likelihood o' another Porteous-mob coming to rabble us again—the law will haud her ain now, neighbour, and that ye'll find to your cost."

"What do you mean by that, sir?" retorted Butler. "You must mistake me for some other person. My name is Reuben Butler, preacher of the gospel."

"I ken that weel eneugh," said the turnkey.

"Well then, if you know me, I have a right to know from you in return, what warrant you have for detaining me; that, I know, is the right of every British subject."

"Warrant?" said the jailor—"the warrant's awa to Libberton wi' twa sheriff officers seeking ye. If ye had staid at hame, as honest men should do, ye wad hae seen the warrant; but if ye come to be incarcerated of your ain accord, wha can help it, my jo?"

"So I cannot see Effie Deans, then," said Butler; "and you are determined not to let me out?"

"Troth will I no, neighbour," answered the old man, doggedly; "as for Effie Deans, ye'll hae aneugh ado to mind your ain business, and let her mind hers; and for letting you out, that maun be as the magistrate will determine. And fare ye weel for a bit, for I maun see Deacon Sawyers put on ane or twa o' the doors that your quiet folk broke down yesternight, Mr Butler."

There was something in this exquisitely provoking, but there was also something darkly alarming. To be imprisoned, even on a false accusation, has something in it disagreeable and menacing even to men of more constitutional courage than Butler had to boast, for although he had much of that resolution which arises from a sense of duty and an honourable desire to discharge it, yet as his imagination was lively, and his frame of body delicate, he was far from possessing that cool insensibility to danger which is the happy portion of men of stronger health, more firm nerves, and less acute sensibility. An indistinct idea of peril, which he could neither understand nor ward off, seemed to float before his eyes. He tried to think over the events of the preceding night, in hopes of discovering some means of explaining or vindicating his conduct for appearing among the mob, since it immediately occurred to him that his detention must be founded on that circumstance. And it was with anxiety that he found he could not recollect to have been under the observation of any disinterested witness in the attempts that he made from time to time to expostulate with the rioters, and to prevail on them to release him. The distress of Deans's family, the dangerous rendezvous which Jeanie had formed, and which he could not now hope to interrupt, had also their share in his unpleasant reflections. Yet impatient as he was to receive an eclaircissement upon the cause of his confinement, and if possible to obtain his liberty, he was affected with a trepidation which seemed no good omen; when, after remaining an hour in this solitary apartment, he received a summons to attend the sitting magistrate. He was conducted from prison strongly guarded by a party of soldiers, with a parade of precaution, that, however ill-timed and unnecessary, is generally displayed *after* an event, which such precaution, if used in time, might have prevented.

He was introduced into the Council Chamber, as the place is called where the magistrates hold their sittings, and which was then at a little distance from the prison. One or two of the senators of the city were present, and seemed about to engage in the examination of an individual who was brought forward to the foot of the long green-covered table round which the council usually assembled. "Is that the preacher?" said one of the magistrates, as the city officer in attendance introduced Butler. The man answered in the affirmative. "Let him sit down there for an instant; we will finish this man's business very briefly."

"Shall we remove Mr Butler?" queried the assistant.

"It is not necessary—Let him remain where he is."

Butler accordingly sate down on a bench at the bottom of the apartment, attended by one of his keepers.

It was a large room, partially and imperfectly lighted, but by chance, or the skill of the architect, who might happen to remember the advantage which might occasionally be derived from such an arrangement, one window was so placed as to throw a strong light at the foot of the table at which prisoners were usually posted for examination, while the upper end, where the examinants sate, was thrown into shadow. Butler's eyes were instantly fixed on the person whose examination was at present proceeding, in the idea that he might recognize some one of the conspirators of the former night. But though the features of this man were sufficiently marked and striking, he could not recollect that he had ever seen them before.

The complexion of this person was dark, and his age somewhat advanced. He wore his own hair, combed smooth down, and cut very short. It was jet black, slightly curled by nature, and already mottled with grey. The man's face expressed rather knavery than vice, and a disposition to sharpness, cunning, and roguery, more than the traces of stormy and indulged passions. His sharp, quick black eyes, acute features, ready sardonic smile, promptitude, and effrontery, gave him altogether what is called among the vulgar a *knowing* look, which generally implies a tendency to knavery. At a fair or market, you could not for a moment have doubted that he was a horse-jockey, intimate with all the tricks of his trade; yet had you met him on a moor, you would not have apprehended any violence from him. His dress was also that of a horse-dealer—a close-buttoned jockey-coat, or wrap-rascal, as it was then termed, with huge metal buttons, coarse blue upper stockings, called boot-hose, because supplying the place of boots, and a slouched hat. He wanted only a loaded whip under his arm, and a spur upon one heel, to complete the dress of the character he seemed to represent.

"Your name is James Ratcliffe?"[3] said the magistrate.

"Ay—always wi' your honour's leave."

"That is to say, you could find me another name, if I did not like that one?"

"Twenty to pick and chuse upon, always with your honour's leave," resumed the respondent.

"But James Ratcliffe is your present name?—what is your trade?"

"I canna just say, distinctly, that I have what ye wad ca' preceesely a trade."

"But," repeated the magistrate, "what are your means of living—your occupation?"

"Hout tout—your honour, wi' your leave, kens that as weel as I do," replied the examined.

"No matter, I want to hear you describe it," said the examinant.

"Me describe?—and to your honour?—far be it from Jemmie Ratcliffe," responded the prisoner.

"Come, sir, no trifling—I insist on an answer."

"Weel, sir," replied the declarant, "I maun make a clean breast, for ye see, (wi' your leave) I am looking for favour—Describe my occupation, quo' ye?—troth it will be ill to do that, in a feasible way, in a place like this—but what is't again that the aught command says?"

"Thou shalt not steal," answered the magistrate.

"Are ye sure o' that?" replied the accused.—"Troth, then, my occupation, and that command, are sair at odds, for I aye read it, thou *shalt* steal, and that makes an unco difference, though there's but ae wee bit word left out."

"To cut the matter short, Ratcliffe, you have been a most notorious thief," said the examinant.

"I believe Highlands and Lowlands ken that, sir, forbye England and Holland," replied Ratcliffe, with the greatest composure and effrontery.

"And what d'ye think the end o' your calling will be?" said the magistrate.

"I could have gien a braw guess yesterday—but I dinna ken sae weel the day," answered the prisoner.

"And what would you have said would have been your end, had you been asked the question yesterday?"

"Just the gallows," replied Ratcliffe, with the same composure.

"You are a daring rascal, sir," said the magistrate; "and how dare you hope times are mended with you to-day?"

"Dear, your honour," answered Ratcliffe, "there's muckle difference between lying in prison under sentence of death, and staying there of ane's ain proper accord, when it would have cost a man naething to get up and rin awa—what was to hinder me from stepping out quietly, when the rabble walked awa wi' Jock Porteous yestreen?—and does your honour really think I staid on purpose to be hanged?"

"I do not know what you may have proposed to yourself; but I know," said the magistrate, "what the law proposes for you, and that is to hang you next Wednesday eight days."[4]

"Na, na, your honour," said Ratcliffe firmly, "craving your honour's pardon, I'll ne'er believe that till I see it. I have kend the Law this mony a year, and mony a thrawart job I hae had wi' her first and last; but the auld jaud is no sae ill as that comes to—I aye fand her bark waur than her bite."

"And if you do not expect the gallows, to which you are condemned, (for the fourth time to my knowledge) may I beg the favour to know," said the magistrate, "what it is that you *do* expect in consideration of your not having taken your flight with the rest of the jail-birds, which I will admit was a line of conduct little to have been expected from you?"

"I would never have thought for a moment of staying in that auld gousty toom house," answered Ratcliffe, "but that use and wont had just gien me a fancy to the place, and I'm just expecting a bit post in't."

"A post!" exclaimed the magistrate; "a whipping-post, I suppose, you mean?"

"Na, na, sir, I had nae thoughts o' a whuppin-post. After having been four times doomed to hang by the neck till I was dead, I think I am far beyond being whuppit."

"Then, in Heaven's name, what *did* you expect?"

"Just the post of under-turnkey, for I understand there's a vacancy," said the prisoner; "I wadna think of asking the lockman's* place ower his head; it wadna suit me sae weel as ither folk, for I never could pit a beast out o' the way, much less deal wi' a man."

"That's something in your favour," said the magistrate, making exactly the inference to which Ratcliffe was desirous to lead him, though he mantled his art with an affectation of oddity. "But," continued the magistrate, "how do you think you can be trusted with a charge in the prison, when you have broken at your own hand half the jails in Scotland?"

"Wi' your honour's leave," said Ratcliffe, "if I kend sae weel how to wun out mysell, it's like I wad be a' the better a hand to keep other

---

* *Hangman*, so called from the small quantity of meal (Scottice, *lock*) which he was entitled to take out of every boll exposed to market in the city. In Edinburgh the duty has been very long commuted; but in Dumfries the finisher of the law still exercises, or did lately exercise, his privilege, the quantity taken being regulated by a small iron ladle, which he uses as the measure of his perquisite. The expression *lock* for a small quantity of any readily divisible dry substance, as corn, meal, flax, or the like, is still preserved, not only popularly, but in a legal description, as the *lock* and *gowpen*, or small quantity and handful, payable in thirlage cases, as in-town multure.

folks in. I think they wad ken their business weel that held me in when I wanted to be out, or wan out when I wanted to haud them in."

The remark seemed to strike the magistrate, but he made no further immediate observation, only desired Ratcliffe to be removed.

When this daring, and yet sly free-booter was out of hearing, the magistrate asked the city-clerk, "what he thought of the fellow's assurance?"

"It's no for me to say, sir," replied the clerk; "but if James Ratcliffe be inclined to turn to good, there is not a man e'er came within the ports of the burgh could be of sae muckle use to the Good Town in the thief and lock-up line of business. I'll speak to Mr Sharpitlaw about him."[5]

Upon Ratcliffe's retreat, Butler was placed at the table for examination. The magistrate conducted his enquiry civilly, but yet in a manner which gave him to understand that he laboured under strong suspicion. With a frankness which at once became his calling and character, Butler avowed his involuntary presence at the murder of Porteous, and, at the request of the magistrate, entered into a minute detail of the circumstances which attended that unhappy affair. All the particulars, such as we have narrated, were taken minutely down by the clerk from Butler's dictation.

When the narrative was concluded the cross-examination commenced, which it is a painful task even for the most candid witness to undergo, since a story, especially if connected with agitating and alarming incidents, can scarce be so clearly and distinctly told, but that some ambiguity and doubt may be thrown upon it by a string of successive and minute interrogatories.

The magistrate commenced, by observing, that Butler had said his object was to return to the village of Libberton, but that he was interrupted by the mob at the West-Port. "Is the West-Port your usual way of leaving town when you go to Libberton?" said the magistrate with a sneer.

"No, certainly," answered Butler, with the haste of a man anxious to vindicate the accuracy of his evidence; "but I chanced to be nearer that port than any other, and the hour of shutting the gates was on the point of striking."

"That was unlucky," said the magistrate drily. "Pray, being, as you say, under coercion and fear of the lawless multitude, and compelled to accompany them through scenes disagreeable to all men of humanity, and more especially irreconcileable to the profession of a minister, did you not attempt to struggle, resist, or escape from their violence?"

Butler replied, "that their numbers prevented him from attempting resistance, and their vigilance from effecting his escape."

"That was unlucky," again repeated the magistrate, in the same dry inacquiescent tone of voice and manner. He proceeded with decency and politeness, but with a stiffness which argued his continued suspicion, to ask many questions concerning the behaviour of the mob, the manners and dress of the ringleaders; and when he conceived that the caution of Butler, if he was deceiving him, must be lulled asleep, the magistrate suddenly and artfully returned to former parts of his declaration, and required a new recapitulation of the circumstances, to the minutest and most trivial point which attended each part of the melancholy scene. No confusion or contradiction, however, occurred, that could countenance the suspicion which he seemed to have adopted against Butler. At length the train of his interrogatories reached Madge Wildfire, at whose name the magistrate and town-clerk exchanged significant glances. If the fate of the Good Town had depended on her careful magistrate's knowing the features and dress of this personage, his enquiries could not have been more particular. But Butler could say almost nothing of this person's features, which were disguised apparently with red paint and soot, like an Indian going to battle, besides the projecting shade of a curch or coif, which muffled the hair of the supposed female. He declared that he thought he could not know this Madge Wildfire, if placed before him in a different dress, but that he believed he might recognize his voice.[6]

The magistrate requested him again to state by what gate he left the city.

"By the Cowgate Port," replied Butler.

"Was that the nearest road to Libberton?"

"No," answered Butler, with embarrassment; "but it was the nearest way to extricate myself from the mob."

The clerk and magistrate again exchanged glances.

"Is the Cowgate Port a nearer way to Libberton from the Grassmarket, than Bristo Port?"

"No," replied Butler; "but I had to visit a friend."

"Indeed?" said the interrogator— "You were in a hurry to tell the sight you had witnessed, I suppose?"

"Indeed I was not," replied Butler; "nor did I speak on the subject the whole time I was at Saint Leonard's Crags."

"Which road did you take to Saint Leonard's Crags?"

"By the foot of Salisbury Crags," was the reply.

"Indeed?—you seem partial to circuitous routes," again said the magistrate. "Whom did you see after you left the city?"

One by one he obtained a description of every one of the groups which had passed Butler, as already noticed, their number, demeanour, and appearance; and, at length, came to the circumstance of the mysterious stranger in the King's Park. On this subject Butler would fain have remained silent. But the magistrate had no sooner got a slight hint concerning the incident, than he seemed bent to possess himself of the most minute particulars.

"Look ye, Mr Butler," said he, "you are a young man, and bear an excellent character; so much I will myself testify in your favour. But we are aware there has been, at times, a sort of bastard and fiery zeal in some of your order, and those, men irreproachable in other points, which has led them into doing and countenancing great irregularities, by which the peace of the country is liable to be shaken.—I will deal plainly with you. I am not at all satisfied with this story, of your setting out again and again to seek your dwelling by two several roads, which were both circuitous. And, to be frank, no one whom we have examined on this unhappy affair could trace in your appearance any thing like your acting under compulsion. Moreover, the waiters at the Cowgate Port observed something like the trepidation of guilt in your conduct, and declare that you were the first to command them to open the gate, in a tone of authority, as if still presiding over the guards and outposts of the rabble, who had besieged them the whole night."

"God forgive them!" said Butler; "I only asked free passage for myself; they must have much misunderstood, if they did not wilfully misrepresent me."

"Well, Mr Butler," resumed the magistrate, "I am inclined to judge the best and hope the best, as I am sure I wish the best; but you must be frank with me, if you wish to secure my good opinion, and lessen the risk of inconvenience to yourself. You have allowed you saw another individual in your passage through the King's Park to Saint Leonard's Crags—I must know every word which passed betwixt you."

Thus closely pressed, Butler, who had no reason for concealing what passed at that meeting, unless because Jeanie Deans was concerned in it, thought it best to tell the whole truth from beginning to end.

"Do you suppose," said the magistrate, pausing, "that the young woman will accept an invitation so mysterious?"

"I fear she will," replied Butler.

"Why do you use the word *fear* it?" said the magistrate.

"Because I am apprehensive for her safety, in meeting, at such a time and place, one who had something of the manner of a desperado, and whose message was of a character so inexplicable."

"Her safety shall be cared for," said the magistrate. "Mr Butler, I am concerned I cannot immediately discharge you from confinement, but I hope you will not be long detained.—Remove Mr Butler, and let him be provided with decent accommodation in all respects."

He was conducted back to the prison accordingly; but, in the food offered to him, as well as in the apartment in which he was lodged, the recommendation of the magistrate was strictly attended to.

CHAPTER 14

Dark and eerie was the night,
And lonely was the way,
As Janet, wi' her green mantell,
To Miles' Cross she did gae.
Old Ballad

LEAVING Butler to all the uncomfortable thoughts attached to his new situation, among which the most predominant was his feeling that he was, by his confinement, deprived of all possibility of assisting the family at Saint Leonard's in their greatest need, we return to Jeanie Deans, who had seen him depart, without an opportunity of further explanation, in all that agony of mind with which the female heart bids adieu to the complicated sensations so well described by Coleridge,[1]—

Hopes, and fears that kindle hope,
An undistinguishable throng;
And gentle wishes long subdued—
Subdued and cherish'd long.

It is not the firmest heart (and Jeanie, under her russet rokelay, had one that would not have disgraced Cato's daughter,) that can most easily bid adieu to these soft and mingled emotions. She wept for a few minutes bitterly, and without attempting to refrain from this indulgence of passion. But a moment's recollection induced her to check herself for a grief selfish and proper to her own affections, while her father and sister were plunged into such deep and irretrievable affliction. She drew from her pocket the letter which had been that morning flung into her apartment through an open window, and the contents of which were as singular as the expression was violent and energetic. "If she would save a human being from the most damning guilt, and all its desperate consequences,—if she desired the life and honour of her sister to be saved from the bloody fangs of an unjust law,—if she desired not to forfeit peace of mind here, and happiness hereafter," such was the frantic style of the conjuration, "she was entreated to give a sure, secret, and solitary meeting to the writer. She alone could rescue him," so ran the letter, "and he only could rescue her." He was in such circumstances, the billet farther informed her, that an attempt to bring any witness of their conference, or even to mention to her father, or any other person whatsoever, the letter which requested it, would inevitably prevent its taking place, and insure the destruction of her sister. The letter concluded with incoherent but violent protestations, that in obeying this summons she had nothing to fear personally.

The message delivered to her by Butler from the stranger in the Park tallied exactly with the contents of the letter, but assigned a later hour and a different place of meeting. Apparently the writer of the letter had been compelled to let Butler so far into his confidence, for the sake of announcing this change to Jeanie. She was more than once on the point of producing the billet, in vindication of herself from her lover's half-hinted suspicions. But there is something in stooping to justification which the pride of innocence does not at all times willingly submit to, besides that the threats contained in the letter, in case of her betraying the secret, hung heavy on her heart. It is probable, however, that had they remained longer together, she might have taken the resolution to submit the whole matter to Butler, and be guided by him as to the line of conduct which she should adopt. And when, by the sudden interruption of their conference, she lost the opportunity of doing so, she felt as if she had been unjust to a friend, whose advice might have been highly useful, and whose attachment deserved her full and unreserved confidence.

To have recourse to her father upon this occasion, she considered as highly imprudent. There was no possibility of conjecturing in what light the matter might strike old David, whose manner of acting and thinking in extraordinary circumstances depended upon feelings and principles peculiar to himself, the operation of which could not be calculated upon even by those best acquainted with him. To have requested some female friend to have accompanied her to the place of rendezvous, would perhaps have been the most eligible expedient; but the threats of the writer, that betraying his secret would prevent their meeting (on which her sister's safety was said to depend,) from taking place at all, would have deterred her from making such a confidence, even had she known a person in whom she thought it could with safety have been reposed. But she knew none such. Their acquaintance with the cottagers in the vicinity had been very slight, and limited to trifling acts of good neighbourhood. Jeanie knew little of them, and what she knew did not greatly incline her to trust any of them. They were of the order of loquacious good-humoured gossips usually found in their situation of life; and their conversation had at all times few charms for a young woman, to whom nature and the circumstance of a solitary life had given a depth of thought and force of character superior to the frivolous part of her sex, whether in high or low degree.

Left alone and separated from all earthly counsel, she had recourse to a friend and adviser, whose ear is open to the cry of the poorest and most afflicted of his people. She knelt, and prayed with fervent sincerity, that God would please to direct her what course to follow in her arduous and distressing situation. It was the belief of the time and sect to which she belonged, that special answers to prayer, differing little in their character from divine inspiration, were, as they expressed it, "borne in upon their minds" in answer to their earnest petitions in a crisis of difficulty. Without entering into an abstruse point of divinity, one thing is plain; namely, that the person who lays open his doubts and distresses in prayer, with feeling and sincerity, must necessarily, in the act of doing so, purify his mind from the dross of worldly passions and interests, and bring it into that state, when the resolutions adopted are likely to be selected rather from a sense of duty, than from any inferior motive. Jeanie arose from her devotions, with her heart fortified to endure affliction, and encouraged to face difficulties.

"I will meet this unhappy man," she said to herself—"unhappy he must be, since I doubt he has been the cause of poor Effie's misfortune—but I will meet him, be it for good or ill. My mind shall never cast up to me, that, for fear of what might be said or done to myself, I left that undone that might even yet be the rescue of her."

With a mind greatly composed since the adoption of this resolution, she went to attend her father. The old man, firm in the principles of his youth, did not, in outward appearance at least, permit a thought of his family distress to interfere with the stoical reserve of his countenance and manners. He even chid his daughter for having neglected, in the distress of the morning, some trifling domestic duties which fell under her department.

"Why, what meaneth this, Jeanie?" said the old man—"The brown four-year-auld's milk is not seiled yet, nor the bowies put up on the bink. If ye neglect your warldly duties in the day of affliction, what confidence have I that ye mind the greater matters that concern salvation? God knows, our bowies, and our pipkins, and our draps o' milk, and our bits o' bread, are nearer and dearer to us than the bread of life."

Jeanie, not unpleased to hear her father's thoughts thus expand themselves beyond the sphere of his immediate distress, obeyed him, and proceeded to put her household matters in order; while old David moved from place to place about his ordinary employments, scarce shewing, unless by a nervous impatience at remaining long stationary, an occasional convulsive sigh, or twinkle of the eye-lid, that he was labouring under the yoke of such bitter affliction.

The hour of noon came on, and the father and child sat down to their homely repast. In his petition for a blessing on the meal, the poor old man added to his usual supplication, a prayer that the bread eaten in sadness of heart, and the bitter waters of Merah,[2] might be made as nourishing as those which had been poured forth from a full cup and a plentiful basket and store;[3] and having concluded his benediction, and resumed the bonnet which he had laid "reverently aside,"[4] he proceeded to exhort his daughter to eat, not by example indeed, but at least by precept.

"The man after God's own heart,"[5] he said, "washed and anointed himself, and did eat bread, in order to express his submission under a dispensation of suffering,[6] and it did not become a Christian man or woman so to cling to creature-comforts of wife or bairns,"—(here the words became too great, as it were, for his utterance)—"as to forget the first duty—submission to the Divine will."

To add force to his precept, he took a morsel on his plate, but nature proved too strong even for the powerful feelings with which he endeavoured to bridle it. Ashamed of his weakness, he started up, and ran out of the house, with haste very unlike the deliberation of his usual movements. In less than five minutes he returned, having successfully struggled to recover his ordinary composure of mind and countenance, and affected to colour over his late retreat, by muttering that he thought he heard the "young staig loose in the byre."

He did not again trust himself with the subject of his former conversation, and his daughter was glad to see that he seemed to avoid further discourse on that agitating topic. The hours glided on, as on they must, and pass whether winged with joy or laden with affliction. The sun set beyond the dusky eminence of the Castle, and the screen of western hills, and the close of evening summoned David Deans and his daughter to the family duty of the night. It came bitterly upon Jeanie's recollection, how often, when this hour of worship approached, she used to watch the lengthening shadows, and look out from the door of the house, to see if she could spy her sister's return homeward. Alas! this idle and thoughtless waste of time, to what evils had it not finally led? and was she altogether guiltless, who, noticing Effie's turn to idle and light society, had not called in her father's authority to restrain her?—But I acted for the best, she again reflected, and who could have expected such a growth of evil, from one grain of human leaven, in a disposition so kind, and candid, and generous?

As they sate down to the "exercise," as it is called, a chair happened accidentally to stand in the place which Effie usually occupied. David Deans saw his daughter's eyes swim in tears as they were directed towards this object, and pushed it aside, with a gesture of some impatience, as if desirous to destroy every memorial of earthly interest when about to address the Deity. The portion of Scripture was read, the psalm was sung, the prayer was made; and it was remarkable that, in discharging these duties, the old man avoided all passages and expressions, of which Scripture affords so many, that might be considered as applicable to his own domestic misfortunes. In doing so it was perhaps his intention to spare the feelings of his daughter, as well as to maintain, in outward show at least, that stoical appearance of patient endurance of all the evil which earth could bring, which was, in his opinion, essential to the character of one who rated all earthly things at their own just estimate of nothingness. When he had finished the duty of the evening, he came up to his daughter, wished her good-night, and, having done so, continued to hold her by the hands for half a minute; then drawing her towards him, kissed her forehead, and ejaculated, "The God of Israel bless you, even with the blessings of the promise,[7] my dear bairn!"

It was not either in the nature or habits of David Deans to seem a fond father; nor was he often observed to experience, or at least to evince, that fullness of the heart which seeks to expand itself in tender expressions or caresses even to those who were dearest to him. On the contrary, he used to censure this as a degree of weakness in several of his neighbours, and particularly in poor Widow Butler. It followed, however, from the rarity of such emotions in this self-denied and reserved man, that his children attached to occasional marks of his affection and approbation a degree of high interest and solemnity; well considering them as evidences of feelings which were only expressed when they became too intense for suppression or concealment.

With deep emotion, therefore, did he bestow, and his daughter receive, this benediction and paternal caress. "And you, my dear father," exclaimed Jeanie, when the door had closed upon the venerable old man, "may you have purchased and promised blessings[8] multiplied upon you—upon *you*, who walk in this world as though you were not of the world,[9] and hold all that it can give or take away but as the *midges* that the sun-blink brings out, and the evening wind sweeps away!"

She now made preparation for her night-walk. Her father slept in another part of the dwelling, and, regular in all his habits, seldom or never left his apartment when he had betaken himself to it for the evening. It was therefore easy for her to leave the house unobserved, so soon as the time approached at which she was to keep her appointment. But the step she was about to take had difficulties and terrors in her own eyes, though she had no reason to apprehend her father's interference. Her life had been spent in the quiet, uniform, and regular seclusion of their peaceful and monotonous household. The very hour which some damsels of the present day, as well of her own as of higher degree, would consider as the natural period of commencing an evening of pleasure, brought, in her opinion, awe and solemnity in it; and the resolution she had taken had a strange, daring, and adventurous character, to which she could hardly reconcile herself when the moment approached for putting it into execution. Her hands trembled as she snooded her fair hair beneath the ribband, then the only ornament or cover which young unmarried women wore on their head, and as she adjusted the scarlet tartan screen or muffler made of plaid, which the Scottish women wore, much in the fashion of the black silk veils still a part of female dress in the Netherlands. A sense of impropriety as well as of danger pressed upon her as she lifted the latch of her paternal mansion to leave it on so wild an expedition, and at so late an hour, unprotected and without the knowledge of her natural guardian.

When she found herself abroad and in the open fields, additional subjects of apprehension crowded upon her. The dim cliffs and scattered rocks, interspersed with greensward, through which she had to pass to the place of appointment, as they glimmered before her in a clear autumn night, recalled to her memory many a deed of violence, which, according to tradition, had been done and suffered among them. In earlier days they had been the haunt of robbers and assassins, the memory of whose crimes is preserved in the various edicts which the council of the city, and even the parliament of Scotland, had passed for dispersing their bands, and insuring safety to the lieges, so near the precincts of the city. The names of these criminals, and of their atrocities, were still remembered in traditions of the scattered cottages and the neighbouring suburb. In latter times, as we have already noticed, the sequestered and broken character of the ground rendered it a fit theatre for duels and rencontres among the fiery youth of the period. Two or three of these incidents, all sanguinary, and one of them fatal in its termination, had happened since Deans came to live at Saint Leonard's. His daughter's recollections, therefore, were of blood and horror as she pursued the small scarce-tracked solitary path, every step of which conveyed her to a greater distance from help, and deeper into the ominous seclusion of these unhallowed precincts.

As the moon began to peer forth on the scene with a doubtful, flitting, and solemn light, Jeanie's apprehensions took another turn, too peculiar to her rank and country to remain unnoticed. But to trace its origin will require another chapter.

CHAPTER 15

——The spirit I have seen
May be the devil. And the devil has power
To assume a pleasing shape.

Hamlet

WITCHCRAFT and dæmonology, as we have had already occasion to remark, were at this period believed in by almost all ranks, but more especially among the stricter classes of presbyterians, whose government, when their party were at the head of the state, had been much sullied by their eagerness to enquire into, and persecute these imaginary crimes.[1] Now, in this point of view also, Saint Leonard's Crags and the adjacent Chase[2] were a dreaded and ill-reputed district. Not only had witches held their meetings there, but even of very late years the enthusiast, or impostor, mentioned in the Pandæmonium of Richard Bovet, Gentleman,[*] had, among the recesses of these romantic cliffs, found his way into the hidden retreats where the fairies revel in the bowels of the earth.

With all these legends Jeanie Deans was too well acquainted, to escape that strong impression which they usually make on the imagination. Indeed, relations of this ghostly kind had been familiar to her from her infancy, for they were the only relief which her father's conversation afforded from controversial argument, or the gloomy history of the strivings and testimonies, escapes, captures, tortures, and executions of those martyrs of the Covenant, with whom it was his chiefest boast to say he had been acquainted. In the recesses of mountains, in caverns, and in morasses, to which these persecuted enthusiasts were so ruthlessly pursued, they conceived they had often to contend with the visible assaults of the Enemy of Mankind, as in the cities, and in the cultivated fields, they were exposed to those of the tyrannical government and their soldiery. Such were the terrors which made one of their gifted seers exclaim,[3] when his companion returned to him, after having left him alone in a haunted cavern in Sorn in Galloway, "It is hard living in this world—incarnate devils

[* See p. 562 for the note, "The Fairy Boy of Leith".]

above the earth, and devils under the earth! Satan has been here since ye went away, but I have dismissed him by resistance; we will be no more troubled with him this night." David Deans believed this, and many other such ghostly encounters and victories, on the faith of the Ansars, or auxiliaries of the banished prophets. This event was beyond David's remembrance. But he used to tell with great awe, yet not without a feeling of proud superiority to his auditors, how he himself had been present at a field-meeting at Crochmade, when the duty of the day was interrupted by the apparition of a tall black man, who, in the act of crossing a ford to join the congregation, lost ground, and was carried down apparently by the force of the stream. All were instantly at work to assist him, but with so little success, that ten or twelve stout men, who had hold of the rope which they had cast in to his aid, were rather in danger to be dragged into the stream, and lose their own lives, than likely to save that of the supposed perishing man. "But famous John Semple[4] of Carsphairn," David Deans used to say with exultation, "saw the whaup in the rape,—'Quit the tow,' he cried to us, (for I that was but a callant had a haud o' the rape mysell;) 'it is the Great Enemy; he will burn, but not drown; his design is to disturb the good wark, by raising wonder and confusion in your minds; to put off from your spirits all that ye hae heard and felt.'— Sae we let go the rape," said David, "and he went adown the water screeching and bullering like a Bull of Bashan,[5] as he is ca'd in Scripture."[*]

Trained in these and similar legends, it was no wonder that Jeanie began to feel an ill-defined apprehension, not merely of the phantoms which might beset her way, but of the quality, nature, and purpose of the being who had thus appointed her a meeting, at a place and hour of horror, and at a time when her mind must be necessarily full of those tempting and ensnaring thoughts of grief and despair, which were supposed to lay sufferers particularly open to the temptations of the Evil One. If such an idea had crossed even Butler's well-informed mind, it was calculated to make a much stronger impression upon hers. Yet firmly believing the possibility of an encounter so terrible to flesh and blood, Jeanie, with a degree of resolution of which we cannot sufficiently estimate the merit, because the incredulity of the age has rendered us strangers to the nature and extent of her feelings, persevered in her determination not to omit an opportunity of doing

[* See p. 564 for the note, "Intercourse of the Covenanters with the Invisible World."]

something towards saving her sister, although in the attempt to avail herself of it she might be exposed to dangers so dreadful to her imagination. So, like Christiana in the Pilgrim's Progress,[6] when traversing with a timid yet resolved step the terrors of the Valley of the Shadow of Death,[7] she glided on by rock and stone, "now in glimmer and now in gloom,"[8] as her path lay through moonlight or shadow, and endeavoured to overpower the suggestions of fear, sometimes by fixing her mind upon the distressed condition of her sister, and the duty she lay under to afford her aid, should that be in her power; and more frequently by recurring in mental prayer to the protection of that Being to whom night is as noon-day.[9]

Thus drowning at one time her fears by fixing her mind on a subject of overpowering interest, and arguing them down at others by referring herself to the protection of the Deity, she at length approached the place assigned for this mysterious conference.

It was situated in the depth of the valley behind Salisbury Crags, which has for a back-ground the north-western shoulder of the mountain called Arthur's Seat, on whose descent still remain the ruins of what was once a chapel, or hermitage, dedicated to Saint Anthony the Eremite.[10] A better site for such a building could hardly have been selected; for the chapel, situated among the rude and pathless cliffs, lies in a desert, even in the immediate vicinity of a rich, populous, and tumultuous capital: and the hum of the city might mingle with the orisons of the recluses, conveying as little of worldly interest as if it had been the roar of the distant ocean. Beneath the steep ascent on which these ruins are still visible, was, and perhaps is still pointed out, the place where the wretch Nicol Muschat, who has been already mentioned in these pages, had closed a long scene of cruelty towards his unfortunate wife, by murdering her with circumstances of uncommon barbarity.[*] The execration in which the man's crime was held extended itself to the place where it was perpetrated, which was marked by a small *cairn*, or heap of stones, composed of those which each chance passenger had thrown there in testimony of abhorrence, and on the principle, it would seem, of the ancient British malediction, "May you have a cairn for your burial-place!"[11]

As our heroine approached this ominous and unhallowed spot, she paused and looked to the moon, now rising broad in the north-west, and shedding a more distinct light than it had afforded during her

[* See p. 561 for the note to Chapter 11, "Muschat's Cairn".]

walk thither. Eyeing the planet[12] for a moment, she then slowly and fearfully turned her head towards the cairn, from which it was at first averted. She was at first disappointed. Nothing was visible beside the little pile of stones, which shone grey in the moonlight. A multitude of confused suggestions rushed on her mind. Had her correspondent deceived her, and broken his appointment?—was he too tardy at the appointment he had made?—or had some strange turn of fate prevented him from appearing as he proposed?—or if he were an unearthly being, as her secret apprehensions suggested, was it his object merely to delude her with false hopes, and put her to unnecessary toil and terror, according to the nature, as she had heard, of those wandering dæmons?—or did he propose to blast her with the sudden horrors of his presence when she had come close to the place of rendezvous? These anxious reflections did not prevent her approaching to the cairn with a pace that, though slow, was determined.

When she was within two yards of the heap of stones, a figure rose suddenly up from behind it, and Jeanie scarce forbore to scream aloud at what seemed the realization of the most frightful of her anticipations. She constrained herself to silence, however, and, making a dead pause, suffered the figure to open the conversation, which he did, by asking, in a voice which agitation rendered tremulous and hollow, "Are you the sister of that ill-fated young woman?"

"I am—I am the sister of Effie Deans!" exclaimed Jeanie. "And as ever you hope God will hear you at your need, tell me, if you can tell, what can be done to save her!"

"I do *not* hope God will hear me at my need," was the singular answer. "I do not deserve—I do not expect he will." This desperate[13] language he uttered in a tone calmer than that with which he had at first spoken, probably because the shock of first addressing her was what he felt most difficult to overcome. Jeanie remained mute with horror to hear language expressed so utterly foreign to all which she had ever been acquainted with, that it sounded in her ears rather like that of a fiend than of a human being. The stranger pursued his address to her without seeming to notice her surprise. "You see before you a wretch, predestined to evil here and hereafter."[14]

"For the sake of Heaven, that hears and sees us," said Jeanie, "dinna speak in this desperate fashion! The gospel is sent to the chief of sinners[15]—to the most miserable among the miserable."

"Then should I have my own share therein," said the stranger, "if you call it sinful to have been the destruction of the mother that bore me—of the friend that loved me—of the woman that trusted me—of the innocent child that was born to me. If to have done all this is to be a sinner, and to survive it is to be miserable, then am I most guilty and most miserable indeed."

"Then you are the wicked cause of my sister's ruin?" said Jeanie, with a natural touch of indignation expressed in her tone of voice.

"Curse me for it, if you will," said the stranger; "I have well deserved it at your hand."

"It is fitter for me," said Jeanie, "to pray to God to forgive you."

"Do as you will, how you will, or what you will," he replied, with vehemence; "only promise to obey my directions, and save your sister's life."

"I must first know," said Jeanie, "the means you would have me use in her behalf."

"No!—you must first swear—solemnly swear, that you will employ them, when I make them known to you."

"Surely, it is needless to swear that I will do all that is lawful to a Christian, to save the life of my sister?"

"I will have no reservation!" thundered the stranger; "lawful or unlawful, Christian or heathen, you shall swear to do my hest, and act by my counsel, or—you little know whose wrath you provoke!"

"I will think on what you have said," said Jeanie, who began to get much alarmed at the frantic vehemence of his manner, and disputed in her own mind, whether she spoke to a maniac, or an apostate spirit incarnate[16]—"I will think on what you say, and let you ken to-morrow."

"To-morrow?" exclaimed the man, with a laugh of scorn—"And where will I be to-morrow?—or, where will you be to-night, unless you swear to walk by my counsel?—There was one accursed deed done at this spot before now; and there shall be another to match it, unless you yield up to my guidance body and soul."

As he spoke, he offered a pistol at the unfortunate young woman. She neither fled nor fainted, but sunk on her knees, and asked him to spare her life.

"Is that all you have to say?" said the unmoved ruffian.

"Do not dip your hands in the blood of a defenceless creature that has trusted to you," said Jeanie, still on her knees.

"Is that all you can say for your life?—Have you no promise to give?—Will you destroy your sister, and compel me to shed more blood?"

"I can promise nothing," said Jeanie, "which is unlawful for a Christian."

He cocked the weapon, and held it towards her.

"May God forgive you!" she said, pressing her hands forcibly against her eyes.

"D—n!" muttered the man; and, turning aside from her, he uncocked the pistol, and replaced it in his pocket—"I am a villain," he said, "steeped in guilt and wretchedness, but not wicked enough to do you any harm! I only wished to terrify you into my measures—She hears me not—she is gone!—Great God! what a wretch am I become!"

As he spoke, she recovered herself from an agony which partook of the bitterness of death;[17] and, in a minute or two, through the strong exertion of her natural sense and courage, collected herself sufficiently to understand he intended her no personal injury.

"No!" he repeated; "I would not add to the murder of your sister, and of her child, that of any one belonging to her!—Mad, frantic, as I am, and unrestrained by either fear or mercy, given up to the possession of an evil being, and forsaken by all that is good, I would not hurt you, were the world offered me for a bribe! But, for the sake of all that is dear to you, swear you will follow my counsel. Take this weapon, shoot me through the head, and with your own hand revenge your sister's wrongs, only follow the course—the only course, by which her life can be saved."

"Alas! is she innocent or guilty?"

"She is guiltless—guiltless of every thing, but of having trusted a villain!—Yet had it not been for those that were worse than I am—yes, worse than I, though I am bad indeed—this misery had not befallen."

"And my sister's child—does it live?" said Jeanie.

"No; it was murdered—the new-born infant was barbarously murdered," he uttered in a low, yet stern and sustained voice;—"but," he added hastily, "not by her knowledge or consent."

"Then, why cannot the guilty be brought to justice, and the innocent freed?"

"Torment me not with questions which can serve no purpose," he sternly replied—"The deed was done by those who are far enough from pursuit, and safe enough from discovery!—No one can save Effie but yourself."

"Woes me! how is it in my power?" asked Jeanie, in despondency.

"Hearken to me!—You have sense—you can apprehend my meaning—I will trust you—Your sister is innocent of the crime charged against her"——

"Thank God for that!" said Jeanie.

"Be still, and hearken!—The person who assisted her in her illness, murdered the child; but it was without the mother's knowledge or consent—She is therefore guiltless, as guiltless as the unhappy innocent, that but gasped a few minutes in this unhappy world—the better was its hap to be so soon at rest. She is innocent as that infant, and yet she must die—it is impossible to clear her of the law!"

"Cannot the wretches be discovered and given up to punishment?" said Jeanie.

"Do you think, you will persuade those who are hardened in guilt, to die to save another?—Is that the reed you would lean to?"

"But you said there was a remedy," again gasped out the terrified young woman.

"There is," answered the stranger, "and it is in your own hands. The blow which the law aims cannot be broken by directly encountering it, but it may be turned aside. You saw your sister during the period preceding the birth of her child—what is so natural as that she should have mentioned her condition to you? The doing so would, as their cant goes, take the case from under the statute, for it removes the quality of concealment. I know their jargon, and have had sad cause to know it; and the quality of concealment is essential to this statutory offence.[*][18] Nothing is so natural as that Effie should have mentioned her condition to you—think—reflect—I am positive that she did."

"Woes me!" said Jeanie, "she never spoke to me on the subject, but grat sorely when I spoke to her about her altered looks, and the change on her spirits."

"You asked her questions on the subject?" he said, eagerly. "You *must* remember her answer was, a confession that she had been ruined by a villain—yes, lay a strong emphasis on that—a cruel, false villain called—the name is unnecessary; and that she bore under her bosom the consequences of his guilt and her folly; and that he had assured her he would provide safely for her approaching illness.—Well he kept his word!" These last words he spoke as it were to himself, and with a violent gesture of self-accusation, and then calmly proceeded, "You will remember all this?—That is all that is necessary to be said."

[* See p. 566 for the note, "Child Murder".]

"But I cannot remember," answered Jeanie, with simplicity, "that which Effie never told me."

"Are you so dull—so very dull of apprehension!" he exclaimed, suddenly grasping her arm, and holding it firm in his hand. "I tell you," (speaking between his teeth, and under his breath, but with great energy,) "you *must* remember that she told you all this, whether she ever said a syllable of it or no. You must repeat this tale, in which there is no falsehood, except in so far as it was not told to you till now, before these Justices—Justiciary—whatever they call their blood-thirsty court, and save your sister from being murdered, and them from becoming murderers. Do not hesitate—I pledge life and salvation, that in saying what I have said, you will only speak the simple truth."

"But," replied Jeanie, whose judgment was too accurate not to see the sophistry of this argument, "I shall be man-sworn in the very thing in which my testimony is wanted, for it is the concealment for which poor Effie is blamed, and you would make me tell a falsehood anent it."

"I see," he said, "my first suspicions of you were right, and that you will let your sister, innocent, fair, and guiltless, except in trusting a villain, die the death of a murdress, rather than bestow the breath of your mouth and the sound of your voice to save her."

"I wad ware the best blood in my body to keep her skaithless," said Jeanie, weeping in bitter agony, "but I canna change right into wrang, or make that true which is false."

"Foolish, hard-hearted girl," said the stranger, "are you afraid of what they may do to you? I tell you, even the retainers of the law, who course life as greyhounds do hares, will rejoice at the escape of a creature so young—so beautiful; that they will not suspect your tale; that, if they did suspect it, they would consider you as deserving, not only of forgiveness, but of praise for your natural affection."

"It is not man I fear," said Jeanie, looking upward; "the God, whose name I must call on to witness the truth of what I say, he will know the falsehood."

"And he will know the motive," said the stranger, eagerly; "he will know that you are doing this—not for lucre of gain, but to save the life of the innocent, and prevent the commission of a worse crime than that which the law seeks to avenge."

"He has given us a law," said Jeanie, "for the lamp of our path;[19] if we stray from it, we err against knowledge—I may not do evil, even that good may come out of it. But you—you that ken all this to be true, which I must take on your word,—you that, if I understood what you said e'en now, promised her shelter and protection in her travail, why do not *you* step forward, and bear leal and soothfast evidence in her behalf, as ye may with a clear conscience?"

"To whom do you talk of a clear conscience, woman?" said he, with a sudden fierceness which renewed her terrors,—"to *me*?—I have not known one for many a year. Bear witness in her behalf?—a proper witness, that, even to speak these few words to a woman of so little consequence as yourself, must chuse such an hour and such a place as this. When you see owls and bats fly abroad, like larks, in the sunshine, you may expect to see such as I am in the assemblies of men.—Hush—listen to that."

A voice was heard to sing one of those wild and monotonous strains so common in Scotland, and to which the natives of that country chaunt their old ballads. The sound ceased—then came nearer, and was renewed; the stranger listened attentively, still holding Jeanie by the arm, (as she stood by him in motionless terror) as if to prevent her interrupting the strain by speaking or stirring. When the sounds were renewed, the words were distinctly audible:

> "When the gledd's in the blue cloud,
> The lavrock lies still;
> When the hound's in the green-wood,
> The hind keeps the hill."[20]

The person who sung kept a strained and powerful voice at its highest pitch, so that it could be heard at a very considerable distance. As the song ceased, they might hear a stifled sound, as of steps and whispers of persons approaching them. The song was again raised, but the tune was changed:

> "O sleep ye sound, Sir James, she said,
> When ye suld rise and ride?
> There's twenty men, wi' bow and blade,
> Are seeking where ye hide."[21]

"I dare stay no longer," said the stranger; "return home, or remain till they come up—you have nothing to fear—but do not tell you saw me—your sister's fate is in your hands." So saying, he turned from her, and with a swift, yet cautiously noiseless step, plunged into the darkness on the side most remote from the sounds which they heard approaching, and was soon lost to her sight. Jeanie remained by the cairn terrified beyond expression, and uncertain whether she ought to fly homeward with all the speed she could exert, or wait the approach of those who were advancing towards her. This uncertainty detained her so long, that she now distinctly saw two or three figures already so near to her, that a precipitate flight would have been equally fruitless and impolitic.

CHAPTER 16

―――She speaks things in doubt,
That carry but half sense: her speech is nothing,
Yet the unshaped use of it doth move
The hearers to collection; they aim at it,
And botch the words up fit to their own thoughts.
                                        Hamlet

LIKE the digressive poet Ariosto,[1] I find myself under the necessity of connecting the branches of my story, by taking up the adventures of another of the characters, and bringing them down to the point at which we have left those of Jeanie Deans. It is not, perhaps, the most artificial way of telling a story, but it has the advantage of sparing the necessity of resuming what a knitter (if stocking-looms have left such a person in the land,) might call our "dropped stitches;" a labour in which the author generally toils much, without getting credit for his pains.

"I could risk a sma' wad," said the clerk to the magistrate, "that this rascal Ratcliffe, if he was once insured of his neck's safety, could do more than ony ten of our police-people and constables, to help us to get out of this scrape of Porteous. He is weel acquent wi' a' the smugglers, thieves, and banditti about Edinburgh; and, indeed, he may be called the father of a' the misdoers in Scotland, for he has passed amang them for these twenty years by the name Daddie Rat."

"A bonny sort of a scoundrel," replied the magistrate, "to expect a place under the city!"

"Begging your honour's pardon," said the city's procurator-fiscal, upon whom the duties of superintendant of police devolved, "Mr Fairscrieve is perfectly in the right. It is just sic as Ratcliffe that the town needs in my department; an it sae be that he's disposed to turn his knowledge to the city service, ye'll no find a better man.―Ye'll get nae saints to be searchers for uncustomed goods, or for thieves and sic like;―and your decent sort of men, religious professors, and broken tradesmen, that are put into the like o' sic trust, can do nae gude ava. They are feared for this, and they are scrupulous about that, and they

are na free to tell a lie, though it may be for the benefit of the city; and
they dinna like to be out at irregular hours, and in a dark cauld night,
and they like a clout ower the croun far waur; and sae between the fear
o' God, and the fear o' man, and the fear o' getting a sair throat, or sair
banes, there's a dozen o' our city-folks, baith waiters, and officers, and
constables, that can find out naething but a wee-bit skulduddery for
the benefit of the Kirk-treasurer.[2] Jock Porteous, that's stiff and stark,
puir fallow, was worth a dozen o' them; for he never had ony fears, or
scruples, or doubts, or conscience, about ony thing your honours bade
him."

"He was a gude servant o' the town," said the Baillie, "though he
was an ower free-living man. But if you really think this rascal
Ratcliffe could do us ony service in discovering these malefactors, I
would insure him life, reward, and promotion. It's an awsome thing
this mischance for the city, Mr Fairscrieve. It will be very ill taen wi'
abune stairs. Queen Caroline, God bless her, is a woman—at least I
judge sae, and it's nae treason to speak my mind sae far—and ye
maybe ken as weel as I do, for ye hae a housekeeper, though ye are nae
married man, that women are wilfu', and downa bide a slight. And it
will sound ill in her ears, that sic a confused mistake suld come to
pass, and naebody sae muckle as to be put in the Tolbooth about it."

"If ye thought that, sir," said the procurator-fiscal, "we could easily
clap into the prison a few blackguards upon suspicion. It will have a
gude active look, and I hae aye plenty on my list, that wad na be a hair
the waur of a week or twa's imprisonment; and if ye thought it no
strictly just, ye could be just the easier wi' them the neist time they
did ony thing to deserve it; they arena the sort to be lang o' gieing ye
an opportunity to clear scores wi' them on that account."

"I doubt that will hardly do in this case, Mr Sharpitlaw," returned
the town-clerk; "they'll run their letters,[*][3] and be a' adrift again,
before ye ken where ye are."

"I will speak to the Lord Provost," said the magistrate, "about
Ratcliffe's business. Mr Sharpitlaw, you will go with me and receive
instructions—something may be made too out of this story of Butler's
and his unknown gentleman—I know no business any man has to
swagger about in the King's Park, and call himself the devil, to the
terror of honest folks, who dinna care to hear mair about the devil

[* A Scottish form of procedure, answering, in some respects, to the English Habeas
Corpus.]

than is said from the pulpit on the Sabbath. I cannot think the preacher himsell wad be heading the mob, though the time has been, they hae been as forward in a bruilzie as their neighbours."

"But these times are lang bye," said Mr Sharpitlaw. "In my father's time, there was mair search for silenced ministers about the Bowhead and the Covenant Close, and all the tents of Kedar,[4] as they ca'd the dwellings o' the godly in those days, than there's now for thieves and vagabonds in the Laigh Calton and the back o' the Canongate. But that time's weel bye, an it bide. And if the Baillie will get me directions and authority from the Provost, I'll speak wi' Daddie Rat mysell; for I'm thinking I'll make mair out o' him than ye'll do."

Mr Sharpitlaw, being necessarily a man of high trust, was accordingly empowered, in the course of the day, to make such arrangements, as might seem in the emergency most advantageous for the Good Town. He went to the jail accordingly, and saw Ratcliffe in private.

The relative positions of a police-officer and a professed thief bear a different complexion, according to circumstances. The most obvious simile of a hawk pouncing upon his prey, is often least applicable. Sometimes the guardian of justice has the air of a cat watching a mouse, and, while he suspends his purpose of springing upon the pilferer, takes care so to calculate his motions that he shall not get beyond his power. Sometimes, more passive still, he uses the art of fascination ascribed to the rattle-snake, and contents himself with glaring on the victim, through all his devious flutterings; certain that his terror, confusion, and disorder of ideas, will bring him into his jaws at last. The interview between Ratcliffe and Sharpitlaw had an aspect different from all these. They sate for five minutes silent, on opposite sides of a small table, and looked fixedly at each other, with a sharp, knowing, and alert cast of countenance, not unmingled with an inclination to laugh, and resembled, more than any thing else, two dogs, who, preparing for a game at romps, are seen to couch down, and remain in that posture for a little time, watching each other's movements, and waiting which shall begin the game.

"So, Mr Ratcliffe," said the officer, conceiving it suited his dignity to speak first, "you give up business, I find?"

"Yes, sir," replied Ratcliffe; "I shall not be on that lay nae mair—and I think that will save your folk some trouble, Mr Sharpitlaw?"

"Which Jock Dalgleish"[5] (then finisher of the law in the Scottish metropolis,) "wad save them as easily," returned the procurator-fiscal.

"Ay; if I waited in the Tolbooth here to have him fit my cravat—but that's an idle way o' speaking, Mr Sharpitlaw."

"Why, I suppose you know you are under sentence of death, Mr Ratcliffe?" replied Mr Sharpitlaw.

"Ay, so are a', as that worthy minister said in the Tolbooth Kirk the day Robertson wan off; but naebody kens when it will be executed. Gude faith, he had better reason to say sae than he dreamed of, before the play was played out that morning."

"This Robertson," said Sharpitlaw, in a lower, and something like a confidential tone, "d'ye ken, Rat—that is, can ye gie us ony inkling where he is to be heard tell o'?"

"Troth, Mr Sharpitlaw, I'll be frank wi' ye; Robertson is rather a cut abune me—a wild deevil he was, and mony a daft prank he played; but except the Collector's job that Wilson led him into, and some tuilzies about run goods wi' the gaugers and the waiters, he never did ony thing that came near our line o' business."

"Umph! that's singular, considering the company he kept."

"Fact, upon my honour and credit," said Ratcliffe, gravely. "He keepit out o' our little bits of affairs, and that's mair than Wilson did; I hae dune business wi' Wilson afore now. But the lad will come on in time; there's nae fear o' him; naebody will live the life he has led, but what he'll come to sooner or later."

"Who or what is he, Ratcliffe? you know, I suppose?" said Sharpitlaw.

"He's better born, I judge, than he cares to let on; he's been a soldier, and he has been a play-actor, and I wat na what he has been or has na been, for as young as he is, sae that it had daffing and nonsense about it."

"Pretty pranks he has played in his time, I suppose?"

"Ye may say that," said Ratcliffe, with a sardonic smile; "and," (touching his nose,) "a deevil amang the lasses."

"Like enough," said Sharpitlaw. "Weel, Ratcliffe, I'll no stand niffering wi' ye; ye ken the way that favour's gotten in my office; ye maun be usefu'."

"Certainly, sir, to the best of my power—naething for naething—I ken the rule of the office," said the ex-depredator.

"Now the principal thing in hand e'en now," said the official person, "is this job of Porteous's; an ye can gie us a lift—why, the inner turnkey's office to begin wi', and the captainship in time—ye understand my meaning?"

"Ay, troth do I, sir; a wink's as gude as a nod to a blind horse;[6] but Jock Porteous's job—Lord help ye, I was under sentence the haill time. God! but I could na help laughing when I heard Jock skirling for mercy in the lads's hands! Mony a het skin ye hae gien me, neighbour, thought I, tak ye what's gaun; time about's fair play;[7] ye'll ken now what hanging's gude for."

"Come, come, this is all nonsense, Rat," said the procurator. "Ye canna creep out at that hole, lad; you must speak to the point—the point, you understand me, if you want favour; gif-gaf makes gude friends,[8] ye ken."

"But how can I speak to the point, as your honour ca's it," said Ratcliffe, demurely, and with an air of great simplicity, "when ye ken I was under sentence, and in the strong-room a' the while the job was gaun on?"

"And how can we turn you loose on the public again, Daddie Rat, unless ye do or say something to deserve it?"

"Well then, d—n it!" answered the criminal, "since it maun be sae, I saw Geordie Robertson amang the boys that brake the jail; I suppose that will do me some gude?"

"That's speaking to the purpose, indeed," said the office-bearer; "and now, Rat, where think ye we'll find him?"

"Deil haet o' me kens," said Ratcliffe; "he'll no likely gang back to ony o' his auld howffs; he'll be off the country by this time. He has gude friends some gate or other, for a' the life he's led; he's been weel educate."

"He'll grace the gallows the better," said Mr Sharpitlaw; "a desperate dog, to murther an officer of the city for doing his duty! Wha kens wha's turn it might be next?—But you saw him plainly?"

"As plainly as I see you."

"How was he dressed?" said Sharpitlaw.

"I couldna weel see; something of a woman's bit mutch on his head; but ye never saw sic a ca'-throw. Ane couldna hae een to a' thing."

"But did he speak to no one?" said Sharpitlaw.

"They were a' speaking and gabbling through other," said Ratcliffe, who was obviously unwilling to carry his evidence farther than he could possibly help.

"This will not do, Ratcliffe," said the procurator; "you must speak *out—out—out*," tapping the table emphatically as he repeated that impressive monosyllable.

"It's very hard, sir," said the prisoner; "and but for the under-turnkey's place"——

"And the reversion of the captaincy—the captaincy of the Tolbooth, man—that is, in case of gude behaviour."

"Ay, ay," said Ratcliffe, "gude behaviour!—there's the deevil. And then it's waiting for dead folk's shoon[9] into the bargain."

"But Robertson's head will weigh something," said Sharpitlaw; "something gay and heavy, Rat; the town maun show cause—that's right and reason—and then ye'll hae freedom to enjoy your gear honestly."

"I dinna ken," said Ratcliffe; "it's a queer way of beginning the trade of honesty—but deil ma care. Weel, then, I heard and saw him speak to the wench Effie Deans, that's up there for child-murder."

"The deil ye did? Rat, this is finding a mare's nest wi' a witness.[10]—And the man that spoke to Butler in the Park, and that was to meet wi' Jeanie Deans at Muschat's Cairn—whew! lay that and that thegither. As sure as I live he's been the father of the lassie's wean."

"There hae been waur guesses than that, I'm thinking," observed Ratcliffe, turning his quid of tobacco in his cheek, and squirting out the juice. "I heard something a while syne about his drawing up wi' a bonny quean about the Pleasaunts, and that it was a' Wilson could do to keep him frae marrying her."

Here a city officer entered, and told Sharpitlaw that they had the woman in custody whom he had directed them to bring before him.

"It's little matter now," said he, "the thing is taking another turn; however, George, ye may bring her in."

The officer retired, and introduced upon his return, a tall, strapping wench of eighteen or twenty, dressed fantastically, in a sort of blue riding jacket, with tarnished lace, her hair clubbed like that of a man, a Highland bonnet, and a bunch of broken feathers, a riding skirt (or petticoat,) of scarlet camlet, embroidered with tarnished flowers. Her features were coarse and masculine, yet at a little distance, by dint of very bright wild-looking black eyes, an aquiline nose, and a commanding profile, appeared rather handsome. She flourished the switch she held in her hand, dropped a curtsey as low as a lady at a birth-night introduction, recovered herself seemingly according to Touchstone's directions to Audrey,[11] and opened the conversation without waiting till any questions were asked.

"God gie your honour gude e'en, and mony o' them, bonny Mr Sharpitlaw—Gude e'en to ye, Daddie Ratton—they tauld me ye were hanged, man; or did ye get out o' John Dalgleish's hands like half-hangit Maggie Dickson?"[12]

"Whisht, ye daft jaud," said Ratcliffe, "and hear what's said to ye."

"Wi' a' my heart, Ratton. Great preferment for poor Madge to be brought up the street wi' a grand man, wi' a coat a' passemented wi' worset-lace, to speak wi' provosts, and baillies, and town-clerks, and prokitors, at this time o' day—and the haill town looking at me too—This is honour on earth for anes!"

"Ay, Madge," said Mr Sharpitlaw, in a coaxing tone; "and ye're dressed out in your braws, I see; these are not your every-days' claiths ye have on."

"Deil be in my fingers,[13] then," said Madge—"Eh, sirs!" (observing Butler come into the apartment,) "there's a minister in the Tolbooth—wha will ca' it a graceless place, now?—I'se warrant he's in for the gude auld cause—but it's be nae cause o' mine," and off she went into song.

"Hey for cavaliers, ho for cavaliers,
Dub a dub, dub a dub;
Have at old Beelzebub,—
Oliver's squeaking for fear."—[14]

"Did you ever see that mad-woman before?" said Sharpitlaw to Butler.

"Not to my knowledge, sir," replied Butler.

"I thought as much," said the procurator-fiscal, looking towards Ratcliffe, who answered his glance with a nod of acquiescence and intelligence.

"But that is Madge Wildfire, as she calls herself," said the man of law to Butler.

"Ay, that I am," said Madge, "and that I have been ever since I was something better—Heigh ho"—(and something like melancholy dwelt on her features for a minute)—"But I canna mind when that was—it was lang syne, at ony rate, and I'll ne'er fash my thumb about it.—

I glance like the wildfire through country and town;
I'm seen on the causeway—I'm seen on the down;
The lightning that flashes so bright and so free,
Is scarcely so blithe or so bonny as me."[15]

"Haud your tongue, ye skirling limmer," said the officer, who had acted as master of the ceremonies to this extraordinary performer, and who was rather scandalized at the freedom of her demeanour before a person of Mr Sharpitlaw's importance—"haud your tongue, or I'se gie ye something to skirl for."

"Let her alone, George," said Sharpitlaw; "dinna put her out o' tune; I hae some questions to ask her—But first, Mr Butler, take another look of her."

"Do sae, minister—do sae," cried Madge; "I am as weel worth looking at as ony book in your aught.—And I can say the single carritch, and the double carritch, and justification, and effectual calling, and the assembly of divines[16] at Westminster, that is," (she added in a low tone) "I could say them anes—but it's lang syne—and ane forgets, ye ken." And poor Madge heaved another deep sigh.

"Weel, sir," said Mr Sharpitlaw to Butler, "what think ye now?"

"As I did before," said Butler; "that I never saw the poor demented creature in my life before."

"Then she is not the person whom you said the rioters last night described as Madge Wildfire?"

"Certainly not," said Butler. "They may be near the same height, for they are both tall, but I see little other resemblance."

"Their dress, then, is not alike?" said Sharpitlaw.

"Not in the least," said Butler.

"Madge, my bonny woman," said Sharpitlaw, in the same coaxing manner, "what did ye do wi' your ilka-day's claise yesterday?"

"I dinna mind," said Madge.

"Where was ye yesterday at e'en, Madge?"

"I dinna mind ony thing about yesterday," answered Madge; "ae day is aneugh for ony body to win ower wi' at a time, and ower muckle sometimes."

"But maybe, Madge, ye wad mind something about it, if I was to gie ye this half-crown?" said Sharpitlaw, taking out the piece of money.

"That might gar me laugh, but it couldna gar me mind."

"But, Madge," continued Sharpitlaw, "were I to send you to the wark-house in Leith Wynd,[17] and gar Jock Dalgleish lay the tawse on your back"—

"That wad gar me greet," said Madge, sobbing, "but it couldna gar me mind, ye ken."

"She is ower far past reasonable folk's motives, sir," said Ratcliffe, "to mind siller, or John Dalgleish, or the cat and nine tails either; but I think I could gar her tell us something."

"Try her then, Ratcliffe," said Sharpitlaw, "for I am tired of her crazy prate, and be d—d to her."

"Madge," said Ratcliffe, "hae ye ony joes now?"

"An onybody ask ye, say ye dinna ken.—Set him up to be speaking of my joes, auld Daddie Ratton!"

"I dare say, ye hae deil ane?"

"See if I haena then," said Madge, with the toss of the head of affronted beauty—"there's Rob the Ranter, and Will Fleming, and then there's Geordie Robertson, lad—that's Gentleman Geordie— what think ye o' that?"

Ratcliffe laughed, and, winking to the procurator-fiscal, pursued the enquiry in his own way. "But, Madge, the lads only like ye when ye hae on your braws—they wadna touch you wi' a pair o' tangs when you are in your auld ilka-day rags."

"Ye're a leeing auld sorrow then," said Madge indignantly; "for Gentle Geordie Robertson put my ilka-day's claise on his ain bonnie sell yestreen, and gaed a' through the town wi' them; and gawsie and grand he lookit, like ony queen in the land."

"I dinna believe a word o't," said Ratcliffe, with another wink to the procurator. "Thae duds were a' o' the colour o' moonshine in the water, I'm thinking, Madge—The gown wad be a sky-blue scarlet, I'se warrant ye?"

"It was nae sic thing," said Madge, whose unretentive memory let out, in the eagerness of contradiction, all that she would have most wished to keep concealed, had her judgment been equal to her inclination. "It was neither scarlet nor sky-blue, but my ain auld brown threshie-coat[18] of a short gown, and my mother's auld mutch, and my red rokelay—and he gaed me a croun and a kiss for the use o' them, blessing on his bonnie face—though it's been a dear ane to me."

"And where did he change his clothes again, hinnie?" said Sharpit-law, in his most conciliatory manner.

"The procurator's spoiled a'," observed Ratcliffe, drily.

And it was even so; for the question, put in so direct a shape, immediately awakened Madge to the propriety of being reserved upon those very topics on which Ratcliffe had indirectly seduced her to become communicative.

"What was't ye were speering at us, sir?" she resumed, with an appearance of stolidity so speedily assumed, as shewed there was a good deal of knavery mixed with her folly.

"I asked you," said the procurator, "at what hour, and to what place, Robertson brought back your clothes."

"Robertson?—Lord haud a care o' us, what Robertson?"

"Why, the fellow we were speaking of, Gentle Geordie, as you call him."

"Geordie Gentle?" answered Madge, with well-feigned amazement—"I dinna ken naebody they ca' Geordie Gentle."

"Come, my jo," said Sharpitlaw, "this will not do; you must tell us what you did with these clothes of yours."

Madge Wildfire made no answer, unless the question may seem connected with the snatch of a song with which she indulged the embarrassed investigator:—

> "What did ye wi' the bridal ring—bridal ring—bridal ring?
> What did ye wi' your wedding ring, ye little cutty quean, O?
> I gied it till a sodger, a sodger, a sodger,
> I gied it till a sodger, an auld true love o' mine, O."[19]

Of all the mad-women who have sung and said, since the days of Hamlet the Dane, if Ophelia be the most affecting,[20] Madge Wildfire was the most provoking.

The procurator-fiscal was in despair. "I'll take some measure with this d—d Bess of Bedlam," said he, "that shall make her find her tongue."

"Wi' your favour, sir," said Ratcliffe, "better let her mind settle a little—Ye have aye made out something."

"True," said the official person; "a brown short-gown, mutch, red rokelay—that agrees with your Madge Wildfire, Mr Butler?" Butler agreed that it did so. "Yes, there was a sufficient motive for taking this crazy creature's dress and name, while he was about such a job."

"And I am free to say *now*," said Ratcliffe——

"When you see it has come out without you," interrupted Sharpitlaw.

"Just sae, sir," reiterated Ratcliffe. "I am free to say now, since it's come out otherwise, that these were the clothes I saw Robertson wearing last night in the jail, when he was at the head of the rioters."

"That's direct evidence," said Sharpitlaw; "stick to that, Rat—I will report favourably of you to the provost, for I have business for you to-night. It wears late; I must home and get a snack, and I'll be back in the evening. Keep Madge with you, Ratcliffe, and try to get her into a good tune again." So saying, he left the prison.

CHAPTER 17

And some they whistled—and some they sang,
   And some did loudly say,
Whenever Lord Barnard's horn it blew,
   "Away, Musgrave, away!"—

Ballad of Little Musgrave

WHEN the man of office returned to the Heart of Mid-Lothian, he resumed his conference with Ratcliffe, of whose experience and assistance he now held himself secure. "You must speak with this wench, Rat—this Effie Deans—you must sift her a wee bit; for as sure as a tether[1] she will ken Robertson's haunts—till her, Rat—till her, without delay."

"Craving your pardon, Mr Sharpitlaw," said the turnkey elect, "that's what I am not free to do."

"Free to do, man? what the deil ails ye now?—I thought we had settled a' that."

"I dinna ken, sir," said Ratcliffe; "I hae spoken to this Effie—she's strange to this place and to its ways, and to a' our ways, Mr Sharpitlaw; and she greets, the silly tawpie, and she's breaking her heart already about this wild chield; and were she the means o' taking him, she wad break it outright."

"She wunna hae time, lad," said Sharpitlaw; "the woodie will hae his ain o' her before that—a woman's heart takes a lang time o' breaking."[2]

"That's according to the stuff they are made o', sir," replied Ratcliffe—"But to make a lang tale short, I canna undertake the job. It gangs against my conscience."

"*Your* conscience, Rat?" said Sharpitlaw, with a sneer, which the reader will probably think very natural upon the occasion.

"Ou ay, sir," answered Ratcliffe calmly, "just *my* conscience; a'body has a conscience, though it may be ill wunnin at it. I think mine's as weel out o' the gate as maist folks' are; and yet it's just like the noop of my elbow, it whiles gets a bit dirl on a corner."

"Weel, Rat," replied Sharpitlaw, "since ye are nice, I'll speak to the hussey mysell."

Sharpitlaw, accordingly, caused himself to be introduced into the little dark apartment tenanted by the unfortunate Effie Deans. The poor girl was seated on her little flock-bed, plunged in a deep reverie. Some food stood on the table, of a quality better than is usually supplied to prisoners, but it was untouched. The person under whose care she was more particularly placed, said, "that sometimes she tasted naething from the tae end of the four-and-twenty hours to the t'other, except a drink of water."

Sharpitlaw took a chair, and, commanding the turnkey to retire, he opened the conversation, endeavouring to throw into his tone and countenance as much commiseration as they were capable of expressing, for the one was sharp and harsh, the other sly, acute, and selfish.

"How's a' wi' ye, Effie?—How d'ye find yoursell, hinny?"

A deep sigh was the only answer.

"Are the folk civil to ye, Effie?—it's my duty to enquire."

"Very civil, sir," said Effie, compelling herself to answer, yet hardly knowing what she said.

"And your victuals," continued Sharpitlaw, in the same condoling tone—"do you get what you like?—or is there ony thing you would particularly fancy, as your health seems but silly?"

"It's a' very weel, sir, I thank ye," said the poor prisoner, in a tone how different from the sportive vivacity of those of the Lily of Saint Leonard's!—"it's a' very gude—ower gude for me."

"He must have been a great villain, Effie, who brought you to this pass," said Sharpitlaw.

The remark was dictated partly by a natural feeling, of which even he could not divest himself, though accustomed to practise on the passions of others, and keep a most heedful guard[3] over his own, and partly by his wish to introduce the sort of conversation which might best serve his immediate purpose. Indeed, upon the present occasion, these mixed motives of feeling and cunning harmonized together wonderfully; for, said Sharpitlaw to himself, the greater rogue Robertson is, the more will be the merit of bringing him to justice. "He must have been a great villain, indeed," he again reiterated; "and I wish I had the skelping o' him."

"I may blame mysell mair than him," said Effie; "I was bred up to ken better, but he, poor fellow,"——(She stopped.)

"Was a thorough blackguard a' his life, I dare say," said Sharpitlaw. "A stranger he was in this country, and a companion of that lawless vagabond, Wilson, I think, Effie."

"It wad hae been dearly telling[4] him that he had ne'er seen Wilson's face."

"That's very true that you are saying, Effie," said Sharpitlaw. "Where was't that Robertson and you were used to howff thegither? Somegate about the Laigh Calton, I am thinking."

The simple and dispirited girl had thus far followed Mr Sharpitlaw's lead, because he had artfully adjusted his observations to the thoughts he was pretty certain must be passing through her own mind, so that her answers became a kind of thinking aloud, a mood into which those who are either constitutionally absent in mind, or are rendered so by the temporary pressure of misfortune, may be easily led by a skilful train of suggestions. But the last observation of the procurator-fiscal was too much of the nature of a direct interrogatory, and it broke the charm[5] accordingly.

"What was it that I was saying?" said Effie, starting up from her reclining posture, seating herself upright, and hastily shading her dishevelled hair back from her wasted, but still beautiful countenance. She fixed her eyes boldly and keenly upon Sharpitlaw;—"You are too much of a gentleman, sir—too much of an honest man, to take any notice of what a poor creature like me says, that can hardly ca' my senses my ain—God help me!"

"Advantage!—I would be of some advantage to you if I could," said Sharpitlaw, in a soothing tone; "and I ken naething sae likely to serve ye, Effie, as gripping this rascal, Robertson."

"O dinna misca' him, sir, that never misca'd you!—Robertson?—I am sure I had naething to say against ony man o' the name, and naething will I say."

"But if you do not heed your own misfortune, Effie, you should mind what distress he has brought on your family," said the man of law.

"O, Heaven help me!" exclaimed poor Effie—"My poor father—my dear Jeanie—O, that's sairest to bide of a'! O, sir, if you hae ony kindness—if ye hae ony touch of compassion—for a' the folk I see here are as hard as the wa'-stanes—If ye wad but bid them let my sister Jeanie in the next time she ca's! for when I hear them put her awa frae the door, and canna climb up to that high window to see sae muckle as her gown-tail, it's like to pit me out o' my judgment." And she looked on him with a face of entreaty so earnest, yet so humble, that she fairly shook the steadfast purpose of his mind.

"You shall see your sister," he began, "if you'll tell me,"—then interrupting himself, he added, in a more hurried tone,—"no, d—n it, you shall see your sister whether you tell me any thing or no." So saying, he rose up and left the apartment.

When he had rejoined Ratcliffe, he observed, "You are right, Ratton; there's no making much of that lassie. But ae thing I have cleared—that is, that Robertson has been the father of the bairn, and so I will wager a boddle it will be him that's to meet wi' Jeanie Deans this night at Muschat's Cairn, and there we'll nail him, Rat, or my name is not Gideon Sharpitlaw."

"But," said Ratcliffe, perhaps because he was in no hurry to see any thing which was like to be connected with the discovery and apprehension of Robertson, "an that were the case, Mr Butler wad hae kend the man in the King's Park to be the same person wi' him in Madge Wildfire's claise, that headed the mob."

"That makes nae difference, man," replied Sharpitlaw—"the dress, the light, the confusion, and maybe a touch o' a blackit cork, or a slake o' paint—hout, Ratton, I have seen ye dress your ainsell, that the deevil ye belang to durstna hae made oath t'ye."

"And that's true, too," said Ratcliffe.

"And besides, ye donnard carle," continued Sharpitlaw triumphantly, "the minister *did* say, that he thought he knew something of the features of the birkie that spoke to him in the Park, though he could not charge his memory where or when he had seen them."

"It's evident, then, your honour will be right," said Ratcliffe.

"Then, Rat, you and I will go with the party oursells this night, and see him in grips or we are done wi' him."

"I seena muckle use I can be o' to your honour," said Ratcliffe, reluctantly.

"Use?" answered Sharpitlaw—"You can guide the party—you ken the ground. Besides, I do not intend to quit sight o' you, my good friend, till I have him in hand."

"Weel, sir," said Ratcliffe, but in no joyful tone of acquiescence; "Ye maun hae it your ain way—but mind he's a desperate man."

"We shall have that with us," answered Sharpitlaw, "will settle him, if it is necessary."

"But, sir," answered Ratcliffe, "I am sure I couldna undertake to guide you to Muschat's Cairn in the night-time; I ken the place, as mony ane does, in fair day-light, but how to find it by moonshine, amang sae mony crags and stanes, as like to each other as the collier to the deil,[6] is mair than I can tell. I might as soon seek moonshine in water."[7]

"What's the meaning o' this, Ratcliffe?" said Sharpitlaw, while he fixed his eye on the recusant, with a fatal and ominous expression,— "Have you forgotten that you are still under sentence of death?"

"No, sir," said Ratcliffe, "that's a thing no easily put out o' memory; and if my presence be judged necessary, nae doubt I maun gang wi' your honour. But I was gaun to tell your honour of ane that has mair skeel o' the gate than me, and that's e'en Madge Wildfire."

"The devil she has!—Do you think me as mad as she is, to trust to her guidance on such an occasion?"

"Your honour is best judge," answered Ratcliffe; "but I ken I can keep her in tune, and gar her haud the straight path—she aften sleeps out or rambles about amang thae hills the haill simmer night, the daft limmer."

"Well, Ratcliffe," replied the procurator-fiscal, "if you think she can guide us the right way—but take heed to what you are about— your life depends on your behaviour."

"It's a sair judgment on a man," said Ratcliffe, "when he has ance gane sae far wrang as I hae done, that deil a bit he can be honest, try't whilk way he will."

Such was the reflection of Ratcliffe, when he was left for a few minutes to himself, while the retainer of justice went to procure a proper warrant, and give the necessary directions.

The rising moon saw the whole party free from the walls of the city, and entering upon the open ground.[8] Arthur's Seat, like a couchant lion of immense size—Salisbury Crags, like a huge belt or girdle of granite,[9] were dimly visible. Holding their path along the southern side of the Canongate, they gained the Abbey of Holyroodhouse, and from thence found their way by step and stile into the King's Park. They were at first four in number—an officer of justice and Sharpitlaw, who were well armed with pistols and cutlasses; Ratcliffe, who was not trusted with weapons, lest he might, peradventure, have used them on the wrong side; and the female. But at the last stile, when they entered the Chase, they were joined by other two officers, whom Sharpitlaw, desirous to secure sufficient force for his purpose, and at the same time to avoid observation, had directed to wait for him at this place. Ratcliffe saw this accession of strength with some disquietude, for he had hitherto thought it likely that Robertson, who was a bold, stout, and active young fellow, might have made his escape from Sharpitlaw and the single officer, by force or agility, without his being implicated in the matter. But the present strength of the followers of justice was overpowering, and the only mode of saving Robertson, (which the old sinner was well disposed to do, providing always he could accomplish his purpose without compromising his own safety), must be by contriving that he should have some signal of their approach. It was probably with this view that Ratcliffe had requested the addition of Madge to the party, having considerable confidence in her propensity to exert her lungs. Indeed, she had already given them so many specimens of her clamorous loquacity, that Sharpitlaw half determined to send her back with one of the officers, rather than carry forward in his company a person so extremely ill qualified to be a guide in a secret expedition. It seemed, too, as if the open air, the approach to the hills, and the ascent of the moon, supposed to be so portentous over those whose brain is infirm, made her spirits rise in a degree tenfold more loquacious than she had hitherto exhibited. To silence her by fair means seemed impossible; authoritative commands and coaxing entreaties she set alike at defiance, and threats only made her sulky, and altogether intractable.

"Is there no one of you," said Sharpitlaw, impatiently, "that knows the way to this accursed place—this Nicol Muschat's Cairn—excepting this mad clavering idiot?"

"Deil ane o' them kens it, except mysell," exclaimed Madge; "how suld they, the poor fule cowards? But I hae sat on the grave frae bat-fleeing time till cock-crow, and had mony a fine crack wi' Nicol Muschat and Ailie Muschat, that are lying sleeping below."

"The devil take your crazy brain," said Sharpitlaw; "will you not allow the men to answer a question?"

The officers, obtaining a moment's audience while Ratcliffe diverted Madge's attention, declared that, though they had a general knowledge of the spot, they could not undertake to guide the party to it by the uncertain light of the moon, with such accuracy as to insure success to their expedition.

"What shall we do, Ratcliffe?" said Sharpitlaw; "if he sees us before we see him,—and that's what he is certain to do, if we go strolling about, without keeping the straight road,—we may bid gude day to the job; and I wad rather lose one hundred pounds, baith for the credit of the police, and because the Provost says somebody maun be hanged for this job o' Porteous, come o't what likes."

"I think," said Ratcliffe, "we maun just try Madge; and I'll see if I can get her keepit in ony better order. And at ony rate, if he suld hear her skirling her auld ends o' sangs, he's no to ken for that that there's ony body wi' her."

"That's true," said Sharpitlaw; "and if he thinks her alone he's as like to come towards her as to rin frae her. So set forward—we hae lost ower muckle time already—see to get her to keep the right road."

"And what sort o' house does Nicol Muschat and his wife keep now?" said Ratcliffe to the mad-woman, by way of humouring her vein of folly; "they were but thrawn folk lang syne, an a' tales be true."

"Ou, ay, ay, ay—but a's forgotten now," replied Madge, in the confidential tone of a gossip giving the history of her next-door neighbour—"Ye see I spoke to them mysell, and tauld them byganes suld be byganes—her throat's sair misguggled and mashackered though; she wears her corpse-sheet drawn weel up to hide it, but that canna hinder the bluid seiping through, ye ken. I wussed her to wash it in St Anthony's Well, and that will cleanse, if ony thing can—But they say bluid never bleaches out o' linen claith—Deacon Sanders's new cleansing draps[10] winna do't—I tried them mysell on a bit rag we hae at hame that was mailed wi' the bluid of a bit skirling wean that was hurt some gate, but out it winna come—Weel, ye'll say that's queer; but I will bring it out to St Anthony's blessed Well ae braw night just like this, and I'll cry up Ailie Muschat, and she and I will hae's a grand bouking-washing, and bleach our claise in the beams of the bonny Lady Moon, that's far pleasanter to me than the sun—the sun's ower het, and ken ye, cummers, my harns are het aneugh already. But the moon, and the dew, and the night-wind, they are just like a caller kail-blade laid on my brow; and whiles I think the moon just shines on purpose to pleasure me, when naebody sees her but mysell."

This raving discourse she continued with prodigious volubility, walking on at a great pace, and dragging Ratcliffe along with her, while he endeavoured, in appearance at least, if not in reality, to induce her to moderate her voice.

All at once, she stopped short upon the top of a little hillock, gazed upward fixedly, and said not one word for the space of five minutes. "What the devil is the matter with her now?" said Sharpitlaw to Ratcliffe—"Can you not get her forward?"

"Ye maun just take a grain o' patience wi' her, sir," said Ratcliffe. "She'll no jee a foot faster than she likes hersell. She'll take her ain time."

"D—n her," said Sharpitlaw, "I'll take care she has her time in Bedlam or Bridewell, or both, for she's both mad and mischievous." In the meanwhile, Madge, who had looked very pensive when she first stopped, suddenly burst into a vehement fit of laughter, then paused and sighed bitterly,—then was seized with a second fit of laughter,—then fixing her eyes on the moon, lifted up her voice, and sung,—

> "Good even, good fair moon, good even to thee;
> I prithee, dear moon, now show to me
> The form and the features, the speech and degree,
> Of the man that true lover of mine shall be.[11]

"But I need not ask that of the bonny Lady Moon—I ken that weel aneugh mysell—*true*-love though he wasna—But naebody shall say that I ever tauld a word about the matter—But whiles I wish the bairn had lived[12]—Weel, God guide us, there's a heaven aboon us a'"—(here she sighed bitterly) "and a bonny moon, and sterns in it forbye," (and here she laughed once more).

"Are we to stand here all night?" said Sharpitlaw, very impatiently. "Drag her forward."

"Ay, sir," said Ratcliffe, "if we kend whilk way to drag her, that would settle it at ance.—Come, Madge, hinny," addressing her, "we'll no be in time to see Nicol and his wife, unless ye show us the road."

"In troth and that I will, Ratton," said she, seizing him by the arm, and resuming her route with huge strides, considering it was a female who took them. "And I'll tell ye, Ratton, blithe will Nicol Muschat be to see ye, for he says he kens weel there is nae sic a villain out o' hell as ye are, and he wad be ravished to hae a crack wi' you—like to like, ye ken—it's a proverb never fails—and ye are baith a pair o' the deevil's peats,[13] I trow—hard to ken whilk deserves the hettest corner o' his ingle-side."

Ratcliffe was conscience-struck, and could not forbear making an involuntary protest against this classification. "I never shed blood," he replied.

"But ye hae sauld it, Ratton—ye hae sauld blood mony a time. Folk kill wi' the tongue as weel as wi' the hand—wi' the word as weel as wi' the gulley,—

> It is the bonny butcher lad,
> That wears the sleeves of blue,
> He sells the flesh on Saturday,
> On Friday that he slew."[14]

"And what is this that I am doing now?" thought Ratcliffe. "But I'll hae nae wyte of Robertson's young bluid, if I can help it;" then speaking

apart to Madge, he asked her, "Whether she did na remember ony
o' her auld sangs?"

"Mony a dainty ane," said Madge; "and blithely can I sing them,
for lightsome sangs make merry gate." And she sang,—

> "When the gledd's in the blue cloud,
>   The lavrock lies still;
> When the hound's in the green-wood,
>   The hind keeps the hill."

"Silence her cursed noise, if you should throttle her," said Sharpitlaw; "I see somebody yonder.—Keep close, my boys, and creep round
the shoulder of the height. George Poinder, stay you with Ratcliffe
and that mad yelling bitch; and you other two, come with me round
under the shadow of the brae."

And he crept forward with the stealthy pace of an Indian savage,
who leads his band to surprise an unsuspecting party of some hostile
tribe. Ratcliffe saw them glide off, avoiding the moonlight, and
keeping as much in the shade as possible. "Robertson's done up," said
he to himself; "thae young lads are aye sae thoughtless. What deevil
could he hae to say to Jeanie Deans, or to ony woman on earth, that he
suld gang awa and get his neck raxed for her? And this mad quean,
after cracking like a pen-gun, and skirling like a pea-hen for the haill
night, behoves just to hae hadden her tongue when her clavers might
have done some gude! But it's aye the way wi' women; if they ever
haud their tongues ava', ye may swear it's for mischief. I wish I could
set her on again without this bloodsucker kenning what I am doing.
But he's as gleg as Mackeachan's elshin,[15] that ran through sax plies
of bend-leather and half an inch into the king's heel."

He then began to hum, but in a very low and suppressed tone, the
first stanza of a favourite ballad of Wildfire's, the words of which bore
some distant analogy with the situation of Robertson, trusting that the
power of association would not fail to bring the rest to her mind:

> "There's a bloodhound ranging Tinwald Wood,
>   There's harness glancing sheen;
> There's a maiden sits on Tinwald brae,
>   And she sings loud between."

Madge had no sooner received the catch-word, than she vindicated
Ratcliffe's sagacity by setting off at score with the song:

"O sleep ye sound, Sir James, she said,
    When ye suld rise and ride?
There's twenty men, wi' bow and blade,
    Are seeking where ye hide."

Though Ratcliffe was at a considerable distance from the spot called Muschat's Cairn, yet his eyes, practised like those of a cat to penetrate darkness, could mark that Robertson had caught the alarm. George Poinder, less keen of sight, or less attentive, was not aware of his flight any more than Sharpitlaw and his assistants, whose view, though they were considerably nearer to the cairn, was intercepted by the broken nature of the ground under which they were screening themselves. At length, however, after the interval of five or six minutes, they also perceived that Robertson had fled, and rushed hastily towards the place, while Sharpitlaw called out aloud, in the harshest tones of a voice which resembled a saw-mill at work, "Chase, lads—chase—haud the brae—I see him on the edge of the hill." Then hollowing back to the rear-guard of his detachment, he issued his farther orders: "Ratcliffe, come here, and detain the woman—George, run and kepp the stile at the Duke's Walk—Ratcliffe, come here directly—but first knock out that mad bitch's brains."

"Ye had better rin for it, Madge," said Ratcliffe, "for it's ill dealing wi' an angry man."

Madge Wildfire was not so absolutely void of common sense as not to understand this inuendo; and while Ratcliffe, in all the seemingly anxious haste of obedience, hastened to the spot where Sharpitlaw waited to deliver up Jeanie Deans to his custody, she fled with all the dispatch she could exert in an opposite direction. Thus the whole party were separated, and in rapid motion of flight or pursuit, excepting Ratcliffe and Jeanie, whom, although making no attempt to escape, he held fast by the cloak, and who remained standing by Muschat's Cairn.

CHAPTER 18

You have paid the heavens your function, and the prisoner the very debt of
your calling.

Measure for Measure

JEANIE Deans,—for here our story unites itself with that part of the
narrative which broke off at the end of chapter 15,—while she
watched, in terror and amazement, the hasty advance of three or four
men towards her, was yet more startled at their suddenly breaking
asunder, and giving chase in different directions to the late object of
her terror, who became at that moment, though she could not well
assign a reasonable cause, rather the object of her interest. One of the
party (it was Sharpitlaw,) came straight up to her, and saying, "Your
name is Jeanie Deans, and you are my prisoner," immediately added,
"but if you will tell me which way he ran I will let you go."

"I dinna ken, sir," was all the poor girl could utter; and indeed it is
the phrase which rises most readily to the lips of any person in her
rank, as the readiest reply to any embarrassing question.

"But," said Sharpitlaw, "ye *ken* wha it was ye were speaking wi',
my leddy, on the hill side, and midnight sae near; ye surely ken *that*,
my bonny woman?"

"I dinna ken, sir," again iterated Jeanie, who really did not comprehend in her terror the nature of the questions which were so hastily put
to her in this moment of surprise.

"We will try to mend your memory by and by, hinny," said
Sharpitlaw, and shouted, as we have already told the reader, to
Ratcliffe, to come up and take charge of her, while he himself directed
the chase after Robertson, which he still hoped might be successful.
As Ratcliffe approached, Sharpitlaw pushed the young woman towards
him with some rudeness, and betaking himself to the more important
object of his quest, began to scale crags and scramble up steep banks,
with an agility of which his profession and his general gravity of
demeanour would previously have argued him incapable. In a few
minutes there was no one within sight, and only a distant halloo from
one of the pursuers to the other, faintly heard on the side of the hill,

argued that there was any one within hearing. Jeanie Deans was left in the clear moonlight, standing under the guard of a person of whom she knew nothing, and, what was worse, concerning whom, as the reader is well aware, she could have learned nothing that would not have increased her terror.

When all in the distance was silent, Ratcliffe for the first time addressed her, and it was in that cold sarcastic indifferent tone familiar to habitual depravity, whose crimes are instigated by custom rather than by passion. "This is a braw night for ye, dearie," he said, attempting to pass his arm across her shoulder, "to be on the green hill wi' your jo." Jeanie extricated herself from his grasp, but did not make any reply. "I think lads and lasses," continued the ruffian, "dinna meet at Muschat's Cairn at midnight to crack nuts," and he again attempted to take hold of her.

"If ye are an officer of justice, sir," said Jeanie, again eluding his attempt to seize her, "ye deserve to have your coat stripped from your back."

"Very true, hinny," said he, succeeding forcibly in his attempt to get hold of her, "but suppose I should strip your cloak off first?"

"Ye are more a man, I am sure, than to hurt me, sir," said Jeanie; "for God's sake, have pity on a half-distracted creature!"

"Come, come," said Ratcliffe, "you're a good-looking wench, and should not be cross-grained. I was going to be an honest man—but the devil has this very day flung first a lawyer, and then a woman, in my gate. I'll tell you what, Jeanie, they are out on the hill-side—if you'll be guided by me, I'll carry you to a wee bit corner in the Pleasance, that I ken o' in an auld wife's, that a' the prokitors o' Scotland wot naething o', and we'll send Robertson word to meet us in Yorkshire, for there is a set o' braw lads about the mid-land counties, that I hae dune business wi' before now, and sae we'll leave Mr Sharpitlaw to whistle on his thumb."

It was fortunate for Jeanie, in an emergency like the present, that she possessed presence of mind and courage, so soon as the first hurry of surprise had enabled her to rally her recollection. She saw the risk she was in from a ruffian, who not only was such by profession, but had that evening been stupifying, by means of strong liquors, the internal aversion which he felt at the business on which Sharpitlaw had resolved to employ him.

"Dinna speak sae loud," said she, in a low voice, "he's up yonder."

"Who?—Robertson?" said Ratcliffe, eagerly.

"Ay," replied Jeanie; "up yonder;" and she pointed to the ruins of the hermitage and chapel.

"By G—d, then!" said Ratcliffe, "I'll make my ain of him, either one way or other—wait for me here."

But no sooner had he set off, as fast as he could run, towards the chapel, than Jeanie started in an opposite direction, over high and low, on the nearest path homeward. Her juvenile exercise as a herds-woman, had put "life and mettle" in her heels,[1] and never had she followed Dustiefoot, when the cows were in the corn, with half so much speed as she now cleared the distance betwixt Muschat's Cairn and her father's cottage at Saint Leonard's. To lift the latch—to enter—to shut, bolt, and double bolt the door—to draw against it a heavy article of furniture, (which she could not have moved in a moment of less energy,) so as to make yet farther provision against violence, was almost the work of a moment, yet done with such silence as equalled the celerity.

Her next anxiety was upon her father's account, and she drew silently to the door of his apartment, in order to satisfy herself whether he had been disturbed by her return. He was awake,—probably had slept but little; but the constant presence of his own sorrows, the distance of his apartment from the outer-door of the house, and the precautions which Jeanie had taken to conceal her departure and return, had prevented him from being sensible of either. He was engaged in his devotions, and Jeanie could distinctly hear him use these words: "And for the other child thou hast given me to be a comfort and stay to my old age, may her days be long in the land, according to the promise thou hast given to those who shall honour father and mother;[2] may all purchased and promised blessings[3] be multiplied upon her; keep her in the watches of the night, and in the uprising of the morning, that all in this land may know thou hast not utterly hid thy face from those that seek thee in truth and in sincerity." He was silent, but probably continued his petition in the strong fervency of mental devotion.

His daughter retired to her apartment, comforted, that while she was exposed to danger, her head had been covered by the prayers of the just as by an helmet, and under the strong confidence, that while she walked worthy of the protection of Heaven, she would experience its continuance.[4] It was in that moment that a vague idea first darted across her mind, that something might yet be achieved for her sister's safety, conscious as she now was of her innocence of the unnatural murther with which she stood charged. It came, as she described it, on her mind like a sun-blink on a stormy sea;[5] and although it instantly vanished, yet she felt a degree of composure which she had not experienced for many days, and could not help being strongly persuaded, that, by some means or other, she would be called upon, and directed, to work out her sister's deliverance. She went to bed, not forgetting her usual devotions, the more fervently made on account of her late deliverance, and she slept soundly in spite of her agitation.

We must return to Ratcliffe, who had started, like a greyhound from the slips[6] when the sportsman cries halloo, so soon as Jeanie had pointed to the ruins. Whether he meant to aid Robertson's escape, or to assist his pursuers, may be very doubtful; perhaps he did not himself know, but had resolved to be guided by circumstances. He had no opportunity, however, of doing either; for he had no sooner surmounted the steep ascent, and entered under the broken arches of the ruins, than a pistol was presented at his head, and a harsh voice commanded him, in the king's name, to surrender himself prisoner.

"Mr Sharpitlaw," said Ratcliffe, surprised, "is this your honour?"

"Is it only you, and be d—d to you?" answered the fiscal, still more disappointed—"what made you leave the woman?"

"She told me she saw Robertson go into the ruins, so I made what haste I could to cleek the callant."

"It's all over now," said Sharpitlaw; "we shall see no more of him to-night; but he shall hide himself in a bean-hool, if he remains on Scottish ground without my finding him.—Call back the people, Ratcliffe."

Ratcliffe hollowed to the dispersed officers, who willingly obeyed the signal; for probably there was no individual among them who would have been much desirous of a rencontre hand to hand, and at a distance from his comrades, with such an active and desperate fellow as Robertson.

"And where are the two women?" said Sharpitlaw.

"Both made their heels serve them, I suspect," replied Ratcliffe, and he hummed the end of the old song—

> "Then hey play up the rin-awa' bride,
> For she has taen the gee."[7]

"One woman," said Sharpitlaw,—for, like all rogues, he was a great calumniator of the fair sex,[*]—"one woman is enough to dark

[* See p. 566 for the note, "Calumniator of the Fair Sex".]

the fairest ploy that ever was planned; and how could I be such an ass as to expect to carry through a job that had two in it? But we know how to come by them both, if they are wanted, that's one good thing."

Accordingly, like a defeated general, sad and sulky, he led back his discomfited forces to the metropolis, and dismissed them for the night.

The next morning early he was under the necessity of making his report to the sitting magistrate of the day. The gentleman who occupied the chair of office on this occasion (for the baillies, *Anglice* aldermen, take it by rotation) chanced to be the same by whom Butler was committed, a person very generally respected among his fellow-citizens. Something he was of a humourist, and rather deficient in general education; but acute, patient, and upright, possessed of a fortune acquired by honest industry, which made him perfectly independent; and, in short, very happily qualified to support the respectability of the office which he held.

Mr Middleburgh[8] had just taken his seat, and was debating, in animated manner, with one of his colleagues, the doubtful chances of a game at golf which they had played the day before, when a letter was delivered to him, addressed "For Baillie Middleburgh; These: to be forwarded with speed." It contained these words:—

"SIR,

"I know you to be a sensible and a considerate magistrate, and one who, as such, will be content to worship God, though the devil bid you.[9] I therefore expect that, notwithstanding the signature of this letter acknowledges my share in an action, which, in a proper time and place, I would not fear either to avow or to justify, you will not on that account reject what evidence I place before you. The clergyman, Butler, is innocent of all but involuntary presence at an action which he wanted spirit to approve of, and from which he endeavoured, with his best set phrases, to dissuade us. But it was not for him that it is my hint to speak.[10] There is a woman in your jail, fallen under the edge of a law so cruel, that it has hung by the wall, like unscoured armour,[11] for twenty years, and is now brought down and whetted to spill the blood of the most beautiful and most innocent creature whom the walls of a prison ever girdled in. Her sister knows of her innocence, as she communicated to her that she was betrayed by a villain.—O that high Heaven

Would put in every honest hand a whip,
To scourge me such a villain through the world.[12]

"I write distractedly—But this girl—this Jeanie Deans, is a peevish puritan, superstitious and scrupulous after the manner of her sect; and I pray your honour, for so my phrase must go, to press upon her, that her sister's life depends upon her testimony. But though she should remain silent, do not dare to think that the young woman is guilty— far less to permit her execution. Remember the death of Wilson was fearfully avenged; and those yet live who can compel you to drink the dregs of your poisoned chalice.[13]—I say, remember Porteous,—and say that you had good counsel from

"ONE OF HIS SLAYERS."

The magistrate read over this extraordinary letter twice or thrice. At first he was tempted to throw it aside as the production of a madman, so little did "the scraps from play-books," as he termed the poetical quotations, resemble the correspondence of a rational being. On a re-perusal, however, he thought that, amid its incoherence, he could discern something like a tone of awakened passion, though expressed in a manner quaint and unusual.

"It is a cruelly severe statute," said the magistrate to his assistant, "and I wish the girl could be taken from under the letter of it. A child may have been born, and it may have been conveyed away while the mother was insensible, or it may have perished for want of that relief which the poor creature herself,—helpless, terrified, distracted, despairing, and exhausted,—may have been unable to afford to it. And yet it is certain, if the woman is found guilty under the statute, execution will follow. The crime has been too common, and examples are become necessary."

"But if this other wench," said the city-clerk, "can speak to[14] her sister communicating her situation, it will take the case from under the statute."

"Very true, Mr Fairscrieve," replied the Baillie; "and I will walk out one of these days to St Leonard's, and examine the girl myself. I know something of their father Deans—an old true-blue Cameronian, who would see house and family go to wreck ere he would disgrace his testimony by a sinful complying with the defections of the times; and such he will probably uphold the taking an oath before a civil magistrate. If they are to go on and flourish in their bull-headed obstinacy, the legislature must pass an act to take their affirmations, as in the case of Quakers. But surely neither a father nor a sister will scruple in a case of this kind. As I said before, I will go speak with them myself, when the hurry of this Porteous investigation is somewhat over; their pride and spirit of contradiction will be far less alarmed, than if they were called into a court of justice at once."

"And I suppose Butler is to remain incarcerated?" said the city-clerk.

"For the present, certainly," said the magistrate. "But I hope soon to set him at liberty upon bail."

"Do you rest upon the testimony of that light-headed letter?" asked the clerk.

"Not very much," answered the baillie; "and yet there is something striking about it too—it seems the letter of a man beside himself, either from great agitation, or some great sense of guilt."

"Yes," said the town-clerk, "it is very like the letter of a mad strolling play-actor, who deserves to be hanged with all the rest of his gang, as your honour justly observes."

"I was not quite so blood-thirsty," continued the magistrate. "But to the point. Butler's private character is excellent; and I am given to understand, by some enquiries I have been making this morning, that he did actually arrive in town only the day before yesterday, so that it was impossible he could have been concerned in any previous machinations of these unhappy rioters, and it is not likely that he should have joined them on a suddenty."

"There's no saying anent that—zeal catches fire at a slight spark as fast as a brunstane match," observed the secretary. "I hae kend a minister wad be fair gude-day and fair gude-e'en wi' ilka man in the parochine, and hing just as quiet as a rocket on a stick, till ye mentioned the word abjuration-oath, or patronage, or sic-like, and then—whiz—he was off, and up in the air an hundred miles beyond common manners, common sense, and common comprehension."

"I do not apprehend," answered the burgher-magistrate, "that the young man Butler's zeal is of so inflammable a character. But I will make further investigation. What other business is there before us?"

And they proceeded to minute investigations concerning the affair of Porteous's death, and other affairs through which this history has no occasion to trace them.

In the course of their business they were interrupted by an old woman of the lower rank, extremely haggard in looks, and wretched in her apparel, who thrust herself into the council-room.

"What do you want, gudewife?—Who are you?" said Baillie Middleburgh.

"What do I want!" replied she, in a sulky tone—"I want my bairn, or I want naething frae nane o' ye, for as grand's ye are." And she went on muttering to herself, with the wayward spitefulness of age—"They maun hae lordships and honours nae doubt—set them up, the gutter-bloods! and deil a gentleman amang them."—Then again addressing the sitting magistrate, "Will *your honour* gie me back my puir crazy bairn?—*His* honour!—I hae kend the day when less wad ser'd him, the oe of a Campvere¹⁵ skipper."

"Good woman," said the magistrate to this shrewish supplicant,—"tell us what it is you want, and do not interrupt the court."

"That's as muckle as till say, Bark, Bawtie, and be dune wi't!—I tell ye," raising her termagant voice, "I want my bairn! is na that braid Scots?"

"Who *are* you?—who is your bairn?" demanded the magistrate.

"Wha am I?—wha suld I be, but Meg Murdockson, and wha suld my bairn be but Magdalen Murdockson?—Your guard-soldiers, and your constables, and your officers, ken us weel aneugh when they rive the bits o' duds aff our backs, and take what penny o' siller we hae, and harle us to the Correction-house in Leith Wynd, and pettle us up wi' bread and water, and siclike sunkets."

"Who is she?" said the magistrate, looking round to some of his people.

"Other than a gude ane, sir," said one of the city-officers, shrugging his shoulders and smiling.

"Will ye say sae?" said the termagant, her eye gleaming with impotent fury; "an I had ye amang the Frigate-Whins, wadna I set my ten talents¹⁶ in your wuzzent face for that very word?" and she suited the word to the action, by spreading out a set of claws resembling those of Saint George's dragon on a country sign-post.

"What does she want here?" said the impatient magistrate—"Can she not tell her business or go away?"

"It's my bairn!—it's Magdalen Murdockson I'm wantin'," answered the beldame, screaming at the highest pitch of her cracked and mistuned voice—"havena I been tellin' ye sae this half-hour? and if ye are deaf, what deevil needs ye sit cockit up there, and keep folks scraughin' t'ye this gate?"

"She wants her daughter, sir," said the same officer whose interference had given the hag such offence before—"her daughter, who was taken up last night—Madge Wildfire, as they ca' her."

"Madge HELLFIRE, as they ca' her!" echoed the beldame; "and what business has a blackguard like you to ca' an honest woman's bairn out o' her ain name?"

"An *honest* woman's bairn, Maggie!" answered the peace-officer, smiling and shaking his head with an ironical emphasis on the adjective, and a calmness calculated to provoke to madness the furious old shrew.

."If I am no honest now, I was honest anes," she replied; "and that's mair than ye can say, ye born beggar and bred thief, that never kend ither folk's gear frae your ain since the day ye was cleckit. Honest, say ye?—ye pykit your mother's pouch o' twalpennies Scots when ye were five years auld, just as she was taking leave o' your father at the fit o' the gallows."

"She has you there, George," said the assistants, and there was a general laugh; for the wit was fitted for the meridian of the place where it was uttered. This general applause somewhat gratified the angry passions of the old hag; "the grim feature"[17] smiled, and even laughed—but it was a laugh of bitter scorn. She condescended, however, as if appeased by the success of her sally, to explain her business more distinctly, when the magistrate, commanding silence, again desired her either to speak out her errand, or to leave the place.

"Her bairn," she said, "*was* her bairn, and she came to fetch her out of ill haft and waur guiding. If she was na sae wise as ither folks, few ither folks had suffered as muckle as she had done; forbye that she could fend the waur for hersell within the four wa's of a jail. She could prove by fifty witnesses, and fifty to that, that her daughter had never seen Jock Porteous, alive or dead, since he had gien her a loundering wi' his cane, the neger that he was, for driving a dead cat at the provost's wig on the Elector of Hanover's[18] birth-day."

Notwithstanding the wretched appearance and violent demeanour of this woman, the magistrate felt the justice of her argument, that her child might be as dear to her as to a more fortunate and more amiable mother. He proceeded to investigate the circumstances which had led to Madge Murdockson's (or Wildfire's,) arrest, and as it was clearly shown that she had not been engaged in the riot, he contented himself with directing that an eye should be kept upon her by the police, but that for the present she should be allowed to return home with her mother. During the interval of fetching Madge from the jail, the magistrate endeavoured to discover whether her mother had been privy to the change of dress betwixt that young woman and Robertson.

But on this point he could obtain no light. She persisted in declaring, that she had never seen Robertson since his remarkable escape during service-time; and that if her daughter had changed clothes with him, it must have been during her absence at a hamlet about two miles out of town, called Duddingstone, where she could prove that she passed that eventful night. And, in fact, one of the town-officers, who had been searching for stolen linen at the cottage of a washer-woman in that village, gave his evidence, that he had seen Maggie Murdockson there, whose presence had considerably increased his suspicion of the house in which she was a visitor, in respect that he considered her as a person of no good reputation.

"I tauld ye sae," said the hag; "see now what it is to hae a character, gude or bad!—Now, maybe after a', I could tell ye something about Porteous that you council-chamber bodies never could find out, for as muckle stir as ye mak."

All eyes were turned towards her—all ears were alert. "Speak out," said the magistrate.

"It will be for your ain gude," insinuated the town-clerk.

"Dinna keep the baillie waiting," urged the assistants.

She remained doggedly silent for two or three minutes, casting around a malignant and sulky glance, that seemed to enjoy the anxious suspense with which they waited her answer. And then she broke forth at once,—"A' that I ken about him is, that he was neither soldier nor gentleman, but just a thief and a blackguard, like maist o' yoursells, dears—What will ye gie me for that news now?—He wad hae served the gude town lang or provost or baillie wad hae fund that out, my joe!"

While these matters were in discussion, Madge Wildfire entered, and her first exclamation was, "Eh! see if there isna our auld ne'er-do-weel deevil's buckie o' a mither—Hegh, sirs! but we are a hopefu' family, to be twa o' us in the Guard at anes—But there were better days wi' us anes—were there na, mither?"

Old Maggie's eyes had glistened with something like an expression of pleasure when she saw her daughter set at liberty. But either her natural affection, like that of the tigress, could not be displayed without a strain of ferocity, or there was something in the ideas which Madge's speech awakened, that again stirred her cross and savage temper. "What signifies what we were, ye street-raking limmer!" she exclaimed, pushing her daughter before her to the door, with no gentle degree of violence. "I'se tell thee what thou is now—thou's a crazed hellicat Bess o' Bedlam, that sall taste naething but bread and water for a fortnight, to serve ye for the plague ye hae gien me, and ower gude for ye, ye idle tawpie."

Madge, however, escaped from her mother at the door, ran back to the foot of the table, dropped a very low and fantastic curtsey to the judge, and said, with a giggling laugh,—"Our minnie's sair mis-set, after her ordinar,[19] sir—She'll hae had some quarrel wi' her auld gudeman—that's Satan, ye ken, sirs." This explanatory note she gave in a low confidential tone, and the spectators of that credulous generation did not hear it without an involuntary shudder. "The gudeman and her disna aye gree weel, and then I maun pay the piper; but my back's broad aneugh to bear't a'—an' if she hae nae havings, that's nae reason why wiser folk suld na hae some." Here another deep curtsey, when the ungracious voice of her mother was heard.

"Madge, ye limmer! If I come to fetch ye."

"Hear till her," said Madge. "But I'll wun out a gliff the night for a' that, to dance in the moonlight, when her and the gudeman will be whirrying through the blue lift on a broom-shank, to see Jean Jap,[20] that they hae putten intill the Kirkcaldy tolbooth—ay, they will hae a merry sail ower Inchkeith, and ower a' the bits o' bonny waves that are poppling and plashing against the rocks in the gowden glimmer o' the moon, ye ken.—I'm coming, mother—I'm coming," she concluded, on hearing a scuffle at the door betwixt the beldame and the officers, who were endeavouring to prevent her re-entrance. Madge then waved her hand wildly towards the ceiling, sung, at the topmost pitch of her voice,—

> "Up in the air,
> On my bonnie grey mare,
> And I see, and I see, and I see her yet,"[21]

and with a hop, skip, and jump, sprung out of the room, as the witches of Macbeth used, in less refined days, to seem to fly upwards from the stage.

Some weeks intervened before Mr Middleburgh, agreeably to his benevolent resolution, found an opportunity of taking a walk towards Saint Leonard's, in order to discover whether it might be possible to obtain the evidence hinted at in the anonymous letter respecting Effie Deans.

In fact, the anxious perquisitions made to discover the murderers of Porteous, occupied the attention of all concerned with the administration of justice.

In the course of these enquiries, two circumstances happened material to our story. Butler, after a close investigation of his conduct, was declared innocent of accession to the death of Porteous; but, as having been present during the whole transaction, was obliged to find bail not to quit his usual residence at Libberton, that he might appear as a witness when called upon. The other incident regarded the disappearance of Madge Wildfire and her mother from Edinburgh. When they were sought, with the purpose of subjecting them to some further interrogatories, it was discovered by Mr Sharpitlaw that they had eluded the observation of the police, and left the city so soon as dismissed from the council-chamber. No efforts could trace the place of their retreat.

In the meanwhile the excessive indignation of the Council of Regency,[22] at the slight put upon their authority by the murder of Porteous, had dictated measures, in which their own extreme desire of detecting the actors in that conspiracy was consulted, in preference to the temper of the people, and the character of their churchmen. An act of parliament[23] was hastily passed, offering two hundred pounds reward to those who should inform against any person concerned in the deed, and the penalty of death, by a very unusual and severe enactment, was denounced against those who should harbour the guilty. But what was chiefly accounted exceptionable, was a clause, appointing the act to be read in churches by the officiating clergyman, on the first Sunday of every month, for a certain period, immediately before the sermon. The ministers who should refuse to comply with this injunction were declared, for the first offence, incapable of sitting or voting in any church judicature, and for the second, incapable of holding any ecclesiastical preferment in Scotland.

This last order united in a common cause those who might privately rejoice in Porteous's death, though they dared not vindicate the manner of it, with the more scrupulous presbyterians, who held that even pronouncing the name of the "Lords Spiritual" in a Scottish pulpit was, *quodammodo*, an acknowledgment of prelacy, and that the injunction of the legislature was an interference of the civil government with the *jus divinum* of presbytery, since to the General Assembly alone, as representing the invisible head of the kirk,[24] belonged the sole and exclusive right of regulating whatever pertained to public worship. Very many also of different political or religious sentiments, and therefore not much moved by these considerations, thought they saw, in so violent an act of parliament, a more vindictive spirit than became the legislature of a great country, and something like an attempt to trample upon the rights and independence of Scotland. The various steps adopted[25] for punishing the city of Edinburgh, by taking away her charter and liberties, for what a violent and over-mastering mob had done within her walls, were resented by many, who thought a pretext was too hastily taken for degrading the ancient metropolis of Scotland. In short, there was much heart-burning, discontent, and disaffection, occasioned by these ill-considered measures.[*]

Amidst these heats and dissensions, the trial of Effie Deans, after she had been many weeks imprisoned, was at length about to be brought forward, and Mr Middleburgh found leisure to enquire into the evidence concerning her. For this purpose he chose a fine day for his walk towards her father's house.

The excursion into the country was somewhat distant, in the opinion of a burgess of those days, although many of the present inhabit suburban villas[27] considerably beyond the spot to which we allude. Three quarters of an hour's walk, however, even at a pace of magisterial gravity, conducted our benevolent office-bearer to the Crags of St Leonard, and the humble mansion of David Deans.

The old man was seated on the deas, or turf-seat, at the end of his cottage, busied in mending his cart-harness with his own hands; for in those days any sort of labour which required a little more skill than usual fell to the share of the goodman himself, and that even when he was well to pass in the world. With stern and austere gravity he persevered in his task, after having just raised his head to notice the advance of the stranger. It would have been impossible to have discovered, from his countenance and manner, the internal feelings of agony with which he contended. Mr Middleburgh waited an instant, expecting Deans would in some measure acknowledge his presence, and lead into conversation; but, as he seemed determined to remain silent, he was himself obliged to speak first.

[* The Magistrates were closely interrogated before the House of Peers, concerning the particulars of the Mob, and the *patois* in which these functionaries made their answers, sounded strange in the ears of the Southern nobles. The Duke of Newcastle having demanded to know with what kind of shot the guard which Porteous commanded had loaded their muskets, was answered naïvely, "Ow, just sic as ane shoots *dukes and fools*[26] with." This reply was considered as a contempt of the House of Lords, and the Provost would have suffered accordingly, but that the Duke of Argyle explained, that the expression, properly rendered into English, meant *ducks and water-fowl*.]

"My name is Middleburgh—Mr James Middleburgh, one of the present magistrates of the city of Edinburgh."

"It may be sae," answered Deans laconically, and without interrupting his labour.

"You must understand," he continued, "that the duty of a magistrate is sometimes an unpleasant one."

"It may be sae," replied David; "I hae naething to say in the contrair;" and he was again doggedly silent.

"You must be aware," pursued the magistrate, "that persons in my situation are often obliged to make painful and disagreeable enquiries at individuals, merely because it is their bounden duty."

"It may be sae," again replied Deans; "I hae naething to say anent it, either the tae way or the t'other. But I do ken there was ance in a day a just and God-fearing magistracy in yon town o' Edinburgh, that did not bear the sword in vain,[28] but were a terror to evil-doers, and a praise to such as kept the path. In the glorious days of auld worthy faithfu' Provost Dick,[*][29] when there was a true and faithfu' General Assembly of the Kirk, walking hand in hand with the real noble-Scottish-hearted barons, and with the magistrates of this and other towns, gentles, burgesses, and commons of all ranks, seeing with one eye, hearing with one ear, and upholding the ark[30] with their united strength—And then folk might see men deliver up their silver to the states' use, as if it had been as muckle sclate stanes. My father saw them toom the sacks of dollars out o' Provost Dick's window intill the carts that carried them to the army at Dunse Law; and if ye winna believe his testimony, there is the window itsell still standing in the Luckenbooths—I think it's a claith-merchant's booth the day[†]—at the airn stanchells, five doors abune Gossford's Close—But now we haena sic spirit amang us; we think mair about the warst wally-draigle in our ain byre, than about the blessing which the angel of the covenant gave to the Patriarch even at Peniel and Mahanaim,[32] or the binding obligation of our national vows;[33] and we wad rather gie a pund Scots to buy an unguent to clear our auld rannell-trees and our beds o' the English bugs[34] as they ca' them, than we wad gie a plack to rid the land of the swarm of Arminian caterpillars, Socinian

[* See p. 567 for the note, "Sir William Dick of Braid".]
[† I think so too—But if the reader be curious he may consult Mr Chambers'[31] Traditions of Edinburgh.]

pismires, and deistical Miss Katies, that have ascended out of the bottomless pit,[35] to plague this perverse, insidious, and lukewarm generation."[36]

It happened to David Deans on this occasion as it has done to many other habitual orators; when once he became embarked on his favourite subject, the stream of his own enthusiasm carried him forward in spite of his mental distress, while his well exercised memory supplied him amply with all the types and tropes of rhetoric peculiar to his sect and cause.

Mr Middleburgh contented himself with answering—"All this may be very true, my friend; but, as you said just now, I have nothing to say to it at present, either one way or other.—You have two daughters, I think, Mr Deans?"

The old man winced, as one whose smarting sore is suddenly galled, but instantly composed himself, resumed the work which, in the heat of his declamation, he had laid down, and answered with sullen resolution, "Ae daughter, sir—only *ane*."

"I understand you," said Mr Middleburgh; "you have only one daughter here at home with you—but this unfortunate girl who is a prisoner—she is, I think, your youngest daughter?"

The presbyterian sternly raised his eyes. "After the world, and according to the flesh, she *is* my daughter; but when she became a child of Belial,[37] and a company-keeper,[38] and a trader in guilt and iniquity, she ceased to be bairn of mine."

"Alas, Mr Deans," said Middleburgh, sitting down by him, and endeavouring to take his hand, which the old man proudly withdrew, "we are ourselves all sinners; and the errors of our offspring, as they ought not to surprise us, being the share which they derive of a common portion of corruption inherited through us, so they do not entitle us to cast them off because they have lost themselves."

"Sir," said Deans, impatiently, "I ken a' that as weel as—I mean to say," he resumed, checking the irritation he felt at being schooled,—a discipline of the mind, which those most ready to bestow it on others, do themselves most reluctantly submit to receive—"I mean to say, that what ye observe may be just and reasonable—But I hae nae freedom to enter into my ain private affairs wi' strangers—And now, in this great national emergency, when there's the Porteous' Act has come doun frae London, that is a deeper blow to this poor sinfu' kingdom and suffering kirk, than ony that has been heard of since the foul and fatal Test—at a time like this"——

"But, goodman," interrupted Mr Middleburgh, "you must think of your own household first, or else you are worse even than the infidels."

"I tell ye, Baillie Middleburgh," retorted David Deans, "if ye be a baillie, as there is little honour in being ane in these evil days—I tell ye, I heard the gracious Saunders Peden[39]—I wotna whan it was; but it was in killing time, when the plowers were drawing lang their furrows[40] on the back of the Kirk of Scotland—I heard him tell his hearers, gude and waled Christians they were too, that some o' them wad greet mair for a bit drowned calf or stirk, than for a' the defections and oppressions of the day; and that they were some o' them thinking o' ae thing, some o' anither, and there was Lady Hundelslope[41] thinking o' greeting Jock at the fire-side! And the lady confessed in my hearing, that a drow of anxiety had come ower her for her son that she had left at hame weak of a decay[*]—And what wad he hae said of me, if I had ceased to think of the gude cause for a cast-away—a—it kills me to think of what she is—"

"But the life of your child, goodman—think of that—if her life could be saved," said Middleburgh.

"Her life!" exclaimed David—"I wadna gie ane o' my grey hairs for her life, if her gude name be gane—And yet," said he, relenting and retracting as he spoke, "I wad make the niffer, Mr Middleburgh—I wad gie a' these grey hairs that she has brought to shame and sorrow—I wad gie the auld head they grow on for her life, and that she might hae time to amend and return, for what hae the wicked beyond the breath of their nosthrils?[42]—But I'll never see her mair.—No!—that—that I am determined in—I'll never see her mair." His lips continued to move for a minute after his voice ceased to be heard, as if he were repeating the same vow internally.

"Well, sir," said Mr Middleburgh, "I speak to you as a man of sense; if you would save your daughter's life, you must use human means."

"I understand what you mean; but Mr Novit, who is the procurator and doer of an honourable person, the Laird of Dumbiedikes, is to do what carnal wisdom can do for her in the circumstances. Mysell am not clear to trinquet and traffic wi' courts o' justice, as they are now constituted; I have a tenderness and scruple in my mind anent them."

[* See Life of Peden, p. 111.]

"That is to say," said Middleburgh, "that you are a Cameronian, and do not acknowledge the authority of our courts of judicature or present government?"

"Sir, under your favour," replied David, who was too proud of his own polemical knowledge, to call himself the follower of any one, "ye tak me up before I fall down. I canna see why I suld be termed a Cameronian, especially now that ye hae given the name of that famous and savoury sufferer, not only until a regimental band of souldiers, whereof I am told many can now curse, swear, and use profane language, as fast as ever Richard Cameron could preach or pray; but also because ye have, in as far as it is in your power, rendered that martyr's name vain and contemptible, by pipes, drums, and fifes, playing the vain carnal spring, called the Cameronian Rant,[43] which too many professors of religion dance to—a practice maist unbecoming a professor to dance to any tune whatsoever, more especially promiscuously, that is, with the female sex.[*] A brutish fashion it is, whilk is the beginning of defection with many, as I may hae as muckle cause as maist folk to testify."

"Well, but Mr Deans," replied Mr Middleburgh, "I only meant to say that you were a Cameronian or MacMillanite, one of the society people,[44] in short, who think it inconsistent to take oaths under a government where the Covenant is not ratified."

"Sir," replied the controversialist, who forgot even his present distress in such discussions as these, "you cannot fickle me sae easily as you do opine. I am *not* a MacMillanite, or a Russelite, or a Hamiltonian, or a Harleyite, or a Howdenite[†]—I will be led by the nose by none—I take my name as a Christian from no vessel of clay.[45] I have my own principles and practice to answer for, and am an humble pleader for the gude auld cause in a legal way."[46]

"That is to say, Mr Deans," said Middleburgh, "that you are a *Deanite*, and have opinions peculiar to yourself."

"It may please you to say sae," said David Deans; "but I have maintained my testimony before as great folks, and in sharper times; and though I will neither exalt myself nor pull down others, I wish every man and woman in this land had kept the true testimony, and the middle and straight path, as it were, on the rigg of a hill, where wind and water shears,[47] avoiding right-hand snares and extremes,

[* See p. 559 for the note, "Peter Walker".]
[† All various species of the great genus Cameronian.]

and left-hand way-slidings, as weel as Johnny Dodds of Farthing's Acre,[48] and ae man mair that shall be nameless."

"I suppose," replied the magistrate, "that is as much as to say, that Johnny Dodds of Farthing's Acre, and David Deans of St Leonard's, constitute the only members of the true, real, unsophisticated Kirk of Scotland?"

"God forbid that I suld make sic a vain-glorious speech, when there are sae mony professing Christians," answered David; "but this I maun say, that all men act according to their gifts and their grace, sae that it is nae marvel that"——

"This is all very fine," interrupted Mr Middleburgh, "but I have no time to spend in hearing it. The matter in hand is this—I have directed a citation to be lodged in your daughter's hands—If she appears on the day of trial and gives evidence, there is reason to hope she may save her sister's life—if, from any overstrained scruples about the legality of her performing the office of an affectionate sister and a good subject, by appearing in a court held under the authority of the law and government, you become the means of deterring her from the discharge of this duty, I must say, though the truth may sound harsh in your ears, that you, who gave life to this unhappy girl, will become the means of her losing it by a premature and violent death."

So saying, Mr Middleburgh turned to leave him.

"Bide awee—bide awee, Mr Middleburgh," said Deans, in great perplexity and distress of mind; but the baillie, who was probably sensible that protracted discussion might diminish the effect of his best and most forcible argument, took a hasty leave, and declined entering farther into the controversy.

Deans sunk down upon his seat, stunned with a variety of conflicting emotions. It had been a great source of controversy among those holding his opinions in religious matters, how far the government which succeeded the Revolution could be, without sin, acknowledged by true presbyterians, seeing that it did not recognize the great national testimony of the Solemn League and Covenant?[49] And latterly, those agreeing in this general doctrine, and assuming the sounding title of the Anti-popish, Anti-prelatic, Anti-erastian, Anti-sectarian, true Presbyterian remnant,[50] were divided into many petty sects among themselves, even as to the extent of submission to the existing laws and rulers, which constituted such an acknowledgment as amounted to sin.

At a very stormy and tumultuous meeting, held in 1682, to discuss these important and delicate points, the testimonies of the faithful few were found utterly inconsistent with each other.[*][51] The place where this conference was held was remarkably well adapted for such an assembly. It was a wild and very sequestered dell in Tweeddale, surrounded by high hills, and far remote from human habitation. A small river, or rather a mountain torrent, called the Talla, breaks down the glen with great fury, dashing successively over a number of small cascades, which has procured the spot the name of Talla-Linns. Here the leaders among the scattered adherents to the Covenant, men who, in their banishment from human society, and in the recollection of the severities to which they had been exposed, had become at once sullen in their temper, and fantastic in their religious opinions, met with arms in their hands, and by the side of the torrent discussed, with a turbulence which the noise of the stream could not drown, points of controversy as empty and unsubstantial as its foam.

It was the fixed judgment of most of the meeting, that all payment of cess or tribute[52] to the existing government was utterly unlawful, and a sacrificing to idols. About other impositions and degrees of submission there were various opinions; and perhaps it is the best illustration of the spirit of those military fathers of the church to say, that while all allowed it was impious to pay the cess employed for maintaining the standing army and militia, there was a fierce controversy on the lawfulness of paying the duties levied at ports and bridges, for maintaining roads and other necessary purposes; that there were some who, repugnant to these imposts for turnpikes and pontages, were nevertheless free in conscience to make payment of the usual freight at public ferries, and that a person of exceeding and punctilious zeal, James Russel,[53] one of the slayers of the Archbishop of St Andrews, had given his testimony with great warmth even against this last faint shade of subjection to constituted authority. This ardent and enlightened person and his followers had also great scruples about the lawfulness of bestowing the ordinary names upon the days of the week and the months of the year, which savoured in their nostrils so strongly of paganism, that at length they arrived at the conclusion that they who owned such names as Monday, Tuesday, January, February, and so forth, "served themselves heirs to the same, if not greater punishment,[54] than had been denounced against the idolaters of old."

[* See p. 568 for the note, "Meeting at Talla-Linns".]

David Deans had been present on this memorable occasion, although too young to be a speaker among the polemical combatants. His brain, however, had been thoroughly heated by the noise, clamour, and metaphysical ingenuity of the discussion, and it was a controversy to which his mind had often returned; and though he carefully disguised his vacillation from others, and perhaps from himself, he had never been able to come to any precise line of decision on the subject. In fact, his natural sense had acted as a counterpoise to his controversial zeal. He was by no means pleased with the quiet and indifferent manner in which King William's government slurred over the errors of the times, when, far from restoring the presbyterian Kirk to its former supremacy, they passed an act of oblivion even to those who had been its persecutors, and bestowed on many of them titles, favours, and employments. When, in the first General Assembly which succeeded the Revolution, an overture was made for the revival of the League and Covenant, it was with horror that Douce David heard the proposal eluded by the men of carnal wit and policy, as he called them, as being inapplicable to the present times, and not falling under the modern model of the church. The reign of Queen Anne had increased his conviction, that the Revolution government was not one of the true presbyterian complexion. But then, more sensible than the bigots of his sect, he did not confound the moderation and tolerance of these two reigns with the active tyranny and oppression exercised in those of Charles II. and James II. The presbyterian form of religion, though deprived of the weight formerly attached to its sentences of excommunication, and compelled to tolerate the co-existence of episcopacy, and of sects of various descriptions, was still the National Church; and though the glory of the second temple[55] was far inferior to that which had flourished from 1639 till the battle of Dunbar,[56] still it was a structure that, wanting the strength and the terrors, retained at least the form and symmetry of the original model. Then came the insurrection in 1715, and David Deans's horror for the revival of the popish and prelatical faction reconciled him greatly to the government of King George, although he grieved that that monarch might be suspected of a leaning unto Erastianism. In short, moved by so many different considerations, he had shifted his ground at different times concerning the degree of freedom which he felt in adopting any act of immediate acknowledgment or submission to the present government, which, however mild and paternal, was still uncovenanted; and now he felt himself called upon by the most powerful motive conceivable, to authorize his daughter's giving testimony in a court of justice, which all who have been since called Cameronians, accounted a step of lamentable and direct defection. The voice of nature, however, exclaimed loud in his bosom against the dictates of fanaticism; and his imagination, fertile in the solution of polemical difficulties, devised an expedient for extricating himself from the fearful dilemma, in which he saw, on the one side, a falling off from principle, and, on the other, a scene from which a father's thoughts could not but turn in shuddering horror.

"I have been constant and unchanged in my testimony," said David Deans; "but then who has said it of me, that I have judged my neighbour over closely, because he hath had more freedom in his walk than I have found in mine? I never was a separatist, nor for quarrelling with tender souls about mint, cummin, or other the lesser tithes.[57] My daughter Jean may have a light in this subject that is hid frae my auld een—it is laid on her conscience and not on mine—If she hath freedom to gang before this judicatory and hold up her hand for this poor cast-away, surely I will not say she steppeth over her bounds; and if not"——He paused in his mental argument, while a pang of unutterable anguish convulsed his features, yet, shaking it off, he firmly resumed the strain of his reasoning—"And IF NOT—God forbid that she should go into defection at bidding of mine! I winna fret the tender conscience of one bairn—no, not to save the life of the other."

A Roman would have devoted his daughter to death from different feelings and motives, but not upon a more heroic principle of duty.

CHAPTER 19

To man, in this his trial state,
  The privilege is given,
When tost by tides of human fate,
  To anchor fast on heaven.
                        WATTS's *Hymns*

IT was with a firm step that Deans sought his daughter's apartment, determined to leave her to the light of her own conscience in the dubious point of casuistry in which he supposed her to be placed.

The little room had been the sleeping apartment of both sisters, and there still stood there a small occasional bed which had been made for Effie's accommodation, when, complaining of illness, she had declined to share, as in happier times, her sister's pillow. The eyes of Deans rested involuntarily, on entering the room, upon this little couch, with its dark-green coarse curtains, and the ideas connected with it rose so thick upon his soul as almost to incapacitate him from opening his errand to his daughter. Her occupation broke the ice. He found her gazing on a slip of paper, which contained a citation to her to appear as a witness upon her sister's trial in behalf of the accused. For the worthy magistrate, determined to omit no chance of doing Effie justice, and to leave her sister no apology for not giving the evidence which she was supposed to possess, had caused the ordinary citation, or *sub-pœna*, of the Scottish criminal court, to be served upon her by an officer during his conference with David.

This precaution was so far favourable to Deans, that it saved him the pain of entering upon a formal explanation with his daughter; he only said, with a hollow and tremulous voice, "I perceive ye are aware of the matter."

"O father, we are cruelly sted between God's laws and man's laws—What will we do?—What can we do?"

Jeanie, it must be observed, had no hesitation whatever about the mere act of appearing in a court of justice. She might have heard the point discussed by her father more than once; but we have already noticed, that she was accustomed to listen with reverence to much which she was incapable of understanding, and that subtle arguments of casuistry found her a patient, but unedified hearer. Upon receiving the citation, therefore, her thoughts did not turn upon the chimerical scruples which alarmed her father's mind, but to the language which had been held to her by the stranger at Muschat's Cairn. In a word, she never doubted but she was to be dragged forward into the court of justice, in order to place her in the cruel position of either sacrificing her sister by telling the truth, or committing perjury in order to save her life. And so strongly did her thoughts run in this channel, that she applied her father's words, "Ye are aware of the matter," to his acquaintance with the advice that had been so fearfully enforced upon her. She looked up with anxious surprise, not unmingled with a cast of horror, which his next words, as she interpreted and applied them, were not qualified to remove.

"Daughter," said David, "it has ever been my mind, that in things of ane doubtful and controversial nature, ilk Christian's conscience suld be his ain guide—Wherefore descend into yourself, try your ain mind with sufficiency of soul exercise, and as you sall finally find yourself clear to do in this matter—even so be it."

"But, father," said Jeanie, whose mind revolted at the construction which she naturally put upon his language, "can this—THIS be a doubtful or controversial matter?—Mind, father, the ninth command¹—'Thou shalt not bear false witness against thy neighbour.'"

David Deans paused; for, still applying her speech to his preconceived difficulties, it seemed to him, as if *she*, a woman, and a sister, was scarce entitled to be scrupulous upon this occasion, where *he*, a man, exercised in the testimonies of that testifying period, had given indirect countenance to her following what must have been the natural dictates of her own feelings. But he kept firm his purpose, until his eyes involuntarily rested upon the little settle-bed, and recalled the form of the child of his old age, as she sate upon it, pale, emaciated, and broken-hearted. His mind, as the picture arose before him, involuntarily conceived, and his tongue involuntarily uttered—but in a tone how different from his usual dogmatical precision!—arguments for the course of conduct likely to insure his child's safety.

"Daughter," he said, "I did not say that your path was free from stumbling—and, questionless, this act may be in the opinion of some a transgression, since he who beareth witness unlawfully, and against his conscience, doth in some sort bear false witness against his neighbour.

Yet in matters of compliance, the guilt lieth not in the compliance sae muckle, as in the mind and conscience of him that doth comply; and, therefore, although my testimony hath not been spared upon public defections, I haena felt freedom to separate mysell[2] from the communion of many who have been clear to hear those ministers who have taken the fatal indulgence, because they might get good of them, though I could not."

When David had proceeded thus far, his conscience reproved him, that he might be indirectly undermining the purity of his daughter's faith, and smoothing the way for her falling off from strictness of principle. He, therefore, suddenly stopped, and changed his tone:— "Jeanie, I perceive that our vile affections,[3]—so I call them in respect of doing the will of our Father,—cling too heavily to me in this hour of trying sorrow, to permit me to keep sight of my ain duty, or to airt you to yours. I will speak nae mair anent this over-trying matter.— Jeanie, if ye can, wi' God and gude conscience, speak in favour of this puir unhappy"—(here his voice faultered)—"she is your sister in the flesh—worthless and cast-away as she is, she is the daughter of a saint in Heaven, that was a mother to you, Jeanie, in place of your ain—but if ye are na free in conscience to speak for her in the court of judicature, follow your conscience, Jeanie, and let God's will be done." After this adjuration, he left the apartment, and his daughter remained in a state of great distress and perplexity.

It would have been no small addition to the sorrows of David Deans, even in this extremity of suffering, had he known that his daughter was applying the casuistical arguments which he had been using, not in the sense of a permission to follow her own opinion on a dubious and disputed point of controversy, but rather as an encouragement to transgress one of those divine commandments which Christians of all sects and denominations unite in holding most sacred.

"Can this be?" said Jeanie, as the door closed on her father—"Can these be his words that I have heard, or has the Enemy taken his voice and features to give weight unto the counsel which causeth to perish![4]—A sister's life, and a father pointing out how to save it!—O God deliver me!—this is a fearfu' temptation."

Roaming from thought to thought, she at one time imagined her father understood the ninth commandment literally, as prohibiting false witness *against* our neighbour, without extending the denunciation against falsehood uttered *in favour* of the criminal. But her clear and unsophisticated power of discriminating between good and evil, instantly rejected an interpretation so limited, and so unworthy of the Author of the law. She remained in a state of the most agitating terror and uncertainty—afraid to communicate her thoughts freely to her father, lest she should draw forth an opinion with which she could not comply,—wrung with distress on her sister's account, rendered the more acute by reflecting that the means of saving her were in her power, but were such as her conscience prohibited her from using,—tossed, in short, like a vessel in an open roadstead during a storm, and like that vessel, resting on one only sure cable and anchor,—faith in Providence, and a resolution to discharge her duty.

Butler's affection and strong sense of religion would have been her principal support in these distressing circumstances, but he was still under restraint, which did not permit him to come to Saint Leonard's Crags; and her distresses were of a nature, which, with her indifferent habits of scholarship, she found it impossible to express in writing. She was therefore compelled to trust for guidance to her own unassisted sense of what was right or wrong.

It was not the least of Jeanie's distresses, that, although she hoped and believed her sister to be innocent, she had not the means of receiving that assurance from her own mouth.

The double-dealing of Ratcliffe in the matter of Robertson had not prevented his being rewarded, as double-dealers frequently have been, with favour and preferment. Sharpitlaw, who found in him something of a kindred genius, had been intercessor in his behalf with the magistrates, and the circumstance of his having voluntarily remained in the prison, when the doors were forced by the mob, would have made it a hard measure to take the life which he had such easy means of saving. He received a full pardon; and soon afterwards, James Ratcliffe, the greatest thief and housebreaker in Scotland, was, upon the faith, perhaps, of an ancient proverb,[5] selected as a person fit to be entrusted with the custody of other delinquents.[6]

When Ratcliffe was thus placed in a confidential situation, he was repeatedly applied to by the sapient Saddletree and others, who took some interest in the Deans family, to procure an interview between the sisters; but the magistrates, who were extremely anxious for the apprehension of Robertson, had given strict orders to the contrary, hoping that, by keeping them separate, they might, from the one or the other, extract some information respecting that fugitive. On this subject Jeanie had nothing to tell them: She informed Mr Middleburgh, that she knew nothing of Robertson, except having met him that night by appointment to give her some advice respecting her sister's concern, the purport of which, she said, was betwixt God and her conscience. Of his motions, purposes, or plans, past, present, or future, she knew nothing, and so had nothing to communicate.

Effie was equally silent, though from a different cause. It was in vain that they offered a commutation and alleviation of her punishment, and even a free pardon, if she would confess what she knew of her lover. She answered only with tears; unless, when at times driven into pettish sulkiness by the persecution of the interrogators, she made them abrupt and disrespectful answers.

At length, after her trial had been delayed for many weeks, in hopes she might be induced to speak out on a subject infinitely more interesting to the magistracy than her own guilt or innocence, their patience was worn out, and even Mr Middleburgh finding no ear lent to further intercession in her behalf, the day was fixed for the trial to proceed.

It was now, and not sooner, that Sharpitlaw, recollecting his promise to Effie Deans, or rather being dinned into compliance by the unceasing remonstrances of Mrs Saddletree, who was his next door neighbour, and who declared it was heathen cruelty to keep the twa broken-hearted creatures separate, issued the important mandate, permitting them to see each other.

On the evening which preceded the eventful day of trial, Jeanie was permitted to see her sister—an awful interview, and occurring at a most distressing crisis. This, however, formed a part of the bitter cup[7] which she was doomed to drink, to atone for crimes and follies to which she had no accession; and at twelve o'clock noon, being the time appointed for admission to the jail, she went to meet, for the first time for several months, her guilty, erring, and most miserable sister, in that abode of guilt, error, and utter misery.

CHAPTER 20

——Sweet sister, let me live;
What sin you do to save a brother's life,
Nature dispenses with the deed so far,
That it becomes a virtue.

Measure for Measure

JEANIE Deans was admitted into the jail by Ratcliffe. This fellow, as void of shame as of honesty, as he opened the now trebly secured door, asked her, with a leer which made her shudder, "whether she remembered him?"

A half-pronounced and timid "No," was her answer.

"What! not remember moonlight, and Muschat's Cairn, and Rob and Rat?" said he, with the same sneer;—"Your memory needs redding up, my jo."

If Jeanie's distresses had admitted of aggravation, it must have been to find her sister under the charge of such a profligate as this man. He was not, indeed, without something of good to balance so much that was evil in his character and habits. In his misdemeanours he had never been bloodthirsty or cruel; and in his present occupation, he had shown himself, in a certain degree, accessible to touches of humanity. But these good qualities were unknown to Jeanie, who, remembering the scene at Muschat's Cairn, could scarce find voice to acquaint him, that she had an order from Baillie Middleburgh, permitting her to see her sister.

"I ken that fu' weel, my bonny doo; mair by token, I have a special charge to stay in the ward wi' you a' the time ye are thegither."

"Must that be sae?" asked Jeanie, with an imploring voice.

"Hout, ay, hinny," replied the turnkey; "and what the waur will you and your titty be of Jim Ratcliffe hearing what ye hae to say to ilk other?—Deil a word ye'll say that will gar him ken your kittle sex better than he kens them already; and another thing is, that if ye dinna speak o' breaking the Tolbooth, deil a word will I tell ower again, either to do ye gude or ill."

Thus saying, Ratcliffe marshalled her the way to the apartment where Effie was confined.

Shame, fear, and grief, had contended for mastery in the poor prisoner's bosom during the whole morning, while she had looked forward to this meeting; but when the door opened, all gave way to a confused and strange feeling that had a tinge of joy in it, as, throwing herself on her sister's neck, she ejaculated, "My dear Jeanie!—my dear Jeanie! it's lang since I hae seen ye." Jeanie returned the embrace with an earnestness that partook almost of rapture, but it was only a flitting emotion, like a sun-beam unexpectedly penetrating betwixt the clouds of a tempest, and obscured almost as soon as visible. The sisters walked together to the side of the pallet bed, and sate down side by side, took hold of each other's hands, and looked each other in the face, but without speaking a word. In this posture they remained for a minute, while the gleam of joy gradually faded from their features, and gave way to the most intense expression, first of melancholy, and then of agony, till, throwing themselves again into each other's arms, they, to use the language of Scripture, lifted up their voices and wept[1] bitterly.

Even the hard-hearted turnkey, who had spent his life in scenes calculated to stifle both conscience and feeling, could not witness this scene without a touch of human sympathy. It was shown in a trifling action, but which had more delicacy in it than seemed to belong to Ratcliffe's character and station. The unglazed window of the miserable chamber was open, and the beams of a bright sun fell right upon the bed where the sufferers were seated. With a gentleness that had something of reverence in it, Ratcliffe partly closed the shutter, and seemed thus to throw a veil over a scene so sorrowful.

"Ye are ill, Effie," were the first words Jeanie could utter, "ye are very ill."

"O what wad I gie to be ten times waur, Jeanie!" was the reply— "what wad I gie to be cauld dead afore the ten o'clock bell the morn! And our father—but I am his bairn nae langer now—O I hae nae friend left in the warld!—O that I were lying dead at my mother's side, in Newbattle Kirkyard!"

"Hout, lassie," said Ratcliffe, willing to show the interest which he absolutely felt, "dinna be sae dooms down-hearted as a' that; there's mony a tod hunted that's no killed.[2] Advocate Langtale has brought folk through waur snappers than a' this, and there's no a cleverer agent than Nichil Novit e'er drew a bill of suspension. Hanged or unhanged, they are weel aff has sic an agent and counsel; ane's sure o' fair play. Ye are a bonny lass too, an ye wad busk up your cockernonie a bit; and a bonny lass will find favour wi' judge and jury, when they would strap up a grewsome carle like me for the fifteenth part of a flea's hide and tallow,[3] d——n them."

To this homely strain of consolation the mourners returned no answer; indeed they were so much lost in their own sorrows as to have become insensible of Ratcliffe's presence. "O Effie," said her elder sister, "how could you conceal your situation from me! O, woman, had I deserved this at your hand?—had ye spoke but ae word—sorry we might hae been, and shamed we might hae been, but this awfu' dispensation had never come ower us."

"And what gude wad that hae dune?" answered the prisoner. "Na, na, Jeanie, a' was ower when ance I forgot what I promised when I faulded down the leaf[4] of my Bible. See," she said, producing the sacred volume, "the book opens aye at the place o' itsell. O see, Jeanie, what a fearfu' scripture!"

Jeanie took her sister's Bible, and found that the fatal mark was made at this impressive text[5] in the book of Job: "He hath stripped me of my glory, and taken the crown from my head. He hath destroyed me on every side, and I am gone. And mine hope hath he removed like a tree."

"Isna that ower true a doctrine?" said the prisoner—"Isna my crown, my honour removed? And what am I but a poor wasted wan-thriven tree, dug up by the roots, and flung out to waste in the highway, that man and beast may tread it under foot? I thought o' the bonny bit thorn that our father rooted out o' the yard last May, when it had a' the flush o' blossoms on it; and then it lay in the court till the beasts had trod them a' to pieces wi' their feet. I little thought, when I was wae for the bit silly green bush and its flowers, that I was to gang the same gate mysell."

"O, if ye had spoken a word," again sobbed Jeanie,—"if I were free to swear that ye had said but ae word of how it stude wi' ye, they could nae hae touched your life this day."

"Could they na?" said Effie, with something like awakened interest—for life is dear even to those who feel it as a burthen— "Wha tauld ye that, Jeanie?"

"It was ane that kend what he was saying weel aneugh," replied Jeanie, who had a natural reluctance at mentioning even the name of her sister's seducer.

"Wha was it?—I conjure ye to tell me, Jeanie," said Effie, seating herself upright.—"Wha could tak interest in sic a cast-bye as I am now?—Was it—was it *him*?"

"Hout," said Ratcliffe, "what signifies keeping the poor lassie in a swither?—I'se uphaud it's been Robertson that learned ye that doctrine when ye saw him at Muschat's Cairn."

"Was it him?" said Effie, catching eagerly at his words—"was it him, Jeanie, indeed?—O, I see it was him—poor lad, and I was thinking his heart was as hard as the nether millstane[6]—and him in sic danger on his ain part—poor George!"

Somewhat indignant at this burst of tender feeling towards the author of her misery, Jeanie could not help exclaiming,—"O, Effie, how can ye speak that gate of sic a man as that?"

"We maun forgie our enemies, ye ken," said poor Effie, with a timid look and a subdued voice, for her conscience told her what a different character the feelings with which she still regarded her seducer bore, compared with the Christian charity under which she attempted to veil it.

"And ye hae suffered a' this for him, and ye can think of loving him still?" said her sister, in a voice betwixt pity and blame.

"Love him?" answered Effie—"If I had na loved as woman seldom loves, I had nae been within these wa's this day; and trow ye, that love sic as mine is lightly forgotten?—Na, na—ye may hew down the tree, but ye canna change its bend[7]—And O, Jeanie, if ye wad do good to me at this moment, tell me every word that he said, and whether he was sorry for poor Effie or no."

"What needs I tell ye ony thing about it," said Jeanie. "Ye may be sure he had ower muckle to do to save himsell, to speak lang or meikle about ony body beside."

"That's no true, Jeanie, though a saunt had said it,"[8] replied Effie, with a sparkle of her former lively and irritable temper. "But ye dinna ken, though I do, how far he pat his life in venture to save mine." And looking at Ratcliffe, she checked herself and was silent.

"I fancy," said Ratcliffe, with one of his familiar sneers, "the lassie thinks that naebody has een but hersell—Didna I see when Gentle Geordie was seeking to get other folk out of the Tolbooth forbye Jock Porteous? but ye were of my mind, hinny—better sit and rue, than flit and rue[9]—Ye needna look in my face sae mazed. I ken mair things than that maybe."

"O my God! my God!" said Effie, springing up and throwing herself down on her knees before him—"D'ye ken whare they hae putten my bairn?—O my bairn! my bairn! the poor sackless innocent new-born wee ane—bone of my bone, and flesh of my flesh![10]—O,

man, if ye wad e'er deserve a portion in Heaven, or a broken-hearted
creature's blessing upon earth, tell me whare they hae put my bairn—
the sign of my shame, and the partner of my suffering! tell me wha has
taen't away, or what they hae dune wi't!"

"Hout tout," said the turnkey, endeavouring to extricate himself
from the firm grasp with which she held him, "that's taking me at my
word wi' a witness—Bairn, quo' she? How the deil suld I ken ony
thing of your bairn, huzzy? Ye maun ask that at auld Meg Murdockson,
if ye dinna ken ower muckle about it yoursell."

As his answer destroyed the wild and vague hope which had
suddenly gleamed upon her, the unhappy prisoner let go her hold of
his coat, and fell with her face on the pavement of the apartment in a
strong convulsion fit.

Jeanie Deans possessed, with her excellently clear understanding,
the concomitant advantage of promptitude of spirit, even in the
extremity of distress.

She did not suffer herself to be overcome by her own feelings of
exquisite sorrow, but instantly applied herself to her sister's relief,
with the readiest remedies which circumstances afforded; and which,
to do Ratcliffe justice, he shewed himself anxious to suggest, and alert
in procuring. He had even the delicacy to withdraw to the farthest
corner of the room, so as to render his official attendance upon them
as little intrusive as possible, when Effie was composed enough again
to resume her conference with her sister.

The prisoner once more, in the most earnest and broken tones,
conjured Jeanie to tell her the particulars of the conference with
Robertson, and Jeanie felt it was impossible to refuse her this gratification.

"Do ye mind," she said, "Effie, when ye were in the fever before
we left Woodend, and how angry your mother, that's now in a better
place, was at me for gieing ye milk and water to drink, because ye grat
for it? Ye were a bairn then, and ye are a woman now, and should ken
better than ask what canna but hurt ye—But come weal or woe, I
canna refuse ye ony thing that ye ask me wi' the tear in your ee."

Again Effie threw herself into her arms, and kissed her cheek and
forehead, murmuring, "O, if ye kend how lang it is since I heard his
name mentioned,—if ye but kend how muckle good it does me but to
ken ony thing o' him, that's like goodness or kindness, ye wadna
wonder that I wish to hear o' him."

Jeanie sighed, and commenced her narrative of all that had passed betwixt Robertson and her, making it as brief as possible. Effie listened in breathless anxiety, holding her sister's hand in hers, and keeping her eye fixed upon her face, as if devouring every word she uttered. The interjections of "Poor fellow,"—"poor George," which escaped in whispers, and betwixt sighs, were the only sounds with which she interrupted the story. When it was finished she made a long pause.

"And this was his advice?" were the first words she uttered.

"Just sic as I hae tell'd ye," replied her sister.

"And he wanted you to say something to yon folks, that wad save my young life?"

"He wanted," answered Jeanie, "that I suld be mansworn."

"And you tauld him," said Effie, "that ye wadna hear o' coming between me and the death that I am to die, and me no aughteen year auld yet?"

"I told him," replied Jeanie, who now trembled at the turn which her sister's reflections seemed about to take, "that I daured na swear to an untruth."

"And what d'ye ca' an untruth?" said Effie, again shewing a touch of her former spirit—"Ye are muckle to blame, lass, if ye think a mother would, or could, murder her ain bairn—Murder?—I wad hae laid down my life just to see a blink o' its ee."

"I do believe," said Jeanie, "that ye are as innocent of sic a purpose, as the new-born babe itsell."

"I am glad ye do me that justice," said Effie, haughtily; "it's whiles the faut of very good folk like you, Jeanie, that they think a' the rest of the warld are as bad as the warst temptations can make them."

"I dinna deserve this frae ye, Effie," said her sister, sobbing, and feeling at once the injustice of the reproach, and compassion for the state of mind which dictated it.

"Maybe no, tittie," said Effie. "But ye are angry because I love Robertson—How can I help loving him, that loves me better than body and soul baith?—Here he put his life in a niffer, to break the prison to let me out; and sure am I, had it stood wi' him as it stands wi' you"—here she paused and was silent.

"O, if it stude wi' me to save ye wi' risk of *my* life!" said Jeanie.

"Ay, lass," said her sister, "that's lightly said, but no sae lightly credited, frae ane that winna ware a word for me; and if it be a wrang word, ye'll hae time aneugh to repent o't."

"But that word is a grievous sin, and it's a deeper offence when it's a sin wilfully and presumptuously committed."

"Weel, weel, Jeanie," said Effie, "I mind a' about the sins o' presumption in the questions[11]—we'll speak nae mair about this matter, and ye may save your breath to say your carritch;[12] and for me, I'll soon hae nae breath to waste on ony body."

"I must needs say," interposed Ratcliffe, "that it's d—d hard, when three words of your mouth would give the girl the chance to nick Moll Blood,* that you mak such scrupling about rapping† to them. D—n me, if they would take me, if I would not rap to all Whatd'yecallum—Hyssop's Fables[13] for her life—I am used to't, b—t me, for less matters. Why, I have smacked calf-skin‡[14] fifty times in England for a keg of brandy."

"Never speak mair o't," said the prisoner. "It's just as weel as it is—and gude day, sister; ye keep Mr Ratcliffe waiting on—Ye'll come back and see me I reckon, before"——here she stopped, and became deadly pale.

"And are we to part in this way," said Jeanie, "and you in sic deadly peril? O, Effie, look but up, and say what ye wad hae me do, and I could find in my heart amaist to say that I wad do't."

"No, Jeanie," replied her sister, after an effort, "I am better minded now. At my best, I was never half sae gude as ye were, and what for suld you begin to mak yoursell waur to save me, now that I am na worth saving? God knows, that, in my sober mind, I wadna wuss ony living creature to do a wrang thing to save my life. I might have fled frae this tolbooth on that awfu' night wi' ane wad hae carried me through the warld, and friended me, and fended for me. But I said to them, let life gang when gude fame is gane before it.[15] But this lang imprisonment has broken my spirit, and I am whiles sair left to mysell, and then I wad gie the Indian mines of gold and diamonds, just for life and breath—for I think, Jeanie, I have such roving fits as I used to hae in the fever; but instead of the fiery een, and wolves, and Widow Butler's bull-segg, that I used to see spieling up on my bed, I am thinking now about a high black gibbet, and me standing up, and such seas of faces all looking up at poor Effie Deans, and asking if it be her that George Robertson used to call the Lily of St Leonard's—And then they stretch out their faces, and make mouths, and girn at me, and which ever way I look, I see a face laughing like Meg

* The Gallows.
† Swearing.
‡ Kissed the book.

Murdockson, when she tauld me I had seen the last of my wean. God preserve us, Jeanie, that carline has a fearsome face." She clapped her hands before her eyes as she uttered this exclamation, as if to secure herself against seeing the fearful object she had alluded to.

Jeanie Deans remained with her sister for two hours, during which she endeavoured, if possible, to extract something from her that might be serviceable in her exculpation. But she had nothing to say beyond what she had declared on her first examination, with the purport of which the reader will be made acquainted in proper time and place. "They wad na believe her," she said, "and she had naething mair to tell them."

At length Ratcliffe, though reluctantly, informed the sisters that there was a necessity that they should part. "Mr Novit," he said, "was to see the prisoner, and maybe Mr Langtale too.—Langtale likes to look at a bonny lass, whether in prison or out o' prison."

Reluctantly, therefore, and slowly, after many a tear, and many an embrace, Jeanie retired from the apartment, and heard its jarring bolts turned upon the dear being from whom she was separated. Somewhat familiarized now even with her rude conductor, she offered him a small present in money, with a request he would do what he could for her sister's accommodation. To her surprise Ratcliffe declined the fee. "I wasna bloody when I was on the pad," he said, "and I winna be greedy—that is, beyond what's right and reasonable,—now that I am in the lock.—Keep the siller; and for civility, your sister sall hae sic as I can bestow; but I hope you'll think better on it, and rap an oath for her—deil a hair ill there is in it, if ye are rapping again the crown. I kenn'd a worthy minister, as gude a man, bating the deed they deposed him for, as ever ye heard claver in a pu'pit, that rapped to a hogshead of pigtail tobacco, just for as muckle as filled his spleuchan.[*] But maybe ye are keeping your ain counsel—weel, weel, there's nae harm in that.—As for your sister, I'se see that she gets her meat clean and warm, and I'll try to gar her lie down and take a sleep after dinner, for deil a ee she'll close the night.—I hae gude experience of these matters. The first night is aye the warst o't. I hae never heard o' ane that sleepit the night afore trial, but of mony a ane that sleepit as sound as a tap the night before their necks were straughted. And it's nae wonder—the warst may be tholed when it's kend[16]—Better a finger aff as aye wagging."[17]

[* Tobacco pouch.]

CHAPTER 21

Yet though thou may'st be dragg'd in scorn
To yonder ignominious tree,
Thou shalt not want one faithful friend
To share the cruel fates' decree.
Jemmy Dawson

AFTER spending the greater part of the morning in his devotions, for his benevolent neighbours had kindly insisted upon discharging his task of ordinary labour, David Deans entered the apartment when the breakfast meal was prepared. His eyes were involuntarily cast down, for he was afraid to look at Jeanie, uncertain as he was whether she might feel herself at liberty, with a good conscience, to attend the Court of Justiciary that day, to give the evidence which he understood that she possessed, in order to her sister's exculpation. At length, after a minute of apprehensive hesitation, he looked at her dress to discover whether it seemed to be in her contemplation to go abroad that morning. Her apparel was neat and plain, but such as conveyed no exact intimation of her intentions to go abroad. She had exchanged her usual garb for morning labour, for one something inferior to that with which, as her best, she was wont to dress herself for church, or any more rare occasion of going into society. Her sense taught her, that it was respectful to be decent in her apparel on such an occasion, while her feelings induced her to lay aside the use of the very few and simple personal ornaments, which, on other occasions, she permitted herself to wear. So that there occurred nothing in her external appearance which could mark out to her father, with any thing like certainty, her intentions on this occasion.

The preparations for their humble meal were that morning made in vain. The father and daughter sate, each assuming the appearance of eating, when the other's eyes were turned to them, and desisting from the effort with disgust, when the affectionate imposture seemed no longer necessary.

At length these moments of constraint were removed. The sound of St Giles's heavy toll announced the hour previous to the commencement of the trial; Jeanie arose, and, with a degree of composure for which she herself could not account, assumed her plaid, and made her other preparations for a distant walking. It was a strange contrast between the firmness of her demeanour, and the vacillation and cruel uncertainty of purpose indicated in all her father's motions; and one unacquainted with both could scarcely have supposed that the former was, in her ordinary habits of life, a docile, quiet, gentle, and even timid country-maiden, while her father, with a mind naturally proud and strong, and supported by religious opinions, of a stern, stoical, and unyielding character, had in his time undergone and withstood the most severe hardship, and the most imminent peril, without depression of spirit, or subjugation of his constancy. The secret of this difference was, that Jeanie's mind had already anticipated the line of conduct which she must adopt, with all its natural and necessary consequences; while her father, ignorant of every other circumstance, tormented himself with imagining what the one sister might say or swear, or what effect her testimony might have upon the awful event of the trial.

He watched his daughter, with a faultering and indecisive look, until she looked back upon him, with a look of unutterable anguish, as she was about to leave the apartment.

"My dear lassie," said he, "I will"—His action, hastily and confusedly searching for his worsted *mittans*[*] and staff, shewed his purpose of accompanying her, though his tongue failed distinctly to announce it.

"Father," said Jeanie, replying rather to his action than his words, "ye had better not."

"In the strength of my God," answered Deans, assuming firmness, "I will go forth."[1]

And, taking his daughter's arm under his, he began to walk from the door with a step so hasty, that she was almost unable to keep up with him. A trifling circumstance, but which marked the perturbed state of his mind, checked his course,—"Your bonnet, father?" said Jeanie, who observed he had come out with his grey hairs uncovered. He turned back with a slight blush on his cheek, being ashamed to have been detected in an omission which indicated so much mental confusion, assumed his large blue Scottish bonnet, and with a step slower, but more composed, as if the circumstance had obliged him to

---

[* A kind of worsted gloves used by the lower orders.]

summon up his resolution, and collect his scattered ideas, again placed his daughter's arm under his, and resumed the way to Edinburgh.

The courts of justice[2] were then, and are still held in what is called the Parliament Close, or, according to modern phrase, the Parliament Square, and occupied the buildings intended for the accommodation of the Scottish Estates. This edifice, though in an imperfect and corrupted style of architecture, had then a grave, decent, and, as it were, a judicial aspect, which was at least entitled to respect from its antiquity. For which venerable front, I observed, on my last occasional visit to the metropolis, that modern taste had substituted, at great apparent expence, a pile so utterly inconsistent with every monument of antiquity around, and in itself so clumsy at the same time and fantastic, that it may be likened to the decorations of Tom Errand the porter, in the Trip to the Jubilee,[3] when he appears bedizened with the tawdry finery of Beau Clincher. *Sed transeat cum cæteris erroribus.*[4]

The small quadrangle, or Close, if we may presume still to give it that appropriate, though antiquated title, which at Litchfield, Salisbury, and elsewhere, is properly applied to designate the enclosure adjacent to a cathedral, already evinced tokens of the fatal scene which was that day to be acted. The soldiers of the City Guard were on their posts, now enduring, and now rudely repelling with the butts of their musquets, the motley crew who thrust each other forward, to catch a glance at the unfortunate object of trial, as she should pass from the adjacent prison to the Court in which her fate was to be determined. All must have occasionally observed with disgust, the apathy with which the vulgar gaze on scenes of this nature, and how seldom, unless when their sympathies are called forth by some striking and extraordinary circumstance, the crowd evince any interest deeper than that of callous, unthinking bustle, and brutal curiosity. They laugh, jest, quarrel, and push each other to and fro, with the same unfeeling indifference as if they were assembled for some holiday sport, or to see an idle procession. Occasionally, however, this demeanour, so natural to the degraded populace of a large town, is exchanged for a temporary touch of human affections; and so it chanced on the present occasion.

When Deans and his daughter presented themselves in the Close, and endeavoured to make their way forward to the door of the Courthouse, they became involved in the mob, and subject, of course, to their insolence. As Deans repelled with some force the rude pushes which he received on all sides, his figure and antiquated dress caught the attention of the rabble, who often shew an intuitive sharpness in ascribing the proper character from external appearance.—

> "Ye're welcome, whigs,
> Frae Bothwell briggs,"[5]

sung one fellow, (for the mob of Edinburgh were at that time jacobitically disposed, probably because that was the line of sentiment most diametrically opposite to existing authority.)

> "Mess David Williamson,
> Chosen of twenty,
> Ran up the pu'pit stair,
> And sang Killiecrankie,"[6]

chaunted a syren, whose profession might be guessed by her appearance. A tattered cadie, or errand porter, whom David Deans had jostled in his attempt to extricate himself from the vicinity of these scorners, exclaimed in a strong north-country[7] tone, "Ta deil ding out her Cameronian een—what gies her titles to dunch gentlemans about?"

"Make room for the ruling elder," said yet another; "he comes to see a precious sister glorify God in the Grassmarket."[8]

"Whisht; shame's in ye, sirs," said the voice of a man very loudly, which, as quickly sinking, said in a low but distinct tone, "It's her father and sister."

All fell back to make way for the sufferers; and all, even the very rudest and most profligate, were struck with shame and silence. In the space thus abandoned to them by the mob, Deans stood, holding his daughter by the hand, and said to her, with a countenance strongly and sternly expressive of his internal emotion, "Ye hear with your ears, and ye see with your eyes, where and to whom the back-slidings and defections of professors are ascribed by the scoffers. Not to themselves alone, but to the kirk of which they are members, and to its blessed and invisible Head. Then, weel may we take wi' patience our share and our portion of this out-spreading reproach."

The man who had spoken, no other than our old friend Dumbiedikes, whose mouth, like that of the prophet's ass,[9] had been opened by the emergency of the case, now joined them, and, with his usual taciturnity, escorted them into the Court-house. No opposition was offered to their entrance, either by the guards or door-keepers; and it is even said, that one of the latter refused a shilling of civility-money, tendered him by the Laird of Dumbiedikes, who was of opinion that "siller wad mak a' easy." But this last incident wants confirmation.

Admitted within the precincts of the Court-house, they found the usual number of busy office-bearers, and idle loiterers, who attend on these scenes by choice, or from duty. Burghers gaped and stared; young lawyers sauntered, sneered, and laughed, as in the pit of the theatre; while others apart sat on a bench retired,[10] and reasoned highly, *inter apices juris*, on the doctrines of constructive crime, and the true import of the statute. The bench was prepared for the arrival of the judges; the jurors were in attendance. The crown-counsel, employed in looking over their briefs and notes of evidence, looked grave, and whispered with each other. They occupied one side of a large table placed beneath the bench; on the other, sat the advocates, whom the humanity of the Scottish law (in this particular more liberal[11] than that of the sister country), not only permits, but enjoins, to appear and assist with their advice and skill all persons under trial. Mr Nichil Novit was seen actively instructing the counsel for the pannel, (so the prisoner is called in Scottish law-phraseology,) busy, bustling, and important. When they entered the Court-room, Deans asked the Laird, in a tremulous whisper, "Where will *she* sit?"

Dumbiedikes whispered Novit, who pointed to a vacant space at the bar, fronting the judges, and was about to conduct Deans towards it.

"No!" he said; "I cannot sit by her—I cannot own her—not as yet at least—I will keep out of her sight, and turn mine own eyes elsewhere—better for us baith."

Saddletree, whose repeated interference with the counsel had procured him one or two rebuffs, and a special request that he would concern himself with his own matters, now saw with pleasure an opportunity of playing the person of importance. He bustled up to the poor old man, and proceeded to exhibit his consequence, by securing, through his interest with the bar-keepers and macers, a seat for Deans, in a situation where he was hidden from the general eye by the projecting corner of the bench.

"It's gude to have a friend at court," he said, continuing his heartless harangues to the passive auditor, who neither heard nor replied to them; "few folk but mysell could hae sorted ye out a seat like this—the Lords will be here incontinent, and proceed *instanter* to trial. They winna fence the court as they do at the Circuit—The High Court of Justiciary is aye fenced.—But Lord's sake, what's this o't?—Jeanie, ye are a cited witness—Macer, this lass is a witness—she maun be inclosed—she maun on nae account be at large.—Mr Novit, suld nae Jeanie Deans be inclosed?"

Novit answered in the affirmative, and offered to conduct Jeanie to the apartment, where, according to the scrupulous practice of the Scottish Court, the witnesses remain in readiness to be called into court to give evidence; and separated, at the same time, from all who might influence their testimony, or give them information concerning that which was passing upon the trial.

"Is this necessary?" said Jeanie, still reluctant to quit her father's hand.

"A matter of absolute needcessity," said Saddletree; "wha ever heard of witnesses no being inclosed?"

"It is really a matter of necessity," said the younger counsellor, retained for her sister; and Jeanie reluctantly followed the macer of the court to the place appointed.

"This, Mr Deans," said Saddletree, "is ca'd sequestering a witness; but it's clean different (whilk maybe ye wadna fund out o' yoursel), frae sequestrating ane's estate or effects, as in cases of bankruptcy. I hae aften been sequestered as a witness, for the Sheriff is in the use whiles to cry me in to witness the declarations at precognitions, and so is Mr Sharpitlaw; but I was ne'er like to be sequestrated o' land and gudes but ance, and that was lang syne, afore I was married. But whisht, whisht! here's the Court coming."

As he spoke, the five Lords of Justiciary, in their long robes of scarlet, faced with white, and preceded by their mace-bearer, entered with the usual formalities, and took their places upon the bench of judgment.

The audience rose to receive them; and the bustle occasioned by their entrance was hardly composed, when a great noise and confusion of persons struggling, and forcibly endeavouring to enter at the doors of the Court-room and of the galleries, announced that the prisoner was about to be placed at the bar. This tumult takes place when the doors, at first only opened to those either having right to be present, or to the better and more qualified ranks, are at length laid open to all whose curiosity induces them to be present on the occasion. With inflamed countenances and dishevelled dresses, struggling with, and sometimes tumbling over each other, in rushed the rude multitude, while a few soldiers, forming, as it were, the centre of the tide, could scarce, with all their efforts, clear a passage for the prisoner to the place which she was to occupy. By the authority of the Court, and the exertions of its officers, the tumult among the spectators was at length appeased, and the unhappy girl brought forward, and placed betwixt two sentinels with drawn bayonets, as a prisoner at the bar, where she was to abide her deliverance for good or evil, according to the issue of her trial.

CHAPTER 22

We have strict statutes, and most biting laws—
The needful bits, and curbs for headstrong steeds—
Which, for these fourteen years, we have let sleep,
Like to an o'ergrown lion in a cave,
That goes not out to prey.

Measure for Measure

"EUPHEMIA Deans," said the presiding Judge, in an accent in which pity was blended with dignity, "stand up, and listen to the criminal indictment now to be preferred against you."

The unhappy girl, who had been stupified by the confusion through which the guards had forced a passage, cast a bewildered look on the multitude of faces around her, which seemed to tapestry, as it were, the walls, in one broad slope from the ceiling to the floor, with human countenances, and instinctively obeyed a command, which rung in her ears like the trumpet of the judgment-day.

"Put back your hair, Effie," said one of the macers. For her beautiful and abundant tresses of long fair hair, which, according to the costume of the country, unmarried women were not allowed to cover with any sort of cap, and which, alas! Effie dared no longer confine with the snood or ribband, which implied purity of maiden fame, now hung unbound and dishevelled over her face, and almost concealed her features. On receiving this hint from the attendant, the unfortunate young woman, with a hasty, trembling, and apparently mechanical compliance, shaded back from her face her luxuriant locks, and showed to the whole court, excepting one individual, a countenance, which, though pale and emaciated, was so lovely amid its agony, that it called forth an universal murmur of compassion and sympathy. Apparently the expressive sound of human feeling recalled the poor girl from the stupor of fear, which predominated at first over every other sensation, and awakened her to the no less painful sense of shame and exposure attached to her present situation. Her eye, which had at first glanced wildly around, was turned on the ground; her cheek, at first so deadly pale, began gradually to be overspread with a faint blush, which increased so fast, that, when in an agony of shame she strove to conceal her face, her temples, her brow, her neck, and all that her slender fingers and small palms could not cover, became of the deepest crimson.

All marked and were moved by these changes, excepting one. It was old Deans, who, motionless in his seat, and concealed, as we have said, by the corner of the bench, from seeing or being seen, did nevertheless keep his eyes firmly fixed on the ground, as if determined that, by no possibility whatever, would he be an ocular witness of the shame of his house.

"Ichabod!" he said to himself—"Ichabod! my glory is departed."

While these reflections were passing through his mind, the indictment, which set forth in technical form the crime of which the pannel stood accused, was read as usual, and the prisoner was asked if she was Guilty, or Not Guilty.

"Not guilty of my poor bairn's death," said Effie Deans, in an accent corresponding in plaintive softness of tone to the beauty of her features, and which was not heard by the audience without emotion.

The presiding Judge next directed the counsel to plead to the relevancy; that is, to state on either part the arguments in point of law, and evidence in point of fact, against and in favour of the criminal; after which it is the form of the Court to pronounce a preliminary judgment, sending the cause to the cognizance of the jury or assize.

The counsel for the crown briefly stated the frequency of the crime of infanticide, which had given rise to the special statute under which the pannel stood indicted. He mentioned the various instances, many of them marked with circumstances of atrocity, which had at length induced the King's Advocate, though with great reluctance, to make the experiment, whether by strictly enforcing the Act of Parliament which had been made to prevent such enormities, their occurrence might be prevented. "He expected," he said, "to be able to establish by witnesses, as well as by the declaration of the pannel herself, that she was in the state described by the statute. According to his information, the pannel had communicated her pregnancy to no one, nor did she allege in her own declaration that she had done so. This secrecy was the first requisite in support of the indictment. The same declaration admitted, that she had borne a male child, in circumstances which gave but too much reason to believe it had died by the hands, or at least with the knowledge or consent, of the unhappy mother. It was not, however, necessary for him to bring positive proof that the pannel was accessory to the murther, nay, nor even to prove that the child was murthered at all. It was sufficient to support the indictment, that it could not be found. According to the stern, but necessary severity of this statute, she who should conceal her pregnancy, who should omit to call that assistance which is most necessary on such occasions, was held already to have meditated the death of her offspring, as an event most likely to be the consequence of her culpable and cruel concealment. And if, under such circumstances, she could not alternatively shew by proof that the infant had died a natural death, or produce it still in life, she must, under the construction of the law, be held to have murthered it, and suffer death accordingly."

The counsel for the prisoner, Mr Fairbrother,[1] a man of considerable fame in his profession, did not pretend directly to combat the arguments of the King's Advocate. He began by lamenting[2] that his senior at the bar, Mr Langtale, had been suddenly called to the county of which he was Sheriff, and that he had been applied to, on short warning, to give the pannel his assistance in this interesting case. He had had little time, he said, to make up for his inferiority to his learned brother by long and minute research; and he was afraid he might give a specimen of his incapacity, by being compelled to admit the accuracy of the indictment under the statute. "It was enough for their Lordships," he observed, "to know, that such was the law, and he admitted the Advocate had a right to call for the usual interlocutor of relevancy." But he stated, "that when he came to establish his case by proof, he trusted to make out circumstances which would satisfactorily elide the charge in the libel. His client's story was a short, but most melancholy one. She was bred up in the strictest tenets of religion and virtue, the daughter of a worthy and conscientious person, who in evil times had established a character for courage and religion, by becoming a sufferer for conscience-sake."

David Deans gave a convulsive start at hearing himself thus mentioned, and then resumed the situation, in which, with his face stooped against his hands, and both resting against the corner of the elevated bench on which the Judges sate, he had hitherto listened to the procedure in the trial. The whig lawyers seemed to be interested; the tories put up their lip.[3]

"Whatever may be our difference of opinion," resumed the lawyer, whose business it was to carry his whole audience with him if possible, "concerning the peculiar tenets of these people," (here Deans groaned deeply) "it is impossible to deny them the praise of sound, and even rigid morals, or the merit of training up their children in the fear of God; and yet it was the daughter of such a person whom a jury would shortly be called upon, in the absence of evidence, and upon mere presumptions, to convict of a crime, more properly belonging to an heathen, or a savage, than to a Christian and civilized country. It was true," he admitted, "that the excellent nurture and early instruction which the poor girl had received, had not been sufficient to preserve her from guilt and error. She had fallen a sacrifice to an inconsiderate affection for a young man of prepossessing manners, as he had been informed, but of a very dangerous and desperate character. She was seduced under promise of marriage—a promise, which the fellow might have, perhaps, done her justice by keeping, had he not at that time been called upon by the law to atone for a crime, violent and desperate in itself, but which became the preface to another eventful history, every step of which was marked by blood and guilt, and the final termination of which had not even yet arrived. He believed that no one would hear him without surprise, when he stated that the father of this infant now amissing, and said by the learned Advocate to have been murdered, was no other than the notorious George Robertson, the accomplice of Wilson, the hero of the memorable escape from the Tolbooth Church, and, as no one knew better than his learned friend the Advocate, the principal actor in the Porteous conspiracy."—

"I am sorry to interrupt a counsel in such a case as the present," said the presiding Judge; "but I must remind the learned gentleman, that he is travelling out of the case before us."

The counsel bowed, and resumed. "He only judged it necessary," he said, "to mention the name and situation of Robertson, because the circumstance in which that character was placed, went a great way in accounting for the silence on which his Majesty's counsel had laid so much weight, as affording proof that his client proposed to allow no fair play for its life, to the helpless being whom she was about to bring into the world. She had not announced to her friends that she had been seduced from the path of honour—and why had she not done so?—Because she expected daily to be restored to character, by her seducer doing her that justice which she knew to be in his power, and believed to be in his inclination. Was it natural—was it reasonable—was it fair, to expect that she should, in the interim, become *felo de se* of her own character, and proclaim her frailty to the world, when she had every reason to expect, that, by concealing it for a season, it might be veiled for ever? Was it not, on the contrary, pardonable, that a young woman in such a situation should be found far from disposed to make a confidante of every prying gossip, who, with sharp eyes, and eager ears, pressed upon her for an explanation of suspicious circumstances, which females in the lower—he might say which females of all ranks are so alert in noticing, that they sometimes discover them where they do not exist? Was it strange, or was it criminal, that she should have repelled their inquisitive impertinence, with petulant denials? The sense and feeling of all who heard him, would answer directly in the negative. But although his client had thus remained silent towards those to whom she was not called upon to communicate her situation,—to whom," said the learned gentleman, "I will add, it would have been unadvised and improper in her to have done so; yet, I trust, I shall remove this case most triumphantly from under the statute, and obtain the unfortunate young woman an honourable dismission from your Lordships' bar, by shewing that she did, in due time and place, and to a person most fit for such confidence, mention the calamitous circumstances in which she found herself. This occurred after Robertson's conviction, and when he was lying in prison in expectation of the fate which his comrade Wilson afterwards suffered, and from which he himself so strangely escaped. It was then, when all hopes of having her honour repaired by wedlock vanished from her eyes,—when an union with one in Robertson's situation, if still practicable, might, perhaps, have been regarded rather as an addition to her disgrace—it was *then*, that I trust to be able to prove, that the prisoner communicated and consulted with her sister, a young woman several years older than herself, the daughter of her father, if I mistake not, by a former marriage, upon the perils and distress of her unhappy situation."

"If, indeed, you are able to instruct *that* point, Mr Fairbrother," said the presiding Judge——

"If I am indeed able to instruct that point, my Lord," resumed Mr Fairbrother, "I trust not only to serve my client, but to relieve your Lordships from that which I know you feel the most painful duty of your high office; and to give all who now hear me the exquisite pleasure of beholding a creature so young, so ingenuous, and so beautiful, as she that is now at the bar of your Lordships' Court, dismissed from thence in safety and in honour."

This address seemed to affect many of the audience, and was followed by a slight murmur of applause. Deans, as he heard his

daughter's beauty and innocent appearance appealed to, was involuntarily about to turn his eyes towards her; but, recollecting himself, he
bent them again on the ground with stubborn resolution.

"Will not my learned brother, on the other side of the bar,"
continued the advocate, after a short pause, "share in this general joy,
since I know, while he discharges his duty in bringing an accused
person here, no one rejoices more in their being freely and honourably
sent hence? My learned brother shakes his head doubtfully, and lays
his hand on the pannel's declaration. I understand him perfectly—he
would insinuate that the facts now stated to your Lordships are
inconsistent with the confession of Euphemia Deans herself. I need
not remind your Lordships, that her present defence is no whit to be
narrowed within the bounds of her former confession; and that it is
not by any account which she may formerly have given of herself, but
by what is now to be proved for or against her, that she must
ultimately stand or fall. I am not under the necessity of accounting for
her chusing to drop out of her declaration the circumstance of her
confession to her sister. She might not be aware of its importance; she
might be afraid of implicating her sister; she might even have forgotten
the circumstance entirely, in the terror and distress of mind incidental
to the arrest of so young a creature on a charge so heinous. Any of
these reasons are sufficient to account for her having suppressed the
truth in this instance, at whatever risk to herself; and I incline most to
her erroneous fear of criminating her sister, because I observe she has
had a similar tenderness towards her lover, (however undeserved on
his part), and has never once mentioned Robertson's name from
beginning to end of her declaration.

"But, my Lords," continued Fairbrother, "I am aware the King's
Advocate will expect me to shew, that the proof I offer is consistent
with other circumstances of the case, which I do not and cannot deny.
He will demand of me how Effie Deans's confession to her sister,
previous to her delivery, is reconcileable with the mystery of the
birth,—with the disappearance, perhaps the murder (for I will not
deny a possibility which I cannot disprove), of the infant. My Lords,
the explanation of this is to be found in the placability, perchance, I
may say, in the facility and pliability, of the female sex. The *dulcis
Amaryllidis irae*,[4] as your Lordships well know, are easily appeased;
nor is it possible to conceive a woman so atrociously offended by the
man whom she has loved, but that she will retain a fund of forgiveness,
upon which his penitence, whether real or affected, may draw largely,

with a certainty that his bills will be answered.[5] We can prove, by a letter produced in evidence, that this villain Robertson, from the bottom of the dungeon whence he already probably meditated the escape, which he afterwards accomplished by the assistance of his comrade, contrived to exercise authority over the mind, and to direct the motions, of this unhappy girl. It was in compliance with his injunctions, expressed in that letter, that the pannel was prevailed upon to alter the line of conduct which her own better thoughts had suggested; and, instead of resorting, when her time of travail approached, to the protection of her own family, was induced to confide herself to the charge of some vile agent of this nefarious seducer, and by her conducted to one of those solitary and secret purlieus of villainy, which, to the shame of our police, still are suffered to exist in the suburbs of this city, where, with the assistance, and under the charge, of a person of her own sex, she bore a male-child, under circumstances which added treble bitterness to the woe denounced against our original mother.[6] What purpose Robertson had in all this, it is hard to tell or even to guess. He may have meant to marry the girl, for her father is a man of substance. But, for the termination of the story, and the conduct of the woman whom he had placed about the person of Euphemia Deans, it is still more difficult to account. The unfortunate young woman was visited by the fever incidental to her situation. In this fever she appears to have been deserted by the person that waited on her, and, on recovering her senses, she found that she was childless in that abode of misery. Her infant had been carried off, perhaps for the worst purposes, by the wretch that waited on her. It may have been murdered for what I can tell."

He was here interrupted by a piercing shriek, uttered by the unfortunate prisoner. She was with difficulty brought to compose herself. Her counsel availed himself of the tragical interruption, to close his pleading with effect.

"My Lords," said he, "in that piteous cry you heard the eloquence of maternal affection, far surpassing the force of my poor words— Rachael weeping for her children![7] Nature herself bears testimony in favour of the tenderness and acuteness of the prisoner's parental feelings. I will not dishonour her plea by adding a word more."

"Heard ye ever the like o' that, Laird?" said Saddletree to Dumbiedikes, when the Counsel had ended his speech. "There's a chield can spin a muckle pirn out of a wee tait of tow![8] Deil haet he kens mair about it than what's in the declaration, and a surmise that Jeanie

Deans suld hae been able to say something about her sister's situation, whilk surmise, Mr Crossmyloof says, rests on sma' authority.—And he's cleckit this great muckle bird out o' this wee egg! And when puir Effie skirld, sae clever as he clinkd it intill his pleading! He could wile the very flounders out o' the Firth.—What gard my father no send me to Utrecht?—But whisht, the Court is gaun to pronounce the interlocutor of relevancy."

And accordingly the Judges, after a few words, recorded their judgment, which bore, that the indictment, if proved, was relevant to infer the pains of law: And that the defence, that the pannel had communicated her situation to her sister, was a relevant defence: And, finally, appointed the said indictment and defence to be submitted to the judgment of an assize.

CHAPTER 23

Most righteous judge! a sentence.—Come, prepare.
Merchant of Venice

It is by no means my intention to describe minutely the forms of a Scottish criminal trial, nor am I sure that I could draw up an account so intelligible and accurate as to abide the criticism of the gentlemen of the long robe. It is enough to say that the jury was impannelled, and the case proceeded. The prisoner was again required to plead to the charge, and she again replied, "Not Guilty," in the same heart-thrilling tone as before.

The crown counsel then called two or three female witnesses, by whose testimony it was established, that Effie's situation had been remarked by them, that they had taxed her with the fact, and that her answers had amounted to an angry and petulant denial of what they charged her with. But, as very frequently happens, the declaration of the pannel or accused party herself was the evidence which bore hardest upon her case.

In the event of these Tales ever finding their way across the Border, it may be proper to apprize the southern reader that it is the practice in Scotland, on apprehending a suspected person, to subject him to a judicial examination before a magistrate. He is not compelled to answer any of the questions asked at him, but may remain silent if he sees it his interest to do so. But whatever answers he chuses to give are formally written down, and being subscribed by himself and the magistrate, are produced against the accused in case of his being brought to trial. It is true, that these declarations are not produced as being in themselves evidence properly so called, but only as *adminicles* of testimony, tending to corroborate what is considered as legal and proper evidence. Notwithstanding this nice distinction, however, introduced by lawyers to reconcile this procedure to their own general rule, that a man cannot be required to bear witness against himself, it nevertheless usually happens that these declarations become the means of condemning the accused, as it were, out of their own mouths. The prisoner, upon these previous examinations, has indeed the privilege of remaining silent if he pleases; but every man necessarily feels that a refusal to answer natural and pertinent interrogatories, put by judicial authority, is in itself a strong proof of guilt, and will certainly lead to his being committed to prison; and few can renounce the hope of obtaining liberty, by giving some specious account of themselves, and shewing apparent frankness in explaining their motives and accounting for their conduct. It, therefore, seldom happens that the prisoner refuses to give a judicial declaration, in which, nevertheless, either by letting out too much of the truth, or by endeavouring to substitute a fictitious story, he almost always exposes himself to suspicion and to contradictions, which weigh heavily in the minds of the jury.

The declaration of Effie Deans was uttered on other principles, and the following is a sketch of its contents, given in the judicial form, in which they may still be found in the Books of Adjournal.

The declarant admitted a criminal intrigue with an individual whose name she desired to conceal. "Being interrogated what her reason was for secrecy on this point? She declared, that she had no right to blame that person's conduct more than she did her own, and that she was willing to confess her own faults, but not to say any thing which might criminate the absent. Interrogated, if she confessed her situation to any one, or made any preparation for her confinement? Declares, she did not. And being interrogated, why she forbore to take steps which her situation so peremptorily required? Declares, she was ashamed to tell her friends, and she trusted the person she has mentioned would provide for her and the infant. Interrogated, if he did so? Declares, that he did not do so personally; but that it was not his fault, for that the declarant is convinced he would have laid down his life sooner than the bairn or she had come to harm. Interrogated, what prevented him from keeping his promise? Declares, that it was impossible for him to do so, he being under trouble at the time, and declines farther answer to this question. Interrogated, where she was from the period she left her master, Mr Saddletree's family, until her appearance at her father's, at St Leonard's, the day before she was apprehended? Declares, she does not remember. And, on the interrogatory being repeated, declares, she does not mind muckle about it, for she was very ill. On the question being again repeated, she declares, she will tell the truth, if it should be the undoing of her, so long as she is not asked to tell on other folk; and admits, that she passed that interval of time in the lodging of a woman, an acquaintance of that person who had wished her to that place to be delivered, and that she was there delivered accordingly of a male child. Interrogated, what was the name of that person? Declares and refuses to answer this question. Interrogated, where she lives? Declares, she has no certainty, for that she was taken to the lodging aforesaid under cloud of night. Interrogated, if the lodging was in the city or suburbs? Declares and refuses to answer that question. Interrogated, whether, when she left the house of Mr Saddletree, she went up or down the street? Declares and refuses to answer the question. Interrogated, whether she had ever seen the woman before she was wished to her, as she termed it, by the person whose name she refuses to answer? Declares and replies, not to her knowledge. Interrogated, whether this woman was introduced to her by the said person verbally, or by writing? Declares, she has no freedom to answer this question. Interrogated, if the child was alive when it was born? Declares, that—God help her and it!—it certainly was alive. Interrogated, if it died a natural death after birth? Declares, not to her knowledge. Interrogated, where it now is? Declares, she would give her right hand to ken, but that she never hopes to see mair than the banes of it. And being interrogated, why she supposes it is now dead? the declarant wept bitterly, and made no answer. Interrogated, if the woman, in whose lodging she was, seemed to be a fit person to be with her in that situation? Declares, she might be fit enough for skill, but that she was an hard-hearted bad woman. Interrogated, if there was any other person in the lodging excepting themselves two? Declares, that she thinks there was another woman, but her head was so carried with pain of body and trouble of mind, that she minded her very little. Interrogated, when the child was taken away from her? Declares, that she fell in a fever, and was light-headed, and when she came to her own mind, the woman told her the bairn was dead; and that the declarant answered, if it was dead it had had foul play. That, thereupon, the woman was very sair on her, and gave her much ill-language; and that the deponent was frightened, and crawled out of the house when her back was turned, and went home to Saint Leonard's Crags, as well as a woman in her condition dought.[*] Interrogated, why she did not tell her story to her sister and father, and get force to search the house for her child, dead or alive? Declares, it was her purpose to do so, but she had not time. Interrogated, why she now conceals the name of the woman, and the place of her abode? The declarant remained silent for a time, and then said, that to do so

[* *i.e.* was able to do.]

could not repair the skaith that was done, but might be the occasion of more. Interrogated, whether she had herself, at any time, had any purpose of putting away the child by violence? Declares, Never; so might God be merciful to her—and then again declares Never, when she was in her perfect senses; but what bad thoughts the Enemy might put into her brain when she was out of herself, she cannot answer for. And again solemnly interrogated, declares, that she would have been drawn with wild horses, rather than have touched the bairn with an unmotherly hand. Interrogated, declares, that among the ill language the woman gave her, she did say sure enough that the declarant had hurt the bairn when she was in the brain-fever; but that the declarant does not believe that she said this from any other cause than to frighten her, and make her be silent. Interrogated, what else the woman said to her? Declares, that when the declarant cried loud for her bairn, and was like to raise the neighbours, the woman threatened her, that they that could stop the wean's skirling would stop hers, if she did not keep a' the lounder.[*] And that this threat, with the manner of the woman, made the declarant conclude, that the bairn's life was gone, and her own in danger, for that the woman was a desperate bad woman, as the declarant judged, from the language she used. Interrogated, declares, that the fever and delirium were brought on her by hearing bad news, suddenly told to her, but refuses to say what the said news related to. Interrogated, why she does not now communicate these particulars, which might, perhaps, enable the magistrate to ascertain whether the child is living or dead; and requested to observe, that her refusing to do so, exposes her own life, and leaves the child in bad hands; as also, that her present refusal to answer on such points, is inconsistent with her alleged intention to make a clean breast to her sister? Declares, that she kens the bairn is now dead, or, if living, there is one that will look after it; that for her own living or dying, she is in God's hands, who knows her innocence of harming her bairn with her will or knowledge; and that she has altered her resolution of speaking out, which she entertained when she left the woman's lodging, on account of a matter which she has since learned. And declares, in general, that she is wearied, and will answer no more questions at this time."

Upon a subsequent examination, Euphemia Deans adhered to the declaration she had formerly made, with this addition, that a paper

[* i.e. the quieter.]

found in her trunk being shewn to her, she admitted that it contained the credentials, in consequence of which she resigned herself to the conduct of the woman at whose lodgings she was delivered of the child. Its tenor ran thus:—

"DEAREST EFFIE,

"I have gotten the means to send to you by a woman who is well qualified to assist you in your approaching streight; she is not what I could wish her, but I cannot do better for you in my present condition. I am obliged to trust to her in this present calamity, for myself and you too. I hope for the best, though I am now in a sore pinch; yet thought is free[1]—I think Handie Dandie and I may queer the stifler* for all that is come and gone. You will be angry for me writing this, to my little Cameronian Lily; but if I can but live to be a comfort to you, and a father to your babie, you will have plenty of time to scold.—Once more let none know your counsel—my life depends on this hag, d—n her—she is both deep and dangerous, but she has more wiles and wit than ever were in a beldame's head, and has cause to be true to me. Farewell, my Lily—Do not droop on my account—in a week I will be yours, or no more my own."

Then followed a postscript. "If they must truss me, I will repent of nothing so much, even at the last hard pinch, as of the injury I have done my Lily."

Effie refused to say from whom she had received this letter, but enough of the story was now known, to ascertain that it came from Robertson; and from the date, it appeared to have been written about the time when Andrew Wilson (called for a nickname Handie Dandie) and he were meditating their first abortive attempt to escape, which miscarried in the manner mentioned in the beginning of this history.

The evidence of the Crown being concluded, the counsel for the prisoner began to lead a proof in her defence. The first witnesses were examined upon the girl's character. All gave her an excellent one, but none with more feeling than worthy Mrs Saddletree, who, with the tears on her cheeks, declared, that she could not have had a higher opinion of Effie Deans, or a more sincere regard for her, if she had been her own daughter. All present gave the honest woman credit for

---

* Avoid the gallows.

her goodness of heart, excepting her husband, who whispered to Dumbiedikes, "That Nichil Novit of yours is but a raw hand at leading evidence, I'm thinking. What signified his bringing a woman here to snotter and snivel, and bather their Lordships? He should hae ceeted me, sir, and I should hae gien them sic a screed o' testimony, they shouldna hae touched a hair o' her head."

"Hadna ye better get up and try't yet?" said the Laird. "I'll mak a sign to Novit."

"Na, na," said Saddletree, "thank ye for naething, neighbour—that would be ultroneous evidence, and I ken what belangs to that; but Nichil Novit suld hae had me ceeted *debito tempore*." And wiping his mouth with his silk handkerchief with great importance, he resumed the port and manner of an edified and intelligent auditor.

Mr Fairbrother now premised, in a few words, "that he meant to bring forward his most important witness, upon whose evidence the cause must in a great measure depend. What his client was, they had learned from the preceding witnesses, and so far as general character, given in the most forcible terms, and even with tears, could interest every one in her fate, she had already gained that advantage. It was necessary, he admitted, that he should produce more positive testimony of her innocence than what arose out of general character, and this he undertook to do by the mouth of the person to whom she had communicated her situation—by the mouth of her natural counsellor and guardian—her sister.—Macer, call into court, Jean, or Jeanie Deans, daughter of David Deans, cowfeeder, at Saint Leonard's Crags."

When he uttered these words, the poor prisoner instantly started up, and stretched herself half-way over the bar, towards the side at which her sister was to enter. And when, slowly following the officer, the witness advanced to the foot of the table, Effie, with the whole expression of her countenance altered, from that of confused shame and dismay, to an eager, imploring, and almost ecstatic earnestness of entreaty, with outstretched hands, hair streaming back, eyes raised eagerly to her sister's face, and glistening through tears, exclaimed, in a tone which went through the heart of all who heard her—"O Jeanie, Jeanie, save me, save me!"

With a different feeling, yet equally appropriate to his proud and self-dependent character, old Deans drew himself back still farther under the cover of the bench, so that when Jeanie, as she entered the court, cast a timid glance towards the place at which she had left him seated, his venerable figure was no longer visible. He sate down on the other side of Dumbiedikes, wrung his hand hard, and whispered, "Ah, Laird, this is warst of a'—if I can but win ower this part—I feel my head unco dizzy; but my Master is strong in his servant's weakness." After a moment's mental prayer, he again started up, as if impatient of continuing in any one posture, and gradually edged himself forward towards the place he had just quitted.

Jeanie in the meantime had advanced to the bottom of the table, when, unable to resist the impulse of affection, she suddenly extended her hand to her sister. Effie was just within the distance that she could seize it with both hers, press it to her mouth, cover it with kisses, and bathe it in tears, with the fond devotion that a Catholic would pay to a guardian saint descended for his safety; while Jeanie, hiding her own face with her other hand, wept bitterly. The sight would have moved a heart of stone, much more those of flesh and blood. Many of the spectators shed tears, and it was some time before the presiding Judge himself could so far subdue his emotion, as to request the witness to compose herself, and the prisoner to forbear those marks of eager affection, which, however natural, could not be permitted at that time, and in that presence.

The solemn oath,—"the truth to tell, and no truth to conceal, as far as she knew or should be asked at," was then administered by the Judge "in the name of God, and as the witness should answer to God at the great day of judgment;" an awful adjuration, which seldom fails to make some impression even on the most hardened character, and to strike with some fear even the most upright. Jeanie, educated in deep and devout reverence for the name and attributes of the Deity, was, by the solemnity of a direct appeal to his person and justice, awed, but at the same time elevated above all considerations, save those which she could, with a clear conscience, call HIM to witness. She repeated the form in a low and reverent, but distinct tone of voice, after the Judge, to whom, and not to any inferior officer of the Court, the task is assigned in Scotland of directing the witness in that solemn appeal, which is the sanction of his testimony.

When the Judge had finished the established form, he added in a feeling, but yet a monitory tone, an advice, which the circumstances appeared to him to call for.

"Young woman," these were his words, "you come before this Court in circumstances, which it would be worse than cruel not to pity and to sympathize with. Yet it is my duty to tell you, that the truth, whatever its consequences may be, the truth is what you owe to your country, and to that God whose word is truth, and whose name you have now invoked. Use your own time in answering the questions that gentleman" (pointing to the counsel) "shall put to you—But remember, that what you may be tempted to say beyond what is the actual truth, you must answer both here and hereafter."

The usual questions were then put to her: Whether any one had instructed her what evidence she had to deliver? Whether any one had given or promised her any good deed, hire, or reward, for her testimony? Whether she had any malice or ill-will at His Majesty's Advocate, being the party against whom she was cited as a witness? To which questions she successively answered by a quiet negative. But their tenor gave great scandal and offence to her father, who was not aware that they are put to every witness as a matter of form.

"Na, na," he exclaimed, loud enough to be heard, "my bairn is no like the widow of Tekoah²—nae man has putten words into her mouth."

One of the Judges, better acquainted, perhaps, with the Books of Adjournal than with the Book of Samuel, was disposed to make some instant enquiry after this Widow Tekoah, who, as he construed the matter, had been tampering with the evidence. But the presiding Judge, better versed in Scripture history, whispered to his learned brother the necessary explanation; and the pause occasioned by this mistake, had the good effect of giving Jeanie Deans time to collect her spirits for the painful task she had to perform.

Fairbrother, whose practice and intelligence were considerable, saw the necessity of letting the witness compose herself. In his heart he suspected that she came to bear false witness in her sister's cause.

"But that is her own affair," thought Fairbrother; "and it is my business to see that she has plenty of time to regain composure, and to deliver her evidence, be it true, or be it false—*valeat quantum.*"

Accordingly, he commenced his interrogatories with uninteresting questions, which admitted of instant reply.

"You are, I think, the sister of the prisoner?"

"Yes, sir."

"Not the full sister, however?"

"No, sir,—we are by different mothers."

"True; and you are, I think, several years older than your sister?"

"Yes, sir," &c.

After the advocate had conceived that, by these preliminary and unimportant questions, he had familiarized the witness with the situation in which she stood, he asked, "whether she had not remarked her sister's state of health to be altered during the latter part of the term, when she had lived with Mrs Saddletree?"

Jeanie answered in the affirmative.

"And she told you the cause of it, my dear, I suppose," said Fairbrother, in an easy, and, as one may say, an inductive sort of tone.

"I am sorry to interrupt my brother," said the Crown Counsel, rising, "but I am in your Lordships' judgment, whether this be not a leading question."

"If this point is to be debated," said the presiding Judge, "the witness must be removed."

For the Scottish lawyers regard with a sacred and scrupulous horror, every question so shaped by the counsel examining, as to convey to a witness the least intimation of the nature of the answer which is desired from him. These scruples, though founded on an excellent principle, are sometimes carried to an absurd pitch of nicety, especially as it is generally easy for a lawyer who has his wits about him, to elude the objection. Fairbrother did so in the present case.

"It is not necessary to waste the time of the Court, my Lord; since the King's Counsel think it worth while to object to the form of my question, I will shape it otherwise.—Pray, young woman, did you ask your sister any question when you observed her looking unwell?—take courage—speak out."

"I asked her," replied Jeanie, "what ailed her."

"Very well—take your own time—and what was the answer she made?" continued Mr Fairbrother.

Jeanie was silent, and looked deadly pale. It was not that she at any one instant entertained an idea of the possibility of prevarication—it was the natural hesitation to extinguish the last spark of hope that remained for her sister.

"Take courage, young woman," said Fairbrother.—"I asked what your sister said ailed her when you inquired?"

"Nothing," answered Jeanie, with a faint voice, which was yet heard distinctly in the most distant corner of the Court-room,—such an awful and profound silence had been preserved during the anxious interval, which had interposed betwixt the lawyer's question and the answer of the witness.

Fairbrother's countenance fell; but with that ready presence of mind, which is as useful in civil as in military emergencies, he immediately rallied.—"Nothing? True; you mean nothing at *first*—but when you asked her again, did she not tell you what ailed her?"

The question was put in a tone meant to make her comprehend the importance of her answer, had she not been already aware of it. The ice was broken, however, and, with less pause than at first, she now replied,—"Alack! alack! she never breathed word to me about it."

A deep groan passed through the Court. It was echoed by one deeper and more agonized from the unfortunate father. The hope, to which unconsciously, and in spite of himself, he had still secretly clung, had now dissolved, and the venerable old man fell forward senseless on the floor of the Court-house, with his head at the foot of his terrified daughter. The unfortunate prisoner, with impotent passion, strove with the guards, betwixt whom she was placed. "Let me gang to my father—I *will* gang to him—I *will* gang to him—he is dead—he is killed—I hae killed him!"—she repeated in frenzied tones of grief, which those who heard them did not speedily forget.

Even in this moment of agony and general confusion, Jeanie did not lose that superiority, which a deep and firm mind assures to its possessor, under the most trying circumstances.

"He is my father—he is our father," she mildly repeated to those who endeavoured to separate them, as she stooped, shaded aside his grey hairs, and began assiduously to chafe his temples.

The Judge, after repeatedly wiping his eyes, gave directions that they should be conducted into a neighbouring apartment, and carefully attended. The prisoner, as her father was borne from the Court, and her sister slowly followed, pursued them with her eyes so earnestly fixed, as if they would have started from their socket. But when they were no longer visible, she seemed to find, in her despairing and deserted state, a courage which she had not yet exhibited.

"The bitterness of it is now past,"[3] she said, and then boldly addressed the Court. "My Lords, if it is your pleasure to gang on wi' this matter, the weariest day will hae its end at last."

The Judge, who, much to his honour, had shared deeply in the general sympathy, was surprised at being recalled to his duty by the prisoner. He collected himself, and requested to know if the pannel's counsel had more evidence to produce. Fairbrother replied, with an air of dejection, that his proof was concluded.

The King's Counsel addressed the jury for the crown. He said in few words, that no one could be more concerned than he was for the distressing scene which they had just witnessed. But it was the necessary consequence of great crimes to bring distress and ruin upon all connected with the perpetrators. He briefly reviewed the proof, in which he showed that all the circumstances of the case concurred with those required by the act under which the unfortunate prisoner was tried: That the counsel for the pannel had totally failed in proving, that Euphemia Deans had communicated her situation to her sister: That, respecting her previous good character, he was sorry to observe, that it was females who possessed the world's good report, and to whom it was justly valuable, who were most strongly tempted, by shame and fear of the world's censure, to the crime of infanticide: That the child was murdered, he professed to entertain no doubt. The vacillating and inconsistent declaration of the prisoner herself, marked as it was by numerous refusals to speak the truth on subjects, when, according to her own story, it would have been natural, as well as advantageous, to have been candid; even this imperfect declaration left no doubt in his mind as to the fate of the unhappy infant. Neither could he doubt that the pannel was a partner in this guilt. Who else had an interest in a deed so inhuman? Surely neither Robertson, nor Robertson's agent, in whose house she was delivered, had the least temptation to commit such a crime, unless upon her account, with her connivance, and for the sake of saving her reputation. But it was not required of him, by the law, that he should bring precise proof of the murder, or of the prisoner's accession to it. It was the very purpose of the statute to substitute a certain chain of presumptive evidence in place of a probation, which, in such cases, it was peculiarly difficult to obtain. The jury might peruse the statute itself, and they had also the libel and interlocutor of relevancy to direct them in point of law. He put it to the conscience of the jury, that under both he was entitled to a verdict of Guilty.

The charge of Fairbrother was much cramped by his having failed in the proof which he expected to lead. But he fought his losing cause with courage and constancy. He ventured to arraign the severity of the statute under which the young woman was tried. "In all other cases," he said, "the first thing required of the criminal prosecutor was, to prove unequivocally that the crime libelled had actually been committed, which lawyers called proving the *corpus delicti*. But this statute, made doubtless with the best intentions, and under the impulse of a just horror for the unnatural crime of infanticide, run the risk of itself occasioning the worst of murders, the death of an innocent person, to atone for a supposed crime which may never have been committed by any one. He was so far from acknowledging the alleged probability of the child's violent death, that he could not even allow that there was evidence of its having ever lived."

The King's Counsel pointed to the woman's declaration; to which the counsel replied—"A production concocted in a moment of terror and agony which approached to insanity," he said, "his learned brother well knew was no sound evidence against the party who emitted it. It was true, that a judicial confession, in presence of the Justices themselves, was the strongest of all proof, in so much that it is said in law, that "*in confitentem nullæ sunt partes judicis.*"[4] But this was true of judicial confession only, by which law meant that which is made in presence of the justices, and the sworn inquest. Of extrajudicial confession, all authorities held with the illustrious Farinaceus, and Mattheus,[5] "*confessio extrajudicialis in se nulla est, et quod nullum est, non potest adminiculari.*"[6] It was totally inept, and void of all strength and effect from the beginning; incapable, therefore, of being bolstered up or supported, or, according to the law-phrase, adminiculated, by other presumptive circumstances. In the present case, therefore, letting the extra-judicial confession go, as it ought to go, for nothing," he contended, "the prosecutor had not made out the second quality of the statute, that a live child had been born; and *that*, at least, ought to be established before presumptions were received that it had been murdered. If any of the assize," he said, "should be of opinion that this was dealing rather narrowly with the statute, they ought to consider that it was in its nature highly penal, and therefore entitled to no favourable construction."

He concluded a learned speech, with an elegant peroration on the scene they had just witnessed, during which Saddletree fell fast asleep.

It was now the presiding Judge's turn to address the jury. He did so briefly and distinctly.

"It was for the jury," he said, "to consider whether the prosecutor had made out his plea. For himself, he sincerely grieved to say, that a shadow of doubt remained not upon his mind concerning the verdict which the inquest had to bring in. He would not follow the prisoner's counsel through the impeachment which he had brought against the statute of King William and Queen Mary. He and the jurors were sworn to judge according to the laws as they stood, not to criticise, or to evade, or even to justify them. In no civil case would a counsel have been permitted to plead his client's case in the teeth of the law; but in the hard situation in which counsel were often placed in the Criminal

Court, as well as out of favour to all presumptions of innocence, he had not inclined to interrupt the learned gentleman, or narrow his plea. The present law, as it now stood, had been instituted by the wisdom of their fathers, to check the alarming progress of a dreadful crime; when it was found too severe for its purpose, it would doubtless be altered by the wisdom of the legislature; at present it was the law of the land, the rule of the court, and, according to the oath which they had taken, it must be that of the jury. This unhappy girl's situation could not be doubted; that she had borne a child, and that the child had disappeared, were certain facts. The learned counsel had failed to show that she had communicated her situation. All the requisites of the case required by the statute were therefore before the jury. The learned gentleman had, indeed, desired them to throw out of consideration the pannel's own confession, which was the plea usually urged, in penury of all others, by counsel in his situation, who usually felt that the declarations of their clients bore hard on them. But that the Scottish law designed that a certain weight should be laid on these declarations, which, he admitted, were *quodammodo* extrajudicial, was evident from the universal practice by which they were always produced and read, as part of the prosecutor's probation. In the present case, no person, who had heard the witnesses describe the appearance of the young woman before she left Saddletree's house, and contrasted it with that of her state and condition at her return to her father's, could have any doubt that the fact of delivery had taken place, as set forth in her own declaration, which was, therefore, not a solitary piece of testimony, but adminiculated and supported by the strongest circumstantial proof.

"He did not," he said, "state the impression upon his own mind with the purpose of biassing theirs. He had felt no less than they had done from the scene of domestic misery which had been exhibited before them; and if they, having God and a good conscience, the sanctity of their oath, and the regard due to the law of the country, before their eyes, could come to a conclusion favourable to this unhappy prisoner, he should rejoice as much as any one in Court; for never had he found his duty more distressing than in discharging it that day, and glad he would be to be relieved from the still more painful task, which would otherwise remain for him."

The jury, having heard the Judge's address, bowed and retired, preceded by a macer of Court, to the apartment destined for their deliberation.

CHAPTER 24

Law, take thy victim—May she find the mercy
In yon mild Heaven, which this hard world denies her.

IT was an hour ere the jurors returned, and as they traversed the
crowd with slow steps, as men about to discharge themselves of a
heavy and painful responsibility, the audience was hushed into profound, earnest, and awful silence.

"Have you agreed on your chancellor, gentlemen?" was the first
question of the Judge.

The foreman, called in Scotland the chancellor of the jury, usually
the man of best rank and estimation among the assizers, stepped
forward, and, with a low reverence, delivered to the Court a sealed
paper, containing the verdict, which, until of late years, that verbal
returns are in some instances permitted, was always couched in
writing. The jury remained standing while the Judge broke the seals
and, having perused the paper, handed it, with an air of mournful
gravity, down to the Clerk of Court, who proceeded to engross in the
record the yet unknown verdict, of which, however, all omened the
tragical contents. A form still remained, trifling and unimportant in
itself, but to which imagination adds a sort of solemnity, from the
awful occasion upon which it is used. A lighted candle was placed on
the table, the original paper containing the verdict was inclosed in a
sheet of paper, and, sealed with the Judge's own signet, was transmitted
to the Crown Office, to be preserved among other records of the same
kind. As all this is transacted in profound silence, the producing and
extinguishing the candle seems a type of the human spark which is
shortly afterwards doomed to be quenched, and excites in the spectators something of the same effect which in England is obtained by the
Judge assuming the fatal cap of judgment. When these preliminary
forms had been gone through, the Judge required Euphemia Deans to
attend to the verdict to be read.

After the usual words of style, the verdict set forth, that the Jury
having made choice of John Kirk, Esq. to be their chancellor, and
Thomas Moore,[1] merchant, to be their clerk, did, by a plurality of

voices, find the said Euphemia Deans GUILTY[2] of the crime libelled; but, in consideration of her extreme youth, and the cruel circumstances of her case, did earnestly entreat that the Judge would recommend her to the mercy of the Crown.

"Gentlemen," said the Judge, "you have done your duty—and a painful one it must have been to men of humanity like you. I will, undoubtedly, transmit your recommendation to the throne. But it is my duty to tell all who now hear me, but especially to inform that unhappy young woman, in order that her mind may be settled accordingly, that I have not the least hope of a pardon being granted in the present case. You know the crime has been increasing[3] in this land, and I know farther, that this has been ascribed to the lenity in which the laws have been exercised, and that there is therefore no hope whatever of obtaining a remission for this offence." The jury bowed again, and, released from their painful office, dispersed among the mass of bystanders.

The Court then asked Mr Fairbrother, whether he had any thing to say, why judgment should not follow on the verdict? The counsel had spent some time in perusing, and reperusing the verdict, counting the letters in each juror's name, and weighing every phrase, nay every syllable, in the nicest scales of legal criticism. But the clerk of the jury had understood his business too well. No flaw was to be found, and Fairbrother mournfully intimated, that he had nothing to say in arrest of judgment.

The presiding Judge then addressed the unhappy prisoner:— "Euphemia Deans, attend to the sentence of the Court now to be pronounced against you."

She rose from her seat, and with a composure far greater than could have been augured from her demeanour during some parts of the trial, abode the conclusion of the awful scene. So nearly does the mental portion of our feelings resemble those which are corporeal, that the first severe blows which we receive bring with them a stunning apathy, which renders us indifferent to those that follow them. Thus said Mandrin,[4] when he was undergoing the punishment of the wheel; and so have all felt, upon whom successive inflictions have descended with continuous and reiterated violence.

"Young woman," said the Judge, "it is my painful duty to tell you, that your life is forfeited under a law, which, if it may seem in some degree severe, is yet wisely so, to render those of your unhappy situation aware what risk they run, by concealing, out of pride or false shame, their lapse from virtue, and making no preparation to save the lives of the unfortunate infants whom they are to bring into the world. When you concealed your situation from your mistress, your sister, and other worthy and compassionate persons of your own sex, in whose favour your former conduct had given you a fair place, you seem to me to have had in your contemplation, at least, the death of the helpless creature, for whose life you neglected to provide. How the child was disposed of—whether it was dealt upon by another, or by yourself—whether the extraordinary story you have told is partly false, or altogether so, is between God and your own conscience. I will not aggravate your distress by pressing on that topic, but I do most solemnly adjure you to employ the remaining space of your time in making your peace with God, for which purpose such reverend clergymen, as you yourself may name, shall have access to you. Notwithstanding the humane recommendation of the jury, I cannot afford to you, in the present circumstances of the country, the slightest hope that your life will be prolonged beyond the period assigned for the execution of your sentence. Forsaking, therefore, the thoughts of this world, let your mind be prepared by repentance for those of more awful moment—for death, judgment, and eternity.—Doomster, read the sentence."[*]

When the Doomster shewed himself, a tall haggard figure, arrayed in a fantastic garment of black and grey, passmented with silver lace, all fell back with a sort of instinctive horror, and made wide way for him to approach the foot of the table. As this office was held by the common executioner,[5] men shouldered each other backward to avoid even the touch of his garment, and some were seen to brush their own clothes, which had accidentally become subject to such contamination. A sound went through the court, produced by each person drawing in their breath hard, as men do when they expect or witness what is frightful, and at the same time affecting. The caitiff villain yet seemed, amid his hardened brutality, to have some sense of his being the object of public detestation, which made him impatient of being in public, as birds of evil omen are anxious to escape from day-light, and from pure air.

Repeating after the Clerk of Court, he gabbled over the words of the sentence, which condemned Euphemia Deans to be conducted back to the Tolbooth of Edinburgh, and detained there until Wednes-

[* See p. 569 for the note, "Doomster, or Dempster, of Court".]

day the —— day of —— ; and upon that day, betwixt the hours of two
and four o'clock afternoon, to be conveyed to the common place of
execution, and there hanged by the neck upon a gibbet. "And this,"
said the Doomster, aggravating his harsh voice, "I pronounce for
doom."

He vanished when he had spoken the last emphatic word, like a foul
fiend after the purpose of his visitation has been accomplished; but the
impression of horror excited by his presence and his errand, remained
upon the crowd of spectators.

The unfortunate criminal,—for so she must now be termed,—with
more susceptibility, and more irritable feelings than her father and
sister, was found, in this emergence, to possess a considerable share of
their courage. She had remained standing motionless at the bar while
the sentence was pronounced, and was observed to shut her eyes when
the Doomster appeared. But she was the first to break silence when
that evil form had left his place.

"God forgive ye, my Lords," she said, "and dinna be angry wi' me
for wishing it—we a' need forgiveness.—As for myself I canna blame
ye, for ye act up to your lights; and if I have na killed my poor infant,
ye may witness a' that hae seen it this day, that I hae been the means
of killing my grey-headed father—I deserve the warst frae man, and
frae God too—But God is mair mercifu' to us than we are to each
other."[6]

With these words the trial concluded. The crowd rushed, bearing
forward and shouldering each other, out of the court, in the same
tumultuary mode in which they had entered; and, in the excitation of
animal motion and animal spirits, soon forgot whatever they had felt
as impressive in the scene which they had witnessed. The professional
spectators, whom habit and theory had rendered as callous to the
distress of the scene as medical men are to those of a surgical
operation, walked homeward in groupes, discussing the general principle of the statute under which the young woman was condemned, the
nature of the evidence, and the arguments of the counsel, without
considering even that of the Judge as exempt from their criticism.

The female spectators, more compassionate, were loud in exclamation against that part of the Judge's speech which seemed to cut off
the hope of pardon.

"Set him up, indeed," said Mrs Howden, "to tell us that the poor
lassie behoved to die, when Mr John Kirk, as civil a gentleman as is
within the ports of the town, took the pains to prigg for her himsell."

"Ay, but neighbour," said Miss Damahoy, drawing up her thin maidenly form to its full height of prim dignity—"I really think this unnatural business of having bastard bairns should be putten a stop to—There is na a hizzy now on this side of thirty that ye can bring within your doors, but there will be chields—writers-lads, prentice-lads, and what not—coming traiking after them for their destruction, and discrediting ane's honest house into the bargain—I hae nae patience wi' them."

"Hout, neighbour," said Mrs Howden, "we suld live and let live— we hae been young oursells, and we are no aye to judge the warst when lads and lasses forgather."

"Young oursells? and judge the warst?" said Miss Damahoy. "I am no sae auld as that comes to, Mrs Howden; and as for what ye ca' the warst, I ken neither good nor bad about the matter, I thank my stars."

"Ye are thankfu' for sma' mercies, then," said Mrs Howden, with a toss of her head; "and as for you and young—I trow ye were doing for yoursell at the last riding of the Scots Parliament, and that was in the gracious year seven, sae ye can be nae sic chicken at ony rate."

Plumdamas, who acted as squire of the body to the two contending dames, instantly saw the hazard of entering into such delicate points of chronology, and being a lover of peace and good neighbourhood, lost no time in bringing back the conversation to its original subject.

"The Judge didna tell us a' he could hae tell'd us, if he had liked, about the application for pardon, neighbours," said he; "there is aye a wimple in a lawyer's clew; but it's a wee bit of a secret."

"And what is't?—what is't, neighbour Plumdamas?" said Mrs Howden and Miss Damahoy at once, the acid fermentation of their dispute being at once neutralized by the powerful alkali implied in the word secret.

"Here's Mr Saddletree can tell ye that better than me, for it was him that tauld me," said Plumdamas as Saddletree came up, with his wife hanging on his arm, and looking very disconsolate.

When the question was put to Saddletree he laughed scornfully. "They speak about stopping the frequency of child murther," said he, in a contemptuous tone; "do ye think our auld enemies of England, as honest Glendook aye ca's them in his printed Statute-book,[7] care a boddle whether we didna kill ane anither, skin and birn, horse and foot, man, woman, and bairns, all and sindry, *omnes et singulos*, as Mr Crossmyloof says? Na, na, it's no that hinders frae pardoning the bit lassie. But here is the pinch of the plea. The king and queen is sae ill pleased wi' that mistak about Porteous, that deil a kindly Scot will they ever pardon again, either by reprieve or remission, if the haill town o' Edinburgh should be a' hanged on ae tow."

"Deil that they were back at their German kale-yard[8] then, as my neighbour MacCroskie ca's it," said Mrs Howden; "an that's the way they're gaun to guide us."

"They say for certain," said Miss Damahoy, "that King George flang his periwig in the fire when he heard o' the Porteous mob."

"He has done that, they say," replied Saddletree, "for less thing."

"Aweel," said Miss Damahoy, "he might keep mair wit in his anger—but it's a' the better for his wig-maker, I'se warrant."

"The queen tore her biggonets[9] for perfect anger,—ye'll hae heard o' that too?" said Plumdamas. "And the king, they say, kickit Sir Robert Walpole[10] for no keeping down the mob of Edinburgh; but I dinna believe he wad behave sae ungenteel."

"It's dooms truth, though," said Saddletree; "and he was for kickin the Duke of Argyle[*] too."

"Kickin the Duke of Argyle!" exclaimed the hearers at once, in all the various combined keys of utter astonishment.

"Ay, but MacCallummore's blood wadna sit down wi' that; there was risk of Andro Ferrara coming in thirdsman."

"The duke is a real Scotsman—a true friend to the country," answered Saddletree's hearers.

"Ay, troth is he, to king and country baith, as ye sall hear," continued the orator, "if ye will come in bye to our house, for it's safest speaking of sic things *inter parietes*."

When they entered his shop he thrust his prentice boy out of it, and, unlocking his desk, took out, with an air of grave and complacent importance, a dirty and crumpled piece of printed paper; he observed, "This is new corn—it's no every body could shew ye the like o' this. It's the duke's speech about the Porteous mob, just promulgated by the hawkers. Ye shall hear what Ian Roy Cean[†] says for himsell. My correspondent bought it in the Palace Yard, that's like just under the king's nose—I think he claws up their mittans.—It came in a letter about a foolish bill of exchange that the man wanted me to renew for him. I wish ye wad see about it, Mrs Saddletree."

Honest Mrs Saddletree had hitherto been so sincerely distressed

---

[* See note to p. 571, "John Duke of Argyle and Greenwich".]

[† Red John the Warrior, a name personal and proper in the Highlands to John Duke of Argyle and Greenwich, as MacCummin was that of his race or dignity.]

about the situation of her unfortunate protégée, that she had suffered her husband to proceed in his own way, without attending to what he was saying. The words *bill* and *renew* had, however, an awakening sound in them; and she snatched the letter which her husband held towards her, and wiping her eyes, and putting on her spectacles, endeavoured, as fast as the dew which collected on her glasses would permit, to get at the meaning of the needful part of the epistle; while her husband, with pompous elocution, read an extract from the speech.[11]

"I am no minister, I never was a minister, and I never will be one"——

"I didna ken his Grace was ever designed for the ministry," interrupted Mrs Howden.

"He disna mean a minister of the gospel, Mrs Howden, but a minister of state," said Saddletree with condescending goodness, and then proceeded: "Time was when I might have been a piece of a minister, but I was too sensible of my own incapacity to engage in any state affair. And I thank God that I had always too great a value for those few abilities which nature has given me, to employ them in doing any drudgery, or any job of what kind soever. I have, ever since I set out in the world, (and I believe few have set out more early,) served my prince with my tongue; I have served him with any little interest I had, and I have served him with my sword, and in my profession of arms. I have held employments which I have lost, and were I to be to-morrow deprived of those which still remain to me, and which I have endeavoured honestly to deserve, I would still serve him to the last acre of my inheritance, and to the last drop of my blood."——

Mrs Saddletree here broke in upon the orator.—"Mr Saddletree, what *is* the meaning of a' this? Here are ye clavering about the Duke of Argyle, and this man Martingale gaun to break on our hands, and lose us gude sixty pounds—I wonder what duke will pay that, quotha—I wish the Duke of Argyle would pay his ain accounts—He is in a thousand punds Scots on thae very books when he was last at Roystoun[12]—I'm no saying but he's a just nobleman, and that it's gude siller—but it wad drive ane daft to be confused wi' deukes and drakes, and thae distressed folk upstairs, that's Jeanie Deans and her father. And then, putting the very callant that was sewing the curpel out o' the shop, to play wi' blackguards in the close—Sit still, neighbours, it's no that I mean to disturb *you*; but what between courts o' law and courts o' state, and upper and under parliaments, and parliament-houses, here and in London, the gudeman's gaen clean gyte, I think."

The gossips understood civility, and the rule of doing as they would be done by, too well, to tarry upon the slight invitation implied in the conclusion of this speech, and therefore made their farewells and departure as fast as possible, Saddletree whispering to Plumdamas that he would meet him at MacCroskie's, (the low-browed shop in the Luckenbooths, already mentioned), "in the hour of cause, and put MacCallummore's speech in his pocket, for a' the gudewife's din."

When Mrs Saddletree saw the house freed of her importunate visitors, and the little boy reclaimed from the pastimes of the wynd to the exercise of the awl, she went to visit her unhappy relative, David Deans, and his elder daughter, who had found in her house the nearest place of friendly refuge.

CHAPTER 25

> *Isab.*   Alas! what poor ability's in me
>   To do him good?
> *Lucio.*   ——Assay the power you have.
>   *Measure for Measure*

WHEN Mrs Saddletree entered the apartment in which her guests had shrouded their misery, she found the window darkened. The feebleness which followed his long swoon had rendered it necessary to lay the old man in bed. The curtains were drawn around him, and Jeanie sate motionless by the side of the bed. Mrs Saddletree was a woman of kindness, nay, of feeling, but not of delicacy. She opened the half-shut window, drew aside the curtain, and taking her kinsman by the hand, exhorted him to sit up, and bear his sorrow like a good man, and a Christian man, as he was. But when she quitted his hand, it fell powerless by his side, nor did he attempt the least reply.

"Is all over?" asked Jeanie, with lips and cheeks as pale as ashes,—"And is there nae hope for her?"

"Nane, or next to nane," said Mrs Saddletree; "I heard the Judge-carle say it with my ain ears—It was a burning shame to see sae mony o' them set up yonder in their red gowns and black gowns, and a' to take the life o' a bit senseless lassie. I had never muckle broo o' my gudeman's gossips, and now I like them waur than ever. The only wiselike thing I heard ony body say was decent Mr John Kirk of Kirk-knowe, and he wussed them just to get the king's mercy, and nae mair about it. But he spake to unreasonable folk—he might just hae keepit his breath to hae blawn on his porridge."[1]

"But *can* the king gie her mercy?" said Jeanie, earnestly. "Some folk tell me he canna gie mercy in cases of mur——in cases like hers."

"*Can* he gie mercy, hinny?—I weel I wot he *can*, when he likes. There was young Singlesword, that stickit the Laird of Ballencleuch, and Captain Hackum, the Englishman, that killed Lady Colgrain's gudeman, and the Master of Saint Clair,[2] that shot the twa Shaws, and mony mair in my time—to be sure they were gentle blude, and had their kin to speak for them—And there was Jock Porteous the other day—I'se warrant there's mercy an folk could win at it."

"Porteous!" said Jeanie; "very true—I forget a' that I suld maist mind.—Fare ye weel, Mrs Saddletree; and may ye never want a friend in the hour o' distress."

"Will ye no stay wi' your father, Jeanie, bairn?—Ye had better," said Mrs Saddletree.

"I will be wanted ower yonder," indicating the Tolbooth with her hand, "and I maun leave him now, or I will never be able to leave him. I fear na for his life—I ken how strong-hearted he is—I ken it," she said, laying her hand on her bosom, "by my ain heart at this minute."

"Weel, hinny, if ye think it's for the best, better he stay here and rest him, than gang back to St Leonard's."

"Muckle better—muckle better—God bless you—God bless you.— At no rate let him gang till ye hear frae me," said Jeanie.

"But ye'll be back belive?" said Mrs Saddletree, detaining her; "they winna let ye stay yonder, hinny."

"But I maun gang to St Leonard's—there's muckle to be dune, and little time to do it in—And I have friends to speak to—God bless you—take care of my father."

She had reached the door of the apartment, when, suddenly turning, she came back, and knelt down by the bedside.—"O father, gie me your blessing—I dare not go till ye bless me. Say but God bless ye, and prosper ye, Jeanie—try but to say that."

Instinctively, rather than by an exertion of intellect, the old man murmured a prayer, that "purchased and promised blessings[3] might be multiplied upon her."

"He has blessed mine errand," said his daughter, rising from her knees; "and it is borne in upon my mind[4] that I shall prosper."

So saying, she left the room.

Mrs Saddletree looked after her, and shook her head. "I wish she binna roving, poor thing—There's something queer about a' thae Deanses. I dinna like folk to be sae muckle better than other folk— seldom comes gude o't. But if she's gaun to look after the kye at St Leonard's, that's another story, to be sure they maun be sorted.— Grizzie, come up here and tak tent to the honest auld man, and see he wants naething.—Ye silly tawpie," (addressing the maid-servant as she entered,) "what gard ye busk up your cockernony that gate?—I think there's been aneugh the day to gie an awfu' warning about your cock-ups and your fal-lal duds—see what they a' come to," &c. &c. &c. &c.

Leaving the good lady to her lecture upon worldly vanities, we must transport our reader to the cell in which the unfortunate Effie Deans was now immured, being restricted of several liberties which she had enjoyed before the sentence was pronounced.

When she had remained about an hour in the state of stupified horror so natural in her situation, she was disturbed by the opening of the jarring bolts of her place of confinement, and Ratcliffe shewed himself. "It's your sister," he said, "wants to speak t'ye, Effie."

"I canna see naebody," said Effie, with the hasty irritability which misery had rendered more acute—"I canna see naebody, and least of a' her—bid her take care o' the auld man—I am naething to any o' them now, nor they to me."

"She says she maun see ye though," said Ratcliffe; and Jeanie, rushing into the apartment, threw her arms round her sister's neck, who writhed to extricate herself from her embrace.

"What signifies coming to greet ower me," said poor Effie, "when you have killed me?—killed me, when a word of your mouth would have saved me—killed me, when I am an innocent creature—innocent of that guilt at least—and me that wad hae wared body and soul to save your finger from being hurt!"

"You shall not die," said Jeanie, with enthusiastic firmness; "say what ye like o' me—think what ye like o' me—only promise—for I doubt your proud heart—that ye winna harm yourself, and you shall not die this shameful death."

"A *shameful* death I will not die, Jeanie, lass. I have that in my heart—though it has been ower kind a ane—that winna bide shame. Gae hame to our father, and think nae mair on me—I have eat my last earthly meal."

"O this was what I feared!" said Jeanie.

"Hout tout, hinnie," said Ratcliffe; "it's but little ye ken o' thae things. Ane aye thinks at the first dinnle o' the sentence, they hae heart aneugh to die rather than bide out the sax weeks; but they aye bide the sax weeks out for a' that. I ken the gate o't weel; I hae fronted the doomster three times, and here I stand, Jim Ratcliffe, for a' that. Had I tied my napkin strait the first time, as I had a great mind till't—and it was a' about a bit grey cowt, was na worth ten punds sterling—where would I have been now?"

"And how *did* you escape?" said Jeanie, the fates of this man, at first so odious to her, having acquired a sudden interest in her eyes from their correspondence with those of her sister.

"*How* did I escape?" said Ratcliffe, with a knowing wink,—"I tell ye I scapit the way that naebody will escape from this tolbooth while I keep the keys."

"My sister shall come out in the face of the sun,"[5] said Jeanie; "I will go to London, and beg her pardon from the king and queen. If they pardoned Porteous, they may pardon her; if a sister asks a sister's life on her bended knees, they *will* pardon her—they *shall* pardon her—and they will win a thousand hearts by it."

Effie listened in bewildered astonishment, and so earnest was her sister's enthusiastic assurance, that she almost involuntarily caught a gleam of hope, but it instantly faded away.

"Ah, Jeanie! the king and queen live in London, a thousand miles from this—far ayont the saut sea;[6] I'll be gane before ye win there."

"You are mistaen," said Jeanie; "it is no sae far, and they go to it by land; I learned something about thae things from Reuben Butler."

"Ah, Jeanie, ye never learned ony thing but what was gude frae the folk ye keepit company wi'; but I—but I"—she wrung her hands, and wept bitterly.

"Dinna think on that now," said Jeanie; "there will be time for that if the present space be redeemed.[7]—Fare ye weel. Unless I die by the road, I will see the King's face that gies grace.[8]—O, sir," (to Ratcliffe) "be kind to her—She ne'er kend what it was to need stranger's kindness till now—Fareweel—fareweel, Effie—Dinna speak to me—I maunna greet now—my head's ower dizzy already."

She tore herself from her sister's arms, and left the cell. Ratcliffe followed her, and beckoned her into a small room. She obeyed his signal, but not without trembling.

"What's the fule thing shaking for?" said he; "I mean nothing but civility to you—D—n me, I respect you, and I can't help it. You have so much spunk, that, d—n me, but I think there's some chance of your carrying the day. But you must not go to the king till you have made some friend; try the duke—try MacCallummore; he's Scotland's friend—I ken that the great folks dinna muckle like him—but they fear him, and that will serve your purpose as weel. D'ye ken naebody wad gie ye a letter to him?"

"Duke of Argyle?" said Jeanie, recollecting herself suddenly—"what was he to that Argyle that suffered[9] in my father's time—in the persecution?"

"His son or grandson, I'm thinking," said Ratcliffe; "but what o' that?"

"Thank God!" said Jeanie, devoutly clasping her hands.

"You whigs are aye thanking God for something," said the ruffian. "But hark ye, hinny, I'll tell ye a secret. Ye may meet wi' rough customers on the Border, or in the Midland, afore ye get to Lunnon. Now deil ane o' them will touch an acquaintance o' Daddie Ratton's; for though I am retired frae public practice, yet they ken I can do a gude or an ill turn yet—and deil a gude fellow that has been but a twelvemonth on the lay, be he ruffler or padder, but he knows my gybe* as well as the jark† of e'er a queer cuffin‡[10] in England—and there's rogue's Latin for you."

It was, indeed, totally unintelligible to Jeanie Deans, who was only impatient to escape from him. He hastily scrawled a line or two on a dirty piece of paper, and said to her, as she drew back when he offered it, "Hey! what the deil—it wunna bite you, my lass—if it does nae gude, it can do nae ill. But I wish you to show it, if you have ony fasherie wi' ony o' St Nicholas's clerks."

"Alas!" said she, "I do not understand what you mean."

"I mean if ye fall among thieves, my precious,—that is a Scripture phrase,[11] if ye will hae ane—the bauldest of them will ken a scart o' my guse feather.—And now awa wi' ye—and stick to Argyle; if ony body can do the job, it maun be him."

He then conducted her to the door of the prison and permitted her to depart.

After casting an anxious look at the grated windows and blackened walls of the old Tolbooth, and another scarce less anxious at the hospitable lodging of Mrs Saddletree, Jeanie turned her back on that quarter, and soon after on the city itself. She reached Saint Leonard's Crags without meeting any one whom she knew, which, in the state of her mind, she considered as a great blessing. "I must do naething," she thought, as she went along, "that can soften or weaken my heart—it's ower weak already for what I hae to do. I will think and act as firmly as I can, and speak as little."

There was an ancient female servant or rather cottar of her father's, who had lived under him for many years, and whose fidelity was worthy of full confidence. She sent for this woman, and explaining to her that the circumstances of her family required that she should

* Pass.
† Seal.
‡ Justice of Peace.

undertake a journey, which would detain her for some weeks from home, she gave her full instructions concerning the management of the domestic affairs in her absence. With a precision, which, upon reflection, she herself could not help wondering at, she described and detailed the most minute steps which were to be taken, and especially such as were necessary for her father's comfort. "It was probable," she said, "that he would return to St Leonard's to-morrow; certain that he would return very soon—all must be in order for him. He had eneugh to distress him, without being fashed about warldly matters."

In the meanwhile she toiled busily, along with May Hettly, to leave nothing unarranged.

It was deep in the night when all these matters were settled; and when they had partaken of some food, the first which Jeanie had tasted on that eventful day, May Hettly, whose usual residence was a cottage at a little distance from Deans's house, asked her young mistress, whether she would not permit her to remain in the house all night? "Ye hae had an awfu' day," she said, "and sorrow and fear are but bad companions in the watches of the night, as I hae heard the gudeman say himsell."

"They are ill companions, indeed," said Jeanie; "but I maun learn to abide their presence, and better begin in the house than in the field."

She dismissed her aged assistant accordingly,—for so slight was the gradation in their rank of life, that we can hardly term May a servant,—and proceeded to make a few preparations for her journey.

The simplicity of her education and country made these preparations very brief and easy. Her tartan screen served all the purposes of a riding-habit, and of an umbrella; a small bundle contained such changes of linen as were absolutely necessary. Barefooted, as Sancho says,[12] she had come into the world, and barefooted she proposed to perform her pilgrimage; and her clean shoes and change of snow-white thread stockings were to be reserved for special occasions of ceremony. She was not aware, that the English habits of *comfort* attach an idea of abject misery to the idea of a barefooted traveller; and if the objection of cleanliness had been made to the practice, she would have been apt to vindicate herself upon the very frequent ablutions to which, with Mahometan scrupulosity, a Scottish damsel of some condition usually subjects herself. Thus far, therefore, all was well.

From an oaken press or cabinet, in which her father kept a few old books, and two or three bundles of papers, besides his ordinary accounts and receipts, she sought out and extracted from a parcel of notes of sermons, calculations of interest, records of dying speeches of the martyrs, and the like, one or two documents which she thought might be of some use to her upon her mission. But the most important difficulty remained behind, and it had not occurred to her until that very evening. It was the want of money, without which it was impossible she could undertake so distant a journey as she now meditated.

David Deans, as we have said, was easy, and even opulent in his circumstances. But his wealth, like that of the patriarchs of old, consisted in his kine and herds, and in two or three sums lent out at interest to neighbours or relatives, who, far from being in circumstances to pay any thing to account of the principal sums, thought they did all that was incumbent on them when, with considerable difficulty, they discharged "the annual rent." To these debtors it would be in vain, therefore, to apply, even with her father's concurrence; nor could she hope to obtain such concurrence, or assistance in any mode, without such a series of explanations and debates as she felt might deprive her totally of the power of taking the step, which, however daring and hazardous, she knew was absolutely necessary for trying the last chance in favour of her sister. Without departing from filial reverence, Jeanie had an inward conviction that the feelings of her father, however just, and upright, and honourable, were too little in unison with the spirit of the time to admit of his being a good judge of the measures to be adopted in this crisis. Herself more flexible in manner, though no less upright in principle, she felt that to ask his consent to her pilgrimage would be to encounter the risk of drawing down his positive prohibition, and under that she believed her journey could not be blessed in its progress and event. Accordingly, she had determined upon the means by which she might communicate to him her undertaking and its purpose, shortly after her actual departure. But it was impossible to apply to him for money without altering this arrangement, and discussing fully the propriety of her journey; pecuniary assistance from that quarter, therefore, was laid out of the question.

It now occurred to Jeanie that she should have consulted with Mrs Saddletree on this subject. But, besides the time that must now necessarily be lost in recurring to her assistance, Jeanie internally revolted from it. Her heart acknowledged the goodness of Mrs Saddletree's general character, and the kind interest she took in their family misfortunes; but still she felt that Mrs Saddletree was a woman of an ordinary and worldly way of thinking, incapable, from habit and temperament, of taking a keen or enthusiastic view of such a resolution as she had formed, and to debate the point with her, and to rely upon her conviction of its propriety for the means of carrying it into execution, would have been gall and wormwood.[13]

Butler, whose assistance she might have been assured of, was greatly poorer than herself. In these circumstances she formed a singular resolution for the purpose of surmounting this difficulty, the execution of which will form the subject of the next chapter.

CHAPTER 26

'Tis the voice of the sluggard, I've heard him complain,
"You have waked me too soon, I must slumber again;"
As the door on its hinges, so he on his bed,
Turns his side, and his shoulders, and his heavy head.

DR WATTS

THE mansion-house of Dumbiedikes, to which we are now to introduce
our readers, lay three or four miles—no matter for the exact
topography[1]—to the southward of St Leonard's. It had once borne
the appearance of some little celebrity; for the "auld laird," whose
humours and pranks were often mentioned in the ale-houses for about
a mile round it, wore a sword, kept a good horse, and a brace of grey-
hounds;[2] brawled, swore, and betted at cock-fights and horse-matches;
followed Somerville of Drum's hawks,[3] and the Lord Ross's hounds,
and called himself *point device* a gentleman. But the line of Dumbiedikes had vailed its splendour in the present proprietor, who cared
for no rustic amusements, and was as saving, timid, and retired, as his
father had been at once grasping and selfishly extravagant,—daring,
wild, and intrusive.

Dumbiedikes was what is called in Scotland a *single* house; that is,
having only one room occupying its whole depth from back to front, each
of which single apartments was illuminated by six or eight cross lights,
whose diminutive panes and heavy frames permitted scarce so much light
to enter as shines through one well-constructed modern window. This
inartificial edifice,[4] exactly such as a child would build with cards, had
a steep roof flagged with coarse grey stones instead of slates; a half-
circular turret, battlemented, or, to use the appropriate phrase, barti-
zan'd on the top, served as a case for a narrow turnpike-stair, by which
an ascent was gained from story to story; and at the bottom of the said
turret, was an entrance-door studded with large-headed nails. There was
no lobby at the bottom of the tower, and scarce a landing-place opposite
to the doors which gave access to the apartments. One or two low and
dilapidated out-houses, connected by a court-yard wall equally ruinous,
surrounded the mansion. The court had been paved, but the flags

being partly displaced, and partly removed, a gallant crop of docks and thistles sprung up between them, and the small garden, which opened by a postern through the wall, seemed not to be in a much more orderly condition. Over the low-arched gateway, which led into the yard, there was a carved stone, exhibiting some attempt at armorial bearings; and above the inner entrance hung, and had hung for many years, the mouldering hatchment, which announced that umquhile Laurence Dumbie, of Dumbiedikes, had been gathered to his fathers in Newbattle kirk-yard. The approach to this palace of pleasure, was by a road formed by the rude fragments of stone gathered from the fields, and it was surrounded by ploughed, but uninclosed[5] land. Upon a baulk, that is an unploughed ridge of land interposed among the corn, the Laird's trusty palfrey was tethered by the head, and picking a meal of grass. The whole argued neglect and discomfort; the consequence, however, of idleness and sluttish indifference, not of poverty.[6]

In this inner court, not without a sense of bashfulness and timidity, stood Jeanie Deans, at an early hour in a fine spring morning. She was no heroine of romance, and therefore looked with some curiosity and interest on the mansion-house and domains, of which, it might at that moment occur to her, a little encouragement, such as women of all ranks know by instinct how to apply, might have made her mistress. Moreover, she was not possessed of taste beyond her time, rank, and country, and certainly thought the house of Dumbiedikes, though inferior to Holyroodhouse, or the palace at Dalkeith,[7] was still a stately structure in its way, and the land a "very bonnie bit, if it were better seen to and done to." But Jeanie Deans was a plain, true-hearted, honest girl, who, while she acknowledged all the splendour of her old admirer's habitation and the value of his property, never for a moment harboured a thought of doing the Laird, Butler, or herself, the injustice, which many ladies of higher rank would not have hesitated to do to all three, on much less temptation.

Her present errand being with the Laird, she looked round the offices to see if she could find any domestic to announce that she wished to see him. As all was silence, she ventured to open one door;—it was the old Laird's dog-kennel, now deserted, unless when occupied, as one or two tubs seemed to testify, as a washing-house. She tried another—it was the roofless shed where the hawks had been once kept, as appeared from a perch or two not yet completely rotten, and a lure and jesses which hung mouldering on the wall. A third door led to the coal-house, which was well stocked. To keep a very good fire, was one of the few points of domestic management in which Dumbiedikes was positively active; in all other matters of domestic economy he was completely passive, and at the mercy of his house-keeper, the same buxom dame whom his father had long since bequeathed to his charge, and who, if fame did her no injustice, had feathered her nest pretty well at his expence.

Jeanie went on opening doors, like the second Calender[8] wanting an eye, in the castle of the hundred obliging damsels, until, like the said prince errant, she came to a stable. The Highland Pegasus, Rory Bean, to which belonged the single entire stall, was her old acquaintance, whom she had seen grazing on the baulk, and she failed not to recognize his lair by the well-known ancient riding furniture and demi-pique saddle, which half hung on the walls, half trailed on the litter. Beyond the "treviss," which formed one side of the stall, stood a cow, who turned her head and lowed when Jeanie came into the stable, an appeal which her habitual occupations enabled her perfectly to understand, and with which she could not refuse complying, by shaking down some fodder to the animal, which had been neglected like most things else in this castle of the sluggard.[9]

While she was accommodating "the milky mother"[10] with the food which she should have received two hours sooner, a slip-shod wench peeped into the stable, and perceiving that a stranger was employed in discharging the task which she, at length, and reluctantly, had quitted her slumbers to perform, ejaculated, "Eh, sirs! the Brownie! the Brownie!"[11] and fled, yelling as if she had seen the devil.

To explain her terror, it may be necessary to notice, that the old house of Dumbiedikes had, according to report, been long haunted by a Brownie, one of those familiar spirits, who were believed in ancient times to supply the deficiencies of the ordinary labourer—

Whirl the long mop, and ply the airy flail.

Certes, the convenience of such a supernatural assistant could have been nowhere more sensibly felt, than in a family where the domestics were so little disposed to personal activity; yet this serving maiden was so far from rejoicing in seeing a supposed aerial substitute discharging a task which she should have long since performed herself, that she proceeded to raise the family by her screams of horror, uttered as thick as if the Brownie had been flaying her. Jeanie, who had immediately resigned her temporary occupation, and followed the yelling damsel into the court-yard, in order to undeceive and appease her, was there met by Mrs Janet Balchristie, the favourite sultana of the last Laird, as scandal went—the house-keeper of the present. The good-looking, buxom woman, betwixt forty and fifty, (for such we described her at the death of the last Laird) was now a fat, red-faced, old dame of seventy, or thereabouts, fond of her place, and jealous of her authority. Conscious that her administration did not rest on so sure a basis as in the time of the old proprietor, this considerate lady had introduced into the family the screamer[12] aforesaid, who added good features and bright eyes to the powers of her lungs. She made no conquest of the Laird, however, who seemed to live as if there was not another woman in the world but Jeanie Deans, and to bear no very ardent or overbearing affection even to her. Mrs Janet Balchristie, notwithstanding, had her own uneasy thoughts upon the almost daily visits to Saint Leonard's Crags, and often, when the Laird looked at her wistfully and paused, according to his custom before utterance, she expected him to say, "Jenny, I am gaun to change my condition;" but she was relieved by "Jenny, I am gaun to change my shoon."

Still, however, Mrs Balchristie regarded Jeanie Deans with no small portion of malevolence, the customary feeling of such persons towards any one who they think has the means of doing them an injury. But she had also a general aversion to any female, tolerably young, and decently well-looking, who shewed a wish to approach the house of Dumbiedikes and the proprietor thereof. And as she had raised her mass of mortality out of bed two hours earlier than usual, to come to the rescue of her clamorous niece, she was in such extreme bad humour against all and sundry, that Saddletree would have pronounced, that she harboured *inimicitiam contra omnes mortales.*

"Wha the deil are ye?" said the fat dame to poor Jeanie, whom she did not immediately recognize, "scouping about a decent house at sic an hour in the morning?"

"It was ane wanting to speak to the Laird," said Jeanie, who felt something of the intuitive terror which she had formerly entertained for this termagant, when she was occasionally at Dumbiedikes on business of her father's.

"Ane?—And what sort of an ane are ye?—hae ye nae name?—D'ye think his honour has naething else to do than to speak wi' ilka idle tramper that comes about the town, and him in his bed yet, honest man?"

"Dear, Mrs Balchristie," replied Jeanie, in a submissive tone, "D'ye no mind me?—d'ye no mind Jeanie Deans?"

"Jeanie Deans!!" said the termagant, in accents affecting the utmost astonishment; then, taking two strides nearer to her, she peered into her face with a stare of curiosity, equally scornful and malignant—"I say Jeanie Deans indeed—Jeanie Deevil, they had better hae ca'd ye!—A bonnie spot o' wark your tittie and you hae made out, murdering ae puir wean, and your light limmer of a sister to be hangit for't, as weel she deserves!—And the like o' you to come to ony honest man's house, and want to be into a decent bachelor gentleman's room at this time in the morning, and him in his bed?—gae wa', gae wa'."

Jeanie was struck mute with shame at the unfeeling brutality of this accusation, and could not even find words to justify herself from the vile construction put upon her visit, when Mrs Balchristie, seeing her advantage, continued in the same tone, "Come, come, bundle up your pipes and tramp awa[13] wi' ye!—ye may be seeking a father to another wean for ony thing I ken. If it waurna that your father, auld David Deans, had been a tenant on our land, I would cry up the men-folk, and hae ye dookit[14] in the burn for your impudence."

Jeanie had already turned her back, and was walking towards the door of the court-yard, so that Mrs Balchristie, to make her last threat impressively audible to her, had raised her stentorian voice to its utmost pitch. But, like many a general, she lost the engagement by pressing her advantage too far.

The Laird had been disturbed in his morning slumbers by the tones of Mrs Balchristie's objurgation, sounds in themselves by no means uncommon, but very remarkable, in respect to the early hour at which they were now heard. He turned himself on the other side, however, in hopes the squall would blow by, when, in the course of Mrs Balchristie's second explosion of wrath, the name of Deans distinctly struck the tympanum of his ear. As he was, in some degree, aware of the small portion of benevolence with which his housekeeper regarded the family at Saint Leonard's, he instantly conceived that some message from thence was the cause of this untimely ire, and getting out of bed, he slipt as speedily as possible into an old brocaded night-gown, and some other necessary integuments, clapped on his head his father's gold-laced hat, (for though he was seldom seen without it, yet it is proper to contradict the popular report, that he slept in it, as Don Quixote did in his helmet[15]), and opening the window of his bed-room, beheld, to his great astonishment, the well-known figure of Jeanie Deans herself retreating from his gate; while his housekeeper, with arms a-kimbo, fist clenched and extended, body erect, and head shaking with rage, sent after her a volley of Billingsgate oaths. His choler rose in proportion to the surprise, and, perhaps, to the disturbance of his repose. "Hark ye," he exclaimed from the window, "ye auld limb of Satan—wha the deil gies you commission to guide an honest man's daughter that gate?"

Mrs Balchristie was completely caught in the manner. She was aware, from the unusual warmth with which the Laird expressed himself, that he was quite serious in this matter, and she knew that, with all his indolence of nature, there were points on which he might be provoked, and that, being provoked, he had in him something dangerous, which her wisdom taught her to fear accordingly.[16] She began, therefore, to retract her false step as fast as she could. "She was but speaking for the house's credit, and she couldna think of disturbing his honour in the morning sae early, when the young woman might as weel wait or call again; and to be sure, she might make a mistake between the twa sisters, for ane o' them wasna sae creditable an acquaintance."

"Haud your peace, ye auld jade," said Dumbiedikes; "the warst quean e'er stude in their shoon may ca' you cousin, an a' be true that I have heard.—Jeanie, my woman, gang into the parlour—but stay, that winna be redd up yet—wait there a minute till I come doun to let ye in—Dinna mind what Jenny says to ye."

"Na, na," said Jenny, with a laugh of affected heartiness, "never mind me, lass—a' the warld kens my bark's waur than my bite[17]—if ye had had an appointment wi' the Laird, ye might hae tauld me—I am nae uncivil person—gang your ways in bye, hinny," and she opened the door of the house with a master-key.

"But I had no appointment wi' the Laird," said Jeanie, drawing back; "I want just to speak twa words to him, and I wad rather do it standing here, Mrs Balchristie."

"In the open court-yard?—Na, na, that wad never do, lass; we maunna guide ye that gate neither—And how's that douce honest man, your father?"

Jeanie was saved the pain of answering this hypocritical question by the appearance of the Laird himself.

"Gang in and get breakfast ready," said he to his housekeeper— "and, d'ye hear, breakfast wi' us yoursell[18]—ye ken how to manage thae porringers of tea-water—and, hear ye, see abune a' that there's a gude fire.—Weel, Jeanie, my woman, gang in bye—gang in bye, and rest ye."

"Na, Laird," Jeanie replied, endeavouring as much as she could to express herself with composure, notwithstanding she still trembled, "I canna gang in—I have a lang day's darg afore me—I maun be twenty mile o' gate the night yet, if feet will carry me."

"Guide and deliver us!—twenty mile—twenty mile on your feet!" ejaculated Dumbiedikes, whose walks were of a very circumscribed diameter,—"Ye maun never think o' that—come in bye."

"I canna do that, Laird," replied Jeanie; "the twa words I hae to say to ye I can say here; forbye that Mrs Balchristie"—

"The deil flee awa wi' Mrs Balchristie," said Dumbiedikes, "and he'll hae a heavy lading o' her. I tell ye, Jeanie Deans, I am a man of few words, but I am laird at hame, as weel as in the field; deil a brute or body about my house but I can manage when I like, except Rory Bean, my powney; but I can seldom be at the plague, an it binna when my bluid's up."

"I was wanting to say to ye, Laird," said Jeanie, who felt the necessity of entering upon her business, "that I was gaun a lang journey, outbye of my father's knowledge."

"Outbye his knowledge, Jeanie!—Is that right?—Ye maun think o't again—it's no right," said Dumbiedikes, with a countenance of great concern.

"If I were anes at Lunnon," said Jeanie, in exculpation, "I am amaist sure I could get means to speak to the queen about my sister's life."

"Lunnon—and the queen—and her sister's life!" said Dumbiedikes, whistling for very amazement—"the lassie's demented."

"I am no out o' my mind," said she, "and, sink or swim, I am determined to gang to Lunnon, if I suld beg my way frae door to door—and so I maun, unless ye wad lend me a small sum to pay my expences—little thing will do it; and ye ken my father's a man of substance, and wad see nae man, far less you, Laird, come to loss by me."

Dumbiedikes, on comprehending the nature of this application, could scarce trust his ears—he made no answer whatever, but stood with his eyes rivetted on the ground.

"I see ye are no for assisting me, Laird," said Jeanie; "sae fare ye weel—and gang and see my poor father as aften as you can—he will be lonely aneugh now."

"Where is the silly bairn gaun?" said Dumbiedikes; and, laying hold of her hand, he led her into the house. "It's no that I didna think o't before," he said, "but it aye stack in my throat."

Thus speaking to himself, he led her into an old-fashioned parlour, shut the door behind them, and fastened it with a bolt. While Jeanie, surprised at this manœuvre, remained as near the door as possible, the Laird quitted her hand, and pressed upon a spring lock fixed in an oak-pannel in the wainscot, which instantly slipped aside. An iron strong-box was discovered in a recess of the wall; he opened this also, and pulling out two or three drawers, shewed that they were filled with leathern bags, full of gold and silver coin.

"This is my bank, Jeanie lass," he said, looking first at her, and then at the treasure, with an air of great complacence,—"nane o' your goldsmith's bills for me,—they bring folk to ruin."[19]

Then suddenly changing his tone, he resolutely said,—"Jeanie, I will make ye Leddy Dumbiedikes afore the sun sets, and ye may ride to Lunnon in your ain coach, if ye like."

"Na, Laird," said Jeanie, "that can never be—my father's grief—my sister's situation—the discredit to you—"

"That's *my* business," said Dumbiedikes; "ye wad say naething about that if ye were na a fule—and yet I like ye the better for't—ae wise body's aneugh in the married state.[20] But if your heart's ower fu', take what siller will serve ye, and let it be when ye come back again—as gude syne as sune."

"But, Laird," said Jeanie, who felt the necessity of being explicit with so extraordinary a lover, "I like another man better than you, and I canna marry ye."

"Another man better than me, Jeanie?" said Dumbiedikes—"how is that possible?—It's no possible, woman—ye hae kend me sae lang."

"Ay but, Laird," said Jeanie, with persevering simplicity, "I hae kend him langer."

"Langer?—It's no possible!" exclaimed the poor Laird. "It canna be; ye were born on the land. O Jeanie woman, ye haena lookit—ye haena seen the half o' the gear." He drew out another drawer—"A' gowd, Jeanie, and there's bands for siller lent—And the rental book, Jeanie—clear three hunder sterling—deil a wadset, heritable band, or burthen—Ye haena lookit at them, woman—And then my mother's wardrope, and my grandmother's forbye—silk gowns wad stand on their ends their lane,[21] pearlin-lace as fine as spiders' webs, and rings and ear-rings to the boot of a' that—they are a' in the chamber of deas—Oh, Jeanie, gang up the stair, and look at them."

But Jeanie held fast her integrity, though beset with temptations, which perhaps the Laird of Dumbiedikes did not greatly err in supposing were those most affecting to her sex.

"It canna be, Laird—I have said it—and I canna break my word till him, if ye wad gie me the haill barony of Dalkeith, and Lugton into the bargain."

"Your word to *him*," said the Laird, somewhat pettishly; "but wha is he, Jeanie?—wha is he?—I haena heard his name yet—Come now, Jeanie, ye are but queering us—I am no trowing that there is sic a ane in the warld—ye are but making fashion—What is he?—wha is he?"

"Just Reuben Butler, that's schule-master at Libberton," said Jeanie.

"Reuben Butler! Reuben Butler!" echoed the Laird of Dumbiedikes, pacing the apartment in high disdain,—"Reuben Butler, the dominie at Libberton—and a dominie-depute too!—Reuben, the son of my cottar!—Very weel, Jeanie lass, wilfu' woman will hae her way[22]—Reuben Butler! he hasna in his pouch the value o' the auld black coat he wears—but it disna signify." And, as he spoke, he shut successively, and with vehemence, the drawers of his treasury. "A fair offer, Jeanie, is nae cause of feud[23]—Ae man may bring a horse to the water, but twenty winna gar him drink—[24] And as for wasting my substance[25] on other folk's joes"——

There was something in the last hint that nettled Jeanie's honest pride.—"I was begging nane frae your honour," she said; "least of a' on sic a score as ye pit it on.—Gude morning to ye, sir; ye hae been kind to my father, and it isna in my heart to think otherwise than kindly of you."

So saying, she left the room without listening to a faint "But, Jeanie—Jeanie—stay, woman!" And traversing the court-yard with a quick step, she set out on her forward journey, her bosom glowing with that natural indignation and shame, which an honest mind feels at having subjected itself to ask a favour, which had been unexpectedly refused. When out of the Laird's ground, and once more upon the public road, her pace slackened, her anger cooled, and anxious anticipations of the consequence of this unexpected disappointment began to influence her with other feelings. Must she then actually beg her way to London? for such seemed the alternative; or must she turn back, and solicit her father for money; and by doing so lose time, which was precious, besides the risk of encountering his positive prohibition respecting her journey? Yet she saw no medium between these alternatives; and, while she walked slowly on, was still meditating whether it were not better to return.

While she was thus in uncertainty, she heard the clatter of a horse's hoofs, and a well-known voice calling her name. She looked round, and saw advancing towards her on a pony, whose bare back and halter assorted ill with the night-gown, slippers, and laced cocked-hat of the rider, a cavalier of no less importance than Dumbiedikes himself. In the energy of his pursuit, he had overcome even the Highland obstinacy of Rory Bean, and compelled that self-willed palfrey to canter the way his rider chose; which Rory, however, performed with all the symptoms of reluctance, turning his head, and accompanying every bound he made in advance with a side-long motion, which indicated his extreme wish to turn round,—a manœuvre which nothing but the constant exercise of the Laird's heels and cudgel could possibly have counteracted.

When the Laird came up with Jeanie, the first words he uttered were,—"Jeanie, they say ane shouldna aye take a woman at her first word?"[26]

"Ay, but ye maun take me at mine, Laird," said Jeanie, looking on the ground, and walking on without a pause.—"I hae but ae word to bestow on ony body, and that's aye a true ane."

"Then," said Dumbiedikes, "at least ye suldna aye take a man at *his* first word. Ye maunna gang this wilfu' gate sillerless, come o't what like."—He put a purse into her hand. "I wad gie you Rory too, but he's as wilfu' as yoursell, and he's ower weel used to a gate that maybe he and I hae gaen ower aften, and he'll gang nae road else."

"But, Laird," said Jeanie, "though I ken my father will satisfy every penny of this siller, whatever there's o't, yet I wadna like to borrow it frae ane that maybe thinks of something mair than the paying o't back again."

"There's just twenty-five guineas o't," said Dumbiedikes, with a gentle sigh, "and whether your father pays or disna pay, I make ye free till't without another word. Gang where ye like—do what ye like—and marry a' the Butlers in the country, gin ye like—And sae, gude morning to you, Jeanie."

"And God bless you, Laird, wi' mony a gude morning," said Jeanie, her heart more softened by the unwonted generosity of this uncouth character, than perhaps Butler might have approved, had he known her feelings at that moment; "and comfort, and the Lord's peace, and the peace of the world, be with you, if we suld never meet again!"

Dumbiedikes turned and waved his hand; and his pony, much more willing to return than he had been to set out, hurried him homewards so fast, that, wanting the aid of a regular bridle, as well as of saddle and stirrups, he was too much puzzled to keep his seat to permit of his looking behind, even to give the parting glance of a forlorn swain. I am ashamed to say, that the sight of a lover, run away with in night-gown and slippers and a laced hat, by a bare-backed Highland pony, had something in it of a sedative, even to a grateful and deserved burst of affectionate esteem. The figure of Dumbiedikes was too ludicrous not to confirm Jeanie in the original sentiments she entertained towards him.

"He's a gude creature," said she, "and a kind—it's a pity he has sae willyard a powney." And she immediately turned her thoughts to the important journey which she had commenced, reflecting with pleasure, that, according to her habits of life and of undergoing fatigue, she was now amply or even superfluously provided with the means of encountering the expences of the road, up and down from London, and all other expences whatever.

CHAPTER 27

What strange and wayward thoughts will slide
  Into a lover's head:
"O mercy!" to myself I cried,
  "If Lucy should be dead!"

WORDSWORTH

IN pursuing her solitary journey, our heroine, soon after passing the house of Dumbiedikes, gained a little eminence, from which, on looking to the eastward down a prattling brook, whose meanders were shaded with straggling willows and alder trees, she could see the cottages of Woodend and Beersheba, the haunts and habitation of her early life, and could distinguish the common on which she had so often herded sheep, and the recesses of the rivulet where she had pulled rushes[1] with Butler, to plait crowns and sceptres for her sister Effie, then a beautiful, but spoiled child, of about three years old. The recollections which the scene brought with them were so bitter, that, had she indulged them, she would have sate down and relieved her heart with tears.

"But I kend," said Jeanie, when she gave an account of her pilgrimage, "that greeting would do but little good, and that it was mair beseeming to thank the Lord, that had shewn me kindness and countenance by means of a man, that mony ca'd a Nabal and churl, but wha was free of his gudes to me as ever the fountain was free of the stream. And I minded the Scripture about the sin of Israel at Meribah,[2] when the people murmured, although Moses had brought water from the dry rock that the congregation might drink and live. Sae, I wad not trust mysell with another look at puir Woodend, for the very blue reek that came out of the lum-head pat me in mind of the sair change of market-days with us."

In this resigned and Christian temper she pursued her journey, until she was beyond this place of melancholy recollections, and not distant from the village where Butler dwelt, which, with its old-fashioned church[3] and steeple, rises among a tuft of trees, occupying the ridge of an eminence to the south of Edinburgh. At a quarter of a mile's distance is a clumsy square tower, the residence of the Laird of

Libberton, who, in former times, with the habits of the predatory chivalry of Germany, is said frequently to have annoyed the city of Edinburgh, by intercepting⁴ the supplies and merchandize which came to the town from the southward.

This village, its tower, and its church, did not lie precisely in Jeanie's road towards England; but they were not much aside from it, and the village was the abode of Butler. She had resolved to see him in the beginning of her journey, because she conceived him the most proper person to write to her father concerning her resolution and her hopes. There was probably another reason latent in her affectionate bosom. She wished once more to see the object of so early and so sincere an attachment, before commencing a pilgrimage, the perils of which she did not disguise from herself, although she did not allow them so to press upon her mind as to diminish the strength and energy of her resolution. A visit to a lover from a young person in a higher rank of life than Jeanie's, would have had something forward and improper in its character. But the simplicity of her rural habits was unacquainted with these punctilious ideas of decorum, and no notion, therefore, of impropriety crossed her imagination, as, setting out upon a long journey, she went to bid adieu to an early friend.

There was still another motive that pressed upon her mind with additional force as she approached the village. She had looked anxiously for Butler in the court-house, and had expected that certainly, in some part of that eventful day, he would have appeared to bring such countenance and support as he could give to his old friend, and the protector of his youth, even if her own claims were laid aside. She knew, indeed, that he was under a certain degree of restraint; but she still had hoped that he would have found means to emancipate himself from it, at least for one day. In short, the wild and wayward thoughts which Wordsworth has described as rising in an absent lover's imagination, suggested as the only explanation of his absence, that Butler must be very ill. And so much had this wrought on her imagination, that when she approached the cottage in which her lover occupied a small apartment, and which had been pointed out to her by a maiden with a milk-pail on her head, she trembled at anticipating the answer she might receive on enquiring for him.

Her fears in this case had, indeed, only hit upon the truth. Butler, whose constitution was naturally feeble, did not soon recover the fatigue of body and distress of mind which he had suffered, in consequence of the tragical events with which our narrative commenced. The painful idea that his character was breathed on by suspicion, was an aggravation to his distress.

But the most cruel addition, was the absolute prohibition laid by the magistrates on his holding any communication with Deans or his family. It had unfortunately appeared likely to them, that some intercourse might be again attempted with that family by Robertson, through the medium of Butler, and this they were anxious to intercept, or prevent if possible. The measure was not meant as a harsh or injurious severity on the part of the magistrates; but, in Butler's circumstances, it pressed cruelly hard. He felt he must be suffering under the bad opinion of the person who was dearest to him, from an imputation of unkind desertion, the most alien to his nature.

This painful thought, pressing on a frame already injured, brought on a succession of slow and lingering feverish attacks, which greatly impaired his health, and at length rendered him incapable even of the sedentary duties of the school, on which his bread depended. Fortunately, old Mr Whackbairn, who was the principal teacher of the little parochial establishment, was sincerely attached to Butler. Besides that he was sensible of his merits and value as an assistant, which had greatly raised the credit of his little school, the ancient pedagogue, who had himself been tolerably educated, retained some taste for classical lore, and would gladly relax after the drudgery of the school was past, by conning over a few pages of Horace or Juvenal with his usher. A similarity of taste begot kindness, and he accordingly saw Butler's increasing debility with great compassion, roused up his own energies to teaching the school in the morning hours, insisted upon his assistant's reposing himself at that period, and, besides, supplied him with such comforts as the patient's situation required, and his means were inadequate to compass.

Such was Butler's situation, scarce able to drag himself to the place where his daily drudgery must gain his daily bread, and racked with a thousand fearful anticipations concerning the fate of those who were dearest to him in the world, when the trial and condemnation of Effie Deans put the cope-stone upon his mental misery.

He had a particular account of these events from a fellow student, who resided in the same village, and who, having been present on the melancholy occasion, was able to place it in all its agony of horrors before his excruciated imagination. That sleep should have visited his eyes, after such a curfew-note, was impossible. A thousand dreadful visions haunted his imagination all night, and in the morning he was awaked from a feverish slumber, by the only circumstance which could have added to his distress—the visit of an intrusive ass.

This unwelcome visitant was no other than Bartoline Saddletree. The worthy and sapient burgher had kept his appointment at Mac-Croskie's, with Plumdamas and some other neighbours, to discuss the Duke of Argyle's speech, the justice of Effie Deans's condemnation, and the improbability of her obtaining a reprieve. This sage conclave disputed high and drank deep,[5] and on the next morning Bartoline felt, as he expressed it, as if his head was like a "confused progress of writts."[6]

To bring his reflective powers to their usual serenity, Saddletree resolved to take a morning's ride upon a certain hackney, which he, Plumdamas, and another honest shopkeeper, combined to maintain by joint subscription, for occasional jaunts for the purpose of business or exercise. As Saddletree had two children boarded with Whackbairn, and was, as we have seen, rather fond of Butler's society, he turned his palfrey's head towards Libberton, and came, as we have already said, to give the unfortunate usher that additional vexation, of which Imogen[7] complains so feelingly when she says,

> I'm sprighted with a fool—
> Sprighted and angered worse.——

If any thing could have added gall to bitterness,[8] it was the choice which Saddletree made of a subject for his prosing harangues, being the trial of Effie Deans, and the probability of her being executed. Every word fell on Butler's ear like the knell of a death-bell, or the note of a screech-owl.[9]

Jeanie paused at the door of her lover's humble abode upon hearing the loud and pompous tones of Saddletree sounding from the inner apartment, "Credit me, it will be sae, Mr Butler.—Brandy cannot save her.[10]—She maun gang down the Bow wi' the lad in the pioted coat[*][11] at her heels.—I am sorry for the puir lassie, but the law, sir, maun hae its course—

> Vivat Rex,
> Currat Lex,[12]

as the poet has it, in whilk of Horace's odes I know not."

[* The executioner, in a livery of black or dark grey and silver, likened by low wit to a magpie.]

Here Butler groaned, in utter impatience of the brutality and ignorance which Bartoline had contrived to amalgamate into one sentence. But Saddletree, like other prosers, was blessed with a happy obtuseness of perception concerning the unfavourable impression which he generally made on his auditors. He proceeded to deal forth his scraps of legal knowledge without mercy, and concluded by asking Butler, with great self-complacency, "Was it na a pity my father didna send me to Utrecht? Havena I missed the chance to turn out as *clarissimus* an *ictus*, as auld Grunwiggin[13] himsell?—Whatfor dinna ye speak, Mr Butler? Wad I no hae been a *clarissimus ictus*?—Eh, man?"

"I really do not understand you, Mr Saddletree," said Butler, thus pushed hard for an answer. His faint and exhausted tone of voice was instantly drowned in the sonorous bray of Bartoline.

"No understand me, man?—*Ictus* is Latin for a lawyer, is it not?"

"Not that ever I heard of," answered Butler, in the same dejected tone.

"The deil ye didna!—See, man, I got the word but this morning out of a memorial of Mr Crossmyloof's—see there it is, *ictus clarissimus et perti—peritissimus*—it's a' Latin, for it's printed in the Italian types."

"O you mean *juris-consultus.*—*Ictus* is an abbreviation for *juris-consultus.*"

"Dinna tell me, man," persevered Saddletree, "there's nae abbreviates except in adjudications; and this is a' about a servitude of water-drap—that is to say, *tillicidian,** (maybe ye'll say that's no Latin neither) in Mary King's Close,[14] in the High Street."

"Very likely," said poor Butler, overwhelmed by the noisy persever-ance of his visitor. "I am not able to dispute with you."

"Few folks are—few folks are, Mr Butler, though I say it, that should na say it," returned Bartoline, with great delight. "Now it will be twa hours yet or ye're wanted in the schule, and as ye are no weel, I'll sit wi' you to divert ye, and explain t'ye the nature of a *tillicidian*. Ye maun ken the pursuer, Mrs Crombie, a very decent woman, is a friend of mine, and I hae stude her friend in this case, and brought her wi' credit into the court, and I doubtna, that in due time she will win out o't wi' credit, win she or lose she. Ye see, being an inferior tenement or laigh house, we grant ourselves to be burthened wi' the *tillicide*, that is, that we are obligated to receive the natural water-drap

---

* He meant, probably, *stillicidium.*

of the superior tenement, sae far as the same fa's frae the heavens on the roof of our neighbour's house, and from thence by the gutters or eaves upon our laigh tenement. But the other night comes a Highland quean of a lass,[15] and she flashes, God kens what,[16] out at the eastmost window of Mrs MacPhail's house, that's the superior tenement. I believe the auld women wad hae greed, for Luckie MacPhail sent down the lass to tell my friend Mrs Crombie that she had made the gardyloo out of the wrang window, from respect for twa Highlandmen that were speaking Gaelic in the close below the right ane. But luckily for Mrs Crombie, I just chanced to come in in time to break aff the communing, for it's a pity the point suldna be tried. We had Mrs MacPhail into the Ten-Mark Court—The hieland limmer of a lass wanted to swear herself free—but haud ye there, says I"—

The detailed account of this important suit might have lasted until poor Butler's hour of rest was completely exhausted, had not Saddletree been interrupted by the noise of voices at the door. The woman of the house where Butler lodged, on returning with her pitcher from the well,[17] whence she had been fetching water for the family, found our heroine Jeanie Deans standing at the door, impatient of the prolix harangue of Saddletree, yet unwilling to enter until he should have taken his leave.

The goodwoman abridged the period of hesitation by enquiring, "Was ye wanting the gudeman or me, lass?"

"I wanted to speak with Mr Butler, if he's at leisure," replied Jeanie.

"Gang in bye then, my woman," answered the goodwife; and opening the door of the room, she announced the additional visitor with, "Mr Butler, here's a lass wants to speak t'ye."

The surprise of Butler was extreme, when Jeanie, who seldom stirred half a mile from home, entered his apartment upon this annunciation.

"Good God!" he said, starting from his chair, while alarm restored to his cheek the colour of which sickness had deprived it; "some new misfortune must have happened."

"None, Mr Reuben, but what you must hae heard of—but O ye are looking ill yoursell!"—for "the hectic of a moment"[18] had not concealed from her affectionate eye the ravages which lingering disease and anxiety of mind had made in her lover's person.

"No: I am well—quite well," said Butler, with eagerness; "if I can do anything to assist you, Jeanie—or your father."

"Ay, to be sure," said Saddletree; "the family may be considered as limited to them twa now, just as if Effie had never been in the tailzie, puir thing. But Jeanie, lass, what brings you out to Libberton sae air in the morning, and your father lying ill in the Luckenbooths?"

"I had a message frae my father to Mr Butler," said Jeanie, with embarrassment; but instantly feeling ashamed of the fiction to which she had resorted, for her love of and veneration for truth was almost quaker-like, she corrected herself—"that is to say, I wanted to speak with Mr Butler about some business of my father's and puir Effie's."

"Is it law business?" said Bartoline; "because if it be, ye had better take my opinion on the subject than his."

"It is not just law business," said Jeanie, who saw considerable inconvenience might arise from letting Mr Saddletree into the secret purpose of her journey; "but I want Mr Butler to write a letter for me."

"Very right," said Mr Saddletree; "and if ye'll tell me what it is about, I'll dictate to Mr Butler as Mr Crossmyloof does to his clerk. Get your pen and ink *in initialibus*, Mr Butler."

Jeanie looked at Butler, and wrung her hands with vexation and impatience.

"I believe, Mr Saddletree," said Butler, who saw the necessity of getting rid of him at all events, "that Mr Whackbairn will be somewhat affronted, if you do not hear your boys called up to their lessons."

"Indeed, Mr Butler, and that's as true; and I promised to ask a half play-day to the schule, so that the bairns might gang and see the hanging, which canna but have a pleasing effect on their young minds, seeing there is no knowing what they may come to themselves.—Odd so, I didna mind ye were here, Jeanie Deans; but ye maun use yoursell to hear the matter spoken o'.—Keep Jeanie here till I come back, Mr Butler; I winna bide ten minutes."

And with this unwelcome assurance of an immediate return, he relieved them of the embarrassment of his presence.

"Reuben," said Jeanie, who saw the necessity of using the interval of his absence in discussing what had brought her there, "I am bound on a lang journey—I am gaun to Lunnon to ask Effie's life at the king and at the queen."

"Jeanie! you are surely not yourself," answered Butler, in the utmost surprise; "*you* go to London—*you* address the king and queen!"

"And what for no, Reuben?" said Jeanie, with all the composed simplicity of her character; "it's but speaking to a mortal man and woman when a' is done. And their hearts maun be made o' flesh and blood like other folk's, and Effie's story wad melt them were they stane. Forbye, I hae heard that they are no sic bad folk as what the jacobites ca's them."

"Yes, Jeanie," said Butler; "but their magnificence—their retinue—the difficulty of getting audience?"

"I have thought of a' that, Reuben, and it shall not break my spirit. Nae doubt their claiths will be very grand, wi' their crowns on their heads, and their sceptres in their hands, like the great King Ahasuerus[19] when he sate upon his royal throne foreanent the gate of his house, as we are told in Scripture. But I have that within me that will keep my heart from failing, and I am amaist sure that I will be strengthened to speak the errand I came for."

"Alas! alas!" said Butler, "the kings now-a-days do not sit in the gate to administer justice, as in patriarchal times. I know as little of courts as you do, Jeanie, by experience; but by reading and report, I know that the King of Britain does every thing by means of his ministers."

"And if they be upright, God-fearing ministers," said Jeanie, "it's sae muckle the better chance for Effie and me."

"But you do not even understand the most ordinary words relating to a court," said Butler; "by the ministry is meant not clergymen, but the king's official servants."

"Nae doubt," returned Jeanie, "he maun hae a great number mair, I daur to say, than the Duchess[20] has at Dalkeith, and great folk's servants[21] are aye mair saucy than themselves. But I'll be decently put on, and I'll offer them a trifle o' siller, as if I came to see the palace. Or if they scruple that, I'll tell them I'm come on a business of life and death, and then they will surely bring me to speech of the king and queen?"

Butler shook his head. "O, Jeanie, this is entirely a wild dream. You can never see them but through some great lord's intercession, and I think it is scarce possible even then."

"Weel, but maybe I can get that too," said Jeanie, "with a little helping from you."

"From me, Jeanie! this is the wildest imagination of all."

"Ay; but it is not, Reuben—Havena I heard you say, that your grandfather (that my father never likes to hear about) did some gude turn langsyne to the forbear of this MacCallummore, when he was Lord of Lorn?"[22]

"He did so," said Butler, eagerly, "and I can prove it.—I will write to the Duke of Argyle—report speaks him a good kindly man, as he is known for a brave soldier and true patriot—I will conjure him to stand between your sister and this cruel fate. There is but a poor chance of success, but we will try all means."

"We *must* try all means," replied Jeanie; "but writing winna do it— a letter canna look, and pray, and beg, and beseech, as the human voice can do to the human heart. A letter's like the music that the ladies have for their spinets—naething but black scores, compared to the same tune played or sung. It's word of mouth maun do it, or naething, Reuben."

"You are right," said Reuben, recollecting his firmness, "and I will hope that Heaven has suggested to your kind heart and firm courage the only possible means of saving the life of this unfortunate girl. But, Jeanie, you must not take this most perilous journey alone; I have an interest in you, and I will not agree that my Jeanie throws herself away. You must even, in the present circumstances, give me a husband's right to protect you, and I will go with you myself on this journey, and assist you to do your duty by your family."

"Alas, Reuben!" said Jeanie in her turn, "this must not be; a pardon will not gie my sister her fair fame again, or make me a bride fitting for an honest man and an usefu' minister. Wha wad mind what he said in the pu'pit, that had to wife the sister of a woman that was condemned for sic wickedness?"

"But, Jeanie," pleaded her lover, "I do not believe, and I cannot believe, that Effie has done this deed."

"Heaven bless you for saying sae, Reuben," answered Jeanie; "but she maun bear the blame o't after all."

"But that blame, were it even justly laid on her, does not fall on you?"

"Ah, Reuben, Reuben," replied the young woman, "ye ken it is a blot that spreads to kith and kin.—Ichabod—as my poor father says—the glory is departed from our house; for the poorest man's house has a glory, where there are true hands, a divine heart, and an honest fame—And the last has gane frae us a'."

"But, Jeanie, consider your word and plighted faith to me; and would ye undertake such a journey without a man to protect you?— and who should that protector be but your husband?"

"You are kind and good, Reuben, and wad tak me wi' a' my shame, I doubt na. But ye canna but own that this is no time to marry or be given in marriage.[23] Na, if that suld ever be, it maun be in another and a better season.—And, dear Reuben, ye speak of protecting me on my journey—Alas! who will protect and take care of you?—your very limbs tremble with standing for ten minutes on the floor; how could you undertake a journey as far as Lunnon?"

"But I am strong—I am well," continued Butler, sinking in his seat totally exhausted, "at least I will be quite well tomorrow."

"Ye see, and ye ken, ye maun just let me depart," said Jeanie, after a pause; and then taking his extenuated hand, and gazing kindly in his face, she added, "It's e'en a grief the mair to me to see you in this way. But ye maun keep up your heart for Jeanie's sake, for if she isna your wife, she will never be the wife of living man. And now gie me the paper for MacCallummore, and bid God speed me on my way."

There was something of romance in Jeanie's venturous resolution; yet, on consideration, as it seemed impossible to alter it by persuasion, or to give her assistance but by advice, Butler, after some farther debate, put into her hands the paper she desired, which, with the muster-roll in which it was folded up, were the sole memorials of the stout and enthusiastic Bible Butler, his grandfather. While Butler sought this document, Jeanie had time to take up his pocket Bible. "I have marked a scripture," she said, as she again laid it down, "with your kylevine pen, that will be useful to us baith. And ye maun tak the trouble, Reuben, to write a' this to my father, for, God help me, I have neither head nor hand for lang letters at ony time, forbye now; and I trust him entirely to you, and I trust you will soon be permitted to see him. And, Reuben, when ye do win to the speech o' him, mind a' the auld man's bits o' ways for Jeanie's sake; and dinna speak o' Latin or English terms to him, for he's o' the auld warld, and downa bide to be fashed wi' them, though I dare say he may be wrang. And dinna ye say muckle to him, but set him on speaking himsell, for he'll bring himsell mair comfort that way. And O, Reuben, the poor lassie in yon dungeon—but I needna bid your kind heart—gie her what comfort ye can as soon as they will let ye see her—tell her—but I winna speak mair about her, for I maunna take leave o' ye wi' the tear in my ee, for that wad na be canny—God bless ye, Reuben!"

To avoid so ill an omen she left the room hastily, while her features yet retained the mournful and affectionate smile which she had compelled them to wear, in order to support Butler's spirits.

It seemed as if the power of sight, of speech, and of reflection, had left him as she disappeared from the room, which she had entered and retired from so like an apparition. Saddletree, who entered immediately afterwards, overwhelmed him with questions, which he answered without understanding them, and with legal disquisitions, which conveyed to him no iota of meaning. At length the learned burgess recollected that there was a Baron Court to be held at Loanhead that day, and though it was hardly worth while, "he might as weel go to see if there was ony thing doing, as he was acquainted with the baron-baillie, who was a decent man, and would be glad of a word of legal advice."

So soon as he departed, Butler flew to the Bible, the last book which Jeanie had touched. To his extreme surprise, a paper, containing two or three pieces of gold, dropped from the book. With a black lead pencil, she had marked the sixteenth and twenty-fifth verses of the thirty-seventh Psalm,[24]—"A little that a righteous man hath, is better than the riches of many wicked."—"I have been young and am now old, yet have I not seen the righteous forsaken, nor his seed begging their bread."

Deeply impressed with the affectionate delicacy which shrouded its own generosity under the cover of a providential supply to his wants, he pressed the gold to his lips with more ardour than ever the metal was greeted with by a miser. To emulate her devout firmness and confidence seemed now the pitch of his ambition, and his first task was to write an account to David Deans of his daughter's resolution and journey southward. He studied every sentiment, and even every phrase, which he thought could reconcile the old man to her extraordinary resolution. The effect which this epistle produced will be hereafter adverted to. Butler committed it to the charge of an honest clown, who had frequent dealings with Deans in the sale of his dairy produce, and who readily undertook a journey to Edinburgh, to put the letter into his own hands.*

---

* By dint of assiduous research I am enabled to certiorate the reader, that the name of this person was Saunders Broadfoot,[25] and that he dealt in the wholesome commodity called kirn-milk, (*Anglice*, butter-milk).—J.C.

CHAPTER 28

"My native land, good night."
LORD BYRON

IN the present day, a journey from Edinburgh to London is a matter
at once safe, brief, and simple, however inexperienced or unprotected
the traveller. Numerous coaches of different rates of charge, and as
many packets, are perpetually passing and repassing[1] betwixt the
capital of Britain and her northern sister, so that the most timid or
indolent may execute such a journey upon a few hours' notice. But it
was different in 1737. So slight and infrequent was then the intercourse
betwixt London and Edinburgh, that men still alive remember that
upon one occasion the mail from the former city arrived at the General
Post-Office in Scotland, with only one letter in it.[*] The usual mode
of travelling was by means of post-horses, the traveller occupying one
and his guide another, in which manner, by relays of horses from stage
to stage, the journey might be accomplished in a wonderfully short
time by those who could endure fatigue. To have the bones shaken to
pieces by a constant change of those hacks, was a luxury for the rich—
the poor were under the necessity of using the mode of conveyance
with which nature had provided them.

With a strong heart, and a frame patient of fatigue, Jeanie Deans,
travelling at the rate of twenty miles a-day, and sometimes farther,
traversed the southern part of Scotland, and advanced as far as
Durham.

Hitherto she had been either among her own country-folks, or those
to whom her bare feet and tartan screen were objects too familiar to
attract much attention. But as she advanced, she perceived that both
circumstances exposed her to sarcasms and taunts, which she might
otherwise have escaped; and, although in her heart she thought it
unkind, and unhospitable, to sneer at a passing stranger on account of
the fashion of her attire, yet she had the good sense to alter those parts
of her dress which attracted ill-natured observation. Her checqued

[* The fact[2] is certain. The single epistle was addressed to the principal director of the
British Linen Company.]

screen was deposited carefully in her bundle, and she conformed to the national extravagance of wearing shoes and stockings for the whole day. She confessed afterwards, that "besides the wastrife, it was lang or she could walk sae comfortably with the shoes as without them, but there was often a bit saft heather by the road-side, and that helped her weel on." The want of the screen, which was drawn over the head like a veil, she supplied by a *bon-grace*, as she called it; a large straw bonnet, like those worn by the English maidens when labouring in the fields. "But I thought unco shame o' mysell," she said, "the first time I put on a married woman's *bon-grace*, and me a single maiden."

With these changes she had little, as she said, to make "her kenspeckle when she didna speak," but her accent and language drew down on her so many jests and gibes, couched in a worse *patois* by far than her own, that she soon found it was her interest to talk as little and as seldom as possible. She answered, therefore, civil salutations of chance passengers with a civil curtsey, and chose, with anxious circumspection, such places of repose as looked at once most decent and most sequestered. She found the common people of England, although inferior in courtesy to strangers, such as was then practised in her own more unfrequented country, yet, upon the whole, by no means deficient in the real duties of hospitality. She readily obtained food, and shelter, and protection at a very moderate rate, which sometimes the generosity of mine host altogether declined, with a blunt apology,—"Thee hast a lang way afore thee, lass; and I'se ne'er take penny out o' single woman's purse; it's the best friend thou canst have o' th' road."

It often happened, too, that mine hostess was struck with "the tidy, nice Scotch body," and procured her an escort or a cast in a waggon for some part of the way, or gave her useful advice and recommendation respecting her resting-places.

At York[3] our pilgrim stopped for the best part of a day, partly to recruit her strength,—partly because she had the good luck to obtain a lodging in an inn kept by a countrywoman,—partly to indite two letters to her father and Reuben Butler; an operation of some little difficulty, her habits being by no means those of literary composition.[4] That to her father was in the following words:

"DEAREST FATHER,

"It makes my present pilgrimage heavy and burthensome, more than through the sad occasion, to reflect that it is without your knowledge, which, God knows, was far contrary to my heart; for

Scripture says, that 'the vow of the daughter should not be binding without the consent of the father,'[5] wherein it may be I have been guilty to tak this wearie journey without your consent. Nevertheless, it was borne in upon my mind that I should be an instrument to help my poor sister in this extremity of needcessity, otherwise I wad not, for wealth or for world's gear, or for the haill lands of Da'keith and Lugton, have done the like o' this, without your free will and knowledge. O, dear father, as ye wad desire a blessing on my journey, and upon your household, speak a word or write a line of comfort to yon poor prisoner. If she has sinned, she has sorrowed and suffered, and ye ken better than me, that we maun forgie others, as we pray to be forgien.[6] Dear father, forgive my saying this muckle, for it doth not become a young head to instruct grey hairs; but I am sae far frae ye, that my heart yearns to ye a', and fain wad I hear that ye had forgien her trespass, and sae I nae doubt say mair than may become me. The folk here are civil, and, like the barbarians unto the holy apostle, hae shown me much kindness;[7] and there are a sort of chosen people in the land, for they hae some kirks without organs that are like ours, and are called meeting-houses, where the minister preaches without a gown.[8] But most of the country are prelatists, whilk is awfu' to think; and I saw twa men that were ministers following hunds, as bauld as Roslin or Driden, the young Laird of Loup-the-dike, or ony wild gallant in Lothian. A sorrowfu' sight to behold! O, dear father, may a blessing be with your down-lying and up-rising, and remember in your prayers your affectionate daughter to command,

"JEAN DEANS."

A postscript bore, "I learned from a decent woman, a grazier's widow, that they hae a cure for the muir-ill in Cumberland, whilk is ane pint, as they ca't, of yill, whilk is a dribble in comparison of our gawsie Scots pint, and hardly a mutchkin, boil'd wi' sope and hartshorn draps, and toomed doun the creature's throat wi' ane whorn. Ye might try it on the bauson-faced year-auld quey; an it does nae gude, it can do nae ill.—She was a kind woman, and seemed skeely about horned beasts. When I reach Lunnon, I intend to gang to our cousin Mistress Glass, the tobacconist, at the sign o' the Thistle, wha is so ceevil as to send you down your spleuchan-fu' anes a-year, and as she must be weel kend in Lunnon, I doubt not easily to find out where she bides."

Being seduced into betraying our heroine's confidence thus far, we will stretch our communication a step beyond, and impart to the reader her letter to her lover.

"Mr Reuben Butler,

"Hoping this will find you better, this comes to say, that I have reached this great town safe, and am not wearied with walking, but the better for it. And I have seen many things which I trust to tell you one day, also the muckle kirk[9] of this place; and all around the city are mills,[10] whilk havena muckle wheels nor mill-dams, but gang by the wind—strange to behold. Ane miller[11] asked me to gang in and see it work, but I wad not, for I am not come to the south to make acquaintance with strangers. I keep the straight road, and just beck if ony body speaks to me ceevilly, and answers naebody with the tong but women of mine ain sect. I wish, Mr Butler, I kend ony thing that wad mak ye weel, for they hae mair medicines in this town of York than wad cure a' Scotland, and surely some of them wad be gude for your complaints. If ye had a kindly motherly body to nurse ye, and no to let ye waste yoursell wi' reading—whilk ye read mair than aneugh with the bairns in the schule—and to gie ye warm milk in the morning, I wad be mair easy for ye. Dear Mr Butler, keep a good heart, for we are in the hands of ane that kens better what is gude for us than we ken what is for oursells. I hae nae doubt to do that for which I am come—I canna doubt it—I winna think to doubt it— because, if I haena full assurance, how shall I bear myself with earnest entreaties in the great folk's presence. But to ken that ane's purpose is right, and to make their heart strong, is the way to get through the warst day's dargue. The bairns' rime says, the warst blast of the borrowing days[*] couldna kill the three silly poor hog-lams. And if it be God's pleasure, we that are sindered in sorrow may meet again in joy, even on this hither side of Gordan.[13] I dinna bid ye mind what I said at our partin' anent my poor father and that misfortunate lassie, for I ken you will do sae for the sake of Christian charity, whilk is mair than the entreaties of her that is your servant to command,

"Jeanie Deans."

This letter also had a postscript. "Dear Reuben, if ye think that it wad hae been right for me to have said mair and kinder things to ye, just

---

[* The three last days of March, old style, are called the Borrowing Days; for as they are remarked to be unusually stormy, it is feigned that March had borrowed them from April, to extend the sphere of his rougher sway. The rhyme on the subject is quoted in Leyden's edition of the Complaynt of Scotland.[12]]

think that I hae written sae, since I am sure that I wish a' that is kind and right to ye and by ye. Ye will think I am turned waster, for I wear clean hose and shoon every day; but it's the fashion here for decent bodies, and ilka land has its ain laugh.[*]¹⁴ Ower and aboon a', if laughing days were e'er to come back again till us, ye wad laugh weel to see my round face at the far end of a strae bongrace, that looks as muckle and round as the middell aisle in Libberton Kirk. But it sheds the sun weel aff, and keeps unceevil folk frae staring as if ane were a worrycow. I sall tell ye by writ how I come on wi' the Duke of Argyle, when I won up to Lunnon. Direct a line, to say how ye are, to me, to the charge of Mrs Margaret Glass, tobacconist, at the sign of the Thistle, Lunnon, whilk, if it assures me of your health, will make my mind sae muckle easier. Excuse bad spelling and writing, as I have ane ill pen."

The orthography of these epistles may seem to the southron to require a better apology than the letter expresses, though a bad pen was the excuse of a certain Galwegian laird for bad spelling; but, on behalf of the heroine, I would have them to know, that, thanks to the care of Butler, Jeanie Deans wrote and spelled fifty times better than half the women of rank in Scotland at that period, whose strange orthography and singular diction form the strongest contrast¹⁵ to the good sense which their correspondence usually intimates.

For the rest, in the tenor of these epistles, Jeanie expressed, perhaps, more hopes, a firmer courage, and better spirits, than she actually felt. But this was with the amiable idea of relieving her father and lover from apprehensions on her account, which she was sensible must greatly add to their other troubles. "If they think me weel, and like to do weel," said the poor pilgrim to herself, "my father will be kinder to Effie, and Butler will be kinder to himsell. For I ken weel that they will think mair o' me, than I do o' mysell."

Accordingly, she sealed her letters carefully, and put them into the post-office with her own hand, after many enquiries concerning the time in which they were likely to reach Edinburgh. When this duty was performed, she readily accepted her landlady's pressing invitation to dine with her, and remain till the next morning. The hostess, as we have said, was her countrywoman, and the eagerness with which Scottish people meet, communicate, and, to the extent of their power, assist each other, although it is often objected to us, as a prejudice and

[* Laugh—Law.]

narrowness of sentiment, seems, on the contrary, to arise from a most justifiable and honourable feeling of patriotism, combined with a conviction, which, if undeserved, would long since have been confuted by experience, that the habits and principles of the nation are a sort of guarantee for the character of the individual. At any rate, if the extensive influence of this national partiality be considered as an additional tie, binding man to man, and calling forth the good offices of such as can render them to the countryman who happens to need them, we think it must be found to exceed, as an active and efficient motive to generosity, that more impartial and wider principle of general benevolence, which we have sometimes seen pleaded[16] as an excuse for assisting no individual whatever.

Mrs Bickerton,[17] lady of the ascendant of the Seven Stars,[18] in the Castle-gate, York, was deeply infected with the unfortunate prejudices of her country. Indeed, she displayed so much kindness to Jeanie Deans, (because, she herself, being a Merse woman, *marched* with Mid-Lothian, in which Jeanie was born,) shewed such motherly regard to her, and such anxiety for her farther progress, that Jeanie thought herself safe, though by temper sufficiently cautious, in communicating her whole story to her.

Mrs Bickerton raised her hands and eyes at the recital, and exhibited much wonder and pity. But she also gave some effectual good advice.

She required to know the strength of Jeanie's purse, reduced by her deposit at Libberton, and the necessary expence of her journey to about fifteen pounds. "This," she said, "would do very well, providing she could carry it a' safe to London."

"Safe?" answered Jeanie; "I'se warrant my carrying it safe, bating the needful expences."

"Ay, but highwaymen, lassie," said Mrs Bickerton; "for ye are come into a more civilized, that is to say, a more roguish[19] country than the north, and how ye are to get forward, I do not profess to know. If ye could wait here eight days, our waggons would go up, and I would recommend you to Joe Broadwheel, who would see you safe to the Swan and two Necks.[20] And dinna sneeze at Joe, if he should be for drawing up wi' you" (continued Mrs Bickerton, her acquired English mingling with her national or original dialect), "he's a handy boy, and a wanter, and no lad better thought o' on the road; and the English make good husbands enough, witness my poor man, Moses Bickerton, as is i' the kirk-yard."

Jeanie hastened to say, that she could not possibly wait for the setting forth of Joe Broadwheel, being internally by no means gratified with the idea of becoming the object of his attention during the journey.

"Aweel, lass," answered the good landlady, "then thou must pickle in thine ain poke-nook,[21] and buckle thy girdle thine ain gate.[22] But take my advice, and hide thy gold in thy stays, and keep a piece or two and some silver, in case thou be'st spoke withal; for there's as wud lads haunt within a day's walk from hence, as on the Braes of Doun in Perthshire. And, lass, thou maunna gang staring through Lunnon, asking wha kens Mrs Glass at the sign o' the Thistle; marry, they would laugh thee to scorn. But gang thou to this honest man," and she put a direction into Jeanie's hand, "he kens maist part of the sponsible Scottish folks in the city, and he will find out your friend for thee."

Jeanie took the little introductory letter with sincere thanks; but, something alarmed on the subject of the highway robbers, her mind recurred to what Ratcliffe had mentioned to her, and briefly relating the circumstances which placed a document so extraordinary in her hands, she put the paper he had given her into the hand of Mrs Bickerton.

The Lady of the Seven Stars did not, indeed, ring a bell, because such was not the fashion of the time, but she whistled on a silver-call, which was hung by her side, and a tight serving-maiden entered the room.

"Tell Dick Ostler to come here," said Mrs Bickerton.

Dick Ostler accordingly made his appearance;—a queer, knowing, shambling animal, with a hatchet-face, a squint, a game-arm, and a limp.

"Dick Ostler," said Mrs Bickerton, in a tone of authority that showed she was (at least by adoption) Yorkshire too, "thou knowest most people and most things o' the road."

"Eye, eye, God help me, mistress," said Dick, shrugging his shoulders betwixt a repentant and a knowing expression—"Eye! I ha' know'd a thing or twa i' ma day, mistress." He looked sharp and laughed—looked grave and sighed, as one who was prepared to take the matter either way.

"Kenst thou this wee bit paper amang the rest, man?" said Mrs Bickerton, handing him the protection which Ratcliffe had given Jeanie Deans.

When Dick had looked at the paper, he winked with one eye, extended his grotesque mouth from ear to ear, like a navigable canal,[23] scratched his head powerfully, and then said, "Ken?—ay—maybe we ken summat, an it werena for harm to him, mistress?"

"None in the world," said Mrs Bickerton; "only a dram of Hollands to thyself, man, an thou will't speak."

"Why then," said Dick, giving the head-band of his breeches a knowing hoist with one hand, and kicking out one foot behind him to accommodate the adjustment of that important habiliment, "I dares to say the pass will be kend weel aneugh on the road, an that be all."

"But what sort of a lad was he?" said Mrs Bickerton, winking to Jeanie, as proud of her knowing ostler.

"Why, what ken I?—Jim the Rat—why he was Cock o' the North[24] within this twelmonth—he and Scotch Wilson, Handie Dandie, as they called him—but he's been out o' this country a while, as I rackon; but ony gentleman, as keeps the road o' this side Stamford, will respect Jim's pass."

Without asking farther questions, the landlady filled Dick Ostler a bumper of Hollands. He ducked with his head and shoulders, scraped with his more advanced hoof, bolted the alcohol, to use the learned phrase, and withdrew to his own domains.

"I would advise thee, Jeanie," said Mrs Bickerton, "an thou meetest with ugly customers o' the road, to show them this bit paper, for it will serve thee, assure thyself."

A neat little supper concluded the evening. The exported Scots-woman, Mrs Bickerton by name, eat heartily of one or two seasoned dishes, drank some sound old ale, and a glass of stiff negus; while she gave Jeanie a history of her gout, admiring how it was possible that she, whose fathers and mothers for many generations had been farmers in Lammermuir, could have come by a disorder so totally unknown to them. Jeanie did not chuse to offend her friendly landlady, by speaking her mind on the probable origin of this complaint, but she thought on the flesh-pots of Egypt,[25] and, in spite of all entreaties to better fare, made her evening meal upon vegetables, with a glass of fair water.

Mrs Bickerton assured her, that the acceptance of any reckoning was entirely out of the question, furnished her with credentials to her correspondent in London, and to several inns upon the road where she had some influence or interest, reminded her of the precautions she should adopt for concealing her money, and as she was to depart early in the morning, took leave of her very affectionately, taking her word that she would visit her on her return to Scotland, and tell her how she had managed, and that *summum bonum* for a gossip, "all how and about it." This Jeanie faithfully promised.

CHAPTER 29

And Need and Misery, Vice and Danger, bind,
In sad alliance, each degraded mind.

As our traveller set out early on the ensuing morning to prosecute her
journey, and was in the act of leaving the inn-yard, Dick Ostler, who
either had risen early or neglected to go to bed, either circumstance
being equally incident to his calling, hollo'd out after her,—"The top
of the morning to you, Moggie. Have a care o' Gunnerby Hill, young
one. Robin Hood's[1] dead and gwone, but there be takers yet in the
vale of Bever." Jeanie looked at him as if to request a further
explanation, but, with a leer, a shuffle, and a shrug, inimitable, (unless
by Emery,[2]) Dick turned again to the raw-boned steed, which he was
currying, and sung as he employed the comb and brush,—

> "Robin Hood was a yeoman right good,
>   And his bow was of trusty yew;
> And if Robin bid stand on the King's lea-land,
>   Pray, why should not we say so too?"

Jeanie pursued her journey without further enquiry, for there was
nothing in Dick's manner that inclined her to prolong their conference.
A painful day's journey[3] brought her to Ferrybridge, the best inn,
then and since, upon the great northern road; and an introduction
from Mrs Bickerton, added to her own simple and quiet manners, so
propitiated the landlady of the Swan[4] in her favour, that the good
dame procured her the convenient accommodation of a pillion and
post-horse then returning to Tuxford, so that she accomplished, upon
the second day after leaving York, the longest journey[5] she had yet
made. She was a good deal fatigued by a mode of travelling to which
she was less accustomed than to walking, and it was considerably later
than usual on the ensuing morning that she felt herself able to resume
her pilgrimage. At noon the hundred-armed Trent, and the blackened
ruins of Newark Castle, demolished in the great civil war, lay before
her. It may easily be supposed, that Jeanie had no curiosity to make
antiquarian researches, but, entering the town, went straight to the inn

to which she had been directed at Ferrybridge. While she procured some refreshment, she observed the girl who brought it to her, looked at her several times with fixed and peculiar interest, and at last, to her infinite surprise, enquired if her name was not Deans, and if she was not a Scotchwoman, going to London upon justice business. Jeanie, with all her simplicity of character, had some of the caution of her country, and, according to Scottish universal custom, she answered the question by another,[6] requesting the girl would tell her why she asked these questions?

The Maritornes of the Saracen's Head,[7] Newark, replied, "Two women had passed that morning, who had made enquiries after one Jeanie Deans, travelling to London on such an errand, and could scarce be persuaded that she had not passed on."

Much surprised, and somewhat alarmed, (for what is inexplicable is usually alarming,) Jeanie questioned the wench about the particular appearance of these two women, but could only learn that the one was aged, and the other young; that the latter was the taller, and that the former spoke most, and seemed to maintain an authority over her companion, and that both spoke with the Scottish accent.

This conveyed no information whatever,[8] and with an indescribable presentiment of evil designed towards her, Jeanie adopted the resolution of taking post-horses for the next stage. In this, however, she could not be gratified; some accidental circumstances had occasioned what is called a run[9] upon the road, and the landlord could not accommodate her with a guide and horses. After waiting some time, in hopes that a pair of horses that had gone southward would return in time for her use, she at length, feeling ashamed of her own pusillanimity, resolved to prosecute her journey in her usual manner.

"It was all plain road," she was assured, "except a high mountain[10] called Gunnerby Hill, about three miles from Grantham, which was her stage for the night."

"I'm glad to hear there's a hill," said Jeanie, "for baith my sight and my very feet are weary o' sic tracks o' level ground—it looks a' the way between this and York as if a' the land had been trenched and levelled, whilk is very wearisome to my Scots een. When I lost sight of a muckle blue hill they ca' Ingleboro',[11] I thought I hadna a friend left in this strange land."

"As for the matter of that, young woman," said mine host, "an you be so fond o' hill, I carena an thou couldst carry Gunnerby away with thee in thy lap, for it's a murther to post-horses. But here's to thy good journey, and mayst thou win well through it, for thou is a bold and a canny lass."

So saying, he took a powerful pull at a solemn tankard of home-brewed ale.[12]

"I hope there is nae bad company on the road, sir?" said Jeanie.

"Why, when it's clean without them I'll thatch Groby pool wi' pancakes.[13] But there arena sae mony now; and since they hae lost Jim the Rat, they hold together no better than the men of Marsham when they lost their common.[14] Take a drop ere thou goest," he concluded, offering her the tankard; "thou wilt get naething at night save Grantham gruel, nine grots and a gallon of water."[15]

Jeanie courteously declined the tankard, and enquired what was her "lawing?"

"Thy lawing? Heaven help thee, wench, what ca'st thou that?"

"It is—I was wanting to ken what was to pay," replied Jeanie.

"Pay? Lord help thee!—why nought, woman—we hae drawn no liquor but a gill o' beer, and the Saracen's Head can spare a mouthful o' meat to a stranger like o' thee, that cannot speak Christian language. So here's to thee once more. The same again, quoth Mark of Bell-grave,"[16] and he took another profound pull at the tankard.

The travellers who have visited Newark more lately, will not fail to remember the remarkably civil and gentlemanly manners of the person who now keeps the principal inn there, and may find some amusement in contrasting them with those of his more rough predecessor. But we believe it will be found that the polish has worn off none of the real worth of the metal.

Taking leave of her Lincolnshire Gaius,[17] Jeanie resumed her solitary walk, and was somewhat alarmed when evening and twilight overtook her in the open ground which extends to the foot of Gunnerby Hill, and is intersected with patches of copse and with swampy spots. The extensive commons on the north road, most of which are now enclosed, and in general a relaxed state of police, exposed the traveller to highway robbery in a degree which is now unknown, excepting in the immediate vicinity of the metropolis.[18] Aware of this circumstance, Jeanie mended her pace when she heard the trampling of a horse behind, and instinctively drew to one side of the road, as if to allow as much room for the rider to pass as might be possible. When the animal came up, she found that it was bearing two women, the one placed on a side-saddle, the other on a pillion behind her, as may still occasionally be seen in England.

"A braw gude night to ye, Jeanie Deans," said the foremost female as the horse passed our heroine; "What think ye o' yon bonny hill yonder, lifting its brow to the moon? Trow ye yon's the gate to Heaven, that ye are sae fain of?—maybe we'll win there the night yet, God sain us, though our minny here's rather driegh in the upgang."

The speaker kept changing her seat in the saddle, and half-stopping the horse, as she brought her body round, while the woman that sate behind her on the pillion seemed to urge her on in words which Jeanie heard but imperfectly.

"Haud your tongue, ye moon-raised b——, what is your business with the —— or with heaven or hell either?"

"Troth, mither, no muckle wi' heaven, I doubt, considering wha I carry ahint me—and as for hell, it will fight its ain battle at its ain time, I'se be bound—Come, naggie, trot awa, man, an as thou wert a broomstick, for a witch rides thee—

> With my curtch on my foot, and my shoe on my hand,[19]
> I glance like the wildfire through brugh and through land."

The tramp of the horse, and the increasing distance, drowned the rest of her song, but Jeanie heard for some time the inarticulate sounds ring along the waste.

Our pilgrim remained stupified with undefined apprehensions. The being named by her name in so wild a manner, and in a strange country, without further explanation or communing, by a person who thus strangely flitted forward and disappeared before her, came near to the supernatural sounds in Comus:[20]—

> The airy tongues, which syllable men's names
> On sands, and shores, and desert wildernesses.

And although widely different in features, deportment, and rank, from the Lady of that enchanting masque, the continuation of the passage may be happily applied to Jeanie Deans upon this singular alarm:—

> These thoughts may startle well, but not astound
> The virtuous mind, that ever walks attended
> By a strong siding champion—Conscience.

In fact, it was, with the recollection of the affectionate and dutiful errand on which she was engaged, her right, if such a word could be applicable, to expect protection in a task so meritorious. She had not advanced much farther, with a mind calmed by these reflections, when she was disturbed by a new and more instant subject of terror. Two men, who had been lurking among some copse, started up as she advanced, and met her on the road in a menacing manner. "Stand and deliver," said one of them, a short stout fellow, in a smock-frock, such as are worn by waggoners.

"The woman," said the other, a tall thin figure, "does not understand the words of action.[21]—Your money, my precious, or your life."

"I have but very little money, gentlemen," said poor Jeanie, tendering that portion which she had separated from her principal stock, and kept apart for such an emergency; "but if you are resolved to have it, to be sure you must have it."

"This won't do, my girl. D—n me, if it shall pass," said the shorter ruffian; "do ye think gentlemen are to hazard their lives on the road to be cheated in this way? We'll have every farthing you have got, or we will strip you to the skin, curse me."

His companion, who seemed to have something like compassion for the horror which Jeanie's countenance now expressed, said, "No, no, Tom, this is one of the precious sisters, and we'll take her word, for once, without putting her to the stripping proof.—Hark ye, my lass, if you'll look up to Heaven, and say, this is the last penny you have about ye, why, hang it, we'll let you pass."

"I am not free," answered Jeanie, "to say what I have about me, gentlemen, for there's life and death depends on my journey; but if you leave me as much as finds me in bread and water, I'll be satisfied, and thank you, and pray for you."

"D—n your prayers," said the shorter fellow, "that's a coin that won't pass with us;" and at the same time made a motion to seize her.

"Stay, gentlemen," said Jeanie, Ratcliffe's pass suddenly occurring to her; "perhaps you know this paper."

"What the devil is she after now, Frank?" said the more savage ruffian—"Do you look at it, for, d—n me, if I could read it, if it were for the benefit of my clergy."

"This is a jark from Jim Ratcliffe," said the taller, having looked at the bit of paper. "The wench must pass by our cutter's law."

"I say no," answered his companion; "Rat has left the lay and turned bloodhound, they say."

"We may need a good turn from him all the same," said the taller ruffian again.

"But what are we to do then?" said the shorter man.—"We promised, you know, to strip the wench, and send her begging back to her own beggarly country, and now you are for letting her go on."

"I did not say that," said the other fellow, and whispered to his companion, who replied, "Be alive about it then, and don't keep chattering till some travellers come up to nab us."

"You must follow us off the road, young woman," said the taller.

"For the love of God!" exclaimed Jeanie, "as you were born of woman, dinna ask me to leave the road; rather take all I have in the world."

"What the devil is the wench afraid of?" said the other fellow. "I tell you you shall come to no harm; but if you will not leave the road and come with us, d—n me, but I'll beat your brains out where you stand."

"Thou art a rough bear, Tom," said his companion.—"An ye touch her, I'll give ye a shake by the collar shall make the Leicester beans rattle in thy guts.[22]—Never mind him, girl, I will not allow him to lay a finger on you, if you walk quietly on with us; but if you keep jabbering there, d—n me, but I'll leave him to settle it with you."

This threat conveyed all that is terrible to the imagination of poor Jeanie, who saw in him that "was of milder mood"[23] her only protection from the most brutal treatment. She, therefore, not only followed him, but even held him by the sleeve, lest he should escape from her; and the fellow, hardened as he was, seemed something touched by these marks of confidence, and repeatedly assured her, that he would suffer her to receive no harm.

They conducted their prisoner in a direction leading more and more from the public road, but she observed that they kept a sort of track or bye-path, which relieved her from part of her apprehensions, which would have been greatly increased had they not seemed to follow a determined and ascertained route. After about half an hour's walking, all three in profound silence, they approached an old barn, which stood on the edge of some cultivated ground, but remote from every thing like habitation. It was itself, however, tenanted, for there was light in the windows.

One of the foot-pads scratched at the door, which was opened by a female, and they entered with their unhappy prisoner. An old woman, who was preparing food by the assistance of a stifling fire of lighted charcoal, asked them, in the name of the devil, what they brought the wench there for, and why they did not strip her and turn her abroad on the common?

"Come, come, Mother Blood," said the tall man, "we'll do what's right to oblige you, and we'll do no more; we are bad enough, but such as you would make us devils incarnate."

"She has got a *jark* from Jim Ratcliffe," said the short fellow, "and Frank here won't hear of our putting her through the mill."

"No, that will I not, by G—d," answered Frank; "but if old Mother Blood could keep her here for a little while, or send her back to Scotland, without hurting her, why, I see no harm in that—not I."

"I'll tell you what, Frank Levitt," said the old woman, "if you call me Mother Blood again, I'll paint this gulley" (and she held a knife up as if about to make good her threat) "in the best blood in your body, my bonnie boy."

"The price of oatmeal must be up in the north," said Frank, "that puts Mother Blood so much out of humour."

Without a moment's hesitation the fury darted her knife at him with the vengeful dexterity of a wild Indian. As he was on his guard, he avoided the missile by a sudden motion of his head, but it whistled past his ear, and stuck deep in the clay wall of a partition behind.

"Come, come, mother," said the robber, seizing her by both wrists, "I shall teach you who's master;" and so saying, he forced the hag backwards by main force, who strove vehemently until she sunk on a bunch of straw, and then letting go her hands, he held up his finger towards her in the menacing posture by which a maniac is intimidated by his keeper. It appeared to produce the desired effect; for she did not attempt to rise from the seat on which he had placed her, or to resume any measures of actual violence, but wrung her withered hands with impotent rage, and brayed and howled like a demoniac.

"I will keep my promise with you, you old devil," said Frank; "the wench shall not go forward on the London road, but I will not have you touch a hair of her head,[24] if it were but for your insolence."

This intimation seemed to compose in some degree the vehement passion of the old hag; and while her exclamations and howls sunk into a low, maundering, growling tone of voice, another personage was added to this singular party.

"Eh, Frank Levitt," said this new-comer, who entered with a hop, step, and jump, which at once conveyed her from the door into the centre of the party, "were ye killing our mother? or were ye cutting the grunter's weasand that Tam brought in this morning? or have ye been reading your prayers backward,[25] to bring up my auld acquaintance the deil amang ye?"

The tone of the speaker was so particular, that Jeanie immediately recognised the woman who had rode foremost of the pair which passed her just before she met the robbers; a circumstance which greatly increased her terror, as it served to shew that the mischief designed against her was premeditated, though by whom, or for what cause, she was totally at a loss to conjecture. From the style of her conversation, the reader also may probably acknowledge in this female, an old acquaintance in the earlier part of our narrative.

"Out, ye mad devil," said Tom, whom she had disturbed in the middle of a draught of some liquor with which he had found means of accommodating himself; "betwixt your Bess of Bedlam pranks, and your dam's frenzies, a man might live quieter in the devil's ken than here."—And he again resumed the broken jug out of which he had been drinking.

"And wha's this o't?" said the madwoman, dancing up to Jeanie Deans, who, although in great terror, yet watched the scene with a resolution to let nothing pass unnoticed which might be serviceable in assisting her to escape, or informing her as to the true nature of her situation, and the danger attending it,—"Wha's this o't!" again exclaimed Madge Wildfire. "Douce Davie Deans, the auld doited whig body's daughter, in a gypsey's barn, and the night setting in; this is a sight for sair een!—Eh sirs, the falling off o' the godly!—And the t'other sister's in the Tolbooth at Edinburgh; I am very sorry for her, for my share—it's my mother wusses ill to her, and no me—though maybe I hae as muckle cause."

"Hark ye, Madge," said the taller ruffian, "you have not such a touch of the devil's blood as the hag your mother, who may be his dam for what I know—take this young woman to your kennel, and do not let the devil enter, though he should ask in God's name."

"Ou ay; that I will, Frank," said Madge, taking hold of Jeanie by the arm, and pulling her along; "for it's no for decent Christian young leddies, like her and me, to be keeping the like o' you and Tyburn Tam company at this time o' night. Sae gude e'en t'ye, sirs, and mony o' them; and may ye a' sleep till the hangman wauken ye, and then it will be weel for the country."

She then, as her wild fancy seemed suddenly to prompt her, walked demurely towards her mother, who, seated by the charcoal fire, with the reflection of the red light on her withered and distorted features marked by every evil passion, seemed the very picture of Hecate at her infernal rites; and suddenly dropping on her knees, said, with the manner of a child six years old, "Mammie, hear me say my prayers before I go to bed, and say God bless my bonny face, as ye used to do lang syne."

"The deil flay the hide o' it to sole his brogues wi'," said the old lady, aiming a buffet at the suppliant, in answer to her duteous request.

The blow missed Madge, who, being probably acquainted by experience with the mode in which her mother was wont to confer her maternal benedictions, slipt out of arm's length with great dexterity and quickness. The hag then started up, and, seizing a pair of old firetongs, would have amended her motion, by beating out the brains either of her daughter or Jeanie, (she did not seem greatly to care which), when her hand was once more arrested by the man whom they called Frank Levitt, who, seizing her by the shoulder, flung her from him with great violence, exclaiming, "What, Mother Damnable—again, and in my sovereign presence!—Hark ye, Madge of Bedlam, get to your hole with your play-fellow, or we shall have the devil to pay here,[26] and nothing to pay him with."

Madge took Levitt's advice, retreating as fast as she could, and dragging Jeanie along with her into a sort of recess, partitioned off from the rest of the barn, and filled with straw, from which it appeared that it was intended for the purpose of slumber. The moonlight shone through an open hole upon a pillion, a pack saddle, and one or two wallets, the travelling furniture of Madge and her amiable mother.—"Now, saw ye e'er in your life," said Madge, "sae dainty a chamber of deas? see as the moon shines down sae caller on the fresh strae! There's no a pleasanter cell in Bedlam, for as braw a place as it is on the outside.—Were ye ever in Bedlam?"

"No," answered Jeanie faintly, appalled by the question, and the way in which it was put, yet willing to sooth her insane companion, being in circumstances so unhappily precarious, that even the society of this gibbering madwoman seemed a species of protection.

"Never in Bedlam!" said Madge, as if with some surprise.—"But ye'll hae been in the cells at Edinburgh?"

"Never," repeated Jeanie.

"Weel, I think thae daft carles the magistrates send naebody to Bedlam but me—they maun hae an unco respect for me, for whenever I am brought to them, they aye hae me back to Bedlam. But troth, Jeanie," (she said this in a very confidential tone,) "to tell ye my private mind about it, I think ye are at nae great loss; for the keeper's a cross patch, and he maun hae it a' his ain gate, to be sure, or he makes the place waur than hell. I often tell him he's the daftest in a' the house.—But what are they making sic a skirling for?—Deil ane o' them's get in here—it wadna be mensefu'! I will sit wi' my back again the door; it winna be that easy stirring me."

"Madge!"—"Madge!"—"Madge Wildfire!"—"Madge devil! what have ye done with the horse?" was repeatedly asked by the men without.

"He's e'en at his supper, puir thing," answered Madge; "deil an ye were at yours too, and it were scauding brimstane, and then we wad hae less o' your din."

"His supper?" answered the more sulky ruffian—"What d'ye mean by that?—Tell me where he is, or I will knock your Bedlam brains out!"

"He's in Gaffer Gabblewood's wheat-close, an ye maun ken."

"His wheat-close, you crazed jilt!" answered the other, with an accent of great indignation.

"O, dear Tyburn Tam, man, what ill will the blades of the young wheat do to the puir naig?"

"That is not the question," said the other robber; "but what the country will say to us to-morrow, when they see him in such quarters.—Go, Tom, and bring him in; and avoid the soft ground, my lad; leave no hoof-track behind you."

"I think you give me always the fag of it, whatever is to be done," grumbled his companion.

"Leap, Laurence, you're long enough,"[27] said the other; and the fellow left the barn accordingly, without farther remonstrance.

In the meanwhile, Madge had arranged herself for repose on the straw; but still in a half-sitting posture, with her back resting against the door of the hovel, which, as it opened inwards, was in this manner kept shut by the weight of her person.

"There's mair shifts bye stealing, Jeanie," said Madge Wildfire; "though whiles I can hardly get our mother to think sae. Whae wad hae thought but mysell of making a bolt of my ain back-bane! But it's no sae strong as thae that I hae seen in the Tolbooth at Edinburgh. The hammermen of Edinburgh are to my mind afore the world for making stancheons, ring-bolts, fetter-bolts, bars, and locks. And they arena that bad at girdles for carcakes neither; though the Cu'ross hammermen have the gree for that. My mother had ance a bonny Cu'ross girdle,[28] and I thought to have baked carcakes on it for my puir wean that's dead and gane, nae fair way—but we maun a' dee, ye ken, Jeanie—You Cameronian bodies ken that brawlies; and ye're for making a hell upon earth that ye may be less unwillin to part wi' it.

But as touching Bedlam that ye were speaking about, I'se ne'er recommend it muckle the tae gate or the tother, be it right—be it wrang. But ye ken what the sang says." And, pursuing the unconnected and floating wanderings of her mind, she sung aloud—

> "In the bonnie cells of Bedlam,
>   Ere I was ane and twenty,
> I had hempen bracelets strong,
> And merry whips, ding-dong,
>   And prayer and fasting plenty.[2]

"Weel, Jeanie, I am something herse the night, and I canna sing muckle mair; and troth, I think, I am gaun to sleep."

She drooped her head on her breast, a posture from which Jeanie, who would have given the world for an opportunity of quiet to consider the means and the probability of her escape, was very careful not to disturb her. After nodding, however, for a minute or two, with her eyes half closed, the unquiet and restless spirit of her malady again assailed Madge. She raised her head, and spoke, but with a lowered tone, which was again gradually overcome by drowsiness, to which the fatigue of a day's journey on horseback had probably given unwonted occasion,—"I dinna ken what makes me sae sleepy—I amaist never sleep till my bonny Lady Moon gangs till her bed—mair by token, when she's at the full, ye ken, rowing aboon us yonder in her grand silver coach—I have danced to her my lane sometimes for very joy— and whiles dead folk came and danced wi' me—the like o' Jock Porteous, or ony body I had kend when I was living—for ye maun ken I was ance dead mysell." Here the poor maniac sung in a low and wild tone,

> "My banes are buried in yon kirk-yard
>   Sae far ayont the sea,
> And it is but my blithesome ghaist
>   That's speaking now to thee.[30]

"But after a', Jeanie, my woman, naebody kens weel wha's living and wha's dead—or wha's gane to Fairyland—there's another question. Whiles I think my puir bairn's dead—ye ken very weel it's buried— but that signifies naething. I have had it on my knee a hundred times, and a hundred till that, since it was buried—and how could that be were it dead, ye ken?—it's merely impossible."—And here, some conviction half-overcoming the reveries of her imagination, she burst into a fit of crying and ejaculation, "Waes me! waes me! waes me!" till at length she moaned and sobbed herself into a deep sleep, which was soon intimated by her breathing hard, leaving Jeanie to her own melancholy reflections and observations.

CHAPTER 30

Bind her quickly; or, by this steel,
I'll tell, although I truss for company.
FLETCHER

THE imperfect light which shone into the window enabled Jeanie to see that there was scarcely any chance of making her escape in that direction, for the aperture was high in the wall, and so narrow, that, could she have climbed up to it, she might well doubt whether it would have permitted her to pass her body through it. An unsuccessful attempt to escape would be sure to draw down worse treatment than she now received, and she, therefore, resolved to watch her opportunity carefully ere making such a perilous effort. For this purpose she applied herself to the ruinous clay partition, which divided the hovel in which she now was from the rest of the waste barn. It was decayed and full of cracks and chinks, one of which she enlarged with her fingers, cautiously and without noise, until she could obtain a plain view of the old hag and the taller ruffian, whom they called Levitt, seated together beside the decayed fire of charcoal, and apparently engaged in close conference. She was at first terrified by the sight, for the features of the old woman had a hideous cast of hardened and inveterate malice and ill-humour, and those of the man, though naturally less unfavourable, were such as corresponded well with licentious habits, and a lawless profession.

"But I remembered," said Jeanie, "my worthy father's tales of a winter evening, how he was confined with the blessed martyr Mr James Renwick, who lifted up the fallen standard of the true reformed Kirk of Scotland, after the worthy and renowned Daniel Cameron, our last blessed banner-man, had fallen among the swords of the wicked at Airds-moss,[1] and how the very hearts of the wicked malefactors and murtherers, whom they were confined withal, were melted like wax at the sound of their doctrine; and I bethought mysell, that the same help that was wi' them in their strait, wad be wi' me in mine, an I could but watch the Lord's time and opportunity for delivering my feet from their snare; and I minded the Scripture of the blessed

Psalmist, whilk he insisteth on, as weel in the forty-second as in the forty-third Psalm, 'Why art thou cast down, O my soul, and why art thou disquieted within me? Hope in God, for I shall yet praise Him, who is the health of my countenance, and my God.'"[2]

Strengthened in a mind naturally calm, sedate, and firm, by the influence of religious confidence, this poor captive was enabled to attend to, and comprehend, a great part of an interesting conversation which passed betwixt those into whose hands she had fallen, notwithstanding that their meaning was partly disguised by the occasional use of cant terms, of which Jeanie knew not the import, by the low tone in which they spoke, and by their mode of supplying their broken phrases by shrugs and signs, as is usual amongst those of their disorderly profession.

The man opened the conversation by saying, "Now, dame, you see I am true to my friend.—I have not forgot that you *planked a chury*,* which helped me through the bars of the Castle of York, and I came to do your work without asking questions, for one good turn deserves another. But now that Madge, who is as loud as Tom of Lincoln,[3] is somewhat still, and this same Tyburn Neddie[4] is shaking his heels after the old nag, why you must tell me what all this is about, and what's to be done—for d—n me if I touch the girl, or let her be touched, and she with Jim Rat's pass too."

"Thou art an honest lad, Frank," answered the old woman, "but e'en too kind for thy trade; thy tender heart will get thee into trouble. I will see ye gang up Holbourn Hill backward,[5] and a' on the word of some silly loon that could never hae rapped to ye had ye drawn your knife across his weasand."

"You may be bilked there, old one," answered the robber; "I have known many a pretty lad cut short in his first summer upon the road, because he was something hasty with his flats and sharps. Besides, a man would fain live out his two years[6] with a good conscience. So, tell me what all this is about, and what's to be done for you that one can do decently."

"Why, you must know, Frank—but first taste a snap of right Hollands." She drew a flask from her pocket, and filled the fellow a large bumper, which he pronounced to be the right thing.—"You must know then, Frank—wunna ye mend your hand?" again offering the flask.

---

* Concealed a knife.

"No, no—when a woman wants mischief from you she always begins by filling you drunk.—D—n all Dutch courage.—What I do I will do soberly—I'll last the longer for that too."

"Well, then, you must know," resumed the old woman, without any farther attempts at propitiation, "that this girl is going to London."

Here Jeanie could only distinguish the word "sister."

The robber answered in a louder tone, "Fair enough that; and what the devil is your business with it?"

"Business enough, I think. If the b—— queers the noose, that silly cull will marry her."

"And who cares if he does?" said the man.

"Who cares, ye donnard Neddie? I care; and I will strangle her with my own hands, rather than she should come to Madge's preferment."

"Madge's preferment! Does your old blind eye see no farther than that? If he is as you say, d'ye think he'll ever marry a moon-calf like Madge? Ecod that's a good one—Marry Madge Wildfire!—Ha! ha! ha!"

"Hark ye, ye crack-rope padder, born beggar and bred thief!" replied the hag, "suppose he never marries the wench, is that a reason he should marry another, and that other to hold my daughter's place, and she crazed, and I a beggar, and all along of him? But I know that of him will hang him—I know that of him will hang him, if he had a thousand lives—I know that of him will hang—hang—hang him!"

She grinned as she repeated and dwelt upon the fatal monosyllable, with the emphasis of a vindictive fiend.

"Then why don't you hang—hang—hang him?" said Frank, repeating her words contemptuously. "There would be more sense in that, than in wreaking yourself here upon two wenches that have done you and your daughter no ill."

"No ill?" answered the old woman—"and he to marry this jail-bird, if ever she gets her foot loose!"

"But as there is no chance of his marrying a bird of your brood, I cannot, for my soul, see what you have to do with all this," again replied the robber, shrugging his shoulders. "Where there is ought to be got, I'll go as far as my neighbours, but I hate mischief for mischief's sake."

"And would you go nae length for revenge?" said the hag—"for revenge, the sweetest morsel to the mouth that ever was cooked in hell!"

"The devil may keep it for his own eating then," said the robber; "for hang me if I like the sauce he dresses it with."

"Revenge!" continued the old woman; "why it is the best reward the devil gives us for our time here and hereafter. I have wrought hard for it—I have suffered for it, and I have sinned for it—and I will have it,—or there is neither justice in heaven nor in hell!"

Levitt had by this time lighted a pipe, and was listening with great composure to the frantic and vindictive ravings of the old hag. He was too much hardened by his course of life to be shocked with them—too indifferent, and probably too stupid, to catch any part of their animation or energy. "But, mother," he said, after a pause, "still I say, that if revenge is your wish, you should take it on the young fellow himself."

"I wish I could," she said, drawing in her breath, with the eagerness of a thirsty person while mimicking the action of drinking—"I wish I could—but no—I cannot—I cannot."

"And why not?—You would think little of peaching and hanging him for this Scotch affair.—Rat me, one might have milled the Bank of England, and less noise about it."

"I have nursed him at this withered breast," answered the old woman, folding her hands on her bosom, as if pressing an infant to it, "and though he has proved an adder to me—though he has been the destruction of me and mine—though he has made me company for the devil, if there be a devil, and food for hell, if there be such a place, yet I cannot take his life—No, I cannot," she continued, with an appearance of rage against herself; "I have thought of it—I have tried it—but, Francis Levitt, I canna gang through wi't!—Na, na—he was the first bairn I ever nurst—ill I had been—but man can never ken what woman feels for the bairn she has held first to her bosom."

"To be sure," said Levitt, "we have no experience; but, mother, they say you ha'nt been so kind to other *bairns* as you call them, that have come in your way.—Nay, d—n me, never lay your hand on the whittle, for I am captain and leader here, and I will have no rebellion."

The hag, whose first motion had been, upon hearing the question, to grasp the haft of a large knife, now unclosed her hand, stole it away from the weapon, and suffered it to fall by her side, while she proceeded with a sort of smile—"Bairns! ye are joking, lad, wha wad touch bairns? Madge, puir thing, had a misfortune wi' ane—and the t'other"—Here her voice sunk so much, that Jeanie, though anxiously upon the watch, could not catch a word she said, until she raised her tone at the conclusion of the sentence—"so Madge, in her daffin', threw it into the Nor'-Loch, I trow."

Madge, whose slumbers, like those of most who labour under mental malady, had been short and were easily broken, now made herself heard from her place of repose.

"Indeed, mother, that's a great lee, for I did nae sic thing."

"Hush, thou hellicat devil," said her mother—"By Heaven! the other wench will be waking too."

"That may be dangerous," said Frank, and he rose and followed Meg Murdockson across the floor.

"Rise," said the hag to her daughter, "or I sall drive the knife between the planks into the Bedlam back of thee!"

Apparently she at the same time seconded her threat, by pricking her with the point of a knife, for Madge, with a faint scream, changed her place, and the door opened.

The old woman held a candle in one hand, and a knife in the other. Levitt appeared behind her; whether with a view of preventing, or assisting her in any violence she might meditate, could not be well guessed. Jeanie's presence of mind stood her friend in this dreadful crisis. She had resolution enough to maintain the attitude and manner of one who sleeps profoundly, and to regulate even her breathing, notwithstanding the agitation of instant terror, so as to correspond with her attitude.

The old woman passed the light across her eyes; and although Jeanie's fears were so powerfully awakened by this movement, that she often declared afterwards, that she thought she saw the figures of her destined murderers through her closed eyelids, she had still the resolution to maintain the feint on which her safety, perhaps, depended.

Levitt looked at her with fixed attention; he then turned the old woman out of the place, and followed her himself. Having regained the outer apartment, and seated themselves, Jeanie heard the highwayman say, to her no small relief, "She's as fast as if she were in Bedfordshire.—Now, old Meg, d—n me, if I can understand a glim of this story of yours, or what good it will do you to hang the one wench, and torment the other; but, rat ye, I will be true to my friend, and serve ye the way ye like it. I see it will be a bad job; but I do think I could get her down to Surfleet on the Wash, and so on board Tom Moonshine's neat lugger, and keep her out of the way three or four weeks, if that will please ye?—But d——n me if any one shall harm her, unless they have a mind to choke on a brace of blue plums.—It's a cruel bad job, and I wish you and it, Meg, were both at the devil."

"Never mind, hinny Levitt," said the old woman; "you are a ruffler, and will have a' your ain gate—She shanna gang to heaven an hour sooner for me; I carena whether she live or die—it's her sister— ay, her sister!"

"Well, we'll say no more about it, I hear Tom coming in. We'll couch a hogshead,*[7] and so better had you." They retired to repose, accordingly, and all was silent in this asylum of iniquity.

Jeanie lay for a long time awake. At break of day she heard the two ruffians leave the barn, after whispering with the old woman for some time. The sense that she was now guarded only by persons of her own sex, gave her some confidence, and irresistible lassitude at length threw her into slumber.

When the captive awakened, the sun was high in heaven, and the morning considerably advanced. Madge Wildfire was still in the hovel which had served them for the night, and immediately bid her good morning, with her usual air of insane glee. "And d'ye ken, lass," said Madge, "there's queer things chanced since ye hae been in the land of Nod.[8] The constables hae been here, woman, and they met wi' my minnie at the door, and they whirled her awa to the Justice's about the man's wheat.—Dear! thae English churles think as muckle about a blade of wheat or grass, as a Scots laird does about his maukins and his muir-poots. Now, lass, if ye like, we'll play them a fine jink; we will awa out and take a walk—they will make an unco wark when they miss us, but we can easily be back by dinner time, or before dark night at ony rate, and it will be some frolic and fresh air.—But maybe ye wad like to take some breakfast, and then lie down again; I ken by mysell, there's whiles I can sit wi' my head on my hand the haill day, and havena a word to cast at a dog[9]—and other whiles that I canna sit still a moment. That's when the folk think me warst, but I am aye canny eneugh—ye needna be feared to walk wi' me."

Had Madge Wildfire been the most raging lunatic, instead of possessing a doubtful, uncertain, and twilight sort of rationality,

---

* Lay ourselves down to sleep.

varying, probably, from the influence of the most trivial causes, Jeanie would hardly have objected to leave a place of captivity where she had so much to apprehend. She eagerly assured Madge that she had no occasion for farther sleep, no desire whatever for eating; and hoping internally that she was not guilty of sin in doing so, she flattered her keeper's crazy humour for walking in the woods.

"It's no a'thegither for that neither," said poor Madge; "but I am judging ye will wun the better out o' thae folks' hands; no that they are a'thegither bad folks neither, but they have queer ways wi' them, and I whiles dinna think it has been ever very weel wi' my mother and me since we kept sic-like company."

With the haste, the joy, the fear, and the hope of a liberated captive, Jeanie snatched up her little bundle, followed Madge into the free air, and eagerly looked round her for a human habitation; but none was to be seen. The ground was partly cultivated, and partly left in its natural state, according as the fancy of the slovenly agriculturists had decided. In its natural state, it was waste, in some places covered with dwarf trees and bushes, in others swamp, and elsewhere firm and dry downs or pasture grounds.

Jeanie's active mind next led her to conjecture which way the high-road lay, whence she had been forced. If she regained that public road, she imagined she must soon meet some person, or arrive at some house, where she might tell her story, and request protection. But after a glance around her, she saw with regret that she had no means whatever of directing her course with any degree of certainty, and that she was still in dependence upon her crazy companion. "Shall we not walk upon the high-road?" said she to Madge, in such a tone as a nurse uses to coax a child. "It's brawer walking on the road than amang thae wild bushes and whins."

Madge, who was walking very fast, stopped at this question, and looked at Jeanie with a sudden and scrutinizing glance that seemed to indicate complete acquaintance with her purpose. "Aha, lass!" she exclaimed, "are ye gaun to guide us that gate?—Ye'll be for making your heels save your hands,[10] I am judging."

Jeanie hesitated for a moment, at hearing her companion thus express herself, whether she had not better take the hint, and try to outstrip and get rid of her. But she knew not in which direction to fly; she was by no means sure that she would prove the swiftest, and perfectly conscious that, in the event of her being pursued and overtaken, she would be inferior to the madwoman in strength. She therefore gave up thoughts for the present of attempting to escape in that manner, and, saying a few words to allay Madge's suspicions, she followed in anxious apprehension the wayward path by which her guide thought proper to lead her. Madge, infirm of purpose,[11] and easily reconciled to the present scene, whatever it was, began soon to talk with her usual diffuseness of ideas.

"It's a dainty thing to be in the woods on a fine morning like this—I like it far better than the town, for there isna a wheen duddie bairns to be crying after ane, as if ane were a warld's wonder, just because ane maybe is a thought bonnier and better put-on than their neighbours—though, Jeanie, ye suld never be proud o' braw claiths, or beauty neither—waes me! they're but a snare.—I anes thought better o' them, and what came o't?"

"Are ye sure ye ken the way ye are taking us?" said Jeanie, who began to imagine that she was getting deeper into the woods, and more remote from the high-road.

"Do I ken the road?—Wasna I mony a day living here, and whatfor shouldna I ken the road?—I might hae forgotten too, for it was afore my accident; but there are some things ane can never forget, let them try it as muckle as they like."

By this time they had gained the deepest part of a patch of woodland. The trees were a little separated from each other, and at the foot of one of them, a beautiful poplar, was a variegated hillock of wild flowers and moss, such as the poet of Grasmere[12] has described in his verses on the Thorn.[13] So soon as she arrived at this spot, Madge Wildfire, joining her hands above her head, with a loud scream that resembled laughter, flung herself all at once upon the ground, and remained lying there motionless.

Jeanie's first idea was to take the opportunity of flight; but her desire to escape yielded for a moment to apprehension for the poor insane being, who, she thought, might perish for want of relief. With an effort, which, in her circumstances, might be termed heroic, she stooped down, spoke in a soothing tone, and endeavoured to raise up the forlorn creature. She effected this with difficulty, and, as she placed her against the tree in a sitting posture, she observed with surprise, that her complexion, usually florid, was now deadly pale, and that her face was bathed in tears. Notwithstanding her own extreme danger, Jeanie was affected by the situation of her companion; and the rather, that through the whole train of her wavering and inconsistent state of mind and line of conduct, she discerned a general colour of kindness towards herself, for which she felt gratitude.

"Let me alane!—let me alane!" said the poor young woman, as her paroxysm of sorrow began to abate—"Let me alane—it does me good to weep. I canna shed tears but maybe anes or twice a-year, and I aye come to wet this turf with them, that the flowers may grow fair, and the grass may be green."

"But what is the matter with you?" said Jeanie—"Why do you weep so bitterly?"

"There's matter enow," replied the lunatic,—"mair than ae puir mind can bear, I trow. Stay a bit, and I'll tell you a' about it; for I like ye, Jeanie Deans—a'body spoke weel about ye when we lived in the Pleasaunts—And I mind aye the drink o' milk ye gae me yon day, when I had been on Arthur's Seat for four-and-twenty hours, looking for the ship that somebody was sailing in."

These words recalled to Jeanie's recollection, that, in fact, she had been one morning much frightened by meeting a crazy young woman near her father's house at an early hour, and that as she appeared to be harmless, her apprehension had been changed into pity, and she had relieved the unhappy wanderer with some food, which she devoured with the haste of a famished person. The incident, trifling in itself, was at present of great importance, if it should be found to have made a favourable and permanent impression on the mind of the object of her charity.

"Yes," said Madge, "I'll tell ye a' about it, for ye are a decent man's daughter—Douce Davie Deans, ye ken—and maybe ye'll can teach me to find out the narrow way, and the strait path,[14] for I have been burning bricks in Egypt, and walking through the weary wilderness of Sinai,[15] for lang and mony a day. But whenever I think about mine errors, I am like to cover my lip[16] for shame."—Here she looked up and smiled.—"It's a strange thing now—I hae spoke mair gude words to you in ten minutes, than I wad speak to my mother in as mony years—it's no that I dinna think on them—and whiles they are just at my tongue's end, but then comes the Devil, and brushes my lips with his black wing, and lays his broad black loof on my mouth—for a black loof it is, Jeanie—and sweeps away a' my gude thoughts, and dits up my gude words, and pits a wheen fule-sangs and idle vanities in their place."

"Try, Madge," said Jeanie,—"try to settle your mind and make your breast clean, and you'll find your heart easier—Just resist the devil, and he will flee from you[17]—and mind that, as my worthy father tells me, there is nae devil sae deceitfu' as our ain wandering thoughts."

"And that's true too, lass," said Madge, starting up; "and I'll gang a gate where the devil daurna follow me; and it's a gate that you will like dearly to gang—but I'll keep a fast haud o' your arm, for fear Apollyon[18] should stride across the path, as he did in the Pilgrim's Progress."

Accordingly she got up, and, taking Jeanie by the arm, began to walk forward at a great pace; and soon, to her companion's no small joy, came into a marked path, with the meanders of which she seemed perfectly acquainted. Jeanie endeavoured to bring her back to the confessional, but the fancy was gone by. In fact, the mind of this deranged being resembled nothing so much as a quantity of dry leaves,[19] which may for a few minutes remain still, but are instantly discomposed and put in motion by the first casual breath of air. She had now got John Bunyan's parable into her head, to the exclusion of every thing else, and on she went with great volubility.

"Did ye never read the Pilgrim's Progress? And you shall be the woman Christiana, and I will be the maiden Mercy, for ye ken Mercy was of the fairer countenance, and the more alluring[20] than her companion—and if I had my little messan dog here, it would be Great-Heart their guide, ye ken, for he was e'en as bauld, that he wad bark at ony thing twenty times his size; and that was e'en the death of him, for he bit Corporal MacAlpine's heels ae morning when they were hauling me to the guard-house, and Corporal MacAlpine killed the bit faithfu' thing wi' his Lochaber axe—deil pike the Highland banes o' him!"

"O fie, Madge," said Jeanie, "ye should not speak such words."

"It's very true," said Madge, shaking her head; "but then I maunna think on my puir bit doggie Snap, when I saw it lying dying in the gutter. But it's just as weel, for it suffered baith cauld and hunger when it was living, and in the grave there is rest for a' things—rest for the doggie, and my puir bairn, and me."

"Your bairn?" said Jeanie, conceiving that by speaking on such a topic, supposing it to be a real one, she could not fail to bring her companion to a more composed temper.

She was mistaken, however, for Madge coloured, and replied with some anger, "*My* bairn? ay, to be sure, *my* bairn. Whatfor shouldna I hae a bairn, and lose a bairn too, as weel as your bonnie tittie, the Lily of St Leonard's?"

The answer struck Jeanie with some alarm, and she was anxious to soothe the irritation she had unwittingly given occasion to. "I am very sorry for your misfortune——"

"Sorry? what wad ye be sorry for?" answered Madge. "The bairn was a blessing—that is, Jeanie, it wad hae been a blessing if it hadna been for my mother; but my mother's a queer woman.—Ye see, there was an auld carle wi' a bit land, and a gude clat o' siller besides, just the very picture of old Mr Feeblemind or Mr Ready-to-halt,[21] that Great-Heart delivered from Slaygood the giant, when he was rifling him, and about to pick his bones, for Slaygood was of the nature of the flesh-eaters—and Great-Heart killed Giant Despair too—but I am doubting Giant Despair's come alive again, for a' the story book—I find him busy at my heart whiles."

"Weel, and so the auld carle," said Jeanie, for she was painfully interested in getting to the truth of Madge's history, which she could not but suspect was in some extraordinary way linked and entwined with the fate of her sister. She was also desirous, if possible, to engage her companion in some narrative which might be carried on in a lower tone of voice, for she was in great apprehension lest the elevated notes of Madge's conversation should direct her mother or the robbers in search of them.

"And so the auld carle," said Madge, repeating her words—"I wish ye had seen him stoiting about, aff ae leg on to the other, wi' a kind o' dot-and-go-one sort o' motion, as if ilk ane o' his twa legs had belanged to sindry folk—But Gentle George could take him aff brawly—Eh as I used to laugh to see George gang hip-hop like him!— I dinna ken, I think I laughed heartier then than what I do now, though maybe no just sae muckle."

"And who was Gentle George?" said Jeanie, endeavouring to bring her back to her story.

"O, he was Geordie Robertson, ye ken, when he was in Edinburgh; but that's no his right name neither—His name is——But what is your business wi' his name?" said she, as if upon sudden recollection. "What have ye to do asking for folk's names?—Have ye a mind I should scour my knife between your ribs, as my mother says?"

As this was spoken with a menacing tone and gesture, Jeanie hastened to protest her total innocence of purpose in the accidental question which she had asked, and Madge Wildfire went on somewhat pacified.

"Never ask folk's names, Jeanie—it's no civil—I hae seen half a dozen o' folk in my mother's at anes, and ne'er ane o' them ca'd the ither by his name; and Daddie Ratton says, it is the most uncivil thing may be, because the baillie bodies are aye asking fashious questions, when ye saw sic a man, or sic a man; and if ye dinna ken their names, ye ken there can be nae mair speerd about it."

In what strange school, thought Jeanie to herself, has this poor creature been bred up, where such remote precautions are taken against the pursuits of justice? What would my father or Reuben Butler think, if I were to tell them there are sic folk in the world? And to abuse the simplicity of this demented creature! O, that I were but safe at hame amang mine ain leal and true people! and I'll bless God, while I have breath, that placed me amongst those who live in his fear, and under the shadow of his wing.[22]

She was interrupted by the insane laugh of Madge Wildfire, as she saw a magpie hop across the path.

"See there—that was the gate my auld joe used to cross the country, but no just sae lightly—he hadna wings to help his auld legs, I trow; but I behoved to have married him for a' that, Jeanie, or my mother wad hae been the dead o' me. But then came in the story of my poor bairn, and my mother thought he wad be deaved wi' its skirling, and she pat it away in below the bit bourock of turf yonder, just to be out o' the gate; and I think she buried my best wits with it, for I have never been just mysell since. And only think, Jeanie, after my mother had been at a' this pains, the auld doited body Johnny Drottle turned up his nose, and wadna hae aught to say to me! But it's little I care for him, for I have led a merry life ever since, and ne'er a braw gentleman looks at me but ye wad think he was gaun to drop off his horse for mere love of me. I have kend some o' them put their hand in their pocket, and gie me as muckle as sixpence[22] at a time, just for my weel-faurd face."

This speech gave Jeanie a dark insight into Madge's history. She had been courted by a wealthy suitor, whose addresses her mother had favoured, notwithstanding the objection of old age and deformity. She had been seduced by some profligate, and, to conceal her shame and promote the advantageous match she had planned, her mother had not hesitated to destroy the offspring of their intrigue. That the consequence should be the total derangement of a mind which was constitutionally unsettled by giddiness and vanity, was extremely natural; and such was, in fact, the history of Madge Wildfire's insanity.

CHAPTER 31

So free from danger, free from fear,
They cross'd the court—right glad they were.
Christabel

PURSUING the path which Madge had chosen, Jeanie Deans observed, to her no small delight, that marks of more cultivation appeared, and the thatched roofs of houses, with their blue smoke arising in little columns, were seen embosomed in a tuft of trees at some distance. The track led in that direction, and Jeanie, therefore, resolved, while Madge continued to pursue it, that she would ask her no questions; having had the penetration to observe, that by doing so she ran the risk of irritating her guide, or awakening suspicions, to the impressions of which, persons in Madge's unsettled state of mind are particularly liable.

Madge, therefore, uninterrupted, went on with the wild disjointed chat which her rambling imagination suggested; a mood in which she was much more communicative respecting her own history, and that of others, than when there was any attempt made, by direct queries, or cross examination, to extract information on these subjects.

"It's a queer thing," she said, "but whiles I can speak about the bit bairn and the rest of it, just as if it had been another body's, and no my ain; and whiles I am like to break my heart about it—Had you ever a bairn, Jeanie?"

Jeanie replied in the negative.

"Ay; but your sister had though—and I ken what came o't too."

"In the name of heavenly mercy," said Jeanie, forgetting the line of conduct which she had hitherto adopted, "tell me but what became of that unfortunate babe, and"——

Madge stopped, looked at her gravely and fixedly, and then broke into a great fit of laughing—"Aha, lass,—catch me if ye can—I think it's easy to gar you trow ony thing.—How suld I ken ony thing o' your sister's wean? Lasses suld hae naething to do wi' weans till they are married—and then a' the gossips and cummers come in and feast as if it were the blithest day in the warld.—They say maidens' bairns[1] are weel guided. I wot that wasna true of your tittie's and mine; but these are sad tales to tell—I maun just sing a bit to keep up my heart—It's a sang that Gentle George made on me lang syne, when I went with him to Lockington[2] wake, to see him act upon a stage, in fine clothes, with the player folk. He might have dune waur than married me that night as he promised—better wed[3] over the mixen* as over the moor, as they say in Yorkshire—he may gang farther and fare waur[4]—But that's a' ane to the sang,[5]—

> I'm Madge of the country, I'm Madge of the town,
> And I'm Madge of the lad I am blithest to own—
> The Lady of Beever[6] in diamonds may shine,
> But has not a heart half so lightsome as mine.
>
> I am Queen of the Wake,[7] and I'm Lady of May,
> And I lead the blithe ring round the May-pole to-day:
> The wild-fire that flashes so fair and so free
> Was never so bright, or so bonnie as me.

"I like that the best o' a' my sangs," continued the maniac, "because *he* made it. I am often singing it, and that's maybe the reason folks ca' me Madge Wildfire. I aye answer to the name, though it's no my ain, for what's the use of making a fash?"

"But ye shouldna sing upon the Sabbath at least," said Jeanie, who, amid all her distress and anxiety, could not help being scandalized at the deportment of her companion, especially as they now approached near to the little village.

"Ay! is this Sunday?" said Madge. "My mother leads sic a life, wi' turning night into day, that ane loses a' count o' the days o' the week, and disna ken Sunday frae Saturday. Besides, it's a' your whiggery—in England, folks sing when they like—And then, ye ken, you are Christiana, and I am Mercy—and ye ken, as they went on their way they sang."—And she immediately raised one of John Bunyan's ditties:—

> "He that is down need fear no fall,
>   He that is low no pride;
> He that is humble ever shall
>   Have God to be his guide.

---

* A homely proverb, signifying, better wed a neighbour than one fetched from a distance.—Mixen, signifies dunghill.

"Fulness to such a burthen is
    That go on pilgrimage;
Here little, and hereafter bliss,
    Is best from age to age.[8]

"And do ye ken, Jeanie, I think there's much truth in that book the Pilgrim's Progress. The boy that sings that song, was feeding his father's sheep in the Valley of Humiliation, and Mr Great-Heart says, that he lived a merrier life, and had more of the herb called hearts-ease in his bosom, than they that wear silk and velvet like me, and are as bonny as I am."

Jeanie Deans had never read the fanciful and delightful parable to which Madge alluded. Bunyan was, indeed, a rigid Calvinist, but then he was also a member of a Baptist congregation, so that his works had no place on David Deans's shelf of divinity. Madge, however, at some time of her life, had been well acquainted, as it appeared, with the most popular of his performances, which, indeed, rarely fails to make a deep impression upon children and people of the lower rank.

"I am sure," she continued, "I may weel say I am come out of the city of Destruction, for my mother is Mrs Bat's-eyes, that dwells at Deadman's Corner; and Frank Levitt, and Tyburn Tam, they may be likened to Mistrust and Guilt, that came galloping up and struck the poor pilgrim to the ground with a great club, and stole a bag of silver, which was most of his spending money, and so have they done to many, and will do to more. But now we will gang to the Interpreter's house, for I ken a man that will play the Interpreter right weel; for he has eyes lifted up to Heaven, the best of books in his hand, the law of truth written on his lips, and he stands as if he pleaded wi' men—O if I had minded what he said to me, I had never been the cast-away creature that I am!—But it is all over now.—But we'll knock at the gate, and then the keeper will admit Christiana, but Mercy will be left out—and then I'll stand at the door trembling and crying, and then Christiana—that's you, Jeanie,—will intercede for me; and then Mercy,—that's me, ye ken,—will faint; and then the Interpreter—yes, the Interpreter, that's Mr Staunton himself, will come out and take me—that's poor, lost, demented me—by the hand, and give me a pomegranate, and a piece of honeycomb, and a small bottle of spirits, to stay my fainting—and then the good times will come back again, and we'll be the happiest folk you ever saw."

In the midst of the confused assemblage of ideas indicated in this speech, Jeanie thought she saw a serious purpose on the part of Madge, to endeavour to obtain the pardon and countenance of some one whom she had offended; an attempt the most likely of all others to bring them once more into contact with law and legal protection. She, therefore, resolved to be guided by her while she was in so hopeful a disposition, and act for her own safety according to circumstances.

They were now close by the village, one of those beautiful scenes which are so often found in merry England,[9] where the cottages, instead of being built in two straight lines, one on each side of a dusty high-road, stand in detached groupes, interspersed not only with large oaks and elms, but with fruit-trees, so many of which were at this time in flourish, that the grove seemed enamelled with their crimson and white blossoms. In the centre of the hamlet stood the parish church and its little Gothic tower, from which at present was heard the Sunday chime of bells.

"We will wait here until the folks are a' in the church—they ca the kirk a church in England, Jeanie, be sure you mind that—for if I was gaun forward amang them, a' the gaitts o' boys and lasses wad be crying at Madge Wildfire's tail, the little hell-rakers, and the beadle would be as hard upon us as if it was our fault. I like their skirling as ill as he does, I can tell him; I'm sure I often wish there was a het peat doun their throats when they set them up that gate."

Conscious of the disorderly appearance of her own dress after the adventure of the preceding night, and of the grotesque habit and demeanour of her guide, and sensible how important it was to secure an attentive and patient audience to her strange story from some one who might have the means to protect her, Jeanie readily acquiesced in Madge's proposal to rest under the trees, by which they were still somewhat screened, until the commencement of service should give them an opportunity of entering the hamlet without attracting a crowd around them. She made the less opposition, that Madge had intimated that this was not the village where her mother was in custody, and that the two squires of the pad[10] were absent in a different direction.

She sate herself down, therefore, at the foot of an oak, and by the assistance of a placid fountain which had been dammed up for the use of the villagers, and which served her as a natural mirror, she began— no uncommon thing with a Scottish maiden of her rank,—to arrange her toilette in the open air, and bring her dress, soiled and disordered as it was, into such order as the place and circumstances admitted.

She soon perceived reason, however, to regret that she had set about this task, however decent and necessary, in the present time and society. Madge Wildfire, who, among other indications of insanity, had a most over-weening opinion of those charms, to which, in fact, she had owed her misery, and whose mind, like a raft upon a lake, was agitated and driven about at random by each fresh impulse, no sooner beheld Jeanie begin to arrange her hair, place her bonnet in order, rub the dust from her shoes and clothes, adjust her neck-handkerchief and mittans, and so forth, than with imitative zeal she began to bedizen and trick herself out with shreds and remnants of beggarly finery, which she took out of a little bundle, and which, when disposed around her person, made her appearance ten times more fantastic and apish than it had been before.

Jeanie groaned in spirit, but dared not interfere in a matter so delicate. Across the man's cap or riding hat which she wore, Madge placed a broken and soiled white feather, intersected with one which had been shed from the train of a peacock. To her dress, which was a kind of riding-habit, she stitched, pinned, and otherwise secured, a large furbelow of artificial flowers, all crushed, wrinkled, and dirty, which had first bedecked a lady of quality, then descended to her Abigail, and dazzled the inmates of the servants' hall. A tawdry scarf of yellow silk, trimmed with tinsel and spangles, which had seen as hard service, and boasted as honourable a transmission, was next flung over one shoulder, and fell across her person in the manner of a shoulder-belt or baldrick. Madge then stripped off the coarse ordinary shoes which she wore, and replaced them by a pair of dirty satin ones, spangled and embroidered to match the scarf, and furnished with very high heels. She had cut a willow switch in her morning's walk, almost as long as a boy's fishing-rod. This she set herself seriously to peel, and when it was transformed into such a wand as the Treasurer or High Steward bears on public occasions, she told Jeanie that she thought they now looked decent, as young women should do, upon the Sunday morning, and that as the bells had done ringing, she was willing to conduct her to the Interpreter's house.

Jeanie sighed heavily, to think it should be her lot on the Lord's day, and during kirk-time too, to parade the street of an inhabited village with so very grotesque a comrade; but necessity had no law,[11] since, without a positive quarrel with the madwoman, which, in the circumstances, would have been very unadvisable, she could see no means of shaking herself free of her society.

As for poor Madge, she was completely elated with personal vanity, and the most perfect satisfaction concerning her own dazzling dress, and superior appearance. They entered the hamlet without being observed, except by one old woman, who, being nearly "high-gravel blind," was only conscious that something very fine and glittering was passing by, and dropped as deep a reverence to Madge as she would have done to a countess. This filled up the measure of Madge's self-approbation. She minced, she ambled, she smiled, she simpered, and waved Jeanie Deans forward with the condescension of a noble *chaperone*, who has undertaken the charge of a country miss on her first journey to the capital.

Jeanie followed in patience, and with her eyes fixed on the ground, that she might save herself the mortification of seeing her companion's absurdities; but she started when, ascending two or three steps, she found herself in the church-yard, and saw that Madge was making straight for the door of the church. As Jeanie had no mind to enter the congregation in such company, she walked aside from the path-way, and said in a decided tone, "Madge, I will wait here till the church comes out—you may go in by yourself, if you have a mind."

As she spoke these words, she was about to seat herself upon one of the grave-stones.

Madge was a little before Jeanie when she turned aside; but suddenly changing her course, she followed her with long strides, and, with every feature inflamed with passion, overtook and seized her by the arm. "Do ye think, ye ungratefu' wretch, that I am gaun to let you sit doun upon my father's grave? The deil settle ye doun, if ye dinna rise and come into the Interpreter's house, that's the house of God, wi' me, but I'll rive every dud aff your back!"

She adapted the action to the phrase; for with one clutch she stripped Jeanie of her straw bonnet and a handful of her hair to boot, and threw it up into an old yew tree, where it stuck fast. Jeanie's first impulse was to scream, but conceiving she might receive deadly harm before she could obtain the assistance of any one, notwithstanding the vicinity of the church, she thought it wiser to follow the madwoman into the congregation, where she might find some means of escape from her, or at least be secured against her violence. But when she meekly intimated her consent to follow Madge, her guide's uncertain brain had caught another train of ideas. She held Jeanie fast with one hand, and with the other pointed to the inscription on the gravestone, and commanded her to read it. Jeanie obeyed, and read these words:—

"THIS MONUMENT WAS ERECTED TO THE MEMORY OF DONALD MUR-
DOCKSON OF THE KING'S XXVI, OR CAMERONIAN REGIMENT, A SINCERE
CHRISTIAN, A BRAVE SOLDIER, AND A FAITHFUL SERVANT, BY HIS GRATE-
FUL AND SORROWING MASTER, ROBERT STAUNTON."

"It's very weel read, Jeanie; it's just the very words," said Madge,
whose ire had now faded into deep melancholy, and with a step,
which, to Jeanie's great joy, was uncommonly quiet and mournful, she
led her companion towards the door of the church.

It was one of those old-fashioned Gothic parish churches which are
frequent in England, the most cleanly, decent, and reverential places
of worship that are, perhaps, any where to be found in the Christian
world. Yet, notwithstanding the decent solemnity of its exterior,
Jeanie was too faithful to the directory[12] of the presbyterian kirk to
have entered a prelatic place of worship, and would, upon any other
occasion, have thought that she beheld in the porch the venerable
figure of her father waving her back from the entrance, and pronouncing in a solemn tone, "Cease, my child, to hear the instruction which
causeth to err from the words of knowledge."[13] But in her present
agitating and alarming situation, she took for safety to this forbidden
place of assembly, as the hunted animal will sometimes seek shelter
from imminent danger in the human habitation, or in other places of
refuge most alien to its nature and habits. Not even the sound of the
organ,[14] and of one or two flutes which accompanied the psalmody,
prevented her from following her guide into the chancel[15] of the
church.

No sooner had Madge put her foot upon the pavement, and become
sensible that she was the object of attention to the spectators, than she
resumed all the fantastic extravagance of deportment which some
transient touch of melancholy had banished for an instant. She swam
rather than walked up the centre aisle, dragging Jeanie after her,
whom she held fast by the hand. She would, indeed, have fain slipped
aside into the pew nearest to the door, and left Madge to ascend in her
own manner and alone to the high places of the synagogue; but this
was impossible, without a degree of violent resistance, which seemed
to her inconsistent with the time and place, and she was accordingly
led in captivity up the whole length of the church by her grotesque
conductress, who, with half-shut eyes, a prim smile upon her lips, and
a mincing motion with her hands, which corresponded with the
delicate and affected pace at which she was pleased to move, seemed to
take the general stare of the congregation, which such an exhibition

necessarily excited, as a high compliment, and which she returned by nods and half curtsies to individuals amongst the audience, whom she seemed to distinguish as acquaintances. Her absurdity was enhanced in the eyes of the spectators by the strange contrast which she formed to her companion, who, with dishevelled hair, downcast eyes, and a face glowing with shame, was dragged as it were in triumph after her.

Madge's airs were at length fortunately cut short by her encountering in her progress the looks of the clergyman, who fixed upon her a glance at once steady, compassionate, and admonitory. She hastily opened an empty pew which happened to be near her, and entered, dragging in Jeanie after her. Kicking Jeanie on the shins, by way of hint that she should follow her example, she sunk her head upon her hand for the space of a minute. Jeanie, to whom this posture of mental devotion was entirely new, did not attempt to do the like, but looked round her with a bewildered stare, which her neighbours, judging from the company in which they saw her, very naturally ascribed to insanity. Every person in their immediate vicinity drew back from this extraordinary couple as far as the limits of their pew permitted, but one old man could not get beyond Madge's reach, ere she had snatched the prayer-book from his hand, and ascertained the lesson of the day.[16] She then turned up the ritual, and, with the most overstrained enthusiasm of gesture and manner, shewed Jeanie the passages as they were read in the service, making at the same time her own responses so loud as to be heard above those of every other person.

Notwithstanding the shame and vexation which Jeanie felt in being thus exposed in a place of worship, she could not and durst not omit rallying her spirits so as to look around her, and consider to whom she ought to appeal for protection so soon as the service should be concluded. Her first ideas naturally fixed upon the clergyman, and she was confirmed in the resolution by observing that he was an aged gentleman, of a dignified appearance and deportment, who read the service with an undisturbed and decent gravity, which brought back to becoming attention those younger members of the congregation who had been disturbed by the extravagant behaviour of Madge Wildfire. To the clergyman, therefore, Jeanie resolved to make her appeal when the service was over.

It is true she felt disposed to be shocked at his surplice,[17] of which she had heard so much, but which she had never seen upon the person of a preacher of the word. Then she was confused by the change of posture adopted in different parts of the ritual, the more so as Madge Wildfire, to whom they seemed familiar, took the opportunity to exercise authority over her, pulling her up and pushing her down with a bustling assiduity, which Jeanie felt must make them both the objects of painful attention. But notwithstanding these prejudices, it was her prudent resolution, in this dilemma, to imitate as nearly as she could what was done around her. The prophet, she thought, permitted Naaman the Syrian to bow even in the house of Rimmon.—Surely if I, in this streight, worship the God of my fathers in mine own language, although the manner thereof be strange to me, the Lord will pardon me in this thing.[18]

In this resolution she became so much confirmed, that, withdrawing herself from Madge as far as the pew permitted, she endeavoured to evince, by serious and undeviating attention to what was passing, that her mind was composed to devotion. Her tormentor would not long have permitted her to remain quiet, but fatigue overpowered her, and she fell fast asleep in the other corner of the pew.

Jeanie, though her mind in her own despite sometimes reverted to her situation, compelled herself to give attention to a sensible, energetic, and well-composed discourse, upon the practical doctrines of Christianity, which she could not help approving, although it was every word written down[19] and read by the preacher, and although it was delivered in a tone and gesture very different from those of Boanerges Stormheaven, who was her father's favourite preacher. The serious and placid attention with which Jeanie listened did not escape the clergyman. Madge Wildfire's entrance had rendered him apprehensive of some disturbance, to provide against which, as far as possible, he often turned his eyes to the part of the church where Jeanie and she were placed, and became soon aware that, although the loss of her head-gear, and the awkwardness of her situation, had given an uncommon and anxious air to the features of the former, yet she was in a state of mind very different from that of her companion. When he dismissed the congregation, he observed her look around with a wild and terrified aspect, as if uncertain what course she ought to adopt, and noticed that she approached one or two of the most decent of the congregation, as if to address them, and then shrunk back timidly, on observing that they seemed to shun and to avoid her. The clergyman was satisfied there must be something extraordinary in all this, and as a benevolent man, as well as a good Christian pastor, he resolved to enquire into the matter more minutely.

CHAPTER 32

——There govern'd in that year
A stern, stout churl—an angry overseer.
                                        CRABBE

WHILE Mr Staunton,[1] for such was this worthy clergyman's name,
was laying aside his gown in the vestry, Jeanie was in the act of
coming to an open rupture with Madge.

"We must return to Mummer's barn directly," said Madge; "we'll
be ower late, and my mother will be angry."

"I am not going back with you, Madge," said Jeanie, taking out a
guinea, and offering it to her; "I am much obliged to you, but I maun
gang my ain road."

"And me coming a' this way out o' my gate to pleasure you, ye
ungratefu' cutty," answered Madge; "and me to be brained by my
mother when I gang hame, and a' for your sake—but I will gar ye as
good"—

"For God's sake!" said Jeanie to a man who stood beside them,
"keep her off—she is mad."

"Ey—ey," answered the boor; "I hae some guess of that, and I
trow thou be'st a bird of the same feather. Howsomever, Madge, I
redd thee keep hand off her, or I'se lend thee a whister-poop."[2]

Several of the lower class of the parishioners now gathered round
the strangers, and the cry arose among the boys, that "there was a-
going to be a fite between mad Madge Murdockson and another Bess
of Bedlam." But while the fry assembled with the humane hope of
seeing as much of the fun as possible, the laced cocked-hat of the
beadle was discerned among the multitude, and all made way for that
person of awful authority. His first address was to Madge.

"What's brought thee back again, thou silly donnot, to plague this
parish? Hast thou brought ony more bastards wi' thee to lay to honest
men's doors? or does thou think to burthen us with this goose, that's
as gare-brained as thysell, as if rates were no up enow? Away wi' thee
to thy thief of a mother; she's fast in the stocks at Barkston town-
end—Away wi' ye out o' the parish, or I'se be at ye with the rattan."

Madge stood sulky for a minute; but she had been too often taught submission to the beadle's authority by ungentle means, to feel courage enough to dispute it.

"And my mother—my puir auld mother, is in the stocks at Barkston!—This is a' your wyte, Miss Jeanie Deans; but I'll be upsides wi' you, as sure as my name's Madge Wildfire—I mean Murdockson—God help me, I forget my very name in this confused waste."

So saying, she turned upon her heel, and went off, followed by all the mischievous imps of the village, some crying, "Madge, canst thou tell thy name yet?" some pulling the skirts of her dress, and all, to the best of their strength and ingenuity, exercising some new device or other to exasperate her into frenzy.

Jeanie saw her departure with infinite delight, though she wished, that, in some way or other, she could have requited the service Madge had conferred upon her.

In the meantime, she applied to the beadle to know, whether "there was any house in the village where she could be civilly entertained for her money, and whether she could be permitted to speak to the clergyman?"

"Ay, ay, we'se ha' reverend care on thee; and I think," answered the man of constituted authority, "that, unless thou answer the Rector all the better, we'se spare thy money, and gie thee lodging at the parish charge,³ young woman."

"Where am I to go, then?" said Jeanie, in some alarm.

"Why, I am to take thee to his Reverence, in the first place, to gie an account o' thysell; and to see thou come na to be a burthen upon the parish."

"I do not wish to burthen any one," replied Jeanie; "I have enough for my own wants, and only wish to get on my journey safely."

"Why, that's another matter," replied the beadle; "an if it be true— and I think thou doest not look so polrumptious as thy play-fellow yonder—thou wouldst be a nittle⁴ lass enow, an thou wert snog and snod⁵ a bit better. Come thou away then—the Rector is a good man."

"Is that the minister," said Jeanie, "who preached"——

"The minister? Lord help thee! What kind o' presbyterian art thou?—Why, 'tis the Rector⁶—the Rector's sell, woman, and there isna the like o' him in the county, nor the four next to it. Come away—away with thee—we munna bide here."

"I am sure I am very willing to go to see the minister," said Jeanie;

"for, though he read his discourse, and wore that surplice, as they call it here, I canna but think he must be a very worthy God-fearing man, to preach the root of the matter[7] in the way he did."

The disappointed rabble, finding that there was like to be no farther sport, had by this time dispersed, and Jeanie, with her usual patience, followed her consequential and surly, but not brutal, conductor towards the Rectory.

This clerical mansion was large and commodious, for the living was an excellent one, and the advowson belonged to a very wealthy family in the neighbourhood, who had usually bred up a son or nephew to the church, for the sake of inducting him, as opportunity offered, into this very comfortable provision. In this manner the Rectory of Willingham had always been considered as a direct and immediate appanage of Willingham-hall; and as the rich baronets to whom the latter belonged, had usually a son, or brother, or nephew settled in the living, the utmost care had been taken to render their habitation not merely respectable and commodious, but even dignified and imposing.

It was situated about four hundred yards from the village, and on a rising ground which sloped gently upward, covered with small enclosures, or closes, laid out irregularly, so that the old oaks and elms which were planted in hedge-rows, fell into perspective and were blended together in beautiful irregularity. When they approached nearer to the house, a handsome gate-way admitted them into a lawn, of narrow dimensions indeed, but which was interspersed with large sweet chesnut trees and beeches, and kept in handsome order. The front of the house was irregular. Part of it seemed very old, and had, in fact, been the residence of the incumbent in Romish times. Successive occupants had made considerable additions and improvements, each in the taste of his own age, and without much regard to symmetry. But these incongruities of architecture were so graduated and happily mingled, that the eye, far from being displeased with the combinations of various styles, saw nothing but what was interesting in the varied and intricate pile which they exhibited. Fruit-trees displayed on the southern wall, outer stair-cases, various places of entrance, a combination of roofs and chimneys of different ages, united to render the front, not indeed beautiful or grand, but intricate, perplexed, or, to use Mr Price's[8] appropriate phrase, picturesque. The most considerable addition was that of the present Rector, who "being a bookish man," as the beadle was at the pains to inform Jeanie, to augment, perhaps, her reverence for the person before whom she was to appear, had built a handsome library and parlour, and no less than two additional bed-rooms.

"Mony men would hae scrupled such expence," continued the parochial officer, "seeing as the living mun go as it pleases Sir Edmund to will it; but his Reverence has a canny bit land of his own, and need not look on two sides of a penny."

Jeanie could not help comparing the irregular yet extensive and commodious pile of building before her, to the "Manses" in her own country, where a set of penurious heritors, professing all the while the devotion of their lives and fortunes to the presbyterian establishment, strain their inventions to discover what may be nipped, and clipped, and pared from a building which forms but a poor accommodation even for the present incumbent, and, despite the superior advantage of stone masonry, must, in the course of forty or fifty years, again burthen their descendants with an expence, which, once liberally and handsomely employed, ought to have freed their estates from a recurrence of it for more than a century at least.

Behind the Rector's house the ground sloped down to a small river, which, without possessing the romantic vivacity and rapidity of a northern stream, was, nevertheless, by its occasional appearance through the ranges of willows and poplars that crowned its banks, a very pleasing accompaniment to the landscape. "It was the best trouting stream," said the beadle, whom the patience of Jeanie, and especially the assurance that she was not about to become a burthen to the parish, had rendered rather communicative, "the best trouting stream in all Lincolnshire, for when you got lower, there was nought to be done wi' fly-fishing."

Turning aside from the principal entrance, he conducted Jeanie towards a sort of portal connected with the older part of the building, which was chiefly occupied by servants, and knocking at the door, it was opened by a servant in grave purple livery, such as befitted a wealthy and dignified clergyman.

"How dost do, Tummas?" said the beadle—"and how's young Measter Staunton?"

"Why, but poorly—but poorly, Measter Stubbs.—Are you wanting to see his Reverence?"

"Ay, ay, Tummas; please to say I ha' brought up the young woman as came to sarvice to-day with mad Madge Murdockson—she seems to be a decentish koind o' body; but I ha' asked her never a question. Only I can tell his Reverence that she is a Scotchwoman, I judge, and as flat as the fens of Holland."

Tummas honoured Jeanie Deans with such a stare, as the pampered domestics of the rich, whether spiritual or temporal, usually esteem it part of their privilege to bestow upon the poor, and then desired Mr Stubbs and his charge to step in till he informed his master of their presence.

The room into which he shewed them was a sort of steward's parlour, hung with a county map or two, and three or four prints of eminent persons connected with the county, as Sir William Monson,[10] James York the blacksmith of Lincoln,[11] and the famous Peregrine, Lord Willoughby,[12] in complete armour, looking as when he said, in the words of the legend below the engraving,—

> Stand to it, noble pikemen,
>   And face ye well about;
> And shoot ye sharp, bold bowmen,
>   And we will keep them out.
> Ye musquet and calliver-men,
>   Do you prove true to me,
> I'll be the foremost man in fight,
>   Said brave Lord Willoughbee.

When they had entered this apartment, Tummas as a matter of course offered, and as a matter of course Mr Stubbs accepted, a "summat" to eat and drink, being the respectable reliques of a gammon of bacon, and a *whole whiskin*, or black pot of sufficient double ale. To these eatables Mr Beadle seriously inclined himself, and (for we must do him justice) not without an invitation to Jeanie, in which Tummas joined, that his prisoner or charge would follow his good example. But although she might have stood in need of refreshment, considering she had tasted no food that day, the anxiety of the moment, her own sparing and abstemious habits, and a bashful aversion to eat in company of the two strangers, induced her to decline their courtesy. So she sate in a chair apart, while Mr Stubbs and Mr Tummas, who had chosen to join his friend in consideration that dinner was to be put back till the afternoon service was over, made a hearty luncheon, which lasted for half an hour, and might not then have concluded, had not his Reverence rung his bell, so that Tummas was obliged to attend his master. Then, and no sooner, to save himself the labour of a second journey to the other end of the house, he announced to his master the arrival of Mr Stubbs, with the other mad-woman, as he chose to designate Jeanie, as an event which had just taken place. He returned with an order that Mr Stubbs and the young woman should be instantly ushered up to the library.

The beadle bolted in haste his last mouthful of fat bacon, washed down the greasy morsel with the last rinsings of the pot of ale, and immediately marshalled Jeanie through one or two intricate passages which led from the ancient to the more modern buildings, into a handsome little hall, or anti-room, adjoining to the library, and out of which a glass door opened to the lawn.

"Stay here," said Stubbs, "till I tell his Reverence you are come."

So saying, he opened a door and entered the library.

Without wishing to hear their conversation, Jeanie, as she was circumstanced, could not avoid it; for as Stubbs stood by the door, and his Reverence was at the upper end of a large room, their conversation was necessarily audible in the anti-room.

"So you have brought the young woman here at last, Mr Stubbs. I expected you some time since. You know I do not wish such persons to remain in custody a moment without some enquiry into their situation."

"Very true, your Reverence," replied the beadle; "but the young woman had eat nought to-day, and soa Measter Tummas did set down a drap of drink and a morsel, to be sure."

"Thomas was very right, Mr Stubbs; and what has become of the other most unfortunate being?"

"Why," replied Mr Stubbs, "I did think the sight on her would but vex your Reverence, and soa I did let her go her ways back to her muther, who is in trouble in the next parish."

"In trouble!—that signifies in prison, I suppose?" said Mr Staunton.

"Ay, truly; something like it, an it like your Reverence."

"Wretched, unhappy, incorrigible woman!" said the clergyman. "And what sort of person is this companion of hers?"

"Why, decent enow, an it like your Reverence," said Stubbs; "for aught I sees of her, there's no harm of her, and she says she has cash enow to carry her out of the county."

"Cash? that is always what you think of, Stubbs—But, has she sense? —has she her wits?—has she the capacity of taking care of herself?"

"Why, your Reverence," replied Stubbs, "I cannot just say—I will be sworn she was not born at Witt-ham;*[13] for Gaffer Gibbs looked at

* A proverbial and punning expression in that county, to intimate that a person is not very clever.

her all the time of sarvice, and he says she could not turn up a single lesson like a Christian, even though she had Madge Murdockson to help her—But then, as to fending for hersell, why, she's a bit of a Scotchwoman, your Reverence, and they say the worst donnot of them can look out for their own turn—and she is decently put on enow, and not behounched like t'other."

"Send her in here then, and do you remain below, Mr Stubbs."

This colloquy had engaged Jeanie's attention so deeply, that it was not until it was over that she observed that the sashed door, which, we have said, led from the anti-room into the garden, was opened, and that there entered, or rather was borne in by two assistants, a young man, of a very pale and sickly appearance, whom they lifted to the nearest couch, and placed there, as if to recover from the fatigue of an unusual exertion. Just as they were making this arrangement, Stubbs came out of the library, and summoned Jeanie to enter it. She obeyed him not without tremor, for besides the novelty of the situation to a girl of her secluded habits, she felt also as if the successful prosecution of her journey was to depend upon the impression she should be able to make on Mr Staunton.

It is true, it was difficult to suppose on what pretext a person travelling on her own business, and at her own charge, could be interrupted upon her route. But the violent detention she had already undergone was sufficient to show that there existed persons at no great distance who had the interest, the inclination, and the audacity forcibly to stop her journey, and she felt the necessity of having some countenance and protection, at least till she should get beyond their reach. While these things passed through her mind, much faster than our pen and ink can record, or even the reader's eye collect the meaning of its traces, Jeanie found herself in a handsome library, and in presence of the Rector of Willingham. The well-furnished presses and shelves which surrounded the large and handsome apartment, contained more books than Jeanie imagined existed in the world, being accustomed to consider as an extensive collection two fir shelves, each about three feet long, which contained her father's treasured volumes, the whole pith and marrow,[14] as he used sometimes to boast, of modern divinity.[15] An orrery, globes, a telescope, and some other scientific implements, conveyed to Jeanie an impression of admiration and wonder not unmixed with fear, for, in her ignorant apprehension, they seemed rather adapted for magical purposes than any other; and a few stuffed animals (as the Rector was fond of natural history,) added to the impressive character of the apartment.

Mr Staunton spoke to her with great mildness. He observed, that although her appearance at church had been uncommon, and in strange, and, he must add, discreditable society, and calculated, upon the whole, to disturb the congregation during divine worship, he wished, nevertheless, to hear her own account of herself before taking any steps which his duty might seem to demand. He was a justice of peace, he informed her, as well as a clergyman.

"His honour" (for she would not say his reverence,) "was very civil and kind," was all that poor Jeanie could at first bring out.

"Who are you, young woman?" said the clergyman, more peremptorily—"and what do you do in this country, and in such company?—We allow no strollers or vagrants here."

"I am not a vagrant or a stroller, sir," said Jeanie, a little roused by the supposition. "I am a decent Scots lass, travelling through the land on my own business and my own expences; and I was so unhappy as to fall in with bad company, and was stopped a' night on my journey. And this puir creature, who is something light-headed, let me out in the morning."

"Bad company!" said the clergyman. "I am afraid, young woman, you have not been sufficiently anxious to avoid them."

"Indeed, sir," returned Jeanie, "I have been brought up to shun evil communication.[16] But these wicked people were thieves, and stopped me by violence and mastery."

"Thieves!" said Mr Staunton; "then you charge them with robbery, I suppose?"

"No, sir; they did not take so much as a boddle from me," answered Jeanie; "nor did they use me ill, otherwise than by confining me."

The clergyman enquired into the particulars of her adventure, which she told him from point to point.

"This is an extraordinary, and not a very probable tale, young woman," resumed Mr Staunton. "Here has been, according to your account, a great violence committed without any adequate motive. Are you aware of the law of this country—that if you lodge this charge you will be bound over to prosecute this gang?"

Jeanie did not understand him, and he explained that the English law, in addition to the inconvenience sustained by persons who have been robbed or injured, has the goodness to entrust to them the care and the expence[17] of appearing as prosecutors.

Jeanie said, "that her business at London was express; all she wanted was, that any gentleman would, out of Christian charity, protect her to some town where she could hire horses and a guide; and, finally," she thought, "it would be her father's mind that she was not free to give testimony in an English court of justice, as the land was not under a direct gospel dispensation."

Mr Staunton stared a little, and asked if her father was a Quaker.

"God forbid, sir," said Jeanie—"He is nae schismatic nor sectary, nor ever treated for sic black commodities[18] as theirs, and that's weel kend o' him."

"And what is his name, pray?" said Mr Staunton.

"David Deans, sir, the cow-feeder at St Leonard's Crags, near Edinburgh."

A deep groan from the anti-room prevented the rector from replying, and, exclaiming, "Good God! that unhappy boy!" he left Jeanie alone, and hastened into the outer apartment.

Some noise and bustle was heard, but no one entered the library for the best part of an hour.

CHAPTER 33

Fantastic passions! maddening brawl!
And shame and terror over all!
Deeds to be hid which were not hid,
Which all confused, I could not know
Whether I suffered or I did,
For all seemed guilt, remorse, or woe;
My own, or other's, still the same
Life-stifling fear, soul-stifling shame.

COLERIDGE

DURING the interval while she was thus left alone, Jeanie anxiously revolved in her mind what course was best for her to pursue. She was impatient to continue her journey, yet she feared she could not safely adventure to do so while the old hag and her assistants were in the neighbourhood, without risking a repetition of their violence. She thought she could collect from the conversation which she had partly overheard, and also from the wild confessions of Madge Wildfire, that her mother had a deep and revengeful motive for obstructing her journey if possible. And from whom could she hope for assistance if not from Mr Staunton? His whole appearance and demeanour seemed to encourage her hopes. His features were handsome, though marked with a deep cast of melancholy; his tone and language were gentle and encouraging; and, as he had served in the army for several years during his youth, his air retained that easy frankness which is peculiar to the profession of arms. He was, besides, a minister of the gospel; and although only a worshipper, according to Jeanie's notions, in the Court of the Gentiles,[1] and so benighted as to wear a surplice; although he read the Common Prayer, and wrote down every word of his sermon[2] before delivering it; and although he was, moreover, in strength of lungs, as well as pith and marrow[3] of doctrine, vastly inferior to Boanerges Stormheaven, Jeanie still thought he must be a very different person from Curate Kiltstoup, and other prelatical divines of her father's earlier days, who used to get drunk in their canonical dress, and hound out the dragoons against the wandering Cameronians. The house seemed to be in some disturbance, but as she could not suppose she was altogether forgotten, she thought it better to remain quiet in the apartment where she had been left, till some one should take notice of her.

The first who entered was, to her no small delight, one of her own sex, a motherly-looking aged person of a house-keeper. To her Jeanie explained her situation in a few words, and begged her assistance.

The dignity of a housekeeper did not encourage too much familiarity with a person who was at the Rectory on justice-business, and whose character might seem in her eyes somewhat precarious; but she was civil, although distant.

"Her young master," she said, "had had a bad accident by a fall from his horse, which made him liable to fainting fits; he had been taken very ill just now, and it was impossible his Reverence could see Jeanie for some time; but that she need not fear his doing all that was just and proper in her behalf the instant he could get her business attended to."—She concluded by offering to show Jeanie a room, where she might remain till his Reverence was at leisure.

Our heroine took the opportunity to request the means of adjusting and changing her dress.

The housekeeper, in whose estimation order and cleanliness ranked high among personal virtues, gladly complied with a request so reasonable; and the change of dress which Jeanie's bundle furnished, made so important an improvement in her appearance, that the old lady hardly knew the spoiled and disordered traveller, whose attire shewed the violence she had sustained, in the neat, clean, quiet-looking little Scotchwoman, who now stood before her. Encouraged by such a favourable alteration in her appearance, Mrs Dalton ventured to invite Jeanie to partake of her dinner, and was equally pleased with the decent propriety of her conduct during that meal.

"Thou canst read this book, canst thou, young woman?" said the old lady when their meal was concluded, laying her hand upon a large Bible.

"I hope sae, madam," said Jeanie, surprised at the question; "my father wad hae wanted mony a thing, ere I had wanted *that* schuling."

"The better sign of him, young woman. There are men here, well to pass in the world, would not want their share of a Leicestershire plover, and that's a bag-pudding,[4] if fasting for three hours would make all their poor children read the Bible from end to end. Take thou the book, then, for my eyes are something dazed, and read where thou listest—it's the only book thou canst not happen wrong in."

Jeanie was at first tempted to turn up the parable of the good Samaritan,[5] but her conscience checked her, as if it were an using of Scripture, not for her own edification, but to work upon the mind of others for the relief of her worldly afflictions; and under this scrupulous sense of duty, she selected, in preference, a chapter of the prophet Isaiah, and read it, notwithstanding her northern accent and tone, with a devout propriety, which greatly edified Mrs Dalton.

"Ah," she said, "an all Scotchwomen were sic as thou!—but it was our luck to get born devils of thy country, I think—every one worse than t'other. If thou knowest of any tidy lass like thysell, that wanted a place, and could bring a good character, and would not go laiking about to wakes and fairs, and wore shoes and stockings all the day round—why, I'll not say but we might find room for her at the Rectory. Hast no cousin or sister, lass, that such an offer would suit?"

This was touching upon a sore point, but Jeanie was spared the pain of replying by the entrance of the same man-servant she had seen before.

"Meester wishes to see the young woman from Scotland," was Tummas's address.

"Go to his Reverence, my dear, as fast as you can, and tell him all your story—his Reverence is a kind man," said Mrs Dalton. "I will fold down the leaf, and make you a cup of tea, with some nice muffin, against you come down, and that's what you seldom see in Scotland, girl."

"Meester's waiting for the young woman," said Tummas impatiently.

"Well, Mr Jack-Sauce, and what is your business to put in your oar?—And how often must I tell you to call Mr Staunton his Reverence, seeing as he is a dignified clergyman, and not be meastering, meastering him, as if he were a little petty squire?"

As Jeanie was now at the door and ready to accompany Tummas, the footman said nothing till he got into the passage, when he muttered, "There are moe masters than one in this house, and I think we shall have a mistress too, an Dame Dalton carries it thus."

Tummas led the way through a more intricate range of passages than Jeanie had yet threaded, and ushered her into an apartment which was darkened by the closing of most of the window-shutters, and in which was a bed with the curtains partly drawn.

"Here is the young woman, sir," said Tummas.

"Very well," said a voice from the bed, but not that of his Reverence; "be ready to answer the bell, and leave the room."

"There is some mistake," said Jeanie, confounded at finding herself in the apartment of an invalid, "the servant told me that the minister"——

"Don't trouble yourself," said the invalid, "there is no mistake. I know more of your affairs than my father, and I can manage them better—Leave the room, Tom." The servant obeyed.—"We must not," said the invalid, "lose time, when we have little to lose. Open the shutter of that window."

She did so, and as he drew aside the curtain of his bed, the light fell on his pale countenance, as, turban'd with bandages, and dressed in a night-gown, he lay seemingly exhausted upon the bed.

"Look at me," he said. "Jeanie Deans, can you not recollect me?"

"No, sir," said she, full of surprise. "I was never in this country before."

"But I may have been in yours. Think—recollect. I would fain not name the name you are most dearly bound to loathe and to detest. Think—remember!"

A terrible recollection flashed on Jeanie, which every tone of the speaker confirmed, and which his next words rendered certainty.

"Be composed—remember Muschat's Cairn, and the moonlight night."

Jeanie sunk down on a chair, with clasped hands, and gasped in agony.

"Yes, here I lie," he said, "like a crushed snake, writhing with impatience at my incapacity of motion—here I lie, when I ought to have been in Edinburgh, trying every means to save a life that is dearer to me than my own.—How is your sister?—how fares it with her?—condemned to death, I know it, by this time! O, the horse that carried me safely on a thousand errands of folly and wickedness, that he should have broke down with me on the only good mission I have undertaken for years! But I must rein in my passion—my frame cannot endure it, and I have much to say. Give me some of the cordial which stands on that table.—Why do you tremble? But you have too good cause.—Let it stand—I need it not."

Jeanie, however reluctant, approached him with the cup into which she had poured the draught, and could not forbear saying, "There is a cordial for the mind, sir, if the wicked will turn from their trangressions,[6] and seek to the Physician of souls."

"Silence!" he said sternly—"and yet I thank you. But tell me, and lose no time in doing so, what you are doing in this country? Remember, though I have been your sister's worst enemy, yet I will serve her with the best of my blood, and I will serve you for her sake; and no one can serve you to such purpose, for no one can know the circumstances so well—so speak without fear."

"I am not afraid, sir," said Jeanie, collecting her spirits. "I trust in God; and if it pleases Him to redeem my sister's captivity, it is all I seek, whosoever be the instrument. But, sir, to be plain with you, I dare not use your counsel, unless I were enabled to see that it accords with the law which I must rely upon."

"The devil take the puritan!" cried George Staunton, for so we must now call him. "I beg your pardon; but I am naturally impatient, and you drive me mad. What harm can it possibly do you to tell me in what situation your sister stands, and your own expectations of being able to assist her? It is time enough to refuse my advice when I offer any which you may think improper. I speak calmly to you, though 'tis against my nature;—but don't urge me to impatience—it will only render me incapable of serving Effie."

There was in the looks and words of this unhappy young man a sort of restrained eagerness and impetuosity which seemed to prey upon itself, as the impatience of a fiery steed fatigues itself with churning[7] upon the bit. After a moment's consideration, it occurred to Jeanie that she was not entitled to withhold from him, whether on her sister's account or her own, the fatal detail of the consequences of the crime which he had committed, nor to reject such advice, being in itself lawful and innocent, as he might be able to suggest in the way of remedy. Accordingly, in as few words as she could express it, she told the history of her sister's trial and condemnation, and of her own journey as far as Newark. He appeared to listen in the utmost agony of mind, yet repressed every violent symptom of emotion, whether by gesture or sound, which might have interrupted the speaker, and, stretched on his couch like the Mexican monarch[8] on his bed of live coals, only the contortions of his cheek, and the quivering of his limbs, gave indication of his sufferings. To much of what she said he listened with stifled groans, as if he were only hearing those miseries confirmed, whose fatal reality he had known before; but when she pursued her tale through the circumstances which had interrupted her journey, extreme surprise and earnest attention appeared to succeed to the symptoms of remorse which he had before exhibited. He questioned Jeanie closely concerning the appearance of the two men, and the conversation which she had overheard between the taller of them and the woman.

When Jeanie mentioned the old woman having alluded to her foster-son—"It is too true," he said; "and the source from which I derived food, when an infant, must have communicated to me the wretched—the fated—propensity to vices[9] that were strangers in my own family.—But go on."

Jeanie passed slightly over her journey in company with Madge, having no inclination to repeat what might be the effect of mere raving on the part of her companion, and therefore her tale was now closed.

Young Staunton lay for a moment in profound meditation, and at length spoke with more composure than he had yet displayed during their interview.—"You are a sensible, as well as a good young woman, Jeanie Deans, and I will tell you more of my story than I have told to any one.—Story did I call it?—it is a tissue of folly, guilt, and misery.—But take notice—I do it because I desire your confidence in return—that is, that you will act in this dismal matter by my advice and direction. Therefore do I speak."

"I will do what is fitting for a sister, and a daughter, and a Christian woman to do," said Jeanie; "but do not tell me any of your secrets—It is not good that I should come into your counsel, or listen to the doctrine which causeth to err."[10]

"Simple fool!" said the young man. "Look at me. My head is not horned, my foot is not cloven, my hands are not garnished with talons; and, since I am not the very devil himself, what interest can any one else have in destroying the hopes with which you comfort or fool yourself? Listen to me patiently, and you will find that, when you have heard my counsel, you may go to the seventh heaven[11] with it in your pocket, if you have a mind, and not feel yourself an ounce heavier in the ascent."

At the risk of being somewhat tedious, as explanations usually prove, we must here endeavour to combine into a distinct narrative, information which the invalid communicated in a manner at once too circumstantial, and too much broken by passion, to admit of our giving his precise words. Part of it, indeed, he read from a manuscript, which he had perhaps drawn up for the information of his relations after his decease.

"To make my tale short—this wretched hag—this Margaret Murdockson, was the wife of a favourite servant of my father;—she had been my nurse;—her husband was dead;—she resided in a cottage near this place;—she had a daughter who grew up, and was then a beautiful but very giddy girl;—her mother endeavoured to promote her marriage with an old and wealthy churl in the neighbourhood;— the girl saw me frequently—She was familiar with me, as our connection seemed to permit—and I—in a word, I wronged her cruelly—It was not so bad as your sister's business, but it was sufficiently villainous—her folly should have been her protection. Soon after this I was sent abroad—To do my father justice, if I have turned out a fiend it is not his fault—he used the best means. When I returned, I found the wretched mother and daughter had fallen into disgrace, and were chased from this country.—My deep share in their shame and misery was discovered—my father used very harsh language—we quarrelled. I left his house, and led a life of strange adventure, resolving never again to see my father or my father's home.

"And now comes the story!—Jeanie, I put my life into your hands, and not only my own life, which, God knows, is not worth saving, but the happiness of a respectable old man, and the honour of a family of consideration. My love of low society, as such propensities as I was cursed with are usually termed, was, I think, of an uncommon kind, and indicated a nature, which, if not depraved by early debauchery, would have been fit for better things. I did not so much delight in the wild revel, the low humour, the unconfined liberty of those with whom I associated, as in the spirit of adventure, presence of mind in peril, and sharpness of intellect which they displayed in prosecuting their maraudings upon the revenue, or similar adventures.——Have you looked round this rectory?—is it not a sweet and pleasant retreat?"

Jeanie, alarmed at this sudden change of subject, replied in the affirmative.

"Well! I wish it had been ten thousand fathom under ground, with its church-lands, and tythes, and all that belongs to it. Had it not been for this cursed rectory I should have been permitted to follow the bent of my own inclinations and the profession of arms, and half the courage and address that I have displayed among smugglers and deer-stealers would have secured me an honourable rank among my contemporaries. Why did I not go abroad when I left this house?—Why did I leave it at all?—Why—But it came to that point with me that it is madness to look back, and misery to look forward."

He paused, and then proceeded with more composure.

"The chances of a wandering life brought me unhappily to Scotland,

to embroil myself in worse and more criminal actions than I had yet
been concerned in. It was now I became acquainted with Wilson, a
remarkable man in his station of life; quiet, composed, and resolute,
firm in mind, and uncommonly strong in person, gifted with a sort of
rough eloquence which raised him above his companions. Hitherto I
had been

> As dissolute as desperate, yet through both
> Were seen some sparkles of a better hope.[12]

But it was this man's misfortune, as well as mine, that, notwithstanding
the difference of our rank and education, he acquired an extraordinary
and fascinating influence over me, which I can only account for by the
calm determination of his character being superior to the less sustained
impetuosity of mine. Where he led I felt myself bound to follow; and
strange was the courage and address which he displayed in his
pursuits. While I was engaged in desperate adventures, under so wild
and dangerous a preceptor, I became acquainted with your unfortunate
sister at some sports of the young people in the suburbs, which she
frequented by stealth—and her ruin proved an interlude to the tragic
scenes in which I was now deeply engaged. Yet this let me say—the
villainy was not premeditated, and I was firmly resolved to do her all
the justice which marriage could do, so soon as I should be able to
extricate myself from my unhappy course of life, and embrace some
one more suited to my birth.—I had wild visions—visions of conducting her as if to some poor retreat, and introducing her at once to rank
and fortune she never dreamt of. A friend, at my request, attempted a
negociation with my father, which was protracted for some time, and
renewed at different intervals. At length, and just when I expected my
father's pardon, he learned by some means or other my infamy,
painted in even exaggerated colours, which was, God knows,
unnecessary—He wrote me a letter—how it found me out, I know
not—enclosing me a sum of money, and disowning me for ever.—I
became desperate—I became frantic—I readily joined Wilson in a
perilous smuggling adventure in which we miscarried, and was willingly blinded by his logic to consider the robbery of the officer of the
customs in Fife, as a fair and honourable reprisal. Hitherto I had
observed a certain line in my criminality, and steered free of assaults
upon personal property, but now I felt a wild pleasure in disgracing
myself as much as possible.

"The plunder was no object to me. I abandoned that to my

comrades, and only asked the post of danger. I remember well, that when I stood with my drawn sword guarding the door while they committed the felony, I had not a thought of my own safety. I was only meditating on my sense of supposed wrong from my family, my impotent thirst of vengeance, and how it would sound in the haughty ears of the family of Willingham, that one of their descendants, and the heir apparent of their honours, should perish by the hands of the hangman for robbing a Scottish gauger of a sum not equal to one-fifth part of the money I had in my pocket-book. We were taken—I expected no less. We were condemned—that also I looked for. But death, as he approached nearer, looked grimly; and the recollection of your sister's destitute condition determined me on an effort to save my life.—I forgot to tell you, that in Edinburgh I again met the woman Murdockson and her daughter.—She had followed the camp when young, and had now, under pretence of a trifling traffic, resumed predatory habits, with which she had already been too familiar. Our first meeting was stormy; but I was liberal of what money I had, and she forgot, or seemed to forget, the injury her daughter had received. The unfortunate girl herself seemed hardly even to know her seducer, far less to retain any sense of the injury she had received. Her mind is totally alienated,[13] which, according to her mother's account, is some-times the consequence of an unfavourable confinement. But it was *my doing*. Here was another stone knitted round my neck to sink me into the pit of perdition. Every look—every word of this poor creature—her false spirits—her imperfect recollections—her allusions to things which she had forgotten, but which were recorded in my conscience, were stabs of a poniard—stabs did I say?—they were tearing with hot pincers, and scalding the raw wound with burning sulphur—they were to be endured, however, and they *were* endured.—I return to my prison thoughts.

"It was not the least miserable of them that your sister's time approached. I knew her dread of you and of her father—She often said she would die a thousand deaths ere you should know her shame—yet her confinement must be provided for.—I knew this woman Murdockson was an infernal hag, but I thought she loved me, and that money would make her true. She had procured a file for Wilson, and a spring-saw for me; and she undertook readily to take charge of Effie during her illness, in which she had skill enough to give the necessary assistance.—I gave her the money which my father had sent me—It was settled that she should receive Effie into her house in the meantime, and wait for farther directions from me, when I should effect my escape. I communicated this purpose, and recommended the old hag to poor Effie by a letter, in which I recollect that I endeavoured to support the character of Macheath under condemnation[14]—a firm, gay, bold-faced ruffian, who is game to the last—Such, and so wretchedly poor, was my ambition! Yet I had resolved to forsake the courses I had been engaged in, should I be so fortunate as to escape the gibbet. My design was to marry your sister, and go over to the West Indies. I had still a considerable sum of money left, and I trusted to be able in one way or other to provide for myself and my wife.

"We made the attempt to escape, and by the obstinacy of Wilson, who insisted upon going first, it totally miscarried. The undaunted and self-denied manner in which he sacrificed himself to redeem his error, and accomplish my escape from the Tolbooth-Church, you must have heard of—all Scotland rang with it. It was a gallant and extraordinary deed—All men spoke of it—all men, even those who most condemned the habits and crimes of this self-devoted man, praised the heroism of his friendship. I have many vices, but cowardice, or want of gratitude, are none of the number. I resolved to requite his generosity, and even your sister's safety became a secondary consideration with me for the time. To effect Wilson's liberation was my principal object, and I doubted not to find the means.

"Yet I did not forget Effie neither. The bloodhounds of the law[15] were so close after me, that I dared not trust myself near any of my old haunts, but old Murdockson met me by appointment, and informed me that your sister had happily been delivered of a boy. I charged the hag to keep her patient's mind easy, and let her want for nothing that money could purchase, and I retreated to Fife, where, among my old associates of Wilson's gang, I hid myself in those places of concealment where the men engaged in that desperate trade are used to find security for themselves and their uncustomed goods. Men who are disobedient both to human and divine laws, are not always insensible to the claims of courage and generosity. We were assured that the mob of Edinburgh, strongly moved with the hardship of Wilson's situation, and the gallantry of his conduct, would back any bold attempt that might be made to rescue him even from the foot of the gibbet. Desperate as the attempt seemed, upon my declaring myself ready to lead the onset on the guard, I found no want of followers who engaged to stand by me, and returned to Lothian, soon joined by some steady associates, prepared to act whatever the occasion might require.

"I have no doubt I should have rescued him from the very noose that dangled over his head," he continued with animation, which seemed a flash of the interest which he had taken in such exploits; "but amongst other precautions, the magistrates had taken one, suggested, as we afterwards learned, by the unhappy wretch Porteous, which effectually disconcerted my measures. They anticipated, by half an hour,[16] the ordinary period for execution; and, as it had been resolved amongst us, that, for fear of observation from the officers of justice, we should not show ourselves upon the street until the time of action approached, it followed that all was over before our attempt at a rescue commenced. It did commence, however, and I gained the scaffold and cut the rope with my own hand. It was too late! The bold, stout-hearted, generous criminal was no more—and vengeance was all that remained to us—a vengeance, as I then thought, doubly due from my hand, to whom Wilson had given life and liberty when he could as easily have secured his own."

"O, sir," said Jeanie, "did the Scripture[17] never come into your mind, 'Vengeance is mine, saith the Lord, and I will repay it?'"

"Scripture? Why, I had not opened a Bible for five years," answered Staunton.

"Waes me, sirs," said Jeanie—"and a minister's son too!"

"It is natural for you to say so; yet do not interrupt me, but let me finish my most accursed history. The beast, Porteous, who kept firing on the people long after it had ceased to be necessary, became the object of their hatred for having over-done his duty, and of mine for having done it too well. We—that is, I and the other determined friends of Wilson—resolved to be avenged; but caution was necessary. I thought I had been marked by one of the officers, and therefore continued to lurk about the vicinity of Edinburgh, but without daring to venture within the walls. At length I visited, at the hazard of my life, the place where I hoped to find my future wife and my son—they were both gone. Dame Murdockson informed me that so soon as Effie heard of the miscarriage of the attempt to rescue Wilson, and the hot pursuit after me, she fell into a brain fever; and that being one day obliged to go out on some necessary business and leave her alone, she had taken that opportunity to escape, and she had not seen her since. I loaded her with reproaches, to which she listened with the most provoking and callous composure; for it is one of her attributes, that, violent and fierce as she is upon most occasions, there are some in which she shews the most imperturbable calmness. I threatened her with justice; she said I had more reason to fear justice than she had. I felt she was right, and was silenced. I threatened her with vengeance; she replied in nearly the same words, that, to judge by injuries received, I had more reason to fear her vengeance, than she to dread mine. She was again right, and I was left without an answer. I flung myself from her in indignation, and employed a comrade to make enquiry in the neighbourhood of Saint Leonard's concerning your sister; but ere I received his answer, the opening quest of a well-scented terrier of the law[18] drove me from the vicinity of Edinburgh to a more distant and secluded place of concealment. A secret and trusty emissary at length brought me the account of Porteous's condemnation, and of your sister's imprisonment on a criminal charge; thus astounding one of mine ears, while he gratified the other.

"I again ventured to the Pleasance—again charged Murdockson with treachery to the unfortunate Effie and her child, though I could conceive no reason, save that of appropriating the whole of the money I had lodged with her. Your narrative throws light on this, and shews another motive, not less powerful because less evident—the desire of wreaking vengeance on the seducer of her daughter,—the destroyer at once of her reason and reputation. Great God! how I wish that, instead of the revenge she made choice of, she had delivered me up to the cord!"

"But what account did the wretched woman give of Effie and the bairn?" said Jeanie, who, during this long and agitating narrative, had firmness and discernment enough to keep her eye on such points as might throw light on her sister's misfortunes.

"She would give none," said Staunton; "she said the mother made a moonlight flitting from her house, with the infant in her arms—that she had never seen either of them since—that the lass might have thrown the child into the North Loch or the Quarry Holes, for what she knew, and it was like enough she had done so."

"And how came you to believe that she did not speak the fatal truth?" said Jeanie, trembling.

"Because, on this second occasion, I saw her daughter, and I understood from her, that, in fact, the child had been removed or destroyed during the illness of the mother. But all knowledge to be got from her is so uncertain and indirect, that I could not collect any farther circumstances. Only the diabolical character of old Murdockson makes me augur the worst."

"The last account agrees with that given by my poor sister," said Jeanie; "but gang on wi' your ain tale, sir."

"Of this I am certain," said Staunton, "that Effie, in her senses, and with her knowledge, never injured living creature—But what could I do in her exculpation?—Nothing—and, therefore, my whole thoughts were turned towards her safety. I was under the cursed necessity of suppressing my feelings towards Murdockson; my life was in the hag's hand—that I cared not for; but on my life hung that of your sister. I spoke the wretch fair; I appeared to confide in her; and to me, so far as I was personally concerned, she gave proofs of extraordinary fidelity. I was at first uncertain what measures I ought to adopt for your sister's liberation, when the general rage excited among the citizens of Edinburgh on account of the reprieve of Porteous, suggested to me the daring idea of forcing the jail, and at once carrying off your sister from the clutches of the law, and bringing to condign punishment a miscreant, who had tormented the unfortunate Wilson, even in the hour of death, as if he had been a wild Indian taken captive by an hostile tribe. I flung myself among the multitude in the moment of fermentation—so did others among Wilson's mates, who had, like me, been disappointed in the hope of glutting their eyes with Porteous's execution. All was organized, and I was chosen for the captain. I felt not—I do not now feel, compunction for what was to be done, and has since been executed."

"O God forgive ye, sir, and bring you to a better sense of your ways!" exclaimed Jeanie, in horror at the avowal of such violent sentiments.

"Amen," replied Staunton, "if my sentiments are wrong. But I repeat, that, although willing to aid the deed, I could have wished them to have chosen another leader; because I foresaw that the great and general duty of the night would interfere with the assistance which I proposed to render Effie. I gave a commission, however, to a trusty friend[19] to protect her to a place of safety, so soon as the fatal procession had left the jail. But for no persuasions which I could use in the hurry of the moment, or which my comrade employed at more length, after the mob had taken a different direction, could the unfortunate girl be prevailed upon to leave the prison. His arguments were all wasted upon the infatuated victim, and he was obliged to leave her in order to attend to his own safety. Such was his account; but, perhaps, he persevered less steadily in his attempt to persuade her than I would have done."

"Effie was right to remain," said Jeanie; "and I love her the better for it."

"Why will you say so?" said Staunton.

"You cannot understand my reasons, sir, if I should render them," answered Jeanie, composedly; "they that thirst for the blood of their enemies have no taste for the well-spring of life."[20]

"My hopes," said Staunton, "were thus a second time disappointed. My next efforts were to bring her through her trial by means of yourself. How I urged it, and where, you cannot have forgotten. I do not blame you for your refusal; it was founded, I am convinced, on principle, and not on indifference to your sister's fate. For me, judge of me as a man frantic; I knew not what hand to turn to, and all my efforts were unavailing. In this condition, and close beset on all sides, I thought of what might be done by means of my family, and their influence. I fled from Scotland—I reached this place—my miserably wasted and unhappy appearance procured me from my father that pardon, which a parent finds it so hard to refuse, even to the most undeserving son. And here I have awaited in anguish of mind, which the condemned criminal might envy, the event of your sister's trial."

"Without taking any steps for her relief?" said Jeanie.

"To the last I hoped her case might terminate more favourably; and it is only two days since that the fatal tidings reached me. My resolution was instantly taken. I mounted my best horse with the purpose of making the utmost haste to London, and there compounding with Sir Robert Walpole[21] for your sister's safety, by surrendering to him, in the person of the heir of the family of Willingham, the notorious George Robertson, the accomplice of Wilson, the breaker of the Tolbooth prison, and the well-known leader of the Porteous mob."

"But would that save my sister?" said Jeanie, in astonishment.

"It would, as I should drive my bargain," said Staunton. "Queens love revenge as well as their subjects—Little as you seem to esteem it, it is a poison which pleases all palates, from the prince to the peasant. Prime ministers love no less the power of pleasing sovereigns by gratifying their passions. The life of an obscure village girl? Why, I might ask the best of the crown-jewels for laying the head of such an insolent conspiracy at the foot of her majesty, with a certainty of being gratified. All my other plans have failed, but this could not—Heaven is just, however, and would not honour me with making this voluntary atonement for the injury I have done your sister. I had not rode ten miles, when my horse, the best and most sure-footed animal in this country, fell with me on a level piece of road, as if he had been struck by a cannon-shot. I was greatly hurt, and was brought back here in the miserable condition in which you now see me."

As young Staunton had come to this conclusion, the servant opened the door, and, with a voice which seemed intended rather for a signal, than merely the announcing of a visit, said, "His Reverence, sir, is coming up stairs to wait upon you."

"For God's sake, hide yourself, Jeanie," exclaimed Staunton, "in that dressing closet!"

"No, sir," said Jeanie; "as I am here for nae ill, I canna take the shame of hiding mysell frae the master o' the house."

"But, good Heavens!" exclaimed George Staunton, "do but consider"——

Ere he could complete the sentence, his father entered the apartment.

CHAPTER 34

And now, will pardon, comfort, kindness, draw
The youth from vice? will honour, duty, law?

CRABBE

JEANIE arose from her seat, and made her quiet reverence, when the elder Mr Staunton entered the apartment. His astonishment was extreme at finding his son in such company.

"I perceive, madam," he said, "I have made a mistake respecting you, and ought to have left the task of interrogating you, and of righting your wrongs, to this young man, with whom, doubtless, you have been formerly acquainted."

"It's unwitting on my part that I am here," said Jeanie; "the servant told me his master wished to speak with me."

"There goes the purple coat over my ears," murmured Tummas. "D—n her, why must she needs speak the truth, when she could have as well said any thing else she had a mind?"

"George," said Mr Staunton, "if you are still—as you have ever been—lost to all self-respect, you might at least have spared your father, and your father's house, such a disgraceful scene as this."

"Upon my life—upon my soul, sir!" said George, throwing his feet over the side of the bed, and starting from his recumbent posture.

"Your life, sir!" interrupted his father, with melancholy sternness,—"What sort of life has it been?—Your soul! alas! what regard have you ever paid to it? Take care to reform both ere offering either as pledges of your sincerity."

"On my honour, sir, you do me wrong," answered George Staunton; "I have been all you can call me that's bad, but in the present instance you do me injustice. By my honour, you do!"

"Your honour!"[1] said his father, and turned from him, with a look of the most upbraiding contempt, to Jeanie. "From you, young woman, I neither ask nor expect any explanation; but, as a father alike and as a clergyman, I request your departure from this house. If your romantic story has been other than a pretext to find admission into it, (which, from the society in which you first appeared, I may be permitted to doubt,) you will find a justice of peace within two miles, with whom, more properly than with me, you may lodge your complaint."

"This shall not be," said George Staunton, starting up to his feet. "Sir, you are naturally kind and humane—you shall not become cruel and inhospitable on my account—Turn out that eaves-dropping rascal," pointing to Thomas, "and get what hartshorn drops, or what better receipt you have against fainting, and I will explain to you in two words the connection betwixt this young woman and me. She shall not lose her fair character through me—I have done too much mischief to her family already, and I know too well what belongs to the loss of fame."

"Leave the room, sir," said the Rector to the servant; and when the man had obeyed, he carefully shut the door behind him. Then addressing his son, he said sternly, "Now, sir, what new proof of your infamy have you to impart to me?"

Young Staunton was about to speak, but it was one of those moments when persons, who, like Jeanie Deans, possess the advantage of a steady courage and unruffled temper, can assume the superiority over more ardent but less determined spirits.

"Sir," she said to the elder Staunton, "ye have an undoubted right to ask your ain son to render a reason of his conduct. But respecting me, I am but a way-faring traveller, no ways obligated or indebted to you, unless it be for the meal of meat which, in my ain country, is willingly gien by rich or poor, according to their ability, to those who need it; and for which, forbye that, I am willing to make payment, if I didna think it would be an affront to offer siller in a house like this— only I dinna ken the fashions of the country."

"This is all very well, young woman," said the Rector, a good deal· surprised, and unable to conjecture whether to impute Jeanie's language to simplicity or impertinence—"this may be all very well—but let me bring it to a point. Why do you stop this young man's mouth, and prevent his communicating to his father and his best friend, an explanation (since he says he has one) of circumstances which seem in themselves not a little suspicious?"

"He may tell of his ain affairs what he likes," answered Jeanie; "but my family and friends have nae right to hae ony stories told anent them without their express desire; and, as they canna be here to speak for themselves, I entreat ye wadna ask Mr George Rob—I mean Staunton, or whatever his name is, ony questions anent me or my folk;

for I maun be free to tell you, that he will neither have the bearing of a Christian or a gentleman, if he answers you against my express desire."

"This is the most extraordinary thing I ever met with," said the Rector, as, after fixing his eyes keenly on the placid, yet modest countenance of Jeanie, he turned them suddenly upon his son. "What have you to say, sir?"

"That I feel I have been too hasty in my promise, sir," answered George Staunton; "I have no title to make any communications respecting the affairs of this young person's family without her assent."

The elder Mr Staunton turned his eyes from one to the other with marks of surprise.

"This is more, and worse, I fear," he said, addressing his son, "than one of your frequent and disgraceful connections—I insist upon knowing the mystery."

"I have already said, sir," replied his son, rather sullenly, "that I have no title to mention the affairs of this young woman's family without her consent."

"And I hae nae mysteries to explain, sir," said Jeanie, "but only to pray you, as a preacher of the gospel and a gentleman, to permit me to go safe to the next public house on the Lunnon road."

"I shall take care of your safety," said young Staunton; "you need ask that favour from no one."

"Do you say so before my face?" said the justly incensed father. "Perhaps, sir, you intend to fill up the cup of disobedience and profligacy by forming a low and disgraceful marriage? But let me bid you beware."

"If you were feared for sic a thing happening wi' me, sir," said Jeanie, "I can only say, that not for all the land that lies between the twa ends of the rainbow wad I be the woman that should wed your son."

"There is something very singular in all this," said the elder Staunton; "follow me into the next room, young woman."

"Hear me speak first," said the young man. "I have but one word to say. I confide entirely in your prudence; tell my father as much or as little of these matters as you will, he shall know neither more nor less from me."

His father darted at him a glance of indignation, which softened into sorrow as he saw him sink down on the couch, exhausted with the scene he had undergone. He left the apartment and Jeanie followed him, George Staunton raising himself as she passed the door-way, and pronouncing the word, "Remember!" in a tone as monitory as it was uttered by Charles I.[2] upon the scaffold. The elder Staunton led the way into a small parlour, and shut the door.

"Young woman," said he, "there is something in your face and appearance that marks both sense and simplicity, and if I am not deceived, innocence also—Should it be otherwise, I can only say, you are the most accomplished hypocrite I have ever seen.—I ask to know no secret that you have unwillingness to divulge, least of all those which concern my son. His conduct has given me too much unhappiness to permit me to hope comfort or satisfaction from him. If you are such as I suppose you, believe me, that whatever unhappy circumstances may have connected you with George Staunton, the sooner you break them through the better."

"I think I understand your meaning, sir," replied Jeanie; "and as ye are sae frank as to speak o' the young gentleman in sic a way, I must needs say that it is but the second time of my speaking wi' him in our lives, and what I hae heard frae him on these twa occasions has been such that I never wish to hear the like again."

"Then it is your real intention to leave this part of the country, and proceed to London?" said the Rector.

"Certainly, sir; for I may say, in one sense, that the avenger of blood[3] is behind me; and if I were but assured against mischief by the way——"

"I have made enquiry," said the clergyman, "after the suspicious characters you described. They have left their place of rendezvous; but as they may be lurking in the neighbourhood, and as you say you have special reason to apprehend violence from them, I will put you under the charge of a steady person, who will protect you as far as Stamford, and see you into a light coach, which goes from thence to London."

"A coach is not for the like of me, sir," said Jeanie; to whom the idea of a stage-coach was unknown, as indeed they were then only used in the neighbourhood of London.

Mr Staunton briefly explained that she would find that mode of conveyance more commodious, cheaper, and more safe than travelling on horseback. She expressed her gratitude with so much singleness of heart, that he was induced to ask her whether she wanted the pecuniary means of prosecuting her journey. She thanked him, but said she had enough for her purpose; and indeed she had husbanded her stock with great care. This reply served also to remove some doubts, which naturally enough still floated in Mr Staunton's mind, respecting her character and real purpose, and satisfied him, at least, that money did not enter into her scheme of deception, if an impostor she should prove. He next requested to know what part of the city she wished to go to.

"To a very decent merchant, a cousin o' my ain, a Mrs Glass, sir, that sells snuff and tobacco, at the sign o' the Thistle, somegate in the town."

Jeanie communicated this intelligence with a feeling that a connection so respectable ought to give her consequence in the eyes of Mr Staunton; and she was a good deal surprised when he answered,

"And is this woman your only acquaintance in London, my poor girl? and have you really no better knowledge where she is to be found?"

"I was gaun to see the Duke of Argyle, forbye Mrs Glass," said Jeanie; "and if your honour thinks it would be best to go there first, and get some of his Grace's folks to show me my cousin's shop——"

"Are you acquainted with any of the Duke of Argyle's people?" said the Rector.

"No, sir."

"Her brain must be something touched[4] after all, or it would be impossible for her to rely on such introductions.—Well," said he aloud, "I must not enquire into the cause of your journey, and so I cannot be fit to give you advice how to manage it. But the landlady of the house where the coach stops, is a very decent person; and, as I use her house sometimes, I will give you a recommendation to her."

Jeanie thanked him for his kindness with her best curtsey, and said, "That with his honour's line, and ane from worthy Mrs Bickerton, that keeps the Seven Stars at York, she did not doubt to be well taken out in Lunnon."

"And now," said he, "I presume you will be desirous to set out immediately."

"If I had been in an inn, sir, or any suitable resting-place," answered Jeanie, "I wad not have presumed to use the Lord's day for travelling; but as I am on a journey of mercy, I trust my doing so will not be imputed."[5]

"You may, if you chuse, remain with Mrs Dalton for the evening; but I desire you will have no further correspondence with my son, who is not a proper counsellor for a person of your age, whatever your difficulties may be."

"Your honour speaks ower truly in that," said Jeanie; "it was not with my will that I spoke wi' him just now, and—not to wish the gentleman ony thing but gude—I never wish to see him between the een again."

"If you please," added the Rector, "as you seem to be a seriously-disposed young woman, you may attend family worship in the hall this evening."

"I thank your honour," said Jeanie; "but I am doubtful if my attendance would be to edification."

"How!" said the Rector; "so young, and already unfortunate enough to have doubts upon the duties of religion!"[6]

"God forbid, sir," replied Jeanie; "it is not for that; but I have been bred in the faith of the suffering remnant of the presbyterian doctrine in Scotland, and I am doubtful if I can lawfully attend upon your fashion of worship, seeing it has been testified against by many precious souls of our kirk, and specially by my worthy father."

"Well, my good girl," said the Rector, with a good-humoured smile, "far be it from me to put any force upon your conscience; and yet you ought to recollect that the same divine grace dispenses its streams to other kingdoms as well as to Scotland. As it is as essential to our spiritual, as water to our earthly wants, its springs, various in character, yet alike efficacious in virtue, are to be found in abundance throughout the Christian world."

"Ah, but," said Jeanie, "though the waters may be alike, yet, with your worship's leave, the blessing upon them may not be equal. It would have been in vain for Naaman[7] the Syrian leper to have bathed in Pharpar and Abana, rivers of Damascus, when it was only the waters of Jordan that were sanctified for the cure."

"Well," said the Rector, "we will not enter upon the great debate betwixt our national churches at present. We must endeavour to satisfy you, that, at least, amongst our errors, we preserve Christian charity, and a desire to assist our brethren."

He then ordered Mrs Dalton into his presence, and consigned Jeanie to her particular charge, with directions to be kind to her, and with assurances, that, early in the morning, a trusty guide and a good horse should be ready to conduct her to Stamford. He then took a serious and dignified, yet kind leave of her, wishing her full success in the objects of her journey, which he said he doubted not were laudable, from the soundness of thinking which she had displayed in conversation.

Jeanie was again conducted by the housekeeper to her own apartment. But the evening was not destined to pass over without further torment from young Staunton. A paper was slipped into her hand by the faithful Tummas, which intimated his young master's desire, or rather demand, to see her instantly, and assured her he had provided against interruption.

"Tell your young master," said Jeanie, openly, and regardless of all the winks and signs by which Tummas strove to make her comprehend that Mrs Dalton was not to be admitted into the secret of the correspondence, "that I promised faithfully to his worthy father that I would not see him again."

"Tummas," said Mrs Dalton, "I think you might be much more creditably employed, considering the coat you wear, and the house you live in, than to be carrying messages between your young master and girls that chance to be in this house."

"Why, Mrs Dalton, as to that, I was hired to carry messages, and not to ask any questions about them; and it's not for the like of me to refuse the young gentleman's bidding, if he were a little wildish or so.—If there was harm meant, there's no harm done, you see."

"However," said Mrs Dalton, "I gie you fair warning, Tummas Ditton, that an I catch thee at this work again, his Reverence shall make a clear house of you."

Tummas retired, abashed and in dismay. The rest of the evening past away without any thing worthy of notice.

Jeanie enjoyed the comforts of a good bed and a sound sleep with grateful satisfaction, after the perils and hardships of the preceding day; and such was her fatigue, that she slept soundly until six o'clock, when she was awakened by Mrs Dalton, who acquainted her that her guide and horse were ready, and in attendance. She hastily rose, and, after her morning devotions, was soon ready to resume her travels. The motherly care of the housekeeper had provided an early breakfast, and, after she had partaken of this refreshment, she found herself safe seated on a pillion behind a stout Lincolnshire peasant, who was, besides, armed with pistols, to protect her against any violence which might be offered.

They trudged on in silence for a mile or two along a country road, which conducted them, by hedge and gate-way, into the principal highway, a little beyond Grantham. At length her master of the horse asked her whether her name was not Jean, or Jane Deans. She answered in the affirmative, with some surprise. "Then here's a bit of

a note as concerns you," said the man, handing it over his left
shoulder. "It's from young master, as I judge, and every man about
Willingham is fain to pleasure him either for love or fear; for he'll
come to be landlord at last, let them say what they like."

Jeanie broke the seal of the note, which was addressed to her, and
read as follows:

"You refuse to see me. I suppose you are shocked at my character:
but, in painting myself such as I am, you should give me credit for my
sincerity. I am, at least, no hypocrite. You refuse, however, to see me,
and your conduct may be natural—but is it wise? I have expressed my
anxiety to repair your sister's misfortunes at the expence of my
honour,—my family's honour—my own life; and you think me too
debased to be admitted even to sacrifice what I have remaining of
honour, fame, and life, in her cause. Well, if the offerer be despised,
the victim is still equally at hand; and perhaps there may be justice in
the decree of Heaven, that I shall not have the melancholy credit of
appearing to make this sacrifice out of my own free good-will. You, as
you have declined my concurrence, must take the whole upon yourself.
Go, then, to the Duke of Argyle, and, when other arguments fail you,
tell him you have it in your power to bring to condign punishment the
most active conspirator in the Porteous mob. He will hear you on this
topic, should he be deaf on every other. Make your own terms, for
they will be at your own making. You know where I am to be found;
and you may be assured I will not give you the dark side of the hill, as
at Muschat's Cairn; I have no thoughts of stirring from the house I
was born in; like the hare,[8] I shall be worried in the seat I started
from. I repeat it—make your own terms. I need not remind you to ask
your sister's life, for that you will do of course; but make terms of
advantage for yourself—ask wealth and reward—office and income for
Butler—ask any thing—you will get any thing—and all for delivering
to the hands of the executioner a man most deserving of his office;—
one who, though young in years, is old in wickedness, and whose most
earnest desire is, after the storms of an unquiet life, to sleep and be at
rest."

This extraordinary letter was subscribed with the initials G.S.

Jeanie read it over once or twice with great attention, which the
slow pace of the horse, as he stalked through a deep lane, enabled her
to do with facility.

When she had perused this billet, her first employment was to tear
it into as small pieces as possible, and disperse these pieces in the air

by a few at a time, so that a document containing so perilous a secret might not fall into any other person's hand.

The question how far, in point of extremity, she was entitled to save her sister's life by sacrificing that of a person who, though guilty towards the state, had done her no injury, formed the next earnest and most painful subject of consideration. In one sense, indeed, it seemed as if denouncing the guilt of Staunton, the cause of her sister's errors and misfortunes, would have been an act of just, and even providential retribution. But Jeanie, in the strict and severe tone of morality in which she was educated, had to consider not only the general aspect of a proposed action, but its justness and fitness in relation to the actor, before she could be, according to her own phrase, free to enter upon it. What right had she to make a barter between the lives of Staunton and of Effie, and to sacrifice the one for the safety of the other? His guilt—that guilt for which he was amenable to the laws—was a crime against the public indeed, but it was not against her.

Neither did it seem to her that his share in the death of Porteous, though her mind revolted at the idea of using violence to any one, was in the relation of a common murder, against the perpetrator of which every one is called to aid the public magistrate. That violent action was blended with many circumstances, which, in the eyes of those of Jeanie's rank in life, if they did not altogether deprive it of the character of guilt, softened, at least, its most atrocious features. The anxiety of the government to obtain conviction of some of the offenders, had but served to increase the public feeling which connected the action, though violent and irregular, with the idea of ancient national independence. The rigorous procedure adopted or proposed against the city of Edinburgh, the ancient metropolis of Scotland—the extremely unpopular and injudicious measure of compelling the Scottish clergy, contrary to their principles and sense of duty, to promulgate from the pulpit the reward offered for the discovery of the perpetrators of this slaughter, had produced on the public mind the opposite consequences from what were intended; and Jeanie felt conscious, that whoever should lodge information concerning that event, and for whatsoever purpose it might be done, it would be considered as an act of treason against the independence of Scotland. With the fanaticism of the Scotch presbyterians, there was always mingled a glow of national feeling, and Jeanie trembled at the idea of her name being handed down to posterity with that of the "fause Monteath,"[9] and one or two others, who, having deserted and betrayed the cause of their country, are damned to perpetual remembrance and execration among its peasantry. Yet, to part with Effie's life once more, when a word spoken might save it, pressed severely on the mind of her affectionate sister.

"The Lord support and direct me," said Jeanie, "for it seems to be his will to try me with difficulties far beyond my ain strength."

While this thought passed through Jeanie's mind, her guard, tired of silence, began to show some inclination to be communicative. He seemed a sensible steady peasant, but not having more delicacy or prudence than is common to those in his situation, he, of course, chose the Willingham family as the subject of his conversation. From this man Jeanie learned some particulars of which she had hitherto been ignorant, and which we will briefly recapitulate for the information of the reader.

The father of George Staunton had been bred a soldier, and during service in the West Indies,[10] had married the heiress of a wealthy planter. By this lady he had an only child, George Staunton, the unhappy young man who has been so often mentioned in this narrative. He passed the first part of his early youth under the charge of a doting mother, and in the society of negro slaves, whose study it was to gratify his every caprice. His father was a man of worth and sense; but as he alone retained tolerable health among the officers of the regiment he belonged to, he was much engaged with his duty. Besides, Mrs Staunton was beautiful and wilful, and enjoyed but delicate health; so that it was difficult for a man of affection, humanity, and a quiet disposition, to struggle with her on the point of her over-indulgence to an only child. Indeed, what Mr Staunton did do towards counteracting the baneful effects of his wife's system, only tended to render it more pernicious, for every restraint imposed on the boy in his father's presence, was compensated by treble license during his absence. So that George Staunton acquired, even in childhood, the habit of regarding his father as a rigid censor, from whose severity he was desirous of emancipating himself as soon and absolutely as possible.

When he was about ten years old, and when his mind had received all the seeds of those evil weeds which afterwards grew apace, his mother died, and his father, half heart-broken, returned to England. To sum her imprudence and unjustifiable indulgence, she had contrived to place a considerable part of her fortune at her son's exclusive controul or disposal. George Staunton had not been long in England till he learned his independence, and how to abuse it. His father had endeavoured to rectify the defects of his education by placing him in a well-regulated seminary. But although he showed some capacity for learning, his riotous conduct soon became intolerable to his teachers. He found means (too easily afforded[11] to all youths who have certain expectations) of procuring such a command of money as enabled him to anticipate in boyhood the frolics and follies of a more mature age, and, with these accomplishments, he was returned on his father's hands as a profligate boy, whose example might ruin an hundred.

The elder Mr Staunton, whose mind, since his wife's death, had been tinged with a melancholy, which certainly his son's conduct did not tend to dispel, had taken orders, and was inducted by his brother Sir William Staunton into the family living of Willingham. The revenue was a matter of consequence to him, for he derived little advantage from the estate of his late wife; and his own fortune was that of a younger brother.

He took his son to reside with him at the rectory, but he soon found that his disorders rendered him an intolerable inmate. And as the young men of his own rank would not endure the purse-proud insolence of the Creole, he fell into that taste for low society, which is worse than "pressing to death, whipping, or hanging."[12] His father sent him abroad, but he only returned wilder and more desperate than before. It is true, this unhappy youth was not without his good qualities. He had lively wit, good temper, reckless generosity, and manners which, while he was under restraint, might pass well in society. But all these availed him nothing. He was so well acquainted with the turf, the gaming-table, the cock-pit, and every worse rendez-vous of folly and dissipation, that his mother's fortune was spent before he was twenty-one, and he was soon in debt and in distress. His early history may be concluded in the words of our British Juvenal,[13] when describing a similar character:—

> Headstrong, determined in his own career,
> He thought reproof unjust and truth severe.
> The soul's disease was to its crisis come,
> He first abused and then abjured his home;
> And when he chose a vagabond to be,
> He made his shame his glory, "I'll be free."

"And yet 'tis pity on Measter George, too," continued the honest boor, "for he has an open hand, and winna let a poor body want an he has it."

The virtue of profuse generosity, by which, indeed, they themselves are most directly advantaged, is readily admitted by the vulgar as a cloak for many sins.

At Stamford our heroine was deposited in safety by her communicative guide. She obtained a place in the coach, which, although termed a light one, and accommodated with no fewer than six horses, only reached London on the afternoon of the second day. The recommendation of the elder Mr Staunton procured Jeanie a civil reception at the inn where the carriage stopped, and, by the aid of Mrs Bickerton's correspondent, she found out her friend and relative Mrs Glass, by whom she was kindly received and hospitably entertained.

CHAPTER 35

My name is Argyle, you may well think it strange,
To live at the court and never to change.

Ballad

FEW names deserve more honourable mention in the history of
Scotland during this period, than that of John, Duke of Argyle and
Greenwich.[1] His talents as a statesman and a soldier were generally
admitted; he was not without ambition, but "without the illness that
attends it"[2]—without that irregularity of thought and aim, which
often excites great men, in his peculiar situation, (for it was a very
peculiar one) to grasp the means of raising themselves to power, at the
risk of throwing a kingdom into confusion. Pope[3] has distinguished
him as

> Argyle, the state's whole thunder born to wield,
> And shake alike the senate and the field.

He was alike free from the ordinary vices of statesmen, falsehood,
namely, and dissimulation, and from those of warriors, inordinate and
violent thirst after self-aggrandizement.[4]

Scotland, his native country, stood at this time in a very precarious
and doubtful situation. She was indeed united to England, but the
cement had not had time to acquire consistence. The irritation of
ancient wrongs still subsisted, and betwixt the fretful jealousy of the
Scottish, and the supercilious disdain of the English, quarrels repeatedly occurred, in the course of which the national league, so important
to the safety of both, was in the utmost danger of being dissolved.
Scotland had, besides, the disadvantage of being divided into intestine
factions, which hated each other bitterly, and waited but a signal to
break forth into action.

In such circumstances, another man, with the talents and rank of
Argyle, but without a mind so happily regulated, would have sought to
rise from the earth in the whirlwind, and direct its fury.[5] He chose a
course more safe and more honourable.

Soaring above the petty distinctions of faction, his voice was raised, whether in office or opposition, for those measures which were at once just and lenient. His high military talents enabled him, during the memorable year 1715,[6] to render such services to the house of Hanover, as, perhaps, were too great to be either acknowledged or repaid.[7] He had employed, too, his utmost influence in softening the consequences of that insurrection to the unfortunate gentlemen, whom a mistaken sense of loyalty had engaged in the affair, and was rewarded by the esteem and affection of his country in an uncommon degree. This popularity, with a discontented and warlike people, was supposed to be a subject of jealousy at court, where the power to become dangerous is sometimes of itself obnoxious, though the inclination is not united with it. Besides, the Duke of Argyle's independent and somewhat haughty mode of expressing himself in parliament, and acting in public, were ill calculated to attract royal favour. He was, therefore, always respected, and often employed, but he was not a favourite of George the Second, his consort, or his ministers. At several different periods in his life, the Duke might be considered as in absolute disgrace at court, although he could hardly be said to be a declared member of opposition. This rendered him the dearer to Scotland, because it was usually in her cause that he incurred the displeasure of his sovereign; and upon this very occasion of the Porteous mob, the animated and eloquent opposition which he had offered to the severe measures which were about to be adopted towards the city of Edinburgh, was the more gratefully received in that metropolis, as it was understood that the Duke's interposition had given personal offence to Queen Caroline.

His conduct upon this occasion, as indeed that of all the Scottish members of the legislature, with one or two unworthy exceptions, had been in the highest degree spirited. The popular tradition, concerning his reply to Queen Caroline, has been given already,[8] and some fragments[9] of his speech against the Porteous Bill are still remembered. He retorted upon the Chancellor, Lord Hardwicke,[10] the insinuation that he had stated himself in this case rather as a party than as a judge:—"I appeal," said Argyle, "to the House—to the nation, if I can be justly branded with the infamy of being a jobber, or a partizan. Have I been a briber of votes?—a buyer of boroughs?—the agent of corruption for any purpose, or on behalf of any party?—Consider my life; examine my actions in the field and in the cabinet, and see where there lies a blot that can attach to my honour. I have shewn myself the friend of my country—the loyal subject of my king.

I am ready to do so again, without an instant's regard to the frowns or smiles of a court. I have experienced both, and am prepared with indifference for either. I have given my reasons for opposing this bill, and have made it appear that it is repugnant to the international treaty of union, to the liberty of Scotland, and, reflectively, to that of England, to common justice, to common sense, and to the public interest. Shall the metropolis of Scotland, the capital of an independent nation, the residence of a long line of monarchs, by whom that noble city was graced and dignified—shall such a city, for the fault of an obscure and unknown body of rioters, be deprived of its honours and its privileges—its gates and its guards?—and shall a native Scotsman tamely behold the havoc? I glory, my Lords, in opposing such unjust rigour, and reckon it my dearest pride and honour to stand up in defence of my native country, while thus laid open to undeserved shame, and unjust spoliation."

Other statesmen and orators, both Scottish and English, used the same arguments, the bill was gradually stripped of its most oppressive and obnoxious clauses, and at length ended in a fine upon the city of Edinburgh in favour of Porteous's widow. So that, as somebody observed at the time,[11] the whole of these fierce debates ended in making the fortune of an old cook-maid, such having been the good woman's original capacity.

The court, however, did not forget the baffle they had received in this affair, and the Duke of Argyle, who had contributed so much to it, was thereafter considered as a person in disgrace. It is necessary to place these circumstances under the reader's observation, because they are connected both with the preceding and subsequent part of our narrative.

The Duke was alone in his study, when one of his gentlemen acquainted him, that a country-girl, from Scotland, was desirous of speaking with his Grace.

"A country-girl, and from Scotland!" said the Duke; "what can have brought the silly fool to London?—Some lover pressed and sent to sea, or some stock sunk in the South-Sea[12] funds, or some such hopeful concern, I suppose, and then nobody to manage the matter but MacCallummore.—Well, this same popularity has its inconveniences.—However, show our countrywoman up, Archibald—it is ill manners to keep her in attendance."

A young woman of rather low stature, and whose countenance might be termed very modest and pleasing in expression, though sun-burnt, somewhat freckled, and not possessing regular features, was ushered into the splendid library.[13] She wore the tartan plaid of her country, adjusted so as partly to cover her head, and partly to fall back over her shoulders. A quantity of fair hair, disposed with great simplicity and neatness, appeared in front of her round and good-humoured face, to which the solemnity of her errand, and her sense of the Duke's rank and importance, gave an appearance of deep awe, but not of slavish fear, or fluttered bashfulness. The rest of Jeanie's dress was in the style of Scottish maidens of her own class; but arranged with that scrupulous attention to neatness and cleanliness, which we often find united with that purity of mind, of which it is a natural emblem.

She stopped near the entrance of the room, made her deepest reverence, and crossed her hands upon her bosom, without uttering a syllable. The Duke of Argyle advanced towards her; and if she admired his graceful deportment and rich dress, decorated with the orders which had been deservedly bestowed on him, his courteous manner, and quick and intelligent cast of countenance, he on his part was not less, or less deservedly, struck with the quiet simplicity and modesty expressed in the dress, manners, and countenance of his humble countrywoman.

"Did you wish to speak with me, my bonnie lass?" said the Duke, using the encouraging epithet which at once acknowledged the connection betwixt them as country-folks; "or, did you wish to see the Duchess?"

"My business is with your honour, my Lord—I mean your Lordship's Grace."

"And what is it, my good girl?" said the Duke, in the same mild and encouraging tone of voice. Jeanie looked at the attendant. "Leave us, Archibald," said the Duke, "and wait in the anti-room." The domestic retired. "And now sit down, my good lass," said the Duke; "take your breath—take your time, and tell me what you have got to say. I guess by your dress, you are just come up from poor old Scotland—Did you come through the streets in your tartan plaid?"

"No, sir," said Jeanie; "a friend brought me in ane o' their street coaches—a very decent woman," she added, her courage increasing as she became familiar with the sound of her own voice in such a presence; "your Lordship's Grace kens her—it's Mrs Glass, at the sign o' the Thistle."

"O my worthy snuff-merchant—I have always a chat with Mrs

Glass when I purchase my Scots high-dried.—Well, but your business, my bonnie woman—time and tide, you know, wait for no one."[14]

"Your honour—I beg your Lordship's pardon—I mean your Grace," for it must be noticed, that this matter of addressing the Duke by his appropriate title had been anxiously inculcated upon Jeanie by her friend Mrs Glass, in whose eyes it was a matter of such importance, that her last words, as Jeanie left the coach, were, "Mind to say your Grace;" and Jeanie, who had scarce ever in her life spoke to a person of higher quality than the Laird of Dumbiedikes, found great difficulty in arranging her language according to the rules of ceremony.

The Duke, who saw her embarrassment, said, with his usual affability, "Never mind my grace, lassie; just speak out a plain tale,[15] and shew you have a Scots tongue in your head."[16]

"Sir, I am muckle obliged—Sir, I am the sister of that poor unfortunate criminal, Effie Deans, who is ordered for execution at Edinburgh."

"Ah!" said the Duke, "I have heard of that unhappy story, I think—a case of child murder, under a special act of parliament—Duncan Forbes[17] mentioned it at dinner the other day."

"And I was come up frae the north, sir, to see what could be done for her in the way of getting a reprieve or pardon, sir, or the like of that."

"Alas! my poor girl," said the Duke, "you have made a long and a sad journey to very little purpose—Your sister is ordered for execution."

"But I am given to understand that there is law for reprieving her, if it is in the king's pleasure," said Jeanie.

"Certainly there is," said the Duke; "but that is purely in the king's breast. The crime has been but too common—the Scots crown-lawyers think it is right there should be an example. Then the late disorders in Edinburgh have excited a prejudice in government against the nation at large, which they think can only be managed by measures of intimidation and severity. What argument have you, my poor girl, except the warmth of your sisterly affection, to offer against all this?—What is your interest?—What friends have you at court?"

"None, excepting God and your Grace," said Jeanie, still keeping her ground resolutely, however.

"Alas!" said the Duke, "I could almost say with old Ormond,[18] that there could not be any, whose influence was smaller with kings and ministers. It is a cruel part of our situation, young woman—I mean of the situation of men in my circumstances, that the public ascribe to them influence which they do not possess; and that individuals are led to expect from them assistance, which we have no means of rendering. But candour and plain-dealing is in the power of every one, and I must not let you imagine you have resources in my influence, which do not exist, to make your distress the heavier—I have no means of averting your sister's fate—She must die."

"We must a' die, sir," said Jeanie; "it is our common doom for our father's transgression;[19] but we shouldna hasten ilk other out o' the world, that's what your honour kens better than me."

"My good young woman," said the Duke, mildly, "we are all apt to blame the law under which we immediately suffer; but you seem to have been well educated in your line of life, and you must know that it is alike the law of God and man, that the murderer shall surely die."[20]

"But, sir, Effie—that is my poor sister, sir—canna be proved to be a murderer; and if she be not, and the law take her life notwithstanding, wha is it that is the murderer then?"

"I am no lawyer," said the Duke; "and I own I think the statute a very severe one."

"You are a law-maker, sir, with your leave; and, therefore, ye have power over the law," answered Jeanie.

"Not in my individual capacity," said the Duke; "though, as one of a large body,[21] I have a voice in the legislation. But that cannot serve you—nor have I at present, I care not who knows it, so much personal influence with the sovereign, as would entitle me to ask from him the most insignificant favour. What could tempt you, young woman, to address yourself to me?"

"It was yoursell, sir."

"Myself?" he replied—"I am sure you have never seen me before."

"No, sir; but a' the world kens that the Duke of Argyle is his country's friend and the poor man's friend; and that ye fight for the right, and speak for the right, and that there's nae name like yours in our present Israel, and so they that think themselves wranged draw to refuge under your shadow; and if ye winna stir to save the blood of an innocent countrywoman of your ain, what should we expect frae southerns and strangers? And maybe I had another reason for troubling your honour."

"And what is that?" asked the Duke.

"I hae understood frae my father, that your honour's house, and especially your gudesire and his father,[22] laid down their lives on the scaffold in the persecuting time. And my father was honoured to gie his testimony baith in the cage[23] and in the pillory, as is specially mentioned in the books of Peter Walker the packman,[24] that your honour, I dare say, kens, for he uses maistpartly the west-land of Scotland. And, sir, there's ane that takes concern in me, that wished me to gang to your Grace's presence, for his gudesire had done your gracious gudesire some good turn, as ye will see frae these papers."

With these words, she delivered to the Duke the little parcel which she had received from Butler. He opened it, and, in the envelope, read with some surprise, "Muster-roll of the men serving in the troop of that godly gentleman, Captain Salathiel Bangtext.—Obadiah Muggleton, Sin-Despise Double-knock, Stand-fast-in-faith Gipps, Turn-to-the-right Thwack-away[25]—What the deuce is this? A list of Praise-God Barebone's[26] Parliament I think, or of old Noll's evangelical army[27]—that last fellow should understand his wheelings to judge by his name.—But what does all this mean, my girl?"

"It was the other paper, sir," said Jeanie, somewhat abashed at the mistake.

"O, this is my unfortunate grandfather's hand sure enough—'To all who may have friendship for the house of Argyle, these are to certify, that Benjamin Butler, of Monk's regiment of dragoons, having been, under God, the means of saving my life from four English troopers who were about to slay me, I, having no other present means of recompense in my power, do give him this acknowledgment, hoping that it may be useful to him or his during these troublesome times; and do conjure my friends, tenants, kinsmen, and whoever will do aught for me, either in the Highlands or Lowlands, to protect and assist the said Benjamin Butler, and his friends or family, on their lawful occasions, giving them such countenance, maintenance, and supply, as may correspond with the benefit he hath bestowed on me; witness my hand—

'LORNE.'[28]

"This is a strong injunction—This Benjamin Butler was your grandfather I suppose?—You seem too young to have been his daughter."

"He was nae akin to me, sir—he was grandfather to ane—to a neighbour's son—to a sincere well-wisher of mine, sir," dropping her little curtsey as she spoke.

"O, I understand," said the Duke—"a true-love affair. He was the grandsire of one you are engaged to?"

"One I *was* engaged to, sir," said Jeanie, sighing; "but this unhappy business of my poor sister"——

"What!" said the Duke, hastily,—"he has not deserted you on that account, has he?"

"No, sir; he wad be the last to leave a friend in difficulties," said Jeanie; "but I maun think for him, as weel as for mysell. He is a clergyman, sir, and it would not beseem him to marry the like of me, wi' this disgrace on my kindred."

"You are a singular young woman," said the Duke. "You seem to me to think of every one before yourself. And have you really come up from Edinburgh on foot, to attempt this hopeless solicitation for your sister's life?"

"It was not a'thegether on foot, sir," answered Jeanie; "for I sometimes got a cast in a waggon, and I had a horse from Ferrybridge, and then the coach"——

"Well, never mind all that," interrupted the Duke.—"What reason have you for thinking your sister innocent?"

"Because she has not been proved guilty, as will appear from looking at these papers."

She put into his hand a note of the evidence, and copies of her sister's declaration. These papers Butler had procured after her departure, and Saddletree had them forwarded to London, to Mrs Glass's care, so that Jeanie found the documents, so necessary for supporting her suit, lying in readiness at her arrival.

"Sit down in that chair, my good girl," said the Duke, "until I glance over the papers."

She obeyed, and watched with the utmost anxiety each change in his countenance as he cast his eye through the papers briefly, yet with attention, and making memoranda as he went along. After reading them hastily over, he looked up, and seemed about to speak, yet changed his purpose, as if afraid of committing himself by giving too hasty an opinion, and read over again several passages which he had marked as being most important. All this he did in shorter time than can be supposed by men of ordinary talents; for his mind was of that acute and penetrating character which discovers with the glance of intuition what facts bear on the particular point that chances to be subjected to consideration. At length he rose after a few minutes' deep reflection.—"Young woman," said he, "your sister's case must certainly be termed a hard one."[29]

"God bless you, sir, for that very word," said Jeanie.

"It seems contrary to the genius of British law," continued the Duke, "to take that for granted which is not proved, or to punish with death for a crime, which, for aught the prosecutor has been able to show, may not have been committed at all."

"God bless you, sir," again said Jeanie, who had risen from her seat, and, with clasped hands, eyes glittering through tears, and features which trembled with anxiety, drank in every word which the Duke uttered.

"But alas! my poor girl," he continued, "what good will my opinion do you, unless I could impress it upon those in whose hands your sister's life is placed by the law? Besides, I am no lawyer; and I must speak with some of our Scottish gentlemen of the gown about the matter."

"O but, sir, what seems reasonable to your honour, will certainly be the same to them," answered Jeanie.

"I do not know that," replied the Duke; "ilka man buckles his belt[30] his ain gate—you know our old Scots proverb?—But you shall not have placed this reliance on me altogether in vain. Leave these papers with me, and you shall hear from me to-morrow or next day. Take care to be at home at Mrs Glass's, and ready to come to me at a moment's warning. It will be unnecessary for you to give Mrs Glass the trouble to attend you;—and, by the by, you will please to be dressed just as you are at present."

"I wad hae putten on a cap, sir," said Jeanie, "but your honour kens it isna the fashion of my country for single women; and I judged that being sae mony hundred miles frae hame, your Grace's heart wad warm to the tartan," looking at the corner of her plaid.

"You judged quite right," said the Duke. "I know the full value of the snood; and MacCallummore's heart will be as cold as death can make it, when it does *not* warm to the tartan. Now, go away, and don't be out of the way when I send."

Jeanie replied,—"There is little fear of that, sir, for I have little heart to go to see sights amang this wilderness of black houses. But if I might say to your gracious honour, that if ye ever condescend to speak to ony ane that is of greater degree than yoursell, though maybe it is nae civil in me to say sae, just if you would think there can be nae sic odds between you and them, as between poor Jeanie Deans from Saint Leonard's and the Duke of Argyle; and so dinna be chappit back or cast down wi' the first rough answer."

"I am not apt," said the Duke, laughing, "to mind rough answers much—Do not you hope too much from what I have promised. I will do my best, but God has the hearts of Kings[31] in his own hand."

Jeanie curtsied reverently and withdrew, attended by the Duke's gentleman, to her hackney-coach, with a respect which her appearance did not demand, but which was perhaps paid to the length of the interview with which his master had honoured her.

CHAPTER 36

——ascend,
While radiant summer opens all its pride,
Thy hill, delightful Shene! Here let us sweep
The boundless landscape.

THOMSON

FROM her kind and officious, but somewhat gossipping friend, Mrs Glass, Jeanie underwent a very close catechism on their road to the Strand, where the Thistle of the good lady flourished in full glory, and, with its legend of *Nemo me impune*, distinguished a shop then well known to all Scottish folks of high and low degree.

"And were you sure aye to say *your Grace* to him?" said the good old lady; "for ane should make a distinction between MacCallummore and the bits o' southern bodies that they ca' lords here—there are as mony o' them, Jeanie, as would gar ane think they maun cost but little fash in the making—some of them I wadna trust wi' saxpennies worth of black rappee—some of them I wadna gie mysell the trouble to put up a hapnyworth in brown paper for—But I hope you showed your breeding to the Duke of Argyle, for what sort of folks would he think your friends in London, if you had been lording him, and him a Duke?"

"He didna seem muckle to mind," said Jeanie; "he kend that I was landward bred."

"Weel, weel," answered the good lady. "His Grace kens me weel; so I am the less anxious about it. I never fill his snuff-box but he says, 'How d'ye do, good Mrs Glass?—How are all our friends in the North?' or it maybe—'Have ye heard from the North lately?' And you may be sure, I make my best curtsey, and answer, 'My Lord Duke, I hope your Grace's noble Duchess, and your Grace's young ladies, are well; and I hope the snuff continues to give your Grace satisfaction.' And then ye will see the people in the shop begin to look about them; and if there's a Scotsman there, as may be there are half a dozen, aff go the hats, and mony a look after him, and 'there goes the Prince of Scotland, God bless him!' But ye have not told me yet the very words he said t'ye."

Jeanie had no intention to be quite so communicative. She had, as the reader may have observed, some of the caution and shrewdness, as well as of the simplicity of her country. She answered generally, that the Duke had received her very compassionately, and had promised to interest himself in her sister's affair, and to let her hear from him in the course of the next day, or the day after. She did not chuse to make any mention of his having desired her to be in readiness to attend him, far less of his hint, that she should not bring her landlady. So that honest Mrs Glass was obliged to remain satisfied with the general intelligence above mentioned, after having done all she could to extract more.

It may easily be conceived, that, on the next day, Jeanie declined all invitations and inducements, whether of exercise or curiosity, to walk abroad, and continued to inhale the close, and somewhat professional atmosphere of Mrs Glass's small parlour. The latter flavour it owed to a certain cupboard, containing, among other articles, a few cannisters of real Havannah, which, whether from respect to the manufacture, or out of a reverent fear of the exciseman, Mrs Glass did not care to trust in the open shop below, and which communicated to the room a scent, that, however fragrant to the nostrils of the connoisseur, was not very agreeable to those of Jeanie.

"Dear sirs," she said to herself, "I wonder how my cousin's silk manty, and her gowd watch, or ony thing in the world, can be worth sitting sneezing all her life in this little stifling room, and might walk on green braes if she liked."

Mrs Glass was equally surprised at her cousin's reluctance to stir abroad, and her indifference to the fine sights of London. "It would always help to pass away the time," she said, "to have something to look at, though ane *was* in distress." But Jeanie was unpersuadable.

The day after her interview with the Duke was spent in that "hope delayed, which maketh the heart sick."[1] Minutes glided after minutes—hours fled after hours—it became too late to have any reasonable expectation of hearing from the Duke that day; yet the hope which she disowned, she could not altogether relinquish, and her heart throbbed, and her ears tingled, with every casual sound in the shop below. It was in vain. The day wore away in the anxiety of protracted and fruitless expectation.

The next morning commenced in the same manner. But before noon, a well-dressed gentleman entered Mrs Glass's shop, and requested to see a young woman from Scotland.

"That will be my cousin, Jeanie Deans, Mr Archibald," said Mrs Glass, with a curtsey of recognizance. "Have you any message for her from his Grace the Duke of Argyle, Mr Archibald? I will carry it up to her in a moment."

"I believe I must give her the trouble of stepping down, Mrs Glass."

"Jeanie—Jeanie Deans!" said Mrs Glass, screaming at the bottom of the little stair-case, which ascended from the corner of the shop to the higher regions. "Jeanie—Jeanie Deans, I say, come down stairs instantly; here is the Duke of Argyle's groom of the chambers desires to see you directly." This was announced in a voice so loud, as to make all who chanced to be within hearing, aware of the important communication.

It may easily be supposed, that Jeanie did not tarry long in adjusting herself to attend the summons, yet her feet almost failed her as she came down stairs.

"I must ask the favour of your company a little way," said Archibald, with civility.

"I am quite ready, sir," said Jeanie.

"Is my cousin going out, Mr Archibald? then I will hae to go wi' her no doubt.—James Rasper—Look to the shop, James.—Mr Archibald," pushing a jar towards him, "you take his Grace's mixture, I think. Please to fill your box, for old acquaintance sake, while I get on my things."

Mr Archibald transposed a modest parcel of snuff from the jar to his own mull, but said he was obliged to decline the pleasure of Mrs Glass's company, as his message was particularly to the young person.

"Particularly to the young person?" said Mrs Glass; "is not that uncommon, Mr Archibald? But his Grace is the best judge; and you are a steady person, Mr Archibald. It is not every one that comes from a great man's house, I would trust my cousin with. But, Jeanie, you must not go through the streets with Mr Archibald with your tartan what d'ye call it there, upon your shoulders, as if you had come up with a drove of Highland cattle.[2] Wait till I bring down my silk cloak. Why we'll have the mob after you!"

"I have a hackney-coach in waiting, madam," said Mr Archibald, interrupting the officious old lady, from whom Jeanie might otherwise have found it difficult to escape, "and, I believe, I must not allow her time for any change of dress."

So saying, he hurried Jeanie into the coach, while she internally praised and wondered at the easy manner in which he shifted off Mrs Glass's officious offers and enquiries, without mentioning his master's orders, or going into any explanation whatever.

On entering the coach, Mr Archibald seated himself in the front seat, opposite to our heroine, and they drove on in silence. After they had proceeded nearly half an hour, without a word on either side, it occurred to Jeanie, that the distance and time did not correspond with that which had been occupied by her journey on the former occasion to, and from, the residence of the Duke of Argyle. At length she could not help asking her taciturn companion, "Whilk way they were going?"

"My Lord Duke will inform you himself, madam," answered Archibald, with the same solemn courtesy which marked his whole demeanour. Almost as he spoke, the hackney-coach drew up, and the coachman dismounted and opened the door. Archibald got out and assisted Jeanie to get down. She found herself in a large turnpike road, without the bounds of London, upon the other side of which road was drawn up a plain chariot and four horses, the pannels without arms, and the servants without liveries.

"You have been punctual, I see, Jeanie," said the Duke of Argyle, as Archibald opened the carriage door. "You must be my companion for the rest of the way. Archibald will remain here with the hackney-coach till your return."

Ere Jeanie could make answer, she found herself, to her no small astonishment, seated by the side of a duke, in a carriage which rolled forward at a rapid yet smooth rate, very different in both particulars from the lumbering, jolting vehicle which she had just left; and which, lumbering and jolting as it was, conveyed to one who had seldom been in a coach before, a certain feeling of dignity and importance.

"Young woman," said the Duke, "after thinking as attentively on your sister's case as is in my power, I continue to be impressed with the belief that great injustice may be done by the execution of her sentence. So are one or two liberal and intelligent lawyers of both countries whom I have spoken with.—Nay, pray hear me out before you thank me.—I have already told you my personal conviction is of little consequence, unless I could impress the same upon others. Now I have done for you, what I would certainly not have done to serve any purpose of my own—I have asked an audience of a lady whose interest with the king is deservedly very high. It has been allowed me, and I am desirous that you should see her and speak for yourself. You have no occasion to be abashed; tell your story simply as you did to me."

"I am much obliged to your Grace," said Jeanie, remembering Mrs Glass's charge, "and I am sure since I have had the courage to speak to your Grace, in poor Effie's cause, I have less reason to be shame-faced in speaking to a leddy. But, sir, I would like to ken what to ca' her, whether your grace, or your leddyship, as we say to lairds' leddies in Scotland, and I will take care to mind it; for I ken leddies are full mair particular than gentlemen about their titles of honour."

"You have no occasion to call her any thing but Madam. Just say what you think is likely to make the best impression—look at me from time to time—if I put my hand to my cravat so—(shewing her the motion)—you will stop; but I shall only do this when you say any thing that is not likely to please."

"But, sir, your Grace," said Jeanie, "if it wasna ower muckle trouble, wad it na be better to tell me what I should say, and I could get it by heart?"

"No, Jeanie, that would not have the same effect—that would be like reading a sermon you know, which we good presbyterians think has less unction than when spoken without book," replied the Duke. "Just speak as plainly and boldly to this lady, as you did to me the day before yesterday; and if you can gain her consent, I'll wad ye a plack, as we say in the north, that you get the pardon from the king."

As he spoke, he took a pamphlet from his pocket, and began to read. Jeanie had good sense and tact, which constitute betwixt them that which is called natural good breeding. She interpreted the Duke's manœuvre as a hint that she was to ask no more questions, and she remained silent accordingly.

The carriage rolled rapidly onwards through fertile meadows, orna-mented with splendid old oaks, and catching occasionally a glance of the majestic mirror of a broad and placid river. After passing through a pleasant village, the equipage stopped on a commanding eminence,[3] where the beauty of English landscape was displayed in its utmost luxuriance. Here the Duke alighted, and desired Jeanie to follow him. They paused for a moment on the brow of a hill, to gaze on the unrivalled landscape which it presented. A huge sea of verdure, with crossing and intersecting promontories of massive and tufted groves, was tenanted by numberless flocks and herds, which seemed to wander unrestrained and unbounded through the rich pastures. The Thames, here turretted with villas, and there garlanded with forests, moved on slowly and placidly, like the mighty monarch[4] of the scene, to whom all its other beauties were but accessories, and bore on his bosom an hundred barks and skiffs, whose white sails and gaily fluttering penons gave life to the whole.

The Duke of Argyle was, of course, familiar with this scene; but to a man of taste, it must be always new. Yet, as he paused and looked on this inimitable landscape, with the feeling of delight which it must give to the bosom of every admirer of nature, his thoughts naturally reverted to his own more grand, and scarce less beautiful, domains of Inverary.—"This is a fine scene," he said to his companion, curious, perhaps, to draw out her sentiments; "we have nothing like it in Scotland."

"It's braw rich feeding for the cows, and they have a fine breed o' cattle here," replied Jeanie; "but I like just as weel to look at the craigs of Arthur's Seat, and the sea coming in ayont them, as at a' thae muckle trees."

The Duke smiled at a reply equally professional and national, and made a signal for the carriage to remain where it was. Then adopting an unfrequented footpath, he conducted Jeanie, through several complicated mazes, to a postern-door in a high brick wall.[5] It was shut; but as the Duke tapped slightly at it, a person in waiting within, after reconnoitring through a small iron-grate contrived for the purpose, unlocked the door, and admitted them. They entered, and it was immediately closed and fastened behind them. This was all done quickly, the door so instantly closing, and the person who had opened it so suddenly disappearing, that Jeanie could not even catch a glimpse of his exterior.

They found themselves at the extremity of a deep and narrow alley, carpetted with the most verdant and close-shaven turf, which felt like velvet under their feet, and screened from the sun by the branches of the lofty elms which united over the path, and caused it to resemble, in the solemn obscurity of the light which they admitted, as well as from the range of columnar stems, and intricate union of their arched branches, one of the narrow side aisles in an ancient Gothic cathedral.

CHAPTER 37

——I beseech you——
These tears beseech you, and these chaste hands woo you,
That never yet were heaved but to things holy——
Things like yourself——You are a God above us;
Be as a God, then, full of saving mercy!

The Bloody Brother

ENCOURAGED as she was by the courteous manners of her noble countryman, it was not without a feeling of something like terror that Jeanie felt herself in a place apparently so lonely, with a man of such high rank. That she should have been permitted to wait on the Duke in his own house, and have been there received to a private interview, was in itself an uncommon and distinguished event in the annals of a life so simple as hers; but to find herself his travelling companion in a journey, and then suddenly to be left alone with him in so secluded a situation, had something in it of awful mystery. A romantic heroine might have suspected and dreaded the power of her own charms; but Jeanie was too wise to let such a silly thought intrude on her mind. Still, however, she had a most eager desire to know where she now was, and to whom she was to be presented.

She remarked that the Duke's dress, though still such as indicated rank and fashion, (for it was not the custom of men of quality at that time to dress themselves like their own coachmen or grooms,) was nevertheless plainer than that in which she had seen him upon a former occasion, and was divested, in particular, of all those badges of external decoration which intimated superior consequence. In short, he was attired as plainly as any gentleman of fashion could appear in the streets of London in a morning; and this circumstance helped to shake an opinion which Jeanie began to entertain, that, perhaps, he intended she should plead her cause in the presence of royalty itself. "But, surely," said she to herself, "he wad hae putten on his braw star and garter,[1] an he had thought o' coming before the face of Majesty—and after a', this is mair like a gentleman's policy than a royal palace."

There was some sense in Jeanie's reasoning; yet she was not sufficiently mistress either of the circumstances of etiquette, or the particular relations which existed betwixt the government and the Duke of Argyle, to form an accurate judgment. The Duke, as we have said, was at this time in open opposition to the administration of Sir Robert Walpole,[2] and was understood to be out of favour with the royal family,[3] to whom he had rendered such important services. But it was a maxim of Queen Caroline, to bear herself towards her political friends with such caution, as if there was a possibility of their one day being her enemies, and towards political opponents with the same degree of circumspection, as if they might again become friendly to her measures. Since Margaret of Anjou,[4] no queen-consort had exercised such weight in the political affairs of England, and the personal address which she displayed on many occasions, had no small share in reclaiming from their political heresy many of those determined tories, who, after the reign of the Stuarts had been extinguished in the person of Queen Anne, were disposed rather to transfer their allegiance to her brother the Chevalier de St George,[5] than to acquiesce in the settlement of the crown on the Hanover family. George II., her husband, whose most shining quality was courage in the field of battle,[6] and who endured the office of King of England, without ever being able to acquire English habits, or any familiarity with English dispositions, found the utmost assistance from the address of his partner, and while he jealously affected to do every thing according to his own will and pleasure, was in secret prudent enough to take and follow the advice of his more adroit consort. He entrusted to her the delicate office of determining the various degrees of favour necessary to attach the wavering, or to confirm such as were already friendly, or to regain those whose good-will had been lost.

With all the winning address of an elegant, and, according to the times, an accomplished woman, Queen Caroline possessed the masculine soul of the other sex. She was proud by nature, and even her policy could not always temper her expressions of displeasure, although few were more ready at repairing any false step of this kind, when her prudence came up to the aid of her passions. She loved the real possession of power, rather than the shew of it, and whatever she did herself that was either wise or popular, she always desired that the king should have the full credit as well as the advantage of the measure, conscious that by adding to his respectability, she was most likely to maintain her own. And so desirous was she to comply with all his tastes, that, when threatened with the gout, she had repeatedly had recourse to checking the fit, by the use of the cold bath, thereby endangering her life that she might be able to attend the king in his walks.

It was a very consistent part of Queen Caroline's character, to keep up many private correspondences with those to whom in public she seemed unfavourable, or who, for various reasons, stood ill with the court. By this means she kept in her hands the thread of many a political intrigue, and, without pledging herself to any thing, could often prevent discontent from becoming hatred, and opposition from exaggerating itself into rebellion. If by any accident her correspondence with such persons chanced to be observed or discovered, which she took all possible pains to prevent, it was represented as a mere intercourse of society, having no reference to politics; an answer with which even the prime minister, Sir Robert Walpole, was compelled to remain satisfied, when he discovered that the Queen had given a private audience to Pulteney,[7] afterwards Earl of Bath, his most formidable and most inveterate enemy.

In thus maintaining occasional intercourse with several persons who seemed most alienated from the crown, it may readily be supposed, that Queen Caroline had taken care not to break entirely with the Duke of Argyle. His high birth, his great talents, the estimation in which he was held in his own country, the great services which he had rendered the house of Brunswick in 1715, placed him high in that rank of persons who were not to be rashly neglected. He had, almost by his single and unassisted talents, stopped the irruption of the banded force of all the Highland chiefs; there was little doubt, that with the slightest encouragement, he could put them all in motion, and renew the civil war; and it was well known that the most flattering overtures had been transmitted to the Duke from the court of St Germains. The character and temper of Scotland was still little known, and it was considered as a volcano, which might, indeed, slumber for a series of years, but was still liable, at a moment the least expected, to break out into a wasteful eruption. It was, therefore, of the highest importance to retain some hold over so important a personage as the Duke of Argyle, and Caroline preserved the power of doing so by means of a lady, with whom, as wife of George II., she might have been supposed to be on less intimate terms.

It was not the least instance of the Queen's address, that she had contrived that one of her principal attendants, Lady Suffolk,[8] should unite in her own person the two apparently inconsistent characters of her husband's mistress, and her own very obsequious and complaisant confidante. By this dexterous management the Queen secured her power against the danger which might most have threatened it—the thwarting influence of an ambitious rival; and if she submitted to the mortification of being obliged to connive at her husband's infidelity, she was at least guarded against what she might think its most dangerous effects, and was besides at liberty, now and then, to bestow a few civil insults upon "her good Howard," whom, however, in general, she treated with great decorum.[*] Lady Suffolk lay under strong obligations to the Duke of Argyle, for reasons[9] which may be collected from Horace Walpole's Reminiscences[10] of that reign, and through her means the Duke maintained some occasional correspondence with Queen Caroline, much interrupted,[11] however, since the part he had taken in the debate concerning the Porteous mob, an affair which the Queen, though somewhat unreasonably, was disposed to resent, rather as an intended and premeditated insolence to her own person and authority, than as a sudden ebullition of popular vengeance. Still, however, the communication remained open betwixt them, though it had been of late disused on both sides. These remarks will be found necessary to understand the scene which is about to be presented to the reader.

From the narrow alley which they had traversed, the Duke turned into one of the same character, but broader and still longer. Here, for the first time since they had entered these gardens, Jeanie saw persons approaching them.

They were two ladies; one of whom walked a little behind the other, yet not so much as to prevent her from hearing and replying to whatever observation was addressed to her by the lady who walked foremost, and that without her having the trouble to turn her person. As they advanced very slowly, Jeanie had time to study their features and appearance. The Duke also slackened his pace, as if to give her time to collect herself, and repeatedly desired her not to be afraid. The lady who seemed the principal person had remarkably good features, though somewhat injured[12] by the small-pox, that venomous scourge which each village Esculapius[13] (thanks to Jenner,[14]) can now tame as easily as their tutelary deity[15] subdued the Python. The lady's eyes were brilliant, her teeth good, and her countenance formed to express

[* See Horace Walpole's Reminiscences.]

at will either majesty or courtesy. Her form, though rather *en-bon-point*, was nevertheless graceful; and the elasticity and firmness of her step gave no room to suspect, what was actually the case, that she suffered occasionally from a disorder[16] the most unfavourable to pedestrian exercise. Her dress was rather rich than gay, and her manner commanding and noble.

Her companion[17] was of lower stature, with light-brown hair and expressive blue eyes. Her features, without being absolutely regular, were perhaps more pleasing than if they had been critically handsome. A melancholy, or at least a pensive expression, for which her lot gave too much cause, predominated when she was silent, but gave way to a pleasing and good-humoured smile when she spoke to any one.

When they were within twelve or fifteen yards of these ladies, the Duke made a sign that Jeanie should stand still, and stepping forward himself, with the grace which was natural to him, made a profound obeisance, which was formally, yet in a dignified manner, returned by the personage whom he approached.

"I hope," she said, with an affable and condescending smile, "that I see so great a stranger at court, as the Duke of Argyle has been of late, in as good health as his friends there and elsewhere could wish him to enjoy."

The Duke replied, "That he had been perfectly well;" and added, "that the necessity of attending to the public business before the House, as well as the time occupied by a late journey to Scotland, had rendered him less assiduous in paying his duty at the levee and drawing-room than he could have desired."

"When your Grace *can* find time for a duty so frivolous," replied the Queen, "you are aware of your title to be well received. I hope my readiness to comply with the wish which you expressed yesterday to Lady Suffolk, is a sufficient proof that one of the royal family, at least, has not forgotten ancient and important services, in resenting something which resembles recent neglect." This was said apparently with great good-humour, and in a tone which expressed a desire of conciliation.

The Duke replied, "That he would account himself the most unfortunate of men, if he could be supposed capable of neglecting his duty, in modes and circumstances when it was expected, and would have been agreeable. He was deeply gratified by the honour which her Majesty was now doing to him personally; and he trusted she would soon perceive, that it was in a matter essential to his Majesty's interest that he had the boldness to give her this trouble."

"You cannot oblige me more, my Lord Duke," replied the Queen, "than by giving me the advantage of your lights and experience on any point of the King's service. Your Grace is aware, that I can only be the medium[18] through which the matter is subjected to his Majesty's superior wisdom; but if it is a suit which respects your Grace personally, it shall lose no support by being preferred through me."

"It is no suit of mine, madam," replied the Duke; "nor have I any to prefer for myself personally, although I feel in full force my obligation to your Majesty. It is a business which concerns his Majesty, as a lover of justice and of mercy, and which I am convinced may be highly useful in conciliating the unfortunate irritation which at present subsists among his Majesty's good subjects in Scotland."

There were two parts of this speech disagreeable to Caroline. In the first place, it removed the flattering notion she had adopted, that Argyle designed to use her personal intercession in making his peace with the administration, and recovering the employments[19] of which he had been deprived; and next, she was displeased that he should talk of the discontents in Scotland as irritations to be conciliated, rather than suppressed.

Under the influence of these feelings, she answered hastily, "That his Majesty has good subjects in England, my Lord Duke, he is bound to thank God and the laws—that he has subjects in Scotland, I think he may thank God and his sword."

The Duke, though a courtier, coloured slightly, and the Queen, instantly sensible of her error, added, without displaying the least change of countenance, and as if the words had been an original branch of the sentence—"And the swords of those real Scotchmen who are friends to the House of Brunswick, particularly that of his Grace of Argyle."

"My sword, madam," replied the Duke, "like that of my fathers, has been always at the command of my lawful king, and of my native country—I trust it is impossible to separate their real rights and interests. But the present is a matter of more private concern, and respects the person of an obscure individual."

"What is the affair, my Lord?" said the Queen. "Let us find out what we are talking about, lest we should misconstrue and misunderstand each other."

"The matter, madam," answered the Duke of Argyle, "regards the fate of an unfortunate young woman in Scotland, now lying under sentence of death, for a crime of which I think it highly probable that she is innocent. And my humble petition to your Majesty is, to obtain your powerful intercession with the King for a pardon."

It was now the Queen's turn to colour, and she did so over cheek and brow—neck and bosom. She paused a moment, as if unwilling to trust her voice with the first expression of her displeasure; and assuming an air of dignity and an austere regard of controul,[20] she at length replied, "My Lord Duke, I will not ask your motives for addressing to me a request, which circumstances have rendered such an extraordinary one. Your road to the King's closet, as a peer and a privy-counsellor entitled to request an audience, was open, without giving me the pain of this discussion. *I*, at least, have had enough of Scotch pardons."

The Duke was prepared for this burst of indignation, and he was not shaken by it. He did not attempt a reply while the Queen was in the first heat of displeasure, but remained in the same firm, yet respectful posture, which he had assumed during the interview. The Queen, trained from her situation to self-command, instantly perceived the advantage she might give against herself by yielding to passion; and added, in the same condescending and affable tone in which she had opened the interview, "You must allow me some of the privileges of the sex, my Lord; and do not judge uncharitably of me, though I am a little moved at the recollection of the gross insult and outrage done in your capital city to the royal authority, at the very time when it was vested in my unworthy person. Your Grace cannot be surprised that I should both have felt it at the time, and recollected it now."

"It is certainly a matter not speedily to be forgotten," answered the Duke. "My own poor thoughts of it have been long before your Majesty, and I must have expressed myself very ill if I did not convey my detestation of the murder which was committed under such extraordinary circumstances. I might, indeed, be so unfortunate as to differ with his Majesty's advisers on the degree in which it was either just or politic to punish the innocent instead of the guilty. But I trust your Majesty will permit me to be silent on a topic in which my sentiments have not the good fortune to coincide with those of more able men."

"We will not prosecute a topic on which we may probably differ," said the Queen. "One word, however, I may say in private—You know our good Lady Suffolk is a little deaf[21]—the Duke of Argyle, when disposed to renew his acquaintance with his master and mistress, will hardly find many topics on which we should disagree."

"Let me hope," said the Duke, bowing profoundly to so flattering an intimation, "that I shall not be so unfortunate as to have found one on the present occasion."

"I must first impose on your Grace the duty of confession," said the Queen, "before I grant you absolution. What is your particular interest in this young woman? She does not seem (and she scanned Jeanie as she said this with the eye of a connoisseur) much qualified to alarm my friend the Duchess's jealousy."

"I think your Majesty," replied the Duke, smiling in his turn, "will allow my taste may be a pledge for me on that score."

"Then, though she has not much the air *d'une grande dame*, I suppose she is some thirtieth cousin in the terrible chapter of Scottish genealogy?²²"

"No, madam," said the Duke; "but I wish some of my nearer relations had half her worth, honesty, and affection."

"Her name must be Campbell at least?" said Queen Caroline.

"No, madam; her name is not quite so distinguished, if I may be permitted to say so," answered the Duke.

"Ah! but she comes from Inverara or Argyleshire?" said the Sovereign.

"She has never been farther north in her life than Edinburgh, madam."

"Then my conjectures are all ended," said the Queen, "and your Grace must yourself take the trouble to explain the affair of your protégée."

With that precision and easy brevity which is only acquired by habitually conversing in the higher ranks of society, and which is the diametrical opposite of that protracted style of disquisition,

Which squires call potter, and which men call prose,²³

the Duke explained the singular law under which Effie Deans had received sentence of death, and detailed the affectionate exertions which Jeanie had made in behalf of a sister, for whose sake she was willing to sacrifice all but truth and conscience.

Queen Caroline listened with attention; she was rather fond, it must be remembered, of an argument, and soon found matter in what the Duke told her for raising difficulties to his request.

"It appears to me, my Lord," she replied, "that this is a severe law. But still it is adopted upon good grounds, I am bound to suppose, as the law of the country, and the girl has been convicted under it. The very presumptions which the law construes into a positive proof of guilt exist in her case; and all that your Grace has said concerning the possibility of her innocence may be a very good argument for annulling the Act of Parliament, but cannot, while it stands good, be admitted in favour of any individual convicted upon the statute."

The Duke saw and avoided the snare, for he was conscious, that, by replying to the argument, he must have been inevitably led to a discussion, in the course of which the Queen was likely to be hardened in her own opinion, until she became obliged out of mere respect to consistency, to let the criminal suffer. "If your Majesty," he said, "would condescend to hear my poor countrywoman herself, perhaps she may find an advocate in your own heart, more able than I am to combat the doubts suggested by your understanding."

The Queen seemed to acquiesce, and the Duke made a signal for Jeanie to advance from the spot where she had hitherto remained watching countenances, which were too long accustomed to suppress all apparent signs of emotion, to convey to her any interesting intelligence. Her Majesty could not help smiling at the awe-struck manner in which the quiet demure figure of the little Scotchwoman advanced towards her, and yet more at the first sound of her broad northern accent. But Jeanie had a voice low and sweetly toned, an admirable thing in woman,[24] and she besought "her Leddyship to have pity on a poor misguided young creature," in tones so affecting, that, like the notes of some of her native songs, provincial vulgarity was lost in pathos.

"Stand up, young woman," said the Queen, but in a kind tone, "and tell me what sort of a barbarous people your countryfolks are, where child-murther is become so common as to require the restraint of laws like yours?"

"If your Leddyship pleases," answered Jeanie, "there are mony places besides Scotland where mothers are unkind to their ain flesh and blood."

It must be observed, that the disputes[25] between George the Second, and Frederick, Prince of Wales, were then at the highest, and that the good-natured part of the public laid the blame on the Queen. She coloured highly, and darted a glance of a most penetrating character first at Jeanie, and then at the Duke. Both sustained it unmoved; Jeanie from total unconsciousness of the offence she had given, and the Duke from his habitual composure. But in his heart he thought, My unlucky protégée has, with this luckless answer, shot dead, by a kind of chance-medley,[26] her only hope of success.

Lady Suffolk, good-humouredly and skilfully, interposed in this awkward crisis. "You should tell this lady," she said to Jeanie, "the particular causes which render this crime common in your country."

"Some thinks it's the Kirk-Session—that is—it's the—it's the cutty-stool, if your Leddyship pleases," said Jeanie, looking down, and curtseying.

"The what?" said Lady Suffolk, to whom the phrase was new, and who besides was rather deaf.

"That's the stool of repentance, madam, if it please your Leddyship," answered Jeanie, "for light life and conversation,[27] and for breaking the seventh command."[28] Here she raised her eyes to the Duke, saw his hand at his chin, and, totally unconscious of what she had said out of joint, gave double effect to the innuendo, by stopping short and looking embarrassed.

As for Lady Suffolk, she retired like a covering party, which, having interposed betwixt their retreating friends and the enemy, have suddenly drawn on themselves a fire unexpectedly severe.

The deuce take the lass, thought the Duke of Argyle to himself; there goes another shot—and she has hit with both barrels right and left.

Indeed the Duke had himself his share of the confusion, for, having acted as master of ceremonies to this innocent offender, he felt much in the circumstances of a country squire, who, having introduced his spaniel into a well-appointed drawing-room, is doomed to witness the disorder and damage which arises to china and to dress-gowns, in consequence of its untimely frolics. Jeanie's last chance-hit, however, obliterated the ill impression which had arisen from the first; for her Majesty had not so lost the feelings of a wife in those of a Queen, but what she could enjoy a jest at the expence of "her good Suffolk." She turned towards the Duke of Argyle with a smile, which marked that she enjoyed the triumph, and observed, "the Scotch are a rigidly moral people." Then again applying herself to Jeanie, she asked, how she travelled up from Scotland.

"Upon my foot mostly, madam," was the reply.

"What, all that immense way upon foot?—How far can you walk in a day?"

"Five and twenty miles and a bittock."

"And a what?" said the Queen, looking towards the Duke of Argyle.

"And about five miles more," replied the Duke.

"I thought I was a good walker," said the Queen, "but this shames me sadly."

"May your Leddyship never hae sae weary a heart, that ye canna be sensible of the weariness of the limbs," said Jeanie.

That came better off, thought the Duke; it's the first thing she has said to the purpose.

"And I didna just a'thegether walk the haill way neither, for I had whiles the cast of a cart; and I had the cast of a horse from Ferrybridge—and divers other easements," said Jeanie, cutting short her story, for she observed the Duke made the sign he had fixed upon.

"With all these accommodations," answered the Queen, "you must have had a very fatiguing journey, and, I fear, to little purpose; since, if the King were to pardon your sister, in all probability it would do her little good, for I suppose your people of Edinburgh would hang her out of spite."

She will sink herself now outright, thought the Duke.

But he was wrong. The shoals on which Jeanie had hitherto touched in this delicate conversation lay under ground, and were unknown to her; this rock was above water, and she avoided it.

"She was confident," she said, "that baith town and country wad rejoice to see his Majesty taking compassion on a poor unfriended creature."

"His Majesty has not found it so in a late instance," said the Queen; "but I suppose my Lord Duke would advise him to be guided by the votes of the rabble themselves, who should be hanged and who spared?"

"No, madam," said the Duke; "but I would advise his Majesty to be guided by his own feelings and those of his royal consort; and then, I am sure, punishment will attach itself only to guilt, and even then with cautious reluctance."

"Well, my Lord," said her Majesty, "all these fine speeches do not convince me of the propriety of so soon showing any mark of favour to your—I suppose I must not say rebellious?—but, at least, your very disaffected and intractable metropolis. Why, the whole nation is in a league to screen the savage and abominable murtherers of that unhappy man; otherwise, how is it possible but that, of so many perpetrators, and engaged in so public an action for such a length of time, one at least must have been recognized? Even this wench, for aught I can tell, may be a depositary of the secret. Hear you, young woman; had you any friends engaged in the Porteous mob?"

"No, madam," answered Jeanie, happy that the question was so framed that she could, with a good conscience, answer it in the negative.

"But I suppose," continued the Queen, "if you were possessed of such a secret, you would hold it matter of conscience to keep it to yourself?"

"I would pray to be directed and guided what was the line of duty, madam," answered Jeanie.

"Yes, and take that which suited your own inclinations," replied her Majesty.

"If it like you, madam," said Jeanie, "I would hae gaen to the end of the earth to save the life of John Porteous, or any other unhappy man in his condition; but I might lawfully doubt how far I am called upon to be the avenger of his blood, though it may become the civil magistrate to do so. He is dead and gane to his place,[29] and they that have slain him must answer for their ain act. But my sister—my puir sister Effie, still lives, though her days and hours are numbered!—She still lives, and a word of the King's mouth might restore her to a broken-hearted auld man, that never, in his daily and nightly exercise, forgot to pray that his Majesty might be blessed with a long and a prosperous reign, and that his throne, and the throne of his posterity, might be established in righteousness. O, madam, if ever ye kend what it was to sorrow for and with a sinning and a suffering creature, whose mind is sae tossed that she can be neither ca'd fit to live or die, have some compassion on our misery!—Save an honest house from dishonour, and an unhappy girl, not eighteen years of age, from an early and dreadful death! Alas! it is not when we sleep soft and wake merrily ourselves that we think on other people's sufferings. Our hearts are waxed high within us then, and we are for righting our ain wrangs and fighting our ain battles. But when the hour of trouble comes to the mind or to the body—and seldom may it visit your Leddyship—and when the hour of death comes, that comes to high and low—lang and late may it be yours—O, my Leddy, then it isna what we hae dune for oursells, but what we hae dune for others, that we think on maist pleasantly. And the thoughts that ye hae intervened to spare the puir thing's life will be sweeter in that hour, come when it may, than if a word of your mouth could hang the haill Porteous mob at the tail of ae tow."

Tear followed tear down Jeanie's cheeks, as, her features glowing and quivering with emotion, she pleaded her sister's cause with a pathos which was at once simple and solemn.

"This is eloquence," said her Majesty to the Duke of Argyle. "Young woman," she continued, addressing herself to Jeanie, "*I* cannot grant a pardon to your sister—but you shall not want my warm intercession with his Majesty. Take this housewife case," she continued, putting a small embroidered needle-case into Jeanie's hands; "do not open it now, but at your leisure you will find something in it which will remind you that you have had an interview with Queen Caroline."

Jeanie, having her suspicions thus confirmed, dropped on her knees, and would have expanded herself in gratitude; but the Duke, who was upon thorns lest she should say more or less than just enough, touched his chin once more.

"Our business is, I think, ended for the present, my Lord Duke," said the Queen, "and, I trust, to your satisfaction. Hereafter I hope to see your Grace more frequently, both at Richmond and St James's.— Come, Lady Suffolk, we must wish his Grace good morning."

They exchanged their parting reverences, and the Duke, so soon as the ladies had turned their backs, assisted Jeanie to rise from the ground, and conducted her back through the avenue, which she trod with the feeling of one who walks in her sleep.

CHAPTER 38

So soon as I can win the offended King
I will be known your advocate.

Cymbeline

THE Duke of Argyle led the way in silence to the small postern by which they had been 'admitted into Richmond Park,[1] so long the favourite residence of Queen Caroline. It was opened by the same half-seen janitor, and they found themselves beyond the precincts of the royal demesne. Still not a word was spoken on either side. The Duke probably wished to allow his rustic protégée time to recruit her faculties, dazzled and sunk with colloquy sublime;[2] and betwixt what she had guessed, had heard, and had seen, Jeanie Deans's mind was too much agitated to permit her to ask any questions.

They found the carriage of the Duke in the place where they had left it; and when they resumed their places, soon began to advance rapidly on their return to town.

"I think, Jeanie," said the Duke, breaking silence, "you have every reason to congratulate yourself on the issue of your interview with her Majesty."

"And that leddy *was* the Queen hersell?" said Jeanie; "I misdoubted it when I saw that your honour didna put on your hat—And yet I can hardly believe it, even when I heard her speak it hersell."

"It was certainly Queen Caroline," replied the Duke. "Have you no curiosity to see what is in the little pocket-book?"

"Do you think the pardon will be in it, sir?" said Jeanie, with the eager animation of hope.

"Why, no," replied the Duke; "that is unlikely. They seldom carry these things about them, unless they were likely to be wanted; and besides, her Majesty told you it was the King, not she, who was to grant it."

"That is true too," said Jeanie; "but I am so confused in my mind—But does your honour think there is a certainty of Effie's pardon then?" continued she, still holding in her hand the unopened pocket-book.

"Why, kings are kittle cattle to shoe behind,[3] as we say in the north," replied the Duke; "but his wife knows his trim, and I have not the least doubt that the matter is quite certain."

"O God be praised! God be praised!" ejaculated Jeanie; "and may the gude leddy never want the heart's ease she has gien me at this moment—And God bless you too, my Lord! without your help I wad ne'er hae won near her."

The Duke let her dwell upon this subject for a considerable time, curious, perhaps, to see how long the feelings of gratitude would continue to supersede those of curiosity. But so feeble was the latter feeling in Jeanie's mind, that his Grace, with whom, perhaps, it was for the time a little stronger, was obliged once more to bring forward the subject of the Queen's present. It was opened accordingly. In the inside of the case were the usual assortment of silk and needles, with scissars, tweazers, &c.; and in the pocket was a bank-bill[4] for fifty pounds.

The Duke had no sooner informed Jeanie of the value of this last document, for she was unaccustomed to see notes for such sums, than she expressed her regret at the mistake which had taken place. "For the hussy itsell," she said, "was a very valuable thing for a keepsake, with the Queen's name written in the inside with her ain hand doubtless—*Caroline*—as plain as could be, and a crown drawn aboon it."

She therefore tendered the bill to the Duke, requesting him to find some mode of returning it to the royal owner.

"No, no, Jeanie," said the Duke, "there is no mistake in the case. Her Majesty knows you have been put to great expence, and she wishes to make it up to you."

"I am sure she is even ower gude," said Jeanie, "and it glads me muckle that I can pay back Dumbiedikes his siller, without distressing my father, honest man."

"Dumbiedikes? What, a freeholder of Mid-Lothian is he not?" said his Grace, whose occasional residence in that county made him acquainted with most of the heritors, as landed persons are termed in Scotland—"He has a house not far from Dalkeith, wears a black wig and a laced hat?"

"Yes, sir," answered Jeanie, who had her reasons for being brief in her answers upon this topic.

"Ah! my old friend Dumbie!" said the Duke; "I have thrice seen him fou, and only once heard the sound of his voice—Is he a cousin of yours, Jeanie?"

"No, sir,—my Lord."

"Then he must be a well-wisher, I suspect?"

"Ye—yes,—my Lord, sir," answered Jeanie, blushing, and with hesitation.

"Aha! then, if the Laird starts, I suppose my friend Butler must be in some danger?"

"O no, sir," answered Jeanie much more readily, but at the same time blushing much more deeply.

"Well, Jeanie," said the Duke, "you are a girl may be safely trusted with your own matters, and I shall enquire no further about them. But as to this same pardon, I must see to get it passed through the proper forms; and I have a friend in office who will, for auld lang syne, do me so much favour. And then, Jeanie, as I shall have occasion to send an express down to Scotland, who will travel with it safer and more swiftly than you can do, I will take care to have it put into the proper channel; meanwhile you may write to your friends by post of your good success."

"And does your Honour think," said Jeanie, "that will do as weel as if I were to take my tap in my lap, and slip my ways hame again on my ain errand?"[5]

"Much better, certainly," said the Duke. "You know the roads are not very safe for a single woman to travel."

Jeanie internally acquiesced in this observation.

"And I have a plan for you besides. One of the Duchess's attendants, and one of mine—your acquaintance Archibald—are going down to Inverara in a light calash, with four horses I have bought, and there is room enough in the carriage for you to go with them as far as Glasgow, where Archibald will find means of sending you safely to Edinburgh—And in the way, I beg you will teach the woman as much as you can of the mystery of cheese-making, for she is to have a charge in the dairy, and I dare swear you are as tidy about your milk-pail as about your dress."

"Does your Honour like cheese?" said Jeanie, with a gleam of conscious delight as she asked the question.

"Like it?" said the Duke, whose good-nature anticipated what was to follow,—"cakes and cheese are a dinner for an emperor, let alone a Highlandman."

"Because," said Jeanie, with modest confidence, and great and evident self-gratulation, "we have been thought particular in making cheese that some folk think is as gude as the real Dunlop; and if your

Honour's Grace[6] wad but accept a stane or twa, blythe, and fain, and proud it wad make us. But maybe ye may like the ewe-milk, that is, the Buckholmside[*][7] cheese better; or maybe the gait-milk, as ye come frae the Highlands—and I canna pretend just to the same skeel o' them; but my cousin Jean, that lives at Lockermachus in Lammermuir, I could speak to her, and"——

"Quite unnecessary," said the Duke; "the Dunlop is the very cheese of which I am so fond, and I will take it as the greatest favour you can do me to send one to Caroline-Park.[8] But remember, be on honour with it, Jeanie, and make it all yourself, for I am a real good judge."

"I am not feared," said Jeanie confidently, "that I may please your Honour; for I am sure you look as if you could hardly find fault wi' ony body that did their best; and weel is it my part, I trow, to do mine."

This discourse introduced a topic upon which the two travellers, though so different in rank and education, found each a good deal to say. The Duke, besides his other patriotic qualities, was a distinguished agriculturist, and proud of his knowledge in that department. He entertained Jeanie with his observations on the different breeds of cattle in Scotland, and their capacity for the dairy, and received so much information from her practical experience in return, that he promised her a couple of Devonshire cows in reward of the lesson. In short, his mind was so transported back to his rural employments and amusements, that he sighed when his carriage stopped opposite to the old hackney-coach, which Archibald had kept in attendance at the place where they had left it. While the coachman again bridled his lean cattle, which had been indulged with a bite of musty hay,[9] the Duke cautioned Jeanie not to be too communicative to her landlady concerning what had passed. "There is," he said, "no use in speaking of matters till they are actually settled; and you may refer the good lady to Archibald, if she presses you hard with questions. She is his old acquaintance, and he knows how to manage with her."

He then took a cordial farewell of Jeanie, and told her to be ready in the ensuing week to return to Scotland—saw her safely established in her hackney-coach, and rolled off in his own carriage, humming a stanza of the ballad which he is said to have composed:—

[* The hilly pastures of Buckholm, which the author now surveys,

> Not in the frenzy of a dreamer's eye,

are famed for producing the best ewe-milk cheese in the south of Scotland.]

"At the sight of Dumbarton once again,
I'll cock up my bonnet and march amain,
With my claymore hanging down to my heel,
To whang at the bannocks of barley meal."[10]

Perhaps one ought to be actually a Scotchman to conceive how ardently, under all distinctions of rank and situation, they feel their mutual connexion[11] with each other as natives of the same country. There are, I believe, more associations common to the inhabitants of a rude and wild, than of a well cultivated and fertile country; their ancestors have more seldom changed their place of residence; their mutual recollection of remarkable objects is more accurate; the high and the low are more interested in each other's welfare; the feelings of kindred and relationship are more widely extended, and, in a word, the bonds of patriotic affection, always honourable even when a little too exclusively strained, have more influence on men's feelings and actions.

The rumbling hackney-coach which tumbled over the (then) execrable London pavement, at a rate very different from that which had conveyed the ducal carriage to Richmond, at length deposited Jeanie Deans and her attendant at the national sign of the Thistle. Mrs Glass, who had been in long and anxious expectation, now rushed, full of eager curiosity and open-mouthed interrogation, upon our heroine, who was positively unable to sustain the overwhelming cataract of her questions which burst forth with the sublimity of a grand gardyloo:—— "Had she seen the Duke, God bless him—the Duchess—the young ladies?—Had she seen the King, God bless him—the Queen—the Prince of Wales—the Princess—or any of the rest of the royal family?—Had she got her sister's pardon?—Was it out and out—or was it only a commutation of punishment?—How far had she gone—where had she driven to—whom had she seen—what had been said—what had kept her so long?"

Such were the various questions huddled upon each other by a curiosity so eager, that it could hardly wait for its own gratification. Jeanie would have been more than sufficiently embarrassed by this over-bearing tide of interrogations, had not Archibald, who had probably received from his master a hint to that purpose, advanced to her rescue. "Mrs Glass," said Archibald, "his Grace desired me particularly to say, that he would take it as a great favour if you would ask the young woman no questions, as he wishes to explain to you more distinctly than she can do how her affairs stand, and consult you on some matters which she cannot altogether so well understand. The Duke will call at the Thistle to-morrow or next day for that purpose."

"His Grace is very condescending," said Mrs Glass, her zeal for enquiry slaked for the present by the dexterous administration of this sugar-plumb—"his Grace is sensible that I am in a manner accountable for the conduct of my young kinswoman, and no doubt his Grace is the best judge how far he should entrust her or me with the management of her affairs."

"His Grace is quite sensible of that," answered Archibald with national gravity, "and will certainly trust what he has to say to the most discreet of the two; and therefore Mrs Glass, his Grace relies you will say nothing to Mrs Jean Deans, either of her own affairs or her sister's, until he sees you himself. He desired me to assure you, in the mean while, that all was going on as well as your kindness could wish, Mrs Glass."

"His Grace is very kind—very considerate, certainly, Mr Archibald—his Grace's commands shall be obeyed, and——But you have had a far drive, Mr Archibald, as I guess by the time of your absence, and I guess" (with an engaging smile) "you winna be the waur of a glass of the right Rosa Solis."

"I thank you, Mrs Glass," said the great man's great man,[12] "but I am under the necessity of returning to my Lord directly." And making his adieus civilly to both cousins, he left the shop of the Lady of the Thistle.

"I am glad your affairs have prospered so well, Jeanie, my love," said Mrs Glass; "though indeed there was little fear of them so soon as the Duke of Argyle was so condescending as to take them into hand. I will ask you no questions about them, because his Grace, who is most considerate and prudent in such matters, intends to tell me all that you ken yourself, dear, and doubtless a great deal more; so that any thing that may lie heavily on your mind may be imparted to me in the meantime, as you see it is his Grace's pleasure that I should be made acquainted with the whole matter forthwith, and whether you or he tells it, will make no difference in the world, ye ken. If I ken what he is going to say beforehand, I will be much more ready to give my advice, and whether you or he tell me about it, cannot much signify after all, my dear. So you may just say whatever you like, only mind I ask you no questions about it."

Jeanie was a little embarrassed. She thought that the communication she had to make was perhaps the only means she might have in her power to gratify her friendly and hospitable kinswoman. But her prudence instantly suggested that her secret interview with Queen Caroline, which seemed to pass under a certain sort of mystery, was not a proper subject for the gossip of a woman like Mrs Glass, of whose heart she had a much better opinion than of her prudence. She, therefore, answered in general, that the Duke had had the extraordinary kindness to make very particular enquiries into her sister's bad affair, and that he thought he had found the means of putting it a' straight again, but that he proposed to tell all that he thought about the matter to Mrs Glass herself.

This did not quite satisfy the penetrating Mistress of the Thistle. Searching as her own small rappee, she, in spite of her promise, urged Jeanie with still further questions. "Had she been a' that time at Argyle-house?[13] Was the Duke with her the whole time? and had she seen the Duchess? and had she seen the young ladies—and specially Lady Caroline Campbell?"[14]—To these questions Jeanie gave the general reply, that she knew so little of the town that she could not tell exactly where she had been; that she had not seen the Duchess, to her knowledge; that she had seen two ladies, one of whom she understood bore the name of Caroline; and more, she said, she could not tell about the matter.

"It would be the Duke's eldest daughter, Lady Caroline Campbell—there is no doubt of that," said Mrs Glass; "but, doubtless, I shall know more particularly through his Grace.—And so, as the cloth is laid in the little parlour above stairs, and it is past three o'clock, for I have been waiting this hour for you, and I have had a snack myself, and, as they used to say in Scotland in my time—I do not ken if the word be used now—there is ill talking between a full body and a fasting."[15]

CHAPTER 39

Heaven first sent letters to some wretch's aid—
Some banished lover or some captive maid.
POPE

BY dint of unwonted labour with the pen, Jeanie Deans contrived to indite, and give to the charge of the postman on the ensuing day, no less than three letters,[1] an exertion altogether strange to her habits; insomuch so, that, if milk had been plenty, she would rather have made thrice as many Dunlop cheeses. The first of them was very brief. It was addressed to George Staunton, Esq. at the Rectory, Willingham, by Grantham; the address being part of the information which she had extracted from the communicative peasant who rode before her to Stamford. It was in these words:—

"SIR,

"To prevent farder mischieves, whereof there hath been enough, comes these: Sir, I have my sister's pardon from the Queen's Majesty, whereof I do not doubt you will be glad, having had to say naut of matters whereof you know the purport. So, sir, I pray for your better welfare in bodie and soul, and that it will please the fisycian[2] to visit you in His good time. Alwaies, sir, I pray you will never come again to see my sister, whereof there has been too much. And so, wishing you no evil, but even your best good, that you may be turned from your iniquity, (for why suld ye die?[3]) I rest your humble servant to command.

"*Ye ken wha.*"

The next letter was to her father. It is too long altogether for insertion, so we only give a few extracts.[4] It commenced—

"*Dearest and truly honoured Father,*

"This comes with my duty to inform you, that it has pleased God to bring back that captivitie[5] of my poor sister, in respect the Queen's blessed Majesty, for whom we are ever bound to pray, hath redeemed her soul from the slayer, granting the ransom of her blood, whilk is ane pardon or reprieve. And I spoke with the Queen face to face, and yet live;[6] for she is not muckle differing from other grand leddies, saving that she hath a stately presence, and een like a blue huntin' hawk's, whilk gaed throu' and throu' me like a Hieland durk—And all this good was, alway under the Great Giver, to whom all are but instruments, wrought forth for us by the Duk of Argile, wha is ane native true-hearted Scotsman, and not pridefu', like other folks we ken of—and likewise skeely enow in bestial, whereof he has promised to gie me twa Devonshire kye, of which he is enamoured, although I do still haud by the real hawkit Airshire breed—and I have promised him a cheese; and I wad wuss ye, if Gowans, the brockit cow, has a quey, that she suld suck her fill of milk, as I am given to understand he has none of that breed, and is not scornfu', but will take a thing frae a puir body, that it may lighten their heart of the loading of debt that they awe him. Also his Honour the Duke will accept ane of our Dunlop cheeses, and it sall be my faut if a better was ever yearned in Lowden."—[Here follow some observations respecting the breed of cattle, and the produce of the dairy, which it is our intention to forward to the Board of Agriculture.[7]]—"Nevertheless, these are but matters of the after-harvest in respect of the great good which Providence hath gifted us with—and, in especial, poor Effie's life. And O, my dear father, since it hath pleased God to be merciful to her, let her not want your free pardon, whilk will make her meet to be ane vessel of grace, and also a comfort to your ain graie hairs. Dear father, will ye let the Laird ken that we have had friends strangely raised up to us, and that the talent[8] whilk he lent me will be thankfully repaid. I hae some of it to the fore; and the rest of it is not knotted up in ane purse or napkin, but in ane wee bit paper, as is the fashion heir, whilk I am assured is gude for the siller.[9] And, dear father, through Mr Butler's means I had gude friendship with the Duke, for there had been kindness between their forbears in the auld troublesome time bye-past. And Mrs Glass has been kind like my very mother. She has a braw house here, and lives bien and warm, wi' twa servant lasses, and a man and a callant in the shop. And she is to send you doun a pound of her hie-dried, and some other tobaka, and we maun think of some propine for her, since her kindness hath been great. And the Duk is to send the pardun doun by an express messenger, in respect that I canna travel sae fast; and I am to come doun in company wi' twa of his Honour's servants—that is, John Archibald, a decent elderly gentleman, that says he has seen you lang syne when ye were buying beasts in the west frae the Laird of Aughtermuggitie[10]—but maybe ye winna mind him—ony way, he's a ceevil man—and Mrs Dolly Dutton,[11] that is to be dairy-maid at Inverara; and they bring me on as far as Glasgo', whilk will make it nae pinch to win hame, whilk I desire of all things. May the Giver of all good things keep ye in your outgauns and incomings,[12] whereof devoutly prayeth your loving dauter,

"JEAN DEANS."

The third letter was to Butler, and its tenor as follows:—

"MASTER BUTLER.

"SIR,—It will be pleasure to you to ken, that all I came for is, thanks be to God, weel dune and to the gude end, and that your forbear's letter was right welcome to the Duk of Argile, and that he wrote your name down with a kylevine pen in a leathern book, whereby it seems like he will do for you either wi' a scule or a kirk; he has enow of baith,[13] as I am assured. And I have seen the Queen, which gave me a hussy-case out of her own hand. She had not her crown and skeptre, but they are laid bye for her, like the bairns' best claise, to be worn when she needs them. And they are keppit in a tour,[14] whilk is not like the tour of Libberton,[15] nor yet Craigmillar, but mair like to the castell of Edinburgh, if the buildings were taen and set down in the midst of the Nor'-Loch. Also the Queen was very bounteous, giving me a paper worth fiftie pounds, as I am assured, to pay my expences here and back agen—Sae, Master Butler, as we were aye neebours bairns, forbye ony thing else that may hae been spoken between us, I trust you winna skrimp yoursell for what is needfu' for your health, since it signifies not muckle whilk o' us has the siller, if the other wants it. And mind this is no meant to haud ye to ony thing whilk ye wad rather forget, if ye suld get a charge of a kirk or a scule, as above said. Only I hope it will be a scule, and not a kirk, because of these difficulties anent aiths and patronages,[16] whilk might gang ill doun wi' my honest father. Only if ye could compas a harmonious call frae the parish of Skreegh-me-dead, as ye anes had hope of, I trow it wad please him weel; since I hae heard him say, that the root of the matter[17] was mair deeply hafted in that wild muirland parish than in the Canogate of Edinburgh. I wish I kend whaten books ye wanted, Mr Butler, for they hae haill houses of them here, and they are obliged to set sum out in the street, whilk are sauld cheap,[18] doubtless, to get them safely out of the weather. It is a muckle place, and I hae seen sae muckle of it, that my poor head turns round—And ye ken langsyne I am nae great pen-woman—and it is near eleven o'clock o' the night. I am cumming down to my native land in good company, and safe—and I had troubles in gaun up, whilk makes me blyther of travelling hame wi' kend folk. My cousin, Mrs Glass, has a braw house here, but a' thing is sae poisoned wi' snuff, that I am like to be scomfished whiles. But what signifies these things, in comparison of the great deliverance whilk has been vouchsafed to my father's house, in whilk you, as our auld and dear well-wisher, will, I dout not, rejoice and be exceedingly glad.[19] And I am, dear Mr Butler, your sincere well-wisher in temporal and eternal things,

"J.D."

After these labours of an unwonted kind, Jeanie retired to her bed, yet scarce could sleep a few minutes together, so often was she awakened by the heart-stirring consciousness of her sister's safety, and so powerfully urged to deposit her burthen of joy, where she had before laid her doubts and sorrows, in the warm and sincere exercises of devotion.

All the next, and all the succeeding day, Mrs Glass fidgetted about her shop in the agony of expectation, like a pea (to use a vulgar simile which her profession renders appropriate,) upon one of her own tobacco-pipes. With the third morning came the expected coach, with four servants clustered behind on the foot-board, in dark-brown and yellow liveries; the Duke in person, with laced coat, gold-headed cane, star and garter,[20] all, as the story-book says, very grand.[21]

He enquired for his little countrywoman at Mrs Glass, but without requesting to see her, probably because he was unwilling to give an appearance of personal intercourse betwixt them, which scandal might have misinterpreted. "The Queen," he said to Mrs Glass, "had taken the case of her kinswoman into her gracious consideration, and being specially moved by the affectionate and resolute character of the elder sister, had condescended to use her powerful intercession with his Majesty, in consequence of which a pardon had been dispatched to Scotland to Effie Deans, on condition of her banishing herself forth of Scotland for fourteen years. The King's Advocate had insisted," he said, "upon this qualification of the pardon, having pointed out to his Majesty's ministers that within the course of only seven years, twenty-one instances[22] of child murther had occurred in Scotland."

"Weary on him!" said Mrs Glass, "what for needed he to have told that of his ain country, and to the English folk abune a'? I used aye to think the Advocate a douce decent man,[*] but it is an ill bird[23]—begging your Grace's pardon for speaking of such a coorse bye-word. And then what is the poor lassie to do in a foreign land?— Why, waes me, it's just sending her to play the same pranks ower again, out of sight or guidance of her friends."

"Pooh! pooh!" said the Duke, "that need not be anticipated. Why, she may come up to London, or she may go over to America, and marry well for all that is come and gone."

"In troth, and so she may, as your Grace is pleased to intimate," replied Mrs Glass; "and now I think upon it, there is my old correspondent in Virginia, Ephraim Buckskin, that has supplied the Thistle this forty years with tobacco, and it is not a little that serves our turn, and he has been writing to me this ten years to send him out a wife. The carle is not above sixty, and hale and hearty, and well to pass in the world, and a line from my hand would settle the matter, and Effie Deans's misfortune (forbye that there is no special occasion to speak about it) would be thought little of there."

"Is she a pretty girl?" said the Duke, "her sister does not get beyond a good comely sonsy lass."

"Oh, far prettier is Effie than Jeanie," said Mrs Glass; "though it is long since I saw her mysell, but I hear of the Deanses by all my Lowden friends when they come—your Grace kens we Scots are clannish bodies."

"So much the better for us," said the Duke, "and the worse for those who meddle with us, as your good old-fashioned Scots sign says,[24] Mrs Glass. And now I hope you will approve of the measures I have taken for restoring your kinswoman to her friends." These he detailed at length, and Mrs Glass gave her unqualified approbation, with a smile and a curtsey at every sentence. "And now, Mrs Glass, you must tell Jeanie, I hope she will not forget my cheese when she gets down to Scotland. Archibald has my orders to arrange all her expences."

"Begging your Grace's humble pardon," said Mrs Glass, "it's a pity to trouble yourself about them; the Deanses are wealthy people in their way, and the lass has money in her pocket."

"That's all very true," said the Duke; "but you know, where

[* The celebrated Duncan Forbes, soon afterwards Lord President of the College of Justice, was at this time Lord Advocate.]

MacCallanmore travels he pays all; it is our highland privilege to take from all what *we* want, and to give to all what *they* want."

"Your Grace's better at giving than taking," said Mrs Glass.

"To shew you the contrary," said the Duke, "I will fill my box out of this canister without paying you a bawbee;" and again desiring to be remembered to Jeanie, with his good wishes for her safe journey, he departed, leaving Mrs Glass uplifted in heart and in countenance, the proudest and happiest of tobacco and snuff dealers.

Reflectively, his Grace's good humour and affability had a favourable effect upon Jeanie's situation. Her kinswoman, though civil and kind to her, had acquired too much of London breeding to be perfectly satisfied with her cousin's rustic and national dress, and was, besides, something scandalized at the cause of her journey to London. Mrs Glass might, therefore, have been less sedulous in her attentions towards Jeanie, but for the interest which the foremost of the Scottish nobles (for such, in all men's estimation, was the Duke of Argyle) seemed to take in her fate. Now, however, as a kinswoman whose virtues and domestic affections had attracted the notice and approbation of royalty itself, Jeanie stood to her relative in a light very different and much more favourable, and was not only treated with kindness, but with actual observance and respect.

It depended upon herself alone to have made as many visits, and seen as many sights, as lay within Mrs Glass's power to compass. But, excepting that she dined abroad with one or two "far-away kinsfolk," and that she paid the same respect, on Mrs Glass's strong urgency, to Mrs Deputy Dabby, wife of the Worshipful Mr Deputy Dabby,[25] of Farringdon Without, she did not avail herself of the opportunity. As Mrs Dabby was the second lady of great rank whom Jeanie had seen in London, she used sometimes afterwards to draw a parallel betwixt her and the Queen, in which she observed, that "Mrs Dabby was dressed twice as grand, and was twice as big, and spoke twice as loud, and twice as muckle as the Queen did, but she hadna the same goss-hawk glance that makes the skin creep, and the knee bend; and though she had very kindly gifted her with a loaf of sugar and twa punds of tea, yet she hadna a'thegether the sweet look that the Queen had when she put the needle-book into her hand."

Jeanie might have enjoyed the sights and novelties of this great city more, had it not been for the qualification added to her sister's pardon, which greatly grieved her affectionate disposition. On this subject, however, her mind was somewhat relieved by a letter which she received in return of post, in answer to that which she had written to her father. With his affectionate blessing, it brought his full approbation of the step which she had taken, as one inspired by the immediate dictates of Heaven, and which she had been thrust upon in order that she might become the means of safety to a perishing household.

"If ever a deliverance was dear and precious, this," said the letter, "is a dear and precious deliverance—and if life saved can be made more sweet and savoury, it is when it cometh by the hands of those whom we hold in the ties of affection. And do not let your heart be disquieted within you,[26] that this victim, who is rescued from the horns of the altar,[27] whereuntil she was fast bound by the chains of human law, is now to be driven beyond the bounds of our land. Scotland is a blessed land to those who love the ordinances of Christianity, and it is a fair land to look upon, and dear to them who have dwelt in it a' their days; and weel said that judicious Christian, worthy John Livingstone,[28] a skipper in Borrowstounness, as the famous Patrick Walker reporteth his words, that howbeit he thought Scotland was a Gehennah of wickedness when he was at home, yet, when he was abroad, he accounted it ane paradise; for the evils of Scotland he found everywhere, and the good of Scotland he found nowhere. But we are to hold in remembrance that Scotland, though it be our native land, and the land of our fathers, is not like Goshen, in Egypt, on whilk the sun of the heavens and of the gospel shineth allenarly,[29] and leaveth the rest of the world in utter darkness. Therefore, and also because this increase of profit at Saint Leonard's Crags may be a cauld waff of wind blawing from the frozen land of earthly self, where never plant of grace took root or grew, and because my concerns make me take something ower muckle a grip of the gear of the warld in mine arms,[30] I receive this dispensation anent Effie as a call to depart out of Haran,[31] as righteous Abraham of old, and leave my father's kindred and my mother's house, and the ashes and mould of them who have gone to sleep before me, and which wait to be mingled with these auld crazed bones of mine own. And my heart is lightened to do this, when I call to mind the decay of active and earnest religion in this land, and survey the height and the depth, the length and the breadth of national defections, and how the love of many is waxing lukewarm and cold; and I am strengthened in this resolution to change my domicile, likewise, as I hear that store-farms are to be set at an easy mail in Northumberland, where there are many precious souls that are of our true, though suffering persuasion. And sic part of the kye or stock as I judge it fit to keep, may be driven thither without incommodity—say about Wooler, or that gate—keeping aye a shouther to the hills, and the rest may be sauld here to gude profit and advantage, if we had grace weel to use and guide these gifts of the warld. The Laird has been a true friend on our unhappy occasions, and I have paid him back the siller for Effie's misfortune, whereof Mr Nichil Novit returned him no balance, as the Laird and I did expect he wad hae done. But law licks up a',[32] as the common folks say.—I have had the siller to borrow out of sax purses. Mr Saddletree advised to give the Laird of Lounsbeck a charge on his band[33] for a thousand merks. But I hae nae broo' of charges, since that awfu' morning that a tout of a horn, at the cross[34] of Edinburgh, blew half the faithfu' ministers of Scotland out of their pulpits.— However I sall raise an adjudication, whilk Mr Saddletree says comes instead of the auld apprisings, and will not lose weel-won gear with the like of him if it may be helped. As for the Queen, and the credit that she hath done to a poor man's daughter, and the mercy and the grace ye found with her, I can only pray for her[35] weel-being here and hereafter, for the establishment of her house now and for ever, upon the throne of these kingdoms.[36] I doubt not but what you told her Majesty, that I was the same David Deans of whom there was a sport at the Revolution when I noited thegither the heads of twa false prophets, these ungracious Graces the prelates, as they stood on the Hie-street, after being expelled from the Convention-parliament.[*][37] The Duke of Argyle is a noble and true-hearted nobleman, who pleads the cause of the poor, and those who have none to help them; verily his reward shall not be lacking unto him. I have been writing of many things, but not of that whilk lies nearest mine heart. I have seen the misguided lassie; she will be at freedom the morn, on enacted caution that she shall leave Scotland in four weeks. Her mind is in an evil frame,—casting her eye backward[38] on Egypt, I doubt, as if the bitter waters of the wilderness were harder to endure than the brick furnaces, by the side of which there were savoury flesh-pots.[39] I need not bid you make haste down, for you are, excepting always my Great Master, my only comfort in these straights. I charge you to withdraw your feet from the delusion of that Vanity-fair[40] in whilk ye are a

[* See p. 573 for the note, "Expulsion of the Bishops from the Scottish Convention".]

sojourner, and not to go to their worship, whilk is but an ill-mumbled mass, as it was weel termed by James the Sext,[41] though he afterwards, with his unhappy son, strove to bring it ower back and belly into his native kingdom, wherethrough their race have been cut off as foam upon the water, and shall be as wanderers among the nations—see the prophecies of Hosea, ninth and seventeeth,[42] and the same, tenth and seventh. But us and our house, let us say with the same prophet; 'Let us return to the Lord, for he hath torn and he will heal us—He hath smitten, and he will bind us up.'"

He proceeded to say, that he approved of her proposed mode of returning by Glasgow, and entered into sundry minute particulars not necessary to be quoted. A single line in the letter, but not the least frequently read by the party to whom it was addressed, intimated, that "Reuben Butler had been as a son to him in his sorrows." As David Deans scarce ever mentioned Butler before, without some gibe, more or less direct, either at his carnal gifts and learning, or at his grandfather's heresy,[43] Jeanie drew a good omen from no such qualifying clause being added to this sentence respecting him.

A lover's hope resembles the bean in the nursery tale,—let it once take root, and it will grow so rapidly, that in the course of a few hours the giant Imagination builds a castle on the top, and by and by comes Disappointment with the "curtal axe,"[44] and hews down both the plant and the superstructure. Jeanie's fancy, though not the most powerful of her faculties, was lively enough to transport her to a wild farm in Northumberland, well stocked with milk-cows, yeald beasts and sheep; a meeting-house hard by, frequented by serious presbyterians, who had united in a harmonious call to Reuben Butler to be their spiritual guide;—Effie restored, not to gaiety, but to cheerfulness at least;—their father, with his grey hairs smoothed down, and spectacles on his nose;—herself, with the maiden snood exchanged for a matron's curch—all arranged in a pew in the said meeting-house, listening to words of devotion, rendered sweeter and more powerful by the affectionate ties which combined them with the preacher. She cherished such visions from day to day, until her residence in London began to become unsupportable and tedious to her, and it was with no ordinary satisfaction that she received a summons from Argyle-house, requiring her in two days to be prepared to join their northward party.

CHAPTER 40

One was a female, who had grievous ill
Wrought in revenge, and she enjoyed it still;
Sullen she was, and threatening; in her eye
Glared the stern triumph that she dared to die.

CRABBE

THE summons of preparation arrived after Jeanie Deans had resided in the metropolis about three weeks.

On the morning appointed she took a grateful farewell of Mrs Glass, as that good woman's attention to her particularly required, placed herself and her moveable goods, which purchases and presents had greatly increased, in a hackney-coach, and joined her travelling companions in the housekeeper's apartment at Argyle-house. While the carriage was getting ready, she was informed that the Duke wished to speak with her; and being ushered into a splendid saloon, she was surprised to find that he wished to present her to his lady and daughters.[1]

"I bring you my little countrywoman, Duchess," these were the words of the introduction. "With an army of young fellows, as gallant and steady as she is, and a good cause, I would not fear two to one."

"Ah, papa!" said a lively young lady,[2] about twelve years old, "remember you were full one to two at Sheriff-muir,[3] and yet," (singing the well-known ballad[4])—

"Some say that we wan, and some say that they wan,
    And some say that nane wan at a', man;
But of ae thing I'm sure, that on Sheriff-muir
    A battle there was that I saw, man."

"What, little Mary turned Tory on my hands?—This will be fine news for our countrywoman to carry down to Scotland!"

"We may all turn Tories for the thanks we have gotten for remaining Whigs," said the second young lady.

"Well, hold your peace, you discontented monkies, and go dress your babies; and as for the Bob of Dumblane,[5]

If it wasna weel bobbit, weel bobbit, weel bobbit,
If it wasna weel bobbit, we'll bobb it again."

"Papa's wit is running low," said Lady Mary; "the poor gentleman is repeating himself—he sang that on the field of battle, when he was told the Highlanders had cut his left wing to pieces with their claymores."

A pull by the hair was the repartee to this sally.

"Ah! brave Highlanders and bright claymores," said the Duke, "well do I wish them, 'for a' the ill they hae done me yet,' as the song goes.[6]—But come, madcaps, say a civil word to your countrywoman—I wish you had half her canny hamely sense; I think you may be as leal and true-hearted."

The Duchess advanced, and, in few words, in which there was as much kindness as civility, assured Jeanie of the respect which she had for a character so affectionate, and yet so firm, and added, "When you get home, you will perhaps hear from me."

"And from me—" "And from me—" "And from me, Jeanie—," added the young ladies one after the other, "for you are a credit to the land we love so well."

Jeanie, overpowered with these unexpected compliments, and not aware that the Duke's investigation had made him acquainted with her behaviour on her sister's trial, could only answer by blushing, and curtseying round and round, and uttering at intervals, "Mony thanks! mony thanks!"

"Jeanie," said the Duke, "you must have *doch an' dorroch*, or you will be unable to travel."

There was a salver with cake and wine on the table. He took up a glass, drank "to all true hearts that lo'ed Scotland," and offered a glass to his guest.

Jeanie, however, declined it, saying, "that she had never tasted wine in her life."

"How comes that, Jeanie?" said the Duke,—"wine maketh glad the heart,[7] you know."

"Ay, sir, but my father is like Jonadab the son of Rechab,[8] who charged his children that they should drink no wine."

"I thought your father would have had more sense," said the Duke, "unless, indeed, he prefers brandy. But, however, Jeanie, if you will not drink, you must eat, to save the character of my house."

He thrust upon her a large piece of cake, nor would he permit her to break off a fragment, and lay the rest on the salver. "Put it in your pouch, Jeanie," said he; "you will be glad of it before you see St Giles's steeple. I wish to heaven I were to see it as soon as you! and so my best service to all my friends at and about Auld Reekie, and a blithe journey to you."

And, mixing the frankness of a soldier with his natural affability, he shook hands with his protégée, and committed her to the charge of Archibald, satisfied that he had provided sufficiently for her being attended to by his domestics, from the unusual attention with which he had himself treated her.

Accordingly, in the course of her journey, she found both her companions disposed to pay her every possible civility, so that her return, in point of comfort and safety, formed a strong contrast to her journey to London.

Her heart also was disburthened of the weight of grief, shame, apprehension, and fear, which had loaded her before her interview with the Queen at Richmond. But the human mind is so strangely capricious, that, when freed from the pressure of real misery, it becomes open and sensitive to the apprehension of ideal calamities. She was now much disturbed in mind, that she had heard nothing from Reuben Butler, to whom the operation of writing was so much more familiar than it was to herself.

"It would have cost him sae little fash," she said to herself; "for I hae seen his pen gang as fast ower the paper, as ever it did ower the water when it was in the grey goose's wing. Waes me! maybe he may be badly—but then my father wad likely hae said something about it—Or maybe he may hae taen the rue, and kens na how to let me wot of his change of mind. He needna be at muckle fash about it,"—she went on, drawing herself up, though the tear of honest pride and injured affection gathered in her eye, as she entertained the suspicion,—"Jeanie Deans is no the lass to pu' him by the sleeve, or put him in mind of what he wishes to forget. I shall wish him weel and happy a' the same; and if he has the luck to get a kirk in our country, I sall gang and hear him just the very same, to show that I bear nae malice." And as she imagined the scene, the tear stole over her eye.

In these melancholy reveries, Jeanie had full time to indulge herself; for her travelling companions, servants in a distinguished and fashionable family, had, of course, many topics of conversation, in which it was absolutely impossible she could have either pleasure or portion.

She had, therefore, abundant leisure for reflection, and even for self-tormenting, during the several days which, indulging the young horses the Duke was sending down to the North with sufficient ease and short stages, they occupied in reaching the neighbourhood of Carlisle.

In approaching the vicinity of that ancient city, they discerned a considerable crowd upon an eminence at a little distance from the high road, and learned from some passengers who were gathering towards that busy scene from the southward, that the cause of the concourse was, the laudable public desire "to see a domned Scotch witch and thief get half of her due[9] upo' Haribee-broo' yonder, for she was only to be hanged; she should hae been boorned aloive, an' cheap on't."

"Dear Mr Archibald," said the dame of the dairy elect, "I never seed a woman hanged in a' my life, and only four men, as made a goodly spectacle. Now, do let us see the sight!"

Mr Archibald, however, was a Scotchman, and promised himself no exuberant pleasure in seeing his countrywoman undergo "the terrible behests of law."[10] Moreover, he was a man of sense and delicacy in his way, and the late circumstances of Jeanie's family, with the cause of her expedition to London, were not unknown to him; so that he answered drily, it was impossible to stop, as he must be early at Carlisle on some business of the Duke's, and he accordingly bid the postillions get on.

The road at that time passed at about a quarter of a mile's distance from the eminence, called Haribee or Harabee-brow, which, though it is very moderate in size and height, is nevertheless seen from a great distance around, owing to the flatness of the country through which the Eden flows. Here many an outlaw, and border-rider of both kingdoms, had wavered in the wind during the wars, and scarce less hostile truces, between the two countries. Upon Harabee, in latter days, other executions had taken place with as little ceremony as compassion; for the frontier provinces remained long unsettled, and even at the time of which we write, were ruder than those in the centre of England.

The postillions drove on, wheeling, as the Penrith road led them, round the verge of the rising ground. Yet still the eyes of Mrs Dolly Dutton, which, with the head and substantial person to which they belonged, were all turned towards the scene of action, could discern plainly the outline of the gallows-tree, relieved against the clear sky, the dark shade formed by the persons of the executioner and the criminal upon the light rounds of the tall aerial ladder, until one of the objects, launched into the air, gave unequivocal signs of mortal agony, though appearing in the distance not larger than a spider dependent at the extremity of his invisible thread, while the remaining form descended from its elevated situation, and regained with all speed an undistinguished place among the crowd. This termination of the tragic scene drew forth of course a squall from Mrs Dutton, and Jeanie, with instinctive curiosity, turned her head in the same direction.

The sight of a female culprit in the act of undergoing the fatal punishment from which her beloved sister had been so recently rescued, was too much, not perhaps for her nerves, but for her mind and feelings. She turned her head to the other side of the carriage, with a sensation of sickness, of loathing, and of fainting. Her female companion overwhelmed her with questions, with proffers of assistance, with requests that the carriage might be stopped—that a doctor might be fetched—that drops might be gotten—that burnt feathers and assafœtida, fair water and hartshorn, might be procured, all at once, and without one instant's delay. Archibald, more calm and considerate, only desired the carriage to push forward, and it was not till they had got beyond sight of the fatal spectacle, that, seeing the deadly paleness of Jeanie's countenance, he stopped the carriage, and jumping out himself, went in search of the most obvious and most easily procured of Mrs Dutton's pharmacopeia—a draught, namely, of fair water.

While Archibald was absent on this good-natured piece of service, damning the Cumbrian brooks as ditches which produced nothing but mud, and thinking upon the thousand bubbling springlets of his own mountains, the attendants on the execution began to pass the stationary vehicle in their way back to Carlisle.

From their half-heard and half-understood words, Jeanie, whose attention was involuntarily rivetted by them, as that of children is by ghost stories, though they know the pain with which they will afterwards remember them, Jeanie, I say, could discern that the present victim of the law had died *game*, as it is termed by those unfortunates, that is, sullen, reckless, and impenitent, neither fearing God nor regarding man.

"A sture woife, and a dour," said one Cumbrian peasant, as he clattered by in his wooden brogues, with a noise like the trampling of a dray-horse.

"She has gone to ho master, with ho's name in her mouth," said another; "Shame the country should be harried wi' Scotch witches and Scotch bitches this gate—but I say hang and drown."

"Ay, ay, Gaffer Tramp," replied a third peasant; "take awa yealdon, take awa low[11]—hang the witch, and there will be less scathe amang us; myne owsen hae been reckan this twomont."

"And mine bairns hae been crining too, mon," replied his neighbour.

"Silence wi' your fule tongues, ye churles," said an old woman, who hobbled past them, as they stood talking near the carriage; "this was nae witch, but a bluidy fingered thief and murtheress."

"Ay? was it e'en sae, Dame Hinchup?" said one in a civil tone, and stepping out of his place to let the old woman pass along the foot-path[12]—"Nay, you know best, sure—but at ony rate, we hae but tint a Scot of her, and that's a thing better lost than found."[13]

The old woman passed on without making any answer.

"Ay, ay, neighbour," said Gaffer Tramp, "seest thou how one witch will speak for t'other?—Scots or English, the same to them."

His companion shook his head, and replied in the same subdued tone, "Ay, ay, when a Sark-foot wife gets on her broomstick, the dames of Allonby[14] are ready to mount, just as sure as the bye-word[15] gangs o' the hills,

> If Skiddaw hath a cap,
> Criffel wots full weel of that."

"But," continued Gaffer Tramp, "thinkest thou the daughter o'yon hangit body isna as rank a witch as ho?"

"I kenna clearly," returned the fellow, "but the folk are speaking o' swimming her[16] i' the Eden." And they passed on their several roads, after wishing each other good morning.

Just as the clowns left the place, and as Mr Archibald returned with some fair water, a crowd of boys and girls, and some of the lower rabble of more mature age, came up from the place of execution, grouping themselves with many a yell of delight around a tall female fantastically dressed, who was dancing, leaping, and bounding in the midst of them. A horrible recollection pressed on Jeanie as she looked on this unfortunate creature, and the reminiscence was mutual, for by a sudden exertion of great strength and agility, Madge Wildfire broke out of the noisy circle of tormentors who surrounded her, and clinging fast to the door of the calash, uttered, in a sound betwixt laughter and screaming, "Eh, d'ye ken, Jeanie Deans, they hae hangit our mother?" Then suddenly changing her tone to that of the most piteous entreaty, she added, "O gar them let me gang to cut her down!—let me but cut her down!—she is my mother, if she was waur than the deil, and she'll be nae mair kenspeckle than half-hangit Maggie Dickson,[17] that cried saut mony a day after she had been hangit; her voice was roupit and hoarse, and her neck was a wee agee, or ye wad hae kend nae odds on her frae ony other saut-wife."

Mr Archibald, embarrassed by the madwoman's clinging to the carriage, and detaining around them her noisy and mischievous attendants, was all this while looking out for a constable or beadle, to whom he might commit the unfortunate creature. But seeing no such person of authority, he endeavoured to loosen her hold from the carriage, that they might escape from her by driving on. This, however, could hardly be achieved without some degree of violence; Madge held fast, and renewed her frantic entreaties to be permitted to cut down her mother. "It was but a tenpenny tow lost," she said, "and what was that to a woman's life?" There came up, however, a parcel of savage-looking fellows, butchers and graziers chiefly, among whose cattle there had been of late a very general and fatal distemper, which their wisdom imputed to witchcraft. They laid violent hands on Madge, and tore her from the carriage, exclaiming—"What, doest stop folk o' king's highway? Hast no done mischief enow already, wi' thy murders and thy witcherings?"

"Oh Jeanie Deans—Jeanie Deans!" exclaimed the poor maniac, "save my mother, and I will take ye to the Interpreter's house again,—and I will teach ye a' my bonnie sangs,—and I will tell ye what came o' the——" The rest of her entreaties were drowned in the shouts of the rabble.

"Save her, for God's sake!—save her from those people!" exclaimed Jeanie to Archibald; "she is mad, but quite innocent."

"She is mad, gentlemen," said Archibald; "do not use her ill, take her before the Mayor."

"Ay, ay, we'se hae care enow on her," answered one of the fellows; "gang thou thy gate, man, and mind thine own matters."

"He's a Scot by his tongue," said another; "and an he will come out o' his whirligig there, I'se gie him his tartan plaid fu' o' broken banes."

It was clear nothing could be done to rescue Madge, and Archibald, who was a man of humanity, could only bid the postillions hurry on to Carlisle, that he might obtain some assistance to the unfortunate woman. As they drove off, they heard the hoarse roar with which the mob preface acts of riot or cruelty, yet even above that deep and dire note, they could discern the screams of the unfortunate victim. They were soon out of hearing of the cries, but had no sooner entered the streets of Carlisle, than Archibald, at Jeanie's earnest and urgent entreaty, went to a magistrate, to state the cruelty which was likely to be exercised on this unhappy creature.

In about an hour and a half he returned and reported to Jeanie, that the magistrate had very readily gone in person, with some assistants, to the rescue of the unfortunate woman, and that he had himself accompanied him; that when they came to the muddy pool, in which the mob were ducking her, according to their favourite mode of punishment, the magistrate succeeded in rescuing her from their hands, but in a state of insensibility, owing to the cruel treatment which she had received. He added, that he had seen her carried to the work-house, and understood that she had been brought to herself, and was expected to do well.

This last averment was a slight alteration in point of fact, for Madge Wildfire was not expected to survive the treatment she had received; but Jeanie seemed so much agitated, that Mr Archibald did not think it prudent to tell her the worst at once. Indeed she appeared so fluttered and disordered by this alarming incident, that, although it had been their intention to proceed to Longtown that evening, her companions judged it most advisable to pass the night at Carlisle.

This was particularly agreeable to Jeanie, who resolved, if possible, to procure an interview with Madge Wildfire. Connecting some of her wild flights with the narrative of George Staunton, she was unwilling to omit the opportunity of extracting from her, if possible, some information concerning the fate of that unfortunate infant which had cost her sister so dear. Her acquaintance with the disordered state of poor Madge's mind did not permit her to cherish much hope that she could acquire from her any useful intelligence; but then, since Madge's mother had suffered her deserts, and was silent for ever, it was her only chance of obtaining any kind of information, and she was loth to lose the opportunity.

She coloured her wish to Mr Archibald by saying, that she had seen Madge formerly, and wished to know, as a matter of humanity, how she was attended to under her present misfortunes. That complaisant person immediately went to the work-house, or hospital, in which he had seen the sufferer lodged, and brought back for reply, that the medical attendants positively forbade her seeing any one. When the application for admittance was repeated next day, Mr Archibald was informed that she had been very quiet and composed, insomuch that the clergyman, who acted as chaplain to the establishment, thought it expedient to read prayers beside her bed, but that her wandering fit of mind had returned soon after his departure; however, her country-woman might see her if she chose it. She was not expected to live above an hour or two.

Jeanie had no sooner received this information, than she hastened to the hospital, her companions attending her. They found the dying person in a large ward, where there were ten beds, of which the patient's was the only one occupied.

Madge was singing when they entered—singing her own wild snatches of songs and obsolete airs, with a voice no longer overstrained by false spirits, but softened, saddened, and subdued by bodily exhaustion. She was still insane, but was no longer able to express her wandering ideas in the wild notes of her former state of exalted imagination. There was death in the plaintive tones of her voice, which yet, in this moderated and melancholy mood, had something of the lulling sound with which a mother sings her infant asleep. As Jeanie entered, she heard first the air, and then a part of the chorus and words, of what had been, perhaps, the song of a jolly harvest-home:

> "Our work is over—over now,
> The goodman wipes his weary brow,
> The last long wain wends slow away,
> And we are free to sport and play.
>
> "The night comes on when sets the sun,
> And labour ends when day is done.
> When Autumn's gone and Winter's come,
> We hold our jovial harvest-home."

Jeanie advanced to the bed-side when the strain was finished, and addressed Madge by her name. But it produced no symptom of recollection. On the contrary, the patient, like one provoked by interruption, changed her posture, and called out, with an impatient tone, "Nurse—nurse, turn my face to the wa', that I may never answer to that name ony mair, and never see mair of a wicked world."

The attendant on the hospital arranged her in her bed as she desired, with her face to the wall, and her back to the light. So soon as she was quiet in this new position, she began again to sing in the same low and modulated strains, as if she was recovering the state of abstraction which the interruption of her visitants had disturbed. The strain, however, was different, and rather resembled the music of the Methodist hymns, though the measure of the song was similar to that of the former.

> "When the fight of grace is fought,—
> When the marriage vest is wrought,—
> When Faith hath chased cold Doubt away,
> And Hope but sickens at delay,—
> When Charity, imprisoned here,
> Longs for a more expanded sphere,
> Doff thy robes of sin and clay:
> Christian, rise, and come away."

The strain was solemn and affecting, sustained as it was by the pathetic warble of a voice which had naturally been a fine one, and which weakness, if it diminished its power, had improved in softness. Archibald, though a follower of the court, and therefore a poco-curante by profession, was confused, if not affected; the dairy-maid blubbered; and Jeanie felt the tears rise spontaneously to her eyes. Even the nurse, accustomed to all modes in which the spirit can pass, seemed considerably moved.

The patient was evidently growing weaker, as was intimated by an apparent difficulty of breathing, which seized her from time to time, and by the utterance of low listless moans, intimating that nature was succumbing in the last conflict. But the spirit of melody, which must originally have so strongly possessed this unfortunate young woman, seemed, at every interval of ease, to triumph over her pain and weakness. And it was remarkable, that there could always be traced in her songs something appropriate, though perhaps only obliquely or collaterally so, to her present situation. Her next seemed to be the fragment of some old ballad:

> "Cauld is my bed, Lord Archibald,
>   And sad my sleep of sorrow;
> But thine sall be as sad and cauld,
>   My fause true-love! to-morrow.
>
> "And weep ye not, my maidens free,
>   Though death your mistress borrow;
> For he for whom I die to-day,
>   Shall die for me to-morrow."[18]

Again she changed the tune to one wilder, less monotonous, and less regular. But of the words only a fragment or two could be collected by those who listened to this singular scene.

> "Proud Maisie is in the wood,
>   Walking so early;
> Sweet Robin sits on the bush,
>   Singing so rarely.
>
> "'Tell me, thou bonny bird,
>   When shall I marry me?'
> 'When six braw gentlemen
>   Kirkward shall carry ye.'

*   *   *

> "'Who makes the bridal bed,
>   Birdie, say truly?'
> 'The gray-headed sexton
>   That delves the grave duly.'

*   *   *

> "The glow-worm o'er grave and stone
>   Shall light thee steady;
> The owl from the steeple sing,
>   'Welcome, proud lady.' "[19]

Her voice died away with the last notes, and she fell into a slumber, from which the experienced attendant assured them, that she would never awake at all, or only in the death-agony.

The nurse's prophecy proved true. The poor maniac parted with existence, without again uttering a sound of any kind. But our travellers did not witness this catastrophe. They left the hospital so soon as Jeanie had satisfied herself that no elucidation of her sister's misfortunes was to be hoped from the dying person.[*]

[* See p. 575 for the note, "Madge Wildfire".]

CHAPTER 41

Wilt thou go on with me?
The moon is bright, the sea is calm,
And I know well the ocean-paths . . . .
Thou wilt go on with me.

Thalaba

THE fatigue and agitation of these various scenes had agitated Jeanie so much, notwithstanding her robust strength of constitution, that Archibald judged it necessary that she should have a day's repose at the village of Longtown. It was in vain that Jeanie herself protested against any delay. The Duke of Argyle's man of confidence was of course consequential; and as he had been bred to the medical profession in his youth, (at least he used this expression to describe his having, thirty years before, pounded for six months in the mortar of old Mungo Mangelman, the surgeon at Greenock), he was obstinate whenever a matter of health was in question.

In this case he discovered febrile symptoms, and having once made a happy application of that learned phrase to Jeanie's case, all farther resistance became in vain; and she was glad to acquiesce, and even to go to bed, and drink water-gruel, in order that she might possess her soul in quiet, and without interruption.

Mr Archibald was equally attentive in another particular. He observed that the execution of the old woman, and the miserable fate of her daughter, seemed to have had a more powerful effect upon Jeanie's mind, than the usual feelings of humanity might naturally have been expected to occasion. Yet she was obviously a strong-minded, sensible young woman, and in no respect subject to nervous affections; and therefore Archibald, being ignorant of any special connection between his master's protégée and these unfortunate persons, excepting that she had seen Madge formerly in Scotland, naturally imputed the strong impression these events had made upon her, to her associating them with the unhappy circumstances in which her sister had so lately stood. He became anxious, therefore, to prevent any thing occurring which might recall these associations to Jeanie's mind.

Archibald had speedily an opportunity of exercising this precaution. A pedlar brought to Longtown that evening, amongst other wares, a large broadside-sheet, giving an account of the "Last Speech[1] and Execution of Margaret Murdockson, and of the barbarous Murder of her Daughter, Magdalene or Madge Murdockson, called Madge Wildfire; and of her pious Conversation with his Reverence Arch-deacon Fleming;" which authentic publication had apparently taken place on the day they left Carlisle, and being an article of a nature peculiarly acceptable to such country-folks as were within hearing of the transactions, the itinerant bibliopolist had forthwith added them to his stock in trade. He found a merchant sooner than he expected; for Archibald, much applauding his own prudence, purchased the whole lot for two shillings and ninepence; and the pedlar, delighted with the profit of such a wholesale transaction, instantly returned to Carlisle to supply himself with more.

The considerate Mr Archibald was about to commit his whole purchase to the flames, but it was rescued by the yet more considerate dairy-damsel, who said, very prudently, it was a pity to waste so much paper, which might crêpe hair, pin up bonnets, and serve many other useful purposes; and who promised to put the parcel into her own trunk, and keep it carefully out of the sight of Mrs Jeanie Deans: "Though by the bye she had no great notion of folks being so very nice. Mrs Deans might have had enough to think about the gallows all this time to endure a sight of it, without all this to do about it."

Archibald reminded the dame of the dairy of the Duke's very particular charge, that they should be attentive and civil to Jeanie; as also that they were to part company soon, and consequently would not be doomed to observing any one's health or temper[2] during the rest of the journey. With which answer Mrs Dolly Dutton was obliged to hold herself satisfied.

On the morning they resumed their journey, and prosecuted it successfully, travelling through Dumfries-shire and part of Lanarkshire, until they arrived at the small town of Rutherglen, within about four miles of Glasgow. Here an express brought letters to Archibald from the principal agent of the Duke of Argyle in Edinburgh.

He said nothing of their contents that evening; but when they were seated in the carriage the next day, the faithful squire informed Jeanie, that he had received directions from the Duke's factor, to whom his Grace had recommended her, to carry her, if she had no objection, for a stage or two beyond Glasgow. Some temporary causes of discontent had occasioned tumults in that city and the neighbourhood, which would render it unadviseable for Mrs Jeanie Deans to travel alone and unprotected betwixt that city and Edinburgh; whereas by going forward a little farther, they would meet one of his Grace's sub-factors, who was coming down from the Highlands to Edinburgh with his wife, and under whose charge she might journey with comfort and in safety.

Jeanie remonstrated against this arrangement. "She had been lang," she said, "frae hame—her father and her sister behoved to be very anxious to see her—there were other friends she had that werena weel in health. She was willing to pay for man and horse at Glasgow, and surely naebody wad middle wi' sae harmless and feckless a creature as she was.—She was muckle obliged by the offer; but never hunted deer langed for its resting-place as she did to find herself at Saint Leon-ard's."

The groom of the chambers exchanged a look with his female companion, which seemed so full of meaning, that Jeanie screamed aloud—"O Mr Archibald—Mrs Dutton, if ye ken of ony thing that has happened at Saint Leonard's, for God's sake—for pity's sake, tell me, and dinna keep me in suspense!"

"I really know nothing, Mrs Deans," said the groom of the chamber.

"And I—I—I am sure, I knows as little," said the dame of the dairy, while some communication seemed to tremble on her lips, which, at a glance of Archibald's eye, she appeared to swallow down, and compressed her lips thereafter into a state of extreme and vigilant firmness, as if she had been afraid of its bolting out before she was aware.

Jeanie saw that there was to be something concealed from her, and it was only the repeated assurances of Archibald that her father—her sister—all her friends were, so far as he knew, well and happy, that at all pacified her alarm. From such respectable people as those with whom she travelled, she could apprehend no harm, and yet her distress was so obvious, that Archibald, as a last resource, pulled out, and put into her hand, a slip of paper, on which these words were written:—

"JEANIE DEANS—You will do me a favour by going with Archibald and my female domestic a day's journey beyond Glasgow, and asking them no questions, which will greatly oblige your friend,

"ARGYLE & GREENWICH."

Although this laconic epistle, from a nobleman to whom she was bound by such inestimable obligations, silenced all Jeanie's objections to the proposed route, it rather added to than diminished the eagerness of her curiosity. The proceeding to Glasgow seemed now no longer to be an object with her fellow-travellers. On the contrary, they kept the left-hand side of the river Clyde, and travelled through a thousand beautiful and changing views down the side of that noble stream, till ceasing to hold its inland character, it began to assume that of a navigable river.

"You are not for gaun intill Glasgow then?" said Jeanie, as she observed that the drivers made no motion for inclining their horses' heads towards the ancient bridge which was then the only mode of access to St Mungo's capital.[3]

"No," replied Archibald; "there is some popular commotion, and as our Duke is in opposition to the court, perhaps we might be too well received; or they might take it in their heads to remember that the Captain of Carrick came down upon them with his highlandmen in the time of Shawfield's mob in 1725, and then we would be too ill received.[*] And at any rate, it is best for us, and for me in especial, who may be supposed to possess his Grace's mind upon many particulars, to leave the good people of the Gorbals to act according to their own imaginations, without either provoking or encouraging them by my presence."

To reasoning of such tone and consequence, Jeanie had nothing to reply, although it seemed to her to contain fully as much self-importance as truth.

The carriage meantime rolled on; the river expanded itself, and gradually assumed the dignity of an æstuary, or arm of the sea. The influence of the advancing and retiring tides became more and more evident, and in the beautiful words of him of the laurel wreath,[4] the river waxed

A broader and a broader stream.

* * * *

[* In 1725, there was a great riot in Glasgow on account of the malt-tax. Among the troops brought in to restore order, was one of the independent companies of Highlanders levied in Argyleshire, and distinguished, in a lampoon of the period, as "Campbell of Carrick and his Highland thieves." It was called Shawfield's Mob, because much of the popular violence was directed against Daniel Campbell, Esq, of Shawfield, M.P., Provost of the town.]

> The Cormorant stands upon its shoals,
> His black and dripping wings
> Half open'd to the wind.[5]

"Which way lies Inverary?" said Jeanie, gazing on the dusky ocean of Highland hills, which now, piled above each other, and intersected by many a lake,[6] stretched away on the opposite side of the river to the northward. "Is yon high castle the Duke's hoose?"

"That, Mrs Deans?—Lud help thee," replied Archibald, "that's the old Castle of Dumbarton, the strongest place in Europe, be the other what it may. Sir William Wallace was governor of it in the old wars with the English, and his Grace is governor just now. It is always entrusted to the best man in Scotland."

"And does the Duke live on that high rock, then?" demanded Jeanie.

"No, no, he has his deputy-governor who commands in his absence; he lives in the white house you see at the bottom of the rock—His Grace does not reside there himself."

"I think not indeed," said the dairy-woman, upon whose mind the road, since they had left Dumfries, had made no very favourable impression; "for if he did, he might go whistle for a dairy-woman, an he were the only duke in England. I did not leave my place and my friends to come down to see cows starve to death upon hills as they be at that pig-stye of Elfinfoot,[7] as you call it, Mr Archibald, or to be perched up on the top of a rock, like a squirrel in his cage, hung out of a three pair of stairs window."

Inwardly chuckling that these symptoms of recalcitration had not taken place until the fair malcontent was, as he mentally termed it, under his thumb, Archibald coolly replied, "That the hills were none of his making, nor did he know how to mend them; but as to lodging, they would soon be in a house of the Duke's in a very pleasant island called Roseneath,[8] where they went to wait for shipping to take them to Inverary, and would meet the company with whom Jeanie was to return to Edinburgh."

"An island?" said Jeanie, who in the course of her various and adventurous travels had never quitted terra firma, "then I am doubting we maun gang in ane of these boats; they look unco sma', and the waves are something rough, and"—

"Mr Archibald," said Mrs Dutton, "I will not consent to it; I was never engaged to leave the country, and I desire you will bid the boys drive round by the other way to the Duke's house."

"There is a safe pinnace belonging to his Grace, ma'am, close by," replied Archibald, "and you need be under no apprehensions whatso-ever."

"But I *am* under apprehensions," said the damsel; "and I insist upon going round by land, Mr Archibald, were it ten miles about."

"I am sorry I cannot oblige you, madam, as Roseneath happens to be an island."

"If it were ten islands," said the incensed dame, "that's no reason why I should be drowned in going over the seas to it."

"No reason why you should be drowned, certainly ma'am," an-swered the unmoved groom of the chambers, "but an admirable good one why you cannot proceed to it by land." And, fixed his master's mandates to perform,[9] he pointed with his hand, and the drivers, turning off the high-road, proceeded towards a small hamlet of fishing huts, where a shallop, somewhat more gaily decorated than any which they had yet seen, having a flag which displayed a boar's-head, crested with a ducal coronet,[10] waited with two or three seamen, and as many Highlanders.

The carriage stopped, and the men began to unyoke their horses, while Mr Archibald gravely superintended the removal of the baggage from the carriage to the little vessel. "Has the Caroline been long arrived?" said Archibald to one of the seamen.

"She has been here in five days from Liverpool, and she's lying down at Greenock," answered the fellow.

"Let the horses and carriage go down to Greenock then," said Archibald, "and be embarked there for Inverary when I send notice—they may stand in my cousin's, Duncan Archibald the stabler's.—Ladies," he added, "I hope you will get yourselves ready, we must not loss the tide."

"Mrs Deans," said the Cowslip of Inverary, "you may do as you please—but I will sit here all night, rather than go into that there painted egg-shell—Fellow—fellow" (this was addressed to a High-lander who was lifting a travelling trunk) "that trunk is *mine*, and that there band-box, and that pillion mail, and those seven bundles, and the paper bag, and if you venture to touch one of them, it shall be at your peril."

The Celt kept his eye fixed on the speaker, then turned his head towards Archibald, and receiving no countervailing signal, he shoul-dered the portmanteau, and without farther notice of the distressed damsel, or paying any attention to remonstrances, which probably he did not understand, and would certainly have equally disregarded whether he understood them or not, moved off with Mrs Dutton's wearables, and deposited the trunk containing them safely in the boat.

The baggage being stowed in safety, Mr Archibald handed Jeanie out of the carriage, and, not without some tremor on her part, she was transported through the surf and placed in the boat. He then offered the same civility to his fellow servant, but she was resolute in her refusal to quit the carriage, in which she now remained in solitary state, threatening all concerned or unconcerned with actions for wages and board-wages, damages and expences, and numbering on her fingers the gowns and other habiliments, from which she seemed in the act of being separated for ever. Mr Archibald did not give himself the trouble of making many remonstrances, which, indeed, seemed only to aggravate the damsel's indignation, but spoke two or three words to the Highlanders in Gaelic; and the wily mountaineers, approaching the carriage cautiously, and without giving the slightest intimation of their intention, at once seized the recusant so effectually fast that she could neither resist nor struggle, and hoisting her on their shoulders in nearly an horizontal posture, rushed down with her to the beach, and through the surf, and, with no other inconvenience than ruffling her garments a little, deposited her in the boat; but in a state of surprise, mortification, and terror at her sudden transportation, which rendered her absolutely mute for two or three minutes. The men jumped in themselves; one tall fellow remained till he had pushed off the boat, and then tumbled in upon his companions. They took their oars and began to pull from the shore, then spread their sail, and drove merrily across the firth.

"You Scotch villain," said the infuriated damsel to Archibald, "how dare you use a person like me in this way?"

"Madam," said Archibald, with infinite composure, "it's high time you should know you are in the Duke's country, and that there is not one of these fellows, but would throw you out of the boat as readily as into it, if such were his Grace's pleasure."

"Then the Lord have mercy on me!" said Mrs Dutton. "If I had had any on myself, I would never have engaged with you."

"It's something of the latest to think of that now, Mrs Dutton," said Archibald; "but I assure you, you will find the Highlands have their pleasures. You will have a dozen of cow-milkers under your own authority at Inverary, and you may throw any of them into the lake, if you have a mind, for the Duke's head people are almost as great as himself."

"This is a strange business, to be sure, Mr Archibald," said the lady; "but I suppose I must make the best on't.—Are you sure the boat will not sink? it leans terribly to one side, in my poor mind."

"Fear nothing," said Mr Archibald, taking a most important pinch of snuff; "this same ferry on Clyde knows us very well, or we know it, which is all the same; no fear of any of our people meeting with any accident. We should have crossed from the opposite shore,[11] but for the disturbances[12] at Glasgow, which made it improper for his Grace's people to pass through the city."

"Are you not afeard, Mrs Deans," said the dairy-vestal, addressing Jeanie, who sat, not in the most comfortable state of mind, by the side of Archibald, who himself managed the helm;—"Are you not afeard of these wild men with their naked——knees, and of this nut-shell of a thing, that seems bobbing up and down like a skimming-dish in a milk-pail?"

"No—no—madam," answered Jeanie, with some hesitation, "I am not feared; for I hae seen Hielandmen before, though I never was sae near them; and for the danger of the deep waters, I trust there is a Providence by sea as well as by land."

"Well," said Mrs Dutton, "it is a beautiful thing to have learned to write and read, for one can always say such fine words whatever should befall them."

Archibald, rejoicing in the impression which his vigorous measure had made upon the intractable dairy-maid, now applied himself, as a sensible and good-natured man, to secure by fair means the ascendancy which he had obtained by some wholesome violence; and he succeeded so well in representing to her the idle nature of her fears, and the impossibility of leaving her upon the beach, enthroned in an empty carriage, that the good understanding of the party was completely revived ere they landed at Roseneath.

CHAPTER 42

⸻Did Fortune guide,
Or rather Destiny, our bark, to which
We could appoint no port, to this blest place?
                                        FLETCHER

THE islands in the Firth of Clyde, which the daily passage of so many smoke-pennoned steam-boats now renders so easily accessible, were, in our fathers' times, secluded spots, frequented by no travellers, and few visitants of any kind. They are of exquisite, yet varied beauty. Arran, a mountainous region, or Alpine island, abounds with the grandest and most romantic scenery. Bute is of a softer and more woodland character. The Cumrays, as if to exhibit a contrast to both, are green, level, and bare, forming the links of a sort of natural bar, which is drawn along the mouth of the Firth, leaving large intervals, however, of ocean. Roseneath, a smaller isle,[1] lies much higher up the Firth, and towards its western shore, near the opening of the lake called the Gare-Loch, and not far from Loch-Long and Loch-Seant, or the Holy-Loch, which wind from the mountains of the western Highlands to join the æstuary of the Clyde.

In these isles the severe frost winds, which tyrannize over the vegetable creation during a Scottish spring, are comparatively little felt; nor, excepting the gigantic strength of Arran, are they much exposed to the Atlantic storms, lying land-locked and protected to the westward by the shores of Argyllshire. Accordingly, the weeping-willow, the weeping-birch, and other trees of early and pendulous shoots, flourish in these favoured recesses in a degree unknown in our eastern districts; and the air is also said to possess that mildness which is favourable to consumptive cases.

The picturesque beauty of the island of Roseneath, in particular, had such recommendations, that the Earls and Dukes of Argyle, from an early period, made it their occasional residence, and had their temporary accommodation in a fishing or hunting-lodge, which succeeding improvements have since transformed into a palace.[2] It was in its original simplicity, when the little bark, which we left traversing the

Firth at the end of the last chapter, approached the shores of the isle.

When they touched the landing-place, which was partly shrouded by some old low but wide-spreading oak-trees, intermixed with hazel-bushes, two or three figures were seen as if awaiting their arrival. To these Jeanie paid little attention, so that it was with a shock of surprise almost electrical, that, upon being carried by the rowers out of the boat to the shore, she was received in the arms of her father!

It was too wonderful to be believed—too much like a happy dream to have the stable feeling of reality—She extricated herself from his close and affectionate embrace, and held him at arm's length to satisfy her mind that it was no illusion. But the form was indisputable[3]—Douce David Deans himself, in his best light-blue Sunday's coat, with broad metal-buttons, and waistcoat and breeches of the same, his strong gramashes or leggins of thick grey cloth—the very copper buckles—the broad Lowland blue bonnet, thrown back as he lifted his eyes to Heaven in speechless gratitude—the grey locks that straggled from beneath it down his weather-beaten "haffets"—the bald and furrowed forehead—the clear blue eye, that, undimmed by years, gleamed bright and pale from under its shaggy grey pent-house—the features, usually so stern and stoical, now melted into the unwonted expression of rapturous joy, affection, and gratitude—were all those of David Deans; and so happily did they assort together, that, should I ever again see my friends[4] Wilkie[5] or Allan,[6] I will beg, borrow or steal from them a sketch of this very scene.

"Jeanie—my ain Jeanie—my best—my maist dutiful bairn—the Lord of Israel be thy father, for I am hardly worthy of thee! Thou hast redeemed our captivity—brought back the honour of our house—Bless thee, my bairn, with mercies promised and purchased!—But He *has* blessed thee in the good of which He has made thee the instrument."

These words broke from him not without tears, though David was of no melting mood.[7] Archibald had, with delicate attention, withdrawn the spectators from the interview, so that the wood and setting sun alone were witnesses of the expansion of their feelings.

"And Effie?—and Effie, dear father!" was an eager interjectional question which Jeanie repeatedly threw in among her expressions of joyful thankfulness.

"Ye will hear—ye will hear," said David hastily, and ever and anon renewed his grateful acknowledgments to Heaven for sending Jeanie safe down from the land of prelatic deadness and schismatic heresy;[8] and for having delivered her from the dangers of the way, and the lions that were in the path.[9]

"And Effie?" repeated her affectionate sister again and again. "And—and—(fain would she have said Butler, but she modified the direct enquiry)—and Mr and Mrs Saddletree—and Dumbiedikes—and a' friends?"

"A' weel—a' weel, praise to His name."

"And—and Mr Butler—he wasna weel when I gaed awa?"

"He is quite mended—quite weel," replied her father.

"Thank God—but O, dear father, Effie?—Effie?"

"You will never see her mair, my bairn," answered Deans in a solemn tone—"You are the ae and only leaf left now on the auld tree—heal be your portion."

"She is dead!—She is slain!—It has come ower late!" exclaimed Jeanie, wringing her hands.

"No, Jeanie," returned Deans, in the same grave melancholy tone. "She lives in the flesh, and is at freedom from earthly restraint, if she were as much alive in faith, and as free from the bonds of Satan."

"The Lord protect us!" said Jeanie.—"Can the unhappy bairn hae left you for that villain?"

"It is ower truly spoken," said Deans—"She has left her auld father, that has wept and prayed for her—She has left her sister, that travailed and toiled for her like a mother—She has left the bones of her mother, and the land of her people, and she is ower the march wi' that son of Belial—She has made a moonlight flitting of it." He paused, for a feeling betwixt sorrow and strong resentment choked his utterance.

"And wi' that man?—that fearfu' man?" said Jeanie. "And she has left us to gang aff wi' him?—O Effie, Effie, wha could hae thought it, after sic a deliverance as you had been gifted wi'!"

"She went out from us, my bairn, because she was not of us,"[10] replied David. "She is a withered branch will never bear fruit of grace[11]—a scape-goat gone forth into the wilderness of the world,[12] to carry wi' her, as I trust, the sins of our little congregation. The peace of the warld gang wi' her, and a better peace when she has the grace to turn to it. If she is of His elected,[13] His ain hour will come. What would her mother have said, that famous and memorable matron, Rebecca MacNaught, whose memory is like a flower of sweet savour in Newbattle, and a pot of frankincense in Lugton?[14]—But be it sae—

let her part—let her gang her gate—let her bite on her ain bridle[15]—
The Lord kens his time—She was the bairn of prayers, and may not
prove an utter castaway. But never, Jeanie—never more let her name
be spoken between you and me—She hath passed from us like the
brook which vanisheth when the summer waxeth warm, as patient
Job[16] saith—let her pass, and be forgotten."

There was a melancholy pause which followed these expressions.
Jeanie would fain have asked more circumstances relating to her
sister's departure, but the tone of her father's prohibition was positive.
She was about to mention her interview with Staunton at his father's
rectory; but, on hastily running over the particulars in her memory,
she thought that, on the whole, they were more likely to aggravate
than diminish his distress of mind. She turned, therefore, the discourse
from this painful subject, resolving to suspend farther enquiry until
she should see Butler, from whom she expected to learn the particulars
of her sister's elopement.

But when was she to see Butler? was a question she could not
forbear asking herself, especially while her father, as if eager to escape
from the subject of his youngest daughter, pointed to the opposite
shore of Dumbartonshire, and asking Jeanie "if it werena a pleasant
abode?" declared to her his intention of removing his earthly tabernacle[17] to that country, "in respect he was solicited by his Grace the
Duke of Argyle, as one well skilled in country-labour, and a' that
appertained to flocks and herds, to superintend a store-farm, whilk his
Grace had taen into his ain hand for the improvement of stock."[18]

Jeanie's heart sunk within her at this declaration. "She allowed it
was a goodly and pleasant land, and sloped bonnily to the western sun;
and she doubtedna that the pasture might be very gude, for the grass
looked green, for as drouthy as the weather had been. But it was far
frae hame, and she thought she wad be often thinking on the bonny
spots of turf, sae fu' of gowans and yellow king-cups, amang the
Craigs at St Leonard's."

"Dinna speak on't, Jeanie," said her father; "I wish never to hear it
named mair—that is, after the rouping is ower, and the bills paid. But
I brought a' the beasts ower bye that I thought ye wad like best.
There is Gowans, and there's your ain brockit cow, and the wee
hawkit ane, that ye ca'd—I needna tell ye how ye ca'd it—but I
couldna bid them sell the pettled creature, though the sight o't may
sometimes gie us a sair heart—it's no the poor dumb creature's
fault—And ane or twa beasts mair I hae reserved, and I caused them

to be driven before the other beasts, that men might say, as when the son of Jesse returned from battle, 'This is David's spoil.'"[19]

Upon more particular enquiry, Jeanie found new occasion to admire the active beneficence of her friend the Duke of Argyle. While establishing a sort of experimental farm[20] on the skirts of his immense[21] Highland estates, he had been somewhat at a loss to find a proper person in whom to vest the charge of it. The conversation his Grace had upon country matters with Jeanie Deans during their return from Richmond, had impressed him with a belief that the father, whose experience and success she so frequently quoted, must be exactly the sort of person whom he wanted. When the condition annexed to Effie's pardon rendered it highly probable that David Deans would chuse to change his place of residence, this idea again occurred to the Duke more strongly, and as he was an enthusiast equally in agriculture and in benevolence, he imagined he was serving the purposes of both, when he wrote to the gentleman in Edinburgh entrusted with his affairs, to enquire into the character of David Deans, cow-feeder, and so forth, at St Leonard's Crags; and if he found him such as he had been represented, to engage him without delay, and on the most liberal terms, to superintend his fancy-farm in Dumbartonshire.

The proposal was made to old David by the gentleman so commissioned, on the second day after his daughter's pardon had reached Edinburgh. His resolution to leave St Leonard's had been already formed; the honour of an express invitation from the Duke of Argyle to superintend a department where so much skill and diligence was required, was in itself extremely flattering; and the more so, because honest David, who was not without an excellent opinion of his own talents, persuaded himself that, by accepting this charge, he would in some sort repay the great favour he had received at the hands of the Argyle family. The appointments, including the right of sufficient grazing for a small stock of his own, were amply liberal; and David's keen eye saw that the situation was convenient for trafficking to advantage in Highland cattle. There was risk of "her'ship"[*] from the neighbouring mountains, indeed; but the awful name of the Duke of Argyle would be a great security, and a trifle of *black-mail* would, David was aware, assure his safety.

[* Her'ship, a Scottish word which may be said to be now obsolete; because, fortunately, the practice of "plundering by armed force," which is its meaning, does not require to be commonly spoken of.]

Still, however, there were two points on which he boggled. The first was the character of the clergyman with whose worship he was to join; and on this delicate point he received, as we will presently show the reader, perfect satisfaction. The next obstacle was the condition of his younger daughter, obliged as she was to leave Scotland for so many years.

The gentleman of the law smiled, and said, "There was no occasion to interpret that clause very strictly—that if the young woman left Scotland for a few months, or even weeks, and came to her father's new residence by sea from the western side of England, nobody would know of her arrival, or at least nobody who had either the right or inclination to give her disturbance. The extensive heritable jurisdictions[22] of his Grace excluded the interference of other magistrates with those living on his estates, and they who were in immediate dependence on him would receive orders to give the young woman no disturbance. Living on the verge of the Highlands, she might, indeed, be said to be out of Scotland, that is, beyond the bounds of ordinary law and civilization."

Old Deans was not quite satisfied with this reasoning; but the elopement of Effie, which took place on the third night after her liberation, rendered his residence at St Leonard's so detestable to him, that he closed at once with the proposal which had been made him, and entered with pleasure into the idea of surprising Jeanie, as had been proposed by the Duke, to render the change of residence more striking to her. The Duke had apprized Archibald of these circumstances, with orders to act according to the instructions he should receive from Edinburgh, and by which accordingly he was directed to bring Jeanie to Roseneath.

The father and daughter communicated these matters to each other, now stopping, now walking slowly towards the Lodge, which showed itself among the trees, at about half a mile's distance from the little bay in which they had landed.

As they approached the house, David Deans informed his daughter, with somewhat like a grim smile, which was the utmost advance he ever made towards a mirthful expression of visage, that "there was baith a worshipful gentleman, and ane reverend gentleman, residing therein. The worshipful gentleman was his honour the Laird of Knocktarlitie,[23] who was baillie of the lordship under the Duke of Argyle, ane Hieland gentleman, tarr'd wi' the same stick," David doubted, "as mony of them, namely, a hasty and choleric temper, and a neglect of the higher things that belong to salvation, and also a gripping unto the things of this world, without muckle distinction of property—but, however, ane gude hospitable gentleman, with whom it would be a part of wisdom to live on a gude understanding—for Hielandmen were hasty, ower hasty.—As for the reverend person of whom he had spoken, he was candidate by favour of the Duke of Argyle (for David would not for the universe have called him presentee[24]) for the kirk of the parish in which their farm was situated, and he was likely to be highly acceptable unto the Christian souls of the parish, who were hungering for spiritual manna, having been fed but upon sour Hieland sowens by Mr Duncan MacDonought, the last minister, who began the morning duly, Sunday and Saturday, with a mutchkin of usquebaugh. But I need say the less about the present lad," said David, again grimly grimacing, "as I think ye may hae seen him afore; and here he is come to meet us."

She had indeed seen him before, for it was no other than Reuben Butler himself.

CHAPTER 43

No more shalt thou behold thy sister's face;
Thou hast already had her last embrace.
Elegy on Mrs Anne Killigrew

THIS second surprise had been accomplished for Jeanie Deans by the rod of the same benevolent enchanter,[1] whose power had transplanted her father from the crags of St Leonard's to the banks of the Gare-Loch. The Duke of Argyle was not a person to forget the hereditary debt of gratitude, which had been bequeathed to him by his grand-father, in favour of the grandson of old Bible Butler. He had internally resolved to provide for Reuben Butler in this kirk of Knocktarlitie, of which the incumbent had just departed this life. Accordingly, his agent received the necessary instructions for that purpose, under the qualifying condition always that the learning and character of Mr Butler should be found proper for the charge. Upon enquiry, these were found as highly satisfactory as had been reported in the case of David Deans himself.

By this preferment, the Duke of Argyle more essentially benefited his friend and protégée, Jeanie, than he himself was aware of, since he contributed to remove objections in her father's mind to the match, which he had no idea had been in existence.

We have already noticed that Deans had something of a prejudice against Butler, which was, perhaps, in some degree owing to his possessing a sort of consciousness that the poor usher looked with eyes of affection upon his elder daughter. This, in David's eyes, was a sin of presumption, even although it should not be followed by any overt act, or actual proposal. But the lively interest which Butler had displayed in his distresses, since Jeanie set forth on her London expedition, and which, therefore, he ascribed to personal respect for himself individually, had greatly softened the feelings of irritability with which David had sometimes regarded him. And, while he was in this good disposition towards Butler, another incident took place which had great influence on the old man's mind.

So soon as the shock of Effie's second elopement was over, it was

Deans's early care to collect and refund to the Laird of Dumbiedikes the money which he had lent for Effie's trial, and for Jeanie's travelling expences. The Laird, the pony, the cocked hat, and the tobacco-pipe, had not been seen at Saint Leonard's Crags for many a day; so that, in order to pay this debt, David was under the necessity of repairing in person to the mansion of Dumbiedikes.

He found it in a state of unexpected bustle. There were workmen pulling down some of the old hangings, and replacing them with others, altering, repairing, scrubbing, painting, and white-washing. There was no knowing the old house, which had been so long the mansion of sloth and silence. The Laird himself seemed in some confusion, and his reception, though kind, lacked something of the reverential cordiality with which he used to greet David Deans. There was a change also, David did not very well know of what nature, about the exterior of this landed proprietor—an improvement in the shape of his garments, a spruceness in the air with which they were put on, that were both novelties. Even the old hat looked smarter; the cock had been newly pointed, the lace had been refreshed, and instead of slouching backward or forward on the Laird's head, as it happened to be thrown on, it was adjusted with a knowing inclination over one eye.

David Deans opened his business, and told down the cash. Dumbiedikes steadily inclined his ear to the one, and counted the other with great accuracy, interrupting David, while he was talking of the redemption of the captivity of Judah, to ask him whether he did not think one or two of the guineas looked rather light. When he was satisfied on this point, had pocketted his money, and had signed a receipt, he addressed David with some little hesitation,—"Jeanie wad be writing ye something, gudeman?"

"About the siller?" replied David—"Nae doubt, she did."

"And did she say nae mair about me?" asked the Laird.

"Nae mair but kind and Christian wishes—what suld she hae said?" replied David, fully expecting that the Laird's long courtship (if his dangling after Jeanie deserves so active a name,) was now coming to a point. And so indeed it was, but not to that point which he wished or expected.

"Aweel, she kens her ain mind best—Gudeman, I hae made a clean house o' Jenny Balchristie and her niece. They were a bad pack—steal'd meat and mault, and loot the carters magg the coals— I'm to be married the morn, and kirkit on Sunday."

Whatever David felt, he was too proud and too steady-minded to show any unpleasant surprise in his countenance and manners.

"I wuss ye happy, sir, through Him that gies happiness—marriage is an honourable state."

"And I am wedding into an honourable house, David—the Laird of Lickpelf's youngest daughter—she sits next us in the kirk, and that's the way I came to think on't."

There was no more to be said, but again to wish the Laird joy, to taste a cup of his liquor,[2] and to walk back again to St Leonard's, musing on the mutability of human affairs and human resolutions. The expectation that, one day or other, Jeanie would be Lady Dumbiedikes, had, in spite of himself, kept a more absolute possession of David's mind than he himself was aware of. At least, it had hitherto seemed an union at all times within his daughter's reach, whenever she might chuse to give her silent lover any degree of encouragement, and now it was vanished for ever. David returned, therefore, in no very gracious humour for so good a man. He was angry with Jeanie for not having encouraged the Laird—he was angry with the Laird for requiring encouragement—and he was angry with himself for being angry at all on the occasion.

On his return he found the gentleman who managed the Duke of Argyle's affairs was desirous of seeing him, with a view to completing the arrangement between them. Thus, after a brief repose, he was obliged to set off anew for Edinburgh, so that old May Hettly declared, "That a' this was to end with the master just walking himsel aff his feet."

When the business respecting the farm had been talked over and arranged, the professional gentleman acquainted David Deans, in answer to his enquiries concerning the state of public worship, that it was the pleasure of the Duke to put an excellent young clergyman, called Reuben Butler, into the parish, which was to be his future residence.

"Reuben Butler!" exclaimed David—"Reuben Butler, the usher at Libberton?"

"The very same," said the Duke's commissioner; "his Grace has heard an excellent character of him, and has some hereditary obligations to him besides—few ministers will be so comfortable as I am directed by his Grace to make Mr Butler."

"Obligations?—The Duke?—Obligations to Reuben Butler!— Reuben Butler a placed minister of the Kirk of Scotland!" exclaimed David, in interminable astonishment, for somehow he had been led by the bad success which Butler had hitherto met with in all his undertakings, to consider him as one of those step-sons of Fortune, whom she treats with unceasing rigour, and ends with disinheriting altogether.

There is, perhaps, no time at which we are disposed to think so highly of a friend,[3] as when we find him standing higher than we expected in the esteem of others. When assured of the reality of Butler's change of prospects, David expressed his great satisfaction at his success in life, which, he observed, was entirely owing to himself (David). "I advised his puir grandmother, who was but a silly woman, to breed him up to the ministry; and I prophesied that, with a blessing on his endeavours, he would become a polished shaft in the temple. He may be something ower proud o' his carnal learning, but a gude lad, and has the root of the matter[4]—as ministers gang now, where ye'll find ane better, ye'll find ten waur than Reuben Butler."

He took leave of the man of business, and walked homeward, forgetting his weariness in the various speculations to which this wonderful piece of intelligence gave rise. Honest David had now, like other great men, to go to work to reconcile his speculative principles with existing circumstances;[5] and, like other great men, when they set seriously about that task, he was tolerably successful.

"Ought Reuben Butler in conscience to accept of this preferment in the Kirk of Scotland, subject as David at present thought that establishment was to the Erastian encroachments of the civil power?" This was the leading question, and he considered it carefully. "The Kirk of Scotland was shorn of its beams,[6] and deprived of its full artillery and banners of authority; but still it contained zealous and fructifying pastors, attentive congregations, and, with all her spots and blemishes,[7] the like of this Kirk was no where else to be seen upon earth."

David's doubts had been too many and too critical to permit him ever unequivocally to unite himself with any of the dissenters, who, upon various accounts, absolutely seceded[8] from the national church. He had often joined in communion with such of the established clergy as approached nearest to the old presbyterian model and principles of 1640.[9] And although there were many things to be amended in that system, yet he remembered that he, David Deans, had himself ever been a humble pleader for the good old cause in a legal way,[10] but without rushing into right-hand excesses,[11] divisions, and separations. But, as an enemy to separation, he might join the right hand of fellowship with a minister of the Kirk of Scotland in its present model. *Ergo*, Reuben Butler might take possession of the parish of Knocktarlitie, without forfeiting his friendship or favour—Q.E.D. But, secondly, came the trying point of lay-patronage,[12] which David Deans had ever maintained to be a coming in by the window, and over the wall,[13] a cheating and starving the souls of a whole parish, for the purpose of clothing the back and filling the belly of the incumbent.[14]

This presentation, therefore, from the Duke of Argyle, whatever was the worth and high character of that nobleman, was a limb of the brazen image, a portion of the evil thing,[15] and with no kind of consistency could David bend his mind to favour such a transaction. But if the parishioners themselves joined in a general call to Reuben Butler to be their pastor, it did not seem quite so evident that the existence of this unhappy presentation was a reason for his refusing them the comforts of his doctrine. If the presbytery admitted him to the kirk, in virtue rather of that act of patronage, than of the general call of the congregation, that might be their error, and David allowed it was a heavy one. But if Reuben Butler accepted of the cure as tendered to him by those whom he was called to teach, and who had expressed themselves desirous to learn, David, after considering and reconsidering the matter, came, through the great virtue of IF, to be of opinion that he might safely so act in that matter.

There remained a third stumbling-block—the oaths[16] to government exacted from the established clergymen, in which they acknowledge an Erastian king and parliament, and homologate the incorporating Union between England and Scotland, through which the latter kingdom had become part and portion of the former, wherein Prelacy, the sister of Popery, had made fast her throne, and elevated the horns of her mitre.[17] These were symptoms of defection which had often made David cry out, "My bowels—my bowels!—I am pained at the very heart!"[18] And he remembered that a godly Bow-head matron had been carried out of the Tolbooth Church in a swoon, beyond the reach of brandy and burnt feathers, merely on hearing these fearful words, "It is enacted by the Lords *spiritual* and temporal," pronounced from a Scottish pulpit, in the proem to the Porteous Proclamation. These oaths were, therefore, a deep compliance[19] and dire abomination—a sin and a snare, and a danger and a defection. But this Shibboleth was not always exacted. Ministers had respect to their own tender consciences, and those of their brethren; and it was not till a later period that the reins of discipline were taken up tight by the General Assemblies and Presbyteries. The peace-making particle came again to David's assistance. *If* an incumbent was not called upon to make such compliances, and *if* he got a right entry into the church without intrusion, and by orderly appointment, why, upon the whole, David Deans came to be of opinion, that the said incumbent might lawfully enjoy the spirituality and temporality of the cure of souls at Knocktarlitie, with stipend, manse, glebe, and all thereunto appertaining.

The best and most upright-minded men are so strongly influenced by existing circumstances, that it would be somewhat cruel to enquire too nearly what weight paternal affection gave to these ingenious trains of reasoning. Let David Deans's situation be considered. He was just deprived of one daughter, and his eldest, to whom he owed so much, was cut off, by the sudden resolution of Dumbiedikes, from the high hope which David had entertained, that she might one day be mistress of that fair lordship. Just while this disappointment was bearing heavy on his spirits, Butler comes before his imagination—no longer the half-starved thread-bare usher, but fat and sleek and fair, the beneficed minister of Knocktarlitie, beloved by his congregation,—exemplary in his life,—powerful in his doctrine,—doing the duty of the kirk as never Highland minister did it before,—turning sinners as a colley dog turns sheep,[20]—a favourite of the Duke of Argyle, and drawing a stipend of eight hundred punds Scots, and four chalders of victual.[21] Here was a match, making up, in David's mind, in a tenfold degree, the disappointment in the case of Dumbiedikes, in so far as the Goodman of St Leonard's held a powerful minister in much greater admiration than a mere landed proprietor. It did not occur to him, as an additional reason in favour of the match, that Jeanie might herself have some choice in the matter; for the idea of consulting her feelings never once entered into the honest man's head, any more than the possibility that her inclination might perhaps differ from his own.

The result of his meditations was, that he was called upon to take the management of the whole affair into his own hand, and give, if it should be found possible without sinful compliance, or backsliding, or defection of any kind,[22] a worthy pastor to the kirk of Knocktarlitie. Accordingly, by the intervention of the honest dealer in butter-milk who dwelt in Libberton, David summoned to his presence Reuben Butler. Even from this worthy messenger he was unable to conceal certain swelling emotions of dignity, in so much, that, when the carter had communicated his message to the usher, he added, that "Certainly the Gudeman of St Leonard's had some grand news to tell him, for he was as uplifted as a midden-cock upon pattens."

Butler, it may readily be conceived, immediately obeyed the summons. His was a plain character, in which worth and good sense and simplicity were the principal ingredients; but love, on this occasion, gave him a certain degree of address. He had received an intimation of the favour designed him by the Duke of Argyle, with what feelings those only can conceive, who have experienced a sudden prospect of being raised to independence and respect, from penury and toil. He resolved, however, that the old man should retain all the consequence of being, in his own opinion, the first to communicate the important intelligence. At the same time, he also determined that in the expected conference he would permit David Deans to expatiate at length upon the proposal, in all its bearings, without irritating him either by interruption or contradiction. This last plan was the most prudent he could have adopted; because, although there were many doubts which David Deans could himself clear up to his own satisfaction, yet he might have been by no means disposed to accept the solution of any other person; and to engage him in an argument would have been certain to confirm him at once and for ever in the opinion which Butler chanced to impugn.

He received his friend with an appearance of important gravity, which real misfortune had long compelled him to lay aside, and which belonged to those days of awful authority in which he predominated over Widow Butler, and dictated the mode of cultivating the crofts at Beersheba. He made known to Reuben with great prolixity the prospect of his changing his present residence for the charge of the Duke of Argyle's stock-farm in Dumbartonshire, and enumerated the various advantages of the situation with obvious self-congratulation; but assured the patient hearer, that nothing had so much moved him to acceptance, as the sense that, by his skill in bestial, he could render the most important services to his Grace the Duke of Argyle, to whom, "in the late unhappy circumstance," (here a tear dimmed the sparkle of pride in the old man's eye,) he had been sae muckle obliged.

"To put a rude Hielandman into sic a charge," he continued, "what could be expected but that he suld be sic a chiefest herdsman, as wicked Doeg the Edomite;[23] whereas, while this grey head is to the fore, not a clute o' them but sall be as weel cared for as if they were the fatted kine of Pharoah.[24]—And now, Reuben, lad, seeing we maun remove our tent[25] to a strange country, ye will be casting a dolefu' look after us, and thinking with whom ye are to hold council anent your government in thae slippery and backsliding times; and nae doubt remembering, that the auld man, David Deans, was made the instrument to bring you out of the mire of schism and heresy, wherein your father's house delighted to wallow;[26] aften also, nae doubt, when ye are pressed wi' ensnaring trials and tentations and heart-plagues, you, that are like a recruit that is marching for the first time to the took of drum, will miss the auld bauld and experienced veteran soldier, that has felt the brunt of mony a foul day, and heard the bullets whistle as aften as he has hairs left on his auld pow."

It is very possible that Butler might internally be of opinion, that the reflection on his ancestor's peculiar tenets might have been spared, or that he might be presumptuous enough even to think, that, at his years and with his own lights, he might be able to hold his course without the pilotage of honest David. But he only replied, by expressing his regret, that any thing should separate him from an ancient, tried, and affectionate friend.

"But how can it be helped, man?" said David, twisting his features into a sort of smile—"How can we help it?—I trow ye canna tell me that—Ye maun leave that to ither folk—to the Duke of Argyle and me, Reuben. It's a gude thing to hae friends in this warld—how muckle better to hae an interest beyond it!"

And David, whose piety, though not always quite rational, was as sincere as it was habitual and fervent, looked reverentially upward, and paused. Mr Butler intimated the pleasure with which he would receive his friend's advice on a subject so important, and David resumed.

"What think ye now, Reuben, of a kirk—a regular kirk under the present establishment?—Were sic offered to ye, wad ye be free to accept it, and under whilk provisions?—I am speaking but by way of query."

Butler replied, "That if such a prospect were held out to him, he would probably first consult whether he was likely to be useful to the parish he should be called to; and if there appeared a fair prospect of his proving so, his friend must be aware, that, in every other point of view, it would be highly advantageous for him."

"Right, Reuben, very right, lad," answered the monitor, "your ain conscience is the first thing to be satisfied—for how sall he teach others that has himself sae ill learned the Scriptures, as to grip for the lucre[27] of foul earthly preferment, sic as gear and manse, money and victual, that which is not his in a spiritual sense—or wha makes his kirk a stalking-horse from behind which he may tak aim at his stipend?[28] But I look for better things of you—and specially ye maun be minded not to act altogether on your ain judgment, for therethrough comes sair mistakes, backslidings, and defections, on the left and on the right. If there were sic a day of trial put to you, Reuben, you, who are a young lad, although it may be ye are gifted wi' the carnal tongues, and those whilk were spoken at Rome, whilk is now the seat of the scarlet abomination,[29] and by the Greeks, to whom the gospel was as foolishness,[30] yet nae-the-less ye may be entreated by your weel-wisher to take the counsel of those prudent and resolved and weather-withstanding professors, wha hae kend what it was to lurk in banks and in mosses, in bogs and in caverns,[31] and to risk the peril of the head rather than renunce the honesty of the heart."

Butler replied, "That certainly, possessing such a friend as he hoped and trusted he had in the goodman himself, who had seen so many changes in the preceding century, he should be much to blame if he did not avail himself of his experience and friendly counsel."

"Eneugh said—eneugh said, Reuben," said David Deans, with internal exultation; "and say that ye were in the predicament whereof I hae spoken, of a surety I would deem it my duty to gang to the rute o' the matter, and lay bare to you the ulcers and imposthumes, and the sores and the leprosies,[32] of this our time, crying aloud and sparing not."[33]

David Deans was now in his element. He commenced his examination of the doctrines and belief of the Christian Church with the very Culdees, from whom he passed to John Knox,[34]—from John Knox to the recusants[35] in James the Sixth's time,—Bruce, Black, Blair, Livingstone,[36]—from them to the brief, and at length triumphant period[37] of the presbyterian church's splendour, until it was over-run by the English Independents. Then followed the dismal times of prelacy, the indulgences, seven[38] in number, with all their shades and bearings, until he arrived at the reign of King James the Second, in which he himself had been, in his own mind, neither an obscure actor nor an obscure sufferer. Then was Butler doomed to hear the most detailed and annotated edition of what he had so often heard before—David Deans's confinement, namely, in the iron cage[39] in the Canongate Tolbooth, and the cause thereof.

We should be very unjust to our friend David Deans, if we should "pretermit," to use his own expression, a narrative[40] which he held essential to his fame. A drunken trooper of the Royal Guards, Francis Gordon by name, had chased five or six of the skulking Whigs, among whom was our friend David; and after he had compelled them to stand, and was in the act of brawling with them, one of their number fired a pocket-pistol, and shot him dead. David used to sneer and shake his head when any one asked him whether *he* had been the instrument of removing this wicked persecutor from the face of the earth. In fact, the merit of the deed lay between him and his friend Patrick Walker, the pedlar, whose works he was so fond of quoting. Neither of them cared directly to claim the merit of silencing Mr Francis Gordon of the Life Guards, there being some wild cousins of his about Edinburgh who might have been even yet addicted to revenge, but yet neither of them chose to disown or yield to the other the merit of this active defence of their religious rites. David said, that if he had fired a pistol then, it was what he never did after or before. And as for Mr Patrick Walker, he has left it upon record, that his great surprise was, that so small a pistol could kill so big a man. These are the words of that venerable biographer, whose trade had not taught him by experience, that an inch was as good as an ell.[41] "He," (Francis Gordon,) "got a shot in his head out of a pocket-pistol, rather fit for diverting a boy than killing such a furious, mad, brisk man, which notwithstanding killed him dead!"[*]

Upon the extensive foundation which the history of the kirk afforded, during its short-lived triumph and long tribulation, David, with length of breath and of narrative, which would have astounded any one but a lover of his daughter, proceeded to lay down his own rules for guiding the conscience of his friend, as an aspirant to serve in the ministry. Upon this subject, the good man went through such a variety of nice and casuistical problems, supposed so many extreme cases, made the distinctions so critical and nice betwixt the right hand and the left hand—betwixt compliance and defection—holding back and stepping aside—slipping and stumbling—snares and errors—that at length, after having limited the path of truth to a mathematical line, he was brought to the broad admission, that each man's conscience, after he had gained a certain view of the difficult navigation which he was to encounter, would be the best guide for his pilotage. He stated the examples and arguments for and against the acceptance of a kirk on the present revolution model, with much more impartiality to Butler than he had been able to place them before his own view. And he concluded, that his young friend ought to think upon these things, and be guided by the voice of his own conscience, whether he could take such an awful trust as the charge of souls, without doing injury to his own internal conviction of what is right or wrong.

[* See p. 579 for the note, "Death of Francis Gordon".]

When David had finished his very long harangue, which was only interrupted by monosyllables, or little more, on the part of Butler, the orator himself was greatly astonished to find that the conclusion, at which he very naturally wished to arrive, seemed much less decisively attained than when he had argued the case in his own mind.

In this particular, David's current of thinking and speaking only illustrated the very important and general proposition concerning the excellence of the publicity of debate. For, under the influence of any partial feeling, it is certain, that most men can more easily reconcile themselves to any favourite measure, when agitating it in their own mind, than when obliged to expose its merits to a third party, when the necessity of seeming impartial procures for the opposite arguments a much more fair statement than that which they afford it in tacit meditation. Having finished what he had to say, David thought himself obliged to be more explicit in point of fact, and to explain that this was no hypothetical case, but one on which, (by his own influence and that of the Duke of Argyle,) Reuben Butler would soon be called to decide.

It was even with something like apprehension that David Deans heard Butler announce, in return to this communication, that he would take that night to consider on what he had said with such kind intentions, and return him an answer the next morning. The feelings of the father mastered David on this occasion. He pressed Butler to spend the evening with him—He produced, most unusual at his meals, one, nay, two bottles of aged strong ale.[42]—He spoke of his daughter—of her merits—her housewifery—her thrift—her affection. He led Butler so decidedly up to a declaration of his feelings towards Jeanie, that, before night-fall, it was distinctly understood she was to be the bride of Reuben Butler; and if they thought it indelicate to abridge the period of deliberation which Reuben had stipulated, it seemed to be sufficiently understood betwixt them, that there was a strong probability of his becoming minister of Knocktarlitie,[43] providing the congregation were as willing to accept of him, as the Duke to grant him the presentation. The matter of the oaths,[44] they agreed, it was time enough to dispute about, whenever the Shibboleth should be tendered.

Many arrangements were adopted that evening, which were afterwards ripened by correspondence with the Duke of Argyle's man of business, who intrusted Deans and Butler with the benevolent wish of his principal, that they should all meet with Jeanie, on her return from England, at the Duke's hunting-lodge in Roseneath.

This retrospect, so far as the placid loves of Jeanie Deans and Reuben Butler are concerned, forms a full explanation of the preceding narrative up to their meeting on the island as already mentioned.

CHAPTER 44

> "I come," he said, "my love, my life,
> And—nature's dearest name—my wife:
> Thy father's house and friends resign,
> My home, my friends, my sire are thine."
>
> LOGAN

THE meeting of Jeanie and Butler, under circumstances promising to crown an affection so long delayed, was rather affecting from its simple sincerity than from its uncommon vehemence of feeling. David Deans, whose practice was sometimes a little different from his theory, appalled them at first, by giving them the opinion of sundry of the suffering preachers and champions of his younger days, that marriage, though honourable by the laws of Scripture, was yet a state over-rashly coveted by professors, and specially by young ministers, whose desire, he said, was at whiles too inordinate for kirks, stipends, and wives, which had frequently occasioned over-ready compliance with the general defections of the times. He endeavoured to make them aware also, that hasty wedlock had been the bane of many a savoury professor—that the unbelieving wife had too often reversed the text,[1] and perverted the believing husband—that when the famous Donald Cargill, being then hiding in Lee-Wood, in Lanarkshire, it being killing-time, did, upon importunity, marry Robert Marshal of Starry Shaw, he had thus expressed himself: "What hath induced Robert to marry this woman? her ill will overcome his good—he will not keep the way long—his thriving days are done." To the sad accomplishment of which prophecy David said he was himself a living witness, for Robert Marshal, having fallen into foul compliances with the enemy, went home and heard the curates, declined into other steps of defection, and became lightly esteemed. Indeed he observed, that the great upholders of the standard, Cargill, Peden, Cameron, and Renwick, had less delight in tying the bonds of matrimony than in any other piece of their ministerial work; and although they would neither dissuade the parties, nor refuse their office, they considered the being called to it as an evidence of indifference, on the part of those between whom it was solemnized, to the many grievous things of the day. Notwithstanding, however, that marriage was a snare unto many, David was of opinion (as, indeed, he had showed in his practice), that it was in itself honourable, especially if times were such that honest men could be secure against being shot, hanged, or banished,[2] and had ane competent livelihood to maintain themselves, and those that might come after them. "And therefore," as he concluded something abruptly, addressing Jeanie and Butler, who, with faces as high-coloured as crimson, had been listening to his lengthened argument for and against the holy state of matrimony, "I will leave ye to your ain cracks."

As their private conversation, however interesting to themselves, might probably be very little so to the reader, so far as it respected their present feelings and future prospects, we shall pass it over, and only mention the information which Jeanie received from Butler concerning her sister's elopement, which contained many particulars that she had been unable to extract from her father.

Jeanie learned, therefore, that, for three days after her pardon had arrived, Effie had been the inmate of her father's house at St Leonard's—that the interviews betwixt David and his erring child, which had taken place before she was liberated from prison, had been touching in the extreme; but Butler could not suppress his opinion, that, when he was freed from the apprehension of losing her in a manner so horrible, her father had tightened the bands of discipline, so as, in some degree, to gall the feelings and aggravate the irritability of a spirit naturally impatient and petulant, and now doubly so from the sense of merited disgrace.

On the third night, Effie disappeared from St Leonard's, leaving no intimation whatever of the route she had taken. Butler, however, set out in pursuit of her, and with much trouble traced her towards a little landing-place, formed by a small brook which enters the sea betwixt Musselburgh and Edinburgh. This place, which has been since made into a small harbour, surrounded by many villas and lodging-houses, is now termed Portobello. At this time it was surrounded by a waste common, covered with furze, and unfrequented, save by fishing-boats, and now and then a smuggling lugger. A vessel of this description had been hovering in the Firth at the time of Effie's elopement, and, as Butler ascertained, a boat had come ashore in the evening on which the fugitive had disappeared, and had carried on board a female. As the vessel made sail immediately, and landed no part of their cargo, there seemed little doubt that they were accomplices of the notorious Robertson, and that the vessel had only come into the Firth to carry off his paramour.

This was made clear by a letter which Butler himself soon afterwards received by post, signed E.D., but without bearing any date of place or time. It was miserably ill written and spelt; sea-sickness having apparently aided the derangement of Effie's very irregular orthography and mode of expression. In this epistle, however, as in all that that unfortunate girl said or did, there was something to praise as well as much to blame. She said, in her letter, "That she could not endure that her father and sister should go into banishment, or be partakers of her shame—that if her burthen was a heavy one, it was of her own binding, and she had the more right to bear it alone,—that in future they could not be a comfort to her, or she to them, since every look and word of her father put her in mind of her transgression, and was like to drive her mad,—that she had nearly lost her judgment during the three days she was at St Leonard's—her father meant weel by her, and all men, but he did not know the dreadful pain he gave her in casting up her sins. If Jeanie had been at hame, it might hae dune better—Jeanie was ane, like the angels in Heaven, that rather weep for sinners, than reckon their transgressions. But she should never see Jeanie ony mair, and that was the thought that gave her the sairest heart of a' that had come and gane yet. On her bended knees would she pray for Jeanie, night and day, baith for what she had done, and what she had scorned to do, in her behalf; for what a thought would it have been to her at that moment o' time, if that upright creature had made a fault to save her. She desired her father would give Jeanie a' the gear—her ain (*i.e.* Effie's) mother's and a'—She had made a deed, giving up her right, and it was in Mr Novit's hand—Warld's gear was henceforward the least of her care, nor was it likely to be muckle her mister—She hoped this would make it easy for her sister to settle;" and immediately after this expression, she wished Butler himself all good things, in return for his kindness to her. "For herself," she said, "she kend her lot would be a waesome ane but it was of her own framing, sae she deserved the less pity. But, for her friends' satisfaction, she wished them to know that she was gaun nae ill gate—that they who had done the maist wrong were now willing to do her what justice was in their power; and she would, in some warldly respects, be far better off than she deserved. But she desired her family to remain satisfied with this assurance, and give themselves no trouble in making further enquiries after her."

To David Deans and to Butler this letter gave very little comfort; for what was to be expected from this unfortunate girl's uniting her fate to that of a character so notorious as Robertson, who they readily guessed was alluded to in the last sentence, excepting that she should become the partner and victim of his future crimes. Jeanie, who knew George Staunton's character and real rank, saw her sister's situation under a ray of better hope. She augured well of the haste he had shewn to reclaim his interest in Effie, and she trusted he had made her his wife. If so, it seemed improbable that, with his expected fortune, and high connections, he should again resume the life of criminal adventure which he had led, especially since, as matters stood, his life depended upon his keeping his own secret, which could only be done by an entire change of his habits, and particularly by avoiding all those who had known the heir of Willingham under the character of the audacious, criminal, and condemned Robertson.

She thought it most likely that the couple would go abroad for a few years, and not return to England until the affair of Porteous was totally forgotten. Jeanie, therefore, saw more hopes for her sister than Butler or her father had been able to perceive; but she was not at liberty to impart the comfort which she felt in believing that she would be secure from the pressure of poverty, and in little risk of being seduced into the paths of guilt. She could not have explained this without making public what it was essentially necessary for Effie's chance of comfort to conceal, the identity namely of George Staunton and George Robertson. After all, it was dreadful to think that Effie had united herself to a man condemned for felony, and liable to trial for murder, whatever might be his rank in life, and the degree of his repentance. Besides, it was melancholy for Jeanie to reflect, that, she herself being in possession of the whole dreadful secret, it was most probable he would, out of regard to his own feelings, and fear for his safety, never again permit her to see poor Effie. After perusing and re-perusing her sister's valedictory letter, she gave ease to her feelings in a flood of tears, which Butler in vain endeavoured to check by every soothing attention in his power. She was obliged, however, at length, to look up and wipe her eyes, for her father, thinking he had allowed the lovers time enough for conference, was now advancing towards them from the Lodge, accompanied by the Captain of Knockdunder,[3] or, as his friends called him for brevity's sake, Duncan Knock, a title which some youthful exploits had rendered peculiarly appropriate.

This Duncan of Knockdunder was a person of first-rate importance in the island of Roseneath, and the continental parishes of Knocktarli-tie, Kilmun, and so forth; nay, his influence extended as far as Cowal, where, however, it was obscured by that of another factor. The Tower of Knockdunder still occupies, with its remains, a cliff overhanging the Holy-Loch.[4] Duncan swore it had been a royal castle; if so, it was one of the smallest, the space within only forming a square of sixteen feet, and bearing therefore a ridiculous proportion to the thickness of the walls, which was ten feet at least. Such as it was, however, it had long given the title of Captain, equivalent to that of Chatellain, to the ancestors of Duncan, who were retainers of the house of Argyle, and held a hereditary jurisdiction under them, of little extent indeed, but which had great consequence in their own eyes, and was usually administered with a vigour somewhat beyond the law.

The present representative of that ancient family was a stout short man about fifty, whose pleasure it was to unite in his own person the dress of the Highlands and Lowlands, wearing on his head a black tie-wig, surmounted by a fierce cocked-hat, deeply guarded with gold lace, while the rest of his dress consisted of the plaid and philabeg. Duncan superintended a district which was partly Highland, partly Lowland, and therefore might be supposed to combine their national habits, in order to show his impartiality to Trojan or Tyrian.[5] The incongruity, however, had a whimsical and ludicrous effect, as it made his head and body look as if belonging to different individuals; or, as some one said who had seen the executions of the insurgent prisoners in 1715, it seemed as if some Jacobite enchanter, having recalled the sufferers to life, had clapped, in his haste, an Englishman's head on a Highlander's body. To finish the portrait, the bearing of the gracious Duncan was brief, bluff, and consequential, and the upward turn of his short copper-coloured nose indicated that he was somewhat ad-dicted to wrath and usquebaugh.

When this dignitary had advanced up to Butler and to Jeanie, "I take the freedom, Mr Deans," he said, in a very consequential manner "to salute your daughter, whilk I presume this young lass to be—I kiss every pretty girl that comes to Roseneath, in virtue of my office." Having made this gallant speech, he took out his quid, saluted Jeanie with a hearty smack, and bade her welcome to Argyle's country. Then addressing Butler, he said, "Ye maun gang ower and meet the carle ministers yonder the morn, for they will want to do your job, and synd it down with usquebaugh doubtless—they seldom make dry wark in this kintra."

"And the Laird"—said David Deans, addressing Butler in further explanation,—

"The Captain, man," interrupted Duncan; "folk winna ken wha ye are speaking aboot, unless ye gie shentlemens their proper title."[6]

"The Captain, then," said David, "assures me that the call is unanimous on the part of the parishioners—a real harmonious call, Reuben."

"I pelieve," said Duncan, "it was as harmonious as could pe expected, when the tae half o' the bodies were clavering Sassenach, and the t'other skirling Gaelic, like sea-maws and claik-geese before a storm. Ane wad hae needed the gift of tongues[7] to ken preceesely what they said—but I pelieve the best end of it was, 'Long live MacCallummore and Knockdunder.'—And as to its being an unanimous call, I wad be glad to ken fat business the carles have to call ony thing or ony body but what the Duke and mysell likes."

"Nevertheless," said Mr Butler, "if any of the parishioners have any scruples, which sometimes happen in the mind of sincere professors, I should be happy of an opportunity of trying to remove———"

"Never fash your peard about it, man," interrupted Duncan Knock—"Leave it a' to me.—Scruple! deil ane o' them has been bred up to scruple ony thing that they're bidden do—And if sic a thing suld happen as ye speak o', ye sall see the sincere professor, as ye ca' him, towed at the stern of my boat for a few furlongs.—I'll try if the water of the Haly-Loch winna wash off scruples as weel as fleas—Cot tamn!———"

The rest of Duncan's threat was lost in a growling, gurgling sort of sound, which he made in his throat, and which menaced recusants with no gentle means of conversion. David Deans would certainly have given battle in defence of the right of the Christian congregation to be consulted in the choice of their own pastor, which, in his estimation, was one of the choicest and most inalienable of their privileges; but he had again engaged in close conversation with Jeanie, and, with more interest than he was in use to take in affairs foreign alike to his occupation and to his religious tenets, was inquiring into the particulars of her London journey. This was, perhaps, fortunate for the new formed friendship betwixt him and the Captain of Knockdunder, which rested, in David's estimation, upon the proofs he had given of his skill in managing stock, but, in reality, upon the special charge transmitted to Duncan from the Duke and his agent, to behave with the utmost attention to Deans and his family.

"And now, sirs," said Duncan, in a commanding tone, "I am to pray ye a' to come in to your supper, for yonder is Mr Archibald half famished, and a Saxon woman, that looks as if her een were fleeing out o' her head wi' fear and wonder, as if she had never seen a shentleman in a philabeg pefore."

"And Reuben Butler," said David, "will doubtless desire instantly to retire, that he may prepare his mind for the exercise of to-morrow, that his work may suit the day, and be an offering of a sweet savour in the nostrils of the reverend presbytery."

"Hout tout, man, it's but little ye ken about them," interrupted the Captain. "Teil a ane o' them wad gie the savour of the hot venison pasty which I smell (turning his squab nose up in the air), a' the way frae the lodge, for a' that Mr Putler, or you either, can say to them."

David groaned, but judging he had to do with a Gallio, as he said, did not think it worth his while to give battle. They followed the Captain to the house, and arranged themselves with great ceremony round a well-loaded supper-table. The only other circumstance of the evening worthy to be recorded is, that Butler pronounced the blessing, that Knockdunder found it too long, and David Deans censured it as too short, from which the charitable reader may conclude it was exactly the proper length.

CHAPTER 45

Now turn the Psalms of David ower,
    And lilt wi' holy clangor;
Of double verse come gie us four,
    And skirl up the Bangor.

                                    BURNS

THE next was the important day, when, according to the forms and ritual of the Scottish Kirk, Reuben Butler was to be ordained minister of Knocktarlitie by the Presbytery of ———.[1] And so eager were the whole party, that all, excepting Mrs Dutton, the destined Cowslip of Inverary, were stirring at an early hour.

Their host, whose appetite was as quick and keen as his temper, was not long in summoning them to a substantial breakfast,[2] where there were at least a dozen of different preparations of milk, plenty of cold meat boiled and roasted, scores of eggs, a huge cag of butter, half a firkin herrings boiled and broiled, fresh and salt, and tea and coffee for them that liked it, which, as their landlord assured them, with a nod and a wink, pointing, at the same time, to a little cutter which seemed dodging under the lee of the island, cost them little beside the fetching ashore.

"Is the contraband trade[3] permitted here so openly?" said Butler. "I should think it very unfavourable to the people's morals."

"The Duke, Mr Putler, had gien nae orders concerning the putting of it down," said the magistrate, and seemed to think that he had said all that was necessary to justify his connivance.

Butler was a man of prudence, and aware that real good can only be obtained by remonstrance when remonstrance is well-timed; so for the present he said nothing more on the subject.

When breakfast was half over, in flounced Mrs Dolly as fine as a blue sacque and cherry-coloured ribbands could make her.

"Good morrow to you, madam," said the master of ceremonies; "I trust your early rising will not skaith ye."

The dame apologized to Captain Knockunder, as she was pleased to term their entertainer; "but, as we say in Cheshire," she added, "I was like the Mayor of Altringham, who lies in bed while his breeches are mending,[4] for the girl did not bring up the right bundle to my room, till she had brought up all the others by mistake one after t'other.—Well, I suppose we are all for church to-day, as I understand—Pray may I be so bold as to ask, if it is the fashion for you North-country gentlemen to go to church in your petticoats, Captain Knockunder?"

"Captain of Knockdunder, madam, if you please, for I knock under to no man; and in respect of my garb, I shall go to church as I am, at your service, madam; for if I were to lie in bed, like your Major What-d'ye-callum, till my preeches were mended, I might be there all my life, seeing I never had a pair of them on my person but twice in my life, which I am pound to remember, it peing when the Duke brought his Duchess here, when her Grace pehoved to be pleasured, so I e'en porrowed the minister's trews for the twa days her Grace was pleased to stay—but I will put myself under sic confinement again for no man on earth, or woman either, but her Grace being always excepted, as in duty pound."

The mistress of the milking-pail stared, but, making no answer to this round declaration, immediately proceeded to show, that the alarm of the preceding evening had in no degree injured her appetite.

When the meal was finished, the Captain proposed to them to take boat, in order that Mistress Jeanie might see her new place of residence, and that he himself might enquire whether the necessary preparations had been made, there and at the Manse, for receiving the future inmates of these mansions.

The morning was delightful, and the huge mountain-shadows slept upon the mirror'd wave[5] of the Firth, almost as little disturbed as if it had been an inland lake. Even Mrs Dutton's fears no longer annoyed her. She had been informed by Archibald, that there was to be some sort of junketting after the sermon, and that was what she loved dearly; and as for the water, it was so still that it would look quite like a pleasuring on the Thames.

The whole party being embarked, therefore, in a large boat, which the captain called his coach and six, and attended by a smaller one termed his gig,[6] the gallant Duncan steered strait upon the little tower of the old-fashioned church of Knocktarlitie, and the exertions of six stout rowers sped them rapidly on their voyage. As they neared the land, the hills appeared to recede from them, and a little valley, formed by the descent of a small river from the mountains, evolved

itself as it were upon their approach. The style of the country on each
side was simply pastoral, and resembled, in appearance and character,
the description of a forgotten Scottish poet,[7] which runs nearly
thus:[8]—

> The water gently down a level slid,
> With little din, but couthy what it made;
> On ilka side the trees grew thick and lang,
> And wi' the wild birds' notes were a' in sang;
> On either side, a full bow-shot and mair,
> The green was even, gowany, and fair;
> With easy slope on every hand the braes
> To the hills' feet with scattered bushes raise;
> With goats and sheep aboon, and kye below,
> The bonnie banks all in a swarm did go.*

They landed in this Highland Arcadia, at the mouth of the small
stream which watered the delightful and peaceable valley. Inhabitants
of several descriptions came to pay their respects to the Captain of
Knockdunder, an homage which he was very peremptory in exacting,
and to see the new settlers. Some of these were men after David
Deans's own heart,[9] elders of the kirk-session, zealous professors, from
the Lennox, Lanarkshire, and Ayrshire, to whom the preceding Duke
of Argyle had given *rooms* in this corner of his estate, because they had
suffered for joining his father the unfortunate Earl during his ill-fated
attempt in 1686.[10] These were cakes of the right leaven for David
regaling himself with; and had it not been for this circumstance, he
has been heard to say, "that the Captain of Knockdunder would have
swore him out of the country in twenty-four hours, sae awsome it was
to ony thinking soul to hear his imprecations, upon the slightest
temptation that crossed his humour."

Besides these, there were a wilder set of parishioners, mountaineers
from the upper glen and adjacent hill, who spoke Gaelic, went about
armed, and wore the Highland dress. But the strict commands of the
Duke had established such good order in this part of his territories,
that the Gael and Saxons lived upon the best possible terms of good
neighbourhood.

They first visited the Manse, as the parsonage is termed in Scotland.
It was old, but in good repair, and stood snugly embosomed in a grove
of sycamore, with a well-stocked garden in front, bounded by the

* Ross's Fortunate Shepherdess. Edit. 1778, p. 23.

small river, which was partly visible from the windows, partly concealed by the bushes, trees, and bounding hedge. Within, the house looked less comfortable than it might have been, for it had been neglected by the late incumbent; but workmen had been labouring under the directions of the Captain of Knockdunder, and at the expence of the Duke of Argyle, to put it into some order. The old "plenishing" had been removed, and neat, but plain household furniture had been sent down by the Duke in a brig[11] of his own, called the Caroline, and was now ready to be placed in order in the apartments.

The gracious Duncan, finding matters were at a stand among the workmen, summoned before him the delinquents, and impressed all who heard him with a sense of his authority, by the penalties with which he threatened them for their delay. Mulcting them in half their charge, he assured them, would be the least of it; for, if they were to neglect his pleasure and the Duke's, "he would be tamn'd if he paid them the t'other half either, and they might seek law for it where they could get it." The work-people humbled themselves before the offended dignitary, and spake him soft and fair; and at length, upon Mr Butler recalling to his mind, that it was the ordination-day, and that the workmen were probably thinking of going to church, Knockdunder agreed to forgive them out of respect to their new minister.

"But an I catch them neglecking my duty again, Mr Putler, the teil pe in me if the kirk shall be an excuse; for what has the like o' them rapparees to do at the kirk ony day put Sundays, or then either, if the Duke and I has the necessitous uses for them?"

It may be guessed with what feelings of quiet satisfaction and delight Butler looked forward to spending his days, honoured and useful as he trusted to be in this sequestered valley, and how often an intelligent glance was exchanged betwixt him and Jeanie, whose good-humoured face looked positively handsome, from the expression of modesty, and, at the same time, of satisfaction, which she wore when visiting the apartments of which she was soon to call herself mistress. She was left at liberty to give more open indulgence to her feelings of delight and admiration, when, leaving the Manse, the company proceeded to examine the destined habitation of David Deans.

Jeanie found with pleasure that it was not above a musket-shot from the Manse; for it had been a bar to her happiness to think she might be obliged to reside at a distance from her father, and she was aware that there were strong objections to his actually living in the same house with Butler. But this brief distance was the very thing which she could have wished.

The farm-house was on the plan of an improved cottage, and contrived with great regard to convenience; an excellent little garden, an orchard, and a set of offices complete, according to the best ideas of the time, combined to render it a most desirable habitation for the practical farmer, and far superior to the hovel at Woodend, and the small house at Saint Leonard's Crags. The situation was considerably higher than that of the Manse, and fronted to the west. The windows commanded an enchanting view of the little vale over which the mansion seemed to preside, the windings of the stream, and the Firth, with its associated lakes and romantic islands. The hills of Dumbarton-shire, once possessed by the fierce clan of MacFarlanes, formed a crescent behind the valley, and far to the right were seen the dusky and more gigantic mountains of Argyleshire, with a seaward view of the shattered and thunder-splitten peaks of Arran.

But to Jeanie, whose taste for the picturesque, if she had any by nature, had never been awakened or cultivated, the sight of the faithful old May Hettly, as she opened the door to receive them in her clean toy, Sunday's russet-gown, and blue apron, nicely smoothed down before her, was worth the whole varied landscape. The raptures of the faithful old creature at seeing Jeanie were equal to her own, as she hastened to assure her that "baith the gudeman and the beasts had been as weel seen after as she possibly could contrive." Separating her from the rest of the company, May then hurried her young mistress to the offices, that she might receive the compliments she expected for her care of the cows. Jeanie rejoiced, in the simplicity of her heart, to see her charge once more; and the mute favourites of our heroine, Gowans, and the others, acknowledged her presence by lowing, turning round their broad and decent brows when they heard her well-known "Pruh, my leddy—pruh, my woman," and, by various indications, known only to those who have studied the habits of the milky mothers,[12] shewing sensible pleasure as she approached to caress them in their turn.

"The very brute beasts are glad to see ye again," said May; "but nae wonder, Jeanie, for ye were aye kind to beast and body. And I maun learn to ca' ye *mistress* now, Jeanie, since ye hae been up to Lunnon, and seen the Duke, and the King, and a' the braw folk. But wha kens," added the old dame slily, "what I'll hae to ca' ye forbye mistress, for I am thinking it winna lang be Deans."

"Ca' me your ain Jeanie, May, and then ye can never gang wrang."

In the cow-house which they examined, there was one animal which Jeanie looked at till the tears gushed from her eyes. May, who had watched her with a sympathizing expression, immediately observed, in an under tone, "The gudeman aye sorts that beast himsell, and is kinder to it than ony beast in the byre; and I noticed he was that way e'en when he was angriest, and had maist cause to be angry.—Eh sirs! a parent's heart's a queer thing!—Mony a warstle he has had for that puir lassie—I am thinking he petitions mair for her than for yoursell, hinny; for what can he plead for you but just to wish you the blessing ye deserve? And when I sleepit ayont the hallan, when we came first here, he was often earnest a' night, and I could hear him come ower and ower again wi', 'Effie—puir blinded misguided thing!' it was aye 'Effie! Effie!'—If that puir wandering lamb comena into the sheepfauld in the Shepherd's ain time, it will be an unco wonder, for I wot she has been a child of prayers.[13] O, if the puir prodigal wad return, sae blithely as the gudeman wad kill the fatted calf![14]—though Brockie's calf will no be fit for killing this three weeks yet."

And then, with the discursive talent of persons of her description, she got once more afloat in her account of domestic affairs, and left this delicate and affecting topic.

Having looked at every thing in the offices and the dairy, and expressed her satisfaction with the manner in which matters had been managed in her absence, Jeanie rejoined the rest of the party, who were surveying the interior of the house, all excepting David Deans and Butler, who had gone down to the church to meet the kirk-session and the clergymen of the presbytery, and arrange matters for the duty of the day.

In the interior of the cottage all was clean, neat, and suitable to the exterior. It had been originally built and furnished by the Duke, as a retreat for a favourite domestic of the higher class, who did not long enjoy it, and had been dead only a few months, so that every thing was in excellent taste and good order. But in Jeanie's bedroom was a neat trunk, which had greatly excited Mrs Dutton's curiosity, for she was sure that the direction, "For Mrs Jean Deans, at Auchingower,[15] parish of Knocktarlitie," was the writing of Mrs Semple, the Duchess's own woman. May Hettly produced the key in a sealed parcel, which bore the same address, and attached to the key was a label, intimating that the trunk and its contents were "a token of remembrance to Jeanie Deans, from her friends the Duchess of Argyle and the young ladies." The trunk, hastily opened as the reader will not doubt, was found to be full of wearing apparel of the best quality, suited to Jeanie's rank in life; and to most of the articles the names of the particular donors were attached, as if to make Jeanie sensible not only of the general, but of the individual interest she had excited in the noble family. To name the various articles by their appropriate names, would be to attempt things unattempted yet in prose or rhyme;[16] besides, that the old-fashioned terms of manteaus, sacques, kissing-strings, and so forth, would convey but little information even to the milliners of the present day. I shall deposit, however, an accurate inventory of the contents of the trunk with my kind friend, Miss Martha Buskbody,[17] who has promised, should the public curiosity seem interested in the subject, to supply me with a professional glossary and commentary. Suffice it to say, that the gift was such as became the donors, and was suited to the situation of the receiver; that every thing was handsome and appropriate, and nothing forgotten which belonged to the wardrobe of a young person in Jeanie's situation in life, the destined bride of a respectable clergyman.

Article after article was displayed, commented upon, and admired, to the wonder of May, who declared, "she didna think the Queen had mair or better claise," and somewhat to the envy of the northern Cowslip. This unamiable, but not very unnatural, disposition of mind, broke forth in sundry unfounded criticisms to the disparagement of the articles, as they were severally exhibited. But it assumed a more direct character, when, at the bottom of all, was found a dress of white silk, very plainly made, but still of white silk, and French silk to boot, with a paper pinned to it, bearing, that it was a present from the Duke of Argyle to his travelling companion, to be worn on the day when she should change her name.

Mrs Dutton could forbear no longer, but whispered into Mr Archibald's ear, that it was a clever thing to be a Scotchwoman; "She supposed all *her* sisters, and she had half a dozen, might have been hanged, without any one sending her a present of a pocket-handkerchief."

"Or without your making any exertion to save them, Mrs Dolly," answered Archibald drily.—"But I am surprised we do not hear the bell yet," said he, looking at his watch.

"Fat ta teil, Mr Archibald," answered the Captain of Knockdunder, "wad ye hae them ring the bell before I am ready to gang to kirk?—I wad gar the bedral eat the bell-rope, if he took ony sic freedom. But if ye want to hear the bell, I will just shew mysell on the knowe-head, and it will begin jowing forthwith."

Accordingly, so soon as they sallied out, and the gold-laced hat of the Captain was seen rising like Hesper above the dewy verge of the rising ground, the clash (for it was rather a clash than a clang) of the bell was heard from the old moss-grown tower, and the clapper continued to thump its cracked sides all the while they advanced towards the kirk, Duncan exhorting them to take their own time, "for teil ony sport wad be till he came."[*]

Accordingly, the bell only changed to the final and impatient chime when they crossed the stile; and "rang in," that is, concluded its mistuned summons, when they had entered the Duke's seat in the little kirk, where the whole party arranged themselves with Duncan at their head, excepting David Deans, who already occupied a seat among the elders.

The business of the day, with a particular detail of which it is unnecessary to trouble the reader, was gone through according to the established form, and the sermon pronounced upon the occasion had the good fortune to please even the critical David Deans, though it was only an hour and a quarter long, which David termed a short allowance of spiritual provender.

The preacher, who was a divine that held many of David's opinions, privately apologized for his brevity by saying, "That he observed the Captain was gaunting grievously, and that if he had detained him longer, there was no knowing how long he might be in paying the next term's victual stipend."[18]

David groaned to find that such carnal motives could have influence upon the mind of a powerful preacher. He had, indeed, been scandalized by another circumstance during the service.

So soon as the congregation were seated after prayers, and the clergyman had read his text, the gracious Duncan, after rummaging the leathern-purse which hung in front of his petticoat, produced a short tobacco-pipe made of iron, and observed, almost aloud, "I hae forgotten my spleuchan—Lachlan, gang down to the Clachan, and bring me up a pennyworth of twist." Six arms, the nearest within reach, presented, with an obedient start, as many tobacco-pouches to the man of office. He made choice of one with a nod of acknowledgment, filled his pipe, lighted it with the assistance of his pistol-flint,

[* See p. 581 for the note "Tolling to Service in Scotland".]

and smoked with infinite composure during the whole time of the sermon. When the discourse was finished he knocked the ashes out of his pipe, replaced it in his sporran, returned the tobacco-pouch or spleuchan to its owner, and joined in the prayer with decency and attention.

At the end of the service, when Butler had been admitted minister of the kirk of Knocktarlitie, with all its spiritual immunities and privileges, David, who had frowned, groaned, and murmured at Knockdunder's irreverent demeanour, communicated his plain thoughts of the matter to Isaac Meiklehose, one of the elders, with whom a reverential aspect and huge grizzle wig had especially disposed him to seek fraternization. "It didna become a wild Indian," David said, "much less a Christian, and a gentleman, to sit in the kirk puffing tobacco reek, as if he were in a change-house."

Meiklehose shook his head, and allowed it was "far frae beseeming—But what will ye say? The Captain's a queer hand, and to speak to him about that or ony thing else that crosses the maggot, wad be to set the kiln a-low.[19] He keeps a high hand ower the country, and we couldna deal wi' the Hielandmen without his protection, sin' a' the keys o' the kintray hings at his belt; and he's no an ill body in the main, and maistry, ye ken, maws the meadows doun."[20]

"That may be a' very true, neighbour," said David; "but Reuben Butler isna the man I take him to be, if he disna learn the Captain to fuff his pipe some other gate than in God's house, or the quarter be ower."

"Fair and softly gangs far,"[21] said Meiklehose; "and if a fule may gie a wise man a counsel,[22] I wad hae him think twice or he mells wi' Knockdunder—He suld hae a lang-shankit spune that wad sup kail wi' the deil.[23] But they are a' away to their dinner to the change-house, and if we dinna mend our pace, we'll come short at meal-time."

David accompanied his friend without answer; but began to feel from experience, that the glen of Knocktarlitie, like the rest of the world, was haunted by its own special subjects of regret and discontent. His mind was so much occupied by considering the best means of converting Duncan of Knock to a sense of reverent decency during public worship, that he altogether forgot to enquire, whether Butler was called upon to subscribe the oaths to government.

Some have insinuated, that his neglect on this head was, in some degree, intentional; but I think this explanation inconsistent with the simplicity of my friend David's character. Neither have I ever been able by the most minute enquiries to know, whether the *formula*, at which he so much scrupled, had been exacted from Butler, aye or no. The books of the kirk-session might have thrown some light on this matter; but unfortunately they were destroyed in the year 1746,[24] by one Donacha Dhu na Dunaigh, at the instance, it was said, or at least by the connivance, of the gracious Duncan of Knock, who had a desire to obliterate the recorded foibles of a certain Kate Finlayson.

CHAPTER 46

Now butt and ben the change-house fills
    Wi' yill-caup commentators,—
Here's crying out for bakes and gills,
    And there the pint-stoup clatters,
Wi' thick and thrang, and loud and lang,—
    W' logic and wi' scripture,
They raise a din that in the end
    Is like to breed a rupture,
                    O' wrath that day.
                                    BURNS

A PLENTIFUL entertainment, at the Duke of Argyle's cost, regaled the reverend gentlemen who had assisted at the ordination of Reuben Butler, and almost all the respectable part of the parish. The feast was, indeed, such as the country itself furnished; for plenty of all the requisites for "a rough and round" dinner were always at Duncan of Knock's command. There was the beef and mutton on the braes, the fresh and salt-water fish in the lochs, the brooks, and firth; game of every kind, from the deer to the leveret, were to be had for the killing, in the Duke's forests, moors, heaths, and mosses; and for liquor, home-brewed ale flowed as freely as water; brandy and usquebaugh both were had in those happy times without duty; even white wine and claret were got for nothing, since the Duke's extensive rights of admiralty gave him a title to all the wine in cask, which is drifted ashore on the western coast and isles of Scotland, when shipping have suffered by severe weather. In short, as Duncan boasted, the entertainment did not cost MacCallanmore a plack out of his sporran, and was nevertheless not only liberal, but overflowing.

The Duke's health was solemnized in a *bona fide* bumper, and David Deans himself added perhaps the first huzza that his lungs had ever uttered, to swell the shout with which the pledge was received. Nay, so exalted in heart was he upon this memorable occasion, and so much disposed to be indulgent, that he expressed no dissatisfaction[1] when three bag-pipers struck up, "The Campbells are coming."[2] The health of the reverend minister of Knocktarlitie was received with similar honours; and there was a roar of laughter, when one of his brethren slyly subjoined the addition of, "A good wife to our brother, to keep the Manse in order." On this occasion David Deans was delivered of his first-born joke; and apparently the parturition was accompanied with many throes, for sorely did he twist about his physiognomy, and much did he stumble in his speech, before he could express his idea, "That the lad being new wedded to his spiritual bride, it was hard to threaten him with ane temporal spouse in the saam day." He then laughed a hoarse and brief laugh, and was suddenly grave and silent, as if abashed at his own vivacious effort.

After another toast or two, Jeanie, Mrs Dolly, and such of the female natives as had honoured the feast with their presence, retired to David's new dwelling at Auchingower, and left the gentlemen to their potations.

The feast proceeded with great glee. The conversation, where Duncan had it under his direction, was not indeed always strictly canonical, but David Deans escaped any risk of being scandalized, by engaging with one of his neighbours in a recapitulation of the sufferings of Ayrshire and Lanarkshire, during what was called the invasion of the Highland Host;[3] the prudent Mr Meiklehose cautioning them from time to time to lower their voices, for "that Duncan Knock's father had been at that onslaught, and brought back muckle gude plenishing, and that Duncan was no unlikely to hae been there himsell, for what he kend."

Meanwhile, as the mirth and fun grew fast and furious,[4] the graver members of the party began to escape as well as they could. David Deans accomplished his retreat, and Butler anxiously watched an opportunity to follow him. Knockdunder, however, desirous, he said, of knowing what stuff was in the new minister, had no intention to part with him so easily, but kept him pinned to his side, watching him sedulously, and with obliging violence filling his glass to the brim, so often as he could seize an opportunity of doing so. At length, as the evening was wearing late,[5] a venerable brother chanced to ask Mr Archibald when they might hope to see the Duke, *tam carum caput*,[6] as he would venture to term him, at the Lodge of Roseneath. Duncan of Knock, whose ideas were somewhat conglomerated, and who, it may be believed, was no great scholar, catching up some imperfect sound of the words, conceived the speaker was drawing a parallel between the Duke and Sir Donald Gorme of Sleat; and being of opinion that such comparison was odious,[7] snorted thrice, and prepared himself to be in a passion.

To the explanation of the venerable divine, the Captain answered, "I heard the word Gorme myself, sir, with my ain ears. D'ye think I do not know Gaelic from Latin?"

"Apparently not, sir;"—so the clergyman, offended in his turn, and taking a pinch of snuff, answered with great coolness.

The copper nose of the gracious Duncan now became heated like the bull of Phalaris, and while Mr Archibald mediated betwixt the offended parties, and the attention of the company was engaged by their dispute, Butler took an opportunity to effect his retreat.

He found the females at Auchingower, very anxious for the breaking up of the convivial party; for it was a part of the arrangement, that although David Deans was to remain at Auchingower, and Butler was that night to take possession of the Manse, yet Jeanie, for whom complete accommodations were not yet provided in her father's house, was to return for a day or two to the Lodge at Roseneath, and the boats had been held in readiness accordingly. They waited, therefore, for Knockdunder's return, but twilight came, and they still waited in vain. At length Mr Archibald, who, as a man of decorum, had taken care not to exceed in his conviviality, made his appearance, and advised the females strongly to return to the island under his escort; observing, that from the humour in which he had left the Captain, it was a great chance whether he budged out of the public-house that night, and it was absolutely certain that he would not be very fit company for ladies. The gig was at their disposal, he said, and there was still pleasant twilight for a party on the water.

Jeanie, who had considerable confidence in Archibald's prudence, immediately acquiesced in this proposal; but Mrs Dolly positively objected to the small boat. If the big boat could be gotten, she agreed to set out, otherwise she would sleep on the floor, rather than stir a step. Reasoning with Dolly was out of the question, and Archibald did not think the difficulty so pressing as to require compulsion. He observed, it was not using the Captain very politely to deprive him of his coach and six; "but as it was in the ladies' service," he gallantly said, "he would use so much freedom—besides the gig would serve the Captain's purpose better, as it could come off at any hour of the tide; the large boat should, therefore, be at Mrs Dolly's command."

They walked to the beach accordingly, accompanied by Butler. It was some time before the boatmen could be assembled, and ere they were well embarked, and ready to depart, the pale moon was come over the hill, and flinging a trembling reflection on the broad and glittering waves. But so soft and pleasant was the night, that Butler, in bidding farewell to Jeanie, had no apprehension for her safety; and what is yet more extraordinary, Mrs Dolly felt no alarm for her own. The air was soft, and came over the cooling wave with something of summer fragrance. The beautiful scene of headlands, and capes, and bays, around them, with the broad blue chain of mountains, were dimly visible in the moonlight; while every dash of the oars made the waters glance and sparkle with the brilliant phenomenon called the sea-fire.[8]

This last circumstance filled Jeanie with wonder, and served to amuse the mind of her companion, until they approached the little bay, which seemed to stretch its dark and wooded arms into the sea as if to welcome them.

The usual landing-place was at a quarter of a mile's distance from the Lodge, and although the tide did not admit of the large boat coming quite close to the jetty of loose stones which served as a pier, Jeanie, who was both bold and active, easily sprung ashore; but Mrs Dolly positively refusing to commit herself to the same risk, the complaisant Mr Archibald ordered the boat round to a more regular landing-place, at a considerable distance along the shore. He then prepared to land himself, that he might, in the meanwhile, accompany Jeanie to the Lodge. But as there was no mistaking the woodland lane, which led from thence to the shore, and as the moonlight shewed her one of the white chimneys rising out of the wood which embosomed the building, Jeanie declined this favour with thanks, and requested him to proceed with Mrs Dolly, who being "in a country where the ways were strange to her, had mair need of countenance."

This, indeed, was a fortunate circumstance, and might even be said to save poor Cowslip's life, if it was true, as she herself used solemnly to aver, that she must positively have expired for fear, if she had been left alone in the boat with six wild Highlanders in kilts.

The night was so exquisitely beautiful, that Jeanie, instead of immediately directing her course towards the Lodge, stood looking after the boat as it again put off from the side, and rowed out into the little bay, the dark figures of her companions growing less and less distinct as they diminished in the distance, and the jorram, or melancholy boat-song of the rowers, coming on the ear with softened and sweeter sound, until the boat rounded the headland, and was lost to her observation.

Still Jeanie remained in the same posture, looking out upon the sea.

It would, she was aware, be some time ere her companions could reach the Lodge, as the distance by the more convenient landing place was considerably greater than from the point where she stood, and she was not sorry to have an opportunity to spend the interval by herself.

The wonderful change which a few weeks had wrought in her situation, from shame and grief, and almost despair, to honour, joy, and a fair prospect of future happiness, passed before her eyes with a sensation which brought the tears into them. Yet they flowed at the same time from another source. As human happiness is never perfect, and as well constructed minds are never more sensible of the distresses of those whom they love, than when their own situation forms a contrast with them, Jeanie's affectionate regrets turned to the fate of her poor sister—the child of so many hopes—the fondled nursling of so many years—now an exile, and, what was worse, dependent on the will of a man, of whose habits she had every reason to entertain the worst opinion, and who, even in his strongest paroxysms of remorse, had appeared too much a stranger to the feelings of real penitence.

While her thoughts were occupied with these melancholy reflections, a shadowy figure seemed to detach itself from the copse-wood on her right hand. Jeanie started, and the stories of apparitions and wraiths, seen by solitary travellers in wild situations, at such times, and in such an hour, suddenly came full upon her imagination. The figure glided on, and as it came betwixt her and the moon, she was aware that it had the appearance of a woman. A soft voice twice repeated, "Jeanie—Jeanie!"—Was it indeed—could it be the voice of her sister?—Was she still among the living, or had the grave given up its tenant?—Ere she could state these questions to her own mind, Effie, alive, and in the body, had clasped her in her arms, and was straining her to her bosom, and devouring her with kisses. "I have wandered here," she said, "like a ghaist, to see you, and nae wonder you take me for ane—I thought but to see you gang by, or to hear the sound of your voice; but to speak to yoursell again, Jeanie, was mair than I deserved, and mair than I durst pray for."

"O Effie! how came ye here alone, and at this hour, and on the wild sea-beach?—Are you sure it's your ain living sell?"

There was something of Effie's former humour in her practically answering the question by a gentle pinch, more beseeming the fingers of a fairy than of a ghost. And again the sisters embraced, and laughed and wept by turns.

"But ye maun gang up wi' me to the Lodge, Effie," said Jeanie, "and tell me a' your story—I hae gude folk there that will make ye welcome for my sake."

"Na, na, Jeanie," replied her sister sorrowfully,—"ye hae forgotten what I am—a banished outlawed creature, scarce escaped the gallows by your being the bauldest and the best sister that ever lived—I'll gae near nane o' your grand friends, even if there was nae danger to me."

"There is nae danger—there shall be nae danger," said Jeanie eagerly. "O Effie, dinna be wilfu'—be guided for anes—we will be sae happy a'thegither!"

"I have a' the happiness I deserve on this side of the grave, now that I hae seen you," answered Effie; "and whether there were danger to mysell or no, naebody shall ever say that I come with my cheat-the-gallows face to shame my sister amang her grand friends."

"I hae nae grand friends," said Jeanie; "nae friends but what are friends of yours—Reuben Butler and my father.—O, unhappy lassie, dinna be dour, and turn your back on your happiness again! We wunna see another acquaintance—Come hame to us, your ain dearest friends—it's better sheltering under an auld hedge than under a new planted wood."[9]

"It's in vain speaking, Jeanie—I maun drink as I hae brewed[10]—I am married, and I maun follow my husband, for better for worse."

"Married, Effie!" exclaimed Jeanie—"Misfortunate creature! and to that awfu'——"

"Hush, hush," said Effie, clapping one hand on her mouth, and pointing to the thicket with the other, "he is yonder."

She said this in a tone which shewed that her husband had found means to inspire her with awe, as well as affection. At this moment a man issued from the wood.

It was young Staunton. Even by the imperfect light of the moon, Jeanie could observe that he was handsomely dressed, and had the air of a person of rank.

"Effie," he said, "our time is well nigh spent—the skiff will be aground in the creek, and I dare not stay longer—I hope your sister will allow me to salute her." But Jeanie shrunk back from him with a feeling of internal abhorrence. "Well," said he, "it does not much signify; if you keep up the feeling of ill-will, at least you do not act upon it, and I thank you for your respect to my secret, when a word (which in your place I would have spoken at once) would have cost me my life. People say, you should keep from the wife of your bosom the secret that concerns your neck[11]—my wife and her sister both know mine, and I shall not sleep a wink the less sound."

"But are you really married to my sister, sir?" asked Jeanie, in great doubt and anxiety; for the haughty careless tone in which he spoke seemed to justify her worst apprehensions.

"I really am legally married, and by my own name," replied Staunton, more gravely.

"And your father—and your friends?—"

"And my father and my friends must just reconcile themselves to that which is done and cannot be undone," replied Staunton. "However, it is my intention, in order to break off dangerous connections, and to let my friends come to their temper, to conceal my marriage for the present, and stay abroad for some years. So that you will not hear of us for some time, if ever you hear of us again at all. It would be dangerous, you must be aware, to keep up the correspondence, for all would guess that the husband of Effie was the—what shall I call myself?—the slayer of Porteous."

Hard-hearted light man! thought Jeanie—to what a character she has intrusted her happiness!—She has sown the wind, and maun reap the whirlwind.[12]

"Dinna think ill o' him," said Effie, breaking away from her husband, and leading Jeanie a step or two out of hearing,—"dinna think *very* ill o' him—he's gude to me, Jeanie—as gude as I deserve— And he is determined to gie up his bad courses.—Sae, after a', dinna greet for Effie; she is better off than she has wrought for.—But you— O you!—how can you be happy eneugh!—never till ye get to Heaven, where a' body is as gude as yoursel.—Jeanie, if I live and thrive, ye shall hear of me—if not, just forget that sic a creature ever lived to vex ye—fare ye weel—fare—fare ye weel!"

She tore herself from her sister's arms, rejoined her husband—they plunged into the copsewood, and she saw them no more. The whole scene had the effect of a vision, and she could almost have believed it such, but that, very soon after they quitted her, she heard the sound of oars, and a skiff was seen on the Firth, pulling swiftly towards the small smuggling sloop which lay in the offing. It was on board of such a vessel that Effie had embarked at Portobello, and Jeanie had no doubt that the same conveyance was destined, as Staunton had hinted, to transport them to a foreign country.

Although it was impossible to determine whether this interview, while it was passing, gave more pain or pleasure to Jeanie Deans, yet the ultimate impression which remained on her mind was decidedly favourable. Effie was married—made, according to the common phrase, an honest woman—that was one main point; it seemed also as if her husband were about to abandon the path of gross vice, in which he had run so long and so desperately—that was another;—for his final and effectual conversion, he did not want understanding, and God knew his own hour.

Such were the thoughts with which Jeanie endeavoured to console her anxiety respecting her sister's future fortune. On her arrival at the Lodge, she found Archibald in some anxiety at her stay, and about to walk out in quest of her. A headache served as an apology for retiring to rest, in order to conceal her visible agitation of mind from her companions.

By this secession also, she escaped another scene of a different sort. For as if there were danger in all gigs, whether by sea or land, that of Knockdunder had been run down by another boat, an accident owing chiefly to the drunkenness of the captain, his crew, and passengers. Knockdunder, and two or three guests, whom he was bringing along with him to finish the conviviality of the evening at the Lodge, got a sound ducking, but, being rescued by the crew of the boat which endangered them, there was no ultimate loss, excepting that of the Captain's laced hat, which, greatly to the satisfaction of the Highland part of the district, as well as to the improvement of the conformity of his own personal appearance, he replaced by a smart Highland bonnet next day. Many were the vehement threats of vengeance which, on the succeeding morning, the gracious Duncan threw out against the boat which had upset him; but as neither she, nor the small smuggling vessel to which she belonged, was any longer to be seen in the Firth, he was compelled to sit down with the affront. This was the more hard, he said, as he was assured the mischief was done on purpose, these scoundrels having lurked about after they had landed every drop of brandy, and every bag of tea they had on board; and he understood the coxswain had been on shore, making particular enquiries concerning the time when his boat was to cross over, and to return, and so forth.

"Put the neist time they meet me on the Firth," said Duncan, with great majesty, "I will teach the moonlight rapscallions and vagabonds to keep their ain side of the road, and be tamn'd to them."

CHAPTER 47

Lord! who would live turmoiled in a court,
And may enjoy such quiet walks as these?

SHAKESPEARE

WITHIN a reasonable time after Butler was safely and comfortably settled in his living, and Jeanie had taken up her abode at Auchingower with her father,—the precise extent of which interval we request each reader to settle according to his own sense of what is decent and proper upon the occasion,—and after due proclamation of banns, and all other formalities, the long wooing of this worthy pair was ended by their union in the holy bands of matrimony. On this occasion, David Deans stoutly withstood the iniquities of pipes, fiddles, and promiscuous dancing, to the great wrath of the Captain of Knockdunder, who said, if he "had guessed it was to be sic a tamned Quakers' meeting, he wad hae seen them peyont the cairn before he wad hae darkened their doors."

And so much rancour remained on the spirits of the gracious Duncan upon this occasion, that various "picqueerings," as David called them, took place upon the same and similar topics; and it was only in consequence of an accidental visit of the Duke to his Lodge at Roseneath, that they were put a stop to. But upon that occasion his Grace shewed such particular respect to Mr and Mrs Butler, and such favour even to old David, that Knockdunder held it prudent to change his course towards the latter. He, in future, used to express himself among friends, concerning the minister and his wife, as "very worthy decent folk, just a little over strict in their notions; put it was pest for thae plack cattle to err on the safe side." And respecting David, he allowed that "he was an excellent judge of nowte and sheep, and a sensible aneugh carle, an it werena for his tamned Cameronian nonsense, whilk it is not worth while of a shentleman to knock out of an auld silly head, either by force of reason, or otherwise." So that, by avoiding topics of dispute, the personages of our tale lived in great good habits with the gracious Duncan, only that he still grieved David's soul, and set a perilous example to the congregation, by sometimes bringing his pipe to the church on a cold winter-day, and almost always sleeping during sermon in the summer-time.

Mrs Butler, whom we must no longer, if we can help it, term by the familiar name of Jeanie, brought into the married state the same firm mind and affectionate disposition,—the same natural and homely good sense, and spirit of useful exertion,—in a word, all the domestic good qualities of which she had given proof during her maiden life. She did not indeed rival Butler in learning; but then no woman more devoutly venerated the extent of her husband's erudition. She did not pretend to understand his expositions of divinity; but no minister of the presbytery had his humble dinner so well arranged, his clothes and linen in equal good order, his fire-side so neatly swept, his parlour so clean, and his books so well dusted.

If he talked to Jeanie òf what she did not understand,—and (for the man was mortal, and had been a schoolmaster,) he sometimes did harangue more scholarly and wisely than was necessary,—she listened in placid silence; and whenever the point referred to common life, and was such as came under the grasp of a strong natural understanding, her views were more forcible, and her observation more acute, than his own. In acquired politeness of manners, when it happened that she mingled a little in society, Mrs Butler was, of course, judged deficient. But then she had that obvious wish to oblige, and that real and natural good-breeding depending on good sense and good humour, which, joined to a considerable degree of archness and liveliness of manner, rendered her behaviour acceptable to all with whom she was called upon to associate. Notwithstanding her strict attention to all domestic affairs, she always appeared the real clean well-dressed mistress of the house, never the sordid household drudge. When complimented on this occasion by Duncan Knock, who swore "that he thought the fairies must help her, since her house was always clean, and nobody ever saw any body sweeping it," she modestly replied, "That much might be dune by timing ane's turns."

Duncan replied, "He heartily wished she could teach that art to the huzzies at the Lodge, for he could never discover that the house was washed at a', except now and then by breaking his shins over the pail—Cot tamn the jauds!"

Of lesser matters there is not occasion to speak much. It may easily be believed that the Duke's cheese was carefully made, and so graciously accepted, that the offering became annual. Remembrances and acknowledgments of past favours were sent to Mrs Bickerton and

Mrs Glass, and an amicable intercourse maintained from time to time
with these two respectable and benevolent persons.

It is especially necessary to mention, that in the course of five years,
Mrs Butler had three children, two boys and a girl, all stout healthy
babes of grace, fair-haired, blue-eyed, and strong-limbed. The boys
were named David and Reuben, an order of nomenclature which was
much to the satisfaction of the old hero of the Covenant, and the girl,
by her mother's special desire, was christened Euphemia, rather
contrary to the wish both of her father and husband, who nevertheless
loved Mrs Butler too well, and were too much indebted to her for
their hours of happiness, to withstand any request which she made
with earnestness, and as a gratification to herself. But from some
feeling, I know not of what kind, the child was never distinguished by
the name of Effie, but by the abbreviation of Femie, which in
Scotland is equally commonly applied to persons called Euphemia.

In this state of quiet and unostentatious enjoyment, there were,
besides the ordinary rubs and ruffles which disturb even the most
uniform life, two things which particularly chequered Mrs Butler's
happiness. "Without these," she said to our informer, "her life would
have been but too happy; and perhaps," she added, "she had need of
some crosses in this world to remind her that there was a better to
come behind it."

The first of these related to certain polemical skirmishes betwixt her
father and her husband, which, notwithstanding the mutual respect
and affection they entertained for each other, and their great love for
her,—notwithstanding also their general agreement in strictness, and
even severity of Presbyterian principle,—often threatened unpleasant
weather between them. David Deans, as our readers must be aware,
was sufficiently opinionative and intractable, and having prevailed on
himself to become a member of a kirk-session under the established
church, he felt doubly obliged to evince, that in so doing, he had not
compromised any whit of his former profession, either in practice or
principle. Now Mr Butler, doing all credit to his father-in-law's
motives, was frequently of opinion that it were better to drop out of
memory points of division and separation, and to act in the manner
most likely to attract and unite all parties who were serious in religion.
Moreover, he was not pleased, as a man and a scholar, to be always
dictated to by his unlettered father-in-law; and as a clergyman, he did
not think it fit to seem for ever under the thumb of an elder of his own
kirk-session. A proud but honest thought carried his opposition now

and then a little farther than it would otherwise have gone. "My brethren," he said, "will suppose I am flattering and conciliating the old man for the sake of his succession, if I defer and give way to him on every occasion; and, besides, there are many on which I neither can nor will conscientiously yield to his notions. I cannot be always persecuting old women for witches, or ferretting out matter of scandal among the young ones,[1] which might otherwise have remained concealed."

From this difference of opinion it happened, that in many cases of nicety, such as in owning certain defections, and failing to testify against certain backslidings of the time, in not always severely tracing forth little matters of scandal and *fama clamosa*, which David called a loosening of the reins of discipline, and in neglecting to demand clear testimonies in other points of controversy which had, as it were, drifted to leeward with the change of times, Butler incurred the censure of his father-in-law; and sometimes the disputes betwixt them became eager and almost unfriendly. In all such cases Mrs Butler was a mediating spirit, who endeavoured, by the alkaline smoothness of her own disposition, to neutralize the acidity[2] of theological controversy. To the complaints of both she lent an unprejudiced and attentive ear, and sought always rather to excuse than absolutely to defend the other party.

She reminded her father that Butler had not "his experience of the auld and wrastling times, when folk were gifted wi' a far look into eternity,[3] to make up for the oppressions whilk they suffered here below in time. She freely allowed that many devout ministers and professors in times past had enjoyed downright revelation, like the blessed Peden,[4] and Lundie,[5] and Cameron,[6] and Renwick,[7] and John Caird the tinkler, wha entered into the secrets,[8] and Elizabeth Melvill, Lady Culross,[9] wha prayed in her bed, surrounded by a great many Christians in a large room, in whilk it was placed on purpose, and that for three hours' time, with wonderful assistance; and Lady Robertland,[10] whilk got sic rare outgates of grace, and mony other in times past; and of a specialty, Mr John Scrimgeour,[11] minister of Kinghorn, who having a beloved child sick to death of the crewels,* was free to expostulate with his Maker with such impatience of displeasure, and complaining so bitterly, that at length it was said unto him, that he was heard for this time, but that he was requested to use no such boldness

* Kings-evil.

in time coming; so that when he returned he found the child sitting up in the bed hale and fair, with all its wounds closed, and supping its parritch, whilk babe he had left at the point of death. But though these things might be true in these needful times, she contended that those ministers who had not seen such vouchsafed and especial mercies, were to seek their rule in the records of ancient times; and therefore Reuben was carefu' both to search the Scriptures and the books written by wise and good men of old; and sometimes in this way it wad happen that twa precious saints might pu' sundry wise, like twa cows riving at the same hay-band."

To this David used to reply, with a sigh, "Ah, hinny, thou kenn'st little o't; but that saam John Scrimgeour, that blew open the gates of heaven as an it had been wi' a sax-pund cannon-ball, used devoutly to wish that most part of books were burned except the Bible.[12] Reuben's a gude lad and a kind—I have aye allowed that; but as to his not allowing enquiry anent the scandal of Margery Kittlesides and Rory MacRand, under pretence that they have southered sin wi' marriage, it's clear again the Christian discipline o' the kirk. And then there's Aily MacClure of Deepheugh,[13] that practises her abominations, spaeing folks' fortunes wi' egg-shells and mutton-banes,[14] and dreams and divinations, whilk is a scandal to ony Christian land to suffer a witch to live;[15] and I'll uphaud that in a' judicatures, civil or ecclesiastical."

"I dare say ye are very right, father," was the general style of Jeanie's answer; "but ye maun come down to the Manse to your dinner the day. The bits o' bairns, puir things, are wearying to see their luckie-dad; and Reuben never sleeps weel, nor I neither, when you and he hae had ony bit outcast."

"Nae outcast, Jeanie; God forbid I suld cast out wi' thee, or aught that is dear to thee." And he put on his Sunday's coat, and came to the Manse accordingly.

With her husband, Mrs Butler had a more direct conciliatory process. Reuben had the utmost respect for the old man's motives, and affection for his person, as well as gratitude for his early friendship. So that, upon any such occasion of accidental irritation, it was only necessary to remind him with delicacy of his father-in-law's age, of his scanty education, strong prejudices, and family distresses. The least of these considerations always inclined Butler to measures of conciliation, in so far as he could accede to them without compromising principle; and thus our simple and unpretending heroine had the merit of those peace-makers, to whom it is pronounced[16] as a benediction, that they shall inherit the earth.

The second Crook in Mrs Butler's Lot,[17] to use the language of her father, was the distressing circumstance, that she had never heard of her sister's safety, or of the circumstances in which she found herself, though betwixt four and five years had elapsed since they had parted on the beach of the island of Roseneath. Frequent intercourse was not to be expected—not to be desired, perhaps, in their relative situations; but Effie had promised, that, if she lived and prospered, her sister should hear from her. She must then be no more, or sunk into some abyss of misery, since she had never redeemed her pledge. Her silence seemed strange and portentous, and wrung from Jeanie, who could never forget the early years of their intimacy, the most painful anticipation concerning her fate. At length, however, the veil was drawn aside.

One day, as the Captain of Knockdunder had called in at the Manse, on his return from some business in the Highland part of the parish, and had been accommodated, according to his special request, with a mixture of milk, brandy,[18] honey, and water, which he said Mrs Butler compounded "petter than ever a woman in Scotland,"— for, in all innocent matters, she studied the taste of every one around her,—he said to Butler, "Py the pye, minister, I have a letter here either for your canny pody of a wife or you, which I got when I was last at Glasco; the postage[19] comes to fourpence, which you may either pay me forthwith, or give me tooble or quitts in a hitt at pack-cammon."

The playing at back-gammon and draughts had been a frequent amusement of Mr Whackbairn, Butler's principal, when at Libberton school. The minister, therefore, still piqued himself on his skill at both games, and occasionally practised them, as strictly canonical,[20] although David Deans, whose notions of every kind were more rigorous, used to shake his head, and groan grievously, when he espied the tables lying in the parlour, or the children playing with the dice-boxes or back-gammon men. Indeed Mrs Butler was sometimes chidden for removing these implements of pastime into some closet or corner out of sight. "Let them be where they are, Jeanie," would Butler say upon such occasions; "I am not conscious of following this, or any other trifling relaxation, to the interruption of my more serious studies, and still more serious duties. I will not therefore, have it supposed, that I am indulging by stealth, and against my conscience, in an amusement which, using it so little as I do, I may well practise openly, and without any check of mind—*Nil conscire sibi*, Jeanie, that is my motto; which signifies, my love, the honest and open confidence which a man ought to entertain, when he is acting openly, and without any sense of doing wrong."

Such being Butler's humour, he accepted the Captain's defiance to a twopenny-hit at back-gammon, and handed the letter to his wife, observing, the post-mark was York, but, if it came from her friend Mrs Bickerton, she had considerably improved her hand-writing, which was uncommon at her years.

Leaving the gentlemen to their game, Mrs Butler went to order something for supper, for Captain Duncan had proposed kindly to stay the night with them, and then carelessly broke open her letter. It was not from Mrs Bickerton, and, after glancing over the first few lines, she soon found it necessary to retire into her own bedroom, to read the document at leisure.

CHAPTER 48

Happy thou art! then happy be,
    Nor envy me my lot;
Thy happy state I envy thee,
    And peaceful cot.
                    LADY C— C—L

THE letter, which Mrs Butler, when retired into her own apartment, perused with anxious wonder, was certainly from Effie, although it had no other signature than the letter E.; and although the orthography, style, and penmanship, were very far superior not only to any thing which Effie could produce, who, though a lively girl, had been a remarkably careless scholar, but even to her more considerate sister's own powers of composition and expression. The manuscript was a fair Italian hand, though something stiff and constrained—the spelling and the diction those of a person who had been accustomed to read good composition and mix in good society.

The tenor of the letter was as follows:

"MY DEAREST SISTER,

"At many risks I venture to write to you, to inform you that I am still alive, and, as to worldly situation, that I rank higher than I could expect or merit. If wealth, and distinction, and an honourable rank, could make a woman happy, I have them all; but you, Jeanie, whom the world might think placed far beneath me in all these respects, are far happier than I am. I have had means of hearing of your welfare, my dearest Jeanie, from time to time—I think I should have broken my heart otherwise. I have learned with great pleasure of your increasing family. We have not been worthy of such a blessing; two infants have been successively removed, and we are now childless— God's will be done. But, if we had a child, it would perhaps divert him from the gloomy thoughts which make him terrible to himself and others. Yet do not let me frighten you, Jeanie; he continues to be kind, and I am far better off than I deserve. You will wonder at my better scholarship; but when I was abroad, I had the best teachers, and I worked hard because my progress pleased him. He is kind, Jeanie, only he has much to distress him, especially when he looks backward. When I look backward myself, I have always a ray of comfort; it is in the generous conduct of a sister, who forsook me not when I was forsaken by every one. You have had your reward. You live happy in the esteem and love of all who know you, and I drag on the life of a miserable impostor, indebted for the marks of regard I receive to a tissue of deceit and lies, which the slightest accident may unravel. He has produced me to his friends, since the estate opened to him, as the daughter of a Scotchman of rank, banished on account of the Viscount of Dundee's wars—that is, our Fr's old friend Clavers,[1] you know— and he says I was educated in a Scotch convent; indeed I lived in such a place long enough to enable me to support the character. But when a countryman approaches me, and begins to talk, as they all do, of the various families engaged in Dundee's affair, and to make enquiries into my connections, and when I see *his* eye bent on mine with such an expression of agony, my terror brings me to the very risk of detection. Good-nature and politeness have hitherto saved me, as they prevented people from pressing on me with distressing questions. But how long—O how long, will this be the case!—And if I bring this disgrace on him, he will hate me—he will kill me, for as much as he loves me; he is as jealous of his family honour now, as ever he was careless about it. I have been in England four months, and have often thought of writing to you; and yet, such are the dangers that might arise from an intercepted letter, that I have hitherto forborne. But now I am obliged to run the risk. Last week I saw your great friend, the D. of A. He came to my box, and sate by me; and something in the play put him in mind of you—Gracious Heaven! he told over your whole London journey to all who were in the box, but particularly to the wretched creature who was the occasion of it all. If he had known—if he could have conceived, beside whom he was sitting, and to whom the story was told!—I suffered with courage, like an Indian at the stake, while they are rending his fibres and boring his eyes,[2] and while he smiles applause at each well-imagined contrivance of his torturers. It was too much for me at last, Jeanie—I fainted; and my agony was imputed partly to the heat of the place, and partly to my extreme sensibility; and, hypocrite all over, I encouraged both opinions—any thing but discovery. Luckily *he* was not there. But the incident has led to more alarms. I am obliged to meet your great man often; and he seldom sees me without talking of E.D. and J.D., and R.B. and D.D., as persons in whom my amiable sensibility[3] is interested. My amiable sensibility!!!—And then the cruel tone of light indifference with which persons in the fashionable world speak together on the most affecting subjects! To hear my guilt, my folly, my agony, the foibles and weaknesses of my friends—even your heroic exertions, Jeanie, spoken of in the drolling style which is the present tone in fashionable life—Scarce all that I formerly endured is equal to this state of irritation—then it was blows and stabs—now it is pricking to death with needles and pins.—He—I mean the D.—goes down next month to spend the shooting-season[4] in Scotland—he says, he makes a point of always dining one day at the Manse—be on your guard, and do not betray yourself, should he mention me—Yourself, alas! *you* have nothing to betray—nothing to fear—you, the pure, the virtuous, the heroine of unstained faith, unblemished purity, what can you have to fear from the world or its proudest minions?—It is E. whose life is once more in your hands—it is E. whom you are to save from being plucked of her borrowed plumes, discovered, branded, and trodden down, first by him, perhaps, who has raised her to this dizzy pinnacle!—The inclosure will reach you twice a-year—do not refuse it—it is out of my own allowance, and may be twice as much when you want it. With you it may do good—with me it never can.

"Write to me soon, Jeanie, or I shall remain in the agonizing apprehension that this has fallen into wrong hands—Address simply to L.S., under cover, to the Reverend George Whiterose,[5] in the Minster-Close, York. He thinks I correspond with some of my noble Jacobite relations who are in Scotland. How high-church and jacobitical zeal would burn in his cheeks, if he knew he was the agent, not of Euphemia Setoun, of the honourable house of Winton,[6] but of E.D., daughter of a Cameronian cow-feeder!—Jeanie, I can laugh yet sometimes—but God protect you from such mirth.—My father—I mean your father, would say it was like the idle crackling of fire among thorns;[7] but the thorns keep their poignancy, they remain unconsumed.[8]—Farewell, my dearest Jeanie—Do not show this even to Mr Butler, much less to any one else—I have every respect for him, but his principles are over strict, and my case will not endure severe handling.—I rest your affectionate sister, E."

In this long letter there was much to surprise as well as to distress Mrs Butler. That Effie—her sister Effie, should be mingling freely in society, and apparently on not unequal terms, with the Duke of

Argyle, sounded like something so extraordinary, that she even doubted if she read truly. Nor was it less marvellous, that, in the space of four years, her education should have made such progress. Jeanie's humility readily allowed that Effie had always, when she chose it, been smarter at her book than she herself was, but then she was very idle, and, upon the whole, had made much less proficiency. Love, or fear, or necessity, however, had proved an able school-mistress, and completely supplied all her deficiencies.

What Jeanie least liked in the tone of the letter was a smothered degree of egotism. "We should have heard little about her," said Jeanie to herself, "but that she was feared the Duke might come to learn wha she was, and a' about her puir friends here; but Effie, puir thing, aye looks her ain way, and folks that do that think mair o' themselves than of their neighbours.——I am no clear about keeping her siller," she added, taking up a 50l. note which had fallen out of the paper to the floor. "We hae aneugh, and it looks unco like theft-boot, or hush-money, as they ca' it; she might hae been sure that I wad say naething wad harm her, for a' the gowd in Lunnon. And I maun tell the minister about it. I dinna see that she suld be sae feared for her ain bonnie bargain o' a gudeman, and that I shouldna reverence Mr Butler just as much; and sae I'll e'en tell him, when that tippling body the Captain has ta'en boat in the morning.——But I wonder at my ain state of mind," she added, turning back, after she had made a step or two to the door to join the gentlemen; "surely I am no sic a fule as to be angry that Effie's a braw lady, while I am only a minister's wife?—— and yet I am as petted as a bairn, when I should bless God, that has redeemed her from shame, and poverty, and guilt, as ower likely she might hae been plunged into."

Sitting down upon a stool at the foot of the bed, she folded her arms upon her bosom, saying within herself, "From this place will I not rise till I am in a better frame of mind;" and so placed, by dint of tearing the veil from the motives of her little temporary spleen against her sister, she compelled herself to be ashamed of them, and to view as blessings the advantages of her sister's lot, while its embarrassments were the necessary consequences of errors long since committed. And thus she fairly vanquished the feeling of pique which she naturally enough entertained, at seeing Effie, so long the object of her care and her pity, soar suddenly so high above her in life, as to reckon amongst the chief objects of her apprehension the risk of their relationship being discovered.

When this unwonted burst of *amour propre* was thoroughly subdued, she walked down to the little parlour where the gentlemen were finishing their game, and heard from the Captain a confirmation of the news intimated in her letter, that the Duke of Argyle was shortly expected at Roseneath.

"He'll find plenty of moor-pouts and plack-cock on the moors of Auchingower, and he'll pe nae doubt for taking a late dinner, and a ped at the Manse, as he has done pefore now."

"He has a gude right, Captain," said Jeanie.

"Teil ane petter to ony ped in the kintra," answered the Captain. "And ye had petter tell your father, puir pody, to get his beasts a' in order, and put his tamned Cameronian nonsense out o' his head for twa or three days, if he can pe so opliging; for fan I speak to him apout prute pestial, he answers me out o' the Pible, whilk is not using a shentleman weel, unless it pe a person of your cloth, Mr Putler."

No one understood better than Jeanie the merit of the soft answer, which turneth away wrath;[9] and she only smiled, and hoped that his Grace would find every thing that was under her father's care to his entire satisfaction.

But the Captain, who had lost the whole postage of the letter at back-gammon, was in the pouting mood not unusual to losers, and which, says the proverb,[10] must be allowed to them.

"And, Master Putler, though you know I never meddle with the things of your kirk-sessions, yet I must pe allowed to say that I will not pe pleased to allow Ailie MacClure of Deepheugh to be poonished as a witch, in respect she only spaes fortunes, and does not lame, or plind, or pedevil any persons, or coup cadgers' carts, or ony sort of mischief; put only tells people good fortunes, as anent our poats killing so many seals and doug-fishes, whilk is very pleasant to hear."

"The woman," said Butler, "is, I believe, no witch, but a cheat;[11] and it is only on that head that she is summoned to the kirk-session, to cause her to desist in future from practising her impostures upon ignorant persons."

"I do not know," replied the gracious Duncan, "what her practices or her postures are, but I pelieve that if the poys take hould on her to duck her in the Clachan-purn, it will be a very sorry practice—and I pelieve, moreover, that if I come in thirdsman among you at the kirk-sessions, you will pe all in a tamn'd pad posture indeed."

Without noticing this threat, Mr Butler replied, "That he had not attended to the risk of ill usage which the poor woman might undergo at the hands of the rabble, and that he would give her the necessary admonition in private, instead of bringing her before the assembled session."

"This," Duncan said, "was speaking like a reasonable shentleman;" and so the evening passed peaceably off.

Next morning, after the Captain had swallowed his morning draught of Athole brose, and departed in his coach and six, Mrs Butler anew deliberated upon communicating to her husband her sister's letter. But she was deterred by the recollection, that in doing so she would unveil to him the whole of a dreadful secret, of which, perhaps, his public character might render him an unfit depositary. Butler already had reason to believe that Effie had eloped with that same Robertson who had been a leader in the Porteous mob, and who lay under sentence of death for the robbery at Kirkcaldy. But he did not know his identity with George Staunton, a man of birth and fortune, who had now apparently reassumed his natural rank in society. He did not know this fact and no good could come to any one from imparting it to him. Jeanie had respected Staunton's own confession as sacred, and upon reflection she considered the letter of her sister as equally so, and resolved to mention the contents to no one.

On reperusing the letter, she could not help observing the staggering and unsatisfactory condition of those who have risen to distinction by undue paths, and the outworks and bulwarks of fiction and falsehood, by which they are under the necessity of surrounding and defending their precarious advantages. But she was not called upon, she thought, to unveil her sister's original history—it would restore no right to any one, for she was usurping none—it would only destroy her happiness, and degrade her in the public estimation. Had she been wise, Jeanie thought she would have chosen seclusion and privacy, in place of public life and gaiety; but the power of choice might not be hers. The money she thought could not be returned without her seeming haughty and unkind. She resolved, therefore, upon reconsidering this point, to employ it as occasion should serve, either in educating her children better than her own means could compass, or for their future portion. Her sister had enough, was strongly bound to assist Jeanie by any means in her power, and the arrangement was so natural and proper, that it ought not to be declined out of fastidious or romantic delicacy. Jeanie accordingly wrote to her sister, acknowledging her letter, and requesting to hear from her as often as she could. In entering into her own little details of news, chiefly respecting domestic affairs, she experienced a singular vacillation of ideas; for sometimes she apologized for mentioning things unworthy the notice of a lady of rank, and then recollected that every thing which concerned her should be interesting to Effie. Her letter, under the cover of Mr Whiterose, she committed to the post-office at Glasgow, by the intervention of a parishioner who had business at that city.

The next week brought the Duke to Roseneath, and shortly afterwards he intimated his intention of sporting in their neighbourhood, and taking his bed at the Manse, an honour which he had once or twice done to its inmates on former occasions.

Effie proved to be perfectly right in her anticipations. The Duke had hardly set himself down at Mrs Butler's right hand, and taken upon himself the task of carving the excellent "barn-door chucky," which had been selected as the high dish upon this honourable occasion, before he began to speak of Lady Staunton of Willingham in Lincolnshire, and the great noise which her wit and beauty made in London. For much of this Jeanie was, in some measure, prepared— but Effie's wit! that would never have entered into her imagination, being ignorant how exactly raillery in the higher rank resembles flippancy among their inferiors.

"She has been the ruling belle—the blazing star—the universal toast of the winter," said the Duke; "and is really the most beautiful creature that was seen at court upon the birth-day."[12]

The birth-day! and at court!—Jeanie was annihilated, remembering well her own presentation, all its extraordinary circumstances, and particularly the cause of it.

"I mention this lady particularly to you, Mrs Butler," said the Duke, "because she has something in the sound of her voice, and cast of her countenance, that reminded me of you—not when you look so pale though—you have over-fatigued yourself—you must pledge me in a glass of wine."

She did so, and Butler observed, "It was dangerous flattery in his Grace to tell a poor minister's wife that she was like a court-beauty."

"Oho! Mr Butler," said the Duke, "I find you are growing jealous; but it's rather too late in the day, for you know how long I have admired your wife. But seriously, there is betwixt them one of those inexplicable likenesses which we see in countenances, that do not otherwise resemble each other."

"The perilous part of the compliment has flown off," thought Mr Butler.

His wife, feeling the awkwardness of silence, forced herself to say, "That, perhaps, the lady might be her countrywoman, and the language might make some resemblance."

"You are quite right," replied the Duke. "She is a Scotchwoman, and speaks with a Scotch accent, and now and then a provincial word drops out so prettily, that it is quite Doric, Mr Butler."

"I should have thought," said the clergyman, "that would have sounded vulgar in the great city."

"Not at all," replied the Duke; "you must suppose it is not the broad coarse Scotch that is spoke in the Cowgate of Edinburgh, or in the Gorbals.[13] This lady has been very little in Scotland, in fact—She was educated in a convent abroad, and speaks that pure court-Scotish[14] which was common in my younger days; but it is so generally disused now, that it sounds like a different dialect, entirely distinct from our modern *patois*."

Notwithstanding her anxiety, Jeanie could not help admiring within herself, how the most correct judges of life and manners can be imposed on by their own preconceptions, while the Duke proceeded thus: "She is of the unfortunate house of Wintoun, I believe; but, being bred abroad, she had missed the opportunity of learning her own pedigree, and was obliged to me for informing her, that she must certainly come of the Setons of Windygoul.[15] I wish you could have seen how prettily she blushed at her own ignorance. Amidst her noble and elegant manners, there is now and then a little touch of bashfulness and conventual rusticity, if I may call it so, that makes her quite enchanting. You see at once the rose that has bloomed untouched amid the chaste precincts of the cloister, Mr Butler."

True to the hint, Mr Butler failed not to start with his

"Ut flos in septis secretus nascitur hortis,"[16] &c.

while his wife could hardly persuade herself that all this was spoken of Effie Deans, and by so competent a judge as the Duke of Argyle; and had she been acquainted with Catullus, would have thought the fortunes of her sister had reversed the whole passage.[17]

She was, however, determined to obtain some indemnification for the anxious feelings of the moment, by gaining all the intelligence she could; and therefore ventured to make some enquiry about the husband of the lady his Grace admired so much.

"He is very rich," replied the Duke; "of an ancient family, and has good manners; but he is far from being such a general favourite as his wife.—Some people say he can be very pleasant—I never saw him so; but should rather judge him reserved, and gloomy, and capricious. He was very wild in his youth, they say, and has bad health;[18] yet he is a good-looking man enough—a great friend of your Lord High Commissioner of the Kirk, Mr Butler."

"Then he is the friend of a very worthy and honourable nobleman," said Butler.

"Does he admire his lady as much as other people do?" said Jeanie, in a low voice.

"Who—Sir George? They say he is very fond of her," said the Duke; "but I observe she trembles a little when he fixes his eye on her, and that is no good sign—But it is strange how I am haunted by this resemblance of yours to Lady Staunton, in look and tone of voice. One would almost swear you were sisters."

Jeanie's distress became uncontroulable, and beyond concealment. The Duke of Argyle was much disturbed, good-naturedly ascribing it to his having unwittingly recalled to her remembrance her family misfortunes. He was too well-bred to attempt to apologize; but hastened to change the subject, and arrange certain points of dispute which had occurred betwixt Duncan of Knock and the minister, acknowledging that his worthy substitute was sometimes a little too obstinate, as well as too energetic, in his executive measures.

Mr Butler admitted his general merits; but said, "He would presume to apply to the worthy gentleman the words of the poet to Marrucinus Asinius,

Manu——
Non belle uteris in joco atque vino."[19]

The discourse being thus turned on parish-business, nothing farther occurred that can interest the reader.

CHAPTER 49

Upon my head they placed a fruitless crown,
And put a barren sceptre in my gripe,
Thence to be wrench'd by an unlineal hand,
No son of mine succeeding.

Macbeth

AFTER this period, but under the most strict precautions against discovery, the sisters corresponded occasionally, exchanging letters about twice every year. Those of Lady Staunton spoke of her husband's health and spirits as being deplorably uncertain; her own seemed also to be sinking, and one of the topics on which she most frequently dwelt, was their want of family. Sir George Staunton, always violent, had taken some aversion at the next heir, whom he suspected of having irritated his friends against him during his absence; and he declared, he would bequeath Willingham and all its lands to an hospital, ere that fetch-and-carry tell-tale should inherit an acre of it.

"Had he but a child," said the unfortunate wife, "or had that luckless infant survived, it would be some motive for living and for exertion. But Heaven has denied us a blessing which we have not deserved."

Such complaints, in varied form, but turning frequently on the same topic, filled the letters which passed from the spacious but melancholy halls of Willingham, to the quiet and happy parsonage at Knocktarlitie. Years meanwhile rolled on amid these fruitless repinings. John Duke of Argyle and Greenwich died in the year 1743, universally lamented, but by none more than by the Butlers, to whom his benevolence had been so distinguished. He was succeeded by his brother Duke Archibald,[1] with whom they had not the same intimacy; but who continued the protection which his brother had extended towards them. This, indeed, became more necessary than ever; for, after the breaking out and suppression of the rebellion in 1745,[2] the peace of the country, adjacent to the Highlands, was considerably disturbed. Marauders, or men that had been driven to that desperate mode of life, quartered themselves in the fastnesses nearest to the

Lowlands, which were their scene of plunder; and there is scarce a glen in the romantic and now peaceable highlands of Perth, Stirling, and Dumbartonshires, where one or more did not take up their residence.

The prime pest of the parish of Knocktarlitie was a certain Donacha dhu na Dunaigh, or Black Duncan the Mischievous, whom we have already casually mentioned. This fellow had been originally a tinkler or *caird*, many of whom stroll about these districts; but when all police was disorganized by the civil war, he threw up his profession, and from half thief became whole robber; and being generally at the head of three or four active young fellows, and he himself artful, bold, and well acquainted with the passes, he plied his new profession with emolument to himself, and infinite plague to the country.

All were convinced that Duncan of Knock could have put down his namesake Donacha any morning he had a mind; for there were in the parish a set of stout young men, who had joined Argyle's banner[3] in the war under his old friend, and behaved very well upon several occasions. And as for their leader, as no one doubted his courage, it was generally supposed that Donacha had found out the mode of conciliating his favour, a thing not very uncommon in that age and country. This was the more readily believed, as David Deans's cattle (being the property of the Duke) were left untouched, when the minister's cows were carried off by the thieves. Another attempt was made to renew the same act of rapine, and the cattle were in the act of being driven off, when Butler, laying his profession aside in a case of such necessity, put himself at the head of some of his neighbours, and rescued the creagh, an exploit at which Deans attended in person, notwithstanding his extreme old age, mounted on a Highland pony, and girded with an old broadsword, likening himself (for he failed not to arrogate the whole merit of the expedition) to David, the son of Jesse, when he recovered the spoil of Ziklag[4] from the Amalekites. This spirited behaviour had so far a good effect, that Donacha dhu na Dunaigh kept his distance for some time to come; and, though his distant exploits were frequently spoken of, he did not exercise any depredations in that part of the country. He continued to flourish, and to be heard of occasionally, until the year 1751, when, if the fear of the second David had kept him in check, fate released him from that restraint, for the venerable patriarch of St Leonard's was that year gathered to his fathers.

David Deans died full of years and of honour. He is believed, for the exact time of his birth is not known, to have lived upwards of ninety years; for he used to speak of events, as falling under his own knowledge, which happened about the time of the battle of Bothwell-Bridge.[5] It was said that he even bore arms there; for once, when a drunken Jacobite laird wished for a Bothwell-Brigg whig, that "he might stow the lugs out of his head," David informed him with a peculiar austerity of countenance, that if he liked to try such a prank, there was one at his elbow; and it required the interference of Butler to preserve the peace.

He expired in the arms of his beloved daughter, thankful for all the blessings which Providence had vouchsafed to him while in this valley of strife and toil—and thankful also for the trials he had been visited with; having found them, he said, needful to mortify that spiritual pride and confidence in his own gifts, which was the side on which the wily Enemy did most sorely beset him. He prayed in the most affecting manner for Jeanie, her husband, and her family, and that her affectionate duty to the puir auld man might purchase her length of days here, and happiness hereafter; then, in a pathetic petition, too well understood by those who knew his family circumstances, he besought the Shepherd of souls, while gathering his flock, not to forget the little one that had strayed from the fold, and even then might be in the hands of the ravening wolf.—He prayed for the national Jerusalem, that peace might be in her land and prosperity in her palaces—for the welfare of the honourable House of Argyle, and for the conversion of Duncan of Knockdunder. After this he was silent, being exhausted, nor did he again utter any thing distinctly. He was heard indeed to mutter something about national defections, right-hand extremes, and left-hand fallings off;[6] but, as May Hettly observed, his head was carried at the time: and it is probable that these expressions occurred to him merely out of general habit, and that he died in the full spirit of charity with all men. About an hour afterwards he slept in the Lord.

Notwithstanding her father's advanced age, his death was a severe shock to Mrs Butler. Much of her time had been dedicated to attending to his health and his wishes, and she felt as if part of her business in the world was ended, when the good old man was no more. His wealth, which came nearly to fifteen hundred pounds, in disposable capital, served to raise the fortunes of the family at the Manse. How to dispose of this sum for the best advantage of his family, was matter of anxious consideration to Butler.

"If we put it on heritable bond, we shall maybe lose the interest; for there's that bond over Lounsbeck's land, your father could neither get principal nor interest for it—If we bring it into the funds, we shall maybe lose the principal and all, as many did in the South-sea scheme.[7] The little estate of Craigsture is in the market—it lies within two miles of the Manse, and Knock says his Grace has no thought to buy it. But they ask £2,500, and they may, for it is worth the money; and were I to borrow the balance, the creditor might call it up suddenly, or in case of my death my family might be distressed."

"And so, if we had mair siller, we might buy that bonnie pasture-ground, where the grass comes so early?" asked Jeanie.

"Certainly, my dear; and Knockdunder, who is a good judge, is strongly advising me to it.—To be sure it is his nephew that is selling it."

"Aweel, Reuben," said Jeanie, "ye maun just look up a text in Scripture, as ye did when ye wanted siller before—just look up a text in the Bible."

"Ah, Jeanie," said Butler, laughing and pressing her hand at the same time, "the best people in these times can only work miracles once."

"We will see," said Jeanie composedly; and, going to the closet in which she kept her honey, her sugar, her pots of jelly, her vials of the more ordinary medicines, and which served her, in short, as a sort of store-room, she jangled vials and gallipots, till, from out the darkest nook, well flanked by a triple row of bottles and jars, which she was under the necessity of displacing, she brought a cracked brown cann, with a piece of leather tied over the top. Its contents seemed to be written papers, thrust in disorder into this uncommon *secrétaire*. But from among these Jeanie brought an old clasped Bible, which had been David Deans's companion in his earlier wanderings, and which he had given to his daughter when the failure of his eyes had compelled him to use one of a larger print. This she gave to Butler, who had been looking at her motions with some surprise, and desired him to see what that book could do for him. He opened the clasps, and to his astonishment a parcel of £50 bank-notes dropped out from betwixt the leaves, where they had been separately lodged, and fluttered upon the floor. "I didna think to hae tauld you o' my wealth, Reuben," said his wife, smiling at his surprise, "till on my death-bed, or maybe on some family pinch; but it wad be better laid out on yon bonny grass-holms, than lying useless here in this auld pigg."

"How on earth came ye by that siller, Jeanie?—Why, here is more than a thousand pounds," said Butler, lifting up and counting the notes.

"If it were ten thousand, it's a' honestly come by," said Jeanie; "and troth I kenna how muckle there is o't, but it's a' there that ever I got.—And as for how I came by it, Reuben—it's weel come by, and honestly, as I said before—And it's mair folk's secret than mine, or ye wad hae kend about it lang syne; and as for ony thing else, I am not free to answer mair questions about it, and ye maun just ask me nane."

"Answer me but one," said Butler. "Is it all freely and indisputably your own property, to dispose of it as you think fit?—Is it possible no one has a claim in so large a sum except you?"

"It *was* mine, free to dispose of it as I like," answered Jeanie; "and I have disposed of it already, for now it is yours, Reuben—You are Bible Butler now, as weel as your forbear, that my puir father had sic an ill will at. Only if ye like, I wad wish Femie to get a gude share o 't when we are gane."

"Certainly, it shall be as you chuse—But who on earth ever pitched on such a hiding-place for temporal treasures?"

"That is just ane o' my auld-fashioned gates, as you ca' them, Reuben. I thought if Donacha Dhu was to make an outbreak upon us, the Bible was the last thing in the house he wad meddle wi'—but an ony mair siller should drap in, as it is not unlikely, I shall e'en pay it ower to you, and ye may lay it out your ain way."

"And I positively must not ask you how you have come by all this money?" said the clergyman.

"Indeed, Reuben, you must not; for if you were asking me very sair I wad maybe tell you, and then I am sure I would do wrong."

"But tell me," said Butler, "is it any thing that distresses your own mind?"

"There is baith weal and woe come aye wi' warld's gear,[8] Reuben; but ye maun ask me naething mair—This siller binds me to naething, and can never be speered back again."

"Surely," said Mr Butler, when he had again counted over the money, as if to assure himself that the notes were real, "there was never man in the world had a wife like mine—a blessing seems to follow her."

"Never," said Jeanie, "since the enchanted princess in the bairns' fairy tale,[9] that kamed gold nobles out o' the tae side of her haffit locks, and Dutch dollars out o' the tother. But gang away now, minister, and put by the siller, and dinna keep the notes wampishing in your hand that gate, or I shall wish them in the brown pigg again, for fear we get a black cast about them—we're ower near the hills in these times to be thought to hae siller in the house. And, besides, ye maun gree wi' Knockdunder, that has the selling o' the lands; and dinna you be simple and let him ken o' this windfa', but keep him to the very barest penny, as if ye had to borrow siller to make the price up."

In the last admonition Jeanie showed distinctly, that, although she did not understand how to secure the money which came into her hands otherwise than by saving and hoarding it, yet she had some part of her father David's shrewdness, even upon worldly subjects. And Reuben Butler was a prudent man, and went and did even as his wife had advised him.

The news quickly went abroad into the parish that the minister had bought Craigsture; and some wished him joy, and some "were sorry it had gane out of the auld name." However, his clerical brethren, understanding that he was under the necessity of going to Edinburgh about the ensuing Whitsunday, to get together David Deans's cash to make up the purchase-money of his new acquisition, took the opportunity to name him their delegate to the General Assembly, or Convocation of the Scottish Church, which takes place yearly in the latter end of the month of May.

CHAPTER 50

But who is this? what thing of sea or land—
Female of sex it seems—
That so bedeck'd, ornate, and gay,
Comes this way sailing?

MILTON

NOT long after the incident of the Bible and the bank-notes, Fortune showed that she could surprise Mrs Butler as well as her husband. The minister, in order to accomplish the various pieces of business, which his unwonted visit to Edinburgh rendered necessary, had been under the necessity of setting out from home in the latter end of the month of February, concluding justly, that he would find the space betwixt his departure and the term of Whitsunday (24th May) short enough for the purpose of bringing forward those various debtors of old David Deans, out of whose purses a considerable part of the price of his new purchase was to be made good.

Jeanie was thus in the unwonted situation of inhabiting a lonely house, and she felt yet more solitary from the death of the good old man, who used to divide her cares with her husband. Her children were her principal resource, and to them she paid constant attention.

It happened, a day or two after Butler's departure, that, while she was engaged in some domestic duties, she heard a dispute among the young folks, which, being maintained with obstinacy, appeared to call for her interference. All came to their natural umpire with their complaints. Femie, not yet ten years old, charged Davie and Reubie with an attempt to take away her book by force; and David and Reuben replied, the elder, "That it was not a book for Femie to read," and Reuben, "That it was about a bad woman."

"Where did ye get the book, ye little hempie?" said Mrs Butler. "How dare ye touch papa's books when he is away?"

But the little lady, holding fast a sheet of crumpled paper, declared, "It was nane o' papa's books, and May Hettly had taken it off the muckle cheese which came from Inverara;" for, as was very natural to suppose, a friendly intercourse, with interchange of mutual civilities, was kept up from time to time between Mrs Dolly Dutton, now Mrs MacCorkindale, and her former friends.

Jeanie took the subject of contention out of the child's hand, to satisfy herself of the propriety of her studies; but how much was she struck when she read upon the title of the broadside-sheet, "The Last Speech, Confession, and Dying Words of Margaret MacCraw, or Murdockson,[1] executed on Harabee-hill, near Carlisle, the — day of —— 1737." It was, indeed, one of those papers which Archibald had bought at Longtown, when he monopolized the pedlar's stock, which Dolly had thrust into her trunk out of sheer economy. One or two copies, it seems, had remained in her repositories at Inverara, till she chanced to need them in packing a cheese, which, as a very superior production, was sent, in the way of civil challenge, to the dairy at Knocktarlitie.

The title of this paper, so strangely fallen into the very hands from which, in well-meant respect to her feelings, it had been so long detained, was of itself sufficiently startling; but the narrative was so interesting, that Jeanie, shaking herself loose from the children, ran up stairs to her own apartment, and bolted the door, to peruse it without interruption.

The narrative, which appeared to have been drawn up, or at least corrected, by the clergyman who attended this unhappy woman, stated the crime for which she suffered to have been "her active part in that atrocious robbery and murder, committed near two years since near Haltwhistle,[2] for which the notorious Frank Levitt was committed for trial at Lancaster assizes. It was supposed the evidence of the accomplice, Thomas Tuck, commonly called Tyburn Tom, upon which the woman had been convicted, would weigh equally heavy against him; although many were inclined to think it was Tuck himself who had struck the fatal blow, according to the dying statement of Meg Murdockson."

After a circumstantial account of the crime for which she suffered, there was a brief sketch of Margaret's life. It was stated, that she was a Scotchwoman by birth, and married a soldier in the Cameronian regiment—that she long followed the camp, and had doubtless acquired in fields of battle, and similar scenes, that ferocity and love of plunder for which she had been afterwards distinguished—that her husband, having obtained his discharge, became servant to a beneficed clergyman of high situation and character in Lincolnshire, and that she acquired the confidence and esteem of that honourable family. She had lost this many years after her husband's death, it was stated, in consequence of conniving at the irregularities of her daughter with the heir of the family, added to the suspicious circumstances attending the birth of a child, which was strongly suspected to have met with foul play, in order to preserve, if possible, the girl's reputation. After this, she had led a wandering life both in England and Scotland, under colour sometimes of telling fortunes, sometimes of driving a trade in smuggled wares, but, in fact, receiving stolen goods, and occasionally actively joining in the exploits by which they were obtained. Many of her crimes she had boasted of after conviction, and there was one circumstance for which she seemed to feel a mixture of joy and occasional compunction. When she was residing in the suburbs of Edinburgh during the preceding summer, a girl, who had been seduced by one of her confederates, was entrusted to her charge, and in her house delivered of a male infant. Her daughter, whose mind was in a state of derangement ever since she had lost her own child, according to the criminal's account, carried off the poor girl's infant, taking it for her own, of the reality of whose death she at times could not be persuaded.

Margaret Murdockson stated, that she, for some time, believed her daughter had actually destroyed the infant in her mad fits, and that she gave the father to understand so, but afterwards learned that a female stroller had got it from her. She showed some compunction at having separated mother and child, especially as the mother had nearly suffered death, being condemned, on the Scotch law, for the supposed murther of her infant. When it was asked what possible interest she could have had in exposing the unfortunate girl to suffer for a crime she had not committed, she asked, if they thought she was going to put her own daughter into trouble to save another? she did not know what the Scotch law would have done to her for carrying the child away. This answer was by no means satisfactory to the clergyman, and he discovered, by close examination, that she had a deep and revengeful hatred against the young person whom she had thus injured. But the paper intimated, that, whatever besides she had communicated upon this subject, was confided by her in private to the worthy and reverend Arch-Deacon who had bestowed such particular pains in affording her spiritual assistance. The broadside went on to intimate, that after her execution, of which the particulars were given, her daughter, the insane person mentioned more than once, and who was generally known by the name of Madge Wildfire, had been very ill used by the populace, under the belief that she was a sorceress, and an accomplice in her mother's crimes, and had been with difficulty rescued by the prompt interference of the police.

Such (for we omit moral reflections, and all that may seem unnecessary to the explanation of our story,) was the tenor of the broadside. To Mrs Butler it contained intelligence of the highest importance, since it seemed to afford the most unequivocal proof of her sister's innocence respecting the crime for which she had so nearly suffered. It is true, neither she nor her husband, nor even her father, had ever believed her capable of touching her infant with an unkind hand when in possession of her reason; but there was a darkness on the subject, and what might have happened in a moment of insanity was dreadful to think upon. Besides, whatever was their own conviction, they had no means of establishing Effie's innocence to the world, which, according to the tenor of this fugitive publication, was now at length completely manifested by the dying confession of the person chiefly interested in concealing it.

After thanking God for a discovery so dear to her feelings, Mrs Butler began to consider what use she should make of it. To have shown it to her husband would have been her first impulse, but, besides that he was absent from home, and the matter too delicate to be the subject of correspondence by an indifferent penwoman, Mrs Butler recollected that he was not possessed of the information necessary to form a judgment upon the occasion, and that, adhering to the rule which she had considered as most advisable, she had best transmit the information immediately to her sister, and leave her to adjust with her husband the mode in which they should avail themselves of it. Accordingly she dispatched a special messenger to Glasgow, with a packet, inclosing the Confession of Margaret Murdockson, addressed, as usual, under cover, to Mr Whiterose of York. She expected, with anxiety, an answer, but none arrived in the usual course of post, and she was left to imagine how many various causes might account for Lady Staunton's silence. She began to be half sorry that she had parted with the printed paper, both for fear of its having fallen into bad hands, and from the desire of regaining the document, which might be essential to establish her sister's innocence. She was even doubting whether she had not better commit the whole matter to her husband's consideration, when other incidents occurred to divert her purpose.

Jeanie (she is a favourite, and we beg her pardon for still using the familiar title) had walked down to the sea-side with her children one morning after breakfast, when the boys, whose sight was more discriminating than hers, exclaimed, that "the Captain's coach and six was coming right for the shore, with ladies in it." Jeanie instinctively bent her eyes on the approaching boat, and became soon sensible that there were two females in the stern, seated beside the gracious Duncan, who acted as pilot. It was a point of politeness to walk towards the landing-place, in order to receive them, especially as she saw that the Captain of Knockdunder was upon honour and ceremony. His piper was in the bow of the boat, sending forth music, of which one half sounded the better that the other was drowned by the waves and the breeze. Moreover, he himself had his brigadier wig newly frizzed, his bonnet (he had abjured the cocked hat) decorated with Saint George's red cross, his uniform mounted as a captain of militia, the Duke's flag with the boar's head displayed—all intimated parade and gala.

As Mrs Butler approached the landing-place, she observed the Captain hand the ladies ashore with marks of great attention, and the party advanced towards her, the Captain a few steps before the two ladies, of whom the taller and elder leaned on the shoulder of the other, who seemed to be an attendant or servant.

As they met, Duncan, in his best, most important, and deepest tone of Highland civility, "pegged leave to introduce to Mrs Putler, Lady—eh—eh—I hae forgotten your leddyship's name."

"Never mind my name, sir," said the lady; "I trust Mrs Butler will be at no loss. The Duke's letter"——And, as she observed Mrs Butler look confused, she said again to Duncan, something sharply, "Did you not send the letter last night, sir?"

"In troth and I didna, and I crave your leddyship's pardon; but you see, matam, I thought it would do as weel to-tay, pecause Mrs Putler is never taen out o' sorts—never—and the coach was out fishing—and the gig was gaen to Greenock for a cag of prandy—and——Put here's his Grace's letter."

"Give it me, sir," said the lady, taking it out of his hand; "since you have not found it convenient to do me the favour to send it before me, I will deliver it myself."

Mrs Butler looked with great attention, and a certain dubious feeling of deep interest on the lady, who thus expressed herself with authority over the man of authority, and to whose mandates he seemed to submit, resigning the letter with a "Just as your leddyship is pleased to order it."

The lady was rather above the middle size, beautifully made, though something *en bon point*, with a hand and arm exquisitely formed. Her manner was easy, dignified, and commanding, and seemed to evince high birth and the habits of elevated society. She wore a travelling dress—a grey beaver hat, and a veil of Flanders lace. Two footmen, in rich liveries, who got out of the barge, and lifted out a trunk and portmanteau, appeared to belong to her suite.

"As you did not receive the letter, madam, which should have served for my introduction—for I presume you are Mrs Butler—I will not present it to you till you are so good as to admit me into your house without it."

"To pe sure, matam," said Knockdunder, "ye canna doubt Mrs Putler will do that.—Mrs Putler, this is Lady—Lady—these tamn'd Southern names rin out o' my hieland head like a stane trowling down hill—put I pelieve she is a Scottish woman porn—the mair our credit—and I presume her leddyship is of the house of——"

"The Duke of Argyle knows my family very well, sir," said the lady, in a tone which seemed designed to silence Duncan, or, at any rate, which had that effect completely.

There was something about the whole of this stranger's address, and tone and manner, which acted upon Jeanie's feelings like the illusions of a dream, that teaze us with a puzzling approach to reality. Something there was of her sister in the gait and manner of the stranger, as well as in the sound of her voice, and something also, when, lifting her veil, she shewed features, to which, changed as they were in expression and complexion, she could not but attach many remembrances.

The stranger was turned of thirty certainly; but so well were her personal charms assisted by the power of dress, and arrangement of ornament, that she might well have passed for one-and-twenty. And her behaviour was so steady and so composed, that as often as Mrs Butler perceived anew some point of resemblance to her unfortunate sister, so often the sustained self-command and absolute composure of the stranger destroyed the ideas which began to arise in her imagination. She led the way silently towards the Manse, lost in a confusion of reflections, and trusting the letter with which she was to be there entrusted, would afford her satisfactory explanation of what was a most puzzling and embarrassing scene.

The lady maintained in the meanwhile the manners of a stranger of rank. She admired the various points of view like one who has studied nature, and the best representations of art. At length she took notice of the children.

"These are two fine young mountaineers—Yours, madam, I presume?"

Jeanie replied in the affirmative. The stranger sighed, and sighed once more as they were presented to her by name.

"Come here, Femie," said Mrs Butler, "and hold your head up."

"What is your daughter's name, madam?" said the lady.

"Euphemia, madam," answered Mrs Butler.

"I thought the ordinary Scottish contraction of the name had been Effie," replied the stranger in a tone which went to Jeanie's heart; for in that single word there was more of her sister—more of *lang syne* ideas—than in all the reminiscences which her own heart had anticipated, or the features and manner of the stranger had suggested.

When they reached the Manse, the lady gave Mrs Butler the letter which she had taken out of the hands of Knockdunder; and as she gave it she pressed her hand, adding aloud, "Perhaps, madam, you will have the goodness to get me a little milk."

"And me a drap of the grey-peard, if you please, Mrs Putler," added Duncan.

Mrs Butler withdrew, but deputing to May Hettly and to David the supply of the strangers' wants, she hastened into her own room to read the letter. The envelope was addressed in the Duke of Argyle's hand, and requested Mrs Butler's attentions and civility to a lady of rank, a particular friend of his late brother, Lady Staunton of Willingham, who being recommended to drink goats' whey by the physicians, was to honour the Lodge at Roseneath with her residence, while her husband made a short tour in Scotland. But within the same cover, which had been given to Lady Staunton unsealed, was a letter from that lady, intended to prepare her sister for meeting her, and which, but for the Captain's negligence, she ought to have received on the preceding evening. It stated that the news in Jeanie's last letter had been so interesting to her husband, that he was determined to enquire farther into the confession made at Carlisle, and the fate of that poor innocent, and that as he had been in some degree successful, she had by the most earnest entreaties extorted rather than obtained his permission, under promise of observing the most strict incognito, to spend a week or two with her sister, or in her neighbourhood, while he was prosecuting researches, to which (though it appeared to her very vainly) he seemed to attach some hopes of success.

There was a postscript, desiring that Jeanie would trust to Lady S. the management of their intercourse, and be content with assenting to what she should propose. After reading and again reading the letter, Mrs Butler hurried down stairs, divided betwixt the fear of betraying her secret, and the desire to throw herself upon her sister's neck. Effie received her with a glance at once affectionate and cautionary, and immediately proceeded to speak.

"I have been telling Mr——, Captain——, this gentleman, Mrs Butler, that if you could accommodate me with an apartment in your house, and a place for Ellis to sleep, and for the two men, it would suit me better than the Lodge, which his Grace has so kindly placed at my disposal. I am advised I should reside as near where the goats feed as possible."

"I have peen assuring my Lady, Mrs Putler," said Duncan, "that though it could not discommode you to receive any of his Grace's visitors or mine, yet she had mooch petter stay at the Lodge; and for the gaits, the creatures can be fetched there, in respect it is mair fitting they suld wait upon her Leddyship, than she upon the like of them."

"By no means derange the goats for me," said Lady Staunton; "I am certain the milk must be much better here." And this she said with languid negligence, as one whose slightest intimation of humour is to bear down all argument.

Mrs Butler hastened to intimate, that her house, such as it was, was heartily at the disposal of Lady Staunton; but the Captain continued to remonstrate.

"The Duke," he said, "had written"——

"I will settle all that with his Grace"——

"And there were the things had been sent down frae Glasco"——

"Any thing necessary might be sent over to the Parsonage³—She would beg the favour of Mrs Butler to shew her an apartment, and of the Captain to have her trunks, &c. sent over from Roseneath."

So she curtsied off poor Duncan, who departed, saying in his secret soul, "Cot tamn her English impudence!—she takes possession of the minister's house as an it were her ain—and speaks to shentlemens as if they were pounden servants, an pe tamn'd to her!—And there's the deer that was shot too—but we will send it ower to the Manse, whilk will pe put civil, seeing I hae prought worthy Mrs Putler sic a fliskmahoy"—And with these kind intentions, he went to the shore to give his orders accordingly.

In the meantime, the meeting of the sisters was as affectionate as it was extraordinary, and each evinced her feelings in the way proper to her character. Jeanie was so much overcome by wonder, and even by awe, that her feelings were deep, stunning, and almost overpowering. Effie, on the other hand, wept, laughed, sobbed, screamed, and clapped her hands for joy, all in the space of five minutes, giving way at once, and without reserve, to a natural excessive vivacity of temper, which no one, however, knew better how to restrain under the rules of artificial breeding.

After an hour had passed like a moment in their expressions of mutual affection, Lady Staunton observed the Captain walking with impatient steps below the window. "That tiresome Highland fool has returned upon our hands," she said. "I will pray him to grace us with his absence."

"Hout no! hout no!" said Mrs Butler, in a tone of entreaty; "ye mauna affront the Captain."

"Affront?" said Lady Staunton; "nobody is ever affronted at what I do or say, my dear. However, I will endure him, since you think it proper."

The Captain was accordingly graciously requested by Lady Staunton to remain during dinner. During this visit his studious and punctilious complaisance towards the lady of rank was happily contrasted by the cavalier air of civil familiarity in which he indulged towards the minister's wife.

"I have not been able to persuade Mrs Butler," said Lady Staunton to the Captain, during the interval when Jeanie had left the parlour, "to let me talk of making any recompence for storming her house, and garrisoning it in the way I have done."

"Doubtless, matam," said the Captain, "it wad ill pecome Mrs Putler, wha is a very decent pody, to make any such sharge to a lady who comes from my house, or his Grace's, which is the same thing.— And, speaking of garrisons, in the year forty-five, I was poot with a garrison of twenty of my lads in the house of Inver-Garry,[4] whilk had near been unhappily, for"—

"I beg your pardon, sir—But I wish I could think of some way of indemnifying this good lady."

"O, no need of intemnifying at all—no trouble for her, nothing at all—So, peing in the house of Inver-Garry, and the people about it peing uncanny, I doubted the warst, and"—

"Do you happen to know, sir," said Lady Staunton, "if any of these two lads, these young Butlers, I mean, show any turn for the army?"

"Could not say, indeed, my leddy," replied Knockdunder—"So, I knowing the people to pe unchancy, and not to lippen to, and hearing a pibroch in the wood, I pegan to pid my lads look to their flints, and then"—

"For," said Lady Staunton, with the most ruthless disregard to the narrative which she mangled by these interruptions, "if that should be the case, it should cost Sir George but the asking a pair of colours for one of them at the War-office, since we have always supported government, and never had occasion to trouble ministers."

"And if you please, my leddy," said Duncan, who began to find some savour in this proposal, "as I hae a braw weel grown lad of a nevoy, ca'd Duncan MacGilligan, that is as pig as paith the Putler pairns putten thegether, Sir George could ask a pair for him at the same time, and it was pe put ae asking for a'."

Lady Staunton only answered this hint with a well-bred stare, which gave no sort of encouragement.

Jeanie, who now returned, was lost in amazement at the wonderful difference betwixt the helpless and despairing girl, whom she had seen stretched on a flock-bed in a dungeon, expecting a violent and disgraceful death, and last as a forlorn exile upon the midnight beach, and the elegant, well-bred, beautiful woman before her. The features, now that her sister's veil was laid aside, did not appear so extremely different, as the whole manner, expression, look, and bearing. In outside show, Lady Staunton seemed completely a creature too soft and fair for sorrow to have touched; so much accustomed to have all her whims complied with by those around her, that she seemed to expect she should even be saved the trouble of forming them; and so totally unacquainted with contradiction, that she did not even use the tone of self-will, since to breathe a wish was to have it fulfilled. She made no ceremony of ridding herself of Duncan so soon as the evening approached; but complimented him out of the house under pretext of fatigue, with the utmost *non-chalance*.

When they were alone, her sister could not help expressing her wonder at the self-possession with which Lady Staunton sustained her part.

"I dare say you are surprised at it," said Lady Staunton, composedly; "for you, my dear Jeanie, have been truth itself from your cradle upwards; but you must remember that I am a Lie of fifteen years' standing, and therefore must by this time be used to my character."

In fact, during the feverish tumult of feelings excited during the two or three first days, Mrs Butler thought her sister's manner was completely contradictory of the desponding tone which pervaded her correspondence. She was moved to tears, indeed, by the sight of her father's grave, marked by a modest stone, recording his piety and integrity; but lighter impressions and associations had also power over her. She amused herself with visiting the dairy, in which she had so long been assistant, and was so near discovering herself to May Hettly, by betraying her acquaintance with the celebrated receipt for Dunlop cheese, that she compared herself to Bedreddin Hassan,[5] whom the vizier, his father-in-law, discovered by his superlative skill in composing cream-tarts with pepper in them. But when the novelty of such avocations ceased to amuse her, she showed to her sister but too plainly, that the gaudy colouring with which she veiled her unhappiness afforded as little real comfort, as the gay uniform of the soldier when it is drawn over his mortal wound. There were moods and moments, in which her despondence seemed to exceed even that which she herself had described in her letters, and which too well convinced Mrs Butler how little her sister's lot, which in appearance was so brilliant, was, in reality, to be envied.

There was one source, however, from which Lady Staunton derived a pure degree of pleasure. Gifted in every particular with a higher degree of imagination than that of her sister, she was an admirer of the beauties of nature, a taste which compensates many evils to those who happen to enjoy it. Here her character of a fine lady stopped short, where she ought to have

> Scream'd at ilk cleugh, and screech'd at ilka how,
> As loud as she had seen the worrie-cow.[6]

On the contrary, with the two boys for her guides, she undertook long and fatiguing walks[7] among the neighbouring mountains, to visit glens, lakes, water-falls, and whatever scenes of natural wonder or beauty lay concealed among their recesses. It is Wordsworth, I think, who, talking of an old man under difficulties, remarks, with singular attention to nature,

> ——whether it was care that spurred him,
> God only knows; but to the very last,
> He had the lightest foot in Ennerdale.[8]

In the same manner, languid, listless, and unhappy within doors, at times even indicating something which approached near to contempt of the homely accommodations of her sister's house, although she instantly endeavoured, by a thousand kindnesses, to atone for such ebullitions of spleen, Lady Staunton appeared to feel interest and energy while in the open air, and traversing the mountain landscapes in society with the two boys, whose ears she delighted with stories of what she had seen in other countries, and what she had to show them at Willingham Manor. And they, on the other hand, exerted themselves in doing the honours of Dumbartonshire to the lady who seemed so kind, insomuch that there was scarce a glen in the neighbouring hills to which they did not introduce her.

Upon one of these excursions, while Reuben was otherwise employed, David alone acted as Lady Staunton's guide, and promised to show her a cascade in the hills, grander and higher than any they had yet visited. It was a walk of five long miles, and over rough ground, varied, however, and cheered by mountain views, and peeps now of the Firth and its islands, now of distant lakes, now of rocks and precipices. The scene itself, too, when they reached it, amply rewarded the labour of the walk. A single shoot carried a considerable stream over the face of a black rock, which contrasted strongly in colour with the white foam of the cascade, and, at the depth of about twenty feet, another rock intercepted the view of the bottom of the fall. The water, wheeling out far beneath, swept round the crag, which thus bounded their view, and tumbled down the rocky glen in a torrent of foam. Those who love nature always desire to penetrate into its utmost recesses, and Lady Staunton asked David whether there was not some mode of gaining a view of the abyss at the foot of the fall. He said that he knew a station on a shelf on the further side of the intercepting rock, from which the whole waterfall was visible, but that the road to it was steep and slippery and dangerous. Bent, however, on gratifying her curiosity, she desired him to lead the way; and accordingly he did so over crag and stone, anxiously pointing out to her the resting-places where she ought to step, for their mode of advancing soon ceased to be walking, and became scrambling.

In this manner, clinging like sea-birds to the face of the rock, they were enabled at length to turn round it, and came full in front of the fall, which here had a most tremendous aspect, boiling, roaring, and thundering with unceasing din, into a black cauldron, a hundred feet at least below them, which resembled the crater of a volcano. The noise, the dashing of the waters, which gave an unsteady appearance to all around them, the trembling even of the huge crag on which they stood, the precariousness of their footing, for there was scarce room for them to stand on the shelf of rock which they had thus attained, had so powerful an effect on the senses and imagination of Lady Staunton, that she called out to David she was falling, and would in fact have dropped from the crag had he not caught hold of her. The boy was bold and stout of his age—still he was but fourteen years old, and as his assistance gave no confidence to Lady Staunton, she felt her situation become really perilous. The chance was, that, in the appalling novelty of the circumstances, he might have caught the infection of her panic, in which case it is likely that both must have perished. She now screamed with terror, though without hope of calling any one to her assistance. To her amazement, the scream was answered by a whistle from above, of a tone so clear and shrill, that it was heard even amid the noise of the waterfall.

In this moment of terror and perplexity, a human face, black, and having grizzled hair hanging down over the forehead and cheeks, and mixing with moustaches and a beard of the same colour, and as much matted and tangled, looked down on them from a broken part of the rock above.

"It is The Enemy!" said the boy, who had very nearly become incapable of supporting Lady Staunton.

"No, no," she exclaimed, inaccessible to supernatural terrors, and restored to the presence of mind of which she had been deprived by the danger of her situation, "it is a man—for God's sake, my friend, help us!"

The face glared at them, but made no answer; in a second or two afterwards, another, that of a young lad, appeared beside the first, equally swart and begrimed, but having tangled black hair, descending in elf-locks, which gave an air of wildness and ferocity to the whole expression of the countenance. Lady Staunton repeated her entreaties, clinging to the rock with more energy, as she found that from the superstitious terror of her guide he became incapable of supporting her. Her words were probably drowned in the roar of the falling stream, for, though she observed the lips of the younger being whom she supplicated move as he spoke in reply, not a word reached her ear.

A moment afterwards it appeared he had not mistaken the nature of her supplication, which, indeed, was easy to be understood from her situation and gestures. The younger apparition disappeared, and immediately after lowered a ladder of twisted osiers, about eight feet in length, and made signs to David to hold it fast while the lady ascended. Despair gives courage, and finding herself in this fearful predicament, Lady Staunton did not hesitate to risk the ascent by the precarious means which this accommodation afforded; and, carefully assisted by the person who had thus providentially come to her aid, she reached the summit in safety. She did not, however, even look around her until she saw her nephew lightly and actively follow her example, although there was now no one to hold the ladder fast. When she saw him safe she looked round, and could not help shuddering at the place and company in which she found herself.

They were on a sort of platform of rock,[9] surrounded on every side by precipices, or overhanging cliffs, and which it would have been scarce possible for any research to have discovered, as it did not seem to be commanded by any accessible position. It was partly covered by a huge fragment of stone, which, having fallen from the cliffs above, had been intercepted by others in its descent, and jammed so as to serve for a sloping roof to the further part of the broad shelf or platform on which they stood. A quantity of withered moss and leaves, strewed beneath this rude and wretched shelter, shewed the lairs,— they could not be termed the beds,—of those who dwelt in this eyrie, for it deserved no other name. Of these, two were before Lady Staunton. One, the same who had afforded such timely assistance, stood upright before them, a tall, lathy, young savage; his dress a tattered plaid and philabeg, no shoes, no stockings, no hat or bonnet, the place of the last being supplied by his hair twisted and matted like the *glibbe* of the ancient wild Irish, and, like theirs, forming a natural thickset, stout enough to bear off the cut of a sword. Yet the eyes of the lad were keen and sparkling; his gesture free and noble, like that of all savages. He took little notice of David Butler, but gazed with wonder on Lady Staunton, as a being different probably in dress, and superior in beauty, to any thing he had ever beheld. The old man, whose face they had first seen, remained recumbent in the same posture as when he had first looked down on them, only his face was turned towards them as he lay and looked up with a lazy and listless apathy, which belied the general expression of his dark and rugged features. He seemed a very tall man, but was scarce better clad than the younger. He had on a loose Lowland great coat, and ragged tartan trews or pantaloons.

All around looked singularly wild and unpropitious. Beneath the brow of the incumbent rock was a charcoal fire, on which there was a still working, with bellows, pincers, hammers, a moveable anvil, and other smith's tools; three guns, with two or three sacks and barrels, were disposed against the wall of rock, under shelter of the superincumbent crag; a dirk or two, swords, and a Lochaber-axe, lay scattered around the fire, of which the red glare cast a ruddy tinge on the precipitous foam and mist of the cascade. The lad, when he had satisfied his curiosity with staring at Lady Staunton, fetched an earthen jar and a horn cup, into which he poured some spirits, apparently hot from the still, and offered them successively to the lady and to the boy. Both declined, and the young savage quaffed off the draught, which could not amount to less than three ordinary glasses. He then fetched another ladder from the corner of the cavern, if it could be termed so, adjusted it against the transverse rock, which served as a roof, and made signs for the lady to ascend it while he held it fast below. She did so, and found herself on the top of a broad rock, near the brink of the chasm into which the brook precipitates itself. She could see the crest of the torrent flung loose down the rock like the mane of a wild horse, but without having any view of the lower platform from which she had ascended.

David was not suffered to mount so easily; the lad, from sport or love of mischief, shook the ladder a good deal as he ascended, and seemed to enjoy the terror of young Butler, so that, when they had both come up, they looked on each other with no friendly eyes. Neither, however, spoke. The young caird, or tinker, or gypsy, with a good deal of attention, assisted Lady Staunton up a very perilous ascent which she had still to encounter, and they were followed by David Butler, until all three stood clear of the ravine on the side of a mountain, whose sides were covered with heather and sheets of loose shingle. So narrow was the chasm out of which they ascended, that, unless when they were on the very verge, the eye passed to the other side without perceiving the existence of a rent so fearful, and nothing was seen of the cataract, though its deep hoarse voice was still heard.

Lady Staunton, freed from the danger of rock and river, had now a new subject of anxiety. Her two guides confronted each other with angry countenances; for David, though younger by two years at least, and much shorter, was a stout, well-set, and very bold boy.

"You are the black-coat's son of Knocktarlitie," said the young caird; "if you come here again, I'll pitch you down the linn like a football."

"Ay, lad, ye are very short to be sae lang,"[10] retorted young Butler undauntedly, and measuring his opponent's height with an undismayed eye; "I am thinking you are a gillie of Black Donacha; if you come down the glen, we'll shoot you like a wild buck."

"You may tell your father," said the lad, "that the leaf on the timber is the last he shall see—we will hae amends for the mischief he has done to us."

"I hope he will live to see mony simmers, and do ye muckle mair," answered David.

More might have passed, but Lady Staunton stepped between them with her purse in her hand, and, taking out a guinea, of which it contained several, visible through the net-work, as well as some silver in the opposite end, offered it to the caird.

"The white siller, lady—the white siller," said the young savage, to whom the value of gold was probably unknown.

Lady Staunton poured what silver she had into her hand, and the juvenile savage snatched it greedily, and made a sort of half inclination of acknowledgment and adieu.

"Let us make haste now, Lady Staunton," said David, "for there will be little peace with them since they hae seen your purse."

They hurried on as fast as they could; but they had not descended the hill a hundred yards or two before they heard a halloo behind them, and looking back, saw both the old man and the young one pursuing them with great speed, the former with a gun on his shoulder. Very fortunately, at this moment a sportsman, a gamekeeper of the Duke, who was engaged in stalking deer, appeared on the face of the hill. The bandits stopped on seeing him, and Lady Staunton hastened to put herself under his protection. He readily gave them his escort home, and it required his athletic form and loaded rifle[11] to restore to the lady her usual confidence and courage.

Donald[12] listened with much gravity to the account of their adventure; and answered with great composure to David's repeated enquiries, whether he could have suspected that the cairds had been lurking there: "Inteed, Master Tavie, I might hae had some guess that they were there, or thereabout, though maybe I had nane. But I am aften on the hill; and they are like wasps—they stang only them that fashes them; sae, for my part, I make a point not to see them, unless I were ordered out on the preceese errand by MacCallanmore or Knockdunder, whilk is a clean different case."

They reached the Manse late; and Lady Staunton, who had suffered much both from fright and fatigue, never again permitted her love of the picturesque to carry her so far among the mountains without a stronger escort than David, though she acknowledged he had won the stand of colours by the intrepidity he had displayed, so soon as assured he had to do with an earthly antagonist. "I couldna, maybe, hae made muckle o' a bargain wi' yon lang callant," said David, when thus complimented on his valour; "but when ye deal wi' thae folk, it's tyne heart tyne a'."[13]

CHAPTER 51

> ————What see you there,
> That hath so cowarded and chased your blood
> Out of appearance?
>
> *Henry the Fifth*

WE are under the necessity of returning to Edinburgh, where the General Assembly was now sitting. It is well known, that some Scottish nobleman is usually deputed as High Commissioner, to represent the person of the King in this convocation; that he has allowances for the purpose of maintaining a certain outward show and solemnity, and supporting the hospitality of the representative of Majesty. Whoever is distinguished by rank, or office, in or near the capital, usually attend the morning levees of the Lord Commissioner, and walk with him in procession to the place where the Assembly meets.

The nobleman who held this office chanced to be particularly connected with Sir George Staunton, and it was in his train that he ventured to tread the High Street of Edinburgh for the first time since the fatal night of Porteous's execution. Walking at the right-hand of the representative of Sovereignty, covered with lace and embroidery, and with all the paraphernalia of wealth and rank, the handsome though wasted form of the English stranger attracted all eyes. Who could have recognized in a form so aristocratic the plebeian convict, that, disguised in the rags of Madge Wildfire, had led the formidable rioters to their destined revenge! There was no possibility that this could happen, even if any of his ancient acquaintances, a race of men whose lives are so brief, had happened to survive the span commonly allotted to evil-doers.[1] Besides, the whole affair had long fallen asleep, with the angry passions in which it originated. Nothing is more certain than that persons known to have had a share in that formidable riot, and to have fled from Scotland on that account, had made money abroad, returned to enjoy it in their native country, and lived and died undisturbed by the law.* The forbearance of the magistrate was in these instances

* See Arnot's[2] Criminal Trials, 4to ed. p. 235.

wise, certainly, and just; for what good impression could be made on the public mind by punishment, when the memory of the offence was obliterated, and all that was remembered was the recent inoffensive, or perhaps exemplary conduct of the offender?

Sir George Staunton might, therefore, tread the scene of his former audacious exploits, free from the apprehension of the law, or even of discovery or suspicion. But with what feelings his heart that day throbbed, must be left to those of the reader to imagine. It was an object of no common interest which had brought him to encounter so many painful remembrances.

In consequence of Jeanie's letter to Lady Staunton, transmitting the confession, he had visited the town of Carlisle, and had found Archdeacon Fleming still alive, by whom that confession had been received. This reverend gentleman, whose character stood deservedly very high, he so far admitted into his confidence, as to own himself the father of the unfortunate infant which had been spirited away by Madge Wildfire, representing the intrigue as a matter of juvenile extravagance on his own part, for which he was now anxious to atone, by tracing, if possible, what had become of the child. After some recollection of the circumstances, the clergyman was able to call to memory, that the unhappy woman had written a letter to George Staunton, Esq. younger, Rectory, Willingham, by Grantham; that he had forwarded it to the address accordingly, and that it had been returned, with a note from the Reverend Mr Staunton, Rector of Willingham, saying, he knew no such person as him to whom the letter was addressed. As this had happened just at the period when George had, for the last time, absconded from his father's house to carry off Effie, he was at no loss to account for the cause of the resentment, under the influence of which his father had disowned him. This was another instance in which his ungovernable temper had occasioned his misfortune; had he remained at Willingham but a few days longer, he would have received Margaret Murdockson's letter, in which was exactly described the person and haunts of the woman, Annaple Bailzou,[3] to whom she had parted with the infant. It appeared that Meg Murdockson had been induced to make this confession, less from any feelings of contrition, than from the desire of obtaining, through George Staunton or his father's means, protection and support for her daughter Madge. Her letter to George Staunton said, "That, while the writer lived, her daughter would have needed nought from any body, and that she would never have meddled in these affairs, except to pay back the ill that George had done to her and hers. But she was to die, and her daughter would be destitute, and without reason to guide her. She had lived in the world long enough to know that people did nothing for nothing;—so she had told George Staunton all he could wish to know about his wean, in hopes he would not see the demented young creature he had ruined perish for want. As for her motives for not telling them sooner, she had a long account to reckon for in the next world, and she would reckon for that too."

The clergyman said, that Meg had died in the same desperate state of mind, occasionally expressing some regret about the child which was lost, but oftener sorrow that the mother had not been hanged— her mind at once a chaos of guilt, rage, and apprehension for her daughter's future safety; that instinctive feeling of parental anxiety which she had in common with the she-wolf and lioness, being the last shade of kindly affection that occupied a breast equally savage.

The melancholy catastrophe of Madge Wildfire was occasioned by her taking the confusion of her mother's execution, as affording an opportunity of leaving the workhouse to which the clergyman had sent her, and presenting herself to the mob in their fury, to perish in the way we have already seen. When Dr Fleming found the convict's letter was returned from Lincolnshire, he wrote to a friend in Edinburgh, to enquire into the fate of the unfortunate girl whose child had been stolen, and was informed by his correspondent, that she had been pardoned, and that, with all her family, she had retired to some distant part of Scotland, or left the kingdom entirely. And here the matter rested, until, at Sir George Staunton's application, the clergyman looked out, and produced Margaret Murdockson's returned letter, and the other memoranda which he had kept concerning the affair.

Whatever might be Sir George Staunton's feelings in ripping up this miserable history, and listening to the tragical fate of the unhappy girl whom he had ruined, he had so much of his ancient wilfulness of disposition left, as to shut his eyes on every thing, save the prospect which seemed to open itself of recovering his son. It was true it would be difficult to produce him, without telling much more of the history of his birth, and the misfortunes of his parents, than it was prudent to make known. But let him once be found, and, being found, let him but prove worthy of his father's protection, and many ways might be fallen upon to avoid such risk. Sir George Staunton was at liberty to adopt him as his heir, if he pleased, without communicating the secret of his birth; or an act of parliament might be obtained, declaring him legitimate, and allowing him the name and arms of his father. He was, indeed, already a legitimate child according to the law of Scotland, by the subsequent marriage of his parents. Wilful in every thing, Sir George's sole desire now was to see this son, even should his recovery bring with it a new series of misfortunes, as dreadful as those which followed on his being lost.

But where was the youth who might eventually be called to the honours and estates of this ancient family? On what heath was he wandering, and shrouded by what mean disguise? Did he gain his precarious bread by some petty trade, by menial toil, by violence, or by theft? These were questions on which Sir George's anxious investigations could obtain no light. Many remembered that Annaple Bailzou wandered through the country as a beggar and fortune-teller, or spae-wife—some remembered that she had been seen with an infant in 1737 or 1738, but for more than ten years, she had not travelled that district; and that she had been heard to say she was going to a distant part of Scotland, of which country she was a native. To Scotland, therefore, came Sir George Staunton, having parted with his lady at Glasgow, and his arrival at Edinburgh happening to coincide with the sitting of the General Assembly of the Kirk, his acquaintance with the nobleman who held the office of Lord High Commissioner forced him more into public than suited either his views or inclinations.

At the public table of this nobleman, Sir George Staunton was placed next to a clergyman of respectable appearance, and well-bred, though plain demeanour, whose name he discovered to be Butler. It had been no part of Sir George's plan to take his brother-in-law into his confidence, and he had rejoiced exceedingly in the assurances he received from his wife, that Mrs Butler, the very soul of integrity and honour, had never suffered the account he had given of himself at Willingham Rectory to transpire, even to her husband. But he was not sorry to have an opportunity to converse with so near a connection, without being known to him, and to form a judgment of his character and understanding. He saw much, and heard more, to raise Butler very high in his opinion. He found he was generally respected by those of his own profession, as well as by the laity who had seats in the Assembly. He had made several public appearances in the Assembly, distinguished by good sense, candour, and ability; and he was followed and admired as a sound, and, at the same time, an eloquent preacher.

This was all very satisfactory to Sir George Staunton's pride, which had revolted at the idea of his wife's sister being obscurely married. He now began, on the contrary, to think the connection so much better than he expected, that, if it should be necessary to acknowledge it, in consequence of the recovery of his son, it would sound well enough that Lady Staunton had a sister, who, in the decayed state of the family, had married a Scottish clergyman, high in the opinion of his countrymen, and a leader in the church.

It was with these feelings, that, when the Lord High Commissioner's company broke up, Sir George Staunton, under pretence of prolonging some enquiries concerning the constitution of the Church of Scotland, requested Butler to go home to his lodgings in the Lawnmarket, and drink a cup of coffee. Butler agreed to wait upon him, providing Sir George would permit him, in passing, to call at a friend's house where he resided, and make his apology for not coming to partake her tea. They proceeded up the High Street, entered the Krames, and passed the begging-box, placed to remind those at liberty of the distresses of the poor prisoners. Sir George paused there one instant, and next day a L.20 note was found in that receptacle for public charity.

When he came up to Butler again, he found him with his eyes fixed on the entrance of the Tolbooth, and apparently in deep thought.

"That seems a very strong door," said Sir George, by way of saying something.

"It is so, sir," said Butler, turning off and beginning to walk forward, "but it was my misfortune at one time to see it prove greatly too weak."

At this moment, looking at his companion, he asked him whether he felt himself ill, and Sir George Staunton admitted, that he had been so foolish as to eat ice, which sometimes disagreed with him. With kind officiousness, that would not be gainsaid, and ere he could find out where he was going, Butler hurried Sir George into the friend's house, near to the prison, in which he himself had lived since he came to town, being indeed no other than that of our old friend Bartoline Saddletree, in which Lady Staunton had served a short noviciate as a shop-maid. This recollection rushed on her husband's mind, and the blush of shame which it excited overpowered the sensation of fear which had produced his former paleness. Good Mrs Saddletree, however, bustled about to receive the rich English baronet as the friend of Mr Butler, and requested an elderly female in a black gown to sit still, in a way which seemed to imply a wish, that she would clear the way for her betters. In the meanwhile, understanding the state of the case, she ran to get some cordial waters, sovereign, of course, in all cases of faintishness whatsoever. During her absence, her visitor, the female in black, made some progress out of the room, and might have left it altogether without particular observation, had she not stumbled at the threshold, so near Sir George Staunton, that he, in point of civility, raised her and assisted her to the door.

"Mrs Porteous is turned very doited now, puir body," said Mrs Saddletree, as she returned with her bottle in her hand—"She is no sae auld, but she got a sair back-cast wi' the slaughter o' her husband—Ye had some trouble about that job, Mr Butler.—I think, sir," to Sir George, "ye had better drink out the haill glass, for to my een ye look waur than when ye came in."

And indeed he grew as pale as a corpse, on recollecting who it was that his arm had so lately supported—the widow whom he had so large a share in making such.

"It is a prescribed job that case of Porteous now," said old Saddletree, who was confined to his chair by the gout—"clean prescribed and out of date."

"I am not clear of that, neighbour," said Plumdamas, "for I have heard them say twenty years⁴ should rin, and this is but the fifty-ane⁵—Porteous's mob was in thretty-seven."

"Ye'll no teach me law, I think, neighbour—me that has four gaun pleas, and might hae had fourteen, an it hadna been the gudewife. I tell ye if the foremost of the Porteous-mob were standing there where that gentleman stands, the King's Advocate wadna meddle wi' him—it fa's under the negative prescription."

"Haud your din, carles," said Mrs Saddletree, "and let the gentleman sit down and get a dish of comfortable tea."

But Sir George had had quite enough of their conversation; and Butler, at his request, made an apology to Mrs Saddletree, and accompanied him to his lodgings. Here they found another guest waiting Sir George Staunton's return. This was no other than our reader's old acquaintance Ratcliffe.

This man had exercised the office of turnkey with so much vigilance, acuteness, and fidelity, that he gradually rose to be governor, or captain of the Tolbooth. And it is yet remembered in tradition, that young men, who rather sought amusing than select society in their merry meetings, used sometimes to request Ratcliffe's company, in order that he might regale them with legends of his extraordinary feats in the way of robbery and escape.* But he lived and died without resuming his original vocation, otherwise than in his narratives over a bottle.

Under these circumstances, he had been recommended to Sir George Staunton by a man of the law in Edinburgh, as a person likely to answer any questions he might have to ask about Annaple Bailzou, who, according to the colour which Sir George Staunton gave to his cause of enquiry, was supposed to have stolen a child in the west of England, belonging to a family in which he was interested. The gentleman had not mentioned his name, but only his official title; so that Sir George Staunton, when told that the captain of the Tolbooth was waiting for him in his parlour, had no idea of meeting his former acquaintance Jem Ratcliffe.

This, therefore, was another new and most unpleasant surprise, for he had no difficulty in recollecting this man's remarkable features. The change, however, from George Robertson to Sir George Staunton, baffled even the penetration of Ratcliffe, and he bowed very low to the baronet and his guest, hoping Mr Butler would excuse his recollecting that he was an old acquaintance.

"And once rendered my wife a piece of great service," said Mr Butler, "for which she sent you a token of grateful acknowledgment, which I hope came safe and was welcome."

"Deil a doubt o't," said Ratcliffe, with a knowing nod; "but ye are muckle changed for the better since I saw ye, Maister Butler."

"So much so, that I wonder you knew me."

"Aha, then!—Deil a face I see I ever forget," said Ratcliffe; while Sir George Staunton, tied to the stake,[7] and incapable of escaping, internally cursed the accuracy of his memory. "And yet, sometimes," continued Ratcliffe, "the sharpest hand will be taen in. There is a face in this very room, if I might presume to be sae bauld, that if I didna ken the honourable person it belangs to—I might think it had some cast of an auld acquaintance."

"I should not be much flattered," answered the Baronet sternly, and roused by the risk in which he saw himself placed, "if it is to me you mean to apply that compliment."

---

* There seems an anachronism in the history of this person. Ratcliffe, among other escapes from justice, was released by the Porteous-mob when under sentence of death. And he was again under the same predicament when the Highlanders made a similar jail-delivery in 1745. He was too sincere a whig to embrace liberation at the hands of the jacobites, and in reward was made one of the keepers of the Tolbooth. So at least runs a constant tradition.[6]

"By no manner of means, sir," said Ratcliffe, bowing very low; "I am come to receive your honour's commands, and no to trouble your honour wi' my poor observations."

"Well, sir," said Sir George, "I am told you understand police matters—So do I.—To convince you of which, here are ten guineas of retaining fee—I make them fifty when you can find me certain notice of a person, living or dead, whom you will find described in that paper.—I shall leave town presently—you may send your written answer to me to the care of Mr ——," (naming his highly respectable agent,) "or of his Grace the Lord High Commissioner." Ratcliffe bowed and withdrew.

"I have angered the proud peat now," he said to himself, "by finding out a likeness—but if George Robertson's father had lived within a mile of his mother, d—n me if I should not know what to think, for as high as he carries his head."

When he was left alone with Butler, Sir George Staunton ordered tea and coffee, which were brought by his valet, and then, after considering with himself for a minute, asked his guest whether he had lately heard from his wife and family. Butler, with some surprise at the question, replied, "that he had received no letter for some time; his wife was a poor pen-woman."

"Then," said Sir George Staunton, "I am the first to inform you there has been an invasion of your quiet premises since you left home. My wife, whom the Duke of Argyle had the goodness to permit to use Roseneath Lodge, while she was spending some weeks in your country, has sallied across and taken up her quarters in the Manse, as she says, to be nearer the goats, whose milk she is using; but I believe, in reality, because she prefers Mrs Butler's company to that of the respectable gentleman who acts as seneschal on the Duke's domains."

Mr Butler said, "he had often heard the late Duke and the present speak with high respect of Lady Staunton, and was happy if his house could accommodate any friend of theirs—it would be but a very slight acknowledgment of the many favours he owed them."

"That does not make Lady Staunton and myself the less obliged to your hospitality, sir," said Sir George. "May I enquire if you think of returning home soon?"

"In the course of two days," Mr Butler answered, "his duty in the Assembly would be ended; and the other matters he had in town being all finished, he was desirous of returning to Dumbartonshire as soon as he could—but he was under the necessity of transporting a considerable sum in bills and money with him, and therefore wished to travel in company with one or two of his brethren of the clergy."

"My escort will be more safe," said Sir George Staunton, "and I think of setting off to-morrow or next day.—If you will give me the pleasure of your company I will undertake to deliver you and your charge safe at the Manse, provided you will admit me along with you."

Mr Butler gratefully accepted of this proposal; the appointment was made accordingly, and by dispatches with one of Sir George's servants, who was sent forward for the purpose, the inhabitants of the Manse of Knocktarlitie were made acquainted with the intended journey; and the news rung through the whole vicinity, "that the minister was coming back wi' a braw English gentleman, and a' the siller that was to pay for the estate of Craigsture."

This sudden resolution of going to Knocktarlitie had been adopted by Sir George Staunton, in consequence of the incidents of the evening. In spite of his present consequence, he felt he had presumed too far in venturing so near the scene of his former audacious acts of violence, and he knew too well, from past experience, the acuteness of a man like Ratcliffe, again to encounter him. The next two days he kept his lodgings, under pretence of indisposition, and took leave, by writing, of his noble friend, the High Commissioner, alleging the opportunity of Mr Butler's company as a reason for leaving Edinburgh sooner than he had proposed. He had a long conference with his agent on the subject of Annaple Bailzou; and the professional gentleman, who was the agent also of the Argyle family, had directions to collect all the information which Ratcliffe or others might be able to obtain concerning the fate of that woman and the unfortunate child, and, so soon as any thing transpired which had the least appearance of being important, that he should send an express with it instantly to Knocktarlitie. These instructions were backed with a deposit of money, and a request that no expence might be spared; so that Sir George Staunton had little reason to apprehend negligence on the part of the persons entrusted with the commission.

The journey, which the brothers made in company, was attended with more pleasure, even to Sir George Staunton, than he had ventured to expect. His heart lightened in spite of himself when they lost sight of Edinburgh; and the easy, sensible conversation of Butler was well calculated to withdraw his thoughts from painful reflections. He even began to think whether there could be much difficulty in removing his wife's connections to the Rectory of Willingham; it was only on his part procuring some still better preferment for the present incumbent, and on Butler's, that he should take orders according to the English church, to which he could not conceive a possibility of his making objection, and then he had them residing under his wing. No doubt there was pain in seeing Mrs Butler, acquainted, as he knew her to be, with the full truth of his evil history—But then her silence, though he had no reason to complain of her indiscretion hitherto, was still more absolutely ensured. It would keep his lady, also, both in good temper and in more subjection, for she was sometimes trouble-some to him, by insisting on remaining in town when he desired to retire to the country, alleging the total want of society at Willingham. "Madam, your sister is there," would, he thought, be a sufficient answer to this ready argument.

He sounded Butler on this subject, asking what he would think of an English living of twelve hundred pounds yearly, with the burthen of affording his company now and then to a neighbour whose health was not strong, or his spirits equal. "He might meet," he said, "occasionally, a very learned and accomplished gentleman, who was in orders as a Catholic priest,[8] but he hoped that would be no insurmount-able objection to a man of his liberality of sentiment. What," he said, "would Mr Butler think of as an answer, if the offer should be made to him?"

"Simply that I could not accept of it," said Mr Butler. "I have no mind to enter into the various debates between the churches; but I was brought up in mine own, have received her ordination, am satisfied of the truth of her doctrines, and will die under the banner I have enlisted to."

"What may be the value of your preferment?" said Sir George Staunton, "unless I am asking an indiscreet question."

"Probably one hundred a-year, one year with another, besides my glebe and pasture-ground."

"And you scruple to exchange that for twelve hundred a-year, without alleging any damning difference of doctrine betwixt the two churches of England and Scotland?"

"On that, sir, I have reserved my judgment; there may be much good, and there are certainly saving means in both, but every man must act according to his own lights. I hope I have done, and am in the course of doing, my Master's work in this Highland parish; and it would ill become me, for the sake of lucre, to leave my sheep in the wilderness. But, even in the temporal view which you have taken of the matter, Sir George, this hundred pounds a-year of stipend hath fed and clothed us, and left us nothing to wish for; my father-in-law's succession, and other circumstances, have added a small estate of about twice as much more, and how we are to dispose of it I do not know—So I leave it to you, sir, to think if I were wise, not having the wish or opportunity of spending three hundred a-year, to covet the possession of four times that sum."

"This is philosophy," said Sir George; "I have heard of it, but I never saw it before."

"It is common sense," replied Butler, "which accords with philosophy and religion more frequently than pedants or zealots are apt to admit."

Sir George turned the subject, and did not again resume it. Although they travelled in Sir George's chariot, he seemed so much fatigued with the motion, that it was necessary for him to remain for a day at a small town called Mid-Calder, which was their first stage from Edinburgh. Glasgow occupied another day, so slow were their motions.[9]

They travelled on to Dumbarton, where they had resolved to leave the equipage, and to hire a boat to take them to the shores near the Manse, as the Gare-Loch lay betwixt[10] them and that point, besides the impossibility of travelling in that district with wheel-carriages. Sir George's valet, a man of trust, accompanied them, as also a footman; the grooms were left with the carriage. Just as this arrangement was completed, which was about four o'clock in the afternoon, an express arrived from Sir George's agent in Edinburgh, with a packet, which he opened and read with great attention, appearing much interested and agitated by the contents. The packet had been dispatched very soon after their leaving Edinburgh, but the messenger had missed the travellers by passing through Mid-Calder in the night, and over-shot his errand by getting to Roseneath before them. He was now on his return, after having waited more than four-and-twenty hours. Sir George Staunton instantly wrote back an answer, and rewarding the messenger liberally, desired him not to sleep till he placed it in his agent's hands.

At length they embarked in the boat, which had waited for them some time. During their voyage, which was slow, for they were obliged to row the whole way, and often against the tide, Sir George Staunton's enquiries ran chiefly on the subject of the Highland banditti who had infested that country since the year 1745. Butler informed him that many of them were not native Highlanders, but gypsies, tinkers, and other men of desperate fortunes, who had taken advantage of the confusion introduced by the civil war, the general discontent of the mountaineers, and the unsettled state of police, to practise their plundering trade with more audacity. Sir George next enquired into their lives, their habits, whether the violences which they committed were not sometimes atoned for by acts of generosity, and whether they did not possess the virtues, as well as the vices,[11] of savage tribes?

Butler answered, that certainly they did sometimes show sparks of generosity, of which even the worst class of malefactors are seldom utterly divested; but that their evil propensities were certain and regular principles of action, while any occasional burst of virtuous feeling was only a transient impulse not to be reckoned upon, and excited probably by some singular and unusual concatenation of circumstances. In discussing these enquiries, which Sir George pursued with an apparent eagerness that rather surprised Butler, the latter chanced to mention the name of Donacha Dhu na Dunaigh, with which the reader is already acquainted. Sir George caught the sound up eagerly, and as if it conveyed particular interest to his ear. He made the most minute enquiries concerning the man whom he mentioned, the number of his gang, and even the appearance of those who belonged to it. Upon these points Butler could give little answer. The man had a name among the lower class, but his exploits were considerably exaggerated; he had always one or two fellows with him, but never aspired to the command of above three or four. In short, he knew little about him, and the small acquaintance he had had, by no means inclined him to desire more.

"Nevertheless, I should like to see him some of these days."

"That would be a dangerous meeting, Sir George, unless you mean we are to see him receive his deserts from the law, and then it were a melancholy one."

"Use every man according to his deserts, Mr Butler, and who shall escape whipping?[12] But I am talking riddles to you. I will explain them more fully to you when I have spoken over the subject with Lady Staunton.—Pull away, my lads," he added, addressing himself to the rowers; "the clouds threaten us with a storm."

In fact, the dead and heavy closeness of the air, the huge piles of clouds which assembled in the western horizon, and glowed like a furnace under the influence of the setting sun—that awful stillness in which nature seems to expect the thunder-burst, as a condemned soldier waits for the platoon-fire which is to stretch him on the earth,[13] all betokened a speedy storm. Large broad drops fell from time to time, and induced the gentlemen to assume the boat-cloaks; but the rain again ceased, and the oppressive heat, so unusual in Scotland in the end of May, inclined them to throw them aside. "There is something solemn in this delay of the storm," said Sir George; "it seems as if it suspended its peal till it solemnized some important event in the world below."

"Alas!" replied Butler, "what are we, that the laws of nature should correspond in their march with our ephemeral deeds or sufferings? The clouds will burst when surcharged with the electric fluid,[14] whether a goat is falling at that instant from the cliffs of Arran,[15] or a hero expiring on the field of battle he has won."

"The mind delights to deem it otherwise," said Sir George Staunton; "and to dwell on the fate of humanity as on that which is the prime central movement of the mighty machine. We love not to think that we shall mix with the ages that have gone before us, as these broad black rain-drops mingle with the waste of waters, making a trifling and momentary eddy, and are then lost for ever."[16]

"*For ever!*—we are not—we cannot be lost for ever," said Butler, looking upward; "death is to us change, not consummation;[17] and the commencement of a new existence, corresponding in character to the deeds which we have done in the body."

While they agitated these grave subjects, to which the solemnity of the approaching storm naturally led them, their voyage threatened to be more tedious than they had expected, for gusts of wind, which rose and fell with sudden impetuosity, swept the bosom of the Firth, and impeded the efforts of the rowers. They had now only to double a small head-land, in order to get to the proper landing-place in the mouth of the little river; but in the state of the weather, and the boat being heavy, this was like to be a work of time, and in the meanwhile they must necessarily be exposed to the storm.

"Could we not land on this side of the head-land," asked Sir George, "and so gain some shelter?"

Butler knew of no landing-place, at least none affording a convenient or even practicable passage up the rocks which surrounded the shore.

"Think again," said Sir George Staunton; "the storm will soon be violent."

"Hout, ay," said one of the boatmen, "there's the Caird's Cove; but we dinna tell the minister about it, and I am no sure if I can steer the boat to it, the bay is sae fu' o' shoals and sunk rocks."

"Try," said Sir George, "and I will give you half-a-guinea."

The old fellow took the helm, and observed, "that if they could get in, there was a steep path up from the beach, and half-an-hour's walk from thence to the Manse."

"Are you sure you know the bay?" said Butler to the old man.

"I maybe kend it a wee better fifteen years syne, when Dandie Wilson was in the Firth wi' his clean-ganging lugger. I mind Dandie had a wild young Englisher wi' him, that they ca'd——"

"If you chatter so much," said Sir George Staunton, "you will have the boat on the Grindstone—bring that white rock in a line with the steeple."

"By G——," said the veteran, staring, "I think your honour kens the bay as weel as me.—Your honour's nose has been on the Grindstane[18] ere now, I'm thinking."

As they spoke thus they approached the little cove, which, concealed behind crags, and defended on every point by shallows and sunken rocks, could scarce be discovered or approached, except by those intimate with the navigation. An old shattered boat was already drawn up on the beach within the cove, close beneath the trees, and with precautions for concealment.

Upon observing this vessel, Butler remarked to his companion, "It is impossible for you to conceive, Sir George, the difficulty I have had with my poor people, in teaching them the guilt and the danger of this contraband trade[19]—yet they have perpetually before their eyes all its dangerous consequences. I do not know any thing that more effectually depraves and ruins their moral and religious principles."

Sir George forced himself to say something in a low voice, about the spirit of adventure natural to youth, and that unquestionably many would become wiser as they grew older.

"Too seldom, sir," replied Butler. "If they have been deeply engaged, and especially if they have mingled in the scenes of violence and blood to which their occupation naturally leads, I have observed, that, sooner or later, they come to an evil end. Experience, as well as Scripture, teaches us, Sir George, that mischief shall hunt the violent man,[20] and that the bloodthirsty man shall not live half his days[21]— but take my arm to help you ashore."

Sir George needed assistance, for he was contrasting in his altered thought the different feelings of mind and frame with which he had formerly frequented the same place. As they landed, a low growl of thunder was heard at a distance.

"That is ominous, Mr Butler," said Sir George.

"*Intonuit lævum*—it is ominous of good, then," answered Butler, smiling.

The boatmen were ordered to make the best of their way round the head-land to the ordinary landing-place; the two gentlemen, followed by the servant, sought their way by a blind and tangled path[22] through a close copsewood to the Manse of Knocktarlitie, where their arrival was anxiously expected.

The sisters in vain had expected their husbands' return on the preceding day, which was that appointed by Sir George's letter. The delay of the travellers at Calder had occasioned this breach of appointment. The inhabitants of the Manse began even to doubt whether they would arrive on the present day. Lady Staunton felt this hope of delay as a brief reprieve, for she dreaded the pangs which her husband's pride must undergo at meeting with a sister-in-law, to whom the whole of his unhappy and dishonourable history was too well known. She knew, whatever force or constraint he might put upon his feelings in public, that she herself must be doomed to see them display themselves in full vehemence in secret,—consume his health, destroy his temper, and render him at once an object of dread and compassion. Again and again she cautioned Jeanie to display no tokens of recognition, but to receive him as a perfect stranger,—and again and again Jeanie renewed her promise to comply with her wishes.

Jeanie herself could not fail to bestow an anxious thought on the awkwardness of the approaching meeting; but her conscience was ungalled—and then she was cumbered with many household cares of an unusual nature, which, joined to the anxious wish once more to see Butler, after an absence of unusual length, made her extremely desirous that the travellers should arrive as soon as possible. And—why should I disguise the truth?—ever and anon a thought stole across her mind that her gala dinner had now been postponed for two days; and how few of the dishes, after every art of her simple *cuisine* had been exerted to dress them, could with any credit or propriety appear again upon the third; and what was she to do with the rest?—Upon this last subject she was saved the trouble of farther deliberation, by the sudden appearance of the Captain, at the head of half-a-dozen stout fellows, dressed and armed in the Highland fashion.

"Goot-morrow morning to ye, Leddy Staunton, and I hope I hae the pleasure to see ye weel—And goot-morrow to you, goot Mrs Putler—I do peg you will order some victuals and ale and prandy for the lads, for we hae peen out on firth and moor since afore day-light, and a' to no purpose neither—Cot tamn!"

So saying, he sate down, pushed back his brigadier wig, and wiped his head with an air of easy importance; totally regardless of the look of well-bred astonishment by which Lady Staunton endeavoured to make him comprehend that he was assuming too great a liberty.

"It is some comfort, when one has had a sair tassell," continued the Captain, addressing Lady Staunton, with an air of gallantry, "that it is in a fair leddy's service, or in the service of a gentleman whilk has a fair leddy, whilk is the same thing, since serving the husband is serving the wife,[23] as Mrs Putler does very weel know."

"Really, sir," said Lady Staunton, "as you seem to intend this compliment for me, I am at a loss to know what interest Sir George or I can have in your movements this morning."

"O Cot tamn!—this is too cruel, my leddy—as if it was not py special express from his Grace's honourable agent and commissioner at Edinburgh, with a warrant conform, that I was to seek for and apprehend Donacha dhu na Dunaigh, and pring him pefore myself and Sir George Staunton, that he may have his deserts, that is to say, the gallows, whilk he has doubtless deserved, py peing the means of frightening your leddyship, as weel as for something of less importance."

"Frightening me?" said her ladyship; "Why, I never wrote to Sir George about my alarm at the water-fall."

"Then he must have heard it otherwise; for what else can give him sic an earnest tesire to see this rapscallion, that I maun ripe the haill mosses and muirs in the country for him, as if I were to get something for finding him, when the pest o't might pe a pall through my prains?"

"Can it be really true, that it is on Sir George's account that you have been attempting to apprehend this fellow?"

"Py Cot, it is for no other cause that I know than his honour's pleasure; for the creature might hae gone on in a decent quiet way for me, sae lang as he respectit the Duke's pounds—put reason goot he suld be taen, and hangit to poot, if it may pleasure ony honourable shentleman, that is the Duke's friend—Sae I got the express over night, and I caused warn half a score of pretty lads, and was up in the morning pefore the sun, and I garr'd the lads take their kilts and short coats—"

"I wonder you did that, Captain," said Mrs Butler, "when you know the act of parliament[24] against wearing the Highland dress."

"Hout-tout, ne'er fash your thumb, Mrs Putler—The law is put twa-three years auld yet, and is ower young to hae come our length; and pesides, how is the lads to climb the praes wi' thae tamned breekens on them?—it makes me sick to see them—Put ony how, I thought I kend Donacha's haunts gay and weel, and I was at the place where he had rested yestreen; for I saw the leaves the limmers had lain on, and the ashes of their fire; by the same token there was a pit greeshoch purning yet. I am thinking they got some word out o' the island what was intended—I sought every glen and cleuch, as if I had been deer-stalking, but teil a waff of his coat-tail could I see—Cot tamn!"

"He'll be away down the Firth to Cowal," said David; and Reuben, who had been out early that morning a-nutting, observed, "That he had seen a boat making for the Caird's Cove," a place well known to the boys, though their less adventurous father was ignorant of its exist-ence.

"Py Cot," said Duncan, "then I will stay here no longer than to trink this fery horn of prandy and water, for it is very possible they will pe in the wood. Donacha's a clever fellow, and maype thinks it pest to sit next the chimley when the lum reeks.[25] He thought naebody would look for him sae near hand. I peg your leddyship will excuse my aprupt departure, as I will return forthwith, and I will either pring you Donacha in life, or else his head, whilk I dare to say will be as satisfactory. And I hope to pass a pleasant evening with your leddyship; and I hope to have mine revenges on Mr Putler at packgammon, for the four pennies whilk he won, for he will pe surely at home soon, or else he will have a wet journey, seeing it is apout to pe a scud."

Thus saying, with many scrapes and bows, and apologies for leaving them, which were very readily received, and reiterated assurances of his speedy return, (of the sincerity whereof Mrs Butler entertained no doubt, so long as her best greybeard of brandy was upon duty,) Duncan left the Manse, collected his followers, and began to scour the close and entangled wood which lay between the little glen and the Caird's Cove. David, who was a favourite with the Captain, on account of his spirit and courage, took the opportunity of escaping, to attend the investigations of that great man.

CHAPTER 52

———— I did send for thee,
* * * * * * * *
That Talbot's name might be in thee reviv'd,
When sapless age, and weak unable limbs,
Should bring thy father to his drooping chair.
But,—O malignant and ill-boding stars!—

First Part of Henry the Sixth

DUNCAN and his party had not proceeded very far in the direction of the Caird's Cove before they heard a shot, which was quickly followed by one or two others. "Some tamn'd villains among the roe-deer," said Duncan; "look sharp out, lads."

The clash of swords was next heard, and Duncan and his myrmidons hastening to the spot, found Butler and Sir George Staunton's servant in the hands of four ruffians. Sir George himself lay stretched on the ground, with his drawn sword in his hand. Duncan, who was as brave as a lion, instantly fired his pistol at the leader of the band, unsheathed his sword, cried out to his men, *Claymore!* and run his weapon through the body of the fellow whom he had previously wounded, who was no other than Donacha dhu na Dunaigh himself. The other banditti were speedily overpowered, excepting one young lad, who made wonderful resistance for his years, and was at length secured with difficulty.

Butler, so soon as he was liberated from the ruffians, ran to raise Sir George Staunton, but life had wholly left him.

"A creat misfortune," said Duncan; "I think it will pe pest that I go forward to intimate it to the coot leddy.—Tavie, my dear, you hae smelled pouther for the first time this day—take my sword and hack off Donacha's head, whilk will pe coot practice for you against the time you may wish to do the same kindness to a living shentleman—or hould, as your father does not approve, you may leave it alone, as he will pe a greater object of satisfaction to Leddy Staunton to see him entire; and I hope she will do me the credit to pelieve that I can afenge a shentleman's plood fery speedily and well."

Such was the observation of a man too much accustomed to the ancient state of manners in the Highlands, to look upon the issue of such a skirmish, as any thing worthy of wonder or emotion.

We will not attempt to describe the very contrary effect which the unexpected disaster produced upon Lady Staunton, when the bloody corpse of her husband was brought to the house, where she expected to meet him alive and well. All was forgotten, but that he was the lover of her youth; and whatever were his faults to the world, that he had towards her exhibited only those that arose from the inequality of spirits and temper, incident to a situation of unparalleled difficulty. In the vivacity of her grief she gave way to all the natural irritability of her mind; shriek followed shriek, and swoon succeeded to swoon. It required all Jeanie's watchful affection to prevent her from making known, in these paroxysms of affliction, much which it was of the highest importance that she should keep secret.

At length silence and exhaustion succeeded to frenzy, and Jeanie stole out to take counsel with her husband, and to exhort him to anticipate the Captain's interference, by taking possession, in Lady Staunton's name, of the private papers of her deceased husband. To the utter astonishment of Butler, she now, for the first time, explained the relation betwixt herself and Lady Staunton, which authorized, nay, demanded, that he should prevent any stranger from being unnecessarily made acquainted with her family affairs. It was in such a crisis that Jeanie's active and undaunted habits of virtuous exertion were most conspicuous. While the Captain's attention was still engaged by a prolonged refreshment, and a very tedious examination, in Gaelic and English, of all the prisoners, and every other witness of the fatal transaction, she had the body of her brother-in-law undressed and properly disposed.—It then appeared, from the crucifix, the beads, and the shirt of hair which he wore next his person, that his sense of guilt had induced him to receive the dogmata of a religion,[1] which pretends, by the maceration of the body, to expiate the crimes of the soul. In the packet of papers, which the express had brought to Sir George Staunton from Edinburgh, and which Butler, authorized by his connection with the deceased, did not scruple to examine, he found new and astonishing intelligence, which gave him reason to thank God he had taken that measure.

Ratcliffe, to whom all sort of misdeeds and misdoers were familiar, instigated by the promised reward, soon found himself in a condition to trace the infant of these unhappy parents. The woman to whom

Meg Murdockson had sold that most unfortunate child, had made it the companion of her wanderings and her beggary, until he was about seven or eight years old, when, as Ratcliffe learned from a companion of hers, then in the Correction-house of Edinburgh, she sold him in her turn to Donacha dhu na Dunaigh. This man, to whom no act of mischief was unknown, was occasionally an agent in a horrible trade then carried on betwixt Scotland and America, for supplying the plantations with servants, by means of *kidnapping*, as it was termed, both men and women, but especially children under age. Here Ratcliffe lost sight of the boy, but had no doubt that Donacha Dhu could give an account of him. The gentleman of the law, so often mentioned, dispatched therefore an express, with a letter to Sir George Staunton, and another covering a warrant for apprehension of Donacha, with instructions to the Captain of Knockdunder to exert his utmost energy for that purpose.

Possessed of this information, and with a mind agitated by the most gloomy apprehensions, Butler now joined the Captain, and obtained from him with some difficulty a sight of the examinations. These, with a few questions to the elder of the prisoners, soon confirmed the most dreadful of Butler's anticipations. We give the heads of the information without descending into minute details.

Donacha Dhu had indeed purchased Effie's unhappy child, with the purpose of selling it to the American traders, whom he had been in the habit of supplying with human flesh. But no opportunity occurred for some time; and the boy, who was known by the name of "The Whistler," made some impression on the heart and affections even of this rude savage, perhaps because he saw in him flashes of a spirit as fierce and vindictive as his own. When Donacha struck or threatened him—a very common occurrence—he did not answer with complaints and entreaties like other children, but with oaths and efforts at revenge—he had all the wild merit, too, by which Woggarwolfe's[2] arrow-bearing page won the hard heart of his master;

> Like a wild cub, rear'd at the ruffian's feet,
> He could say biting jests, bold ditties sing,
> And quaff his foaming bumper at the board,
> With all the mockery of a little man.*

In short, as Donacha Dhu said, the Whistler was a born imp of Satan, and *therefore* he should never leave him. Accordingly, from his

* Ethwald.

eleventh year forward, he was one of the band, and often engaged in acts of violence. The last of these was more immediately occasioned by the researches which the Whistler's real father made, after him whom he was taught to consider as such. Donacha Dhu's fears had been for some time excited by the strength of the means which began now to be employed against persons of his description. He was sensible he existed only by the precarious indulgence of his namesake, Duncan of Knockdunder, who was used to boast that he could put him down or string him up when he had a mind. He resolved to leave the kingdom by means of one of those sloops which were engaged in the traffic of his old kidnapping friends, and which was about to sail for America; but he was desirous first to strike a bold stroke.

The ruffian's cupidity was excited by the intelligence that a wealthy Englishman was coming to the Manse—he had neither forgotten the Whistler's report of the gold he had seen in Lady Staunton's purse, nor his old vow. of revenge against the minister; and, to bring the whole to a point, he conceived the hope of appropriating the money, which, according to the general report of the country, the minister was to bring from Edinburgh to pay for his new purchase. While he was considering how he might best accomplish his purpose, he received the intelligence from one quarter, that the vessel in which he proposed to embark was to sail immediately from Greenock; from another, that the minister and a rich English lord, with a great many thousand pounds, were expected the next evening at the Manse; and from a third, that he must consult his safety by leaving his ordinary haunts as soon as possible, for that the Captain had ordered out a party to scour the glens for him at break of day. Donacha laid his plans with promptitude and decision. He embarked with the Whistler and two others of his band, (whom, by the bye, he meant to sell to the kidnappers,) and set sail for the Caird's Cove. He intended to lurk till night-fall in the wood adjoining to this place, which he thought was too near the habitation of men to excite the suspicion of Duncan Knock, then break into Butler's peaceful habitation, and flesh at once his appetite for plunder and for revenge. When his villainy was accomplished, his boat was to convey him to the vessel, which, according to previous agreement with the master, was instantly to set sail.

This desperate design would probably have succeeded, but for the ruffians being discovered in their lurking-place by Sir George Staunton and Butler, in their accidental walk from the Caird's Cove towards the

Manse. Finding himself detected, and at the same time observing that the servant carried a casket, or strong-box, Donacha conceived that both his prize and his victims were within his power, and attacked the travellers without hesitation. Shots were fired and swords drawn on both sides; Sir George Staunton offered the bravest resistance, till he fell, as there was too much reason to believe, by the hand of a son,[3] so long sought, and now at length so unhappily met.

While Butler was half-stunned with this intelligence, the hoarse voice of Knockdunder added to his consternation.

"I will take the liperty to take down the pell-ropes, Mr Putler, as I must pe taking order to hang these idle people up to-morrow morning, to teach them more consideration in their doings in future."

Butler entreated him to remember the act abolishing the heritable jurisdictions, and that he ought to send them to Glasgow or Inverara, to be tried by the Circuit. Duncan scorned the proposal.

"The Jurisdiction Act,"[4] he said, "had nothing to do put with the rebels, and specially not with Argyle's country, and he would hang the men up all three in one row before coot Leddy Staunton's windows, which would be a creat comfort to her in the morning to see that the coot gentleman, her husband, had been suitably afenged."

And the utmost length that Butler's most earnest entreaties could prevail, was, that he would reserve "the twa pig carles for the circuit, but as for him they ca'd the Fustler, he should try how he could fustle in a swinging tow, for it suldna be said that a shentleman, friend to the Duke, was killed in his country, and his people didna take at least twa lives for ane."

Butler entreated him to spare the victim, for his soul's sake. But Knockdunder answered, "that the soul of such a scum had been long the tefil's property, and that, Cot tamn! he was determined to gif the tefil his due."

All persuasion was in vain, and Duncan issued his mandate for execution on the succeeding morning. The child of guilt and misery was separated from his companions, strongly pinioned, and committed to a separate room, of which the Captain kept the key.

In the silence of the night, however, Mrs Butler arose, resolved, if possible, to avert, at least to delay, the fate which hung over her nephew, especially if, upon conversing with him, she should see any hope of his being brought to better temper. She had a master-key that opened every lock in the house; and at midnight, when all was still, she stood before the eyes of the astonished young savage, as, hard bound with cords, he lay, like a sheep designed for slaughter, upon a quantity of the refuse of flax which filled a corner in the apartment. Amid features sun-burnt, tawny, grimed with dirt, and obscured by his shaggy hair of a rusted black colour, Jeanie tried in vain to trace the likeness of either of his very handsome parents. Yet how could she refuse compassion to a creature so young and so wretched,—so much more wretched than even he himself could be aware of, since the murder he had too probably committed with his own hand, but in which he had at any rate participated, was in fact a parricide? She placed food on a table near him, raised him, and slacked the cords on his arms, so as to permit him to feed himself. He stretched out his hands, still smeared with blood, perhaps that of his father, and he ate voraciously and in silence.

"What is your first name?" said Jeanie, by way of opening the conversation.

"The Whistler."

"But your Christian name, by which you were baptized?"

"I never was baptized that I know of—I have no other name than the Whistler."

"Poor unhappy abandoned lad!" said Jeanie. "What would ye do if ye could escape from this place, and the death you are to die tomorrow morning?"

"Join wi' Rob Roy,[5] or wi' Serjeant More Cameron,"[6] (noted freebooters at that time,) "and revenge Donacha's death on all and sundry."

"O ye unhappy boy," said Jeanie, "do ye ken what will come o' ye when ye die?"

"I shall neither feel cauld nor hunger more," said the youth doggedly.

"To let him be execute in this dreadful state of mind would be to destroy baith body and soul—and to let him gang I dare not—what will be done?—But he is my sister's son—my own nephew—our flesh and blood—and his hands and feet are yerked as tight as cords can be drawn.—Whistler, do the cords hurt you?"

"Very much."

"But, if I were to slacken them, you would harm me?"

"No, I would not—you never harmed me or mine."

"There may be good in him yet," thought Jeanie—"I will try fair play with him."

She cut his bonds—he stood upright, looked round with a laugh of wild exultation, clapped his hands together, and sprung from the ground, as if in transport on finding himself at liberty. He looked so wild, that Jeanie trembled at what she had done.

"Let me out," said the young savage.

"I wunna, unless you promise"——

"Then I'll make you glad to let us both out."

He seized the lighted candle and threw it among the flax, which was instantly in a flame. Jeanie screamed, and ran out of the room; the prisoner rushed past her, threw open a window in the passage, jumped into the garden, sprung over its enclosure, bounded through the woods like a deer, and gained the sea-shore. Meantime, the fire was extinguished, but the prisoner was sought in vain. As Jeanie kept her own secret, the share she had in his escape was not discovered; but they learned his fate some time afterwards—it was as wild as his life had hitherto been.

The anxious enquiries of Butler at length learned that the youth had gained the ship in which his master, Donacha, had designed to embark. But the avaricious shipmaster,[7] inured by his evil trade to every species of treachery, and disappointed of the rich booty which Donacha had proposed to bring aboard, secured the person of the fugitive, and having transported him to America, sold him as a slave, or indented servant, to a Virginian planter, far up the country. When these tidings reached Butler, he sent over to America a sufficient sum to redeem the lad from slavery, with instructions that measures should be taken for improving his mind, restraining his evil propensities, and encouraging whatever good might appear in his character. But this aid came too late. The young man had headed a conspiracy in which his inhuman master was put to death, and had then fled to the next tribe of wild Indians. He was never more heard of; and it may therefore be presumed that he lived and died after the manner of that savage people, with whom his previous habits had well fitted him to associate.

All hopes of the young man's reformation being now ended, Mr and Mrs Butler thought it could serve no purpose to explain to Lady Staunton a history so full of horror. She remained their guest more than a year, during the greater part of which period her grief was excessive. In the latter months, it assumed the appearance of listlessness and low spirits, which the monotony of her sister's quiet establishment afforded no means of dissipating. Effie, from her earliest youth, was never formed for a quiet low content.[8] Far different from her sister, she required the dissipation of society to divert her sorrow, or enhance her joy.[9] She left the seclusion of Knocktarlitie with tears of sincere affection, and after heaping its inmates with all she could think of that might be valuable in their eyes. But she *did* leave it, and when the anguish of the parting was over, her departure was a relief to both sisters.

The family at the Manse of Knocktarlitie, in their own quiet happiness, heard of the well-dowered and beautiful Lady Staunton resuming her place in the fashionable world. They learned it by more substantial proofs; for David received a commission, and as the military spirit of Bible Butler seemed to have revived in him, his good behaviour qualified the envy of five hundred young Highland cadets, "come of good houses," who were astonished at the rapidity of his promotion. Reuben followed the law, and rose more slowly, yet surely. Euphemia Butler, whose fortune, augmented by her aunt's generosity, and added to her own beauty, rendered her no small prize, married a Highland laird, who never asked the name of her grandfather, and was loaded on the occasion with presents from Lady Staunton, which made her the envy of all the beauties in Dumbarton and Argyle-shires.

After blazing nearly ten years in the fashionable world, and hiding, like many of her compeers, an aching heart with a gay demeanour;— after declining repeated offers of the most respectable kind for a second matrimonial engagement, Lady Staunton betrayed the inward wound by retiring to the continent, and taking up her abode in the convent where she had received her education. She never took the veil, but lived and died in severe seclusion, and in the practice of the Roman Catholic religion, in all its formal observances, vigils, and austerities.

Jeanie had so much of her father's spirit as to sorrow bitterly for this apostacy, and Butler joined in her regret. "Yet any religion, however imperfect," he said, "was better than cold scepticism, or the hurrying din of dissipation, which fills the ear of worldlings, until they care for none of these things."[10]

Meanwhile, happy in each other, in the prosperity of their family, and the love and honour of all who knew them, this simple pair lived beloved, and died lamented.

READER—This tale will not be told in vain, if it shall be found to illustrate the great truth, that guilt, though it may attain temporal splendour, can never confer real happiness; that the evil consequences of our crimes long survive their commission, and, like the ghosts of the murdered, for ever haunt the steps of the malefactor; and that the paths of virtue, though seldom those of worldly greatness, are always those of pleasantness and peace.

L'Envoy, by JEDEDIAH CLEISHBOTHAM

THUS concludeth the Tale of "THE HEART OF MID-LOTHIAN," which hath filled more pages than I opined.[11] The Heart of Mid-Lothian is now no more,[12] or rather it is transferred to the extreme side of the city,[13] even as the Sieur Jean Baptiste Poquelin[14] hath it, in his pleasant comedy called *Le Medecin Malgre lui*,[15] where the simulated doctor wittily replieth to a charge, that he had placed the heart on the right side, instead of the left, "*Cela étoit autrefois ainsi, mais nous avons changé tout cela*."[16] Of which witty speech, if any reader shall demand the purport, I have only to respond, that I teach the French as well as the Classical tongues, at the easy rate of five shillings per quarter, as my advertisements are periodically making known to the public.[17]

SCOTT'S INTRODUCTION AND
NOTES TO THE 1830 EDITION

INTRODUCTION TO
THE HEART OF MID-LOTHIAN

THE author has stated[1] in the preface to the Chronicles of the
Canongate, 1827, that he received from an anonymous correspondent
an account of the incident upon which the following story is founded.
He is now at liberty to say, that the information was conveyed to him
by a late amiable and ingenious lady, whose wit and power of
remarking and judging of character still survive in the memory of her
friends. Her maiden name was Miss Helen Lawson, of Girthhead, and
she was wife of Thomas Goldie, Esq., of Craigmuie, Commissary of
Dumfries.

Her communication was in these words:

"I had taken for summer lodgings a cottage near the old Abbey of
Lincluden. It had formerly been inhabited by a lady who had pleasure
in embellishing cottages, which she found perhaps homely and even
poor enough; mine therefore possessed many marks of taste and
elegance unusual in this species of habitation in Scotland, where a
cottage is literally what its name declares.

"From my cottage door I had a partial view of the old Abbey before
mentioned; some of the highest arches were seen over, and some
through, the trees scattered along a lane which led down to the ruin,
and the strange fantastic shapes of almost all those old ashes accorded
wonderfully well with the building they at once shaded and orna-
mented.

"The Abbey itself from my door was almost on a level with the
cottage; but on coming to the end of the lane, it was discovered to be
situated on a high perpendicular bank, at the foot of which run the
clear waters of the Cluden, where they hasten to join the sweeping
Nith,

'Whose distant roaring swells and fa's.'[2]

As my kitchen and parlour were not very far distant, I one day went in
to purchase some chickens from a person I heard offering them for
sale. It was a little, rather stout-looking woman, who seemed to be
between seventy and eighty years of age; she was almost covered with

a tartan plaid, and her cap had over it a black silk hood, tied under the chin, a piece of dress still much in use among elderly women of that rank of life in Scotland; her eyes were dark, and remarkably lively and intelligent; I entered into conversation with her, and began by asking how she maintained herself, &c.

"She said that in winter she footed stockings, that is, knit feet to countrypeople's stockings, which bears about the same relation to stocking-knitting that cobbling does to shoe-making, and is of course both less profitable and less dignified; she likewise taught a few children to read, and in summer she whiles reared a few chickens.

"I said I could venture to guess from her face she had never been married. She laughed heartily at this, and said, 'I maun hae the queerest face that ever was seen, that ye could guess that. Now, do tell me, madam, how ye cam to think sae?' I told her it was from her cheerful disengaged countenance. She said, 'Mem, have ye na far mair reason to be happy than me, wi' a gude husband and a fine family o' bairns, and plenty o' every thing? for me, I'm the puirest o' a' puir bodies, and can hardly contrive to keep mysell alive in a' thae wee bits o' ways I hae tell't ye.' After some more conversation, during which I was more and more pleased with the old woman's sensible conversation, and the *naïveté* of her remarks, she rose to go away, when I asked her name. Her countenance suddenly clouded, and she said gravely, rather colouring, 'My name is Helen Walker; but your husband kens weel about me.'

"In the evening I related how much I had been pleased, and enquired what was extraordinary in the history of the poor woman. Mr Goldie said, there were perhaps few more remarkable people than Helen Walker. She had been left an orphan, with the charge of a sister considerably younger than herself, and who was educated and maintained by her exertions. Attached to her by so many ties, therefore, it will not be easy to conceive her feelings, when she found that this only sister must be tried by the laws of her country for child-murder, and upon being called as principal witness against her. The counsel for the prisoner told Helen, that if she could declare that her sister had made any preparations, however slight, or had given her any intimation on the subject, that such a statement would save her sister's life, as she was the principal witness against her. Helen said, 'It is impossible for me to swear to a falsehood; and, whatever may be the consequence, I will give my oath according to my conscience.'

"The trial came on, and the sister was found guilty and condemned;

but, in Scotland, six weeks must elapse between the sentence and the execution, and Helen Walker availed herself of it. The very day of her sister's condemnation, she got a petition drawn up, stating the peculiar circumstances of the case, and that very night set out on foot to London.

"Without introduction or recommendation, with her simple (perhaps ill-expressed) petition, drawn up by some inferior clerk of the court, she presented herself, in her tartan plaid and country attire, to the late Duke of Argyle, who immediately procured the pardon she petitioned for, and Helen returned with it, on foot, just in time to save her sister.

"I was so strongly interested by this narrative, that I determined immediately to prosecute my acquaintance with Helen Walker; but as I was to leave the country next day, I was obliged to defer it till my return in spring, when the first walk I took was to Helen Walker's cottage.

"She had died a short time before. My regret was extreme, and I endeavoured to obtain some account of Helen from an old woman who inhabited the other end of her cottage. I enquired if Helen ever spoke of her past history, her journey to London, &c. 'Na,' the old woman said, 'Helen was a wily body, and whene'er ony o' the neebors asked any thing about it, she aye turned the conversation.'

"In short, every answer I received only tended to increase my regret, and raise my opinion of Helen Walker, who could unite so much prudence with so much heroic virtue."

This narrative was enclosed in the following letter to the author, without date or signature:—

"SIR,—The occurrence just related happened to me 26 years ago. Helen Walker lies buried in the churchyard of Irongray, about six miles from Dumfries. I once proposed that a small monument[3] should have been erected to commemorate so remarkable a character, but I now prefer leaving it to you to perpetuate her memory in a more durable manner."

The reader is now able to judge how far the author has improved upon, or fallen short of, the pleasing and interesting sketch of high principle and steady affection displayed by Helen Walker, the proto-type of the fictitious Jeanie Deans. Mrs Goldie was unfortunately dead before the author had given his name to these volumes, so he lost all opportunity of thanking that lady for her highly valuable communica-tion. But her daughter, Miss Goldie, obliged him with the following additional information.

"Mrs Goldie endeavoured to collect further particulars of Helen Walker, particularly concerning her journey to London, but found this nearly impossible; as the natural dignity of her character, and a high sense of family respectability, made her so indissolubly connect her sister's disgrace with her own exertions, that none of her neighbours durst ever question her upon the subject. One old woman, a distant relation of Helen's, and who is still living, says she worked an harvest with her, but that she never ventured to ask her about her sister's trial, or her journey to London; 'Helen,' she added, 'was a lofty body, and used a high style o' language.' The same old woman says, that every year Helen received a cheese from her sister, who lived at Whitehaven, and that she always sent a liberal portion of it to herself or to her father's family. This fact, though trivial in itself, strongly marks the affection subsisting between the two sisters, and the complete conviction on the mind of the criminal, that her sister had acted solely from high principle, not from any want of feeling, which another small but characteristic trait will further illustrate. A gentleman, a relation of Mrs Goldie's, who happened to be travelling in the North of England, on coming to a small inn, was shown into the parlour by a female servant, who, after cautiously shutting the door, said, 'Sir, I'm Nelly Walker's sister.' Thus practically showing that she considered her sister as better known by her high conduct, than even herself by a different kind of celebrity.

"Mrs Goldie was extremely anxious to have a tombstone and an inscription upon it, erected in Irongray churchyard; and if Sir Walter Scott will condescend to write the last, a little subscription could be easily raised in the immediate neighbourhood, and Mrs Goldie's wish be thus fulfilled."

It is scarcely necessary to add, that the request of Miss Goldie will be most willingly complied with, and without the necessity of any tax on the public. Nor is there much occasion to repeat how much the author conceives himself obliged to his unknown correspondent, who thus supplied him with a theme affording such a pleasing view of the moral dignity of virtue, though unaided by birth, beauty, or talent. If the picture has suffered in the execution, it is from the failure of the author's powers to present in detail the same simple and striking portrait, exhibited in Mrs Goldie's letter.

ABBOTSFORD,
April 1, 1830.

POSTSCRIPT

ALTHOUGH it would be impossible to add much to Mrs Goldie's picturesque and most interesting account of Helen Walker, the prototype of the imaginary Jeanie Deans, the Editor may be pardoned for introducing two or three anecdotes respecting that excellent person, which he has collected from a volume entitled, "Sketches from Nature, by John M'Diarmid,"⁴ a gentleman who conducts an able provincial paper in the town of Dumfries.

Helen was the daughter of a small farmer in a place called Dalwhairn, in the parish of Irongray; where, after the death of her father, she continued, with the unassuming piety of a Scottish peasant, to support her mother by her own unremitted labour and privations; a case so common, that even yet, I am proud to say, few of my countrywomen would shrink from the duty.

Helen Walker was held among her equals *pensy*, that is, proud or conceited; but the facts brought to prove this accusation seem only to evince a strength of character superior to those around her. Thus it was remarked, that when it thundered, she went with her work and her Bible to the front of the cottage, alleging that the Almighty could smite in the city as well as in the field.

Mr M'Diarmid mentions more particularly the misfortune of her sister, which he supposes to have taken place previous to 1736. Helen Walker, declining every proposal of saving her relation's life at the expense of truth, borrowed a sum of money sufficient for her journey, walked the whole distance to London barefoot, and made her way to John Duke of Argyle. She was heard to say, that, by the Almighty's strength, she had been enabled to meet the Duke at the most critical moment, which, if lost, would have caused the inevitable forfeiture of her sister's life.

Isabella, or Tibby Walker, saved from the fate which impended over her, was married by the person who had wronged her, (named Waugh,) and lived happily for great part of a century, uniformly acknowledging the extraordinary affection to which she owed her preservation.

Helen Walker died about the end of the year 1791, and her remains are interred in the churchyard of her native parish of Irongray, in a romantic cemetery on the banks of the Cairn.[5] That a character so distinguished for her undaunted love of virtue, lived and died in poverty, if not want, serves only to show us how insignificant, in the sight of Heaven, are our principal objects of ambition upon earth.

NOTE TO PROLEGOMEN

It is an old proverb, that "many a true word is spoken in jest." The existence of Walter Scott, third son of Sir William Scott of Harden, is instructed, as it is called, by a charter under the great seal, Domino Willielmo Scott de Harden Militi, et Waltero Scott suo filio legitimo tertio genito, terrarum de Roberton.* The munificent old gentleman left all his four sons considerable estates, and settled those of Eilrig and Raeburn, together with valuable possessions around Lessudden, upon Walter, his third son, who is ancestor of the Scotts of Raeburn, and of the Author of Waverley. He appears to have become a convert to the doctrine of the Quakers, or Friends, and a great asserter of their peculiar tenets. This was probably at the time when George Fox, the celebrated apostle of the sect, made an expedition into the south of Scotland about 1657, on which occasion he boasts, that "as he first set his horse's feet upon Scottish ground, he felt the seed of grace to sparkle about him like innumerable sparks of fire." Upon the same occasion, probably, Sir Gideon Scott of Highchester, second son of Sir William, immediate elder brother of Walter, and ancestor of the author's friend and kinsman, the present representative of the family of Harden, also embraced the tenets of Quakerism. This last convert, Gideon, entered into a controversy with the Rev. James Kirkton, author of the Secret and True History of the Church of Scotland, which is noticed by my ingenious friend Mr Charles Kirkpatricke Sharpe, in his valuable and curious edition of that work, 4to, 1817. Sir William Scott, eldest of the brothers, remained, amid the defection of his two younger brethren, an orthodox member of the Presbyterian Church, and used such means for reclaiming Walter of Raeburn from his heresy, as savoured far more of persecution than persuasion. In this he was assisted by MacDougal of Makerston, brother to Isabella MacDougal, the wife of the said Walter, and who, like her husband, had conformed to the Quaker tenets.

The interest possessed by Sir William Scott and Makerston was powerful enough to procure the two following acts of the Privy

* See Douglas's Baronage, page 215.

Council of Scotland, directed against Walter of Raeburn as an heretic and convert to Quakerism, appointing him to be imprisoned first in Edinburgh jail, and then in that of Jedburgh; and his children to be taken by force from the society and direction of their parents, and educated at a distance from them, besides the assignment of a sum for their maintenance, sufficient in those times to be burdensome to a moderate Scottish estate.

"Apud Edin. vigesimo Junii 1665.

"The Lords of his Majesty's Privy Council having receaved information that Scott of Raeburn, and Isobel Mackdougall, his wife, being infected with the error of Quakerism, doe endeavour to breid and traine up William, Walter, and Isobel Scotts, their children, in the same profession, doe therefore give order and command to Sir William Scott of Harden, the said Raeburn's brother, to seperat and take away the saids children from the custody and society of the saids parents, and to cause educat and bring them up in his owne house, or any other convenient place, and ordaines letters to be direct at the said Sir William's instance against Raeburn, for a maintenance to the saids children, and that the said Sir Wm. give ane account of his diligence with all conveniency."

"Edinburgh, 5th July 1666.

"Anent a petition presented be Sir Wm. Scott of Harden, for himself and in name and behalf of the three children of Walter Scott of Raeburn, his brother, showing that the Lords of Councill, by ane act of the 22d day of Junii 1665, did grant power and warrand to the petitioner, to separat and take away Raeburn's children, from his family and education, and to breed them in some convenient place, where they might be free from all infection in their younger years, from the principalls of Quakerism, and, for maintenance of the saids children, did ordain letters to be direct against Raeburn; and, seeing the Petitioner, in obedience to the said order, did take away the saids children, being two sonnes and a daughter, and after some paines taken upon them in his owne family, hes sent them to the city of Glasgow, to be bread at schooles, and there to be principled with the knowledge of the true religion, and that it is necessary the Councill determine what shall be the maintenance for which Raeburn's three children may be charged, as likewise that Raeburn himself, being now prisoner in the Tolbooth of Edinburgh, where he dayley converses with all the Quakers who are prisoners there, and others who daily resort to them, whereby he is hardened in his pernitious opinions and principles, without all hope of recovery, unlesse he be separat from such pernitious company, humbly therefore, desyring that the Councell might determine upon the soume of money to be payed be Raeburn, for the education of his children, to the petitioner, who will be countable therefore; and that, in order to his conversion, the place of his imprisonment may be changed. The Lords of his Maj. Privy Councell having at length heard and considered the foresaid petition, doe modifie the soume of two thousand pounds Scots, to be payed yearly at the terme of Whitsunday be the said Walter Scott of Raeburn, furth of his estate to the petitioner, for the entertainment and education of the said children, beginning the first termes payment therof at Whitsunday last for the half year preceding, and so furth yearly, at the said terme of Whitsunday in tym comeing till furder orders; and ordaines the said Walter Scott of Raeburn to be transported from the tolbooth of Edinburgh to the prison of Jedburgh, where his friends and others may have occasion to convert him. And to the effect he may be secured from the practice of other Quakers, the said Lords doe hereby discharge the magistrates of Jedburgh to suffer any persons suspect of these principles to have access to him; and in case any contraveen, that they secure ther persons till they be therfore puneist; and ordaines letters to be direct heirupon in form, as effeirs."

Both the sons, thus harshly separated from their father, proved good scholars. The eldest, William, who carried on the line of Raeburn, was, like his father, a deep Orientalist; the younger, Walter, became a good classical scholar, a great friend and correspondent of the celebrated Dr Pitcairn, and a Jacobite so distinguished for zeal, that he made a vow never to shave his beard till the restoration of the exiled family. This last Walter Scott was the author's great-grandfather.

There is yet another link betwixt the author and the simple-minded and excellent Society of Friends, through a proselyte of much more importance than Walter Scott of Raeburn. The celebrated John Swinton of Swinton, xixth baron in descent of that ancient and once powerful family, was, with Sir William Lockhart of Lee, the person whom Cromwell chiefly trusted in the management of the Scottish affairs during his usurpation. After the Restoration, Swinton was devoted as a victim to the new order of things, and was brought down in the same vessel which conveyed the Marquis of Argyle to Edinburgh, where that nobleman was tried and executed. Swinton was destined to the same fate. He had assumed the habit, and entered into the society of the Quakers, and appeared as one of their number before the Parliament of Scotland. He renounced all legal defence, though several pleas were open to him, and answered, in conformity to the principles of his sect, that at the time these crimes were imputed to him, he was in the gall of bitterness and bond of iniquity; but that God Almighty having since called him to the light, he saw and acknowledged these errors, and did not refuse to pay the forfeit of them, even though, in the judgment of the Parliament, it should extend to life itself.

Respect to fallen greatness, and to the patience and calm resignation with which a man once in high power expressed himself under such a change of fortune, found Swinton friends; family connexions, and some interested considerations of Middleton the Commissioner, joined to procure his safety, and he was dismissed, but after a long imprisonment, and much dilapidation of his estates. It is said, that Swinton's admonitions, while confined in the Castle of Edinburgh, had a considerable share in converting to the tenets of the Friends Colonel David Barclay, then lying there in garrison. This was the father of Robert Barclay, author of the celebrated Apology for the Quakers. It may be observed among the inconsistencies of human nature, that Kirkton, Wodrow, and other Presbyterian authors, who have detailed the sufferings of their own sect for non-conformity with the established church, censure the government of the time for not exerting the civil power against the peaceful enthusiasts we have treated of, and some express particular chagrin at the escape of Swinton. Whatever might be his motives for assuming the tenets of the Friends, the old man retained them faithfully till the close of his life.

Jean Swinton, grand-daughter of Sir John Swinton, son of Judge Swinton, as the Quaker was usually termed, was mother of Anne Rutherford, the author's mother.

And thus, as in the play in the Anti-Jacobin,[1] the ghost of the author's grandmother[2] having arisen to speak the Epilogue, it is full time to conclude, lest the reader should remonstrate that his desire to know the Author of Waverley never included a wish to be acquainted with his whole ancestry.

TOLBOOTH OF EDINBURGH
(*Note, p. 65*)

THE ancient Tolbooth of Edinburgh, situated and described as in the last chapter, was built by the citizens in 1561, and destined for the accommodation of Parliament, as well as of the High Courts of Justice; and at the same time for the confinement of prisoners for debt, or on criminal charges. Since the year 1640, when the present Parliament House was erected, the Tolbooth was occupied as a prison only. Gloomy and dismal as it was, the situation in the centre of the High Street rendered it so particularly well-aired, that when the plague laid waste the city in 1645, it affected none within these melancholy precincts. The Tolbooth was removed, with the mass of buildings in which it was incorporated, in the autumn of the year 1817. At that time the kindness of his old schoolfellow and friend, Robert Johnstone, Esquire, then Dean of Guild of the city, with the liberal acquiescence of the persons who had contracted for the work, procured for the Author of Waverley the stones which composed the gateway, together with the door, and its ponderous fastenings, which he employed in decorating the entrance of his kitchen-court at Abbotsford. "To such base offices may we return."[1] The application of these relics of the Heart of Mid-Lothian to serve as the postern gate to a court of modern offices, may be justly ridiculed as whimsical; but yet it is not without interest, that we see the gateway through which so much of the stormy politics of a rude age, and the vice and misery of later times, had found their passage, now occupied in the service of rural economy. Last year, to complete the change, a tom-tit was pleased to build her nest within the lock of the Tolbooth,—a strong temptation to have committed a sonnet, had the author, like Tony Lumpkin, been in a concatenation accordingly.[2]

It is worth mentioning, that an act of beneficence celebrated the demolition of the Heart of Mid-Lothian. A subscription, raised and applied by the worthy Magistrate above-mentioned, procured the manumission of most of the unfortunate debtors confined in the old jail, so that there were few or none transferred to the new place of confinement.

NOTE TO CHAPTER 7

MEMORIAL CONCERNING THE MURDER OF CAPTAIN PORTEOUS

THE following interesting and authentic account of the enquiries made by Crown Counsel into the affair of the Porteous Mob, seems to have been drawn up by the Solicitor-General. The office was held in 1737 by Charles Erskine, Esq.

I owe this curious illustration to the kindness of a professional friend. It throws, indeed, little light on the origin of the tumult; but shows how profound the darkness must have been, which so much investigation could not dispel.

"Upon the 7th of September last, when the unhappy wicked murder of Captain Porteus was committed, His Majesty's Advocate and Solicitor were out of town; the first beyond Inverness, and the other in Annandale, not far from Carlyle; neither of them knew any thing of the reprieve, nor did they in the least suspect that any disorder was to happen.

"When the disorder happened, the magistrates and other persons concerned in the management of the town, seemed to be all struck of a heap; and whether from the great terror that had seized all the inhabitants, they thought ane immediate enquiry would be fruitless, or whether being a direct insult upon the prerogative of the crown, they did not care rashly to intermeddle; but no proceedings was had by them. Only, soon after, ane express was sent to his Majesties Solicitor, who came to town as soon as was possible for him; but, in the meantime, the persons who had been most guilty, had either run off, or, at least, kept themselves upon the wing until they should see what steps were taken by the Government.

"When the Solicitor arrived, he perceived the whole inhabitants under a consternation. He had no materials furnished him; nay, the inhabitants were so much afraid of being reputed informers, that very few people had so much as the courage to speak with him on the streets. However, having received her Majesties orders, by a letter from the Duke of Newcastle, he resolved to sett about the matter in earnest, and entered upon ane enquiry, groping in the dark. He had no assistance from the magistrates worth mentioning, but called witness after witness in the privatest manner, before himself in his own house, and for six weeks time, from morning to evening, went on in the enquiry without taking the least diversion, or turning his thoughts to any other business.

"He tried at first what he could do by declarations, by engaging secrecy, so that those who told the truth should never be discovered; made use of no clerk, but wrote all the declarations with his own hand, to encourage them to speak out. After all, for some time, he could get nothing but ends of stories which, when pursued, broke off; and those who appeared and knew any thing of the matter, were under the utmost terror, lest it should take air that they had mentioned any one man as guilty.

"During the course of the enquiry, the run of the town, which was strong for the villanous actors, begun to alter a little, and when they saw the King's servants in earnest to do their best, the generality, who before had spoke very warmly in defence of the wickedness, begun to be silent, and at that period more of the criminals begun to abscond.

"At length the enquiry began to open a little, and the Sollicitor was under some difficulty how to proceed. He very well saw that the first warrand that was issued out would start the whole gang; and as he had not come at any one of the most notorious offenders, he was unwilling, upon the slight evidence he had, to begin. However, upon notice given him by Generall Moyle, that one King, a butcher in the Canongate, had boasted in presence of Bridget Knell, a soldier's wife, the morning after Captain Porteus was hanged, that he had a very active hand in the mob, a warrand was issued out, and King was apprehended and imprisoned in the Canongate tolbooth.

"'This obliged the Sollicitor immediately to proceed to take up those against whom he had any information. By a signed declaration, William Stirling, apprentice to James Stirling, merchant in Edinburgh, was charged as haveing been at the Nether-Bow, after the gates were shutt, with a Lochaber ax, or halbert in his hand, and haveing begun a huzza, marched upon the head of the mob towards the Guard.

"James Braidwood, son to a candlemaker in town, was, by a signed declaration, charged as haveing been at the Tolbooth door, giveing directions to the mob about setting fire to the door, and that the mob named him by his name, and asked his advice.

"By another declaration, one Stoddart, a journeyman smith, was charged of haveing boasted publickly, in a smith's shop at Leith, that he had assisted in breaking open the Tolbooth door.

"Peter Traill, a journeyman wright, by one of the declarations, was also accused of haveing lockt the Nether-Bow Port when it was shutt by the mob.

"His Majesties Sollicitor having these informations, imployed privately such persons as he could best rely on, and the truth was, there were very few in whom he could repose confidence. But he was, indeed, faithfully served by one Webster, a soldier in the Welsh fuzileers, recommended to him by Lieutenant Alshton, who, with very great address, informed himself, and really run some risque in getting his information, concerning the places where the persons informed against used to haunt, and how they might be seized. In consequence of which, a party of the Guard from the Canongate was agreed on to march up at a certain hour, when a message should be sent. The Solicitor wrote a letter and gave it to one of the town officers, ordered to attend Captain Maitland, one of the town Captains, promoted to that command since the unhappy accident, who, indeed, was extremely diligent and active throughout the whole; and haveing got Stirling and Braidwood apprehended, dispatched the officer with the letter to the military in the Canongate, who immediately begun their march, and by the time the Sollicitor had half examined the said two persons in the Burrow-room, where the magistrates were present, a party of fifty men, drums beating, marched into the Parliament close, and drew up, which was the first thing that struck a terror, and from that time forward, the insolence was succeeded by fear.

"Stirling and Braidwood were immediately sent to the Castle, and imprisoned. That same night, Stoddart the smith was seized, and he was committed to the Castle also; as was likewise Traill the journeyman wright, who were all severally examined, and denyed the least accession.

"In the meantime, the enquiry was going on, and it haveing cast up in one of the declarations, that a hump'd-backed creature marched with a gun as one of the guards to Porteus when he went up the Lawn Markett, the person who emitted this declaration, was employed to walk the streets to see if he could find him out; at last he came to the Sollicitor and told him he had found him, and that he was in a certain house. Whereupon a warrand was issued out against him, and he was apprehended and sent to the Castle, and he proved to be one Birnie, a helper to the Countess of Weemys's coachman.

"Thereafter, ane information was given in against William M'Lauchlan, ffootman to the said Countess, he haveing been very active in the mob; ffor sometime he kept himself out of the way, but at last he was apprehended and likewise committed to the Castle.

"And these were all the prisoners who were putt under confinement in that place.

"There were other persons imprisoned in the Tolbooth of Edinburgh, and severalls against whom warrands were issued, but could not be apprehended, whose names and cases shall afterwards be more particularly taken notice of.

"The ffriends of Stirling made an application to the Earl of Islay, Lord Justice-Generall, setting furth, that he was seized with a bloody fflux; that his life was in danger; and that upon ane examination of witnesses whose names were given in, it would appear to conviction, that he had not the least access to any of the riotous proceedings of that wicked mob.

"This petition was by his Lordship putt in the hands of his Majesties Sollicitor, who examined the witnesses; and by their testimonies it appeared, that the young man, who was not above eighteen years of age, was that night in company with about half a dozen companions, in a public house in Stephen Law's closs, near the back of the Guard, where they all remained untill the noise came to the house, that the mob had shut the gates and seized the Guard, upon which the company broke up, and he, and one of his companions, went towards his master's house; and, in the course of the after examination, there was a witness who declared, nay, indeed swore, (for the Sollicitor, by this time, saw it necessary to put those he examined upon oath,) that he met him [Stirling] after he entered into the alley where his master lives, going towards his house; and another witness, fellow-prentice with Stirling, declares, that after the mob had seized the Guard, he went home, where he found Stirling before him; and that his master lockt the door, and kept them both at home till after twelve at night: upon weighing of which testimonies, and upon consideration had, That he was charged by the declaration only of one person, who really did not appear to be a witness of the greatest weight, and that his life was in danger from the imprisonment, he was admitted to baill by the Lord Justice-Generall, by whose warrand he was committed.

"Braidwood's friends applyed in the same manner; but as he stood charged by more than one witness, he was not released—tho', indeed, the witnesses adduced for him say somewhat in his exculpation—that he does not seem to have been upon any original concert; and one of the witnesses says he was along with him at the Tolbooth door, and refuses what is said against him, with regard to his having advised the burning of the Tolbooth door. But he remains still in prison.

"As to Traill, the journeyman wright, he is charged by the same witness who declared against Stirling, and there is none concurrs with him; and to say the truth concerning him, he seemed to be the most ingenuous of any of them whom the Solicitor examined, and pointed out a witness by whom one of the first accomplices was discovered, and who escaped when the warrand was to be putt in execution against them. He positively denys his having shutt the gate, and 'tis thought Traill ought to be admitted to baill.

"As to Birnie, he is charged only by one witness, who had never seen him before, nor knew his name; so, tho' I dare say the witness honestly mentioned him, 'tis possible he may be mistaken; and in the examination of above 200 witnesses, there is no body concurrs with him, and he is ane insignificant little creature.

"With regard to M'Lauchlan, the proof is strong against him by one witness, that he acted as a serjeant or sort of commander, for some time, of a Guard, that stood cross between the upper end of the Luckenbooths and the north side of the street, to stop all but friends from going towards the Tolbooth; and by other witnesses, that he was at the Tolbooth door with a link in his hand, while the operation of beating and burning it was going on: that he went along with the mob with a halbert in his hand, untill he came to the gallows stone in the Grassmarket, and that he stuck the halbert into the hole of the gallows stone: that afterwards he went in amongst the mob when Captain Porteus was carried to the dyer's tree; so that the proof seems very heavy against him.

"To sum up this matter with regard to the prisoners in the Castle, 'tis believed there is strong proof against M'Lauchlan; there is also proof against Braidwood. But as it consists only in emission of words said to have been had by him while at the Tolbooth door, and that he is ane insignificant pitifull creature, and will find people to swear heartily in his favours, 'tis at best doubtfull whether a jury will be got to condemn him.

"As to those in the Tolbooth of Edinburgh, John Crawford, who had for some time been employed to ring the bells in the steeple of the new Church of Edinburgh, being in company with a soldier accidentally, the discourse falling in concerning Captain Porteus and his murder, as he appears to be a light-headed fellow, he said, that he knew people that were more guilty than any that were putt in prison.

Upon this information, Crawford was seized, and being examined, it appeared, that when the mob begun, as he was comeing down from the steeple, the mob took the keys from him; that he was that night in several corners, and did indeed delate severall persons whom he saw there, and immediately warrands were dispatched, and it was found they had absconded and fled. But there was no evidence against him of any kind. Nay, on the contrary, it appeared, that he had been with the Magistrates in Clerk's the vintner's, relating to them what he had seen in the streets. Therefore, after haveing detained him in prison ffor a very considerable time, his Majesties Advocate and Sollicitor signed a warrand for his liberation.

"There was also one James Wilson incarcerated in the said Tolbooth, upon the declaration of one witness, who said he saw him on the streets with a gun; and there he remained for some time, in order to try if a concurring witness could be found, or that he acted any part in the tragedy and wickedness. But nothing further appeared against him; and being seized with a severe sickness, he is, by a warrand signed by his Majestie's Advocate and Sollicitor, liberated upon giveing sufficient baill.

"As to King, enquiry was made, and the ffact comes out beyond all exception, that he was in the lodge at the Nether-Bow with Lindsay the waiter, and several other people, not at all concerned in the mob. But after the affair was over, he went up towards the guard, and having met with Sandie the Turk and his wife, who escaped out of prison, they returned to his house at the Abbey, and then 'tis very possible he may have thought fitt in his beer to boast of villany, in which he could not possibly have any share; for that reason he was desired to find baill and he should be set at liberty. But he is a stranger and a fellow of very indifferent character, and 'tis believed it won't be easy for him to find baill. Wherefore, it's thought he must be sett at liberty without it. Because he is a burden upon the Government while kept in confinement, not being able to maintain himself.

"What is above is all that relates to persons in custody. But there are warrands out against a great many other persons who had fled, particularly against one William White, a journeyman baxter, who, by the evidence, appears to have been at the beginning of the mob, and to have gone along with the drum, from the West-Port to the Nether-Bow, and is said to have been one of those who attacked the guard, and probably was as deep as any one there.

"Information was given that he was lurking at Falkirk, where he was born. Whereupon directions were sent to the Sheriff of the County, and a warrand from his Excellency Generall Wade, to the commanding officers at Stirling and Linlithgow, to assist, and all possible endeavours were used to catch hold of him, and 'tis said he escaped very narrowly, having been concealed in some outhouse; and the misfortune was, that those who were employed in the search did not know him personally. Nor, indeed, was it easy to trust any of the acquaintances of so low obscure a fellow with the secret of the warrand to be putt in execution.

"There was also strong evidence found against Robert Taylor, servant to William and Charles Thomsons, periwig-makers, that he acted as ane officer among the mob, and he was traced from the guard to the well at the head of Forrester's Wynd, where he stood and had the appellation of Captain from the mob, and from that walking down the Bow before Captain Porteus, with his Lochaber-axe; and by the description given of one who hawl'd the rope by which Captain Porteus was pulled up, 'tis believed Taylor was the person; and 'tis further probable, that the witness who delated Stirling had mistaken Taylor for him, their stature and age (so far as can be gathered from the description) being much the same.

"A great deal of pains were taken, and no charge was saved, in order to have catched hold of this Taylor, and warrands were sent to the country where he was born; but it appears he had shipt himself off for Holland, where it is said he now is.

"There is strong evidence also against Thomas Burns, butcher, that he was ane active person from the beginning of the mob to the end of it. He lurkt for some time amongst those of his trade; and artfully enough a train was laid to catch him, under pretence of a message that had come from his father in Ireland, so that he came to a blind alehouse in the Flesh-market closs, and a party being ready, was by Webster the soldier, who was upon this exploit, advertised to come down. However, Burns escaped out at a back window, and hid himself in some of the houses which are heaped together upon one another in that place, so that it was not possible to catch him. 'Tis now said he is gone to Ireland to his father, who lives there.

"There is evidence also against one Robert Anderson, journeyman and servant to Colin Alison, wright; and against Thomas Linnen and James Maxwell, both servants also to the said Colin Alison, who all seem to have been deeply concerned in the matter. Anderson is one of those who putt the rope upon Captain Porteus's neck. Linnen seems also to have been very active; and Maxwell (which is pretty remarkable) is proven to have come to a shop upon the Friday before, and charged the journeymen and prentices there to attend in the Parliament close on Tuesday night, to assist to hang Captain Porteus. These three did early abscond, and though warrands had been issued out against them, and all endeavours used to apprehend them, could not be found.

"One Waldie, a servant to George Campbell, wright, has also absconded, and many others, and 'tis informed that numbers of them have shipt themselves off ffor the Plantations; and upon an information that a ship was going off ffrom Glasgow, in which severall of the rogues were to transport themselves beyond seas, proper warrands were obtained, and persons dispatched to search the said ship, and seize any that can be found.

"The like warrands had been issued with regard to ships from Leith. But whether they had been scard, or whether the information had been groundless, they had no effect.

"This is a summary of the enquiry, ffrom which it appears there is no prooff on which one can rely, but against M'Lauchlan. There is a prooff also against Braidwood, but more exceptionable. His Majesties Advocate, since he came to town, has join'd with the Sollicitor, and has done his utmost to gett at the bottom of this matter, but hitherto it stands, as is above represented. They are resolved to have their eyes and their ears open, and to do what they can. But they labour'd exceedingly against the stream; and it may truly be said, that nothing was wanting on their part. Nor have they declined any labour to answer the commands laid upon them to search the matter to the bottom."

THE PORTEOUS MOB

In the preceding chapters, the circumstances of that extraordinary riot and conspiracy, called the Porteous Mob, are given with as much accuracy as the author was able to collect them. The order, regularity, and determined resolution with which such a violent action was devised and executed, were only equalled by the secrecy which was observed concerning the principal actors.

Although the fact was performed by torch-light, and in presence of a great multitude, to some of whom, at least, the individual actors must have been known, yet no discovery was ever made concerning any of the perpetrators of the slaughter.

Two men only were brought to trial for an offence which the government were so anxious to detect and punish. William M'Lauchlan, footman to the Countess of Wemyss, who is mentioned in the report of the Solicitor-General, (page 550), against whom strong evidence had been obtained, was brought to trial in March 1737, charged as having been accessory to the riot, armed with a Lochaberaxe. But this man (who was at all times a silly creature) proved, that he was in a state of mortal intoxication during the time he was present with the rabble, incapable of giving them either advice or assistance, or, indeed, of knowing what he or they were doing. He was also able to prove, that he was forced into the riot, and upheld while there by two bakers, who put a Lochaber-axe into his hand. The jury, wisely judging this poor creature could be no proper subject of punishment, found the panel Not guilty. The same verdict was given in the case of Thomas Linning, also mentioned in the Solicitor's memorial, who was tried in 1738. In short, neither then, nor for a long period afterwards, was any thing discovered relating to the organization of the Porteous Plot.

The imagination of the people of Edinburgh was long irritated, and their curiosity kept awake, by the mystery attending this extraordinary conspiracy. It was generally reported of such natives of Edinburgh as, having left the city in youth, returned with a fortune amassed in foreign countries, that they had originally fled on account of their share in the Porteous Mob. But little credit can be attached to these surmises, as in most of the cases they are contradicted by dates, and in none supported by any thing but vague rumours, grounded on the ordinary wish of the vulgar, to impute the success of prosperous men to some unpleasant source. The secret history of the Porteous Mob has been till this day unravelled; and it has always been quoted as a close, daring, and calculated act of violence, of a nature peculiarly characteristic of the Scottish people.

Nevertheless, the author, for a considerable time, nourished hopes to have found himself enabled to throw some light on this mysterious story. An old man, who died about twenty years ago, at the advanced age of ninety-three, was said to have made a communication to the clergyman who attended upon his death-bed, respecting the origin of the Porteous Mob. This person followed the trade of a carpenter, and had been employed as such on the estate of a family of opulence and condition. His character, in his line of life and amongst his neighbours, was excellent, and never underwent the slightest suspicion.

His confession was said to have been to the following purpose: That he was one of twelve young men belonging to the village of Pathhead, whose animosity against Porteous, on account of the execution of Wilson, was so extreme, that they resolved to execute vengeance on him with their own hands, rather than he should escape punishment. With this resolution they crossed the Forth at different ferries, and rendezvoused at the suburb called Portsburgh, where their appearance in a body soon called numbers around them. The public mind was in such a state of irritation, that it only wanted a single spark to create an explosion; and this was afforded by the exertions of the small and determined band of associates. The appearance of premeditation and order which distinguished the riot, according to his account, had its origin, not in any previous plan or conspiracy, but in the character of those who were engaged in it. The story also serves to show why nothing of the origin of the riot has ever been discovered, since, though in itself a great conflagration, its source, according to this account, was from an obscure and apparently inadequate cause.

I have been disappointed, however, in obtaining the evidence on which this story rests. The present proprietor of the estate on which the old man died, (a particular friend of the author,) undertook to question the son of the deceased on the subject. This person follows his father's trade, and holds the employment of carpenter to the same family. He admits, that his father's going abroad at the time of the Porteous Mob was popularly attributed to his having been concerned in that affair; but adds, that, so far as is known to him, the old man had never made any confession to that effect; and, on the contrary, had uniformly denied being present. My kind friend, therefore, had recourse to a person from whom he had formerly heard the story; but who, either from respect to an old friend's memory, or from failure of his own, happened to have forgotten that ever such a communication was made. So my obliging correspondent (who is a fox-hunter) wrote to me that he was completely *planted*; and all that can be said with respect to the tradition is, that it certainly once existed, and was generally believed.

CARSPHARN JOHN
(*Note, p. 94*)

JOHN Semple, called Carspharn John, because minister of the parish in Galloway so called, was a presbyterian clergyman of singular piety and great zeal, of whom Patrick Walker records the following passage: "That night after his wife died, he spent the whole ensuing night in prayer and meditation in his garden. The next morning, one of his elders coming to see him, and lamenting his great loss and want of rest, he replied,—'I declare I have not, all night, had one thought of the death of my wife, I have been so taken up in meditating on heavenly things. I have been this night on the banks of Ulai, plucking an apple here and there.'"—*Walker's Remarkable Passages of the Life and Death of Mr John Semple.*

PETER WALKER
(Note, p. 103)

THIS personage,[1] whom it would be base ingratitude in the author to pass over without some notice, was by far the most zealous and faithful collector and recorder of the actions and opinions of the Cameronians. He resided, while stationary, at the Bristo Port of Edinburgh, but was by trade an itinerant merchant or pedlar, which profession he seems to have exercised in Ireland as well as Britain. He composed biographical notices of Alexander Peden, John Semple, John Welwood, and Richard Cameron, all ministers of the Cameronian persuasion, to which the last mentioned member gave the name.

It is from such tracts as these, written in the sense, feeling, and spirit of the sect, and not from the sophisticated narratives of a later period, that the real character of the persecuted class is to be gathered. Walker writes with a simplicity which sometimes slides into the burlesque, and sometimes attains a tone of simple pathos, but always expressing the most daring confidence in his own correctness of creed and sentiments, sometimes with narrow-minded and disgusting bigotry. His turn for the marvellous was that of his time and sect; but there is little room to doubt his veracity concerning whatever he quotes on his own knowledge. His small tracts now bring a very high price, especially the earlier and authentic editions.

The tirade against dancing, pronounced by David Deans, is, as intimated in the text, partly borrowed from Peter Walker. He notices, as a foul reproach upon the name of Richard Cameron, that his memory was vituperated "by pipers and fiddlers playing the Cameronian march—carnal vain springs, which too many professors of religion dance to; a practice unbecoming the professors of Christianity to dance to any spring, but somewhat more to this. Whatever," he proceeds, "be the many foul blots recorded of the saints in Scripture, none of them is charged with this regular fit of distraction. We find it has been practised by the wicked and profane, as the dancing at that brutish, base action of the calf-making; and it had been good for that unhappy lass, who danced off the head of John the Baptist, that she had been born a cripple, and never drawn a limb to her. Historians say, that her sin was written upon her judgment, who some time thereafter was dancing upon the ice, and it broke, and snapt the head off her; her head danced above, and her feet beneath. There is ground to think and conclude, that when the world's wickedness was great, dancing at their marriages was practised; but when the heavens above, and the earth beneath, were let loose upon them with that overflowing flood, their mirth was soon staid; and when the Lord in holy justice rained fire and brimstone from heaven upon that wicked people and city Sodom, enjoying fulness of bread and idleness, their fiddle-strings and hands went all in a flame; and the whole people in thirty miles of length, and ten of breadth, as historians say, were all made to fry in their skins; and at the end, whoever are giving in marriages and dancing when all will go in a flame, they will quickly change their note.

"I have often wondered thorow my life, how any that ever knew what it was to bow a knee in earnest to pray, durst crook a hough to fyke and fling at a piper's and fiddler's springs. I bless the Lord that ordered my lot so in my dancing days, that made the fear of the bloody rope and bullets to my neck and head, the pain of boots, thumikens, and irons, cold and hunger, wetness and weariness, to stop the lightness of my head, and the wantonness of my feet. What the never-to-be-forgotten Man of God, John Knox, said to Queen Mary, when she gave him that sharp challenge, which would strike our mean-spirited, tongue-tacked ministers dumb, for his giving public faithful warning of the danger of the church and nation, through her marrying the Dauphine of France, when he left her bubbling and greeting, and came to an outer court, where her Lady Maries were fyking and dancing, he said, 'O brave ladies, a brave world, if it would last, and heaven at the hinder end! But fye upon the knave Death, that will seize upon those bodies of yours; and where will all your fiddling and flinging be then?' Dancing being such a common evil, especially amongst young professors, that all the lovers of the Lord should hate, has caused me to insist the more upon it, especially that foolish spring the Cameronian march!"—*Life and Death of three Famous Worthies, &c. by Peter Walker*, 12mo, p. 59.

It may be here observed, that some of the milder class of Cameronians made a distinction between the two sexes dancing separately, and allowed of it as a healthy and not unlawful exercise; but when men and women mingled in sport, it was then called *promiscuous dancing*, and considered as a scandalous enormity.

MUSCHAT'S CAIRN
(*Note, p. 116*)

NICOL Muschat, a debauched and profligate wretch, having conceived a hatred against his wife, entered into a conspiracy with another brutal libertine and gambler, named Campbell of Burnbank, (repeatedly mentioned in Pennycuick's[1] satirical poems of the time,) by which Campbell undertook to destroy the woman's character, so as to enable Muschat, on false pretences, to obtain a divorce from her. The brutal devices to which these worthy accomplices resorted for that purpose having failed, they endeavoured to destroy her by administering medicine of a dangerous·kind, and in extraordinary quantities.

This purpose also failing, Nicol Muschat, or Muschet, did finally, on the 17th October, 1720, carry his wife under cloud of night to the King's Park, adjacent to what is called the Duke's Walk, near Holyrood Palace, and there took her life by cutting her throat almost quite through, and inflicting other wounds. He pleaded guilty to the indictment, for which he suffered death. His associate, Campbell, was sentenced to transportation for his share in the previous conspiracy. See MacLaurin's Criminal Cases, pages 64 and 738.

In memory, and at the same time execration, of the deed, a *cairn*, or pile of stones, long marked the spot. It is now almost totally removed, in consequence of an alteration on the road in that place.

THE FAIRY BOY OF LEITH
(*Note, p. 153*)

THIS legend was in former editions inaccurately said to exist in Baxter's "World of Spirits;" but is, in fact, to be found in "Pandæmonium, or the Devil's Cloyster; being a further blow to Modern Sadduceism," by Richard Bovet, Gentleman, 12mo, 1684. The work is inscribed to Dr Henry More. The story is entitled, "A remarkable passage of one named the Fairy Boy of Leith, in Scotland, given me by my worthy friend Captain George Burton, and attested under his hand;" and is as follows:—

"About fifteen years since, having business that detained me for some time in Leith, which is near Edenborough, in the kingdom of Scotland, I often met some of my acquaintance at a certain house there, where we used to drink a glass of wine for our refection. The woman which kept the house, was of honest reputation amongst the neighbours, which made me give the more attention to what she told me one day about a Fairy Boy (as they called him) who lived about that town. She had given me so strange an account of him, that I desired her I might see him the first opportunity, which she promised; and not long after, passing that way, she told me there was the Fairy Boy but a little before I came by; and casting her eye into the street, said, 'Look you, sir, yonder he is at play with those other boys,' and designing him to me, I went, and by smooth words, and a piece of money, got him to come into the house with me; where, in the presence of divers people, I demanded of him several astrological questions, which he answered with great subtility, and through all his discourse carried it with a cunning much beyond his years, which seemed not to exceed ten or eleven. He seemed to make a motion like drumming upon the table with his fingers, upon which I asked him, whether he could beat a drum, to which he replied, 'Yes, sir, as well as any man in Scotland; for every Thursday night I beat all points to a sort of people that use to meet under yonder hill' (pointing to the great hill between Edenborough and Leith.) 'How, boy,' quoth I; 'what company have you there?'—'There are, sir,' said he, 'a great company both of men and women, and they are entertained with many sorts of musick besides my drum; they have, besides, plenty variety of meats and wine; and many times we are carried into France or Holland in a night, and return again; and whilst we are there, we enjoy all the pleasures the country doth afford.' I demanded of him, how they got under that hill? To which he replied, 'that there were a great pair of gates that opened to them, though they were invisible to others, and that within there were brave large rooms, as well accommodated as most in Scotland.' I then asked him, how I should know what he said to be true? upon which he told me he would read my fortune, saying I should have two wives, and that he saw the forms of them sitting on my shoulders; that both would be very handsome women.

"As he was thus speaking, a woman of the neighbourhood, coming into the room, demanded of him what her fortune should be? He told her that she had two bastards before she was married; which put her in such a rage, that she desired not to hear the rest. The woman of the house told me that all the people in Scotland could not keep him from the rendezvous on Thursday night; upon which, by promising him some more money, I got a promise of him to meet me at the same place, in the afternoon of the Thursday following, and so dismissed him at that time. The boy came again at the place and time appointed, and I had prevailed with some friends to continue with me, if possible, to prevent his moving that night; he was placed between us, and answered many questions, without offering to go from us, until about eleven of the clock, he was got away unperceived of the company; but I suddenly missing him, hasted to the door, and took hold of him, and so returned him into the same room: we all watched him, and on a sudden he was again got out of the doors. I followed him close, and he made a noise in the street as if he had been set upon; but from that time I could never see him.

"GEORGE BURTON."

INTERCOURSE OF THE COVENANTERS WITH THE INVISIBLE WORLD

(*Note, p. 154*)

THE gloomy, dangerous, and constant wanderings of the persecuted sect of Cameronians, naturally led to their entertaining with peculiar credulity the belief, that they were sometimes persecuted, not only by the wrath of men, but by the secret wiles and open terrors of Satan. In fact, a flood could not happen, a horse cast a shoe, or any other the most ordinary interruption thwart a minister's wish to perform service at a particular spot, than the accident was imputed to the immediate agency of fiends. The encounter of Alexander Peden with the Devil in the cave, and that of John Semple with the demon in the ford, are given by Peter Walker, almost in the language of the text.

CHILD MURDER
(*Note, p. 159*)

THE Scottish Statute Book, anno 1690, chapter 21, in consequence of the great increase of the crime of child murder,[1] both from the temptations to commit the offence and the difficulty of discovery, enacted a certain set of presumptions, which, in the absence of direct proof, the jury were directed to receive as evidence of the crime having actually been committed. The circumstances selected for this purpose were, that the woman should have concealed her situation during the whole period of pregnancy; that she should not have called for help at her delivery; and that, combined with these grounds of suspicion, the child should be either found dead or be altogether missing. Many persons suffered death during the last century under this severe act. But during the author's memory a more lenient course was followed, and the female accused under the act, and conscious of no competent defence, usually lodged a petition to the Court of Justiciary, denying, for form's sake, the tenor of the indictment, but stating, that as her good name had been destroyed by the charge, she was willing to submit to sentence of banishment, to which the crown counsel usually consented. This lenity in practice, and the comparative infrequency of the crime since the doom of public ecclesiastical penance has been generally dispensed with, have led to the abolition of the statute of William and Mary, which is now replaced by another, imposing banishment in those circumstances in which the crime was formerly capital. This alteration took place in 1803.

CALUMNIATOR OF THE FAIR SEX
(*Note, p. 186*)

THE journal of Graves, a Bow-street officer, dispatched to Holland to obtain the surrender of the unfortunate William Brodie,[1] bears a reflection on the ladies somewhat like that put in the mouth of the police-officer Sharpitlaw. It had been found difficult to identify the unhappy criminal; and, when a Scotch gentleman of respectability had seemed disposed to give evidence on the point required, his son-in-law, a clergyman in Amsterdam, and his daughter, were suspected by Graves to have used arguments with the witness to dissuade him from giving his testimony. On which subject the journal of the Bow-street officer proceeds thus:

"Saw then a manifest reluctance in Mr —, and had no doubt the daughter and parson would endeavour to persuade him to decline troubling himself in the matter, but judged he could not go back from what he had said to Mr Rich.—NOTA BENE. *No mischief but a woman or a priest in it*—here both."

SIR WILLIAM DICK OF BRAID
(*Note, p. 196*)

THIS gentleman formed a striking example of the instability of human prosperity. He was once the wealthiest man of his time in Scotland, a merchant in an extensive line of commerce, and a farmer of the public revenue; insomuch that, about 1640, he estimated his fortune at two hundred thousand pounds sterling. Sir William Dick was a zealous Covenanter; and in the memorable year 1641, he lent the Scottish Convention of Estates one hundred thousand merks at once, and thereby enabled them to support and pay their army, which must otherwise have broken to pieces. He afterwards advanced L.20,000 for the service of King Charles, during the usurpation; and having, by owning the royal cause, provoked the displeasure of the ruling party, he was fleeced of more money, amounting in all to L.65,000 sterling.

Being in this manner reduced to indigence, he went to London to try to recover some part of the sums which had been lent on government security. Instead of receiving any satisfaction, the Scottish Crœsus was thrown into prison, in which he died, 19th December, 1655. It is said his death was hastened by the want of common necessaries. But this statement is somewhat exaggerated, if it be true, as is commonly said, that though he was not supplied with bread, he had plenty of pie-crust, thence called "Sir William Dick's necessity."

The changes of fortune are commemorated in a folio pamphlet entitled, "The Lamentable Estate and Distressed Case of Sir William Dick." It contains several copper-plates, one representing Sir William on horseback, and attended with guards as Lord Provost of Edinburgh, superintending the unloading of one of his rich argosies. A second exhibiting him as arrested, and in the hands of the bailiffs. A third presents him dead in prison. The tract is esteemed highly valuable by collectors of prints. The only copy I ever saw upon sale, was rated at L.30.

MEETING AT TALLA-LINNS
(*Note, p. 201*)

THIS remarkable convocation took place upon 15th June, 1682, and an account of its confused and divisive proceedings may be found in Michael Shield's Faithful Contendings Displayed, Glasgow, 1780, p. 21. It affords a singular and melancholy example how much a metaphysical and polemical spirit had crept in amongst these unhappy sufferers, since, amid so many real injuries which they had to sustain, they were disposed to add disagreement and disunion concerning the character and extent of such as were only imaginary.

DOOMSTER, OR
DEMPSTER, OF COURT
(*Note, p. 247*)

THE name of this officer is equivalent to the pronouncer of doom or sentence. In this comprehensive sense, the Judges of the Isle of Man were called Dempsters. But in Scotland the word was long restricted to the designation of an official person, whose duty it was to recite the sentence after it had been pronounced by the Court, and recorded by the clerk; on which occasion the Dempster legalized it by the words of form, "*And this I pronounce for doom.*" For a length of years, the office, as mentioned in the text, was held *in commendam* with that of the executioner; for when this odious but necessary officer of justice received his appointment, he petitioned the Court of Justiciary to be received as their Dempster, which was granted as a matter of course.

The production of the executioner in open court, and in presence of the wretched criminal, had something in it hideous and disgusting to the more refined feelings of later times. But if an old tradition of the Parliament House of Edinburgh may be trusted, it was the following anecdote which occasioned the disuse of the Dempster's office.

It chanced at one time that the office of public executioner was vacant. There was occasion for some one to act as Dempster, and, considering the party who generally held the office, it is not wonderful that a *locum tenens* was hard to be found. At length, one Hume, who had been sentenced to transportation, for an attempt to burn his own house, was induced to consent that he would pronounce the doom on this occasion. But when brought forth to officiate, instead of repeating the doom to the criminal, Mr Hume addressed himself to their lordships in a bitter complaint of the injustice of his own sentence. It was in vain that he was interrupted, and reminded of the purpose for which he had come hither; "I ken what ye want of me weel aneugh," said the fellow, "ye want me to be your Dempster; but I am come to be none of your Dempster, I am come to summon you, Lord T—, and you, Lord E—, to answer at the bar of another world for the injustice you have done me in this." In short, Hume had only made a pretext of complying with the proposal, in order to have an opportunity of reviling the Judges to their faces, or giving them, in the phrase of his country, "a sloan." He was hurried off amid the laughter of the audience, but the indecorous scene which had taken place contributed to the abolition of the office of Dempster. The sentence is now read over by the clerk of court, and the formality of pronouncing doom is altogether omitted.

JOHN DUKE OF ARGYLE
AND GREENWICH
(*Note, p. 250*)

THIS nobleman[1] was very dear to his countrymen, who were justly proud of his military and political talents, and grateful for the ready zeal with which he asserted the rights of his native country. This was never more conspicuous than in the matter of the Porteous Mob, when the Ministers brought in a violent and vindictive bill, for declaring the Lord Provost of Edinburgh incapable of bearing any public office in future, for not foreseeing a disorder which no one foresaw, or interrupting the course of a riot too formidable to endure opposition. The same Bill made provision for pulling down the city gates, and abolishing the city guard,—rather a Hibernian mode of enabling them better to keep the peace within burgh in future.

The Duke of Argyle opposed this bill as a cruel, unjust, and fanatical proceeding, and an encroachment upon the privileges of the royal burghs of Scotland, secured to them by the treaty of Union. "In all the proceedings of that time," said his Grace, "the nation of Scotland treated with the English as a free and independent people; and as that treaty, my Lords, had no other guarantee for the due performance of its articles, but the faith and honour of a British Parliament, it would be both unjust and ungenerous, should this House agree to any proceedings that have a tendency to injure it."

Lord Hardwicke, in reply to the Duke of Argyle, seemed to insinuate, that his Grace had taken up the affair in a party point of view, to which the nobleman replied in the spirited language quoted in the text—Lord Hardwicke apologized. The bill was much modified, and the clauses concerning the dismantling the city, and disbanding the Guard, were departed from. A fine of L.2000 was imposed on the city for the benefit of Porteous's widow. She was contented to accept three-fourths of the sum, the payment of which closed the transaction. It is remarkable, that, in our day, the Magistrates of Edinburgh have had recourse to both those measures, held in such horror by their predecessors, as necessary steps for the improvement of the city.

It may be here noticed, in explanation of another circumstance mentioned in the text, that there is a tradition in Scotland, that George II., whose irascible temper is said sometimes to have hurried him into expressing his displeasure *par voie du fait*, offered to the Duke of Argyle, in angry audience, some menace of this nature, on which he left the presence in high disdain, and with little ceremony. Sir Robert Walpole, having met the Duke as he retired, and learning the cause of his resentment and discomposure, endeavoured to reconcile him to what had happened by saying, "Such was his Majesty's way, and that he often took such liberties with himself without meaning any harm." This did not mend matters in M'Callummore's eyes, who replied, in great disdain, "You will please to remember, Sir Robert, the infinite distance there is betwixt you and me." Another frequent expression of passion on the part of the same monarch, is alluded to in the old Jacobite song—

> The fire shall get both hat and wig,
> As oft times they've got a' that.[2]

EXPULSION OF THE BISHOPS FROM THE SCOTTISH CONVENTION
(*Note, p. 403*)

FOR some time after the Scottish Convention had commenced its sittings, the Scottish prelates retained their seats, and said prayers by rotation to the meeting, until the character of the Convention became, through the secession of Dundee, decidedly Presbyterian. Occasion was then taken on the Bishop of Ross mentioning King James in his prayer, as him for whom they watered their couch with tears—on this the Convention exclaimed, they had no occasion for spiritual lords, and commanded the bishops to depart and return no more, Montgomery of Skelmorley breaking at the same time a coarse jest upon the scriptural expression used by the prelate. Davie Deans's oracle, Patrick Walker, gives this account of their dismission:—"When they came out, some of the Convention said they wished that the honest lads knew that they were put out, for then they would not win away with heal (whole) gowns. All the fourteen gathered together with pale faces, and stood in a cloud in the Parliament Close. James Wilson, Robert Neilson, Francis Hislop, and myself were standing close by them. Francis Hislop with force thrust Robert Neilson upon them; their heads went hard upon one another. But there being so many enemies in the city fretting and gnashing their teeth, waiting for an occasion to raise a mob, where undoubtedly blood would have been shed, and we having laid down conclusions among ourselves to guard against giving the least occasion to all mobs, kept us from tearing of their gowns.

"Their graceless Graces went quickly off, and neither bishop nor curate was seen in the streets: this was a surprising sudden change not to be forgotten. Some of us would have rejoiced more than in great sums to have seen these bishops sent legally down the Bow, that they might have found the weight of their tails in a tow to dry their hosesoles; that they might know what hanging was, they having been active for themselves, and the main instigators to all the mischiefs, cruelties, and bloodshed of that time, wherein the streets of Edinburgh and other places of the land did run with the innocent, precious dear blood of the Lord's people."—*Life and Death of three famous Worthies* (Semple, etc.), by Patrick Walker. Edin. 1727, pp. 72, 73.

MADGE WILDFIRE
(*Note, p. 415*)

IN taking leave of the poor maniac, the author may here observe, that the first conception of the character, though afterwards greatly altered, was taken from that of a person calling herself, and called by others, Feckless Fannie, (weak or feeble Fannie,) who always travelled with a small flock of sheep. The following account, furnished by the persevering kindness of Mr Train, contains probably all that can now be known of her history, though many, among whom is the author, may remember having heard of Feckless Fannie, in the days of their youth.

"My leisure hours," says Mr Train,[1] "for some time past have been mostly spent in searching for particulars relating to the maniac called Feckless Fannie, who travelled over all Scotland and England, between the years 1767 and 1775, and whose history is altogether so like a romance, that I have been at all possible pains to collect every particular that can be found relative to her in Galloway, or in Ayrshire.

"When Feckless Fannie appeared in Ayrshire, for the first time, in the summer of 1769, she attracted much notice, from being attended by twelve or thirteen sheep, who seemed all endued with faculties so much superior to the ordinary race of animals of the same species, as to excite universal astonishment. She had for each a different name, to which it answered when called by its mistress, and would likewise obey in the most surprising manner any command she thought proper to give. When travelling, she always walked in front of her flock, and they followed her closely behind. When she lay down at night in the fields, for she would never enter into a house, they always disputed who should lie next to her, by which means she was kept warm, while she lay in the midst of them; when she attempted to rise from the ground, an old ram, whose name was Charlie, always claimed the sole right of assisting her; pushing any that stood in his way aside, until he arrived right before his mistress; he then bowed his head nearly to the ground that she might lay her hands on his horns, which were very large; he then lifted her gently from the ground by raising his head. If she chanced to leave her flock feeding, as soon as they discovered she was gone, they all began to bleat most piteously, and would continue to do so till she returned; they would then testify their joy by rubbing their sides against her petticoat, and frisking about.

"Feckless Fannie was not, like most other demented creatures, fond of fine dress; on her head she wore an old slouched hat, over her shoulders an old plaid, and carried always in her hand a shepherd's crook; with any of these articles, she invariably declared she would not part for any consideration whatever. When she was interrogated why she set so much value on things seemingly so insignificant, she would sometimes relate the history of her misfortune, which was briefly as follows:

"'I am the only daughter of a wealthy squire in the north of England, but I loved my father's shepherd, and that has been my ruin; for my father, fearing his family would be disgraced by such an alliance, in a passion mortally wounded my lover with a shot from a pistol. I arrived just in time to receive the last blessing of the dying man, and to close his eyes in death. He bequeathed me his little all, but I only accepted these sheep to be my sole companions through life, and this hat, this plaid, and this crook, all of which I will carry until I descend into the grave.'

"This is the substance of a ballad, eighty-four lines of which I copied down lately from the recitation of an old woman in this place, who says she has seen it in print, with a plate on the title-page, representing Fannie with her sheep behind her. As this ballad is said to have been written by Lowe,[2] the author of Mary's Dream, I am surprised that it has not been noticed by Cromek, in his Remains of Nithsdale and Galloway Song; but he perhaps thought it unworthy of a place in his collection, as there is very little merit in the composition; which want of room prevents me from transcribing at present. But if I thought you had never seen it, I would take an early opportunity of doing so.

"After having made the tour of Galloway in 1769, as Fannie was wandering in the neighbourhood of Moffat, on her way to Edinburgh, where, I am informed, she was likewise well known, Old Charlie, her favourite ram, chanced to break into a kale-yard, which the proprietor observing, let loose a mastiff that hunted the poor sheep to death. This was a sad misfortune; it seemed to renew all the pangs which she formerly felt on the death of her lover. She would not part from the side of her old friend for several days, and it was with much difficulty she consented to allow him to be buried; but, still wishing to pay a tribute to his memory, she covered his grave with moss, and fenced it round with osiers, and annually returned to the same spot, and pulled the weeds from the grave and repaired the fence. This is altogether like a romance; but I believe it is really true that she did so. The grave of Charlie is still held sacred even by the schoolboys of the present day in that quarter. It is now, perhaps, the only instance of the law of Kenneth being attended to, which says, 'The grave where anie that is slaine lieth buried, leave untilled for seven years. Repute every grave holie so as thou be well advised, that in no wise with thy feet thou tread upon it.'

"Through the storms of winter, as well as in the milder season of the year, she continued her wandering course, nor could she be prevented from doing so, either by entreaty or promise of reward. The late Dr Fullarton of Rosemount, in the neighbourhood of Ayr, being well acquainted with her father when in England, endeavoured, in a severe season, by every means in his power, to detain her at Rosemount for a few days until the weather should become more mild; but when she found herself rested a little, and saw her sheep fed, she raised her crook, which was the signal she always gave for the sheep to follow her, and off they all marched together.

"But the hour of poor Fannie's dissolution was now at hand, and she seemed anxious to arrive at the spot where she was to terminate her mortal career. She proceeded to Glasgow, and, while passing through that city, a crowd of idle boys, attracted by her singular appearance, together with the novelty of seeing so many sheep obeying her command, began to torment her with their pranks, till she became so irritated that she pelted them with bricks and stones, which they returned in such a manner, that she was actually stoned to death between Glasgow and Anderston.

"To the real history of this singular individual, credulity has attached several superstitious appendages. It is said, that the farmer who was the cause of Charlie's death, shortly afterwards drowned himself in a peat-hag; and that the hand, with which a butcher in Kilmarnock struck one of the other sheep, became powerless, and withered to the very bone. In the summer of 1769, when she was passing by New Cumnock, a young man, whose name was William Forsyth, son of a farmer in the same parish, plagued her so much that she wished he might never see the morn; upon which he went home and hanged himself in his father's barn. And I doubt not many such stories may yet be remembered in other parts where she had been."

So far Mr Train. The author can only add to this narrative, that Feckless Fannie and her little flock were well known in the pastoral districts.

In attempting to introduce such a character into fiction, the author felt the risk of encountering a comparison with the Maria[3] of Sterne; and, besides, the mechanism of the story would have been as much retarded by Feckless Fannie's flock, as the night-march of Don Quixote was delayed by Sancho's tale[4] of the sheep that were ferried over the river.

The author has only to add, that notwithstanding the preciseness of his friend Mr Train's statement, there may be some hopes that the outrage on Feckless Fannie and her little flock was not carried to extremity. There is no mention of any trial on account of it, which, had it occurred in the manner stated, would have certainly taken place; and the author has understood that it was on the Border she was last seen, about the skirts of the Cheviot hills, but without her little flock.

DEATH OF FRANCIS GORDON
(*Note, p. 440*)

THIS exploit seems to have been one in which Patrick Walker prided himself not a little; and there is reason to fear, that that excellent person would have highly resented the attempt to associate another with him, in the slaughter of a King's Life-Guardsman. Indeed, he would have had the more right to be offended at losing any share of the glory, since the party against Gordon was already three to one, besides having the advantage of fire-arms. The manner in which he vindicates his claim to the exploit, without committing himself by a direct statement of it, is not a little amusing. It is as follows:—

"I shall give a brief and true account of that man's death, which I did not design to do while I was upon the stage; I resolve, indeed, (if it be the Lord's will,) to leave a more full account of that and many other remarkable steps of the Lord's dispensations towards me through my life. It was then commonly said, that Francis Gordon was a volunteer out of wickedness of principles, and could not stay with the troop, but was still raging and ranging to catch hiding suffering people. Meldrum and Airly's troops, lying at Lanark upon the first day of March 1682, Mr Gordon and another wicked comrade, with their two servants and four horses, came to Kilcaigow, two miles from Lanark, searching for William Caigow and others under hiding.

"Mr Gordon, rambling throw the town, offered to abuse the women. At night, they came a mile further to the Easter-Seat, to Robert Muir's, he being also under hiding. Gordon's comrade and the two servants went to bed, but he could sleep none, roaring all night for women. When day came, he took only his sword in his hand, and came to Moss-platt, and some new men (who had been in the fields all night) seeing him, they fled, and he pursued. James Wilson, Thomas Young, and myself, having been in a meeting all night, were lying down in the morning. We were alarmed, thinking there were many more than one; he pursued hard, and overtook us. Thomas Young said, 'Sir, what do ye pursue us for?' he said, 'he was come to send us to hell.' James Wilson said, 'that shall not be, for we will defend ourselves.' He said, 'that either he or we should go to it now.' He run his sword furiously throw James Wilson's coat. James fired upon him, but missed him. All this time he cried, Damn his soul! He got a shot in his head out of a pocket pistol, rather fit for diverting a boy than killing such a furious, mad, brisk man, which, notwithstanding, killed him dead. The foresaid William Caigow and Robert Muir came to us. We searched him for papers, and found a long scroll of sufferers' names, either to kill or take. I tore it all in pieces. He had also some Popish books and bonds of money, with one dollar, which a poor man took off the ground; all which we put in his pocket again. Thus, he was four miles from Lanark, and near a mile from his comrade, seeking his own death, and got it. And for as much as we have been condemned for this, I could never see how any one could condemn us that allows of self-defence, which the laws both of God and nature allow to every creature. For my own part, my heart never smote me for this. When I saw his blood run, I wished that all the blood of the Lord's stated and avowed enemies in Scotland had been in his veins. Having such a clear call and opportunity, I would have rejoiced to have seen it all gone out with a gush. I have many times wondered at the greater part of the indulged, lukewarm ministers and professors in that time, who made more noise of murder, when one of these enemies had been killed even in our own defence, than of twenty of us being murdered by them. None of these men present was challenged for this but myself. Thomas Young thereafter suffered at Machline, but was not challenged for this; Robert Muir was banished; James Wilson outlived the persecution; William Caigow died in the Canongate Tolbooth, in the beginning of 1685. Mr Wodrow is misinformed; who says, that he suffered unto death.''

TOLLING TO SERVICE
IN SCOTLAND
(Note, p. 457)

In the old days of Scotland, when persons of property (unless they happened to be non-jurors) were as regular as their inferiors in attendance on parochial worship, there was a kind of etiquette, in waiting till the patron or acknowledged great man of the parish should make his appearance. This ceremonial was so sacred in the eyes of a parish beadle in the Isle of Bute, that the kirk bell being out of order, he is said to have mounted the steeple every Sunday, to imitate with his voice the successive summonses which its mouth of metal used to send forth. The first part of this imitative harmony was simply the repetition of the words *Bell bell, bell bell*, two or three times, in a manner as much resembling the sound as throat of flesh could imitate throat of iron. *Bellùm! bellùm!* was sounded forth in a more urgent manner; but he never sent forth the third and conclusive peal, the varied tone of which is called in Scotland the *ringing-in*, until the two principal heritors of the parish approached, when the chime ran thus:—

> *Bellùm Bellèllum,*
> *Bernera and Knockdow's coming!*
> *Bellùm Bellèllum,*
> *Bernera and Knockdow's coming!*

Thereby intimating, that service was instantly to proceed.

EDITOR'S NOTES

ABBREVIATIONS USED IN
THE NOTES

References to the Bible are given by book, chapter and verse. References to
Shakespeare are given by play, act, scene and line number according to *The
Complete Works: The Pelican Text Revised*, A. Harbage, ed. (1969). Other
frequently cited works are abbreviated as follows:

Child	F.J. Child, ed., *The English and Scottish Popular Ballads*, 5 vols. (Boston, Massachusetts, 1882–98; Dover reprint, New York, 1965)
CSD	M. Robinson, ed., *The Concise Scots Dictionary* (Aberdeen, 1985)
Defoe, *Tour*	Daniel Defoe, *A Tour through the Whole Island of Great Britain* (1724–6; intro. G.D.H. Cole and D.C. Browning, 1962)
DNB	*The Dictionary of National Biography*
Graham	H.G. Graham, *The Social Life of Scotland in the Eighteenth Century* (second edition, 1900)
Grose, *PG*	Francis Grose, *A Provincial Glossary* (1787; Scolar facsimile edition, 1968)
Grose, *VT*	Francis Grose, *A Classical Dictionary of the Vulgar Tongue* (1785; third edition, 1796; 1931, 1963, Eric Partridge, ed.)
Herd	David Herd, *Ancient and Modern Scottish Songs*, 2 vols. (Edinburgh, 1776; reprinted Glasgow, 1869)
Kelly	James Kelly, *A Complete Collection of Scottish Proverbs Explained and Made Intelligible to the English Reader* (1721)
Kinsley	J. Kinsley, ed., *The Poems and Songs of Robert Burns*, 3 vols. (1968)
Kirkton	James Kirkton, *The Secret and True History of the Church of Scotland from the Restoration to 1678*, C.K. Sharpe, ed. (Edinburgh, 1817)
Kirkton Review	Scott's review of Kirkton's *History*, *Quarterly Review* (January 1818, quoted from *MPW*, 19, 213–82)
Letters	Sir Herbert Grierson and others, eds., *The Letters of Sir Walter Scott*, 12 vols. (1932–7; with *Notes and Index* by James C. Corson, 1979)
Lockhart	John Gibson Lockhart, *Memoirs of the Life of Sir Walter*

	Scott, Bart., 7 vols. (1837–8; frequently reprinted, so cited by chapter only)
MPW	*The Miscellaneous Prose Works of Sir Walter Scott*, 24 vols. (1834–6)
Normand	MS notes on Scottish Law in the Waverley Novels, by the late Lord Normand (National Library of Scotland)
OED	*The Oxford English Dictionary*
ODEP	W.G. Smith and F.P. Wilson, *The Oxford Dictionary of English Proverbs* (third edition, 1970)
PP	John Bunyan, *The Pilgrim's Progress*, J.B. Wharey and R. Sharrock, eds. (second edition, 1960)
PW	*The Poetical Works of Sir Walter Scott, Bart.*, 12 vols. (1833–4)
Roughead	W. Roughead, ed., *Trial of Captain Porteous* (Glasgow, 1909)
Six Saints	Patrick Walker, *Six Saints of the Covenant: Peden, Semple, Welwood, Cameron, Cargill, Smith*, D. Hay Fleming, ed., 2 vols. (1901)
SMM	J. Johnson, *The Scots Musical Museum*, 6 vols. (Edinburgh, 1787–1803; Scolar facsimile edition, Aldershot, 1991)
Smout	T.C. Smout, *A History of the Scottish People 1560–1830* (1969; 1972 reprint)
SND	William Grant and David Murison, eds., *The Scottish National Dictionary*, 10 vols. (Edinburgh, 1931–76)
TTM	Allan Ramsay, ed., *The Tea-Table Miscellany*, 4 vols. (Edinburgh, 1723, 1726, 1727, 1737, and frequently reprinted)

PRELIMINARY MATTER

Opposite the title-page of Vol. I of *1818* appeared an advertisement for *Criminal Trials, illustrative of the tale entitled 'The Heart of Mid-Lothian'*, with an epigraph from Ben Jonson (*Sejanus His Fall*, 5, 811–17) commenting on the conduct of the Roman mob: 'quite transported with their cruelty', they dismember the fallen tyrant. The anonymous volume, variously ascribed to Scott and to his friend C.K. Sharpe, reprints a 1737 *Life* of Porteous along with reports of the trials of Wilson, Hall and Robertson, of Porteous himself and of Maclauchlan, the only alleged rioter brought to trial, followed by an account of the Muschett case. No child-murder material is included.

Title-page: For the series title and feigned authorship, see Introduction, p. xx.

Jedediah Cleishbotham: Significant names of fictitious characters, as well as place-names real and invented, are normally treated in the Glossary.

Hear...BURNS: The first stanza of Burns's 'On the Late Captain Grose's Peregrinations thro' Scotland, collecting the Antiquities of that Kingdom' (Kinsley, 494). Francis Grose (1731–91), author of *A Classical Dictionary of the Vulgar Tongue* (1785) and *The Antiquities of Scotland* (1789–91), shared several of Scott's (and Jedediah's) traits and interests; his *Provincial Glossary* (1787) was the source for most of Scott's English dialect and country lore in *The Heart of Mid-Lothian*.

Archibald Constable: (1774–1827), founder of the *Edinburgh Review* in 1802 and publisher of *Marmion* and of most of the Waverley Novels.

Epigraph-page: The passage from Cervantes's *Don Quixote*, in Jervas's 1742 translation, appears as epigraph in all four series of the *Tales* (Penguin Classics edition, 1, 32). In its context it introduces a dispute between the priest, who wishes to burn the two romances found in the trunk, and the landlord, who prefers them to the remaining volume, which contains two biographies. The landlord, like Don Quixote, believes that the romances record the truth; the priest believes in the greater truth of the biography – which is, it is clear, equally fictitious.

PROLEGOMEN

1. *a second story with atticks*: With the gratifying proceeds of the first *Tales of My Landlord*, Scott had pressed on with building the first stage of his new house at Abbotsford.

2. *a new tale and an old song*: The first *Tales of My Landlord*, December 1816, and the poem *Harold the Dauntless*, begun some years before but published anonymously, January 1817.

3. *purchasing... land*: Scott was much taken up in 1818 with arranging to purchase land from his Abbotsford neighbour Nichol Milne.

4. *sought to identify... vain fables*: According to Lockhart, it took less than a week for 'Jedediah' to be generally identified with the still anonymous 'Author of Waverley'; Scott kept up the mystification, himself contributing anonymously to the review of the 1816 *Tales* in the *Quarterly Review* for January 1817 (*MPW*, 19, 11–86).

5. *impeached... veracity... authenticity*: The Rev. Thomas McCrie, in a series of articles in the *Edinburgh Christian Instructor* early in 1817, attacked *Old Mortality*'s alleged misrepresentation of the seventeenth-century Covenanters' language, attitudes, beliefs and conduct; Scott's self-review was in part a defence against McCrie.

6. *extenuation... person*: Cf. 'made my body some way light like my purse' (Walker, for whom see p. 559, *Six Saints*, 1, 4).

7. *1st of April*: All Fools' Day – not in this case to be taken literally.

CHAPTER 1

Epigraph: Adapted from *three* inside passengers in the diligence, or coach, at the romantic old town in the Derbyshire Peak District, in the mock-didactic poem *The Loves of the Triangles* (1798) by Scott's friends Canning, Ellis and Frere, the Tory satirical journalists of *The Anti-Jacobin*. The lines quoted are by Canning. The 'Argument of the First Canto', though not the completed fragments of the poem, introduces a coach-upset.

Readers should note that all chapter epigraphs are annotated in the Editor's Notes, although indicators do not appear in the text for the epigraphs to chapters 2–52.

1. *Peter Pattieson*: Peter, son of Patie, i.e. of any rustic Scotsman; see Introduction, p. xx and n. 14.

2. *twenty or thirty years*: The first mail-coach from Edinburgh to Aberdeen ran in 1798, but in remote areas mail was carried by postal runners until well into the nineteenth century.

3. *Tom Jones*: Fielding's novel of 1749 comments on the regular route of the stage-coach (2, 1), on the overcrowding enforced by the coachman (11, 9) and on the brief but close fellowship of the passengers (18, 1) but not directly on its slowness.

4. *the Stage-Coach*: In the opening scene of *The Stage-Coach* (1704) by George Farquhar (1678–1707), Tom Jolt, the coachman, offers, if duly bribed, to reduce a two-day journey by an hour; the highest bribe, however, is given by the innkeepers, so that desperate travellers will hire their post-horses instead.

5. *Bull and Mouth*: An inn and coaching office in the City of London, on the site in St Martin's le Grand long occupied by the General Post Office (and now by a foreign bank).

6. *Demens. . . equorum*: 'The madman who sought, with gleaming bronze and horses' drumming hoofs, to mimic divine splendour and the inimitable thunder' (Virgil, *Aeneid*, 6, 590–91). While thus challenging Zeus, Salmoneus was struck down by a thunderbolt.

7. *Mr Palmer*: John Palmer (1742–1818), owner of the theatre in Bath in which Scott saw his first play in 1776. He was still alive when *The Heart of Mid-Lothian* appeared and had become a controversial postal reformer in the 1780s, transferring the mails from erratic and insecure post-boys to his newly organized service of fast and regular coaches, which, by 1786, included a London–Edinburgh route.

8. *Mr Pennant*: Thomas Pennant (1726–98), Welsh antiquarian, naturalist and traveller, author of various *Tours* in Scotland and in Wales (1771–81). His *Letter. . . on Mail-Coaches* (1792) argues that the transfer of passenger traffic to Palmer's toll-exempt mail-coaches has disrupted the finance and

maintenance of the rural turnpike roads, and incidentally complains of 'the barbarity with which the poor horses are treated... the very frequent destruction of the passengers' and 'the terror spread along the whole road by the wanton conduct of the profligate guards' who whip and fire on the people as they pass.

9. *Frighted Skiddaw... unscythed car*: Plainly the peaceful modern touring vehicle has little in common with the chariots of Boadicea, but the quotation (if it is one, as well as being *OED's* sole example of 'Unscythed') has so far eluded the editor, though *scythed* cars are found in the poetry of Thomas Warton and in Scott's own *The Black Dwarf*, Chapter 6.

10. *The grand debate... again*: From the reflective poem *The Task* (1785), 4, 30–35, by William Cowper (1731–1800). Scott slightly misquotes at the end, omitting 'once' before 'again'.

11. *cloudy tabernacle*: Exodus 40:34–8.

12. *were dimly seen contending with the tide*: A pentameter line, apparently Scott's own neat version of the Latin that follows.

13. Rari apparent nantes in gurgite vasto: 'They can be seen here and there, swimming in the great swirl of waters' (Virgil, *Aeneid*, 1, 118). Scott quotes this again in his *Journal*, 23 November 1825.

14. Nautæ caupones, stabularii: 'Mariners, innkeepers and stable-keepers' – the first words of Chapter 4, §9, of Justinian's *Digesta* or *Pandectae*, for which see n. 7 on p. 598. The three groups referred to were especially likely to be responsible for property and personal safety, and the section deals with their liability for the actions of their agents and servants.

15. *Wallace-head*: Named after William Wallace (1272?–1305), patriot and Guardian of Scotland in the earlier part of the War of Independence, whose head was exposed on London Bridge after his execution.

16. *complain, like Cowley... Gideon's fleece*: In Judges 6:36–40 God confirms his call to Gideon to save Israel by a double miracle: on the first night the fleece laid out by Gideon is wet with dew, while all around is dry; on the second night dry while all else is wet. In lines 68 to 74 of his 'Complaint' (*c.* 1663) against lack of preferment, the poet Abraham Cowley (1618–67) adapts the story to the uneven distribution of royal patronage: 'And nothing but the Muses Fleece was dry.'

17. *Steele and Addison*: The co-editors of the early periodicals the *Tatler* (1709–11) and the *Spectator* (1711–12, 1714).

18. *nothing can come of nothing*: An ancient axiom (e.g. Lucretius, 1, 155). Scott's phrasing is close to *King Lear*, I, i, 90.

19. *Making good... far from God*: ODEP, 557, proverbial since the fourteenth century, and recurrent in Scott. The wording here resembles the rough draft of Swift's 'A Character... of the Legion Club' (1736), 7–8, quoted in Scott's edition of Swift's *Works* (1814), 10, 548, and describing the Irish Parliament House of 1728, which was built, like the Edinburgh Tolbooth, close against a church.

20. *Red Man*: A member of the City Guard on sentry duty, in the uniform described on p. 34. Signs were used by all trades before literacy and street-numbering became general.

21. *have decreed. . . shall not remain*: 'they are now pulling it down' writes Scott in a letter, 12 November 1816.

22. *Right as my glove*: Not traced.

23. *played. . .lead*: The series of puns ends in the language of card-games.

24. *Last Speech, Confession, and Dying Words*: The conventional form of title in popular criminal biography. Scott owned a 1745 *Lives, Behaviour and Dying Words of the Most Remarkable Convicts*. Cf. the further pastiche of the form in Chapter 50.

25. *dangled. . . west end*: Early nineteenth-century views of the Tolbooth show a flat-roofed extension to the west, presumably used for the modern 'Newgate' style of execution mentioned on p. 27.

26. A well-developed instance of the brief sententious essays on moral and social topics that enrich the novel's texture while somewhat undermining its narrative organization. The parallel between life and prison recurs verbally in Shakespeare from *Richard II*, V, v, and is structurally important in *Measure for Measure*.

27. *honest friend Crabbe*: In 1818 Scott had not yet met George Crabbe (1754–1832), country rector and writer of verse satires and tales, though Scott had known passages of Crabbe by heart since the 1780s and they had been in friendly correspondence since 1812, when Crabbe remarked on the interest of 'brief histories of extraordinary cases'. Later, in 1822, Crabbe stayed with Scott in Edinburgh, and the two writers walked to Muschat's Cairn and St Anthony's Chapel, the setting of Chapter 15 of the novel (Lockhart, Chapter 56). It is not so clear why Hardie should call Crabbe his 'honest friend'.

28. Crabbe, *The Borough* (1810), Letter 20, 76–90.

29. *Stair's Institutes*: *Institutions of the Law of Scotland* (1681), a systematic and comparative summary of Scots law and custom by James Dalrymple, Viscount Stair (1619–95), on whose daughter's story Scott based the plot of *The Bride of Lammermoor*.

30. *Morrison's Decisions*: *Decisions of the Court of Session from Its Institution until. . . 1808* (1811) by W.M. Morison (d. 1821).

31. *within the bar*: King's Counsel.

32. *Pistol*: Coward and braggart, forced to eat a leek as punishment in *Henry V*, V, i.

33. *coinage of his brain*: An echo of Gertrude's words to Hamlet (III, iv, 136).

34. *for many years*: From the fifteenth century, with rebuilding in 1561, until the erection of the Parliament House in 1639.

35. *when the mob*: On 17 December 1596 the Edinburgh trades intervened to protect James VI from a crowd of armed extreme Protestants who sought to interrupt his dealing with a deputation in the Tolbooth.

36. *The sword. . . Gideon*: The battle-cry of Gideon's elite guerrilla force that overthrows the Midianites in Judges 7.

37. *Haman*: In the Book of Esther, a Persian high official who seeks to turn the king against the Jews and who is hanged fifty cubits high on the gallows that he had expected to use for them. The story was read during the 1596 episode and is obviously relevant to Porteous.

38. Causes Celebres *of Caledonia*: Scott's last piece of criticism was his February 1831 review of the first part of R. Pitcairn, *Ancient Criminal Trials in Scotland* (1829–33). Later in the novel Scott refers to Hugo Arnot's earlier collection of 1785, to which his father had subscribed (see p. 669 n. 2).

39. Magna. . . prævalebit: 'Great is truth, and mighty above all things' – the response of the people in the Apocryphya (1 Esdras 4:41) to a folktale of rhetorical contest and comparison in which Truth prevails over Wine, Women and the King. Hardie articulates a programme for the aesthetic and the ethics of the novel that follows.

40. *division of labour*: Hardie ironically applies to crime the leading concept from Adam Smith's *The Wealth of Nations* (1776). The rational historiography of the Scottish Enlightenment underlies the novel's many generalizations on social matters.

41. *Bow Street, Hatton Garden, or the Old Bailey*: All well-known criminal courts in London.

42. *Commentaries*: Four volumes (1790–97) on aspects of Scottish criminal law by David Hume (1757–1838), nephew of the philosopher, a friend of Scott and in 1818 his colleague as principal clerk of the Court of Session.

43. *half-bound and slip-shod*: Half-bound: having leather spines and corners only, in contrast to the full leather bindings applied to books in a gentleman's library. Slip-shod: perhaps in protective loose covers, or well thumbed and worn like an old shoe or slipper.

44. *circulating library*: Introduced by the 1720s, soon denounced as 'an evergreen tree of diabolical knowledge' (Mrs Malaprop in Sheridan, *The Rivals*, 1775), and by the early nineteenth century a crucial medium for the expansion of the reading public and the publishing trade.

45. *pint of claret*: The reader may decide between the imperial pint (0.567 litres) and the Scots pint (1.7 litres).

46. *hereditary jurisdictions*: A feudal arrangement under which the inheritors of sheriffdoms, stewartries, regalities and baronies had the right to try civil and criminal cases and inflict both capital and lesser punishments on their own tenants and their less privileged neighbours. Under the Heritable Jurisdictions Act of 1747 these powers were taken over by the Crown, to the detriment, some thought, of the traditional social structure of the Highlands.

47. perfervidum ingenium Scotorum: The 'over-fiery temperament of the Scots', a phrase applied by the historian George Buchanan (1506–82) to

the expected conduct of the Scottish military leaders at a particular
juncture in 1560 (*Opera*, Edinburgh, 1715, 1, 321) and extended by later
writers (not only lawyers as Scott apparently thought) to the national
character in general.

48. *smelled the battle afar off*: In Job 39:25 it is the horse that does this; the
eagle appears at verse 27.

49. *miry Slough of Despond*: Into which Christian and Pliable sink early in *The
Pilgrim's Progress* (1678–84) by John Bunyan (1628–88), a recurring
reference-point in Scott's novel.

CHAPTER 2

Epigraph: From 'The Thief and the Cordelier', a mock-ballad in the form of a
scaffold dialogue satirizing priestcraft, by the diplomat and wit Matthew
Prior (1664–1721). Scott quotes the poem again in a letter of 18 July 1825.

1. *Tyburn*: The London crossroads later known as Marble Arch, until 1783
the site of a permanent triangular gallows and the principal place of
execution in eighteenth-century London. The Oxford Road, now Oxford
Street, led out of London past the prison of Newgate.

2. Edinburgh Old Town lies astride a 'crag and tail' formation – once a
typical volcano, later scoured by glacial action from the west until the hard
lava core stood exposed and vertical on three sides (north, south and west)
and the softer detritus scraped from the surrounding cone formed a long
ridge descending eastward. On the dramatic high point to the west stands
the Castle. The main street follows the spine of the ridge in gradual
eastward descent, and bore in turn most of the features mentioned in the
novel: the Weigh House, the Lawnmarket, the Parliament House, the
Tolbooth, the High Kirk of St Giles, the High Street, the Netherbow
Port, the Canongate, and, where the ridge descends to the plain, Holyrood-
house and the Watergate from which roads diverged north past the Quarry
Holes to the port of Leith and east towards the heath where Effie
embarked with Staunton. The glacier had divided to flow past the central
rock, and the weight of ice to each side scooped out hollows to the north
(the Nor' Loch at the time of the novel) and to the south (the Grassmarket,
where the narrative now begins). Houses formed long narrow plots running
back from the main street down towards the plain, in a pattern of alleys
and closes resembling the skeleton of a fish; the Cowgate connected the
downhill ends of the southern series to each other and to the Grassmarket.
Towards the higher end, where the gradient on the sides of the ridge was
too steep for a straight street, the zig-zag of the Bow connected the
Grassmarket to the Lawnmarket.

3. *five-and-twenty years*: 'Twenty' in the MS; 'thirty' in *1830*. The last
execution in the Grassmarket took place in 1784, so if Scott is being

careful one must think of Pattieson's manuscript as written within five years of 1809. The block in which the gallows-tree had been mounted remained in position until 1823.

4. *when I was one of their number*: 1778–84, if 'I' denotes Scott and the schoolboys were the 'petulant brood of the High School' mentioned on p. 34.

5. *Parliament-House, or courts of justice*: See n. 2 on p. 625.

6. *similar to that in front of Newgate*: A platform entered directly from the prison, with a trapdoor instead of the ladder or cart formerly used to drop the victim. Newgate Prison, of medieval origin, was rebuilt to designs by George Dance after its destruction in the Gordon Riots of 1780. It was demolished in 1902 to make way for the Central Criminal Court.

7. *7th day of September, 1736*: This was indeed the day on which Porteous was murdered, but, circumstantial though the subsequent description seems, the scene 'at an early hour' is wholly invented – see Introduction, p. xxx.

8. *reigns of George I. and II.*: 1714–27 and 1727–60 respectively.

9. *unaccustomed to imposts*: Duties on ale, beer, whisky and meat, and on imported tobacco, wines and textiles, had been imposed in 1644 to finance Scotland's part in the Civil War. Under the Union of 1707, English rates and articles of duty were introduced, with certain exemptions. The sense of injustice Scott mentions arose especially from the British Parliament's attempts – successful in the end – at ending the exemptions. Similar problems existed in England, where 'the whole country soaked up smuggled goods like a sponge' and issues of civil liberty and public order arose from government use of 'harsh measures, savage punishment and the full authority of the Crown to make the public conform' (J.H. Plumb, *Sir Robert Walpole, The King's Minister*, 1960, 236–9).

10. *Andrew Wilson*: The novel's account of the Wilson part of the affair differs from the factual records only trivially, providing a fourth member of the gang and slightly different detail of events in Kirkcaldy, placing Robertson's escape after, rather than before, the sermon and treating Wilson's conduct as unequivocally altruistic, a view not shared by the most articulate eyewitness, Alexander Carlyle. The historical Robertson apparently escaped to Holland.

11. *Levite in the parable*: Of the Good Samaritan, Luke 10:30–37.

12. *St Giles is now divided*: The cathedral, dating in part from the thirteenth century or earlier, was secularized at the Reformation and partitioned to serve the needs of three Edinburgh congregations; part was used as a prison in the seventeenth century and in Scott's time the building still housed a police office. The partitions were removed during restoration in 1878.

CHAPTER 3

Epigraph: The last stanza of Fergusson's (see n. 5 below) poem of 1772 celebrating the snugness and sociability of Edinburgh city life at the time of the New Year festivities.

1. *Captain John Porteous*: Scott's account follows and judiciously softens the 1737 *Life and Death of Captain John Porteous*, reprinted in the 1818 companion volume of *Criminal Trials* and described by the legal historian Roughead as 'so violently partial as to defeat its own design'.

2. *disturbed year 1715*: Disturbed by riots, an election, treason trials, flights into exile and a threat of invasion as the Whigs consolidated their power under the new Hanoverian monarch, but especially by the Jacobite rising in north-eastern Scotland from September 1715 to February 1716. The Duke of Argyle, who plays a part later in the novel, occupied Stirling, containing most of the insurgent forces north of the River Forth until, after the drawn battle of Sheriffmuir on 13 November, they lost heart and gradually dispersed. Edinburgh was put in defence in October against a Jacobite diversionary column that crossed the Firth of Forth by boat, briefly seized the outlying fort at Leith and compromised the Setons (see n. 6 on p. 666) before making its way into England and eventually surrendering at Preston.

3. *The corps*: Incorporated in 1679 to replace less effective forms of town watch, the City Guard was, well through the eighteenth century, more formidable and more frequently in lethal contact with the citizens than is conveyed by Scott's humorous account of their latter days.

4. *between the Luckenbooths and the Netherbow*: The irony of these limits becomes clear in Chapters 6 and 7. For the two features, see p. 57 and p. 60 respectively.

5. *Poor Fergusson*: Robert Fergusson (1750–74), Edinburgh satirical poet in Scots and English. After attending Edinburgh High School and St Andrews University, he worked as a law-copyist, plunging himself into the city's tavern life and literary clubs, but died in the city asylum in a manic state after an accident.

6. *Gude folk. . . cockad*: From 'Hallow-Fair' (1772), 100–103.

7. *O soldiers. . . bluid*: From 'The King's Birth-Day in Edinburgh' (1772), 61–6.

8. *similar question*: *King Lear*, II, iv, 256. Scott hints at the topic of the treatment of a difficult old father by two of his daughters.

9. *cocked-hat*: The three-cornered brimmed hat of the eighteenth century, not the 'fore-and-aft' ceremonial hat of nineteenth and twentieth century officials.

10. *statue of Charles the Second*: In lead, life-size, equestrian, as Caesar, erected by the city in 1685 and still there.

11. *ancient refuge*: For the old Guard-house, see p. 60.

12. *disbanded*: The local historian Grant takes pleasure in noting that two survivors were present when the foundation stone of the Scott Monument was laid in 1846.

13. *Jockey to the fair*: A lively traditional air (in e.g. W. Chappell, *Popular Music of the Olden Time*, 1859, reprinted 1965, 2, 711–13) – not especially Scottish, though printed in e.g. Oliver and Boyd's *The Scottish Minstrel* (1813), 28. The 'dirge' that replaced it is No. 18 in *SMM*.

14. *manuscripts bequeathed to friends and executors*: A reminder of Pattieson as narrator – but also a topos at least as old as Cervantes. Scott had dedicated *Waverley* to Henry Mackenzie (1745–1831), whose best-known work, *The Man of Feeling* (1771), purports to be the fragments of such a bequest, rescued from use as shot-gun wadding.

15. *John Dhu*: Or Dow, the middle figure in the second etching (dated 1784) in *A Series of Original Portraits and Caricature Etchings by the Late John Kay*, Hugh Paton (1837). The accompanying text, partly derived from Scott, claims that in 1789 Dhu killed, with his Lochaber axe, 'one peculiarly outrageous member of the democracy' who was demonstrating against the City Guard's salute on the king's birthday, but goes on to stress that this mini-Porteous was kind-hearted, gentle, affectionate and obliging. John Kay (1742–1826) was for sixty years a prolific producer of drawings and etchings of Edinburgh characters.

16. *king's birth-day*: Officially 4 June. Throughout the Hanoverian period a day for loyal rejoicing and disloyal counter-demonstration, and in 1792 the occasion of extensive rioting with threats to treat various officials 'as Porteous was', the burning in effigy of Henry Dundas, dragoons on the Edinburgh streets and at least one fatality (K.J. Logue, *Popular Disturbances in Scotland 1780–1815*, 1979, 133–47).

17. This exchange follows the 1737 pamphlet closely, but Scott has introduced the word 'mercy' and elements of symmetry that shift the register towards the New Testament and *Measure for Measure*.

18. *covenant*: See Introduction, p. x.

19. *on occasions something similar*: In all, over twenty Cameronians were executed between November 1680 and October 1681.

20. *a decent grave*: Instead of being hung in chains or anatomized. Wilson was duly buried in Pathhead, Fife.

21. *six or seven*: Porteous's indictment (which did not necessarily include all the victims) charged him with the deaths of seven people.

22. *ere men's temper had time to cool*: The Guard fired on the citizens on 14 April, Porteous's trial began on 5 July, and sentence was passed on 20 July. Again, Scott's summary of the proceedings follows the sources closely.

23. *verdict*: Baron Hume, Scott's colleague (and Hardie's mentor on pp. 21–2 above) thought the jury's verdict doubtful and incomplete in its failure to take account of all extenuating circumstances (Roughead, 62–3).

24. *8th September, 1736*: The date set for the execution is correctly reported
here, but compare p. 27, where the gallows has been erected before dawn
on 7 September and the crowd forms at an early hour.

CHAPTER 4

Epigraph: See Scott's note. Elsewhere he adds, 'The original story is to be
found in Gervase of Tilbury', a twelfth-century recorder of marvels
(*Minstrelsy* in *PW*, 4, 350).

1. *still exhibit. . . the iron cross*: Reputedly installed by later owners to maintain
   their claim to the exemptions enjoyed by the suppressed medieval orders.
2. *The mob of Edinburgh. . . risen repeatedly. . .*: From a large body of relevant
   modern discussion, G. Rudé, *The Crowd in History* (1964) and K.O.
   Logue, *Popular Disturbances in Scotland 1780–1815* (1979) stand out; both
   have bibliographies, and Logue has an introductory chapter on the earlier
   eighteenth century.
3. *reprieve*: The details are historically correct, but they had been common
   knowledge for some days before 7 September.
4. *the Duke of Newcastle*: Thomas Pelham-Holles (1693–1768), one of the two
   Secretaries of State, officially handled Scottish business from 1725 to 1742,
   the separate Scottish secretaryship having been suppressed during factional
   manoeuvres (see A. Murdoch, '*The People Above*', 1980). Later – it is said
   to embarrass Walpole, whose political alliances were starting to break up –
   Newcastle introduced the Bill of Pains and Penalties, which Argyle opposes
   in Chapters 24 and 35.
5. *Queen Caroline*: Caroline of Anspach (1683–1737), described more fully in
   Chapter 37.
6. *absence of George II.*: From 22 May 1736 to 15 January 1737.
7. *wad na stand gude in the auld Scots law*: It was argued that the abolition of
   the Scottish Privy Council after the Union of 1707 left no authority
   competent to grant reprieves valid in Scots law, and it was rejoined that
   the Privy Council of Great Britain was the obvious successor.
8. *oppressed our trade*: A review of Scottish experience with cattle, textiles,
   tobacco-importing and taxation in the generation after the Union leads
   Smout (226) to conclude, 'There was no quick breakthrough anywhere
   along the line. . . the harm that Union did to the Scottish economy is
   usually greatly exaggerated. . . The biggest loss was probably . . . heavy
   expenditure of rents raised in Scotland by noblemen and lairds travelling
   and living in England.' His last point echoes Defoe, *Tour*, 2, 371.
9. *grey mare*: Proverbially, 'the grey mare proves the better horse', i.e. 'the
   good wife is master' (Kelly, T284; *ODEP*, 338).
10. *gentle King Jamie. . . it*: Scott uses almost the same words about James VI
    and I in *Waverley*, Chapter 10.

11. *Butler*: In the MS Butler appears first as Thwackbairn (Smackchild), another aggressive Jonsonian type and (if we remember Pattieson's part in the narration) an improbably close parallel to Cleishbotham – inconsistent, too, with the timorous upright scholarly introvert he later turns out to be. Scott did not substantially revise this introductory dialogue after he changed the character's name and nature.

12. *schoolmaster of a parish*: Scots have long prided themselves on the national system of parish schools introduced in the sixteenth century and gradually and somewhat unevenly implemented thereafter, with its associated relatively high rates of literacy and of access to higher education. Sceptical comparative inquiry, in Scott's time and since, has qualified, but not exploded the traditional account. See M. Lynch, *A New History of Scotland* (1991), 259.

13. *would not have distressed her majesty*: Frederick Louis, Prince of Wales (1707–51), was notoriously on bad terms with both parents on matters of money, temperament and family arrangements, and had them lampooned in pamphlets; even on her deathbed in late 1737 his mother declined to receive him (*DNB*). On this point depends a later dramatic moment in the novel (p. 384).

14. *be the upshot what like o't*: 'Be the result of it what it may.'

15. *Weigh-house to the Water-gate*: Weigh-house: 'at the upper end of this Land-market is a stone building appropriated to several public offices of lesser value; for below stairs are warehouses, with public weights and scales for goods'. Water-gate: 'the east gate by the palace, leading out of the city towards Berwick' (Defoe, *Tour*, 2, 305). Taken together, the terms mean 'from one end of the city to the other'.

16. *ended or mended*: Cf. *PW*, 2, 218, 'this they imagine will either *end them or mend them*'.

CHAPTER 5

Epigraph: Not in the printed works of Sir David Lindsay of the Mount (1486–1555), on whom it was traditional to father orally transmitted (or newly invented) rhymes, epigrams, etc. Compare 'But in these nice sharp quillets of the law, / Good faith, I am no wiser than a daw' (*1 Henry VI*, II, iv, 17–18) partly quoted on p. 107.

1. non omnia possumus . . .: 'We cannot all do everything.' The proverbial phrase for which Saddletree struggles is not, for once, law-Latin, as he thinks, but occurs in Virgil, *Eclogues*, 8, 63, quoted from the earlier writer Lucilius.

2. *Duncan Forbes*: Of Culloden (1685–1747), active on the government side in the Fifteen and the Forty-five and Lord President of the Court of Session from 1737. He took a prominent part in opposing the punishment of Edinburgh after the Porteous Riot.

3. *Arniston*: Robert Dundas, Lord Arniston (1685–1753). Lord Advocate (1720), Dean of the Faculty of Advocates (1721), judge (1737) and successor to Forbes as Lord President (1748); for fifteen years MP for Midlothian, father of Henry Dundas, Viscount Melville (the Tory 'manager' of Scotland in the late eighteenth century and an early patron of Scott) and grandfather of Scott's lifelong friend and patron Robert Dundas, second Viscount Melville.

4. *bend-leather guns*: A light metal barrel was bound with rope and enclosed in a thick leather sheath. Although it was intended to function easily as mobile artillery, this seventeenth-century innovation proved useless at the battles of Dunbar and Worcester (G. Parker, *The Military Revolution*, 1988, 33–4).

5. *ready made out o' Holland*: Even in the fifteenth century, 'lack of native craftsmanship seriously unbalanced Scottish trade. . . exports were almost entirely unprocessed raw materials. . . and Scotland was almost wholly dependent on imports for manufactured goods' (J. Wormald, *Court, King and Community: Scotland 1470–1625*, 1981, 43). Froissart, whom Scott had read, reports the view of French visitors of 1385 in words very similar to those of Saddletree, who blindly tries to turn the defect into a virtue.

6. *import our lawyers from Holland*: In the late seventeenth and early eighteenth centuries it was common for Scottish lawyers to complete their education in Roman Law at the schools of Leiden, Groningen or Utrecht. The practice declined after 1750. See p. 276 and n. 13 on p. 632.

7. *Substitutes and Pandex*: Saddletree garbles the titles of the *Institutes* and *Pandects*, the first two parts of the great *Corpus juris* of ancient legal rules, arguments and decisions compiled by order of Justinian (Emperor of Constantinople, 527–65). (Scots law, like that of other European countries but unlike the English Common Law, is based on 'Roman' legal principles, and aspiring Scots advocates had to pass examinations on both texts, which still appear on the syllabuses of European law schools.) Saddletree goes on to garble the law of entail, in which the institute, the heir originally named in a deed, is by no means synonymous with the substitute, the first heir's subsequent heir or assignee.

8. *Balfour's Practiques*: A manuscript compilation on Scots law by Sir James Balfour of Pittendriech (d. 1583), apparently not printed until 1754.

9. *Dallas of St Martin's Stiles*: *A System of Styles* (1697) by George Dallas (1630–1701), 'for many years indispensable in the office of every Scottish lawyer' (*DNB*). Dallas and Balfour have already appeared together on Bailie Macwheeble's bookshelf in *Waverley*, Chapter 66.

10. *brass. . . Corinthian*: Corinthian brass or bronze was an alloy of gold, silver and copper prized in the ancient world and used for the finest work. Corinth was proverbial for wealth and luxury, and Corinthian, from Shakespeare's time to the middle of the nineteenth century, meant a man-about-town.

11. *Non*... *Corinthum*: *Non cuivis homini contingit adire Corinthum*, 'It is not every man's lot to visit Corinth', Horace's balanced comment on the choice between ease and ambition (*Epistles*, 1, 17, 36) rephrased in the past tense by Butler, refers doubly to Saddletree's ignorance and Butler's own missed opportunity.

12. *Optat ephippia bos piger*: 'The lazy ox desires the trappings of the horse' (Horace, *Epistles*, 1, 14, 43). Butler's 'Nothing new under the sun' is itself a quotation (Ecclesiastes 1:9).

13. *fair-haired girl*: Here, Effie's hair changes from black to fair only with the 1821 printing. It remains brown on p. 98. Her eyelashes are dark (p. 105) and her son's hair is black (p. 529). Her appearance at the trial, however, settles the matter (p. 224). The change abandons an initial contrast with Jeanie, who is fair throughout.

14. *let sorrow come when sorrow maun*: Compare 'Sorrow is soon enough when it comes' (*ODEP*, 754; Kelly, S48) and 'God send you joy, for sorrow will come fast enough' (*ODEP*, 312).

15. *Statute*: See Scott's note, 'Child Murder', on p. 565.

16. *Luckie Smith*: Condemned in March 1679, on circumstantial evidence, to be hanged for murdering a child to which she had been called as midwife. She dissolved the 'stanchells and iron graits' of the Tolbooth with acid, but broke a leg climbing out; the failed attempt was held against her. Her case apparently suggested to the Scottish law officers the 1690 statute, modelled on an English Act of 1623 (21 James I, c. 27) (John Lauder of Fountainhall, 1646–1722, whose papers were known to Scott, *Historical Notices*, 1848, 1, 220, 224).

17. *walked in from Dumfries yesterday*: Well might Butler look white, for the distance was seventy-four miles through hilly country. Butler's summer teaching post has kept him away from the Deanses and their affairs during a critical period for Effie, but the clues provided may lead readers to suspect that he is the father of the missing child.

18. *natural son bred to the Kirk*: In itself an insult by the minor gentry to the community of the godly.

19. *license*: The presbytery's licence to preach is still an essential step preceding the ordination of a Scottish minister.

20. Quos diligit castigat: 'Whom the Lord loveth he chasteneth', Hebrews 12:6.

21. *Seneca*: The Stoic philosopher (*c*. 4 BC–AD 65) touches this topic so often that Butler need have no particular allusion in mind.

22. In the interleaved set, Scott here added the note, 'Child Murder' (p. 565), which in this edition is keyed to p. 159 to correspond with its *1830* position.

CHAPTER 6

Epigraph: Scott here quotes from the current 'common', or broadsheet version, of the ballad (Child, 169B, Stanza 17), although for his own *Minstrelsy of the Scottish Border* he had preferred the allegedly more authentic version from Allan Ramsay's *The Ever Green* (1724), in which these lines do not appear.

1. *ancient prison*: For Scott's note, 'Tolbooth of Edinburgh', once appended to this chapter, see p. 547.

2. *buttress and coign of vantage*: Echoing Banquo's words in *Macbeth*, I, vi, 7.

3. *a ponderous key*: Scott obtained the door, lock and key of the Tolbooth during demolition in 1817. They can still be seen at Abbotsford.

4. Porta adversa ... &c.: Virgil, *Aeneid*, 6, 552–4, describing the entrance to Tartarus, the place of punishment in the pagan afterworld. Dryden's version of Virgil was included in Scott's edition of *The Works of John Dryden* (1808).

5. The first speaker's rather literary English may identify him as 'Robertson', though the biblical phrasing and the separate appearance of the 'Wildfire' character at pp. 60 and 61 suggest otherwise. Scott's conception is still fluid and he does not yet reveal his whole hand to the reader.

6. *hair of your head*: A recurrent phrase in the Bible, often in a context of God's providence (e.g. Matthew 10:30).

7. *right hand nor the left*: Another recurrent biblical contrast much used by David Deans.

8. *all ... a dream*: Perhaps evokes *Measure for Measure*, III, i, 32–4.

9. *should have been called women*: Close to Banquo's words on meeting the Weird Sisters (*Macbeth*, I, iii, 45). Cross-dressing in riots can work both practically as disguise and symbolically as affirmation of disorder.

10. *thousands*: The city population was about 50,000.

11. *Guard-house ... esplanade*: The Guard-house stood near the Tron Kirk, two hundred yards east of St Giles. Scott's 'beautiful esplanade' refers to the open vista of the broad middle part of the High Street, not to the clear ground higher up, between Castle Hill and the Castle, nowadays known as the Esplanade.

12. *ordinary serjeant's guard*: The normal night strength of thirty men was reduced to twenty (by illness and because some who had earlier fired on the crowd were still suspended from duty) – about fourteen were at the Guard-house.

13. *Mr Lindsay*: Patrick Lindsay (d. 1753). Lord Provost of Edinburgh (1729, 1733); as MP (1734–41) spoke strongly against the Porteous Bill; author of *The Interest of Scotland, Considered with Reference to Its Police, Agriculture, Trade, Manufacture and Fishery* (1733) (*DNB*).

14. *Persons are yet living*: Scott among them, of course.

15. *A near relation*: Since Scott's parents and their siblings were infants or unborn in 1736, the most likely source is one of his three long-lived great-aunts (Alison Cockburn, Joanna Keith, Margaret Swinton) or Anne Rutherford, his maternal grandfather's second wife.

16. *the Cardinal Beatoun*: David Beaton (1494–1546), Archbishop of St An-

drews and leading statesman of the Catholic, pro-French faction in Scottish sixteenth-century affairs. His assassination, ostensibly in revenge for his part in the burning of the Protestant George Wishart, was cited as precedent by the assassins of Archbishop Sharp in 1679 – see p. 201 and note.

17. *read the riot-act*: Read the appropriate formula specified in the Act of 1715, requiring assembled persons to disperse to their homes on pain of being treated as felons.

CHAPTER 7

Epigraph: From Shylock's justification of revenge (III, i, 46ff.), evoking Shakespeare's discussions of justice and mercy and those of his plays that turn on legal quibbles.

1. *his heart was merry within him*: Like the drunken Nabal (1 Samuel 25:36), unaware that his life has been spared only through his wife's intercession with David's guerrillas and that the Lord will smite him ten days later.

2. *surely the bitterness of death was past*: Agag's words just before Samuel hews him in pieces before the Lord (1 Samuel 15:32–3). Scott's biblical echoes parallel Porteous's situation, again enunciate the justice and mercy theme, and adapt the Cameronian habits of biblical parallelism. See p. 241 and n. 3 on p. 627.

3. *entertainment. . .supper*: The earlier visitors, for dinner in the early afternoon, are historical, but the interrupted evening supper is, according to Roughead, 'a creation of the novelist's fancy'.

4. *'full of bread,'. . .sins full blown*: Like Hamlet's father, described by Hamlet as he postpones killing Claudius until a suitable and equally damnable moment (IV, iii, 73ff.). The allusions strengthen the reference to sudden death and retributive justice, and anticipate Robertson's obsession with Jacobean drama.

5. *wanted presence of mind*: If anything Porteous, who was warned of the threats against him, showed too much cool confidence in the strength of his position (Roughead, 73–4).

6. *rush to the chimney*: Roughead (83) contradicts this with a seemingly contemporary but unsourced account in which Porteous faces his assailants coolly.

7. *the same whose female disguise*: Robertson again speaks English where others speak Scots – but he adopts the 'biblical' register.

8. *horns of the altar*: Brass or gold covered projections from the altar of the Old Testament Jews, on to which sacrifices were to be bound (Psalms 118:27) and especially appropriate in rituals to expiate sins committed in ignorance by the ruler or the people (Leviticus 4:13ff.), with obvious application to Effie, to Porteous and to his killers.

9. *Let us mete to him. . .*: 'For with the same measure that ye mete withal it shall be measured to you again' (Luke 6:38). The verse occurs thrice in the New Testament, twice in the context of 'Judge not that ye be not judged' – the rioters are perverting it to their own ends. It also launches unequivocally the novel's series of references to *Measure for Measure*.

10. *donnard auld deevil*: Oldbuck uses the same phrase (*The Antiquary*, Chapter 2).

11. *at the ear of the young woman*: As Satan is found beside the sleeping Eve (*Paradise Lost*, 4, 180).

12. *Flee. . . you*: Robertson continues to speak English, but in the MS and *1818* Scott had him speaking Scots. The corrector of *1821* even sought to anglicize 'flee' to 'fly', apparently unaware that it was a distinct English word.

13. *Better. . . good fame*: Not among recorded proverbs, but similar to the series of 'tine *x*/tine *y*' at Kelly, T182–4, and to young David's remark on p. 506.

14. *harm*: Anglicized from *skaith* of MS, *1818*, *1819* via 'violence' in *1821–5*.

15. *Blood must have blood*: Even here Robertson is quoting (*Macbeth*, III, iv, 122).

16. *away with him*: John 19:16 – the Jews' response to Pilate's 'Behold your King!'

17. *escaped. . . struggles*: Scott thus spares his readers the gruesome details of Porteous's last moments, known from reports by witnesses against the only rioters to be brought to trial.

18. *Haddo's-hole*: The north transept of St Giles's Church, used as a prison for Sir John Gordon of Haddo before his execution in 1644.

19. *John, Duke of Argyle*: Argyle, here brought into the novel with seeming casualness, plays an important part later, for which Scott prepares with further anecdotes both in the text and in the note on p. 571. The 'hunting field' threat against the Presbyterian Lowlands, without any . retort, is, however, attributed by seventeenth-century writers to the Duke of York, the future James VII and II, when governing Scotland in 1684–5. For Argyle, see Introduction, pp. xxxvii–xxxix and the notes on pp. 571 and 645.

CHAPTER 8

Epigraph: The 'old song', 'Waly Waly Gin Love be Bony', appeared in *TTM* by 1727 and in other eighteenth-century Scots collections, though the stanza Scott uses may be even older (Child, 204, Appendix). Arthur's Seat is a hill in the King's Park, less than a mile from the centre of Edinburgh, over 800 feet high and still not seriously encroached on by the city; St Anthony's Chapel and Well lie among its north-western ridges.

1. *Salisbury Crags*: The English artist B.R. Haydon claimed in 1827 to have detected Scott's authorship from his echoing and adopting this passage in conversation in 1820 (Wilfred Partington, *The Private Letter-books of Sir Walter Scott*, 1930, 115).

2. *Monk's army*: George Monck, first Duke of Albemarle (1608–70), consolidated English Parliamentarian control over the northern part of Scotland in late 1651 while the main Scottish army was invading England in support of the claims of Charles II, already recognized by the Scottish Estates. His army took Dundee on 1 September, and Cromwell defeated the Scots at Worcester on 3 September; Scotland was then incorporated into the Commonwealth. As commander-in-chief in Scotland, Monck played a decisive part, after Cromwell's death, in the restoration of Charles II in 1660; the separate Scottish Estates (i.e. Parliament) was then re-established. (See F.D. Dow, *Cromwellian Scotland*, 1979.)

3. *Dalkeith*: Six miles south-east of Edinburgh; according to Defoe in the 1720s, 'a pretty large market-town', an interchange for produce from the Border counties *en route* to Edinburgh, lying just outside the park-gates of 'the prettiest and largest new-built house in Scotland' (*Tour*, 2, 360).

4. *weighed. . . wanting*: Like Belshazzar in Daniel 5:27.

5. *Middleton's*: John Middleton (1619–74), a former Parliamentary general who (like politically active Scots in general) supported the agreement reached with Charles I in 1648 and subsequently recognized and fought for Charles II. After the Restoration he was commander-in-chief in Scotland and Lord High Commissioner to the Scottish Estates, until dismissed in 1663 for bribery and misuse of power (apparently the 'trooper' took after him). In the Kirkton Review Scott treats Middleton's Church policy with severity: 'rash' and 'ill-judged', 'it could not but prepare materials for a national convulsion' (250). Cf. n. 34 on p. 653.

6. *Horace's phrase*: Horace tells of a soldier who, when penniless, had been bold enough to capture a strong enemy post but who, urged to a similar feat after being well rewarded in cash, tells his general, 'A man who has lost his money-belt will go wherever you like' (Epistles, 2, 2, 26–40). The parallel with Bible Butler is apparent.

7. *Beersheba*: Where Isaac settled and took a wife when his disputes with the Philistines were over (Genesis 26).

8. *'evil days and evil tongues,'*: Adapted from *Paradise Lost*, 7, 26.

9. *same predicament*: Persecution and neglect suffered by Commonwealth supporters after the Restoration.

10. *fines for non-conformity*: An Act of 1663 punished wilful absence from the parish church on Sundays by a fine (in the case of tenant farmers) of up to a quarter of the offender's 'free movables'.

11. *a vegetable*: Takes up the gentle mockery of Erasmus Darwin's *Loves of the Plants* embodied in the Canning epigraph to Chapter 1.

12. *task-master*: Used in the Bible solely in connection with the Israelites' captivity in Egypt (Exodus 1–14).

13. *1700 and 1701*: Throughout Europe the 1690s were the coldest decade for seven hundred years. Contemporaries such as Patrick Walker refer to King William's Ill Years, 1694–1701, but modern historians such as Ferguson and Smout place the worst of the famine in 1695–9.

14. *Pentland, Bothwell Brigg, or Airdsmoss*: Two battles and a skirmish, respectively, in 1666, 1679 and 1680, between government troops and Covenanters – insurgent in the first two cases, fugitive in the third, where Cameron, who gave his name to the Cameronians, was killed. Scott gives his account of Bothwell Brigg in Chapters 30–32 of *Old Mortality*.

15. The Miser's Deathbed and those who assemble round it is a literary topos at least as old as Horace's *Satires*, 1, 1, and here the apparent echoes of Jonson's *Volpone* and Pope's Euclio (*Moral Essays*, 1, 256–61) could as easily be parallels as sources.

16. *Nichil Novit*: From the Latin *Nihil novit*, 'He knows nothing', the stock formula that enabled an heir to disown, on oath, alleged debts incurred by his predecessor. Nichil Novit junior, mentioned later (p. 135, etc.), was in part of the MS Michel Novit, 'He knows a lot' (Scots *mickle*), but Scott abandoned his joke, perhaps deciding that his profession did not after all improve over the generations. The exasperatingly dilatory Abbotsford neighbour Nichol Milne, who provoked the quip '*Ex Nichilo nihil fit*' (*Letters*, 17 November 1817), also played his part.

17. *no solicitors*: Scottish solicitors, though mentioned as early as 1596, formed a society only in 1784, gaining a royal charter in 1797.

18. *laird . . . earl*: Neither the laird nor the earl has been identified.

19. *from the fowler*: Psalms 91:3.

20. *Curate. . . Prayer-book*: The laird longs for his episcopalian priest, and for traditional written prayers rather than the oral inspirational doctrine of the Presbyterian Church, for which he has perforce been paying since the Revolution.

21. *the curse of Cromwell*: Traditionally directed against Whigs, Protestants and Puritans; the phrase always stands by itself without more specific content.

22. *ye b——*: So in the MS.

23. *Deil stick the minister*: An anti-Presbyterian air of seventeenth-century origin; in 1683 a man was tried at Stirling for inciting a piper to play it in the minister's hearing (Lauder of Fountainhall, *Historical Notices*, 1848, 1, 442). The tune, apparently set for wind instruments, appears in James Oswald's *Caledonian Pocket Companion* (1752), but the words are elusive; those in J. Stokoe and S. Reay, *Songs and Ballads of Northern England* (*c.* 1882, 116–17) (CJH) seem too good-humoured to be the original provocative ones, and must be a redaction of something more sharply satirical.

24. *the original malediction*: With which Adam was expelled from Eden – 'In the sweat of thy face shalt thou eat bread' (Genesis 3:19).

25. *right-hand heats and extremes, and left-hand defections*: Not biblical, but stock phrases from Walker (*Six Saints*, 1, 5, 102, etc.).
26. *great foundation of our covenanted reformation*: Again echoes Walker's phrases (*Six Saints*, 1, 259, 289; 2, 4).
27. *breaking down the carved work*: Psalms 74:6.
28. *aits. . .pease*: 'here and there another division [of infield] for peas and beans. . . Oats was the other and more usual crop on infield. . . the main product. . . more like wild oats than the fat seed of modern husbandry' (Smout, 119–20).
29. *'that singular Christian woman,'*: *Six Saints*, 1, 61 and 158.
30. *name was savoury to all that knew her for a desirable professor*: Cf. 'names are savoury to all who knew them for two desirable Christians' (*Six Saints*, 1, 285).
31. *Hochmagirdle*: A Joycean moment, for the village name, ostensibly indicating something like 'Hitch-my-waistband' or 'Hoist-my-cooking-iron', also irresistibly calls to mind 'Hochmagandy', 'fornication'.

CHAPTER 9

Epigraph: Crabbe, *The Parish Register*, 2, 435–40.
 1. *'parts and portions'*: Stock formula from a Scottish lease.
 2. *Georgics*: An ostensibly didactic poem about agriculture written 30–37 BC, and long a standard element in the classical curriculum.
 3. *Columella and Cato the Censor*: Roman authors of prose treatises on agriculture – much more unusual reading than Virgil.
 4. *Gallio*: Gallio, brother of the philosopher Seneca, was the Roman proconsul of Achaia who declined jurisdiction over 'a question of words and names' when the local Jews accused St Paul of preaching heresy (Acts 18:12–17); he 'cared for none of these things' even when the Greeks beat the ruler of the synagogue. Deans equates the retreat from theocracy to comparative tolerance in the Revolution Settlement with a return to pagan indifference and unspirituality.
 5. *hearts. . . like the nether millstone*: Job 41:24.
 6. *shaft cleanly polished*: Isaiah 49:2 and *Six Saints*, 2, 64.
 7. *body of the kirk*: Colossians 1:18, still a somewhat jocular stock phrase in Scots conversation.
 8. *like the sow, to wallow in the mire*: 2 Peter 2:22.
 9. *heretical extremes and defections*: Walker's phrases – see n. 25 on p. 604.
10. *wings. . . pots*: Psalms 68:13; the pots are the principles of independency.
11. *High School*: Later in the eighteenth century Dalkeith High School was good enough to attract boarders from other parts of the country.
12. *physics and ethics. . . at the time. . . St Andrews*: New subjects and changes in teaching methods were well in hand by the 1720s at Edinburgh

University, Scott's first thought, replaced in MS by the comparatively stagnant St Andrews (A. Chitnis, *The Scottish Enlightenment*, 1976, 132–5).

13. *riding on horseback to hell than ganging barefooted to Heaven*: Not traced.

14. *profane company-keeper*: 1 Corinthians 5 forbids keeping company with fornicators, drunkards, etc.

15. *play-house, or music-house, or dancing-house*: See n. 16 on p. 609.

16. *imposer of aiths, or bonds*: Although lawful oaths were authorized by Chapter 22 of the Westminster Confession, oaths remained objectionable to religious purists for several reasons: because of the injunction 'Swear not at all. . . But let your communication be Yea, yea; Nay, nay' (Matthew 5:34–7); because they were demanded by the state under various Acts of the Restoration period and of the disappointingly uncovenanted Parliament that came in after the Revolution; because they normally incorporated recognition of the monarch as head of the Church, of England if not of Scotland; and because they had been used to elicit capitally punishable doctrinal dissent in the years before 1688, as in the case of Argyle's grandfather, who, taking an oath with a note of reservation, was convicted of treason when his motives were examined and made the subject of a death sentence that was later carried out when he was in custody on another charge. Cf. n. 16 on p. 659.

17. *breathing of a gale upon his spirit*: 'somewhat of a gale of young zeal upon my spirit, fearing no danger upon the right-hand if I held off the left' (*Six Saints*, 1, 286 and 337; 2, 20).

18. *mansion of clay*: Job 4:19.

19. *creature-comforts*: As distinct from the comfort of contemplating the creator.

20. *beatific vision*: The vision of the Divine Being in heaven, the final destiny of the redeemed. Scott's irony works against Dumbiedikes and also tends to check any thought of Jeanie as a Presbyterian saint.

21. *grave-digger's aphorism*: Hamlet, V, i, 53–4.

22. *sole remaining parent*: Grandparent surely, unless Scott is using the word in a very old-fashioned way.

23. *refined gold*: 1 Chronicles 28:18.

24. *father of the fatherless*: Psalms 68:5.

25. *Give honour where it is due*: Romans 13:7.

26. *Alexander Peden*: (?1626–86), an Ayrshireman and graduate of Glasgow, ejected from the charge of New Luce, Galloway, in 1663, lived his remaining twenty-three years as a fugitive Covenanting preacher with reputed prophetic powers, and sometimes as a prisoner. His *Life* by Patrick Walker (for whom see Scott's note on p. 559) appeared in 1724.

27. . . . *ink*: Peden predicted that the 'indulged, luke-warm ministers' would return from exile and hive together like bees in a General Assembly, whereupon the 'bits of papers and drops of blood' cherished by his fellow

sufferers would be 'shot to the door and never a word more of them' (*Six Saints*, 1, 83).

28. *the halt's gane now*: Ballantyne, who often made detailed suggestions on the proof sheets, may have pointed out the discrepancy between Butler's Dumfries walk and his lameness.

29. *the Paip, and again baptizing of bairns*: As an extreme Protestant, old Butler naturally took up his testimony (i.e. spoke or preached) against the Pope. His attitude to infant baptism, however (a controversy going back to the third century AD), was not a necessary part of his position as an Independent in Church government. Deans as a Presbyterian is consistent in rejecting both Independency and Anabaptism, both of which were rejected as unscriptural by the Westminster Assembly in 1647.

30. *outs and ins in the tract of his walk*: Butler's lameness has apparently moved from body to soul. This phrase and 'his gifts will get the heels of his grace' occur together (with 'round-spun Presbyterian', for which see p. 129) in Walker's life of Welwood (*Six Saints*, 1, 207–8).

31. *thinks as muckle about the form of the bicker as he does about the healsomeness of the food*: Not traced.

32. *broider the marriage-garment with lace and passments*: Marriage-garment is Matthew 22:11, the Scots adaptation not traced.

33. *affliction may gie him a jagg*: Walker reports Semple's prayer for a cleric whose sermons were too airy and fine: 'Good Lord, brod him, and let out the wind out of him' (*Six Saints*, 1, 189). For the 'jagg' and what it cures, see Hardy, *Far from the Madding Crowd*, Chapter 21.

34. *a burning and a shining light*: John 5:35, and also Burns's 'Holy Willie's Prayer', 11.

35. Deans's first sentence adapts from Isaiah 57:1; his second draws on Lamentations 3:48, where Jeremiah laments the destruction of Jerusalem through the image of a lost daughter of Zion.

36. *Semple*: For John Semple (1602–77), see Scott's note on p. 558; but he was misled by a clumsy transition in Patrick Walker's narrative, for this story is told of James Welwood, not of Semple (*Six Saints*, 1, 205).

37. *Ulai*: A river beside which Daniel had an apocalyptic vision (Daniel 8).

38. *dairy-farmer*: Defoe in 1724 notes as a gap in the Lothian economy the fact that the 'farmers have no dairies, no butter or cheese' (*Tour*, 2, 290).

39. *sixth*: Hardly so, if he has reviewed the alternatives and waited for a week.

CHAPTER 10

Epigraph: *The Parish Register*, 2, 135–8. In contrast with the previous epigraph, these seemingly positive lines introduce a tale of village seduction followed by unhappy forced marriage.

1. *fascination*: Scott quotes instances of fascination in northern legend in *Letters on Demonology and Witchcraft* (1830), 100.

2. *artes perditæ*: A phrase from the writings of Guido Pancirolli (*fl.* 1599), taken up in Swift's *A Tale of a Tub* (A.C. Guthkelch and Nicol Smith, eds., 1968, 155 and 200).

3. *middle age*: Jeanie, ten years older than Effie (p. 52), must be twenty-six or twenty-seven at this point – though the account of Rebecca's machinations suggests a greater difference in their ages.

4. *Grecian-shaped head*: 'The classic Greek outline, the nose continuing the forehead in almost a straight line, the chin large and firmly shaped', writes David Piper of portraiture of the 1790s (*The English Face*, 1957, 249). The heroine of Ann Radcliffe, *The Italian* (1797) also has 'features. . . of the Grecian outline' (F. Garber, ed., 1968, 6). Scott here projects the neo-Hellenic taste of his young days on to narrative set sixty years earlier.

5. *had no power to shake the stedfast mind*: The phrase, whose Miltonic diction and rhythm work mockingly against Dumbiedikes, anticipates the lines from *Comus* quoted later (p. 294).

6. *common and hereditary guilt and imperfection*: After the Fall, according to the Westminster Confession, Chapter 6, Adam and Eve became 'wholly defiled in all the faculties and parts of soul and body' through the 'original corruption, whereby we are utterly indisposed, disabled and made opposite to all good, and wholly inclined to evil'.

7. *authoress of 'Glenburnie'*: Mrs Elizabeth Hamilton (1758–1816), author of *The Cottagers of Glenburnie: A Tale for the Farmer's Ingle-Nook* (1808), which uses a father-with-contrasted-daughters plot to depict selfishness and domestic anarchy among the novel-reading classes as well as in the 'inferior' McClarty family. (For a recent alert discussion, see Gary Kelly, *English Fiction of the Romantic Period*, 1989, 89–92.) These references again push the supposed date of composition of Pattieson's tale back by some years. The 'editorial' footnote is by Scott.

8. *times of family worship*: Daily in the morning and evening, in theory, although pious writers complained that the practice was not diligently kept up.

9. *in her own conceit*: 'Be not wise in your own conceit', Romans 12:16.

10. *a cottage evening scene*: Although thus placed within the established genre 'representation of common life', the account develops in strong contrast to its conventional beginning, moving away from Burns's 'The Cotter's Saturday Night' and analogous paintings.

11. *The elfin knight. . . nae mair*: Effie's composite ballad verse hints pointedly at sexuality. The first line comes from 'The Elfin Knight' (Child, 2), in which a wise virgin (whose younger sister is already married) fences in riddles with her would-be seducer. The refrain comes from Scott's fragmentary memories of his nurserymaid's singing 'Sheath and Knife' (Child, 16), in which an incestuous brother bitterly regrets having murdered and buried his sister and their newborn babe. Moreover 'gathering broom, in folk-song, is a common metaphor for female sexual adventure' (Kinsley, 1529).

12. *questions . . . lees*: Proverbial (*ODEP*, 20).

13. *Scotch song*:

> I'll trip upon trenchers, I'll dance upon dishes;
> My mither sent me for barm, for barm:
> And through the kirk-yard I met wi' the laird,
> The silly, poor body could do me no harm.
>
> But down i' the park, I met with the clerk,
> And he gaed me my barm, my barm.
>
> ('Fragments of Comic and Humourous Songs' in Herd, 2, 231)

14. *Here the songstress stopped*: Just before completing the stanza with the words that would make the teasing about the laird and the clerk into a much more cruelly and coarsely explicit sexual taunt. Did Scott expect those of his readers who could complete the verse for themselves to assume that Jeanie would do so too? CJH suggests 'knowledge of the context makes Effie's singing the tune within David Deans's hearing an act of recklessness'.

15. *untaught child of nature*: A stock phrase later in the eighteenth century, in the era of Rousseau and the Noble Savage – it gives further colour to the view that Effie is slightly anachronistic.

16. *'Dance?'*: According to the Larger Catechism, Q. 139, 'sins forbidden in the seventh commandment' include 'lascivious songs, books, pictures, dancings, stage plays' and the last two items, lascivious or not, were suspect in themselves to the stricter sects; as late as the 1750s John Home was forced to resign from the ministry of the Church of Scotland because he had written an innocuous historical tragedy.

17. *regular fit of distraction*: Walker's words (from the source for most of the ensuing speech by Deans, quoted in Scott's note, pp. 559–60 and in *Six Saints*, 1, 239–41).

18. *base and brutish. . . Calf. . . unhappy lass. . . born a cripple*: All phrases from Walker, quoted in Scott's note. For the Golden Calf by Mount Sinai, which was worshipped with dancing, see Exodus 32; for the unhappy lass Salome, Matthew 14 and Mark 6. The golden calf at Bethel (1 Kings 12, 13, etc.) had no connection with dancing; is Scott, in adding the extra words to Walker's account, deliberately introducing error into Deans's harangue?

19. *Peter Walker the packman*: To the account in Scott's note should be added Walker's correct first name, Patrick, his dates (?1665–1745) and the view of his 1901 editor, D. Hay Fleming, that the designation as 'pedlar' or 'packman' probably arose from a misunderstood metaphor. Scott's whole imagining of Deans is saturated with Walker's phrases and attitudes.

20. *kingdom of darkness, warring with the kingdom of light*: Pauline thoughts but not specifically biblical wording.

21. *upright walk*: Morality of conduct, evincing understanding (Proverbs 15:21) and attracting God's blessing (Psalms 15:2 and 84:11; Proverbs 2:7, 28:18, etc.).

22. *Tolbooth Kirk*: Cf. p. 30. Its minister in 1736 was John Taylor (c. 1682–1736).

23. *bent the knee unto Baal*: Refers to the idolatry of the Israelites under King Ahab in the time of Elijah, to whom the Lord said, 'Yet have I left me seven thousand in Israel, all the knees which have not bowed unto Baal' (1 Kings 19:18).

24. *national defections. . . oaths*: Walker's words (*Six Saints*, 1, 290). For union and toleration, see Introduction, pp. x–xi; for patronage, see Glossary; for oaths, see n. 16 on p. 606.

25. *breaking down of the carved work*: Psalms 74:6.

26. *legalized formalist*: Cf. *Six Saints*, 1, 144.

27. *Something there was. . .could clear*: Crabbe, *The Borough*, 15, 'Inhabitants of the Alms-house', 39–42.

28. *Holy-Rood. . . perfect*: Two well-known proverbs in unfamiliar form; Holy-Rood was substituted for the Rome of Scott's first MS thought, and in his *Journal* of 27 January 1829 he quotes 'Use makes perfect' from Beaumont's and Fletcher's *The Knight of the Burning Pestle* (c. 1607), 1, 3.

29. *nice sharp quillets*: *1 Henry VI*, II, iv, 17.

30. *it's sad wark but siller will help it*: It's indeed a bad job that money won't improve – proverbial in style, but not in *ODEP*.

31. *Rock of Ages*: Not Toplady's hymn, published in 1775, but a Hebrew attribute of Jehovah cited in the Authorized Version note to Isaiah 26:4.

32. *the promise*: Of eternal life (1 John 2:25).

33. *Zipporah*: The wife Moses married during his exile in Midian; in a cryptic passage closely connected with God's threat to the first-born of Egypt, she seemingly saves Moses's life from an angry God by circumcising their son and denounces Moses as 'a bloody husband' (Exodus 4:24–6).

34. *hand-waled murderers*: *Six Saints*, 1, 238.

35. *push out the lip*: In contempt (Psalms 22:7).

36. *stumbling-block and scandal*: Romans 14:13, 'stumbling-block or an occasion to fall'. The verse opens 'Let us not therefore judge one another any more.'

37. *an eye for an eye . . .*: Exodus 21:23–4, and elsewhere in the Old Testament. At Deuteronomy 19:16–21 the formula concludes the rules for treating false witness – the perjurer is liable to the penalty for the crime of which he sought to convict another.

38. *it's the law of God and it's the law of man*: See Textual Notes. Deans forgets that the formula was specifically revoked by Christ (Matthew 5:38).

CHAPTER 11

Epigraph: *A Midsummer Night's Dream*, III, ii, 198–201, from a speech of Helena, who is beset by two unwanted lovers of doubtful sincerity.

1. *soldier*: 'soldier of Christ' occurs in 2 Timothy 2:3 and is developed through such works as Erasmus's *Manual of the Christian Soldier* (1503).

2. *peace upon earth...*: Luke 2:14.

3. *a strange right of intermeddling*: The Form of Presbyterial Church Government agreed upon by the Westminster Assembly included 'Pastors... And he hath also a ruling power over the flock as a pastor. Of Congregational Assemblies... The ruling officers of a particular congregation have power, authoritatively, to call before them any member of the congregation... to enquire into the knowledge and spiritual estate of the several members of the congregation... to admonish and rebuke.'

4. *in season and out of season*: 2 Timothy 4:2.

5. *'Thou shalt do no* MURDER': Matthew 19:18. Deans has just repeated an Old Testament formula rejected by Christ (p.109), but Butler adopts the New Testament rephrasing of the sixth commandment. To Robertson, the words convey more than Butler realizes.

6. *Cain*: Genesis 4. A fashionable allusion in Romantic and Gothic writing (Byron, Peacock, Maturin) as well as a commonplace in sermons against violence.

7. Duelling was still a live issue in Scott's circle, in which challenges arising out of political quarrels claimed at least one life. Butler's serious religious arguments against it seem closer to those of Scott's time than, say, the worldly-wise mockery used by Steele in the *Spectator*, 25 and 31 (1709).

8. *to disbelieve witchcraft... proof of atheism*: See n. 13 below.

9. *Nicol Muschat's Cairn*: See Scott's note on p. 561.

10. *Roaring Lion*: The Devil (1 Peter 5:8).

11. *those who live in the present day*: In the following purple passage 'Pattieson' (if it is he), supposedly writing *c.* 1809, rejects the literal demonology of the 1730s for sensational details from the stock figures of the 'Gothic' or Byronic demonology of his own day; Robin Mayhew has pointed out the parallels in Byron and in Ann Radcliffe's *The Italian* (1797).

12. *mien, language, and port of the ruined archangel*: Of Satan, as described by Milton in *Paradise Lost*, 1, 590ff:

> care
> Sat on his faded cheek, but under brows
> Of dauntless courage, and considerate pride
> Waiting revenge; cruel his eye, but cast
> Signs of remorse and passion to behold
> The fellows of his crime...condemned...

13. *laws against witchcraft...lately been acted upon*: In fact, sceptical judges were rendering prosecutions ineffective during the later seventeenth century, the last trial took place in 1727, and Westminster repealed the witchcraft legislation in 1736 – developments deplored by conservative

religious groups. Butler's divided attitude of 1736 has become more secular by the time he comes to deal with Ailie McClure in 1750 or so (see p. 479). Graphic detail of the Scottish witch-craze may be found in Graham (486–8) and Smout (184–92), a broad perspective in Keith Thomas, *Religion and the Decline of Magic* (1971) and sustained analysis in Christina Larner, *Enemies of God: The Witch-hunt in Scotland* (1981).

14. *common sense*: A more pointed phrase then than now, and the name of a specific school within Scottish philosophy. Butler's argument from 'the general rules by which the universe is governed' parallels that of David Hume's essay 'Of Miracles' (1748), a view that Hume thought too bold to publish or even to circulate privately in 1737 (E.C. Mossner, *Life of David Hume*, 1954, 111); it must, however, be roughly that on which the abolitionist law officers acted.

CHAPTER 12

Epigraph: 'Sweet William's Ghost' (Child, 77A), printed in the 1740 edition of *TTM* and other eighteenth-century collections. The lover's ghost knocks at Margaret's door (as does Butler in the following sentence) to reclaim the unfulfilled troth-pledge; she returns it, but love prevails and she joins him in the grave.

1. *a bard of that time and country*: Allan Ramsay, *The Gentle Shepherd* (1725), 5, 2, 4; all part of another genre-piece.

2. *Southey*: Robert Southey (1774–1843), the Poet Laureate. The line 'stern to inflict, and stubborn to endure' occurs in his verse 'Epistle' prefixed to A.S. Cottle's *Icelandic Poetry* (1797), p. xxxiv (Lamont). Scott first applied it to Deans in the form 'firm to resolve and stubborn to endure', restoring 'inflict' only in *1830*.

3. Not for the last time Scott appeals to the visual arts, in this contrast between the haunting and impressive character portraits of patriarchs by Rembrandt van Rijn (1606–69), and the symbolic classical figures, heroic poses and grand scale of the painting and sculpture of Michelangelo (1475–1564).

4. *the old ballad*: *Chevy Chase or The Hunting of the Cheviot* (Child, 162B), stanza 37.

5. *a reproach and a hissing*: Both terms occur several times in the Old Testament and the Apocrypha, but not together.

6. *lay saft, fed sweet, and drank deep*: 'the tables better covered, the chambers warmer, and the beds softer than the cold hills and glens' (*Six Saints*, 1, 103).

7. *Donald Cameron*: The name conflates two Covenanters, Donald (or Daniel) Cargill (for whom see pp. 443–4 and n. 2 on p. 661) and Richard Cameron, the young Covenanter field-preacher killed at Airdsmoss in 1680, who was, along with Alexander Peden, the chief subject of Walker's biographical work.

8. *Blackadder*: John Blackadder (1615–86), ejected minister, Covenanter preacher and prisoner; the nickname is in *Six Saints*, 1, 251.

Additional passage in Textual Notes: James Renwick (1662–88), Cameronian organizer, propagandist and field-preacher, the last Covenanter to be hanged in the Grassmarket (February 1688).

9. *crying aloud, and sparing not*: Isaiah 58:1.

10. *nation-wasting. . . Stuarts*: Almost word for word from Walker's *Vindication of Mr Cameron's Name* (*Six Saints*, 1, 270); the 'last woman' is Queen Anne. See n. 24 on p. 610.

11. *'Cry of an Howl in the Desert'*: 'I am like an owl of the desert', Psalms 102: 6. Walker says that 'some of late have written *A Cry of an Howl in the Desert to all Elderships*' (*Six Saints*, 1, 275) but his 1901 editor had never seen a copy, and the work does not appear in the *Eighteenth-century Short Title Catalogue*.

12. *flying stationers*: Chapmen, the book-pedlars who played an important part in the circulation of reading matter before the advent of the cheap newspaper and the railway from the 1830s. Deans's title-page has the conventional imprint of a chapbook.

13. *Saint Jerome*: (*c.* 342–420), one of the fathers of the Church and translator of the Bible into Latin. The passage corresponds in part to 2 Corinthians 6:8.

14. *'Watchman. . .night?'*: Isaiah 21:11, quoted in *Six Saints*, 1, 5.

15. *crook in my lot*: For meaning, see Glossary. *The Crook in the Lot; or The Wisdom and Sovereignty of God Displayed in the Afflictions of Men* (1732) is a tract by Thomas Boston of Ettrick (1676–1732). Cf. p. 473.

16. *polished shaft*: Isaiah 49:2, again.

17. *and meet to be a pillar*: Revelation 3:12. Cf. *Six Saints*, 2, 64.

18. *light. . .kail-worm*: Not traced.

19. *rag of human righteousness*: Isaiah 64:6.

20. *Rochefoucault*: Scott alludes to No. 99 of the cynical *Réflexions, ou sentences et maximes morales* of François, Duc de La Rochefoucauld (1613–80), first published in 1664. Scott's well-stocked library does not seem to have contained a copy, but this item was an eighteenth-century commonplace.

21. *heaven-daring*: From Walker's vocabulary, e.g. *Six Saints*, 1, 22, and 37, etc.

22. *the back is made for the burthen*: Proverbial from 1822 (*ODEP*, 312).

23. *no granter of propositions*: Not traced.

24. *Privy-Council*: The Scots Privy Council had been abolished as a separate body in 1708.

25. *wise after the manner of this world*: 1 Corinthians 3:18.

26. *black hand. . . sworn murtherers*: 'the red-hands with blood, and the black-hands with defection, will be taken by the hand, and the hand given them by our ministers' (*Six Saints*, 1, 83).

27. *numbered the towers. . . marked the bulwarks*: 'Walk about Zion, and go

round about her; tell the towers thereof. Mark ye well her bulwarks, consider her palaces; that ye may tell it to the generation following' (Psalms 48:12–13). The passage is used in Walker's *Vindication of Mr Cameron's Name* (1727) (*Six Saints*, 1, 259); from Walker's and Deans's point of view, the 'generation following' had been betrayed by the Revolution Settlement.

28. *blue-bottle flees... bike*: 'When that day comes, there will a bike of indulged, luke-warm ministers come out of Holland, England and Ireland, together with a bike of them at home, and some young things that know nothing, and they will all hyve together in a General Assembly' (Peden in *Six Saints*, 1, 83).

29. *language of Antichrist*: Latin, because spoken in Rome.

30. *knowledge for pieces of silver*: As Judas sold Christ.

31. *union, toleration, patronages, and Yerastian prelatic oaths*: For the language, compare pp. 118–19; also *Six Saints*, 1, 290: 'these new begun courses of national defections, Union, toleration, patronages, and bundle of Erastian prelatical oaths'. For the substance, see n. 24 on p. 610.

32. *bundle of papers*: The case recounted by Saddletree sounds like a notional theme for student disputation, but an almost identical one was gravely reported from Ballater in February 1819 (*SND*, 7, 172) – perhaps a 'spoof' suggested by the novel.

33. *uncertainty*: Because of the difficulty of converting a customary measure based on the capacity of the plough-team, which would vary locally with soil, gradients, etc., into standard units in the new era of measurement and surveying.

34. *guse's grass*: Not entirely a joke, for Boswell, resolving to withdraw 'a cow's grass', or pasturage, as an element in an employee's wages, values it at £5 per annum (*Journal*, 25 March 1789).

35. Titius, praised for wit by Cicero, and Maevius, denounced by Virgil and Horace, have become stock figures in legal examples. The guse's grass and the crimson horse are also legal fictions – as is Effie's guilt.

36. *ane act*: See Scott's note, 'Child Murder', p. 565.

37. *His will be done*: From the Lord's Prayer, Matthew 6:10.

38. *the very deil is no sae ill as he's ca'd*: Proverbial (*ODEP*, 306; Kelly, T34; *Guy Mannering*, Chapter 32).

39. *glancing-glasses*: Walker (*Six Saints*, 1, 277; 2, 69) uses the phrase 'glazing glancing-glass' to attack his contemporary John Glass, founder of the 'glancing Glassites lately start up in their new lights and flights'.

40. *heathen emperors and popish canons*: Referring to the law's origins in Roman law and in the canon law of the medieval Church.

41. *Titus*: (39–81), conqueror of Jerusalem (70) and emperor of Rome (79–81). See n. 35 above.

42. *round-spun presbyterian*: James Welwood's phrase, according to *Six Saints*, 1, 208. For meaning, see Glossary.

43. *polititious*: 'the publick, witty and polititious, consulting and racking the rules of carnal state-policy' (*Six Saints*, 1, 256).

44. *1715 . . . had the luck to cross the Firth*: They did, but not in enough strength to bring out any but their most committed sympathizers – see n. 21 on p. 594.

45. *Arniston. . .medals. . .Gordon*: For the Dundases of Arniston, see n. 3 on p. 598. The younger Robert (1713–87) had not yet been admitted advocate in 1737 and his father, though famous as a defending lawyer and on the point of becoming a judge, was at fifty-two scarcely a 'chield'; perhaps Saddletree is being pointedly familiar. A kinsman of theirs had been accused, twenty-five years previously, of affronting Queen Anne by urging the Faculty of Advocates to accept into its collections a Jacobite political medal provocatively offered by the Roman Catholic Duchess of Gordon.

46. *in the multitude. . .safety*: Proverbs 11:14; 24:6 (Saddletree tries to bandy scripture with Deans).

47. *young Mackenyie*: Sir George Mackenzie's advocate nephew Simon had in fact been drowned in 1730 at the age of fifty-six.

48. *uncle's practiques. . .*: the legal works (*Pleadings*, a *Discourse* and *Institutions* rather than practiques) of Sir George Mackenzie (1636–91), who as King's Advocate (1677–86, 1688) played a major part in the repression of the Covenanters.

49. *gae down the water*: 'go to wreck or perdition' (*SND*, 'Water' 1, 3, i, a, citing this example).

50. *sectarians*: Deans falls back on his long-standing membership of the national Church, to which Butler's forebears did not belong.

51. *gallant soldier. . . bayonet*: More dignified than the 'butt-end' proposed for the same purpose in Cibber, *The Refusal* (1721).

52. *sun shines. . . unjust*: Matthew 5:45 – Butler characteristically opposes New Testament texts to Deans's Old Testament ones.

53. *pitch. . . defiled*: Ecclesiasticus 13:1 (also *Much Ado about Nothing*, III, iii, 53).

54. *remnant*: Of Israel, a recurrent topic with the later Old Testament prophets.

55. *clifts of the rocks*: God placed Moses in the cleft of a rock to protect him from the sight of His glory (Exodus 33:22); Isaiah sends people there for comfort and shelter (Isaiah 2:21), and so does the preacher Donald Cargill (*Six Saints*, 2, 49).

56. *wi' a wat finger*: Easily. Proverbial since the sixteenth century (*ODEP*, 881).

57. The fact that on this charge, exceptionally, the prosecution does not have to prove the positive fact of the crime may well make Effie's case harder, not easier – Saddletree blunders again.

58. *protestation. . . libel*: Saddletree's jargon apparently bamboozles Dumbiedikes into increasing his contribution.

CHAPTER 13

Epigraph: Adapted from *The Tempest*, I, i, 43. The fellow is safe from drowning because born to be hanged.

1. *Nichil Novit*: See n. 16 on p. 604.

2. *Fugit irrevocabile tempus!*: Time flies, not to be called back – Scott or Butler misquotes Virgil's *Fugit irreparabile tempus* (not to be retrieved) of *Georgics*, 3, 284.

3. *Ratcliffe*: Apparently a wholly fictitious character, despite the care with which his career is developed.

4. *hang you next Wednesday eight days*: Normand remarks that in Ratcliffe's case the jurisdiction to reprieve as well as to sentence lay with the City under its charter of 1482, so that the delayed and complex process of obtaining pardon from the Privy Council was not necessary.

5. *I'll speak to Mr Sharpitlaw about him*: This sentence was substituted in *1818* for a substantial passage of MS cut, probably in proof, and later thriftily reincorporated at pp. 207 and 512–13. See Textual Notes, n. 30 to Introduction and n. 6 on p. 669.

6. *recognize his voice*: Butler has already failed to do so in Chapter 11.

CHAPTER 14

Epigraph: A variant version of 'Tam Linn' (Child, 39, stanza 36 of the *SMM* version there, also Scott's *Minstrelsy* version, stanza 46). Janet, pregnant by a seducer who has himself fallen captive to the fairies, sets out to release him by means of a midnight shape-changing ritual.

1. *Coleridge*: In 'Love' (1799), 73–6.

2. *bitter waters of Merah*: Sweetened for the Israelites by Moses with the Lord's advice, Exodus 15:23ff.

3. *basket and store*: In formulae of blessing and cursing, Deuteronomy 28:5, 17; compare Burns, 'Holy Willie's Prayer', 78 (Kinsley, 74–8).

4. *laid 'reverently aside,'*: Scott quotes and alludes to the evening prayers in stanza 12 of Burns's 'The Cotter's Saturday Night' (1785–6; Kinsley, 145–52), a poem (English rather than Scots) explicitly invoking a Gray's *Elegy* perception of the poor.

5. *'The man after God's own heart'*: David, according to Samuel (1 Samuel 13:14).

6. *washed... suffering*: 2 Samuel 12:20, after the Lord struck the child of David's adulterous union with Uriah's wife.

7. *blessings of the promise*: Of God's promise to Abraham, as recalled by Paul in Hebrews 6:12–15.

8. *purchased and promised blessings*: Those promised to Abraham, and those purchased by Christ's death on the cross – recurrent in Walker (e.g. *Six Saints*, 1, 31 and 85; 2, 99).

9. *walk . . . not of the world*: Jeanie speaks of her father in the words with which Christ commends his apostles to God (John 17:14–18).

CHAPTER 15

Epigraph: *Hamlet*, II, ii, 584–6. The hero ponders the genuineness of his father's ghost.

1. *Witchcraft . . . imaginary crimes*: Scott somewhat exaggerates the prevalence of the belief at the time of the novel. See n. 13 on p. 611, and especially Larner's study.

2. *Chase*: Exaggerates, perhaps deliberately, the wildness of what had long been an enclosed park.

3. *one of their gifted seers exclaim*: Peden, for whom see n. 26 on p. 606. The story is sited in a wild cave in Galloway, not in the specially constructed refuge-cellar in Sorn in Ayrshire where Peden died in 1686 (*Six Saints*, 1, 78–9 and 95).

4. *Semple*: See Scott's note, p. 558, and n. 36 on p. 607. The story is from Walker (*Six Saints*, 1, 195), with a final sentence from Sharpe's edition of Law's *Memorialls* (Anderson).

5. *Bull of Bashan*: Psalms 22:12.

6. *Christiana . . . Progress*: John Bunyan's allegory of 1678–84 – the second reference to a text that gains in significance later in the novel. In Bunyan, Christiana traverses the Valley in daylight (*PP*, 240–46); it was her spouse who went through in darkness.

7. *Valley of the Shadow of Death*: From Psalms 23:4 and Jeremiah 2:6.

8. *'now in glimmer and now in gloom'*: Coleridge, *Christabel* (published 1816), 169. Appropriately, the heroine of Coleridge's unfinished poem is unwittingly introducing into her home a beautiful hypnotic creature, perhaps a vampire, with a loathsome but unspecified deformity under her garments. The shape-changing motif underlying the 'Tamlane' epigraph to Chapter 14 is carried forward. Cf. epigraph to Chapter 31.

9. *night is as noon-day*: E.g. Isaiah 58:10.

10. *Saint Anthony the Eremite*: Scott's praise of the aptness of the site is linked to its patron saint (*fl.* 300), who was first among the Desert Fathers. His lurid sexual temptations, a standard theme in religious art, reinforce the unhallowed imagery from Coleridge and Muschat.

11. *a cairn for your burial-place*: On the other hand, Pennant, visiting the Highlands sixty years earlier, noted that the size of the cairn reflected the honour in which the deceased was held (*Tour in Scotland . . . 1772*, 1776, 1, 209).

12. *planet*: Scott's term for the moon is correct in the classification of his own day and of Jeanie's.

13. *desperate*: Quite literally, deprived of hope.

14. *predestined to evil here and hereafter*: Theologically unsound even among the Calvinists, to whom he has apparently been listening.

15. *chief of sinners*: Paul's description of himself at 1 Timothy 1:15.

16. *apostate spirit incarnate*: One of the angels who revolted with Satan, now a devil made flesh.

17. *bitterness of death*: 1 Samuel 15:32.

18. Scott's note (placed at the end of this chapter in *1830* though originally proposed by him for the end of Chapter 5) omits to mention the final abolition of the crime in 1809.

19. *lamp of our path*: Proverbs 6:23, etc.

20. *When the gledd's . . . the hill*: Apparently remembered or, more probably, composed by Scott.

21. *O sleep . . . hide*: Close to a stanza of 'Young Johnstone' (Child, 88C, stanza 22) taken down in 1825 – a ballad not included by Scott in the *Minstrelsy* (CJH).

CHAPTER 16

Epigraph: *Hamlet*, IV, v, 6–10. A gentleman describes Ophelia.

1. *digressive poet Ariosto*: (1474–1535), author of the intricately plotted romantic epic *Orlando Furioso*.

2. *skulduddery . . . Kirk-treasurer*: Penalties for sexual misbehaviour accrued to the Kirk-session, not to the civil authorities.

3. *run their letters*: Become free by elapse of the period allowed for the prosecution to bring its case. Cf. Scott's footnote.

4. *tents of Kedar*: Psalms 120:5. Kedar was the son of Ishmael, son of Abraham by an Egyptian maidservant – hence in biblical society a rallying-point for outcasts of Jewish origin.

5. *Jock Dalgleish*: As executioner and doomster, succeeded his whipped and banished predecessor in 1722, is recorded as having read Porteous's sentence in court, and presumably appears, though unnamed, on p. 247.

6. *wink . . . horse*: *ODEP*, 575. This unusually double-edged proverb ('No need to labour the point/However explicit you are he won't understand you'), not recorded earlier than the 1790s, is frequent in Scott (*Letters*, 15 November 1818, *The Fortunes of Nigel*, Chapter 25).

7. *time about's fair play*: *ODEP*, 846.

8. *gif-gaf makes gude friends*: *ODEP*, 301, quotes no instance between Kelly, G19, and *The Heart of Mid-Lothian*; Grose, *PG*, which Scott used heavily in Chapters 29–32, has (like Kelly) the form 'Giff-goff makes good fellowship' (E3r).

9. *dead folk's shoon*: *ODEP*, 171, in English, citing Kelly, H172, and *Guy Mannering* for the Scots form.

10. *mare's nest wi' a witness*: Obviously better than an ordinary mare's nest (*ODEP*, 512).

11. *Touchstone's . . . Audrey*: 'Bear your body more seeming, Audrey', *As You Like It*, V, iv, 65.

12. *half-hangit Maggie Dickson*: Tried and hanged in 1728 under the 1690 statute on child-murder, but recovered through the jolting of the cart in which her coffin was travelling, bore several more children and kept an ale-house.

13. *Deil be in my fingers*: Perhaps a witches' imprecation in travesty of some pious prayer such as 'God be in my fingers.'

14. *Hey for cavaliers . . . for fear*: Adapted from the chorus of 'The Cavaliers Song' in Thomas Durfey, *Pills to Purge Melancholy* (1719), 3, 131 (CJH). Scott rings further changes in *Peveril of the Peak*, Chapter 1, and in *Woodstock*, Chapter 5.

15. *I glance. . . bonny as me*: Apparently Scott's own – fragments of the whole song supposedly made for Madge by Robertson recur in Chapters 29 and 31.

16. *say the single carritch . . . and the double carritch, and justification, and effectual calling, and the assembly of divines*: The Shorter Catechism and the Longer Catechism, agreed on by the Scottish and English Assembly of Divines at Westminster in 1647, included questions on specific theological topics, which Madge, having been coached in them in childhood, now ramblingly recalls.

17. *wark-house in Leith Wynd*: The house of correction, in a street running north from outside the Netherbow Port.

18. *threshie-coat*: A coat of rushes, or as green as the rushes, worn by the Scots Cinderella.

19. *What did ye. . . love o' mine, O*: A version of the final stanza of 'The Wren, or Lennox's Love to Blantyre' (*SMM*, 483). CJH observes that the 'wedding ring' idea hints at a sexual relation between Madge and Robertson.

20. *Ophelia be the most affecting*: In *Hamlet*, IV, v.

CHAPTER 17

Epigraph: Close to Child, 81A, stanza 14. Barnard is hastening to surprise his wife in Little Musgrave's bower, while his retinue try to warn the lovers.

1. *as sure as a tether*: Not in *ODEP*, *SND* or *OED*. Apt for the speakers because a tether can also mean a hangman's noose.

2. *a woman's heart takes a lang time o' breaking*: Not in *ODEP* or Kelly, but apparently a misogynous proverb.

3. *keep a most heedful guard*: Hardly his conduct with Madge in the previous chapter or with Effie in this.

4. *wad hae been dearly telling*: Would have been of great advantage to him (Lamont, citing *OED*, 'tell', 22d).

5. *broke the charm*: Either Sharpitlaw repeats with Effie the mistake he has just made with Madge on p. 171 or Scott carelessly repeats an incident.

6. *as like to each other as the collier to the deil*: *ODEP*, 465. Proverbial from the sixteenth century, and in Bunyan.

7. *seek moonshine in water*: *ODEP*, 542. Proverbial in Paston Letters, *Love's Labours Lost* and *Rob Roy*.

8. *open ground*: Only in the relative sense of being outside the city walls; the Canongate had long been closely built up on both sides.

9. *granite*: Teschenite, in fact (G.P. Black, *Arthur's Seat*, 1966, 159).

10. *Deacon Sanders's new cleansing draps*: Not traced.

11. *Good even. . . mine shall be*: Madge's charm parallels one in Grose, *PG*, 54. Reciting the lines while standing over a gate or stile and looking at the new moon will bring a dream of the future husband or wife.

12. *whiles I wish the bairn had lived*: Scott has already thought out his plot, but the reader still takes this bairn to be Effie's.

13. *like to like. . . proverb never fails. . . deevil's peats*: Now the full version of the proverb touched on a few pages before (p. 176), 'Like will to like, quoth the devil to the collier', surfaces in Madge's associative speech.

14. *It is the bonny. . . he slew*: No sources have been found for this and the following two ballad stanzas, which are included as Scott's in most editions of his poems; for the last one, see n. 21 to p. 618.

15. *as gleg as Mackeachan's elshin*: Which, in popular story, thus injured Robert Bruce during running repairs after a battle. (Ramsay of Ochtertyre, quoted by J. Currie, edo, Works of Robert Burns, 1800, 1, 201).

CHAPTER 18

Epigraph: *Measure for Measure*, III, ii, 234–5. Escalus, the sympathetic magistrate, told by the disguised duke that the condemned prisoner has composed himself for death, comments thus, and adds, 'I have laboured for the poor gentlemen to the extremest shore of my modesty, but my brother-justice have I found so severe that he hath forced me to tell him he is indeed Justice.'

1. *'life and mettle' in her heels*: The phrase describes the witches' dance to Auld Nick's piping in ruined Kirk-Alloway in Burns's 'Tam o' Shanter', 118 (Kinsley, 557–64). The poem was first published in Grose's *Antiquities of Scotland* (1791), the work alluded to in the title-page epigraph.

2. *long in the land. . . honour father and mother*: The fourth commandment, Exodus 20:12.

3. *purchased and promised blessings*: See n. 8 on p. 616.

4. *watches. . . uprising. . . utterly hid thy face. . . just. . . prayers. . . helmet. . . continuance*: Recurrent Old Testament phraseology, especially from the Psalms.

5. *a sun-blink on a stormy sea*: 'sun-blink' (but not the whole phrase) recurs in *Six Saints* (1, 157 and 218; 2, 112).

6. *greyhound from the slips*: *Henry V*, III, i, 31.

7. *Then hey... the gee*: 'The Rinaway Bride' in Herd, 2, 87, and *SMM*, 474. The bride decamps before the wedding.

8. *Middleburgh*: Obviously a burgher in a middle social position between the Deanses' world and the Duke of Argyle's, but the name also suggests a connection with the Dutch trade to Middelburg in Zeeland – as Meg Murdockson sneeringly points out on p. 190.

9. *worship God, though the devil bid you*: Adapts *Othello*, I, i, 109–10.

10. *hint to speak*: *Othello*, I, iii, 142.

11. *hung by the wall, like unscoured armour*: *Measure for Measure*, I, ii, 162. Spoken by the condemned youth Claudio with reference to the newly enforced law.

12. *Would put... world*: *Othello*, IV, ii, 142 and paraphrase of 143.

13. *poisoned chalice*: *Macbeth*, I, vii, 11.

14. *to*: As to.

15. *Campvere*: A Dutch seaport five miles from Middelburg, in which the Scots long enjoyed special trading privileges. Cf. n. 8 above.

16. *ten talents*: I.e. fingernails – the printed texts' bowdlerization of MS 'ten commandments' (from *2 Henry VI*, I, iii, 142) has been accepted. Stevenson picks up the phrase in 'A Lodging for the Night' (Tusitala edition, 1, 237).

17. *'the grim feature'*: Milton's term for Death as he scents 'the smell of mortal change on earth' (*Paradise Lost*, 10, 279).

18. *Elector of Hanover's*: In denying the king his British title, Meg shows herself to be at least a Tory, perhaps a Jacobite.

19. *after her ordinar*: 'out of her usual state' (rather than 'after her regular drink').

20. *Jean Jap*: Not in C. Larner et al., *A Sourcebook of Scottish Witchcraft* (1977), which seeks to calendar the recorded cases.

21. *Up in the air... her yet*: In the poem (so titled) in *TTM* (reprinted 1876, 1, 75) the lines sung by Madge are preceded by 'In glens the fairies skip and dance,/And witches wallop o'er to France'.

22. *Council of Regency*: Cf. p. 42.

23. *act of parliament*: 10 Geo. II, cap. 35, conveniently printed in Roughead, Appendix 15.

24. *invisible head of the kirk*: 'The Catholic or universal church, which is invisible... shall be gathered into one, under Christ the head thereof' (Westminster Confession, Chapter 25, 1).

25. *steps adopted*: Those mentioned were proposed in the Bill but, after repeated intervention by Argyle and others, not enacted.

26. dukes and fools: Again Scott seems to have improved a traditional joke, which occurs in simpler form, without its political context and merely as a matter of Scots pronunciation, in Edmund Burt, *Letters from a Gentleman in the North of Scotland* (1754), 1, 21. There, a greasy Edinburgh cook

offers guests 'a Duke, a Fool or a Meer-fool' for dinner. Scott knew Burt's work well and contributed material to Jamieson's new edition in 1818.

27. *suburban villas*: Newington, south of St Leonard's, was developed from 1806 (A.J. Youngson, *The Making of Georgian Edinburgh*, Edinburgh, 1966, 272).

28. *did not bear the sword in vain. . . praise*: Phrases from the opening verses of Romans 13, Paul's advice on Christian attitudes to the civil ruler (cf. Westminster Confession, Chapter 23, 'Of the Civil Magistrate').

29. *Provost Dick*: (1580?–1655), provost in 1638–9. See Scott's note on p. 567. The *DNB* denies that he died in prison. A descendant was still petitioning Parliament for repayment of the Dick fortune as late as 1842.

30. *Seeing with one eye, hearing with one ear, and upholding the ark*: Generally, not specifically, biblical.

31. *Mr Chambers'*: Robert Chambers (1802–71), a protégé of Scott and a rising Edinburgh bookseller, publisher and author; his *Vestiges of Creation* (1844) paved the way for Darwin. His *Traditions of Edinburgh* (1823) adds nothing significant to the account of Dick in Scott's note.

32. *Patriarch. . . Peniel. . . Mahanaim*: Jacob, in Genesis 32, wrestles with God in the night there.

33. *national vows*: The National Covenant of 1638 (see pp. ix–x).

34. *wally-draigle. . . rannell-trees. . . English bugs*: In this vigorous invective (not in Walker and not traced elsewhere) Scott either imitates or quotes the homely and domestic style adopted by some Presbyterian preachers.

35. *bottomless pit*: Revelation *passim*.

36. *perverse. . . generation*: Deuteronomy 32:5, Revelation 3:16; etc.

37. *world. . . flesh. . . Belial*: David takes the distinction between fleshly and spiritual relationships chiefly from St Paul's Epistles; Belial is the Devil, especially as a source of lust (1 Samuel 2:12–24; *Paradise Lost*, 1, 490ff.).

38. *company-keeper*: One who engages in courtship; but Deans also echoes Paul's call to exclude fornicators from social contact with Christians, in 1 Corinthians 5:11.

39. *Saunders Peden*: For Peden, see n. 26 on p. 606. Peden's rebukes to inattentive hearers are reported by Walker among the additional passages in the 1728 edition (*Six Saints*, 1, 124).

40. *drawing lang their furrows*: 'The plowers plowed upon my back, and drew long their furrows', Psalms 129:3; Walker reports Peden's sermon on this text in Kyle in 1682 (*Six Saints*, 1, 59).

41. *Lady Hundelslope*: Apparently the wife of the occupant of Hundleshope, a property three miles south of Peebles.

42. *wicked beyond the breath of their nosthrils*: Uses the Apocryphal Wisdom 2:2, where the ungodly give this as a reason for hedonism.

43. *Cameronian Rant*: A strathspey tune printed in 1771, most easily found (as 'The Battle of Sherra-muir', text by Burns) in *SMM*, 282, and Kinsley, 534. See p. 405.

44. *society people*: Middleburgh blunders by confounding Deans with the

'right-hand extremes' among the factions of the disintegrating Covenanters – all the groups mentioned were illuminist sects, 'positively proclaiming their disowning of the state', refusing to pay taxes, and rejecting the ministry and organization of the Church. Middleburgh displays a later generation's lack of interest in the original fine distinctions. Walker, who insists passionately on the distinction between those of 'the Lord's people, who have any well-balanced zeal' and 'these Dissenters', would have disagreed with Scott's *1830* footnote (*Six Saints*, 1, 142; 2, 69; etc).

45. *vessel of clay*: Traditional image of human weakness deriving from Jeremiah 18:4. Deans's splendid utterance aligns him with the Presbyterian attitude to secular authority – compare Butler's account of the source of his 'commission' in his encounter with Staunton in the King's Park in Chapter 11.

46. *humble pleader for the gude auld cause in a legal way*: Cf. Walker (*Six Saints*, 1, 260), who frequently cites and endorses the 'Humble Pleaders for the Good Old Way' and their writings (1, 29, 244, 263, etc.); see also Glossary under 'cause'.

47. *rigg of a hill, where wind and water shears*: More untraced familiar imagery.

48. *Johnny Dodds of Farthing's Acre*: Not traced.

49. *Solemn League and Covenant*: See Introduction, p. x.

50. *Anti-popish. . . remnant*: Kirkton, 444n.

51. Scott obviously has first-hand knowledge of Talla-Linns itself; his immediate source for the policies discussed there seems to be C.K. Sharpe's biographical note on James Russel, in Kirkton, 399–401, commented on in Kirkton Review, 279–80.

52. *cess or tribute*: Deans 'translates' cess, the Scottish land-tax, into the tribute collected by the Romans from Jews and early Christians (Matthew 17:25; 22:17), emphasizing the Cameronian self-identification with New Testament groups.

53. *James Russel*: Obscure except for his participant's account of the murder of Archbishop Sharp, May 1679, appended to C.K. Sharpe's edition of Kirkton's *History*.

54. *punishment*: Exclusion from the kingdom of God (1 Corinthians 6:9).

55. *second temple*: By analogy with the Temple at Jerusalem, rebuilt in 520 BC after the Babylonian captivity of the Jews.

56. *1639. . . Dunbar*: From Charles I's acceptance of the Covenanters' demands in the Pacification of Berwick, to Cromwell's defeat of the Scots (by then fighting as supporters of Charles II) on 3 September 1650.

57. *mint. . . tithes*: Matthew 23:23.

CHAPTER 19

Epigraph: Not so far traced among the works of Isaac Watts (1674–1748), of which there appears to be no reliably complete edition. In the Introduction

to *Chronicles of the Canongate* (1827) Scott remarks that his epigraphs 'are
sometimes quoted either from reading or from memory, but, in the general
case, are pure invention'; he has 'been entertained when Dr Watts and
other graver authors have been ransacked in vain for stanzas for which the
novelist alone was responsible'. Among the fifty-two epigraphs of *The
Heart of Mid-Lothian*, however, fifty have now been identified as wholly or
partly authentic quotations, the exceptions being those to Chapters 19 and
24.

1. *ninth command*: Exôdus 20:16.
2. *haena felt freedom to separate mysell*: Again Deans is carefully distinguished
   from the extremists among his co-religionists.
3. *vile affections*: Romans 1:26.
4. *counsel which causeth to perish!*: Biblical language but no specific quotation
   here.
5. *ancient proverb*: 'Set a thief to catch a thief' (*ODEP*, 810) seems more
   current in the relevant period, and in the authors Scott read, than 'Old
   poachers make the best gamekeepers' (*ODEP*, 592).
6. *James Ratcliffe. . . delinquents*: The first sentence of the passage cut from p.
   142.
7. *bitter cup*: Recalls a series of biblical usages from Psalms through Jeremiah
   to Christ's last days.

CHAPTER 20

Epigraph: Claudio, the condemned brother, in *Measure for Measure*, III, i,
133–6.

1. *language. . . wept*: Job's comforters in Job 2:12.
2. *mony a tod hunted that's no killed*: Apparently proverbial but not found in
   ODEP or Kelly.
3. *flea's hide and tallow*: To flay a flea for its hide and tallow (*ODEP*, 267)
   recurs in *The Abbot*, Chapter 19.
4. *faulded down the leaf*: Cf. Scott's footnote to p. 103, which stresses the
   solemn and binding intention but not the expectation of predictive content
   in the biblical text.
5. *text*: Job 19:9, 10.
6. *as hard as the nether millstane*: Job 41:24.
7. *ye may hew down the tree, but ye canna change its bend*: 'hew down the tree'
   comes from Daniel 4:10. Effie coins it into one of her original quasi-
   proverbial sayings. Compare the items under 'Bend while it is a twig',
   ODEP, 46.
8. *though a saunt had said it*: Perhaps the first hint of Effie's incipient Roman
   Catholicism.
9. *better sit and rue, than flit and rue*: *ODEP*, 55; Kelly, B27.

10. *bone of my bone, and flesh of my flesh!*: Genesis 2:23, as Adam names Eve.

11. *sins o' presumption in the questions*: Q. 151 of the Larger Catechism includes among aggravated sins those done 'wilfully, presumptuously'.

12. *save. . . carritch*: Effie wittily adapts the proverbial 'Save your breath to cool your parritch' (*ODEP*, 418; Kelly, K34; *Old Mortality*, Chapter 35).

13. *Hyssop's Fables*: Ratcliffe distorts 'Aesop' into the name of the astringent shrub offered to Christ on the cross.

14. *Moll Blood. . . rapping. . . calf-skin*: 'rap' and 'smack calfskin' appear in Grose, *VT*, but 'Moll Blood' is apparently a coinage of Scott's.

15. *let life gang when gude fame is gane before it*: Cf. p. 69 and n. 13 on p. 602.

16. *the warst may be tholed when it's kend*: Similar but not identical phrases at *ODEP*, 435 and Kelly, I180.

17. *Better a finger aff as aye wagging*: *ODEP*, 49; Kelly, B7; *Rob Roy*, Chapter 18; *Redgauntlet*, Chapter 2; and thrice in Scott's *Letters*.

CHAPTER 21

Epigraph: The eleventh stanza of a pastiche street-ballad by William Shenstone (1714–63), which tells of the execution of an English Jacobite youth in 1746 and of his true-love's death from grief. The ballad appears in Percy's *Reliques of Early English Poetry* (1765) and is quoted again on p. 408. Scott had already used this stanza as an epigraph for Chapter 45 of *Guy Mannering* (1815) and recounts the story at length in *Tales of a Grandfather* (1827–9), Chapter 85.

1. *In. . . go forth*: Psalms 71:16, in which the biblical David asks God not to forsake him in old age.

2. *courts of justice*: For the court building, Scott's place of employment, see J. Gifford and others, *The Buildings of Scotland: Edinburgh* (1984), 118ff. Thomas Reid's 'ponderous Adamesque wallpaper' was laid round the outside of the 1630s Parliament House in 1804–11; extensions and remodellings have further altered the buildings since Scott's time.

3. *Trip to the Jubilee*: The alternative title of the farcical comedy *The Constant Couple* (1699) by George Farquhar (1678–1707), often revived in Scott's lifetime.

4. *Sed transeat cum cæteris erroribus*: 'But let it pass away like other aberrations' from *The History of John Bull* (1712) by John Arbuthnot (1667–1735), included in Scott's edition of Swift's works. Bower and Erickson's edition of *John Bull* (1976), 113 and n., finds no specific earlier source for the phrase, something of a favourite of Scott's (e.g. *Letters*, 11 October 1812, 27 July 1823).

5. *'Ye're welcome, whigs,/Frae Bothwell briggs,'*: A song satirizing the language, theology, and alleged sexual and political hypocrisy of the extreme Protestants. 'You lie, you lust, you break your trust. . . Your covenant makes you

a saint,/Although you live a devil' (James Hogg, *Jacobite Relics of Scotland*, Edinburgh, 1819, 18–20).

6. *Mess David Williamson. . . Killiecrankie*: The Covenanting minister David Williamson (1636–1706) was doubly famous – for having been seven times married and for supposedly getting with child a laird's daughter in whose bed he was being hidden from pursuing soldiery. The tale recurs as alleged evidence of the immorality and hypocrisy of the Covenanters: in the satirical tract *Scotch Presbyterian Eloquence Display'd* (1692); in the *Memoirs of Captain John Creighton* (1731), allegedly ghost-written by Swift and annotated by Scott in his edition of Swift's *Works* (1814), 10, 117–18; in Burns's bawdy reworking (*c.* 1790) of a traditional song on the incident; and in various jests in letters between Scott and his Episcopalian friend C.K. Sharpe. In context here it is a cruelly specific taunt. A slightly different version of the stanza, now in the British Library, has a marginal note in Scott's hand (H. Hecht, *Songs from David Herd's Manuscripts*, 1904, 207).

'Killiecrankie' was a pretended song of lament for, but really a satire on, the losers in the battle of the same name in 1689 north of Perth, at which the Williamite Protestant Lowland forces were overwhelmed by a Jacobite Highland charge (in James Hogg, *Jacobite Relics of Scotland*, 1819, 32–3).

7. *north-country*: The first appearance in the novel of mimicked 'Highland English', with its thickened and softened consonants and its distinctive use of pronouns and plurals. (For details and brief critique, see Graham Tulloch, *The Language of Sir Walter Scott*, 1980, 254–6.)

8. *precious sister glorify God in the Grassmarket*: Stock phrases in mockery of the Covenanters' idiom.

9. *prophet's ass*: Balaam's, at Numbers 22:28.

10. *others apart sat on a bench retired*: Adapted from *Paradise Lost*, 2, 557, where the disputing devils produce 'vain reason all, and false philosophy'.

11. *more liberal*: Until 1837 counsel in English criminal courts defending on lesser charges than high treason could only raise points of law; they did not cross-examine witnesses or address the jury.

CHAPTER 22

Epigraph: The duke, in *Measure for Measure*, I, iii, 19–23; a moment later he fears that his reassertion of the laws will prove 'too dreadful'.

1. *Fairbrother*: George Eliot's weak but essentially virtuous clergyman in *Middlemarch* (1871–2) is likewise called Farebrother.

2. *He began by lamenting*: This and the following sentence, both added in *1830*, account for the disappearance of Mr Langtale, previously briefed to appear; it has been suggested that they also allow Scott to escape from the question 'How did Jeanie come to be called as a witness if she had no helpful testimony to give?'

3. *put up their lip*: Sneered.
4. dulcis Amaryllidis irae: Fairbrother adapts, rather than quotes, Virgil's *Eclogues*, 2, 14, to mean 'the sweet sulks', rather than the 'dire rages', of Amaryllis.
5. *bills will be answered*: In modern terms, cheques will be honoured.
6. *woe. . . mother*: 'in sorrow shalt thou bring forth children' (Genesis 3:16).
7. *Rachael. . .children*: Jeremiah 31:15, applied by Matthew 2:18 to the Massacre of the Innocents.
8. *spin a muckle pirn out of a wee tait of tow!*: Not in *ODEP*, but Kelly, G46, has 'Get your spindle and roke ready and God will send you tow.'

CHAPTER 23

Epigraph: Adapted from Shylock expecting his favourable judgment at *The Merchant of Venice*, IV, i, 299, 302.

1. *thought is free*: *ODEP*, 814.
2. *widow of Tekoah*: In 2 Samuel 14, the feigned widow successfully gains access to David and intercedes for Absalom; although she is detected, her mission succeeds.
3. *bitterness. . . past*: Echoes 1 Samuel 15:32, transposes and develops Porteous's thought in the second sentence of Chapter 7, and actually quotes the words of Lord William Russell (condemned to death on political charges) on parting with his family in 1683 (James Anderson, *Sir Walter Scott and History*, 1981, 65). (See Claire Lamont's note in *Scott Newsletter*, 3, 1983, 3–5.)
4. 'in confitentem nullæ sunt partes judicis': 'confronted with a confession, the judge has no rôle', i.e. a confession made without duress or inducement overrides the judge's normal duty to protect the accused by (e.g.) requiring corroborative evidence.
5. *Farinaceus, and Mattheus*: Prosper Farinacci (1544–1613), an Italian writer on criminal jurisprudence; and Anton Matthaeus (1601–54), author of *De criminibus* (Amsterdam, 1644, 1661).
6. 'confessio. . . adminiculari': 'Confession outside the courtroom is nothing in itself, and being nothing cannot be supported by evidence.' In Normand's view this underestimates the value of such a confession if proved in court and corroborated.

CHAPTER 24

Epigraph: Apparently Scott's own.

1. *Kirk. . . Moore*: Common names chosen for solemnity and neutrality rather than for Scott's more usual comic uses.

2. *GUILTY*: Perhaps for the sake of drama, perhaps for accessibility to English readers, Scott streamlines the normal Scottish jury-verdict of 'Proven', which strictly leaves the finding of guilt to the bench as in the trials of Porteous (Chapter 3) and Isobel Walker (W.S. Crockett, *Scott Originals*, 1912, 417–18).

3. *the crime has been increasing*: Hugo Arnot (*Criminal Trials*, 1785) noted that twenty-one cases reached the High Court in Edinburgh between 1700 and 1706. W. Ferguson (*Scotland 1689 to the Present*, 1968, 164) states, without discussing trends, that it is the most frequent crime encountered in the records of the justiciary court. Both commentators blame the fear of public penance and note that the crime apparently declined as penance fell into disuse later in the century.

4. *Mandrin*: Scott owned the *Authentic Memoir of the Remarkable Life and Surprising Exploits of Mandrin, Captain-General of the French Smugglers, &c* (1755), but this detail of Mandrin's dying words is not found therein. Scott returns to the image in *The Betrothed*, Chapter 30, and also in his *Journal* for 3 February 1826 to account for his own indifference to a painful detail of the process of his bankruptcy.

5. *common executioner*: Presumably Dalgleish.

6. *God is . . . each other*: Seemingly another of Effie's original epigrams.

7. *Glendook. . . Statute-book*: Sir Thomas Murray of Glendoick (d. 1684) and his *Laws and Acts of Parliament of Scotland* (1681–3).

8. *kale-yard*: Mrs Howden, still as anti-Hanoverian as she was in Chapter 4, mocks German cabbage-eating.

9. *tore her biggonets*: Creighton's agent, James Gibb, disguised as a Covenanter, 'wherever he came, made the old wives, in their devout fits, tear off their biggonets and mutches' (Swift, *Works*, Scott, ed., 1814, 10, 143).

10. *Sir Robert Walpole*: First Earl of Orford (1676–1745), leading Whig politician and from 1721–42 Prime Minister (not quite in the modern sense); his life by W. Coxe (1798) and the *Memoirs* and *Reminiscences* of his son Horace (1717–97, the Gothicist) are among Scott's sources for the early Georgian court.

11. Argyle's speech: The gist of a paragraph from Argyle's second (and highly effective) speech on the Porteous Bill in the House of Lords on 3 April 1737, broadly as reported in Robert Campbell, *The Life of the Most Illustrious Prince John, Duke of Argyle* (1745), 319, and in Cobbett's *Parliamentary History*, (1812), 10, 246, in both of which contexts it is clear that 'job' means 'corrupt advantage', not mere employment. Scott owned the *Life* but not the *Parliamentary History* and was otherwise deeply read in the period. Variations of wording suggest a possible third source (such as a hawked version, though the Abbotsford Library catalogue does not record one) but, since the passage is in Scott's own normal working hand in MS and there are none of the references to 'paper apart' with which he gave instructions to take in printed material, it seems that he simply

restyled his source towards greater elegance and dignity as he copied it over. See also pp. 361–2.

12. *Roystoun*: Royston House, then on a country estate but now in West Granton Road, Edinburgh, 'a villa of the grandest sort, designed to display the owners' importance... whilst affording the necessary privacy for political intrigue' (J. Gifford and others, *The Buildings of Scotland: Edinburgh*, 1984, 603ff.). Bought by Argyle (actually not until 1739), it was renamed Caroline Park after his eldest daughter, through whom it passed to her son, the third Duke of Buccleuch, Scott's 'chief', early patron and dedicatee of the *Minstrelsy*. Later, confusingly, the name 'Royston' was applied to the building also known as Granton Castle, which was demolished in the 1920s.

CHAPTER 25

Epigraph: Isabella the postulant and Lucio the pimp in *Measure for Measure*, I, iv, 75–6.

1. *breath... porridge*: See n. 12 on p. 625.

2. Singlesword and Hackum are fictitious cases, but the Master of Sinclair's court-martial in 1708 was reprinted by Scott for the Roxburghe Club as 'a wild Scottish story and no bad example of what our lawyers call the *perfervidum ingenium Scotorum*' (letter of 3 December 1828).

3. *purchased... multiplied*: See n. 8 on p. 616.

4. *borne in upon my mind*: Not traced.

5. '*My sister shall come out in the face of the sun*,': Not directly biblical.

6. *a thousand miles... ayont the saut sea*: Travel between Edinburgh and London by sea was normal until the railway age, but Effie's lyrical language distances the journey into folklore.

7. *time... redeemed*: Cf. Ephesians 5:16.

8. *the King's face that gies grace*: According to Scott in *Tales of a Grandfather* (Chapter 26, end), 'an old proverb' quoted by Henry VIII against some callous conduct by James V of Scotland.

9. *Argyle that suffered*: Archibald, the ninth earl, executed 1685; the second duke was his grandson.

10. Scott's footnote glosses apparently come from Grose, *VT*.

11. *Scripture phrase*: Aptly, from the parable of the Good Samaritan at Luke 10:30.

12. *as Sancho says*: Sancho twice refers to himself as born 'naked' (*Don Quixote*, Penguin Classics edition, 201, 814), but his being 'barefoot' has eluded the present editor.

13. *gall and wormwood*: Animal and vegetable substances of intense bitterness, used frequently in a symbolic sense in the Bible and together at Lamentations 3:19.

CHAPTER 26

Epigraph: The opening stanza of 'The Sluggard' in Isaac Watts (1674–1748), *Divine Songs . . . for the Use of Children* (1715).

1. *no matter for the exact topography*: The phrase is in the MS and not, as one might suspect, added in proof as part of Scott's dialogue with Ballantyne – but the *1830* footnote on p. 78 makes a similar point with a heavier hand.

2. *brace of grey-hounds*: Presumably for informal hare-coursing meets as well as day-to-day foraging on his estate.

3. *Somerville of Drum's hawks*: Despite his recent disclaimer, Scott's mind clearly has turned to 'the exact topography' of the country between Edinburgh and Dalkeith. The Somervilles were an ancient family whose William Adam house, The Drum (1726), still stands at Gilmerton (J. Gifford and others, *The Buildings of Scotland: Edinburgh*, 1989, 583–5); Scott had edited their family history, *Memorie of the Somervilles*, in 1815 and the then Lord Somerville was among his 'best neighbours and most beloved friends' (*Letters*, 6, 249). The Lords Ross were Renfrewshire magnates; on the site of their Edinburgh town house, redeveloped as George Square in the 1770s, Scott's father built the house in which the novelist grew up, and their country estate at Melville Castle west of Dalkeith became the property of Scott's friends and patrons Henry and Robert Dundas, successive Viscounts Melville (cf. n. 3 on p. 598).

4. *this inartificial edifice*: The 1843 Abbotsford edition of the novels illustrates Peffermill House in the Craigmillar district of Edinburgh as the 'supposed residence' of Dumbiedikes (3, 495).

5. *ploughed, but uninclosed*: The common, though not universal, state of the land under the older unimproved Scottish agriculture (see e.g. Smout, Chapter 5).

6. *idleness and sluttish indifference, not of poverty*: The standard view of such upper-class critics of rural life as Maria Edgeworth and Elizabeth Hamilton, in contrast with Defoe, who thought "'Tis the poverty of the people makes them indolent' (*Tour*, 2, 324).

7. *palace at Dalkeith*: 'the finest and largest new built house in Scotland' (Defoe, *Tour*, 2, 360); 'an old castle virtually rebuilt by James Smith in 1702–11 . . . the grandest of all early classical houses in Lothian and for that matter in Scotland' 7 (C. McWilliam, *The Buildings of Scotland: Lothian*, 1978, 158).

8. *Calender*: A mendicant dervish. Scott owned several versions of the *Arabian Nights*, including *Tales of the East* (1812), edited by his protégé Henry Weber; for this tale, in which the opening of each door reveals a new voluptuous wonder until the forbidden final one discloses a malign horse that puts out the explorer's eye, see e.g. *The Book of the Thousand Nights and One Night*, J.C. Mardrus and Powys Mathers, eds. (1937), 1, 121–39.

9. *castle of the sluggard*: If there is a particular allusion, it is to *The Castle of*

Indolence (1748), the Spenserean mock-epic by James Thomson (1700–1748).

10. '*the milky mother*': from Dryden's version of Virgil's *Pastorals*, 6, 84. Cf. p. 454.

11. *the Brownie*: The helpful but grudging and reclusive household fairy more fully described in Scott's Introduction to *Minstrelsy of the Scottish Border* (*PW*, 1, 201–6), which prints as Appendix 6, 270–73, the 'Supplementary Stanzas to Collins's Ode on the Superstitions of the Highlands' (1788) by Scott's friend William Erskine Lord Kinedder (1768–1822), including the line 'Trail'st the long mop, or whirl'st the mimic flail'. See too K.M. Briggs, *The Fairies in Tradition and Literature* (1967), Chapter 3.

12. *screamer*: *OED* records only from 1837 the meaning 'a splendid specimen, e.g. a well-grown or beautiful female'.

13. *bundle up your pipes and tramp awa*: See n. 2 on p. 640.

14. *dookit*: Mrs Balchristie's threat prefigures Madge Wildfire's fate.

15. *as Don Quixote did in his helmet*: 'cutting the most ridiculous figure imaginable' in Cervantes's novel (Penguin Classics edition, 39); its knot cannot be untied and Don Quixote will not allow his servants to cut the strap.

16. *had in him. . . dangerous. . . wisdom. . . fear*: Adapted from *Hamlet*, V, i, 249–50.

17. *bark. . .bite*: *ODEP*, 30.

18. *breakfast wi' us yoursell*: As a chaperone.

19. *goldsmith's bills. . . bring folk to ruin*: Again Scott's financial anxieties fleetingly surface, as with Dunover and Saddletree earlier.

20. *ae wise body's aneugh in the married state*: Seemingly proverbial, but no parallel has been found.

21. *gowns wad stand on their ends their lane*: Compare Mrs Glegg's 'brocaded gown that would stand up empty' (*The Mill on the Floss*, Penguin Classics edition, 185).

22. *wilfu' woman will hae her way*: *ODEP*, 90, with *Rob Roy*, Chapter 28, as the source; Kelly has other 'wilful man' proverbs (A7, 8).

23. *A fair offer, Jeanie, is nae cause of feud*: *ODEP*, 239, as Kelly, F63, and here.

24. *Ae man may bring. . .drink*: *ODEP*, 449, cites Johnson in Boswell (14 July 1763) for the strong form exactly parallel to Dumbiedikes's.

25. *wasting my substance*: Like the Prodigal Son, Luke 15:13.

26. *they say ane shouldna aye take a woman at her first word*: *ODEP*, 261, counters with 'Take the first advice of a woman and not the second.'

CHAPTER 27

Epigraph: The last stanza of the first of the 'Lucy' poems, in which a lover's happy journey towards his beloved is clouded by a sudden intimation of her mortality. Where Wordsworth wrote 'fond', Scott has substituted 'strange', the first word of the poem itself.

1. *pulled rushes*: Perhaps an echo of 'We twa hae run about the braes, / And pou'd the gowans fine' in Burns's 'Auld Lang Syne'.

2. *Meribah*: In Exodus 17:7. Scott has Jeanie reverse the order of events in the Bible: the people murmured before, not after, Moses struck the rock.

3. *old-fashioned church*: The church at Liberton was completely rebuilt in 1815 after a fire – the supposed date of Pattieson's narrative is again placed a few years back.

4. *clumsy square tower. . . predatory. . . intercepting*: J. Gifford and others, *The Buildings of Scotland: Edinburgh* (1984), identify Liberton Tower as 'an exceptionally complete medieval tower house' (489) and class it among 'the luxurious suburban retreats of the city patriciate' (50) – but Scott is preparing the ground for his contrast with English village life later in the novel.

5. *disputed high and drank deep*: Cf. 'high dispute', *Paradise Lost*, 8, 55; 'drink deep', *Hamlet*, I, ii, 175.

6. *'confused progress of writts'*: Set of legal documents (especially title-deeds) lacking coherence or regular sequence.

7. *Imogen*: Tactfully reshaped from *Cymbeline*, II, iii, 139–40, where Imogen is both sprighted and frighted.

8. *added gall to bitterness*: Cf. Acts 8:23; and the vinegar mingled with gall given to Christ in Matthew 27:34.

9. *screech-owl*: 'the screech-owl, screeching loud, / Puts the wretch that lies in woe / In remembrance of a shroud', *A Midsummer Night's Dream*, V, i, 365.

10. *Brandy cannot save her*: Presumably Effie is beyond being brought back to life by conventional methods – not a recorded proverb.

11. *lad in the pioted coat*: The executioner – Walker's phrase (*Six Saints*, 1, 321).

12. *Vivat Rex, / Currat Lex*: 'God save the King, and Let the law roll on', certainly not by Horace; the first two words are the Vulgate Latin of 1 Samuel 10:24.

13. *Utrecht. . . Grunwiggin*: See n. 6 on p. 598. It is tempting to credit Saddletree with both taking Groningen to be a jurist rather than a place, and reshaping the name accordingly as though it signified 'Big-Wig'; but Simon Groenwegen (1613–52), editor of the legal works of Grotius, was possibly still remembered.

14. *Mary King's Close*: Now built over by the western part of Edinburgh City Chambers. The ghostly tales recorded by Grant are not relevant to Scott's casual reference.

15. *Highland quean of a lass*: Her mistress too has a surname of Gaelic origin, the gardyloo is misdirected out of respect for other Highlanders, and the lawsuit is promoted by Lowland busybodies.

16. *God kens what*: For the contents of the Edinburgh *gardyloo*, see e.g. Win Jenkins's letter of 18 July in *Humphry Clinker* or Boswell's *Tour to the Hebrides* under 14 August 1773.

17. *woman of the house... pitcher from the well*: The biblical diction reminiscent of Genesis 24 again casts Scottish rural life in Old Testament terms.

18. *'hectic of a moment'*: A passing flush. The phrase is from Sterne, *A Sentimental Journey*, (1768), 'The Monk: Calais: 2' (Penguin Classics edition, 31).

19. *King Ahasuerus*: The Persian king in the Book of Esther, which is full of relevance to the developing conversation and to Jeanie's journey. In a setting of regal splendour, an unworthy wife is set aside as queen; an obscure girl from a minority nation and religion comes to court and gains influence with the monarch; her stiff-necked adoptive father provokes persecution of his antinomian sect; the girl, now queen, persuades the king to mercy; an unjust official is hanged on the gallows he had set up for another.

20. *Duchess*: Of Buccleuch, predecessor of the wife of Scott's own friend and 'chief'. For Dalkeith House, long locally known as Dalkeith Palace, see n. 7 on p. 630.

21. *great folk's servants*: Apparently proverbial, but not in *ODEP*.

22. *the forbear... when he was Lord of Lorn*: Archibald Campbell (1629–85), ninth Earl of Argyle and grandfather to the Argyle of the novel, was (like others of his line) known as Lord Lorn during his father's lifetime.

23. *marry or be given in marriage*: Cf. Matthew 24:38.

24. *Psalm*: Variations from the biblical wording suggest that Scott was quoting from memory, as usual.

25. *Saunders Broadfoot*: Combines a 'country' abbreviation of the Christian name Alexander with a common Lowland surname that also contrives to suggest rusticity.

CHAPTER 28

Epigraph: In *Childe Harold's Pilgrimage* (1812) the refrain of 'Childe Harold's Good Night', the lyric (after 1, 13) in which Harold enthusiastically embraces exile. Byron acknowledged that his poem was suggested by 'Lord Maxwell's Good Night' in Scott's *Minstrelsy of the Scottish Border* (1802). In ironic contrast with Jeanie's reluctant journey, the line marks the beginning of the third main movement of the novel, signalled by the repetition of the travel theme from the opening of Chapter 1.

1. *passing and repassing*: Even by 1786 James Boswell, hastening to an election campaign, could leave London by mail-coach at 8.20 p.m. on 25 November

and reach Carlisle towards 5 a.m. on the 28th (Boswell, *The English Experiment*, 1986, 102).

2. *The fact*: Thomas Somerville, *My Own Life and Times 1741–1814* (1861), 354, recalls hearing a similar account in the 1750s from long-serving postal officials.

3. *York*: For this part of her journey Scott brings Jeanie through the Vale of York rather than by the more westerly (and in his time apparently more direct and regular) route of the Great North Road, which she rejoins at Ferrybridge.

4. *literary composition*: Scott returns to the question of Jeanie's skills and their origin on p. 287 and in Chapter 39. *Humphry Clinker* offered a range of models for non-standard letter-writing, and in the Kirkton Review (270) Scott had drawn attention to Anne Keith's Scots letters printed among Sharpe's notes (Kirkon, 355 ff.).

5. *vow. . . father*: Summarized from Numbers 30.

6. *forgie. . . forgien*: Here (and with 'forgie her trespass' a few lines below) Jeanie uses the language of the Lord's Prayer.

7. *barbarians. . . kindness*: The non-Greek-speaking Maltese kindled a fire for Paul and his companions in shipwreck (Acts 28:2).

8. *chosen people. . . kirks without organs. . . preaches without a gown*: The Protestant Dissenters, spiritual and intellectual descendants of the Presbyterians, Independents and Quakers of the seventeenth century, maintained their distinctiveness through the eighteenth, despite various restrictions on their worship and their political activities.

9. *muckle kirk*: York Minster.

10. *all around the city are mills*: Apparently a feature by Scott's time, though not found worthy of note by Defoe in the 1720s, who says the city has 'no trade except such as depends upon the confluence of the gentry' (*Tour*, 2, 234).

11. *miller*: Proverbial for lechery as well as rapacity.

12. *The rhyme*:

> March said to Aperill,
> I see three hogs upon a hill;
> But lend your three first days to me,
> And I'll be bound to gar them die.
> The first, it sall be wind and weet;
> The next, it sall be snaw and sleet;
> The third, it sall be sic a freeze,
> Sall gar the birds stick to the trees.
> But when the *borrowed* days were gane,
> The three silly hogs came hirplin hame.

(John Leyden, ed., *The Complaynt of Scotland*, 1801, 314)

John Leyden (1775–1811), balladist, physician and collaborator with Scott in the years around 1800, took up oriental languages and died in Java; *The*

Complaynt of Scotland (1550) is an elaborate Scots prose work of uncertain authorship, directed against English encroachments on Scottish life.

13. *hither side of Gordan*: In life, rather than after death.

14. *ilka land has its ain laugh*: A proverb (*ODEP*, 441) of *c*. 1628 goes 'Everie land hes the laich, / Everie corn hes the cafe', i.e. every farm has its area of low-lying ill-drained land, every corn has its chaff and (presumably) nothing is perfect in this world. Kelly, E12, gives 'Every Land hath its own Laugh, and every Corn its own Caff', glossing 'Laugh' as 'Law, Custom'. In *1818* Scott, giving Jeanie 'laugh', has her shrewdly, albeit ignorantly, develop from it her further discussion of laughter. The corrector of *1822* loses that point by changing 'laugh' to 'law'; Scott, in 1828 or 1829, partly restores things by correcting 'law' to 'lauch' (a possible Scots form of 'laugh') but provides a footnote gloss, 'Lauch – Law', which the printers of *1830* transform to 'land-law'. The *1818* reading has been retained.

15. *orthography... strongest contrast*: Graham Tulloch comments, 'Realism of speaking also triumphs over realism of writing in... Jeanie Deans's letters... Scott's a-little-unconvincing comment about Butler's educative skills allows him to use her letters to reflect her normal style of speech... Butler would certainly have aimed to teach Jeanie an English spelling and not the modified Scottish spelling used by the eighteenth-century poets... really an extension of the dialogue rather than any fully developed separate medium of letters' (*The Language of Sir Walter Scott*, 1980, 331). For the wider question ('half the women of rank in Scotland'), see Smout, Chapter 18, and R.A. Houston, *Scottish Literacy and Scottish Identity* (1985), Chapter 6.

16. *general benevolence... sometimes seen pleaded*: 'Giving alms to common beggars is naturally praised... but... we regard that species of charity rather as a weakness than as a virtue' (Hume, *An Inquiry Concerning the Principles of Morals*, 1751, 2, 2); 'it is taken for granted that in the case in question the dictates of benevolence are not contradicted by those of a more extensive, that is enlarged, benevolence' (Bentham, *Introduction to the Principles of Morals and Legislation*, 1789, 10, 37). Novelists from Fielding to Dickens, and satirists such as Canning and Shaw, dramatize this contradiction in early modern social thought.

17. *Bickerton*: The name of a village near York, not necessarily therefore a token of aggressiveness, as its syllables might suggest.

18. *Seven Stars, in the Castle-gate*: Not recorded in contemporary directories or in histories of York; the inn in Castlegate was the Blue Boar, where Dick Turpin's corpse lay in 1739 (C.B. Knight, *History of the City of York*, 1944, 534).

19. *civilized... roguish*: Scott's social paradoxes continue, and are based on fact: 'highwaymen clustered most thickly near London... opportunity was greatest... traffic more frequent... better chances of disposing of stolen

goods and better places of concealment' (H.L. Beales, in A.S. Turberville, ed., *Johnson's England*, 1933, 1, 146).

20. *Swan and two Necks*: (Strictly, nicks, cut on the bills of birds belonging to the Vintners' Company.) An inn and coach office in Gresham Street in the City of London.

21. *pickle. . . poke-nook*: To rely on one's own resources (literally, to peck from the bottom of one's own bag). Despite its proverbial air, the phrase is first recorded in *Rob Roy*, Chapter 26 (1817).

22. *buckle thy girdle thine ain gate*: Proverbial – *ODEP*, 89, citing an English version from Kelly, E8 (from the same page as 'ilka land has its ain laugh', cf. n. 14 on p. 635); in Scots in Burns's letter to Thomson, 1 September 1793. Cf. p. 368.

23. *navigable canal*: A topical simile for the author and his Scottish readers, for the Forth and Clyde Canal was under construction in 1818, but less in keeping with the novel's setting, for extensive canal-building set in only from the 1750s.

24. *Cock o' the North*: Obviously, the fighting champion of the north – but specifically applied to the Marquis of Huntly in some versions of the Sheriffmuir ballad quoted on p. 405.

25. *flesh-pots of Egypt*: Foreign luxuries, Exodus 16:3.

CHAPTER 29

Epigraph: Crabbe, *The Borough* (1810), 18, 352-3. The passage describes a disused warehouse let out to beggars, vagabonds and social outcasts.

1. *Robin Hood's*: The legendary benevolent outlaw of Sherwood Forest, whom Scott introduces into *Ivanhoe* (1819); the verse linking him to later practices of highway-robbery does not occur among the many Robin Hood ballads collected in Child.

2. *Emery*: John Emery (1777–1822), an actor who specialized in 'country parts' and who (among other parts in stage versions of Scott's novels) played Ratcliffe in the 1819 dramatization of *The Heart of Mid-Lothian*.

3. *A painful day's journey*: Of only some twenty-two miles over the low-lying flood-plains of the Wharfe and the Aire, not obviously more formidable than some of Jeanie's earlier travels.

4. *Ferrybridge, the best inn. . . Swan*: Or White Swan, noted by Arthur Young as 'very good and reasonable' (*Six Months' Tour*, 1770, 4, 588). Still listed (with four other Ferrybridge inns) in directories of the 1820s, it seemingly disappeared with the coming of the railways, before the first Ordnance Survey of 1845-9.

5. *Tuxford. . . longest journey*: Some thirty-five miles south of Ferrybridge.

6. *answered the question by another*: At *ODEP*, 405, said to be an Irish trait.

7. *hundred-armed Trent. . .Newark Castle. . . Saracen's Head*: The Trent

branches at Newark, but 'hundred-armed' is an epic epithet applied with epic licence; the castle ruins (unconnected with the Newark Castle on the Yarrow in Selkirkshire, in which *The Lay of the Last Minstrel* is supposedly narrated) have been restored several times since Jeanie's time (and indeed since Scott's); the Saracen's Head, a colonnaded coaching inn of 1721 found 'disagreeable and dear' by Young in 1770 but complimented by Scott on p. 293, survives with a 'Jeanie Deans' inscription, though now occupied by a bank.

8. *no information whatever*: Not at least to Jeanie, but the reader knows what to make of it, thanks to deft organization earlier, and now understands the narrative reason for Jeanie's detour via York.

9. *run*: *OED* (run, sb, 15b) makes this its earliest instance of the sense 'extensive or well-sustained demand' outside banking contexts.

10. *high mountain*: A plain-dweller's description, for Gonerby, at 360 feet above sea level, lies only 200–250 feet above the flats of Gonerby Moor.

11. *they ca' Ingleboro'*: In contrast, this prominent south-western summit of the Yorkshire part of the Pennines rises to 2,373 feet; but, since it lies forty miles west of the nearest point of Jeanie's purported route, the reader may treat her information with caution.

12. *home-brewed ale*: In contrast with modern urban 'table-beer, guiltless of hops and malt, vapid and nauseous' denounced as early as 1771 in *Humphry Clinker* (Penguin edition, 154) as brewing became industrialized.

13. *thatch Groby pool wi' pancakes*: Proverbial – *ODEP*, 809, citing Ray, 1678, and Grose, *PG*, O5v. Groby pool is a sheet of water near Leicester.

14. *men of Marsham when they lost their common*: Scott follows Grose *PG*, O7r, in reading 'Marsham', a village deep in Norfolk ten miles north of Norwich. *ODEP*, 366, and earlier sources give the more local and plausible 'Marham', in the Fens ten miles from King's Lynn.

15. *Grantham gruel . . . water*: *ODEP*, 331 (as *nine grits*), with seventeenth-century citations, and Grose, *PG*, O7r.

16. *the same again, quoth Mark of Bellgrave*: Grose, *PG*, O5r.

17. *Gaius*: 'mine host' to St Paul (Romans 16:23) and Christiana's inn-keeper in *PP*, 258–70.

18. *highway robbery. . . metropolis*: See n. 19 on p. 635.

19. *curtch. . . foot. . . shoe. . . hand*: Cf. n. 25, below, for the witch's inversion of normal relationships. The verse is another fragment of Robertson's song about Madge (cf. pp. 169 and 316).

20. *Comus*: Milton's *A Masque Presented at Ludlow Castle* (1634), 207–11. A lady traveller, abandoned by her companions in a haunted wood, expresses her alarm and her faith.

21. *The woman. . . does not understand the words of action*: Quoted from Jonson, *Every Man in His Humour* (1616), 1, 5, 127 (Lamont).

22. *shake. . . guts*: 'Shake a Leicestershire yeoman by the collar, and you shall hear the beans rattle in his belly' (Grose, *PG*, O3r, from alleged prevalence

of bean crops there); versions at *ODEP*, 718, go back to the fifteenth century.

23. *him that 'was of milder mood'*: Applied to one of the hired murderers in the broadside ballad 'The Children in the Wood' (Percy's *Reliques* and elsewhere), stanza 13 – but he expresses his mildness by killing his comrade and abandoning the children to their deaths.

24. *a hair of her head*: A biblical phrase recurring in escapes (Daniel 3:27) and assurances (Luke 21:18).

25. *reading your prayers backward*: For parallels, see I. Opie and M. Tatem, *A Dictionary of Superstitions* (1989), 316.

26. *the devil to pay here*: *ODEP*, 184, with reference to 'alleged bargains with Satan and the inevitable payment to be made to him in the end'; 'and nothing to pay him with' seems to be Levitt's or Scott's contribution.

27. *'Leap, Lawrence, you're long enough'*: Not traced.

28. *Cu'ross girdle*: Brought together with Lady Culross (for whom see p. 471 and n.) in Kirkton, 181n.

29. *In the bonny cells of Bedlam . . . fasting plenty*: A closely similar verse occurs in 'Tom of Bedlam' in J. Ritson, *Ancient Songs* (1790; third edition revised by W.C. Hazlitt, 1877, 359) (CJH).

30. *My banes are buried . . . now to thee*: Slightly variant version of stanza 9 of 'Sweet William's Ghost' (Child, 77) as it appears in *TTM* (1740) and as no. 363 in *SMM*, part 4 (1792). The stanza following serves as epigraph to Chapter 12 above; see note thereon.

CHAPTER 30

Epigraph: Francis Beaumont (1584–1616) and John Fletcher (1579–1625), *The Coxcomb* (acted 1612), 2, 2, 77–8. Scott supervised the edition of their *Works* (14 vols., Edinburgh, 1812) by his protégé and assistant, Henry Weber. In the play the heroine is waylaid and maltreated by a male and a female criminal who vie with each other in bandying thieves' cant. For Scott's first intention for the epigraph to this chapter, see Textual Note to p. 310.

1. For Renwick and Cameron, see nn. 7 and 8 on pp. 612 and 613; for Airdsmoss, see n. 14 on p. 604.

2. *the forty-second as in the forty-third Psalm*: Psalms 42:5, 11 and 43:5.

3. *as loud as Tom of Lincoln*: 'an extraordinary great bell hanging in one of the towers of Lincoln Minster' according to Grose, *PG*, O6r; *ODEP* 487–8 cites only seventeenth-century occurrences before *The Heart of Mid-Lothian*.

4. *Neddie*: The donkey has gone to fetch the horse.

5. *Holbourn Hill backward*: Condemned men faced backwards in the executioner's cart, en route from Newgate to the gallows at Tyburn (compare

the opening of Chapter 2 above); a phrase from Grose, *PG*, P1v, and *VT* (1963), 190.

6. *two years*: Apparently the life expectation of a highwayman – no source found.

7. *couch a hogshead*: From Grose, *VT* (1963), 98, as is the footnote.

8. *in the land of Nod*: Asleep (from Genesis 4:16).

9. *a word to cast at a dog*: Cf. *As You Like It*, I, iii, 2. Madge has apparently retained some 'scraps from playbooks' from her relationship with Robertson.

10. *heels. . . .hands*: See Textual Notes and *ODEP*, 607, which includes a similar antithesis from *The Monastery*.

11. *infirm of purpose*: *Macbeth*, II, ii, 52.

12. *poet of Grasmere*: Scott's contemporary William Wordsworth (1770–1850).

13. *verses on the Thorn*: In *Lyrical Ballads* (1798), stanzas 4 and 5 include the lines

> A beauteous heap, a hill of moss,
> Just half a foot in height.
> All lovely colours there you see,
> All colours that were ever seen;
> And mossy network too is there,
> As if by hand of lady fair
> The work had woven been;
> And cups, the darlings of the eye,
> So deep is their vermilion dye.
>
> Ah me! what lovely tints are there,
> Of olive green and scarlet bright,
> In spikes, in branches and in stars,
> Green, red, and pearly white!
> This heap of earth o'ergrown with moss. . .
> So fresh in all its beauteous dyes,
> Is like an infant's grave in size. . .

14. *the narrow way, and the strait path*: Matthew 7:13.

15. *burning. . .Sinai*: A general reference to the events of Exodus.

16. *cover my lip*: Micah 3:7.

17. *resist the devil. . .you*: James 4:7.

18. *Apollyon*: *PP*, 56–60, 74–5.

19. *dry leaves*: According to legend, the Cumean Sibyl's prophetic wisdom was offered, inscribed on leaves, to an early king of Rome.

20. *fairer countenance, and the more alluring*: *PP*, 226.

21. *Mr Feeblemind or Mr Ready-to-halt*: *PP*, 266–71, 306–8.

22. *bless. . . wing*: A recurring thought in the Psalms, in particular 63:4–7.

23. *gentleman. . . horse. . . sixpence*: Apparently a reminiscence of the lovers' last encounter in Henryson's *Testament of Cresseid*, 495ff.

CHAPTER 31

Epigraph: Coleridge, *Christabel* (1816), 135–6 and 143–4. The innocent heroine is unwittingly giving shelter to an evil spirit who apparently destroys her life. Cf. n. 8 on p. 617.

1. *maidens' bairns*: Proverbial since the sixteenth century as 'Bachelors' wives and maids' children are well taught' (*ODEP*, 24); in Swift's *Polite Conversation* (1738), which Scott had edited; in Scots as 'Maidens' bairns are aye weel bred' in Allan Ramsay's *Scots Proverbs* (1736); and in *The Cottagers of Glenburnie* (1808).

2. *Lockington*: A village in the north of Leicestershire. Grose, *PG*, O3v, records 'Put up your pipes and go to Lockington-wake' as 'a saying to a troublesome fellow, desiring him to take himself off'. Compare Mrs Balchristie (p. 265).

3. *better wed*: *ODEP*, 57, citing seventeenth-century examples and *The Heart of Mid-Lothian*; a Cheshire proverb in Grose, *PG*, L5r, with a note like Scott's.

4. *gang farther and fare waur*: *ODEP*, 306; in Swift, *Polite Conversation* (1738).

5. *the sang*: Parts have been sung already, on pp. 169, 294.

6. *Lady of Beever*: The Duchess of Rutland, whose seat is Belvoir Castle.

7. *Queen of the Wake, and I'm Lady of May*: Female head of the wake (the annual festival of an English parish) and of the May Day festival.

8. *went on their way... age to age*: *PP*, 208, 238. Scott quotes and praises Bunyan's lines at the end of his 1830 review of Southey's *Life of John Bunyan*, where his estimate of the work's appeal is more positive and less patronizing than it is here. Of the various references in Madge's long speech it is enough to note that the figure 'with eyes lifted... as if he pleaded wi' men' is Bunyan's Evangelist, not the Interpreter himself.

9. *beautiful scenes... merry England*: The novel here launches on a series of cultural contrasts in which Jeanie and the narrative voice support different sides – contrasts from which Scotland perhaps can learn but that are not finally assessed until Butler, in Chapter 51, responds to the offer of a living in this very parish.

10. *squires of the pad*: Takes up a phrase from the Prior epigraph to Chapter 2.

11. *necessity had no law*: *ODEP*, 557.

12. *directory*: *The Directory for the Public Worship of God* (1645), another document of the Westminster Assembly.

13. *Cease... knowledge*: Proverbs 19:27.

14. *organ*: Rather an anachronism in an English village church in the 1730s, though a wealthy patron might have donated one as part of the contemporary movement towards elegance and gentility. Flutes in church are not documented until the 1790s.

15. *chancel*: An unlikely point of entry, and one inconsistent with the characters' later movements.

16. *lesson of the day*: The Prayer-book of the Church of England specifies and prints appropriate readings for each Sunday of the Christian year.
17. *shocked at his surplice*: Scots Presbyterian clergymen did not at that time wear special garments in the pulpit (Graham, 282n.).
18. *The prophet. . . this thing*: Naaman, captain of the host of the king of Syria, cured of leprosy by the Jewish prophet Elisha (2 Kings 5), recognized the supremacy of the Lord but still had to bow down in the temple where his master worshipped. To Jeanie, the Church of England is as the House of Rimmon.
19. *written down*: The Presbyterians preferred extempore preaching, and Walker denounces the delivery of 'legal, formal sermons. . . standing straight up in the pulpit, having all in readiness, and delivering all in a neat fine stile, without once making mention of the sweet name of Jesus' (*Six Saints*, 1, 15).

CHAPTER 32

Epigraph: Crabbe, *The Borough* (1810) 14, 229–30. Fortunately for Jeanie, only the less powerful of the figures of authority in the chapter corresponds to Crabbe's account.

1. *Staunton*: Staunton Hall, at Staunton-in-the-Vale, where Nottinghamshire, Leicestershire and Lincolnshire meet, two miles west of the Great North Road and equidistant from Newark and Grantham, was promptly identified as 'Willingham', and one reviewer objected to 'this use of an existing name and title' (*Monthly Review*, 87, December 1818, 367n.). (Still inhabited by Stauntons, the Hall was notable enough to figure in topographical publications such as *The Beauties of England and Wales*, 1812, 12, 2, 246–7.) Scott made no comment or change, and the 1843 Abbotsford edition of the Waverley Novels (3, 547) illustrates Staunton Hall as Willingham. There is no obvious moment at which Scott might have acquired such relevant local knowledge as he displays, for, though his friend Crabbe lived for ten years as rector of an adjacent parish, the authors did not meet until 1822, and Scott's only recorded visit to the area was to Melton Mowbray nearly twenty miles away; he did of course traverse the Great North Road from time to time, and the compliment to the Newark innkeeper also, however teasingly, implies local knowledge. A Staunton family tradition of his having stayed at the Hall was set down only in 1901 (*Transactions of the Thoroton Society*, 4, 51).
2. *whister-poop*: Given as Exmoor dialect for 'a backhanded blow' in Grose, *PG*, which Scott especially in this chapter quarried for English regional phrases and words such as 'donnot', 'gare-brained', 'polrumptious', 'whole-whiskin' and 'behounched'.
3. *lodging at the parish charge*: Not a friendly offer of free accommodation but a threat of subjection to forced labour in the local workhouse.

4. *nittle*: From MS, for 'mettle' in *1818*. Another word from Grose.

5. *snog and snod*: The words, each independently meaning smooth or sleek, are listed together by Grose; Scott apparently understood Grose's pairing to indicate that they were a regular doublet, and has seemingly been followed by later writers of 'dialect'.

6. *minister. . . Rector*: Jeanie's normal Scots word for a clergyman implicitly denies both the special nature of priesthood and the rank in the English Church hierarchy to which the beadle appeals.

7. *root of the matter*: Job 19:28.

8. *Mr Price's*: Uvedale Price (1747–1829), whose *Essay on the Picturesque* (1794) sought to add to the existing categories of beauty (Reynolds) and sublimity (Burke) and influenced Scott's gardening at Abbotsford.

9. *as flat as the fens of Holland*: Again, flat because not (mentally) sharp. Holland is the Lincolnshire district rather than the Netherlands.

10. *Sir William Monson*: (1569–1643), Elizabethan mariner, Jacobean admiral and naval writer.

11. *James York the blacksmith of Lincoln*: Author of *The Union of Honour* (1640), a treatise on English heraldry with special emphasis on Lincolnshire families.

12. *Peregrine, Lord Willoughby*: Peregrine Bertie, eleventh Lord Willoughby de Eresby, was a military commander of English troops in the Netherlands in 1586–9. The ballad, which survives in seventeenth-century copies, is reprinted in Percy's *Reliques* and in V. de S. Pinto and A.E. Rodway, eds., *The Common Muse* (1957), 40.

13. *not born at Witt-ham*: A Lincolnshire and Essex proverb, according to Grose, *PG*, M8r and O7r. The note is also from Grose.

14. *pith and marrow*: Hamlet, I, iv, 22.

15. *of modern divinity*: *The Marrow of Modern Divinity* (1646) by E.F., an English Independent, was declared heretical by the General Assembly of the Church of Scotland in 1720.

16. *evil communication*: 1 Corinthians 15:33.

17. *inconvenience. . . care. . . expence*: Alleviated in England in the nineteenth century by enabling the police to prosecute, and in the late twentieth by introducing a Crown Prosecution Service.

18. *schismatic nor sectary. . . black commodities*: From the Deanses' point of view the Quakers were indeed schismatic, but it is not clear what improper compromises with government they could have been accused of in the 1730s.

CHAPTER 33

Epigraph: Coleridge, 'The Pains of Sleep', published 1816, 25–32.

1. *Court of the Gentiles*: In the last days in Revelation 11:2.

2. *read. . . sermon*: Cf. Argyle's explanation on p. 374.

3. *pith and marrow*: Cf. nn. 14 and 15 on p. 642.

4. *Leicestershire plover, and that's a bag-pudding*: Grose, *PG*, O5v.

5. *good Samaritan*: Luke 10.

6. *wicked will turn from their transgressions*: A recurring phrase in Ezekiel 18.

7. *churning*: Apparently unique in this sense, but quite clear in MS.

8. *Mexican monarch*: Guatemozin (Cuauhtemoc) successor to Montezuma, tortured after capture in 1521 to appease Cortés's greedy and mutinous officers. The ultimate source for his stoicism and his retort to a complaining fellow sufferer ('Am I now reposing on a bed of flowers?') is the life of Cortés by his secretary F. Lopez de Gómara, but Scott probably knew it through Keating's translation of Bernal Díaz's *True History* (1800, 320–21) or William Robertson's *History of America* (1777, etc., V). Scott returns to the topic, and to a parallel case in sixteenth-century Scotland, in his Kirkton Review (224–5) and in the text and notes of *Ivanhoe* (1819), Chapter 22.

9. *propensity to vices*: Staunton's explanation sounds like a blend of superstition and ideology, but for the medical hazards and psychological wounds of wet-nursing as practised at the time see L. Stone, *The Family, Sex and Marriage in England 1500–1800* (1977), 99–101.

10. *come into your counsel . . . doctrine which causeth to err*: Biblical vocabulary without specific quotation.

11. *seventh heaven*: The 'heaven of heavens' in Babylonian, Jewish and Islamic cosmography – perhaps another echo of Scott's debt to *The Arabian Nights*.

12. *As dissolute . . . hope*: Adapted from *Richard II*, V, iii, 20–21.

13. *mind is totally alienated*: Apparently one of the first modern occurrences of this euphemism for insanity.

14. *Macheath under condemnation*: In John Gay, *The Beggar's Opera* (1728), Airs 60 and 61 have the words 'Since I must swing – I scorn,/I scorn to wince or whine./But now again my Spirits sink:/I'll raise them high with wine.' Gay's plot is tongue-in-cheek, and the highwayman gets his reprieve.

15. *bloodhounds of the law*: The figurative meaning was presumably always available (and cf. p. 181), but this is the earliest modern example in the *OED*; Partridge records criminal use in 1819 with the meaning 'A Bow-street officer'.

16. *anticipated, by half an hour*: Not confirmed by contemporary evidence, although the proceedings were shortened and carried out promptly (Roughead, 165–6).

17. *Scripture*: Romans 12:19.

18. *terrier of the law*: Presumably pursues the fugitive who has gone to earth, as the bloodhound (above) chases the one in open country.

19. *trusty friend*: Scott seems to be meeting the objection that Staunton does not try hard enough, in Chapter 7, to persuade Effie.

20. *well-spring of life*: Proverbs 16:22, where it is identified as understanding.
21. *Walpole*: See n. 10 on p. 628.

CHAPTER 34

Epigraph: *The Borough* (1810), 12, 'Players', 257–8 (an account of a youth whose career partly parallels Staunton's).

1. *Upon my life... Your life... On my honour... Your honour*: Cf. my conscience... your conscience, p. 173, and contrast the reactions. Ramsay of Ochtertyre reports the notorious judge Braxfield in dialogue with a colleague: ' "This is my opinion." "Your opinion!" ' (*Scotland and Scotsmen in the Eighteenth Century*, written 1775–1800, 1888, 1, 385n.).
2. *Remember!... Charles I.*: On 30 January 1649. One of Scott's friends descended from the chaplain to whom was uttered 'the emphatic and enigmatical word *Remember* to which no good clue has ever been found' (*Letters*, 3, 311).
3. *avenger of blood*: Deuteronomy 19:6 and other Old Testament passages in which God establishes sanctuary and the rule of law in place of revenge.
4. *brain must be something touched*: Scott would have us believe that Mr Staunton's English and hierarchic social assumptions quite fail to understand the openness of customary relations among Scots of different classes.
5. *imputed*: Charged by God as a sin. Jeanie's choice of word has further resonances in Protestant theology, but the point is perhaps that she does not fully understand them.
6. *young... religion*: Staunton thinks Jeanie tainted by scepticism, when 'really' she regards his church as laxly ritualistic.
7. *Naaman*: Again see 2 Kings 5.
8. *like the hare*: Quoted as a proverb in *ODEP*, 354, with only one somewhat dissimilar Spanish parallel.
9. *'fause Monteath,'*: Sir John de Menteith, who, in 1305, betrayed William Wallace (for whom see n. 15 on p. 589) to Edward I of England.
10. *West Indies*: The Caribbean figures from time to time in early nineteenth-century literature (Wordsworth's sonnet 'To Toussaint L'Ouverture', Sir Thomas Bertram's voyage in *Mansfield Park*, the origin of the first Mrs Rochester in *Jane Eyre*), marking the role of that colonial economy in British life of the period. For a more specific reason for Robertson/Staunton's 'Creole' origin, see Introduction, p. xliv.
11. *means (too easily afforded...*: Through moneylenders. Byron's early career offers a well-known example.
12. *'pressing to death, whipping, or hanging'*: *Measure for Measure* again – the denouement (V, i, 520–21) when Lucio, the low-living but truth-telling roisterer and pimp, declares marriage to a prostitute to be worse than any of these fates.

13. *British Juvenal*: Crabbe. The quotation (*Borough*, 12, 261–6) follows on from the lines taken as chapter epigraph. Scott had already called Crabbe 'the English Juvenal' in *Waverley*, Chapter 70.

CHAPTER 35

Epigraph: The opening lines of a rhyming monologue (*SMM*, 560) purportedly spoken by Argyle and sometimes taken to be written by him, though as it proceeds its burlesque (if not downright satirical) nature becomes fairly clear. Cf. p. 393.

1. For John, second Duke of Argyle and Greenwich (1678–1743), see Introduction, pp. xxxvii–xxxviii and Scott's note, 'John Duke of Argyle and Greenwich' on p. 571; for Scott's admiring summary of his character and earlier career, see *Tales of a Grandfather*, Chapter 63, but for a judicious (though partisan) and much cooler account, see W. Coxe, *Memoirs of. . . Sir Robert Walpole* (1798), 1, 610–15. Scott owes much of his knowledge and opinions about Argyle to his friend Lady Louisa Stuart (1757–1851), his personal link to the mid-eighteenth century, whose 'Memoir' of the duke is reprinted in *Selections from Her Writings*, J.A. Home, ed. (1899). The only biographies of Argyle (neither of which does justice to the full range of his interest) are the contemporary *Life* by Robert Campbell (1745) and Patricia Dickson, *Red John of the Battles* (1973). Nikolaus Pevsner (*Buildings of England: London 1*, second edition, 1962, pl. 77a) reproduces Roubiliac's fine portrait head from Argyle's huge monument in Westminster Abbey, which looms over Poets' Corner with a bust of Scott nestling in its shadow.

2. *not without. . . attends it*: Adapted from the 'should attend' of Lady Macbeth's first speech (I, v, 117–18).

3. *Pope*: Alexander Pope (1688–1744), in *Epilogue to the Satires* (1738), 2, 86–7.

4. *falsehood. . . self-aggrandizement*: Through Scott's next few paragraphs runs a strong implicit contrast between Argyle and John Churchill, first Duke of Marlborough (1650–1722), whose duplicity and inordinate ambition Scott knew in detail from his editorial work on Swift.

5. *rise from the earth in the whirlwind, and direct its fury*: Pope on Argyle has reminded Scott of Addison on Marlborough, who, 'pleas'd the Almighty's orders to perform, / Rides in the whirlwind, and directs the storm' (*The Campaign*, 1705, 291–2).

6. *memorable year 1715*: See n. 2 on p. 594.

7. *too great to be either acknowledged or repaid*: Perhaps a transposition of 'power too great to keep or to resign' (Johnson, *The Vanity of Human Wishes*, 1749, 134).

8. *already*: See p. 74.

9. *fragments*: Like the passage quoted on p. 251, these are, apparently, authentic speeches of Argyle, lightly reworked for force and effect.

10. *Lord Hardwicke*: Philip Yorke (1690–1764), at the time Lord Chief Justice and later Lord Chancellor and first Earl of Hardwicke.

11. *somebody observed at the time*: 'The generality of mankind, who looked on these great transactions in cool blood, were not a little jocose on the two Houses of Parliament having been employed five months in declaring a man should never again be a magistrate who had never desired to be one, and in raising two thousand pounds on the city of Edinburgh to give the cook-maid widow of Captain Porteous, and make her, with most unconjugal joy, bless the hour in which her husband was hanged' (John Baron Hervey, 1696–1743, *Memoirs*, 1855, 2, 336–7). Unless the quip found its way into print earlier, Scott must have seen the memoirs in MS or heard an oral version, most probably from Lady Louisa Stuart.

12. *South-Sea*: Having survived the notorious 'bubble' of 1720 (cf. n. 7 on p. 667), the South Sea Company again attracted attention to its affairs after 1733; it was alleged that the directors were trading illegally on their own accounts and disregarding the stockholders' interests, but Walpole tried to prevent an inquiry on grounds of national interest (Hervey, *Memoirs*, 1, 224).

13. *splendid library*: Actually added to Argyle House, Argyll Street, W1 (on the site of the present London Palladium) by Duke John's successor; see n. 13 on p. 651.

14. *time and tide, you know, wait for no one*: Proverbial (*ODEP*, 822; Kelly, T3).

15. *plain tale*: Prince Hal at *1 Henry IV*, II, iv, 242.

16. *Scots tongue in your head*: Proverbial (Kelly, Y250).

17. *Duncan Forbes*: See n. 2 on p. 597.

18. *Ormond*: Not Argyle's comrade-in-arms, the second Duke of Ormonde (1665–1745), but his grandfather James Butler, first Duke of Ormonde (1610–88), whose biographer provides the whole exchange: 'he told him, that he had no friend at Court, but God and his Grace. "Alas! poor Cary (replied the Duke) I pity thee; thou couldst not have two friends that have less interest at court, or less respect shown them there"' (Thomas Carte, *A History of the Life of James, Duke of Ormonde*, 1736, 2, 443). Ormonde, having served as royalist general in Ireland and lord lieutenant (1661–9), then underwent the 'seven years of coldness on the king's part and enmity from his courtiers' (*DNB*) from which he has just emerged when Scott introduces him in *Peveril of the Peak*.

19. *our father*: Adam.

20. *shall surely die*: Echoes several verses of Numbers 35, in which various degrees of murder and their penalties are defined.

21. *a large body*: Argyle sat in the House of Lords by right of his English title, Duke of Greenwich, not as one of the 'representative' Scottish peers provided for in the Act of Union.

22. *gudesire and his father*: Archibald, ninth Earl of Argyle (1629–85), and the

Marquis and eighth Earl of Argyle (1598–1661), both executed for opposition to Stuart absolutism.

23. *in the cage*: The 'Canongate iron-house' is mentioned in *Six Saints*, 2, 97–8.

24. *Peter Walker the packman*: See n. 19 on p. 609.

25. *Salathiel. . . Thwack-away*: The muster-roll punningly mingles Old Testament figures, religious slogans, commands from pike-drill and real seventeenth-century names: Salathiel is an obscure descendant of David and ancestor of Joseph; Obadiah, in 1 Kings 18, hides a hundred prophets from Jezebel's persecution; Ludovick Muggleton (1609–98) founded a sect that survived into the twentieth century. Such Tory jesting was licensed by a Sussex jury-list of Commonwealth times printed as a note to Chapter 61 of David Hume's *History of England* (1763) (Anderson).

26. *Praise-God Barebone*: (?1596–1679), a leather-seller, Baptist minister, pamphleteer and in 1653 MP for the City of London.

27. *old Noll's evangelical army*: Cromwell's New Model Army raised (actually by Fairfax) in 1645.

28. *Lorne*: See n. 22 on p. 633.

29. *case. . . a hard one*: The phrase 'hard cases make bad law' is recorded only from 1854 (*OED*, Supp. s. v., Hard adj. 20).

30. *buckles his belt*: Cf. p. 289 and n. 22 on p. 636.

31. *the hearts of Kings*: Unsearchable, according to Proverbs 25:3

CHAPTER 36

Epigraph: James Thomson (1700–1748), 'Summer', 1406–9, among lines added in 1744 to the poem of 1727. Shene was the original name of the manor and palace in Surrey that were renamed Richmond about 1510, and Thomson is buried in the parish church there.

1. *hope. . . sick*: Proverbs 13:12 ('deferred' for 'delayed').

2. *come up with a drove of Highland cattle*: A staple Scottish export of the period.

3. *pleasant village. . . commanding eminence*: The direct road to Richmond crossed the Thames at Putney Bridge (built 1727–9), passed through East Sheen and skirted the northern slopes of Richmond Hill to ascend to what Cherry and Pevsner (*London 2: South*, 1983) still call the 'unmatched landscape' of Richmond Hill and Park. Scott's description of the view to the west and north, from Windsor to Syon House, follows Thomson's verses of 1744 in content and phraseology; the view was frequently painted, for example by Pieter Tillemans in the 1720s (J. Harris, *The Artist and the Country House*, 1979, plate 259), by Zuccarelli and Reynolds later in the century, and by Scott's illustrator Turner, whose 'Richmond Hill on the Prince Regent's Birthday', exhibited in 1819 and therefore

representing an event close to the novel's publication the preceding summer, is still in the Royal Collection (plate 125 in M. Butler and E. Joll, *The Paintings of J. M. W. Turner*, 1977). Scott's 'chiefs', the Buccleuchs, had a house on the river bank below the viewpoint.

4. *mighty monarch*: Milton, *Paradise Regained*, 3, 262.

5. *postern-door in a high brick wall*: The short walk from the top of Richmond Hill and the high wall place the imagined interview in Richmond Park. Queen Caroline's occasional residence was in fact Richmond Lodge, in Richmond Gardens down on river level towards Kew.

CHAPTER 37

Epigraph: From *Rollo Duke of Normandy or the Bloody Brother* by John Fletcher (see epigraph note, Chapter 30) and others (performed *c.* 1616; published 1639), 3, 1, 279–83.

1. *star and garter*: Insignia of the highest order of English knighthood, to which Argyle had been admitted in 1710 for military services as well as for political reasons.

2. *at this time in open opposition to the administration of Sir Robert Walpole*: For Walpole, see n. 10 on p. 628. Scott perhaps compresses events, for opinions differ as to the timing of Argyle's various estrangements. According to Lynch, he was 'a thorn in the side of the London administration' from about 1731 (*A New History of Scotland*, 1991, 318), but others judge that after opposing the legislation against Edinburgh proposed in 1736–7, Argyle moved into opposition only during 1738 (J. Butt, ed., *Poems of Alexander Pope*, Twickenham edition, 1961, 4, 318n.) and finally broke with Walpole only in 1739 (A. Murdoch, *The People Above*, 1980, 32). See also n. 19 below.

3. *out of favour with the royal family*. J.W. Croker denies that any estrangement existed between Argyle and the queen at this earlier time (*Memoirs of John Lord Hervey*, 1848, 2, 317n.). Admittedly, Croker is countering Hervey's hostile account of the Argyle brothers, according to which they had, long before, permanently antagonized the queen by trying to manipulate the king through Lady Suffolk.

4. *Margaret of Anjou*: (1430–82), queen consort of Henry VI, who played a prominent part in the Wars of the Roses.

5. *brother the Chevalier de St George*: Queen Anne's exiled Roman Catholic half-brother, also known as the Old Pretender – James Francis Edward Stuart (1688–1766), son of James II by Mary of Modena.

6. *field of battle*: George II was the last English monarch to lead his troops in battle, at Dettingen in 1743.

7. *Pulteney*: William Pulteney, Earl of Bath (1684–1764), an estranged former ally of Walpole's who led the opposition to him in the 1730s. The particular anecdote has not been traced.

8. *Lady Suffolk*: Henrietta Howard (née Hobart), Countess of Suffolk (1681–1767), had in fact retired from the court in 1734, being succeeded as the queen's attendant by Lady Sundon and as the king's mistress by Madame Walmoden (later Lady Yarmouth, and the occasion of the king's absence in Hanover in 1736) – if indeed Lady Suffolk had actually held the latter office, for Hervey claimed to know many well-informed courtiers who 'doubt the King's ever having entered into any commerce with her, that he might not innocently have had with his daughter' (*Memoirs*, J.W. Croker, ed., 1848, 1, 55–9). Scott himself, having here followed Horace Walpole's account, later read and reviewed Lady Suffolk's *Correspondence* (*Quarterly Review*, January 1824, *MPW*, 19, 185–212) and was no longer so fully persuaded that she had been the king's mistress.

9. *reasons*: In 1726 Mrs Howard, already estranged from her husband and established in the then Prince of Wales's circle, was prevented by protocol from travelling with his household on its retreat to Richmond for the summer, but feared that if she travelled independently she would be seized by her jealous husband. Argyle and his brother Ilay solved the problem by providing a coach and their escort in person. Howard's 'noisy honour' was later bought off (Walpole, 4, 302).

10. *Reminiscences*: Written in 1788 by Horace Walpole (1717–97), the Prime Minister's youngest son, and published in his quarto *Works* (1798), 4, 271–318. By 1818 they had been issued separately twice.

11. *much interrupted*: But see nn. 2 and 3 above.

12. *somewhat injured*: Caroline had small-pox soon after her marriage to George in 1705, but, according to Horace Walpole (4, 304), it did not destroy her personal charms.

13. *Esculapius*: The Latin form of the name of the Greek god of healing, Asclepius, but here used merely to mean any doctor.

14. *Jenner*: Edward Jenner, MD (1749–1823), established in 1796 that cowpox vaccine prevented small-pox.

15. *tutelary deity*: Apollo, the Greek god of healing and disease (also light, music, knowledge, etc.), who slew the dragon Python when taking possession of the shrine at Delphi.

16. *disorder*: Caroline suffered from gout, but she was also concealing the rupture from which she died later in 1737.

17. *Her companion*: The paragraph seems to draw on Walpole, 4, 303.

18. *the medium*: Contemporaries comment on the tact with which Caroline concealed the extent to which the king depended on her judgement.

19. *employments*: The historical Argyle had already been reappointed colonel of the Blues (1733) and gazetted field-marshal (1736); he lost the colonelcy on going into opposition in 1739 (P. Dickson, *Red John of the Battles*, 1973, 218–24).

20. *austere regard of controul*: *Twelfth Night*, II, v, 63 (Lamont).

21. *a little deaf*: Not a polite fiction, an actual disability noted by contemporaries.

22. *terrible chapter of Scottish genealogy*: Scots were considered especially likely to remember and value degrees of kinship that to English readers seemed remote; 'terrible chapter' is a stock phrase recalling the genealogical parts of the Old Testament, such as Genesis 36 and 1 Chronicles 1–8 – cf. 'terrible chapter of Cameronian biography', Kirkton Review, 272.

23. *Which squires call potter, and which men call prose*: Not traced.

24. *voice low and sweetly toned, an admirable thing in woman*: Echoes *King Lear*, V, iii, 273.

25. *disputes*: According to the nineteenth-century editor Croker (on Hervey's *Memoirs*, 1, 236), the original cause of the quarrel is unknown; but by the mid-1730s it had been inflamed by disputes over the size of the prince's payment from the Civil List and by conflicts over the birth and upbringing of his children.

26. *chance-medley*: Swift uses the word of Dr Thomas Sheridan, grandfather of the playwright, who in 1725 inadvertently preached on the text 'Sufficient unto the day is the evil thereof' on the King's birthday (*Prose Works*, Herbert Davis, ed., 1939–68, 5, 223) (Anderson).

27. *conversation*: A recurring term in the Pauline Epistles.

28. *seventh command*: Exodus 20:14, 'Thou shalt not commit adultery.'

29. *gane to his place*: Like Judas in Acts 1:25.

CHAPTER 38

Epigraph: *Cymbeline*, I, i, 75–6. In the play the promise is insincere.

1. *Richmond Park*: See n. 5 on p. 648.

2. *dazzled and sunk with colloquy sublime*: Conflated from *Paradise Lost*, 8, 455–7.

3. *kittle cattle to shoe behind*: *ODEP*, 428, with this as the only example, but the *OED* has an example from 1600.

4. *bank-bill*: With the exception of the purses produced by the backward Dumbiedikes and the over-elegant Lady Staunton, all the money transactions in the novel use paper, reflecting practice during the rapid economic expansion of the early nineteenth century; in 1826 Scott pamphleteered against a challenge to the Scottish banks' right to issue notes.

5. *ain errand*: Cf. 'on my anes errand', i.e. sticking to my specific business (*SND*, 'aince errand').

6. *Honour's Grace*: Jeanie now doubles her forms of address for Argyle.

7. *Buckholmside*: A hillside north of Galashiels, in full view from Scott's house at Abbotsford. The quoted line in the footnote has not been identified, but in thought and cadence it parallels 'As is a landscape to a blind man's eye' in Wordsworth, 'Tintern Abbey', 24.

8. *Caroline-Park*: See note on Roystoun at p. 629.

9. *lean cattle. . . musty hay*: The echo of the Pharaoh's dream (Genesis 41:17–36) gives the contrast between London drought and Scottish pastoral.

10. *At the sight. . . barley meal*: Lines from *SMM*, 560, again, as in the epigraph to Chapter 35.

11. *mutual connexion. . . a rude and wild, than of a well cultivated and fertile country*: Scott's parallels in thought and language to Adam Ferguson, *An Essay on the History of Civil Society* (1767), are discussed in A. Fleishman, *The English Historical Novel*, 1971, Chapter 3; and see Introduction, pp. xi–xii and xlvi, n. 8.

12. *great man's great man*: An echo of Fielding's subversive play with the phrase in his anti-Walpole satire *Jonathan Wild* (1743).

13. *Argyle-house*: In fact this house, with its famous library, was built from *c.* 1735 by the duke's brother, political partner and in 1743 successor, Archibald, Earl of Ilay: Duke John lived in Bruton Street, Mayfair. Cf. n. 13 on p. 646.

14. *Lady Caroline Campbell*: (1717–94), the duke's oldest and favourite daughter, heiress of his English estates, which passed to Scott's 'chiefs' by inheritance after her marriage in 1742 to the heir to the Duke of Buccleuch.

15. *ill talking between a full body and a fasting*: Proverbial (*ODEP*, 293) in Lindsay of Pitscottie's sixteenth-century *Chronicles*, and used by Scott in *Redgauntlet*, Letter 11 ('Wandering Willie's Tales') (D. Murison, *Scots Saws*, 1981, 49).

CHAPTER 39

Epigraph: Pope, *Eloisa to Abelard* (1717), 51–2 (actually, 'taught letters for').

1. *three letters*: See n. 15 on p. 635.

2. *fisycian*: Jesus, in allusion to Matthew 9:12, etc.

3. *turned. . . die*: Ezekiel 33:9, 11, etc.

4. Early in her second letter Jeanie writes in biblical vocabulary, echoing the passages on sanctuary in Deuteronomy and Joshua, but without her father's habit of specific quotation.

5. *bring back that captivitie*: Psalms 14:7.

6. *face to face, and yet live*: Like Jacob's words after meeting God, Genesis 32:30 – Gideon feared death after meeting a mere angel in this way (Judges 6:22).

7. *Board of Agriculture*: An official body founded in 1793 and publisher of e.g. *Communications to the Board of Agriculture on Subjects Relative to the Husbandry and Internal Improvements of the Country*, 7 vols. (1797–1813).

8. *talent*: A Hebrew unit of weight for precious metals – hence, a substantial sum of money, with allusion to the parable in Matthew 25.

9. *wee bit paper. . . gude for the siller*: Is Jeanie teasing her father, or allowing for his old-fashionedness – or is she herself the victim of some London humorist's pun? She explains the bank-note quite clearly to Butler in the letter that follows.

10. *Aughtermuggitie*: Scott burlesques an actual place-name (Auchtermuchty) with his coinage from Gaelic (*uachtar*, 'an upland') and Latin (*mugitus*, 'bellowing').

11. *Dutton*: Also the surname of a quarrelsome and thieving male servant in Tobias Smollett's *Humphry Clinker*.

12. *outgauns and incomings*: Scotticizes the biblical formula 'goings out and comings in', e.g. Ezekiel 43:11.

13. *enow of baith*: A modern historian describes successive Argyles as 'the wealthiest peer' and 'the largest and most influential aristocratic interest' in Scotland in the period (Alexander Murdoch, *The People Above*, 1980, 7–8).

14. *tour*: The Tower of London, which was moated until the 1840s.

15. *tour of Libberton*: Cf. n. 4 on p. 632.

16. *aiths and patronages*: For oaths, see n. 16 on p. 606 and n. 16 on p. 659; for patronage, see n. 24 on p. 658.

17. *root of the matter*: Job 19:28.

18. *sauld cheap*: More play with Jeanie's *naïveté* – she inverts the reason for the cheap books' presence on the outside stalls.

19. *rejoice and be exceedingly glad*: Matthew 5:12, after Christ's blessings to the poor in spirit, the meek, the merciful and the reviled and persecuted.

20. *star and garter*: See n. 1 on p. 648.

21. *all, as the story-book says, very grand*: Not traced to any particular story-book.

22. *seven years, twenty-one instances*: Presumably taken from the 1700–1706 data upholding the liberalizing, anti-clerical argument in Hugo Arnot's *Criminal Trials* (1785), 311.

23. *it is an ill bird*: . . .that fouls its own nest (*ODEP*, 397) – a proverb first found in medieval Latin and used by Scott in *Rob Roy*, Chapter 26.

24. *sign says*: See p. 370 and '*Nemo me impune*' in Glossary.

25. *Worshipful Mr Deputy Dabby, of Farringdon Without*: The deputy alderman of a somewhat unattractive ward in the north-west of the City of London, abutting on Smithfield, Newgate and the recently covered-over Fleet River.

26. *disquieted within you*: Psalms 42:5.

27. *horns of the altar*: See n. 8 on p. 601.

28. *Livingstone*: From *Six Saints*, 1, 290–91, which Deans or Scott considerably sharpens and improves.

29. *Goshen. . .sun. . .shineth. . .allenarly*: 'only in the land of Goshen was there no hail' during the plagues of Egypt (Exodus 9:26).

30. *ower muckle a grip of the gear of the warld in mine arms*: Cf. 'got too much of the world in his arms' (*Six Saints*, 1, 336–7).

31. *Haran*: In Genesis 12, Abraham obeys the Lord's command to depart 'from thy kindred and from thy father's house'.

32. *law licks up a'*: *ODEP*, 446 (thus only in Scott, here and *St Ronan's Well*, 28; in other versions law is a lickpenny, a bottomless pit, etc.).

33. *give the Laird of Lounsbeck a charge on his band*: Formally call in the secured loan to Lounsbeck – the technical meaning of 'charge' ('the

command of the sovereign's letters to perform an act') linking it with the matter of the note that follows.

34. *awfu' morning that a tout of a horn, at the cross*: The words are Alexander Shields's, quoted more than once by Walker (*Six Saints*, 1, 361, 299), the 'awfu' morning' (1 October 1662) the day on which was proclaimed, with the usual ceremonial, Middleton's order in council removing from their parishes all ministers who had failed to obtain endorsement by bishop and patron – in Scott's opinion an 'ill-judged proclamation' that brought twenty-five years of bitter schism and 'the downfall of Episcopacy' (Kirkton Review, 250–51).

35. *pray for her*: A striking concession from Deans.

36. *kingdoms*: Deans appears to accept the union of the crowns but not that of the Parliaments.

37. Scott's note reprints Walker's account, as at *Six Saints*, 1, 253–4.

38. *casting her eye backward*: Like Lot's wife in Genesis 19:26.

39. *bitter waters. . .flesh-pots*: Echo the predicaments and complaints of the Israelites in Exodus 15 and 16.

40. *Vanity-fair*: In *PP*, 88ff.; Deans doubtless agrees in detail with Bunyan's critique of the indiscriminate selling of 'Preferments. . . Kingdoms. . . Wives. . . Souls' in this all-the-year-round market of Beelzebub.

41. *an ill-mumbled mass. . .James the Sext*: Walker's phrase (*Six Saints*, 1, 154; 2, 153) colloquialized from the words 'evill said mass', attributed to James in 1590 by D. Calderwood, *History of the Church of Scotland* (1678), 5, 106.

42. *ninth and seventeenth*: Ninth chapter, seventeenth verse – a regular form of words with Scots preachers into the present century. The immediately preceding verse, poignantly for David, is 'I will slay even the beloved fruit of their womb.' His next quotation is from Hosea 6:1.

43. *heresy*: As a Baptist.

44. *bean. . . 'curtal axe'*: The nursery tale of Jack and the Beanstalk.

CHAPTER 40

Epigraph: Crabbe, *The Borough*, 23, 'Prisons', 209–10, 213–14. The woman described is pregnant, and awaits execution for rick-burning.

1. For the Campbell daughters' careers, see D.M. Stenton, *The English Woman in History* (1957; 1977 edition), 265ff.

2. *lively young lady*: Argyle's fifth daughter, Lady Mary Campbell (1727–1811), later famous both for her decisive withdrawal from an uncongenial marriage to Edward, Viscount Coke, and as dedicatee of Horace Walpole's *The Castle of Otranto* (1765), the first Gothic novel. Lady Louisa Stuart, Scott's link to this eighteenth-century circle, edited Lady Mary's journals and wrote a memoir of her life, introduced by an account of the contrast between her father Argyle and her uncle Ilay.

3. *one to two at Sheriff-muir*: Argyle's regular troops faced about three times their number of Highlanders; the drawn battle left each side able to deny that the other had won (hence Argyle's complaint that Mary was turning Tory) but achieved the government's strategic purpose by keeping the Jacobites north of the Forth.

4. *well-known ballad*: Herd, 1, 104–8, and Joseph Ritson, *Scotish Songs* (1794), 2, 56; (1869), 2, 399.

5. *Bob of Dumblane*: A bob is a dance with a bobbing up-and-down or to-and-fro movement, Dunblane the town nearest to Sheriffmuir, the Bob of Dumblane the title and air of a traditional bawdy song adopted as a nickname for the equivocal battle – on the sardonic suggestion of Argyle himself, if the 'well authenticated' anecdote set down by Burns in the 1790s is to be credited. Most eighteenth-century collections contain only Ramsay's modernized and bowdlerized version. Burns's text and anecdote, first printed in R.H. Cromek, *Reliques of Robert Burns* (1808), 305, and later rejected as spurious until vindicated by the rediscovery of Burns's MS, can be found in J.C. Dick, ed., *Notes on Scottish Song by Robert Burns* (1908) and among the appendices to D.A. Low's 1991 edition of *SMM*.

6. *as the song goes*: The refrain of 'Jocky's gray breeks', in Joseph Ritson, *Scotish Songs* (1794), 1, 212; (1869), 1, 281; and (with a note of Scott's annotations) in H. Hecht, *Songs from David Herd's Manuscripts* (1904), 184.

7. *wine maketh glad the heart*: Psalms 104:15.

8. *Jonadab the son of Rechab*: Jeremiah 35:6.

9. *witch and thief get half of her due*: Hanged for theft, apparently, but not burned as a witch. The acts penalizing witchcraft were repealed in both England and Scotland in 1736, whereupon 'villagers turned to informal violence, counter-magic and the occasional lynching' (Keith Thomas, *Religion and the Decline of Magic*, 1971, 696). Again Scott's unobtrusive informed topicality shows clearly.

10. *'terrible behests of law.'*: Shenstone, 'Jemmy Dawson', stanza 13 (cf. epigraph to Chapter 21 and n.).

11. *take awa yealdon, take awa low*: 'Take away fuel, take away flame.' Proverbial, *ODEP*, 293, citing seventeenth century versions in Standard English. No dialect version appears in Grose, Scott's usual source.

12. In giving way to the supposed witch and speaking her fair, the rustics fall in with advice in Grose, *PG*, 'Superstitions', 29–30.

13. *tint a Scot. . . better lost than found*: Proverbial, *ODEP*, 485, cited as Northumberland both in seventeenth-century collections and in Grose, though in more wordy and less clear versions than Scott's.

14. *Sark-foot. . .Allonby*: Respectively, the mouth of a river forming the border between Scotland and England, eight miles north-north-east of Carlisle, and a (former) fishing village on the English side of the Solway Firth twenty-two miles west-south-west of the city.

15. *bye-word*: The rhyme appears as a Cumberland saying in Grose, *PG*, Mr, and is there applied to Skiddaw and 'Scuffel' (i.e. Sca Fell), prominent tops of the Cumberland Mountains. Grose's note, surprisingly, explains the 'Criffel' version of the rhyme rather than his own: 'These are two very high hills, one in this country, the other in Anan-dale, in Scotland; if the former be capped with clouds or foggy mists, it will not be long before rain falls on the other. It is spoken of such who may expect to sympathize in their sufferings, by reason of the vicinity of their situation.'

16. *swimming her*: Grose, *PG*, 'Superstitions', 27, also describes this technique for persecuting, while supposedly detecting, witches. Scott's more direct source for Madge's fate, however, was the death of Jean Gordon, a Scottish gypsy whose Jacobite views, rashly expressed at Carlisle soon after 1745, gave 'such great offence to the rabble of that city' that 'they inflicted upon poor Jean Gordon no slighter penalty than that of ducking her to death in the Eden'. Scott had known since childhood about Jean and her daughter Madge, and has used aspects of their stories in *Guy Mannering* and in his anonymous contributions to the 1817 *Blackwood's Edinburgh Magazine* series of articles on Scottish gypsies.

17. *half-hangit Maggie Dickson*: See n. 12 on p. 619. Commentators close to Scott's time say that the Maggie who sold salt was a different, later figure of the Edinburgh streets.

18. *Cauld is my bed... for me to-morrow*: The ballad fragment, with its accusing female ghost claiming the life of her betrayer, echoes the situation of David Mallet's 'Margaret's Ghost' (1724 or earlier; reprinted in Percy's *Reliques*).

19. *Proud Maisie... proud lady*: Birds frequently warn in the ballads, and macabre dialogue between them can be found in 'The Twa Corbies', admitted with some reluctance as part of Child, 26; six tall bearers appear to Lady Alice (Child, 85).

In the MS the first three stanzas of 'Proud Maisie' appear to have been written in one stage, with the first in the past tense and the third sharpening its first line to its present form after beginning with a typically balladic repetition of the first line of stanza 2. The gaps between the stanzas are not strongly marked. Later Scott changed 'was' and 'sat' to 'is' and 'sits', inserted the asterisks between the stanzas, and added the fourth and final one.

CHAPTER 41

Epigraph: Slightly adapted from 11, 37, of *Thalaba the Destroyer* (1801), an 'Arabian tale' by Scott's friend and (to some extent) protégé Robert Southey (1774–1843).

1. *Last Speech*: Cf. Scott's request to a correspondent for Dying Speeches (letter of 24 April 1818).

2. *not be doomed to observing any one's health or temper*: There is an underlying threat to Mrs Dutton in this apparent reassurance.

3. *only mode of access to St Mungo's capital*: Two more bridges had been added by 1818.

4. *him of the laurel wreath*: Southey accepted the Poet Laureateship in 1813 after Scott declined it.

5. *A broader. . .wind*: Thalaba the Destroyer, 11, 36.

6. *lake*: So in MS.

7. *Elfinfoot*: Elvanfoot, a hamlet half-way between Carlisle and Glasgow where the road crossed to the left bank of the River Clyde. The version of the word that Mrs Dutton has apparently picked up from Archibald suggests that even he now speaks with soft 'Highland' pronunciation.

8. *island called Roseneath*: The passage reads better if both Scott and Archibald are credited with knowing that Rosneath is a peninsula, joined to the mainland by a slender isthmus several miles to the north of its Clyde shore.

9. *fixed his master's mandates to perform*: Scott repeats the cadence of 'pleased the Almighty's orders to perform' from the suppressed Addison quotation on p. 360.

10. *boar's-head, crested with a ducal coronet*: Still the crest of the Duke of Argyll.

11. *crossed from the opposite shore*: Crossed the Gareloch to Rosneath from the vicinity of modern Helensburgh or Rhu.

12. *disturbances*: Apparently in this case a fiction of Archibald's, or of Scott's.

CHAPTER 42

Epigraph: Fletcher (see epigraph note to Chapter 30), perhaps with Massinger, *The Sea Voyage* (acted 1622), 2, 2, 186–8.

1. *a smaller isle*: The narrator does apparently believe that Rosneath is an island and that the short, almost rectilinear Holy Loch 'wind[s] from the mountains'. Scott saw the intricate coastline of the lower Clyde from sea-level at the end of his cruise with the Northern Lighthouse Commissioners in 1814, and on earlier and later ferry crossings.

2. *hunting-lodge. . . palace*: The ancient castle, much extended during the eighteenth century, burned down in 1802; Bonomi's Italianate palace of 1803–5 was demolished in 1961.

3. *the form was indisputable*: These 'directions to a painter', with their further references to 'The Cotter's Saturday Night' (cf. p. 100) in the mention of the bonnet and the haffets, were not followed out. Though the frontispiece to Volume 11 of *1830* (by J. Burnet) shows Deans in his cottage with

Jeanie, it fell to Wilkie to illustrate other novels of the edition and Allan (who had provided in 1820 a comic scene with Knockdunder) did not contribute at all in 1829–30.

4. *my friends*: Strongly breaks the decorum of the 'Pattieson' persona.

5. *Wilkie*: Sir David Wilkie (1785–1841), a Scottish painter of genre scenes of peasant life in the Dutch manner and (later) of historical subjects. His painting of Scott and the Abbotsford household in peasant garb (1817), now in the Scottish National Portrait Gallery, Edinburgh, was attacked for vulgarity by some English critics, much as *The Heart of Mid-Lothian* was. Wilkie had already offended his patrons among the gentry with the social protest of *Distraining for Rent* (1815, National Gallery of Scotland) and Scott's mention of him here can appear as a gesture of support.

6. *Allan*: Sir William Allan (1782–1850), an Edinburgh-based painter in Scott's circle who travelled in Russia, later painted historical scenes, and illustrated scenes from several Waverley novels in 1820 (including Duncan of Knockdunder at the Manse of Knocktarlitie, but not the Deanses' reunion). His portrait of Scott is in the National Portrait Gallery (London). For both Allan and Wilkie in relation to Scott and his times, see D. and F. Irwin, *Scottish Painting* (1975) and D. Macmillan, *Painting in Scotland* (1986), especially 163–71 (though the composition of *The Heart of Mid-Lothian* is there dated one year too early) and *Scottish Art* (1990).

7. *melting mood*: Othello, V, ii, 349.

8. *prelatic deadness and schismatic heresy*: Not traced.

9. *lions that were in the path*: A lion in the way, Proverbs 22:13; 26:13.

10. *out from us. . . not of us*: 1 John 2:19.

11. *withered branch will never bear fruit of grace*: Phrases from John 15:6–8.

12. *scape-goat. . . into the wilderness of the world*: Leviticus 16:10.

13. *elected*: 'As God hath appointed the elect unto glory, so. hath he. . . foreordained all the means thereunto' (Westminster Confession, 3, 6).

14. *flower. . .Lugton*: Deans may seem to fall into self-parody here, but his heightened prose (more florid and metaphorical than usual, yet at the same time still earthy) is well within the range of Presbyterian eloquence used by, for example, Samuel Rutherford (*c.* 1600–1661), whose letters on spiritual subjects include many addressed to Marion Macknaught.

15. *let her bite on her ain bridle*: Let her fend for herself, let her go hungry (*ODEP*, 62).

16. *patient Job*: At 6:15–17.

17. *earthly tabernacle*: 2 Corinthians 5:1.

18. *store-farm. . .stock*: For a historian's overview of the Argylls' consistent policy of modernization and improvement on their Highland estates, and its motives and results, see E. Cregeen, 'The Changing Role of the House of Argyll in the Scottish Highlands' in N. Phillipson and R. Mitchison, *Scotland in the Age of Improvement* (1970), 5–23.

19. *'This is David's spoil.'*: 1 Samuel 30:20. The son of Jesse is David.

20. *experimental farm*: Cregeen documents a new phase of leasing at this date but not the experimental farm.
21. *immense*: 500 square miles, with feudal rights over 3,000 more.
22. *heritable jurisdictions*: See n. 46 on p. 591.
23. *Knocktarlitie*: Apparently adapted from Kiltarlity in Inverness-shire by substituting the Gaelic *Cnoc*, 'hillock', for *Cil*, 'hermitage'.

The parish is cunningly unlocated among the lochs opening to the north of the Firth of Clyde. Contradictory hints point to Kilmun on the Holy Loch (in the manuscript, but rather far from Rosneath), to Garelochhead (the hinterland has room for the events of Chapter 50 and the Kirk is illustrated in the Abbotsford edition, 1843, though built only in the late eighteenth century; the view of Arran is lacking), to Rosneath itself, and to Cove on the west side of the Rosneath peninsula, which has the views, plausible distances and the modern house of Auchingower, but no church and doubtful hinterland. The site of modern Helensburgh is a further possibility.
24. *candidate. . .presentee*: 'Candidate' (for election by the parish elders) aligns with David's Presbyterian view of Church government; 'presentee' would entail acknowledgement of the Erastian view of the vacancy as a property in the landowner's gift. Argyle's blend of power and influence makes David's fastidiousness dignified but absurd in this case, but conflicts between kirk-sessions and landowners, leading to boycotts, occupations and lawsuits, become frequent and intense in the early nineteenth century and culminated in the Disruption of the Church of Scotland in 1843.

CHAPTER 43

Epigraph: From strophe 9 of Dryden's *Ode* of 1686. The situation – a traveller's arrival across water to the unexpected loss of a sister – parallels Jeanie's.
1. *benevolent enchanter*: The phrase denotes Argyle but became increasingly applicable to Scott, who had already been described as 'the great magician. . . by the Border' ('Chaldee MS', *Blackwood's Edinburgh Magazine*, October 1817) and who was to be known as 'the Wizard of the North' increasingly from 1820–21.
2. *cup of his liquor*: Unless Scott has forgotten David's Rechabite stance, (p. 406), Argyle's guess that he prefers brandy must have been correct.
3. *think so highly of a friend. . .*: A Rochefoucauldian thought, but not apparently an actual quotation from the master.
4. *polished shaft. . . carnal learning. . . root of the matter*: Either Deans or Scott is repeating himself, for these phrases from Walker and the Bible have already been used on pp. 87, 92, 119, 398, etc.
5. *great men. . . reconcile his speculative principles with existing circumstances*:

The eighteenth century abounds with possible instances literary and actual, from Macheath and Jonathan Wild through Dr Pangloss and the three philosophers in *Rasselas* to Hume in the puddle (Ernest Campbell Mossner, *Life*, 563) and even the captive Napoleon himself, but the phrase seems to be Scott's.

6. *shorn of its beams*: Milton, *Paradise Lost*, 1, 596.

7. *spots and blemishes*: Cf. 'of blemish or of spot' (Milton, 'To Mr Cyriack Skinner Upon His Blindness', 2).

8. *dissenters, who, upon various accounts, absolutely seceded*: *CSD*, 820, provides a chart tracing the various schisms of the Scottish Churches from 1690 to the present.

9. *of 1640*: The moment between the First and Second Bishops' Wars when, in Deans's view, Scotland came closest to being a Covenanted theocracy.

10. *humble pleader for the good old cause in a legal way*: Cf. *Humble Pleadings for the Good Old Way* (1713), mentioned by Walker as having 'above all the divided parties in Scotland since the Revolution, had most of the old Covenanters' plea in hand' (*Six Saints*, 1, 29).

11. *right-hand excesses, divisions, and separations*: Walker's language again (*Six Saints*, e.g. 1, 260).

12. *lay-patronage*: See n. 24 on p. 658.

13. *in by the window, and over the wall*: A concealed allusion to John 10:1, 'He that entereth not by the door into the sheepfold, but climbeth up some other way, the same is a thief and a robber'; the expelled Presbyterian ministers and their congregations pointedly left church and pulpit doors barred to compel the 'intruded' successors to enter by force.

14. *cheating. . . incumbent*: 'for the clothing of one back and feeding of one intruding belly, they will starve a thousand souls' (*Six Saints*, 1, 273).

15. *limb of the brazen image, a portion of the evil thing*: Not traced.

16. *the oaths*: For oaths in general, see n. 16 on p. 606. Those required of the clergy, imposed under the Toleration Act of 1712, comprised allegiance to the Crown, assurance of loyalty to the Hanoverian dynasty and abjuration of the Jacobite claim to the throne in terms that restricted succession to members of the Church of England – all objectionable in content or principle to strict Presbyterians and even to moderate ones such as Alexander Carlyle, who describes in Chapter 4 of his *Autobiography* his efforts to avoid subscribing to them when going abroad in 1745.

17. *Prelacy. . .mitre*: David's language invokes the Covenanters' identification of their opponents with the Scarlet Woman of Revelation 17 and her accoutrements.

18. *My bowels. . . heart!*: Jeremiah 4:19

19. *deep compliance*: Cf. foul compliance, *Six Saints*, 1, 54, etc.; the other phrases here are standard pulpit terms of the time.

20. *turning sinners. . . sheep*: Not traced.

21. *eight hundred punds Scots, and four chalders of victual*: £66. 13. 4d and about

four tons of grain, of which three quarters, usually, would be oats – a
typical but moderate stipend for the region and period, whose scale makes
clear the significance of the £50 bank-notes that begin to appear.

22. *sinful compliance, or backsliding, or defection of any kind*: Cf. e.g. 'the
sinfulness of our backslidings and complying courses' (*Six Saints*, 2, 82)
and p. 435.

23. *Doeg the Edomite*: In 1 Samuel 21 and 22, Saul's chief herdsman, who
betrayed and slew the priests who had assisted David.

24. *the fatted kine of Pharaoh*: David is being carried away here – the fatted
calf was killed for the return of the Prodigal Son (Luke 15:23), but
Pharaoh's well-favoured kine existed only in his dream (Genesis 41:2).

25. *remove our tent*: Like Abraham, Genesis 13:18.

26. *mire. . . wallow*: 2 Peter 2:22.

27. *lucre*: Repeatedly used thus in the Epistles of Paul and Peter.

28. *stalking-horse. . . stipend*: Not traced.

29. *Rome. . . abomination*: Revelation 17 again.

30. *Greeks. . foolishness*: 1 Corinthians 1:23.

31. *weather-withstanding professors. . . banks. . . mosses. . . bogs. . . caverns*: Not
traced.

32. *ulcers. . .imposthumes. . .sores. . . leprosies*: Not traced.

33. *crying aloud and sparing not*: Isaiah 58:1.

34. *John Knox*: (*c.* 1513–72), theological and political leader (as well as historian)
of the Protestant Reformation in Scotland, often thought responsible for
the harsh and theocratic directions in which it developed.

35. *commenced. . . Culdees. . . recusants*: Exactly the approach adopted in Kirkton's *History*.

36. *Bruce. . . Livingstone*: Robert Bruce (1554–1631), penalized from 1596 for
resisting royal authority and a ringleader in the Tolbooth incident recalled
by Hardie on p. 20; David Black (d. 1603), minister of St Andrews,
condemned in 1596 for asserting the primacy of ministers of religion over
secular authorities and banished beyond the River Tay; Robert Blair
(1593–1666) and David Livingstone (1603–72) defended similar views in
the 1620s and 1630s and later supported the National Covenant.

37. *brief. . . period*: From the signing of the Covenant in 1638 to the military
defeats at Dunbar (1650) and Worcester (1651).

38. *the indulgences, seven*: a series (actually of five) declarations of limited
toleration of Presbyterian ministers and worship under the Episcopal
constitution, issued in 1669, 1672, 1679 and 1687, and divisive in their
effect on various shades of Presbyterian opinion.

39. *iron cage*: Cf. p. 366 and n. 23 on p. 647.

40. *a narrative*: A pugnacious correction of the Church historian Wodrow, one
of many digressions in Walker's 'Vindication of Cameron's Name' (*Six
Saints*, 1, 349–55ff.), largely included in Scott's note; Walker's account is
appropriated for Deans.

41. *trade. . .an inch was as good as an ell*: *ODEP*, 403, with two instances before 1620 and then this one. If Walker's supposed pedlar's pack contained fabrics and ribbons, his trade would have shown him that an inch was by no means as good as an ell, whatever might be the case in respect of wounds. The passage quoted in Scott's note is in *Six Saints*, 1, 352–5.

42. *aged strong ale*: Not only does Deans drink with Dumbiedikes, he keeps a supply at home!

43. *Knocktarlitie*: In MS, 'Kilmun'.

44. *oaths*: See n. 16, above.

CHAPTER 44

Epigraph: The seemingly positive quatrain about marriage, applicable to Butler and Jeanie, is assembled from different stanzas of 'The Lovers' by John Logan (1748–88), a dialogue-poem full of foreboding (a dirge, an owl, a raven, 'What tears may I have yet to shed?') that is softened only by the prospect of children. The underlying disjunctive meanings, applicable to Staunton and Effie, become clearer as the chapter proceeds.

1. *reversed the text*: 1 Corinthians 7:14 – 'the unbelieving husband is sanctified by the wife, and the unbelieving wife is sanctified by the husband'.

2. *Cargill. . .banished*: Quite closely follows Walker's account of Cargill's attitude (*Six Saints*, 2, 47–8). 'Hearing the curates' was for Covenanters an issue sufficiently grave to receive its own chapter of treatment in Alexander Shields, *A Hind Let Loose* (1687).

3. *Knockdunder*: The text encourages us to explore the puns around Duncan Knock's name. As well as shortening to Knock, it resolves into either *Cnoc* = hillock + dunder = stupid, 'Foolshill'; or into Knocked under = surrendered or defeated. Its bearer can thus be read as both violent and foolish or as a figure of pathos, and the reader is reminded of this at p. 451 when Duncan declares, 'I knock under to no man.'

4. *Tower. . .cliff overhanging the Holy-Loch*: The apparently circumstantial description is a standard type of Highland fortlet. If the tower and Duncan's jurisdiction go together, the whole location of Knocktarlitie is moved away from the Rosneath peninsula itself to Kilmun, which does appear once as an MS first-thought for the location. W.C. Maughan (*Rosneath Past and Present*, 1893, 68n.) plays with two alleged sites for Duncan's house, both conveniently vanished.

5. *Trojan or Tyrian*: As Dido offers to assimilate Aeneas's shipwrecked followers in Carthage (*Aeneid*, 1, 574). (A frequent quotation used in e.g. *Don Quixote*, Penguin Classics edition, 2, 26, and on the title-page of Pennant's *Tour*.)

6. At first Duncan appears to speak Lowland Scots, but at 'shentlemens' he takes to 'Highland English'.

7. *gift of tongues*: An allusion to Acts 2.

CHAPTER 45

Epigraph: The third stanza of Burns's satire 'The Ordination' (1786); the first
line should run 'Mak haste and turn King David owre'.

1. *Presbytery of* ——: Scott's dash keeps the topography in doubt – if Knocktarlitie were Rosneath itself, or Rhu on the opposite shore of the Gareloch,
   Dumbarton would fill the blank; if Kilmun, Dunoon.

2. *substantial breakfast*: Descriptions of Scottish breakfasts are a literary
   topos of the period, from Pennant's citation of James V's hunting banquet
   out of Lindsay of Pitscottie (*Tour*, 1769, 1774 edition, 106–8; also picked
   up by Scott in *Waverley*, Chapter 24) and Smollett (*Humphry Clinker*, 280,
   289) to the many in Scott's novels and to Scott's own as described by
   Hogg and others. According to Annette Hope's survey (*A Caledonian
   Feast*, 1987, Chapter 6), Duncan offered comparatively 'plebeian fare'.

3. *contraband trade*: The very words in which the topic of smuggling is first
   introduced on p. 57 and finally denounced on p. 520.

4. *Mayor of Altringham. . . mending*: *ODEP*, 519, as a seventeenth-century
   Cheshire proverb; also in Grose, *PG*, L6v. Scott quotes it again in a letter
   of late July 1828, presumably while revising *The Heart of Mid-Lothian*.

5. *shadows slept upon the mirror'd wave*: An iambic line recalling words and
   cadences of Wordsworth and of Keats, but not, it seems, a direct quotation.

6. *gig*: Recorded only from 1790 in this sense.

7. *forgotten Scottish poet*: Alexander Ross (1699–1784), schoolmaster of Loch-
   lee, Angus, whose *Helenore or The Fortunate Shepherdess, A Poem in the
   Broad Scotch Dialect* was first published at Aberdeen in 1768.

8. *nearly thus*: The passage (corresponding to lines 410–19 of the text in M.
   Wattie, ed., *The Scottish Works of Alexander Ross*, 1938) has been somewhat
   adapted by either Scott or his printers.

9. *men. . . heart*: Cf. 1 Samuel 13:14, and n. 5 on p. 616.

10. *ill-fated attempt in 1686*: 1685, in fact – an abortive invasion in support of
    Monmouth's claim to succeed Charles II. Argyle was executed on an old
    charge of treason (for taking the test oath with reservations) and his head
    displayed on the Edinburgh Tolbooth.

11. *furniture. . . sent down. . . in a brig*: Presumably from Glasgow, though
    the third duke is known to have had fittings for the castles at Rosneath and
    Inveraray shipped from London to Edinburgh and reshipped from Glasgow
    (Ian G. Lindsay and Mary Cosh, *Inveraray and the Dukes of Argyll*, 1973,
    92). Scott too, in 1818, was importing furniture from London by sea
    (*Letters*, 18 May 1818, etc.).

12. *milky mothers*: For simple 'animal' of *1818* – and see n. 10 on p. 631.

13. *child of prayers*: Who should therefore have been specially holy, as was John the Baptist (Luke 1).

14. *prodigal . . . calf*: Luke 15.

15. *Auchingower*: Gaelic *achaidhean gobhar*, 'goat-pastures'. The name is today borne in Rosneath by a late Victorian mansion on the west side of the peninsula (National Grid reference 214840) in a position consistent with the topographic information on p. 454. Life, however, has imitated art, for no such name appeared on the relevant sheet of the 1860 Ordnance Survey (Dumbartonshire 16).

16. *things unattempted yet in prose or rhyme*: Milton, *Paradise Lost*, 1, 16.

17. *Miss Martha Buskbody*: 'a young lady who has carried on the profession of mantua-making at Gandercleugh. . . for about forty years' and who presses Pattieson to clear up loose ends of narrative in the 'Conclusion' to *Old Mortality*.

18. *next term's victual stipend*: The next quarter's or half-year's delivery of the part of the minister's salary paid in grain, etc.

19. *set the kiln a-low*: 'put the fat in the fire', proverbial, *ODEP*, 424, 617.

20. *maistry, ye ken, maws the meadows doun*: Proverbial, *ODEP*, 518, citing Kelly, M64 – 'spoken when people of power and wealth effect a great business in a short time'.

21. *'Fair and softly gangs far,'*: Proverbial, *ODEP*, 238.

22. *fule may gie a wise man a counsel*: Proverbial, *ODEP*, 274, citing Kelly, A147.

23. *lang-shankit spune. . . deil*: Proverbial, *ODEP*, 480; Scott's version closely follows Ferguson (1641) and *Six Saints*, 1, 329.

24. *1746*: In the aftermath of the Jacobite rising of 1745–6.

CHAPTER 46

Epigraph: Stanza 18 of 'The Holy Fair' (1785), another of Burns's satires on Church ceremonies and the dissension that accompanies them.

1. *expressed no dissatisfaction*: Despite his objections to secular music and Highland culture.

2. *'The Campbells are coming.'*: The traditional march of the Campbells, with words probably associated with their role in the Fifteen (*SMM*, 299).

3. *Highland Host*: As a collective coercion and punishment in 1678, the government quartered some thousands of clansmen and English and Irish soldiers on the people of Ayrshire and the lower Clyde.

4. *mirth and fun grew fast and furious*: As at the witches' sabbath in Burns, 'Tam o' Shanter', 143.

5. *wearing late*: From the same poem, 3.

6. tam carum caput: 'so beloved a person', a tag from Horace, *Odes*, 1, 24. Duncan, confounding the pronunciations of *carum* (carrum) and *Gorme*

(Gurrum; Gaelic 'blue', perhaps 'blue-chinned'), the epithet of successive
chiefs of the MacDonalds of Sleat in southern Skye, objects as a mainland
Whig to his chief's being compared to an island Jacobite.

7. *comparison was odious*: Proverbial, *ODEP*, 138.

8. *sea-fire*: 'At times the ocean appears entirely illuminated around the vessel'
   by phosphorescence (Scott's note to *The Lord of the Isles*, 1, 21).

9. *better sheltering under an auld hedge than under a new planted wood*:
   Proverbial, *ODEP*, 722.

10. *maun drink as I hae brewed*: Proverbial, *ODEP*, 85, citing Kelly, 178, and
    The Cottagers of Glenburnie, Chapter 14.

11. *keep from the wife of your bosom the secret that concerns your neck*: If
    proverbial, in *ODEP*, 808, only in the weak form 'He that tells his wife
    news is but newly married.'

12. *sown the wind, and maun reap the whirlwind*: Hosea 8:7.

CHAPTER 47

Epigraph: 2 *Henry VI*, IV, x, 15–16.

1. *persecuting. . . ferretting. . . young ones*: Compare the attack on 'their busy
   zeal in hunting out after young women whom they suspected of being with
   child, and after old women who lay under the imputation of witchcraft' in
   Hugo Arnot, *Celebrated Criminal Trials in Scotland* (1785), 311 (for whom
   see n. 2 on p. 669).

2. *alkaline. . . acidity*: The earliest figurative use of this opposition in the
   OED, s.v. alkaline, 1. b.

3. *gifted wi' a far look into eternity*: Walker describes the Blink, a period of
   'very astonishing apparitions, both in the firmament and upon the earth'
   before and during the first field-preachings and before the persecution had
   begun (*Six Saints*, 1, 32–4). Scott does not put all his knowledge of the
   period into the surface level of the novel.

4. *blessed Peden*: See n. 26 on p. 606.

5. *Lundie*: Walker's 'Peden' includes an account of Thomas Lundie's deathbed
   vision of 'the Frenches marching with their armies' through a Scotland
   bridle-deep in blood (*Six Saints*, 1, 92–3). Scott owned a 1739 *Predictions
   or Prophecies* of Lundie, Rutherford, Cameron and others.

6. *Cameron*: See n. 7 on p. 612.

7. *Renwick*: See n. 8 on p. 613.

8. *John Caird the tinkler, wha entered into the secrets*: Not found, either in
   Walker or in John Howie's *Biographia Scoticana* (see n. 11 below), the
   other main collection of pious memoirs.

9. *Elizabeth Melvill, Lady Culross*: For accounts of Lady Culross (married by
   1598 and still alive in 1630) and specimens of her allegorical poetry, see G.
   Greer and others, eds., *Kissing the Rod* (1988), 32–8, or C. Kerrigan, ed.,

Anthology of Scottish Women's Poetry (1991), 154–6. On the occasion invoked by Jeanie, Lady Culross, praying privately in a curtained bed, was encouraged to speak out because she was alone, whereupon the room filled with listeners (Kirkton, 16n., and W.K. Tweedie, *Select Biographies*, 1845, 1, 346–7).

10. *Lady Robertland*: Surnamed Fleeming, of Stewarton in Ayrshire (the scene of a religious revival in the 1630s), still alive and spiritually active in 1649; 'often got as rare outgates' as Lady Culross (Kirkton, 19 and n.; W.K. Tweedie, as in n. 9 above).

11. *Mr John Scrimgeour*: Not in Walker. A version of the anecdote appears in John Howie's *Biographia Scoticana or... Scots Worthies*, (third edition, 1796, 114–15). Scott owned the Glasgow 1797 and Leith 1816 editions of this popular collection. Scrimgeour had also in 1620 resisted an attempt by his bishop to deprive him of his ministry for non-compliance.

12. *wish that most part of books were burned except the Bible*: John Howie, *Biographia Scoticana*, 114.

13. *Aily MacClure of Deepheugh*: Alison MacClure of Deep-hollow.

14. *egg-shells and mutton-banes*: For their uses, see entries for Eggshell and Bladebone in I. Opie and M. Tatem, eds., *A Dictionary of Superstitions* (1989), where various Highland sources including Pennant's *Tour* are cited; neither topic occurs in Grose, *PG*, or in Scott's own *Letters on Demonology and Witchcraft* (1830).

15. *suffer a witch to live*: Exodus 22:18. See n. 13 on p. 611.

16. *it is pronounced*: In Matthew 5, but not quite as quoted – the meek are to inherit the earth, the peace-makers to be called the children of God.

17. *Crook in Mrs Butler's Lot*: See n. 15 on p. 613.

18. *brandy*: Not only David's but Jeanie's attitude to drink has softened.

19. *postage*: Often paid by the recipient until Hill's reform of 1840.

20. *strictly canonical*: 'idleness, prodigality and wasteful gaming' are forbidden in the Larger Catechism's analysis of sins forbidden in the eighth commandment, 'Thou shalt not steal' (Q. 142).

CHAPTER 48

Epigraph: The final stanza of 'To the Shepherd of Glen' from p. 32 of *Poems on Several Occasions* by a Lady, Edinburgh (1797) (Lamont), 'Printed but not published' according to an author's inscription in the British Library copy. The refined author half envies the shepherd's lack of sensibility – 'yet all his share of happiness/From rustic ignorance flows'. Lady Charlotte Campbell (1775–1861), youngest daughter of the fifth Duke of Argyll, a literary hostess in Edinburgh early in the century and Lady of the Bedchamber to the Princess of Wales 1809–15, wrote novels and memoirs under her later married name of Bury.

1. *Dundee. . . Clavers*: John Graham of Claverhouse, Viscount Dundee (1648–89), government cavalry commander at Drumclog and Bothwell Brigg, and military and political leader of the repression of the Covenanters until his death at the head of the Jacobite forces at Killiecrankie.

2. *Indian at the stake. . . rending his fibres and boring his eyes. . .* : In his note to *Rokeby*, 3, 2, Scott cites James Adair's account of the cruelty and stoicism of native American warfare (*History of the American Indians*, 1775). Lismahago's experience (*Humphry Clinker*, Penguin edition, 228) also lay to hand, as did Peter Williamson's *French and Indian Cruelty Exemplified* (1757), which Scott owned in the 1759 edition (cf. n. 7 on p. 671).

3. *sensibility*: Effie's language has been seen as anachronistic, but the *OED* documents similar uses of the word in Addison (1711) and Hume (1741).

4. *shooting-season*: First recorded in 1781 (*OED*, Supplement) – here the characters are indeed ahead of their time.

5. *Whiterose*: The Jacobite emblem.

6. *Setoun. . . Winton*: George Seton, fifth Earl of Winton, commanded the Lothian Jacobite cavalry in 1715 but lost his colleagues' confidence through vacillation, escaped from the Tower of London while under sentence of death in 1716 and died abroad without issue, his estates in East Lothian being forfeited. The Windygoul branch (p. 482 and Glossary) appears in a document of 1672 quoted in Kirkton, 166n., but does not figure among the twenty-odd Seaton and Seatoun families in R. Douglas, *The Baronage of Scotland* (1798).

7. *the idle crackling of fire among thorns*: 'as the crackling of thorns under a pot, so is the laughter of the fool': Ecclesiastes 7:6.

8. *they remain unconsumed*: Like the burning bush in which God appeared to Moses in Exodus 3:2 – the verse in Latin (*Nec tamen consumebatur*) has long been the motto of the Church of Scotland.

9. *soft answer, which turneth away wrath*: Proverbs 15:1.

10. *proverb*: Give losers leave to speak (*ODEP*, 485); give losing Gamesters leave to talk (Kelly, G80).

11. *no witch, but a cheat*: Long the stock argument of enlightened officials – cf. R. Scot, *The Discovery of Witchcraft* (1584); *Spectator*, 117, 1711, and n. 13 on p. 611.

12. *birth-day*: Of the monarch.

13. *Gorbals*: At the time of the supposed events of the novel, a medieval village with a few later buildings; by 1818 apparently still a smart modern suburb newly challenged by canal and colliery development. Scott's connotation of 'broad, coarse' speech in 1818 (if not in 1751) seems to conflict with the modern urban historian's account that describes development of the old village beginning only from 1787, 'two elegant very long terraces' under construction in 1802, 'building activity becoming intense' in 1818–21 and the final flight of the middle classes taking place only in the second half of the nineteenth century (A. Gibb, *Glasgow: The Making of a City*, 1983, 100–101).

14. *court-Scotish*: In the light of Jeanie's reflection that follows, it is tempting to suppose that Scott is satirizing 'court-Scotish' as a wishful figment of the genteel imagination. Yet he ends a letter to Constable (25 February 1822) by lamenting the passing of Scots as 'a language . . . spoken by the learned and the wise & witty & the accomplished'.

15. *Wintoun. . . Setons of Windygoul*: See n. 6, above.

16. *'Ut flos. . . hortis,'*: 'As grows a flower within a garden close', Catullus (*c.* 84–*c.* 54 BC), *Carmina*, 62, 39.

17. *reversed the whole passage*: In Catullus's poem, as in Air 6 of Gay's *Beggar's Opera* (1728), which imitates it, the flower thrives in its garden but is despised after being picked and given to the world.

18. *bad health*: Perhaps a euphemism for venereal infection, also connected with the couple's childlessness.

19. *'"Manu. . . vino"'*: 'You make poor use of your hand during our merriment and drinking', Catullus, *Carmina*, 12, 1–2. Butler's point is general, Catullus's specific – his boon companion disconcerts people by purloining their table-napkins.

CHAPTER 49

Epigraph: *Macbeth*, III, i, 62.

1. *Duke Archibald*: Archibald Campbell, formerly Earl of Ilay (1682–1761), commissioner for the Union in 1707, wounded at Sheriffmuir, 'manager' of Scotland through and after the Walpole years, rebuilder of the Argyll seat at Inveraray and inventor of Highland regiments – despite his shadowy presence in this novel, in some ways a more 'historical' figure than his brother.

2. *1745*: The 'Forty-five', the last and most nearly successful of the Jacobite risings, whose forces reached Derby before turning back to face defeat at Culloden (1746) and the subsequent suppression of traditional Highland life. For Scott's account of the episode, see *Waverley* and *Tales of a Grandfather*.

3. *Argyle's banner*: As usual the Campbells were on the Protestant, Hanoverian side – Argyle's clansmen defended their own area and harassed the Jacobite clans' homelands during the campaign. See J. Fergusson, *Argyll in the Forty-five* (1951).

4. *Ziklag*: In 1 Samuel 30.

5. *Bothwell-Bridge*: In 1679; see n. 14 on p. 604.

6. *defections. . . fallings-off*: See n. 25 on p. 604.

7. *the South-sea scheme*: In 1720 an attempt at privatizing the national debt by means of the South Sea Company led to speculative fever followed by a collapse of stock values.

8. *There is baith weal and woe come aye wi' warld's gear*: Again an apparent proverb, only vaguely paralleled by *ODEP*, 873, 'No weal without woe.'

9. *princess. . . fairy tale. . .*: Traced among British folk-tales only in a fragment
in J.F. Campbell, *Popular Tales of the West Highlands* (1890), 1, lxxi,
although the motif (in Stith Thompson, *Motif Index of Folk-Literature*,
1955-8, D. 1454.1) is found in Danish and American sources.

CHAPTER 50

Epigraph: Milton, *Samson Agonistes* (1670), 710-13; the chorus notices the
approach of Delila, seemingly over-dressed for the occasion.

1. *MacCraw, or Murdockson*: The double citation of a woman's maiden and
   married names is still common formal practice in Scotland. Meg's maiden
   name, as well as being a form of MacCrae, reads as 'child of Crow, or of
   Gullet'.
2. *Haltwhistle*: A small town between Carlisle and Newcastle.
3. *Parsonage*: Effie keeps up her incognito by using the English term instead
   of *manse*.
4. *house of Inver-Garry*: The old castle of Invergarry, where a major route
   from the west debouches into the Great Glen south of Fort Augustus, was
   the seat of the MacDonells of Glengarry, whose clansmen fought on the
   Jacobite side in every battle of the Forty-five, and the place at which, after
   Culloden, Charles Edward Stuart parted from his retinue and took to the
   hills. It was duly burned by government forces. The MacDonell of Scott's
   day is said to have provided 'most of the features of Fergus MacIvor in
   Waverley'.
5. *Bedreddin Hassan*: In 'The Tale of the Wazir Nir al-Din', *The Book of the
   Thousand Nights and One Night*, J.C. Mardrus and Powys Mathers, eds.
   (1937), 1, 176-235. Scott owned and doubtless knew Scot's six-volume
   edition of 1811 and his protégé Weber's popular version of 1812.
6. *Scream'd. . .worrie-cow*: From Ross's *Helenore*, 2170-71 (cf. n. 7 on p. 662).
7. *long and fatiguing walks*: The opportunity for these, and the later Dumbartonshire reference, support a Garelochhead location for Knocktarlitie –
   Rosneath, whether as island or as peninsula, has no room for them.
8. *whether. . . Ennerdale*: Wordsworth, 'The Brothers' (1800), 217-19.
9. Donacha's lair may owe something to the description of 'Cluny's Cage', a
   Jacobite fugitive's retreat, in J. Home, *History of the Rebellion* (1802), 381,
   previously cited by Scott in a note to *The Lady of the Lake*, 1, 25. Scott
   also knew Home's conversation.
10. *very short to be sae lang*: 'Ye're unko short, my lass, to be so lang'
    (Alexander Ross, *Helenore*, 1,632).
11. *rifle*: Not recorded by the *OED* in this sense before 1770.
12. *Donald*: Stock name for Highlander, extending on into *Punch* cartoons in
    the second half of the century.
13. *tyne heart tyne a'*: Duncan is varying his aunt's remark on p. 69, and

ODEP, 825, cites eighteenth-century parallels – Kelly, H120, and Ross's *Helenore*, 2,222. The Watson Mazer, an early sixteenth-century cup belonging to the National Museums of Scotland, is inscribed TYNE GEIR TYNE LITIL TYNE HONOUR TYNE MUCKIL TYNE HART TYNE AL.

CHAPTER 51

Epigraph: *Henry V*, II, ii, 74–6. The turning-point of another of the justice-and-mercy debates in Shakespeare, as the king hands to three noblemen, who have just unsuccessfully counselled him against pardoning a drunken slanderer, the documents that in turn convict them of treasonable conspiracy with the French.

1. *span commonly allotted to evil-doers*: Perhaps a reference to Frank Levitt's 'two years' on p. 304, or to Jeremiah 17:11, 'he that getteth riches, and not by right, shall leave them in the midst of his days'.

2. *Arnot's*: Hugo Arnot, *Celebrated Criminal Trials in Scotland* (1785), 229ff., mentions such a return within the past four or five years, as an example in his discussion of the relation of the Roman doctrine of prescription to Scots law and current public policy. Scott's father, along with Pitt, Dundas and Dugald Stewart, appears on the volume's long subscription list.

3. *Annaple Bailzou*: Rather outside Scott's usual practices of naming, realistic or fanciful – a form of Annabel Baillie, or a play on Scots *balou*, lullaby? Cf. 'The Highland Balou' (*SMM*, 472), Burns's half-humorous song about the upbringing of a potential cattle-raider.

4. *twenty years*: Arnot asserts that the twenty years' prescription of Roman law had never been part of the common law of Scotland, and, that if it were to be adopted, certain aggravated crimes should, on grounds of public policy, remain punishable indefinitely (*Celebrated Criminal Trials in Scotland*, 229ff.).

5. The year's being 1751 strains the chronology – we must take David to have died almost at New Year, giving time for Craigsture to come on the market and Butler to be appointed to the Assembly before setting out at the end of February. Also, Plumdamas misdates the Porteous Mob by a year.

6. *This man had exercised ... narratives over a bottle ... constant tradition*: Scott at last finds a place for the remainder of the passage extruded from p. 142 (seemingly because of a change in the division between Volume 1 and Volume 2 of *1818*), which he had already sought to introduce at p. 207. The narrative stance and connection here (especially in the references to anachronism and tradition) seem only slightly less perfunctory.

7. *tied to the stake*: Like Gloucester in *King Lear* (III, vii, 54), like Macbeth (V, vii, 1), like Lismahago's friend Murphy (*Humphry Clinker*, Penguin edition, 228) and like the Indian captive (p. 337).

8. *Catholic priest*: The second hint, in addition to her convent education, that Effie will turn to the Catholic religion.

9. *so slow were their motions*: Like Jeanie's detour through York, the delay at Mid-Calder allows the plot to develop ahead of the principals' movements.

10. *the Gare-Loch lay betwixt*: More hard-to-reconcile topographical information, shifting Knocktarlitie westwards again.

11. *the virtues, as well as the vices, of savage tribes*: Explored in Rousseau's *Discours sur les sciences et les arts* (1750), as well as in Adam Ferguson's *Essay on the History of Civil Society* (1767), which helped mould Scott's thought.

12. *use every man. . . whipping*: *Hamlet*, II, ii, 516–17. Does Staunton think of his strait-laced brother-in-law as Polonius?

13. *thunder-burst. . . platoon-fire. . . stretch him on the earth*: This rather heavy-handed narrative prolepsis does at least keep the reader suspended between lightning and bullet as the instrument of the obviously impending judgement.

14. *electric fluid*: Franklin's term of 1750, embodying his theory.

15. *goat is falling. . . Arran*: An unconscious pun, the chief mountain of Arran being Goat Fell?

16. *something solemn. . . lost for ever*: Staunton's 'pathetic fallacy', in effect unexpectedly similar to Deans's providential outlook, retreating before Butler's Humean rationalism, takes refuge in psychology and in prefiguring the humanist pathos of Burns's 'Or like the snow falls in the river,/A moment white – then melts for ever' ('Tam o' Shanter', 61–2).

17. *change, not consummation*: Cf. Philippians 3:21, 1 Corinthians 15:51 and the Order for the Burial of the Dead in the Book of Common Prayer.

18. *nose has been on the Grindstane*: Proverbial since the sixteenth century (*ODEP*, 578).

19. *the guilt and the danger of this contraband trade*: Butler's tone is very different from the detached manner of the narrator of Chapter 2 (p. 27) and even from his own milder remonstrance that opens Chapter 45 (p. 450).

20. *mischief shall hunt the violent man*: Psalms 140:11, in the metrical version sung in Scotland, quoted by Walker, *Six Saints*, 2, 57.

21. *bloodthirsty. . . days*: Bloody men shall not live out half their days, Psalms 55:23. Cf. n. 1, above.

22. *blind and tangled path*: Allegorical?

23. *serving the husband is serving the wife*: Apparently a *risqué* proverb or catch-phrase, though not traced among the usual collections.

24. *act of parliament*: The Disarming Act of 1746.

25. *sit next the chimley when the lum reeks*: *ODEP*, 738, citing Johnson's *Life of Roscommon*; Scott uses it again in *Woodstock*.

CHAPTER 52 (AND L'ENVOY)

Epigraph: *1 Henry VI*, IV, v, 1, 3–7. The passage continues:

> Now thou art come unto a feast of death,
> A terrible and unavoided danger.

Young Talbot, insisting on sharing his father's danger, is killed in battle, whereupon Old Talbot dies of a broken heart.

1. *a religion*: Roman Catholicism.
2. *Woggarwolfe's*: In *Ethwald* (1802), 1, 2, 5, a play by Scott's friend Joanna Baillie (1762–1851), Woggarwolfe is a captive about to be surreptitiously released.
3. *fell . . by the hand of a son*: The post-Homeric but ancient epic the *Telegonia* told how the aged Odysseus died on the sea-shore, while resisting a pirate raid, by the hand of his unknown son Telegonus, begotten years before during his stay with the enchantress Circe.
4. *Jurisdiction Act*: See n. 46 on p. 591.
5. *Rob Roy*: A judiciously placed reminder of Scott's preceding novel, published for Christmas 1817 and readvertised in July 1818 alongside the new *Tales*; the historical Rob Roy MacGregor (1671–1734) had long been dead when the Whistler spoke, but his sons were convicted of abduction and forced marriage in the early 1750s (*DNB*).
6. *Serjeant More Cameron*: Alan Cameron, again grouped with Rob Roy in *Redgauntlet*, Letter 3.
7. *avaricious shipmaster*: The Whistler's fate may be compared with Peter Williamson's account of being kidnapped in Aberdeen about 1742 and sold as an indentured servant in the American colonies (*French and Indian Cruelty Exemplified*, 1757, summarized in Graham, 14, 4).
8. *quiet low content*: Cf. settled low content, *As You Like It*, II, iii, 68.
9. *divert her sorrow, or enhance her joy*: Cf. 'And moves the sorrows to enhance the joys', Pope, *Homer's Odyssey*, 24, 282.
10. *care for none of these things*: Like Gallio (see n. 4 on p. 605).
11. *filled more pages than I opined*: An open reference to the disproportionately large fourth volume, a covert one to Scott's having sacrificed the Scottish Regalia tale to this one (see Introduction, p. xxxix).
12. *now no more*: Though its doorway, doubtless the one that made Staunton turn pale, survives at Abbotsford.
13. *transferred to the extreme side of the city*: Calton Hill, where a new jail, since mostly demolished, was built 1815–17.
14. *Poquelin*: Better known as the French playwright Molière (1622–73).
15. *Le Medecin Malgre lui*: A comedy of 1666, *A Doctor in Spite of Himself*.
16. *Cela . . . cela*: 'That was once so, but we have altered it all' – from Act 2, Scene 4, of the play.

17. *advertisements are periodically making known to the public*: In the first
    edition, Constable's advertisements dated June 1818 were bound in at the
    beginning or end of many copies of the Tale.

SCOTT'S INTRODUCTION AND
NOTES TO THE 1830 EDITION

INTRODUCTION (p. 537)

1. *has stated*: The passage referred to runs (New Edition, 41, xiv–xv):

> Another debt, which I pay most willingly, I owe to an unknown correspondent (a
> lady), who favoured me with the history of the upright and high-principled female,
> whom, in the Heart of Mid-Lothian, I have termed Jeanie Deans. The circumstance
> of her refusing to save her sister's life by an act of perjury, and undertaking a
> pilgrimage to London to obtain her pardon, are both represented as true by my fair
> and obliging correspondent; and they led me to consider the possibility of rendering
> a fictitious personage interesting by mere dignity of mind and rectitude of principle,
> assisted by unpretending good sense and temper, without any of the beauty, grace,
> talent, accomplishment, and wit, to which a heroine of romance is supposed to have
> a prescriptive right. If the portrait was received with interest by the public, I am
> conscious how much it was owing to the truth and force of the original sketch,
> which I regret that I am unable to present to the public, as it was written with
> much feeling and spirit.

2. *'Whose distant roaring swells and fa's'*: Mrs Goldie quotes Burns's 'Song:
As I Stood by Yon Roofless Tower', 15–16, which refers to Lincluden
Abbey (Kinsley, 832).

3. *monument*: The epitaph composed by Scott for Helen Walker's tombstone
in Irongray Churchyard, Dumfries-shire, and here quoted from the 1871
Centenary Edition of the novel, runs:

THIS STONE WAS ERECTED

BY THE AUTHOR OF WAVERLEY

TO THE MEMORY

OF

HELEN WALKER,

WHO DIED IN THE YEAR OF GOD 1791.

THIS HUMBLE INDIVIDUAL PRACTISED IN REAL LIFE

THE VIRTUES

WITH WHICH FICTION HAS INVESTED

THE IMAGINARY CHARACTER OF

JEANIE DEANS;

REFUSING THE SLIGHTEST DEPARTURE
FROM VERACITY,
EVEN TO SAVE THE LIFE OF A SISTER,
SHE NEVERTHELESS SHOWED HER
KINDNESS AND FORTITUDE,
IN RESCUING HER FROM THE SEVERITY OF THE LAW
AT THE EXPENSE OF PERSONAL EXERTIONS
WHICH THE TIME RENDERED AS DIFFICULT
AS THE MOTIVE WAS LAUDABLE.
RESPECT THE GRAVE OF POVERTY
WHEN COMBINED WITH LOVE OF TRUTH
AND DEAR AFFECTION.
Erected October 1831.

4. *M'Diarmid*: MacDiarmid, editor of the *Dumfries and Galloway Courier*, took up Helen Walker's story more than once between 1818 and 1830; see M. Lascelles, *The Story-teller Retrieves the Past* (1980), Chapter 4. The 'small farmer' he mentions was father of one of his informants, not, as Scott supposed, of Helen Walker herself, who, according to MacDiarmid, was the daughter of 'a labouring man'.

5. *Cairn*: On modern maps, the river at that point is the Cluden.

NOTE TO PROLEGOMEN (p. 543)

1. *play in the Anti-Jacobin*: In No. 30 of *The Anti-Jacobin*, 4 June 1798, appears *The Rovers; or The Double Arrangement*, a collective skit by the Tory wits on contemporary politics and the German drama. The Ghost of the Prologue's grandmother appears and blesses him, but does not speak – and there is no epilogue.

2. *ghost of the author's grandmother*: Cf. 'soul of thy grandam', *Twelfth Night*, IV, ii, 51, 58.

TOLBOOTH OF EDINBURGH (Note, p. 547)

1. *'to such. . . return,'*: Cf. *Hamlet*, V, i, 190.

2. *in a concatenation accordingly*: From the Fourth Shabby Fellow's praise of Tony Lumpkin's song in the second scene of *She Stoops to Conquer* (1773) by Oliver Goldsmith (1728–74).

PETER WALKER (Note, p. 559)

1. See also pp. 103, 579, n. 19 on p. 609 and *Six Saints*, 1, 240–41.

MUSCHAT'S CAIRN (Note, p. 561)

1. *Pennycuik's*: Alexander Pennecuik, (d. 1730), the younger of two Scots poets of that name.

CHILD MURDER (Note, p. 565)

1. See also n. 18 on p. 618.

CALUMNIATOR OF THE FAIR SEX (Note, p. 566)

1. *Brodie*: 'Deacon' Brodie, an Edinburgh councillor executed in 1788 for robbing the Excise Office. The 'Scottish gentleman' was in fact a clergyman who made difficulties about giving evidence on oath. Graves's remark occurs in the quarto edition of William Creech, *An Account of the Trial of William Brodie and George Smith* (1788), 107 (which Scott owned) and in W. Roughead, ed., *The Trial of Deacon Brodie* (1906), Appendix 12.

JOHN DUKE OF ARGYLE AND GREENWICH (Note, p. 571)

1. For Argyle, see also Chapter 35, n. 1 on p. 645 and Introduction, pp. xxxvii–xxxviii.
2. *The fire... a' that*: From the Jacobite version of 'For a' that' ('Though Geordie reigns in Jamie's stead') in *A Collection of Loyal Songs* (1750), 43, and James Hogg, *Jacobite Relics* (1819), 2, 55–7.

MADGE WILDFIRE (Note, p. 415)

1. *Mr Train*: Joseph Train (1779–1852), Scottish poet, exciseman and antiquary who plied Scott with anecdotes and information, some of it useful and stimulating. In November 1818 he sent his account of Feckless Fannie, quite comically wide of the mark as Madge Wildfire's 'original' in any direct sense (in that Fannie was gentle, harmless, rural, law-abiding, a plain dresser, a shepherdess, the victim of a severe father, stoned to death by boys in Glasgow, whereas Madge was violent, formidable, urban, a companion of criminals, an extravagant dresser, a dog-lover, the victim of a seducer and ducked to death by adults in Carlisle like her avowed prototype Jean Gordon – cf. n. 16 to p. 655). Scott was apparently glad enough to print Train's material in *1830* but surrounded it with disclaimers that fall just short of irony.
2. *Lowe*: John Lowe (1750–98), whose other poem appears in R.H. Cromek's volume of 1810.
3. *Maria*: A touching lunatic introduced with her goat and her dog towards the end of both *Tristram Shandy* (1767), vol. 9, and *A Sentimental Journey* (1768) by Laurence Sterne (1713–68).
4. *Sancho's tale*: *Don Quixote*, 1, 20 (Penguin Classics edition, 153–4) – a shaggy-dog story about sheep, in principle almost interminable, and presumably summing up Scott's view of Train's contribution.

TEXTUAL NOTES

Scott habitually wrote out his novels rapidly and directly, in close lines across large sheets of paper folded to form two leaves. No preliminary drafts or jottings survive, but as Scott wrote, or soon afterwards, he would enter corrections and additions between the lines and on the blank reverse of the facing page. The manuscript was transcribed by a confidential secretary to shield Scott's supposed anonymity even from the printers, and set up in type. Scott then revised the proofs, sometimes extensively and normally in more than one stage – he could afford to do this because he virtually owned his printers as well as being closely involved in the financial affairs of his publisher. The corrected proofs were again transcribed, like the manuscript, before the printed version of the novel was produced. Errors as well as additions and improvements arose during these processes.

The early Scottish novels were reprinted in collected editions in 1819, 1821, 1822, 1823 and 1825, with some changes that seem likely to be the unauthorized work of the printers but many (especially in 1823) that on the whole implement policies of correction aligned with Scott's expressed concern and with his own revisions before and after, even if they sometimes go too far or betray misunderstandings of the text they seek to correct. In the late 1820s Scott revised all his fiction by means of a specially prepared interleaved set of the novels (the 1822 printing, in the case of the earlier ones), adding notes and correcting the text sometimes acutely but for the most part in a rather perfunctory way, which is understandable given his failing health and eyesight and his other anxieties. The set was used (again after transcription, this time for convenience rather than secrecy) to produce a New Edition in monthly volumes from 1829 to 1833, which omits some of Scott's own corrections while incorporating many more changes, apparently from proof-sheets that have not on the whole survived. Most later editions of Scott's fiction, reprinted directly or indirectly from the 1829–33 edition, perpetuate its rather formal heavily punctuated proto-Victorian version of the novels, spattered with commas and exclamation marks and weighed down by obtrusive notes between chapters.

In the case of *The Heart of Mid-Lothian* almost all the manuscript, a few pages of a late stage of proof, and the interleaved set with Scott's markings survive. The present Penguin Classics edition bases its text on the first edition of 1818, with its lighter punctuation closer to Scott's manuscript habit and its 'feel' of being a Regency or early nineteenth-century novel rather than a Victorian one. (The 1818 edition, including the few copies claimed probably as a selling stratagem to be 'second' or 'third' editions, appears all to be printed from a single setting of type – a conclusion based on selective checking in several copies, not on exhaustive comparison. The present text derives from a copy lent by Aberdeen University Library.) The wording of the 1818 edition has been modified in cases (i) where it appears to arise from misreading, rather than intentional amendment, during the journey from MS to the first edition of 1818; (ii) where Scott marked the interleaved set for amendment (including markings apparently overlooked in the New Edition of 1830) except where a further amendment in proof to the marked corrections seems probable; (iii) where altered readings in editions from 1819 to 1830 correct actual mistakes or appear to make improvements in line with those that Scott made himself (the most common being 'elegant variation' to eliminate traces of his habit of using the same word several times in close proximity), but not where such changes merely regularize or modernize grammar or expression. 'Wording' as used above includes the choice between English and Scots; the combined effect of the corrections from MS and those from *1830* is slightly to increase the density of Scots forms in the dialogue passages. All changes of wording (thus defined) from the first edition of 1818, and all cases in which the wording of the 1830 edition has been rejected, are listed on pp. 682–722, along with selected variants of interest from the MS and from other editions.

SILENT CORRECTIONS

Chapter numbering has been converted from Roman to Arabic numerals. Each edition down to *1830* begins a new chapter-number sequence with each fresh volume, not always correctly or consistently with each other. The 1818 volume divisions noted below do not match Scott's original intentions, themselves somewhat fluid.

Volume 1 – Chapters 1–12 (but 4 to 12 misnumbered 3 to 11)
Volume 2 – Chapters 13–25 (as 1–13)
Volume 3 – Chapters 26–37 (as 1–12)
Volume 4 – Chapters 38–52 (as 1–14, with a second 14)

Spelling and punctuation generally follow the 1818 edition, with the silent incorporation of (a) correction of some obvious small errors, mostly recognized by the careful proofreaders of *1819*; (b) a few capital letters from MS; (c) some dashes with which Scott marked interrupted speeches in the interleaved set; and (d) a handful of italicizations from *1830*, typically serving to disambiguate dialogue by locating the stress within a phrase or sentence. In certain circumstances, however, when the MS, *1830* and modern usage agree against *1818* they have been allowed to prevail. In particular, for past tenses of Scots verbs and a few other words that are embarrassed by apostrophes in the 1818 printing, unitary forms (*gien, taen, kend, gard, deil*) have been adopted, in accordance with Scott's apparent preference both spontaneous (MS) and considered (*1830*). *An* is printed without apostrophe when it signifies *if*, with one when it is the Scots for *and*. Compound proper names, chiefly those of streets, have usually been modernized from e.g. *High-street, Parliament-house,*

State-trials to *High Street, Parliament House, State Trials* etc, and *Holyrood-house* and *Lawnmarket* have been so standardized to match *Grassmarket*. The varying forms of *gaol/jail, frith/firth, courtesy/curtsey, poney/pony* and *centinel/sentinel* have each been standardized to the second form cited. Scott's sporadic attempts at introducing Nichil Novit's son as *Michel Novit* (he knows a great deal) do not meet the criteria for admission to the text, where the character remains as ignorant as his father; *Bartoline* has been so standardized, to evoke a diminutive jurist rather than the apostle; Scott's late and previously unadopted variation of *MacCallummore* to *MacCallanmore* has been followed when Gaelic speakers are being quoted or reported, but not introduced elsewhere; Grizell Damahoy appears now as *Miss*, now as *Mrs*, according to whether her spinsterhood or her maturity is in question. MS *winna* has been preferred to printed *wunna*, but the seemingly systematic preference of the printed texts for *gaun* over MS *ganging* has been allowed to stand. In dialogue, variation such as *claise, claes* and *claiths* and *Bever/Beever* has been kept as possibly marking individual, regional or class nuances of pronunciation. *Kirk-caldy* and *Gunnerby* have been standardized so. The lay-out of chapter epigraphs, and of their attributions within the novel text, has been made consistent. Displayed verse has been placed between marks of quotation only when it is clearly the utterance of a character in the novel, a matter on which both *1818* and *1830* are internally inconsistent.

Scott's later Introduction and notes, here placed together after the main body of the novel, are (with two exceptions) printed from the New Edition of 1830, with silent correction (from the interleaved set and from bibliographical sources) of a few errors in transcription, in personal names and in titles of books mentioned. The footnote on p. 400 is printed from the interleaved set, which is also the source of the note, 'Expulsion of the Bishops from the Scottish Convention', here printed from the corrected version in the Dryburgh Edition (1893).

For treatment of Scott's footnotes, see p. viii. Throughout, footnote symbols and page numbers of references have been silently adjusted to maintain coherence.

KEY TO THE TEXTUAL NOTES

M = Scott's manuscript of 1818, National Library of Scotland MS 1548.
m = Scott's manuscript corrections of 1828–9, in the interleaved copy of the 1822 edition, National Library of Scotland MSS 23009–10.

18, 19, 21, 22, 23, 25 refer to the editions of 1818, 1819, 1821, 1822, 1823 and 1825 respectively, and 30 to volumes 11, 12 and 13 of the New Edition of 1829–33, published in April, May and June 1830, where the text of *The Heart of Mid-Lothian* is flanked by the closing pages of *Old Mortality* and the opening of

The Bride of Lammermoor. 71 denotes the Centenary, 93 the Dryburgh, editions, which also made textual claims. *1994* refers to the present edition.

In the register of readings, the adopted reading (or its source, from which it may slightly diverge) comes first, usually followed by the rejected alternative. An en-rule linking two sigla indicates that all editions between and including those referred to agree on a reading. The line numbering takes account of every line with type on it on a page, except the running heading.

Penguin P. L.	*Authority for Adopted Reading*	*Rejected Reading*
7· 9	prolegomen M 18 19 23 25	prolegomenon 21 22 30
12	hast had M–25	had 30
12	fulfilled M 18 21 25	filled 19 22 23 30
19	nether 18–30	other M
8· 9	favour 18–30	savour M
16–17	dribble of drink M–21 23 25	Dribble o' Drink 22 30
26	Of a surety m 30	Truly M–25
27	consider m 30	remember M–25
33	still 30	yet M–25
36	Verily m 30	Truly M–25
37	cautelous 18–30	cautious M
9· 2–7	The descendants. . . tyrannical. 23	He whom. . . is desirous. . . his predecessors. . . their power. . . their execution. . . deem them. . . M–22 30
6	those 30	these 18–25 (M *doubtful*)
12	high spirited M	high-spirited 18–30
22	these M	their 18–30
23	opinion M 21 25	opinions 18 19 22 23 30
11· 6	are M	were 18–30
10	credible M 30	creditable 18–25
32	on 30	upon M–25
12·11	passenger has M–21 23 25	passengers had 22 30
13·11	pleasures M 18 21 25 30	pleasure 19 22 23
23–4	resort to m 30	practise M–25
14·32	like M–25	likely 30
33	The M–19 23 30	This 21 22 25
36	was M–25	were 30
15· 5	manifest 21 22 25	

Penguin P. L.	Authority for Adopted Reading	Rejected Reading
15·36	a Scotsman says M	says a Scotchman 18 19 23 30
		a Scotchman says 21 22 25
36	o' 21 22 25	of M–19 23 30
16·17	too 21 22 25	
17	him and M	him. And 18–30
17·15	take any share 23 25	partake M–22 30
29	said the agent 21 22 25	
33	ever 21 22 25	
37	frequently and 23 25	
19·17	misfortune (-s deleted) M	misfortunes 18–30
24	elopement the M	development 18–30
27	such M	
20· 2	those M (secretary's hand and texts of Crabbe)	there 18–30
31	Jamie's M	James's 18–30
39	consolations M 30	consolation 18–25
21·23	very long M	very 18–22 30
		rendered 23 25
35	and M	
39	Scottish M 30	Scotch 18–25
22·11	rested 30	vested M–25
23	that 23 30	this M–22 25
24	pair M–25	pairs 30
37	pair M–21 25	pairs 23 30
23· 2	to M 30	with 18–25
17	Scottish M	Scotch 18–30
20	a prisoner for debt m 30	he M–25
31	advocate's m 30	lawyer's M–25
24· 4	received m 30	had M–25
11	his M 22–5	this 18–21 30
11	for the brief 23 25	
34	providing M 18	provided 19–30
25·11	has 21–5	had M–19 30
22	good m 30	
26· 8	pad, and the M, some copies of 71, and texts of Prior	poet, and 18–30, other copies of 71

Penguin P. L.	Authority for Adopted Reading	Rejected Reading
26·27	five-and-twenty 18–25	twenty m thirty m 30
27· 9	convict 30	pannel M–25
9	stalks m 30	walks M–25
14	ceremonial M	ceremony 18–30
19	On 30	Upon M–25
35	in 23 30	with M–22 25
28·17	suspicious and watchful attention 18 19 30	suspicious attention M suspicions and watchful attention 21–5 71 93
26	Wilson 30	he M–25
28	other two M–19	two other 21–30
29·37	thoughts m thoughts were 30	mind was M–25
30· 1	of the M 23	of 18–22 25 30
15	in consequence of m 30	since M–25
29	feel 23 25	to feel M–22 30
31· 9	as we have already m 30	we have M–25
32· 6	save M–30	hedge *texts of Fergusson*
12	of a tailor m 30	
20	as an officer of police m 30	
23	manners 22 23	habits M–21 25 30
24	other 22 23	
28	They were m 30	It was M–25
31	acting, in short, as an armed police, m 30	
33·12	for the greater part m 30	in general M–25
13	or education and M	education or 18–22 30 education nor 23 25
22	love the M–30	alias *texts of Fergusson*
27	a holyday licensed 30	holiday licenses M–25
37	need one M–22 25 30	need we one 23
34·22	was M–25	were 30
38	object (-s *deleted*) M	objects 18–30
35· 2	topic 23 25	subject M–22 30
15	confided m 30	entrusted M–25
22	on 30	upon M–25

Penguin P. L.	Authority for Adopted Reading	Rejected Reading
35·28	introducing m 30	fetching M–25
29	drawing them up in the m 30	into a M–25
30	sounded 30	struck M–25
37· 2	on 30	upon M–25
2–3	occasions something similar 23 25	the same occasion M–22 30
7	fulfilled 30	executed M–25
16	it for 23	for it M–22 25 30
26	persons 30	people M–25
26	more M	were 18–30
35	at his M	at the 18–30
38· 4–5	the defence founded on these circumstances m 30	this M–25
5	Porteous m 30	he M–25
10	of better condition M	
12	temper M–25	tempers 30
16	absolutely 23	positively M–22 25 30
39· 9	that 30	which M–25
18	on such an occasion, objects 30	objects, on such an occasion, 18–25
27	scorned 30	despised M–25
40· 2	on 30	upon M–25
5	looked 30	gazed M–25
18	a numerous and fluctuating body, that 23 25	which, being a numerous and fluctuating body M–22 30
27	on 30	upon M–25
38	temporary m 30	
41·29	scarce M–25	scarcely 30
36	their 21 25 30	the (for their deleted) M the 18 19 22 23
42·17	seemed M–25	appeared 30
18	appeared M 21–5	seemed 18 19 30
24	New paragraph m 30	
32	an act 23 25	
34	occasion M–19	occasions 21–30

Penguin P. L.	Authority for Adopted Reading	Rejected Reading
44·16	our 18–30	their M
28	hand M	hands 18–30
30	fact that M 18	fact 19–30
45·15	on 30	upon M–25
18	unless 30	unless when M–25
47· 1	the M	
19	gold and M	gold 18–30
48· 4	Mrs M–21 25	Miss 22 23 30
9	-gate 30	-port M–25
12	drinking m 30	taking M–25
49·11	running footman 18–30	flunkie M
17	mears 22 30	mares M–19 23 meres 21 25
20	Weel, weel-weel, weel-weel M	Weel, weel, weel-weel, weel 18–30
26	sae sune M 18	sae soon 19 as soon 21–30
32	ance M	once 18–30
50· 8	broggin 30	brogging M–25
17	had bought. . . have forgot m 30	bought. . . forget 18–25
23	o' M	of 18–30
25	an M–21 25	a 22 23 30
25	a M	
28	ower 21–30	too M–19
39	now are M–19	are now 21–30
51· 1	contigit M–30	contingit text of Horace
3–4	well be M–21 25	be well 22 23 30
22–3	is brawly" said Saddletree readily enough M	is," said Saddletree, "readily enough." 18–30
25	property as M	as properly 18–30
33	you 30	ye M–25
35	hae nae 30	have no M have nae 18–25
52· 7	puir 25 30	poor M–23
8	doun M	down 18–30
14	folks M 22 23 30	folk 18–21 25
16	wark M–25	their work 30

Penguin P. L.	Authority for Adopted Reading	Rejected Reading
52·19	fair 21–30	black M–19
22	kens M	knows 18–30
28	David Deans 21–30	Andrew Howden M Andrew Deans 18 19
30	aulder 22 23 30	elder M–21 25
31	tittie m 30	sister M–25
39–40	Saxteen hundred and ninety, chapter twenty-ane M	sixteen. . . chapter one 18–30 (*with minor variants*)
53· 8	live a week 23 25	be 18–22 30
23	you 30	ye M–25
25–7	, answered. . . curiosity m 30	
30–31	, more collectedly m 30	
31	Black-at-the-bane 18–30	Blacketburn M *deleted and replaced by* Black at the bane
32	on M 18	upon 19–30
54·12	gaun 18–30	ganging M
26	ye are that I should say sae M	ye are 18–30
35	gudewife 21–30	goodwife M–19
40	that M	if 18–30
55· 6	Puir 30	Poor M–25
6	na M–21 25	now 22 23 30
8	born 23 25	
15–16	I am sure. . . gentry murther m 30	I am sure that's the way the gentry murder M–25
16	makes M–21 25	make 22 23 30
22	puir 21 25 30	poor M–19 22 23
56· 5	at M–25	of 30
57· 2	had M 30	have 18–25
9	are M–21 30	were 23 25
58· 2	exscindere M 23–30	exscindire 18–22
4	half an hour more m 30	more time M–25
5	find 30	seek out M–25
9	intervals 23 25	some intervals M–22 30

Penguin P. L.	Authority for Adopted Reading	Rejected Reading
58·14–15	the hour. . . near m 30	he might be near the hour of shutting the gates M–25
59· 6	sent m 30	seen M–25
27	appeared 30	seemed M–25
30	avoid 30	have avoided M–25
30	lead M–19 30	head 21–5
33	appeared 30	seemed M–25
38	their M 21–5	them 18 19 30
60· 8	the multitude m 30	they M–25
10	striking 30	singular M *deleted* 18–25
15	closely m 30	
24	named 30	called M–25
25	separates m 30	divides M–25
29–30	would possess. . . purpose 30 (*developed from version in* m)	totally defeated the purpose of the rioters M–25
61· 5	draw on themselves by a valiant defence 23 25	expose themselves by a valiant defence to M–22 30
17	of doors m 30	
23	the first act of the multitude m 30	the first act 18 19 their first act 21–5
62· 6–7	authority being respected by the craftsmen, m 30	being useful M–25
19	verbal communication m 30	measures M–19 message 21–5
29	accomplish m 30	carry M–25
38	even 23 25 m 30	and even M–22
63· 1	terrified females m 30	ladies M–25
4	street M	streets 18–30
6	vehicles 30	chairs M–25
12	interrupted 23 25	thus interrupted M–22 30
28	door was m 30	doors were M–25
32	iron, studded besides with M	*omitted* 18–30, *which last seeks to mend the sense with effect; for being. . . nails, the door was so secured. . . . 71, 93 make various adjustments without restoring the* M *reading.*

Penguin P. L.	Authority for Adopted Reading	Rejected Reading
63·33	by any degree of violence, M	
34	appeared 30 71	were M 93 seemed 18–25
64·33	Tolbooth door M	Tolbooth 18–25 Tolbooth gate m 30
65· 1	attain M	obtain 18–30
9	speedily 30	soon M–25
12	ferocious faces M–25	ferocious 30
13	countenances m	groupes 18–21 groups 22–30
66·21	overawe m 30	despise and overawe M–25
67·11–13	The latter hastily fled. . . the former. . . awaited 25 93	The former hastily fled. . . the latter. . . awaited M–21 30 71 The former. . . awaited. . . the latter hastily fled. . . 22 23
25	were 30	was M–25
68·25	measured 30	gied M–19 22 23 gave 21 25
27–8	sedate though ferocious, m 30	
28–9	colouring their cruel and revengeful action with m 30	imposing upon their cruel and revengeful action M–25
38	of m 30	of their M–25
40	hidden 30	concealed M–25
69· 1	conceal M–19 30	shrowd 21 shroud 22–5
3	New paragraph m 30	
12	Stay then and be hanged M	Stay there, and be hanged 18–22 Stay there, then, and be hanged 23 Stay there, and be hanged, then 30
14	in female attire m 30	
17–26	Flee. . . flee. . . Flee. . . flee. . . flee. . . M–19 30	Fly throughout 21–5

Penguin P. L.	Authority for Adopted Reading	Rejected Reading
69·19	all 22–30	a' M–19
19	you 21 25 30	ye M–19 22 23
24	own M 21–30	ain 18–19
26	then, 30	after M–25
70·13	the judges' m 30	his M–25
14	for m 30	for your M–25
22	harm 30	skaith M–19 violence 21–5
26	work 21 23 25 30	wark M–19 22
29	shall M 30	should 18–25
29	so 21–30	sae M–19
71· 9	answered 30	said M–25
11	for repentance 23 25	
17	were 23 30	
20	work, far. . . occasion, seemed 23 25	work were so far. . . occasion, that they seemed M–22 30
28	this M–21 25 30	the 22 23
72· 2	got m	kept 18–30
4	object 21–5	purpose M–19 30
25	him M	
73· 9–10	, and could. . . partisans m 30	
12	New paragraph m 30	
12	the fugitive m 30	he M–25
24	the main-gate m 30	one of the leaves of the main-gate M–25
25	beyond m 30	from beyond M–25
74· 6	still hung m 30	remained M–25
8	which were found m 30	and which remained M–25
27	On 30	Upon M–25
75· 8	path m 30	walk M–25
12	now M deleted	
15	islets	isles 18–30
18	picturesque 30	varied and picturesque M–25
20	objects 21 22 25 30	subjects M–19 23
27	near 30	nearer M–23

Penguin P. L.	Authority for Adopted Reading	Rejected Reading
75· n.		*earlier forms*: A beautiful and solid pathway has now been formed round (22, around) these romantic rocks.—1820. (21, 22, 25). The path has of late been completely repaired. (23)
76·19	how 30	by what M–25
22	the 30	that M–25
33	appeared m 30	appear 18–25
40	immediately M–22 25 30	*omitted* 23
77· 2	On 30	Upon M–25
6	be likely ultimately to m 30	ultimately M–25
8	unreverently M	irreverently 18–30
37	independency 30	independence M–25
78· 7	slight 23 25	small M–22 30
19	wedded 30	married M–23
79· 3	may be supposed to entertain 23 25	entertains M–22 30
23	plenishing m 30	
39	they m 30	both M–25
80·16	the following 30	these M–25
19	neibours M	neighbours 18–30
23	you M 23	ye 18–22 25 30
24	Master M	Mr 18 19 22 23 30 Maister 21 25
26	that's but M	that 18–30
81·21	intractable M 21 23–30	untractable 18 19 22
33	Deans M–19	Deanses 21–30
36	his M	her 18–30
36	kind o' 30	
82· 1	drift M	drifts 18–30
20	" replied Dumbiedikes, " 30	replied penitent or impenitent m
33	now of m 30	now M–25
83· 3–4	Southron. . . Southron M	southern. . . southern 18–30

Penguin P. L.	*Authority for Adopted Reading*	*Rejected Reading*
83·10	prepossessions M	professions 18–30
12	and at length m 30	
18	old m 30	
22	her m 30	it was possible her M–25
85·27	fortitude m 30	firmness M–25
34	too m 30	over- M–25
86· 8	little 30	little round M–25
18	lesson M 18	lessons 19–30
20	in that m 30	that M–25
88· 3	possessed m 30	had M–25
13	himself a man M 30	a man himself 18–25
13	Dumbiedikes 30	he M–22
28	ganging M m 30	gaun 18–25
28	he was nae 23	nae M–22 25 30
35	by 30	as M–25
90·27	was little remarked, owing to m 30	less marked from M–25
31–3	On these. . . both. m 30	
39	or other of the m 30	or two M–21 23 25 of our 22
91·35	Deans. . . Davie 30	Davie. . . Deans M–25
19	upon M 19–30	on 18
26	puir 22–5	poor M–21 30
92· 2	in respect of fitting discharge of our duty m 30	
11	aside M–22 25 30	*omitted* 23
14	o' M	of 18–30
27–8	answered the submissive Judith. m 30	
32	said David with solemnity m 30	
34	tract M–22 25	track 23 30
40	enable M	enables 18–30
93· 1	moved M	
12	like M–25	likely 30
13	man m 30	gentleman M–25
94·17	said the sufferer m 30	

Penguin P. L.	Authority for Adopted Reading	Rejected Reading
94·18	well be M	well be said 18–21 25 30 be well said 22 23
28	rapt M	wrapt 18–30
95· 6	then nearly M	nearly 18–25 about 30
39	a M	the 18–30
96·35	principle M	principles 18–30
100·13	and 30	
15	their M 18	her M deleted 19–30
101·19	our 21–30	my M–19
23	prudent 30	prudential M–25
102· 4	her M	the 18–30
11	Effie, lassie 21–5	Effie M–19 30
12	tak M	take 18–30
32	brutish M	brutal 18–30
103·18	diversion M	division 18–30
104·19	commences 30	commenced M–25
105· 8	as he was m 30	
8	as one really endowed with m 30	as possessed M as endowed with 18–25
22	from 30	with M–25
29	departure 30	removal M–25
106· 1	and M–25	omitted 30
3	During the first few weeks 30	The first week or two M–25
29–30	a considerable time 30	about a deleted two months M several months 18–25
108· 4	pains M–19	pain 21–5 trouble 30
7	returned M 18	had returned 19–30
109·14	old 21 25 30	own old M–19 22 23
26	God. . . man M	man. . . God 18–30
110·10	on 30	upon M–25
111· 2	divided by faction m 30	
37	and strong M	
112· 2	look 30	voice M–25
8	Sir, M	

Penguin P. L.	Authority for Adopted Reading	Rejected Reading
112·21	is 23	are M–22 25 30
114· 3	plan of M	
4	spectral appearances M	spectres 18–30
12–13	a man brave. . . constitution m 30	a stout-hearted man M–25
115· 4	imperious 30	peremptory M–25
25	handsome but m 30	whose regular beauty were M whose perfect beauty was 18–25
35	ruined 30	
37	was 93	were M–71
116· 1	spot 21–5	place M–19 30
117·16	reputation 30	character M–25
16	amongst M–19	among 21–30
17	of 18–30	come of M
118· 2	sufferer 21–5	old man M–19 30
3	had yet m 30	
5	an m 30	had an M–25
7	inflict m 30	resolve M–25
34–5	angels. . . cause of a 18–30	M *here reads*: angels afore I was fifteen when I was found worthy to be scourged by the same bloody hands that quarterd the dear body of James Renwick and cut off those hands that were the first to raise up the down-fallen banner of the testimony – and how I was even preferd to stand in the pillory at the Canongate cross for twa hours during a cauld nor-east blast and might hae been hangit by the neck had I been twa years elder for the cause of a
35	deserted M	national 18–30

Penguin P. L.	Authority for Adopted Reading	Rejected Reading
119·14	reverend M	revered 18–30
120·24	were M 30	was 18–25
36	restored M	resolved 18–30
121· 2	puir M (replacing poor deleted)	poor 18–30
4	mysell M	myself 18–30
27	on 30	on the M–25
29	must 30	maun M–25
34	cannot 22 23 30	canna M–21 25
37	yoursell 21–5	yourself M–19 30
122· 1	doun M	down 18–30
4	you M 23 25 30	ye 18–22
33	go M	be 18–30
123· 5	My God M–25	Mercy 30
6	did 30	could M–25
7	next M	
20	propose M 22 23	purpose 18–21 25 30
125· 4	whilk is m 30	that's M–25
27	hand. . . was. . . hand M	hands. . . was. . . hands 18 19 hands. . . were. . . hands 21–30
126· 3	blue-bottle flees m 30	blue-bottles M–25
16	losses M–22 25	loses 23 30
23	turns M	terms 18–30
127· 2	bows m	
34–5	and wearing m sky-blue scarlet pair of breeches m	M–25 have only lying-dogs, without having about him ane—— and 30, 71, 93 misplace and partly omit the m material to read lying-dogs, and wearing a scarlet pair of breeches, without having
39	whereas 71 93	where M–30
128·15	just 21–5	
24	had held M 18	held 21–30
33	wisdom, and a M 25	wisdom, and 18–23 30

Penguin P. L.	Authority for Adopted Reading	Rejected Reading
128·38	to M 30	
129·25	Whulliewhaw M	Whilliewhaw 18–30
36	end M	ends 18–30
130· 1	sae muckle as 21–5	
132· 2	whillywhaing 30	whullying M whillying 18–25
36	directly." 18–30	directly—ocior ventis—ocior Euro—" M *and a fragment of proof (at Yale) on which the Latin is marked for deletion*
134·30	was 23–5	were M–22 30
135· 1	uhu M	uhm 18–30
136· 6	even *deleted* recollection even M	even recollection 18–30
25	proceeding M	proceedings 18–30
137·36	you M 19 23 30	ye 18
138· 9	peril 30	danger M–25
27	which such precaution, if used in time, m 30	which if, used in time such caution M which, if used in time, such precaution 18–25
139·13	he had ever M 30	ever he had 18–25
17	and m 30	more M–25
18	more m 30	
29	wanted only M	wanted 18–25 only wanted m 30
35	one 30	ane M–25
140·14	replied the accused m 30	
14	Troth 18–30	Odd M
15	aye M	
16	ae M	a 18–30
25	braw 30	brave 18–25
141·10–11	from you 21–5	
24	pit 18	put M 19–30
141·n.	*thus* M–25	30 *gathers note to end of chapter and reads* Lockman *for* Hangman *in first line.*

Penguin P. L.	Authority for Adopted Reading	Rejected Reading
142· 4	observation 25 30	remark M–23
11	business 18–30	M *ends the speech here and goes on*: The hint was followed and James Ratcliffe the greatest thief and house-breaker in Scotland was selected upon the faith of an ancient proverb I suppose to be intrusted with the guard of other delinquents He exercized the trust which was at first confided to him under suspicious and jealous precautions with so much vigilance. . .

 M *then continues as a first draft of pp. 512–13 below, from* vigilance *to* over a bottle *including the footnote. The transferred passage originally stood immediately after the closing words of the first sheet of 1818, vol. 2, as finally printed, and must have been cut during the shift of Chapter 13 from Volume 1 to Volume 2, a move apparently settled before the composition of Chapter 16, in which Ratcliffe's fate is still undecided. Late in Chapter 19, at p. 207 below, M shows a first attempt at reintroducing the passage.* |
143·24	his M	her 18–30
144· 4	which 23	who M–22 25 30
30		if *ends leaf 98 of M and the following leaf is missing. On the verso of 98 appear in Scott's hand in reversed*

Penguin P. L.	Authority for Adopted Reading	Rejected Reading
		image, transferred from the lost leaf, the words 'of Vol. I', apparently marking the originally intended end of the volume.
146·24	irretrievable 18–30	irremediable M
147·29	the m 30	and the M–25
39	trifling m 30	little trifling M–25
148·24	this 30	with this M–25
28	myself m 30	me M–25
149·12	usual M	
13	sadness of heart, and the bitter m 30	bitterness, and the M–25
13	Merah M–30 93	Marah 71 and Bible
30	ordinary 30	usual M–25
36	must, and pass 1994	must and pass M must and do pass, 18–30
38–9	evening. . . night. . . 30	evening. . . evening. . . M–21 day. . . evening 23 25
40	this M	the 18–30
150· 7	growth 30	flood M–25
30	observed m 30	known M–25
38	expressed M–19 30	exhibited 21–5
151·39	is 21–5	are M–19 30
153· 9	their party were 30	
14–15	the Pandæmonium of Richard Bovet, Gentleman m 30	Baxter's World of Spirits M–25
154·17	tow 21–5	rope M–19 30
155·23	city 30	capital M–25
37	in M	on 18–30
156·12	propose M 23	purpose 18–22 25 30
157·35	said the unmoved ruffian m 30	
158·23	wrongs M 18	wrong 19–30
28	I M	I am 18–30
28	indeed 30	enough M–25

Penguin P. L.	Authority for Adopted Reading	Rejected Reading
159·33	called—the M	call it—any other 18–30
160· 8	till now 23 25	
9	whatever M 30	whatsoever 18–25
161·24	highest 30	very highest M–25
163· 6	fit to M–25 *and texts of Hamlet*	to fit 30
18	was once M	was 18–25 were 30
20	Porteous M	Porteous's 18–30
29	an' it sae be M	an' if sae be 18–30
30	ye'll. . . man 18–30 *(apparently added in proof to supply an imagined need for a main clause, arising from the misreading of M's conditional an' as standing for connective and)*	
164· 5	'folks M	folk 18–30
18	are nae M–25	arena a 30
21	in M	into 18–30
30	a' M	
165·20	takes 30	taking 18–25
35	not M	
166· 3	a' 30	we a' M–25
167· 5	said the procurator m 30	
6–7	to the point—the point, you M	to the point, you 18–30
12	gaun 21–5	going M–19 30
37	said the prisoner m 30	
169·13	song M	a song 18–30
17	squeaking m 30	rinning M running 18–25
170·39	prate m	pate M–30
171· 1	up M	
12	said Madge indignantly M	replied the fair one m 30
172·17	measure M	measures 18–30
173·22	his M–25	its m 30
175·29–30	said the man of law m 30	
176· 7	him M	he 18–30

Penguin P. L.	Authority for Adopted Reading	Rejected Reading
176·34	will M	that will 18–30
38	ane M	
177·10	best M–25	the best 30
39	single m 30	
178· 6	propensity 19–30	propensities M 18
179· 1	hae 30	have M–25
19	ae M	some 18–30
20	's M	
23	harns M	brains 18–30
36	jee M	gae 18–30
36–7	She'll take her ain time 23 25	
38	said Sharpitlaw 30	
180· 3	fixing 30	fixed M–25
22	is nae M	isna 18–30
37	this M	
181· 1	na M	not 18–30
12	yelling m 30	
182·18	kepp 18 19 30	kep at M
		keep 21–5
24	all the M	
183· 5	here our M 30	her own 18–25
6	chapter 15 1994	II 18 (of Volume 2). The number is repeatedly amended in M, and varies with the division of volumes in each of 19–30. See n. 30 to Introduction, pp. xlix†l.
7	watchd M	waited 18–30
11	object 21–5	cause M–19 30
18	said Sharpitlaw 30	
30	object 30	objects M–25
184·19	get hold of 30	seize M–25
185·28	purchased M	her purchased 18–30
30	thou M	that thou 18–30
38	continuance M	countenance 18–30
186·13	himself know 30	know himself M–25
38	one woman 30	

Penguin P. L.	Authority for Adopted Reading	Rejected Reading
186·38	dark 18–22 30	?durk ?dark M dirk 23 25
187·10	chanced to be the same 18–30	was a different and more intelligent person than him M
17	in M	in an 18–30
188·16	quotations M	quotation 18–30
18	discern M	discover 18–30
28	become M	
32	Mr Fairscrieve m	
32	replied the Baillie m 30	
38	on and flourish in 1994	(two illegible words) in M on and flourish wi/with 18–30
189·10	asked 30	said M–25
14	some M	
32	apprehend M–21 25	comprehend 22 23 understand m 30
39–40	extremely... apparel m 30 (looks m, look 30)	
190· 1	New paragraph m	
1	said Bailie Middleburgh, m 30	
24	gude 30	good M–25
28	talents 18–30	commandments M
36	deevil 21–5	
36	folks M	folk 18–30
191· 9	beggar 1994 (cf. p. 305)	
11	Scots M	Scotch 18–30
17	angry M	
192·31–2	anes... anes M	ance... ance 18–30
193·13	suld na M	shouldna 18–30
14	curtsey, when the 30	curtesy—the M curtsey. The 18–25
25	sung M	and sung 18–30
194·16	was 25	were M–23 30
24	on 30	upon M–25
32	even 23	even the M–22 25 30

Penguin P. L.	Authority for Adopted Reading	Rejected Reading
194.36–7	belonged. . . pertained 30	belonged. . . belonged M–19
		appertained. . . belonged 21–5
195. 9–10	she had been many weeks imprisoned 30	many weeks(') confinement M–25
15	those 23–30	these 18–22 (M doubtful)
196.11	at M–25	of 30
197.23	trader M 21–30	traitor 18–19
24	bairn M	a bairn 18–30
28	share 25	portion M–23 30
198. 7	lang M	alang 18–30
22	wad 30	would M–25
199. 4	was 23 25 30	
6	tak M–25	take 30
27	I 30	and M–25
36	rigg M	ridge 18–30
200.15	overstrained M	constrained 18–30
201. 3	was held 25	took place M–23 30
12	temper M	tempers 18–30
20	those 30	these 18–25 (M doubtful)
26	pontages M 71 93	postages 18–30
204.30	will (from 22). . . can m	will. . . will M–25
		shall. . . can 30
31	hesitation m 30	scruples M–22 25
		scruple 23
207.18	Jeanie's m 30	her M–25
30	fit M	
30	delinquents M–30	M adds And here we may as well insert what we have to add concerning the personal history of this notorious character. He exercized/as in printed papers also take in the Note./ The last twelve words are struck through: cf. textual note on 142.11 above.
208. 8	at times m 30	

Penguin P. L.	Authority for Adopted Reading	Rejected Reading
208·13	or 30	and M–25
209·32	again M	
33	gude M 18	good 19–30
210·31	am his bairn nae langer m 30	am na (amna) his bairn langer M–25
211·26–7	trod them a' to pieces 30	dung them a' to pieces M trod them a' pieces 18–25
38	Jeanie M	
212· 7	George 18–30	Robertson M
25	meikle M	muckle 18–30
34	were M	are 18–30
35	mazed M	amazed 18–30
	whare 18–25	where M 30
213· 8	at M–25	of 30
31	at M–25	wi' 30
214· 1	it as 30	it at the first as M–25
16	daured 30	dared M–25
30	tittie M	sister 18–30
215· 5	when 30	that when M–25
8–9	—Hyssop's Fables m 30	fables M fabbs 18–25
22	na M–25	no 30
216· 1	I had 18–30	she had M
21	Ratcliffe m 30	he M–25
28	pu'pit M 25 30	pulpit 18–23
218·11	hardship M	hardships 18–30
35	a slight m 30	something like a M–25
35	being m 30	as if M–25
219·28	the crowd m 30	they M–25
220·30	our portion M	portion 18–30
221· 8	inter apices juris m 30	
14	more m 30	much more M–25
15	the 30	her M–25
222·18	sequestrating M 23 25	sequestering 18 30
18	, as in cases of bankruptcy m 30	
21	sequestrated M 23 25	sequestered 18 30

Penguin P. L.	Authority for Adopted Reading	Rejected Reading
222·26	the 21–30	their M–19
225· 1	an M 25	
9	whatever 30	whatsoever M–25
19	presiding Judge m 30	Court M–25
31		m *marks an insertion between the sentences but gives no text*
226·12	Mr Fairbrother, m 30	
14–21	He began. . . statute. 30 *revised in proof from* m	
227· 5	or a 18–30	and M
228· 2	that a young woman in such a situation 1994	that in such an emergency she M
		that in such an emergency a young woman, in such a situation, 18–30
13	in 30	to M–25
229·17	circumstance M 18	circumstances 19–30
230·12	those M 21–30	these 18 19
23	deserted M	deceived 18–30
231· 3–4	And when puir Effie. . . pleading! M	
232·18	In the event of these Tales ever finding 30	In case these Tales should ever find M–25
22	at M–25	of 30
233· 8	nevertheless 30	
234·20	he being under trouble at the time, m 30	
12	writing 23 25	word of mouth M–22 30
27	Declares 25	Declared M–23 30
37	now conceals. . . abode? m 30	conceals. . . abode now? M–25
235· 6	for M	
236·11	Dandie m 30	Andie M–25
26	(called for a nickname Handie Dandie) m 30	
34	or M–25	nor 30
237·27	poor prisoner 30	prisoner at the bar M–25

Penguin P. L.	Authority for Adopted Reading	Rejected Reading
237·37	appropriate M 23	appropriated 18–22 25 30
238·15	those of M	
25	some M	
25	character M	characters 18–30
26	some M	
26–7	deep and devout 30	severe M the most devout 18–25
29	same time M 19–30	same 18
31	reverent M 21–30	reverend 18–19
239·20	Widow Tekoah M–25	Widow of Tekoah 30
240· 1	think M–21	thinks 22–30
241·10	forward 30	forwards M–25
24	conducted 30	transported M–25
242·38	run M–22 30	ran 23
40	supposed crime m 30	murder M–25
243· 6	agony which M	agony, and which 18–30
36	jurors M	jury 18–30
244·12	case 21–30	situation M–19
246·15	dispersed 23	dispersed themselves M–22 25 30
17	Mr Fairbrother m 30	of Fairbrother M Fairbrother 18–25
31	corporeal M 21–5 71	corporal 18 19 30 93
33	Thus m 30	So M–25
247·14	clergymen M 25 71	clergyman 18–23 30 93
20	moment M	moments 18–30
23	silver m 30	
248·10	for 30	
249· 4	is na a hizzy M	isna a huzzy 18–25 isna a hussy 30
5	writers-lads M	writer-lads 18–30
33	laughed scornfully M	looked very scornful 18–30
36	honest M	
36	care M 30	cares 18–25
39	hinders M	hinders them 18–30
40	is M	are 18–30
250· 1	wi' 19–30	with M 18

Penguin P. L.	Authority for Adopted Reading	Rejected Reading
250· 2	ever M	
251· 8	elocution M	elevation 18–30
15	Time M	The time 18–30
30	gaun 18–30	ganging M
35	confused M m 30	confeised 18–25
252· 1	gaen M	gane 18–30
253· 2,4	*Isab. Lucio.* 30	
254·36	tak M 71	take 18–30 93
255·12	they M	them 18–30
16	said poor Effie m 30	
256· 2	the M	in 18–30
8	will win 30	shall win M–25
17	keepit company wi' 18–30	keepit wi' M
257·22–3	He then. . . depart. M	
33	female 23 25	
258· 3	affairs 30	concerns M–25
34	a barefooted traveller 18–30	barefooted travelling M
259· 7	could 30	should M–25
20	knew 30 93	felt M–25 71
260·10	chapter 18–30	chapter (*deleted*) Volume. Here the Vol. may end. (*deleted*) M
261·15	of Dumbiedikes 23 25	
16	had vailed its splendour 1994	had vailed of its splendour M
		had been veiled of its splendour 18–30 (vailed 21 23–30)
21	depth from back to front 30	breadth M–25
25	had 21 23–30	having M–19 22
30	an entrance-door 23 25	a door M–22 30
262· 1	removed M 23 25	renewed 18–22 30
10	fields 30	land M–25
15	sluttish 23 25	
22	not possessed 23 25	no person M–22 30
37	had been m 30	were M–25
39	hung M	were 18–30

Penguin P. L.	Authority for Adopted Reading	Rejected Reading
263·11	and 23 25	as M–22 30
12	his lair 23 25	
19	this castle 21–30	the castle 18 19
264· 6	administration 30	place of administration 18–22
		post of administration 23 25
29	scouping 18–30	scraughing M
35	an M	
265· 6	ae M–22 25 30	a 23
6–7	sister. . . hangit M	sister's . . . hanged 18–30
33	bed M	his bed 18–30
35	integuments 30	garments 18–25
266· 1	fist M–25	fists 30
267· 7	o' M 30	of 18–25
17	gaun 18–30	ganging M
37	gaun 18–30	ganging M
39	aye M	
268· 9	complacence M–25	complacency 30
12	Leddy 21 25 30	Lady M–19 22 23
26	hae 23 30	
28	exclaimed the poor Laird m 30	
35	their ends their lane M	their ends, their 18–25
		their ends 30
269·40	in M	in an 18–30
270·16	Laird m 30	
18	body m 30	ane M–25
271· 6	had 30	has M–25
272·19–20	when she gave an account of her pilgrimage m 30	
21	shewn M	shewed 18–21 23 25
		showed 22 30
25	Meribah M 23 30 and Bible	Mirebah 18–22 25
27	puir 22 30	poor M–21 23 25
29	sair 21 25	
273· 1–2	of Libberton m 30	
18	unacquainted m 30	inconsistent M–25

Penguin P. L.	Authority for Adopted Reading	Rejected Reading
274·18	teacher m 30	
24	past 30 93	over M–25 71
29	his 30	his own M–25
275·32	puir 23	
276· 5	generally 30	sometimes M–25
33	pursuer M 18 21 25	prisoner 19 22 23 petitioner 30
277· 1	on M	or 18–30
8	from 30	out of M–25
27	the room M	a room 18–30
278·35–6	at. . . at. . . M–25	of. . . of. . . 30
279· 5	ca's M–23	ca' 30
23	not clergymen, but m 30	
26	daur 30	dare M–25
39	turn M	
280·29	even 30	
39	tak 30	take M–23
281· 7	will M–25	shall 30
9	extenuated M	extended 18–30
33	winna M	maunna 18–30
39	sight M 30	light 18–25
282·15	many M	the 18–30
21	with 30	
283·10	then 30	
28	sarcasms M	sarcasm 18–30
32	checqued 18–22 30	checked M che(c)quered 23 25
284· 3	*text continuous* M 30	*New paragraph* 18–25
14	talk m 30	speak M–25
17	and most M	and 18–30
24	o' single 1994	of single M o' a single 18–30
25	canst have o' th' M	can have on the 18–30
38–9	It makes. . . to reflect M	I make my present pilgrimage more heavy and burthensome, through the sad occasion to reflect 18–30

Penguin P. L.	Authority for Adopted Reading	Rejected Reading
285· 2	without the 30	without M–25
30	a 30	half ane M–25
37	weel M 30	well 18–25
37	bides M	lives 18–30
286·29	Gordan M–25	Jordan 30
287· 4	laugh M–21 23 25	law 22
		lauch m
		m *note* Lauch-Law
		mistakenly included in text
		of 30 *as* land-law
15–16	though. . . spelling 30	
28	himsell M 22	himself 18–21 23–30
288·30	roguish m 30	dangerous M–25
36	or 30	and M–25
289· 4	thy 30	thine M–25
291·14	right good M–25	good 30
16	bid M	said 18–30
292·33	tracks M–23	tracts 25 30
293· 1	good M	
22	remarkably 21 23–30	remarkable M–19 22
32	to M 21 25	to a 18 19 22 23 30
39	still occasionally be 30	be still occasionally M–25
294· 3	we'll M	we will 18–25 71
		we may 30 93
10	the —— m	 18–30
33–5	In fact, it was, with . . . meritorious 18–30	?She ?facd it with. . . engaged and her. . . meritorious M
295·27	said Jeanie M	
29	the 30	
296·22	these M 30	those 18–25
31	like M	like a 18–30
40	but M	but not 18–30
297·10	oatmeal M	ointment 18–30
15	deep 30	
298·38	child six years old 18–25	child of six years old M
		six years old child 30

Penguin P. L.	Authority for Adopted Reading	Rejected Reading
299· 2	suppliant M	suppliant 18–30
300· 6	e'en 30	
7	too 30	
7	and M	an' 18–30
16	naig 30	nag M–25
33	are 19–30	
39	brawlies M–25	brawlie 30
304·28	bilked M	baulked 18–30
305·16	eye M	eyes 18–30
18–19	—Ha! ha! ha! m 30	
21	replied the hag m 30	
306·30	but 30	and M–25
307· 9	lee 30	lie M–25
39	rat ye 18–25	hang ye M rat me 30
308·28	an M	
35	eneugh 23 30	enough M–22 25
309·34	hands M	head 18–30
35	at 18–25	upon M on 30
310·23–5	a variegated. . . the Thorn 30 93	a (little M only) hillock of moss, such as the poet of Grasmere has described in the motto to our chapter M 18–22 a hillock of moss. 23 25 . . . described. So soon. . . 71
27	ground 25	spot M–23 30
40	gratitude M–25	grateful 30
311·21	impression 30	impression in her favour M–25
23	a' M–25	all 30
28	lip M–25	lips 30
313·20	ye M–25 71	you 30 93
22	belanged 18–25	belonged 30
314·13	auld M–25	old 30
16	wad hae 18–25	would have M 30

Penguin P. L.	Authority for Adopted Reading	Rejected Reading
314·16	o' 22 30	of M–21 23 25
20	since 30	yet M–25
315·19	examination M	examinations 18–30
30	ye 18–25	you M 30
316· 5	folk M 30	folks 18–25
24	village 30	village or hamlet M–25
317·28	said M 21 25	had said 18 19 22 23 30
318· 9	straight lines, one M	direct lines 18–30
34	by the 19–30	by M 18
321·19	took M	looked 18–30
322·39	seen 30	witnessed M–25
323· 6	prudent m 30	sensible M–25
14	undeviating 30	composed M–25
17	fast 30	
29	although 30	notwithstanding M–25
31	anxious air 30	wild appearance M–25
34	aspect 23	look M–22 25 30
325·8	waste 18–30	world M
12	new 19–30	
27	thysell 30	thyself M–25
32	doest M–25	dost 30
33	nittle M	mettle 18–30
326· 2	canna M–25	cannot 30
4	farther 30	
33	exhibited 21 25 30	displayed M–19 22 23
327· 8	her 30	us M–25
37	sarvice M 22	service 18–21 23–30
328·33	the afternoon service was over 30 93	after the afternoon service M–22 25 71 the afternoon service 23
329·22	Thomas 30	Mr Thomas M–25
26	muther 18–25	mother M 30
329· n.	intimate 30	express M–19 22 23 indicate 21 25
329· n.	clever 21 m 30	witty M–19 22–5
330· 1	sarvice M–25	service 30
6	behounched M	bechounched 18–30

Penguin P. L.	Authority for Adopted Reading	Rejected Reading
331· 3	and in 30	in M–25
4	add, M 23 30	add, in 18–22 25
15	Scots M–19 22 23 71	Scotch 21 25 30 93
333·26	only M	
29	although 19–30	though 18
334·24	spoiled M–25	soiled 30
36	Leicestershire 18	Leistershire M Leicester 19–30
335· 2	using M	use 18–30
8	Scotchwomen 21 25 30	Scotswomen M–19 22 23
10	any M 19–30	ony 18
16	pain M 25 30	pains 18–23
336·15	would fain not name 94	would faint not name M would faint did I name 18–25 should faint did I name 30
337·11	cried 30	said M–25
24	fatal detail of the 23	fatal account of the M–22 25 account of the fatal 30
338·31	tedious 21 25	heavy M–19 22 23 30
339·30	fathom M–25	fathoms 30
39	proceeded 30	went on M–25
340·15	wild 21 25	strange M–19 22 23 30
36	steerd M	stood 18–30
341· 8–9	of a sum. . . pocket-book m 30	
342· 5	firm M	fine 18–30
9–10	a considerable sum of m 30	some M–25
10	to be able 30	
28	Fife. . . myself in m 30	
30	that m 30	Wilson's M–25
30–31	find security for m 30	hide M–25
34	hardship M–25 71	hardships 30 93
39–40	and. . . require m 30, adopting whatever m against whenever 30 but joined 30 against followed m	

Penguin P. L.	Authority for Adopted Reading	Rejected Reading
343·18	saith the Lord M	
26	the other 30 m	other M–25
345·22	you M 18	ye 19–30
346·30–32	Prime. . . passions m 30 *revising* gratifying. . . gratifying m	
32	village girl 30	villager M–25
40	miserable 30	
347· 1	this M 21 25	the 18 19 22 23 30
348· 8	he said 30	
27	all M	all that 18–30
349·14–15	him. Then 30	him, and then M–25
17	persons 30 93	those M–25 71
350·37	nor 23 25 30	or M–22
39	at M–25	to 30
352·28	kindness 18–30	courtesy M
353·27	Pharpar *Bible*	Pharphar M–30
354·23	Tummas M 30	Thomas 18–25
36	on 30	along M–23
355·22	on M 18	to 19–30
356·27	procedure 30	measures M–25
29–30	Scottish clergy, contrary to. . . duty, 30	clergy M–25 m *marks with 'x'*
31	offered M–30	*partly deleted* m
357·21	and 30	and of M–25
37	sum M	sum up 18–30
39	disposal. George M	disposal, in consequence of which management, George 18–30 (*variously punctuated*)
362·11	Scotsman M 30	Scotchman 18–25
26–7	because. . . connected both with 23	both because. . . connected with M–22 25 30
364· 1, 13, 29	Scots M–25	Scotch 30
365·30	his 30	the M–25
31	and the poor man's friend M	
32	nae name M	nane 18–30

Penguin P. L.	Authority for Adopted Reading	Rejected Reading
365·32	like yours M–19 22 23 30	like you 21 25
36	southerns M–25	southrons 30
39	frae M 18	from 19–30
366· 4	maistpartly M	maist partly 18–30
14	Barebone's M 30	Barebones's 18–25
36	well-wisher M–19 23	weel-wisher 21 22 25 30
369· 5	of the 30	of M–25
370·16	saxpennies worth M	six pennies worth 18–25 sixpennies worth 30
32–33	and if. . . a dozen M	and if there's a Scotsman, as there may be three or half a dozen 18–30
371·18	reverent 21 25 30	reverend M–19 22 23
372· 3	up M	
33	if 30	
373· 3	going into any explanation whatever 30	entering into any explanation M–25
6	proceeded 30	driven M–25
28	seldom 30	never 18 19 22 23 only once 21 so seldom 25
374· 7	lairds leddies M	lairds and leddies 19–30
16	na M–21 25	nae 22 23 no 30
375· 6	taste m 30	genius M–25
9	and m 30	yet M–25
25	had M 18	
26	glimpse 30	glance M–25
377·19	George II., her 23 25	Her M–22 30
28	such as 30	those who M–25
378·33	least expected 21 25 30	most unexpected M least unexpected 18 19 22 23
36	power 30	means M–25
379·13	maintained m	had M–30
16	though somewhat unreasonably, m 30	

Penguin P. L.	Authority for Adopted Reading	Rejected Reading
379·25	gardens *struck out in* m *but not replaced*	
29–30	by the lady. . . her person m 30	
381·17	next m 30	then M–25
382· 5	and M	and on 18–30
384·22	she M	eke 18–30
31	besides M–25	beside 30
385·19	hit m 30	killed M–25
28	what M–25	that 30
386·15	hitherto 23 25	
27	attach itself only M	only attach itself 18–30
387·26	high M	light 18–30
390·29	ower 22 30	over M–21 23 25
391·19	if 23 30	
39	gratulation 30	congratulation M–25
39	thought particular. . .cheese that. . .is as M	thought (accounted 23 25) so particular. . .cheese, that. . .it as 18–30
392· 2	that is 30	or M–25
22	of M–25	for 30
29	use in M	use of 18–30
394· 1	understand 23 25	explain M–22 30
12	say m	speak M–30
396· 2	sent letters to M–30	taught letters for *texts of Pope*
29	bring back m	redeem M–30
397· 1	blood M	
4	hath M–25	has 30
31	had M 18	hae 19–30
31	there M 22–5	their 18–21 30
39	in company m	
398· 3	ceevil m	civil 18–30
18	keppit M	keepit 18–30
35	kend M m	had 18–22 30 had kenn'd 23 25
399· 1	safely m	

Penguin P. L	Authority for Adopted Reading	Rejected Reading
399· 4	to my native land m	
5	hame m	
400· n.	*footnote* m 93	
401· 1	MacCallanmore M m	MacCallummore 18–30
402·17	skipper m	sailor M–22 30 mariner 23 25
403· 4	here M	
30	lassie m	thing 18–30
403· n.	*note* 93 *slightly revising* m 71	
404· 1	but M	
406· 9	hae M–25	've 30
23	around M–25	round 30
407·12	civility 30	attention M–25
13	comfort 30	ease M–25
408· 2	horses 30	horses which M–25
4	neighbourhood 21 25 30	vicinity M–19 22 23
14	Now. . .sight! 21 25	
31	the m	these 18–30
32	those M 19–30	these 18
409·23	fair 30	fresh M–25
25	Cumbrian brooks as m	
410· 1	replied a third peasant m	
3	reckan M–30	?traiking m
3	twomont M–19 22 23	towmont 21 25 30
411·28	she. . . innocent *ends Jeanie's speech in* M, *but begins Archibald's in* 18–93	
412·20	incident M 18	accident 19–30
413·31	symptom M	symptoms 18–30
414·16	therefore M 18	
20	moved 30	affected M–25
415·24	The nurse's prophecy proved 30	Her first prophecy was M–25
416·24	had 30	made M–25
417· 9–10	transactions M	transaction 18–30

Penguin P. L.	Authority for Adopted Reading	Rejected Reading
417·27	that M 21 25 30	
39	her, M	him 18–30
418·33	her M 19–30	his 18
419·19	especial 21 25	particular M–19 22 23 30
420·18	reside m 30	live M–25
40	by M 18	
423·15	naked——knees M	naked knees 18–30
424· 4	blest M 18 21 25	best 19 22 23 30 *and texts of Fletcher*
24	Argyllshire 93	Ayrshire M–71
425· 1	the last M	last 18–30
1	approached 30	was approaching M–25
24	beg M	try to 18–30
36	eager 30	
426· 2	for having delivered 23	had delivered M–22 30 for delivering 25
10	replied her father m 30	
427·31	amang 30	among M–25
38	pettled m	petted 30
429· 1	boggled M	haggled 18–30
5	younger M	youngest 18–30
430· 4	gude 30	good M–25
8	for 30	to M–25
431·25	elder M–25	eldest 30
432·14	of what nature m 30	what M–25
22	steadily m 30	
28	David M 21 22 25	Davie 18 19 23 30
40	manners M–25	manner 30
433·36	by his Grace 21 25	
37	Obligations to m 30	
434· 8	(David) 30	
11	may be m 30	was M–25
435·15	cure M (*uncertain, replacing* call *deleted*) 21–5	care 18–19 30
21–2	acknowledge. . . homologate m 30	acknowledged. . . homologated M–25

Penguin P. L.	Authority for Adopted Reading	Rejected Reading
435·37	of discipline m 30	
436· 2	the said incumbent m 30	he M–25
437·22	made known. . . with 30	acquainted. . . at M 18–25
24	and 30	
31	he continued 30	
438·33	answered the monitor m 30	
38	from behind which he may m 30	to M–25
439· 7	wisher m 30	wishers M–25
9	in M	on 18–30
10	rather than renunce m 30	against M–25
17	rute 18	root M 19–30
18	to you *follows* bare m 30, *but* time 18–25	
28	the Second m 30	
440·20	narrative 30	narration M–25
35	his young friend m 30	he M–25
441· 1	finished 23 m 30	concluded M–22 25
10	more m 30	much more M–25
14	they afford 21 23 25	he affords M–19 22 30
16	in point of fact m 30	
33	Knocktarlitie 18–30	Kilmun M
443·17	endeavoured to make m 30	made M–25
19	reversed 23 25 30	revenged 18–22
33	the parties 30	
444·29	intimation m 30	
32	Musselburgh 21 23–30	Dalkeith M–19 22
33	surrounded by many villas m 30	and surrounded by many small villas M–19 22 23 and surrounded by neat villas 21 25
445· 2	the m 30	that M–25
10	much M	
11	sister M 22 23	her sister 18–21 25 30
20	than m 30	as M–25
34	deserved M	desired 18–30

Penguin P. L.	Authority for Adopted Reading	Rejected Reading
445·36	the M	her 18–30
38	warldly m 30	
446·16	the couple m 30	they M–25
27	might be m 30	were M–25
28	repentance m 30	remorse M–25
28	for Jeanie 23 25	
447·12	own 30	
32	in a very consequential manner m 30	
448· 1–2	addressing Butler in further explanation, — m 30	
10	claik M	clack 18–30
20	ane 21 25 m 30	
21	do M	to do 18–30
450· 2	Now turn the Psalms of M–30	Mak haste and turn King (*text of Burns*)
15	meat boiled and roasted, scores of eggs, a huge 1994	meat boiled and roasted eggs a huge M meat, scores boiled and roasted eggs, a huge 18–30
451·15	her M	his 18–30
33	pleasuring 30	party M–25
454·32	habits of the milky mothers m 30	animals' habits M–25
455· 3	from 30	into M–25
456·13	in M 30	on 18–25
457· 3	and the 93	and that the M–22 30 71 and as the 23
458· 7	When the discourse was finished 30	At the end of the discourse M–25
22	a' M	
34	reverent 30	reverential M–25
459· 6	recorded foibles m 30	records of the foibles M–22 (*in* M, foibles *for* amours *deleted*) record which exposed the foibles 23 records which. . . 25

Penguin P. L.	Authority for Adopted Reading	Rejected Reading
460·22	those 30	this M these 18–25
461· 4	and 30	
7	new M–25	now 30
24	himsell M 21 22 25	himself 18 19 23 30
25	and fun M	
31	so M–19 22 23	as 21 25 30
462·30	Reasoning 30	Reason M–25
36	command 23 25	service M–22 30
465· 4	creature 30	body M–25
6	even 30	
40	the 30	
466·26	that m 30	
469· 1	on 23	during M–22 25 30
19	observation M	observations 18–30
22	and that 30	that M–25
23–5	depending on. . . which, joined to. . . rendered her behaviour 30	which depends on. . . to which she joined. . . so that her behaviour was M–25
27	real clean M–25	clean 30
470·32	profession M	professions 18–30
471· 5	always M	
13	neglecting 23 25	failing M–22 30
17	became 30	turned M–19 22 23 grew 21 25
31	room, in 30	bed, on M–25
33	sic M 18	six 22 23 30
33	rare M	sure 18–30
471· n.	*Kings-evil M	
472· 3	point 23 25	time M–22 30
22	a witch M	sic a wretch 18–30
474· 6	Lady C— C—l m 30	Anonymous M–25
15	those 23	that M–22 30
16	composition M 22 30	compositions 18–21 23 25
477·13–15	you, the pure. . . minions? m 30	
31–2	fire among M	
479· 6	pouts M	fowls 18–30

Penguin P. L.	Authority for Adopted Reading	Rejected Reading
479·10	petter 30	better M–25
480·16–18	He. . .him M	
31	her 30	
481·18	rank 30	ranks M–25
39	thought 30	said M–25
482·10	spoke M–18	spoken 19–30
12	Scotish M	Scotch 18–30
21–2	must certainly come m 30	comes M–25
26	has M	had 18–30
39	general m 30	
483· 3	a m 30	a young M–25
484·15	an M 19–30	a 18
485· 3	-shires M	-shire 18–30
27	person 23 30	person on the occasion M–22 25
31	Ziklag 23 25 30	Ziglag M–22
486·12	toil 30	trial M–25
487· 1, 3	shall 30	will M–25
489· 3	shall 30	will M–25
8	barest M	lowest 18–30
23	yearly M	usually 18–30
491·17	narrative M 23	narrative itself 18–22 25 30
494·18	party M–25	parties 30
495· 2	en bon point M (for plump deleted) –25	embonpoint 30
14	hieland M	
498·17	will m 30	shall M–25
33	unhappily 18–30	unhappy M
499·21	and 23	with M–22 25 30
30	so soon M–19 22 23	as soon 21 25 30
38	Lye M	liar 18–30
500·29	and M	with a 19–30
31	with M 18	with a 19–30
36	within doors 30	
501· 4	traversing 30	amid M–25
5	in 30	and in 18–25
11–12	employed 30	engaged M–25

Penguin P. L.	Authority for Adopted Reading	Rejected Reading
501·39	noise 30	din M–25
502·20	very 30	
504· 3	or two, swords M	and two swords 18–30
505·14	her M	his 18–30
36	MacCallanmore m	MacCallummore M–30
39	again permitted 30	suffered M–25
508· 4	offender 30	sufferer M–25
26	period 25	time M–23 30
511·28	ice M–22 25 30	rice 23
512· 4	without particular observation 30	
29	comfortable 30	
35	See Textual Note on 142·11	
513·22	o' t M	on' t 18–30
514·30	said, he 30	
37	answered 30	said 18–25
515·19–20	knew too well, from. . . Ratcliffe, again 30	knew, from. . . Ratcliffe, too well again 18–25
519·27	had 18	
31	little 30	small M–25
520· 7	bay M	way 18–30
521· 8	the 18	their 19–30
522· 9	tassell M–25	tussell 30
		tussle 93
523· 7	gay M–25	gey 30
9	their fire M	them 18–30
525·12	mind 21 25	temper M–19 22 23 30
526·10	that M 18	but 19–30
527· 4	was M 18	had been 19–30
22	to embark, was to sail 21 25	to sail was to (clear out deleted) sail M
		to sail was to sail 18 19 22 23 30
29	band 30	gang M–25
34	for revenge M	revenge 18–30
528· 7	met 30	discovered M–25
531·31	ear M	ears 18–30

GLOSSARY

Definitions in italic are taken from the glossaries appended to the editions of 1822 and 1830.

a'	*all*
abbreviate	an abstract or abridgement, specifically of a decree of adjudication
Abigail	a lady's maid (1 Samuel 25:24)
a'body	everybody
abjuration-oath	see n. 16 on p. 659
aboon	*above*
aboot	about
abroad	out of doors
abune	*above*
abune stairs	among our employers, i.e. at court
accessories	accompanying circumstances
acquent	acquainted
ad avisandum	for further consideration (of all Scots law phrases, perhaps the one most widely adopted in jocular use)
adjudication	legal seizure of landed property in satisfaction of debt
admire	to marvel
advocate	a professional pleader in a court of justice (the regular Scots term for British–English 'barrister', American–English 'counselor')
Lord Advocate, (also King's Advocate)	the chief law officer of the Crown in Scotland
advowson	the right to appoint to a vacant religious benefice
ae	one (number)
aff	*off*
afore	*before*
aften	*often*
again	against
agane	in readiness for
agee	*awry*
agent	solicitor, attorney
aggravate	to make bad worse
Ahasuerus	see n. 19 on p. 633
ahint	*behind*
Ailie	pet form of the name Alison

ain	*own*
ainsell	*own self*
air	*early*
airn	*iron*
airt	*to direct*, i.e. to orient
aith	oath
aits	*oats*
alane	*alone*
allenarly	exclusively
Allonby	see n. 14 on p. 654
a-low	*a-fire, in a flame*
amaist	*almost*
amang	among
Amazon	a female warrior
amour propre	self-love
an	*if*
as an	as if
anabaptism	rebaptism of adults (as practised by Baptists) on the grounds that infant baptism was invalid and insufficient; no connection with sixteenth century German Anabaptism
ance, anes	once
anes-errand	*of set purpose: sole-errand*; for that specific purpose
Andro Ferrara	the Scottish broadsword; cf. Scott's note to *Waverley*, Chapter 50
ane	a, an (formal or old-fashioned); one (pronoun, only rarely as numeral)
aneath	beneath
anent	*respecting*, concerning
anes	see ance
aneugh	*enough*
Anglice	in English
an' if	if
anither	another
anker	eight-gallon keg
Annaple Bailzou	see n. 3 on p. 669
Ansars	the citizens of Medina who succoured Mohammed when he was driven from Mecca
anticipate	to bring about before due time, to forestall

anticipation	expectation, preconception
Apollyon, Abaddon	Greek and Hebrew names for the Devil as destroyer, from Revelation 9:11
appanage	provision for the maintenance of a younger son; later, a dependency, an adjunct
apprising	valuation and sale of landed property in payment of debt, replaced in 1672 by adjudication, qv
aqua mirabilis	spirit of wine flavoured with spices
aqua-vitae	distilled liquors in general
arena	are not
Arminian	follower of Arminius (1560–1609), a Dutch Protestant who rejected Calvin's rigorous predestination, teaching that God's sovereignty accommodated significant human free-will and that Christ died for all, not only for the elect
Arniston	see n. 3 on p. 598
arriage and carriage	*plough and cart service* due by a tenant to his landlord
artes perditae	forgotten skills (see n. 2 on p. 607)
Arthur's Seat	see note on epigraph to Chapter 8, p. 602
artificial	skilful, according to the rules of art
ascertain	render certain
ashler-work	masonry of squared hewn stones
assafoetida	a pungent-smelling oriental resin used against convulsions and faintness
a'thegither	altogether
Athole brose	whisky mixed with oatmeal or honey
atween	between
aught	anything; *possession*; eighth
aughteen	eighteen
Aughtermuggitie	see n. 10 on p. 652
aughty-nine	eighty-nine, i.e. 1689 and the political and religious events of that year
auld	*old*
auld lang syne	bygone days, (for) old times' sake
Auld Reekie	Old Smoky, i.e. Edinburgh
ava	at all
awa	away

awe	owe
awee	a little
aweel	*well* (interjection)
awmous	*alms*
awmrie	*close cupboard for keeping cold victuals, bread &c*
ay	yes
aye	always
ayont	beyond
baby	a doll
Babylonian jargon	confusion of tongues, as at Babel (Genesis 11)
back and belly	completely, 'lock, stock and barrel'
back-cast	set-back, reverse
back-friend	supporter, retainer
baillie	*alderman or magistrate*
Bailzou	see n. 3 on p. 609
bairn	*child*
baith	*both*
band	*bond*
bandalier	shoulder-belt with cartridge-pockets
bane	*bone*
Bangor	a favourite psalm tune
Baptist	a member of an evangelical Protestant denomination practising baptism by immersion of adult believers only
barkened	tanned (of leather)
Barkston	now Barkestone, a village three miles west-north-west of Belvoir Castle and seven from Staunton
barm	a frothy, whitish form of liquid yeast used as a fermenting agent
Baron Court	local court of civil and criminal jurisdiction under the authority of any owner of freehold estate, by virtue of his grant from the Crown
barony	unit of land held direct from the Crown
bather	bother
bating	except, apart from
bauld	*bold*
bauson-faced	*having a white oblong spot on the face*

bawbee	*halfpenny*
Bawtie	a name for a dog
bean-hool	bean-pod
bear	*barley that has more than two rows of grain in the ear*
beck	curtsy
Bedlam or Bridewell	the lunatic asylum or the reformatory
Bess o' Bedlam	female lunatic vagrant
bedral	*beadle*, sexton
Beever	phonetic form of **Belvoir**, qv
behounched	'trick'd up and made fine . . . in general used ironically' (Grose, *PG*)
behoves, behoved	must, had to, would necessarily
belangs	belongs
beldame	an evil or threatening old woman
Belial	the Devil, especially as the inspirer of lust
belive	*speedily*
Belvoir	a district (the Vale) to the west of Grantham, with a castle, the seat of the Dukes of Rutland
ben	in, into or towards the inner part or best room of a house
bend-leather	*thick sole leather*
Ben Nevis	the highest mountain in Scotland, on the south side of the Great Glen near Fort William
beseem	be fitting for
Bessie Bowie	Bent Betty, Betty the Tub
Bess-Wynd	an alley running south from the Edinburgh High Street near the Tolbooth, removed in 1809
bestial	livestock
Bever	phonetic form of **Belvoir**, qv
bible-aith	oath sworn on the Bible
bibliopolist	bookseller
bicker	*wooden vessel, made by a cooper for holding liquor, brose &c*
bide	*stay; endure; reside*
bien	*wealthy, well-provided*
biggonets	*linen caps of the fashion worn by the Beguine sisterhood*
bike	*a wild-bees' nest*
bilked	baulked, cheated

bill (of exchange)	a written order from A to B to pay A or C a certain sum on a specific date
to renew a bill	to postpone the date on which payment is due
to sign bills with	roughly equivalent to guaranteeing a post-dated cheque, a dubious and potentially fraudulent transaction, especially when done reciprocally
bill of suspension	application for stay of execution of sentence or decree
billet	a note, a short letter
Billingsgate	London fish-market proverbial for strong language
bink	*bench*
binna	*be not*
birkie	*lively young fellow*
birn	'skin and birn', a sheep fully accounted for by producing both the skin and the head with the owner's brand on the nose – hence, the whole of anything
birth-night	court festival to mark a royal birthday
bit	*small, little*
bite and soup	food and drink
Bitem	Deceive them
bittock	*little bit; a short distance*
Black-at-the-bane	gangrenous, or dyed through and through (substituted in proof for the realistic place-name Blacketburn)
black cast	stroke of ill-luck
black cattle	bovine animals as distinct from other livestock; the dark-coloured cattle of the Highlands; clergymen
blackit	*blackened*
black-mail	protection money
blaw	to blow
Blazonbury, Lord Flash and Flame	blazon (a coat of arms) puns on 'blazing' and leads to other words suggesting fire
blude, bluid	*blood*
blue hawk	peregrine falcon or sparrowhawk

blue plums	pistol balls (cf. Latin *plumbum*, lead)
blythe	happy, joyous
Boanerges	Sons of Thunder, Christ's surname for James and John (Mark 3:17)
board-wages	'wages allowed to servants to keep themselves in victual' (*OED*)
bob	dance with an up-and-down movement
bobbit	danced, bobbed
Bob o' Dumblane	see n. 5 on p. 654
boddle	*a copper coin, value the sixth part of an English penny, equal to two doits, or Scottish pennies*
body	person (often in contemptuous or disparaging use)
boggled	demurred, stickled
bona fide	genuine, sincere
bongrace	a broad-brimmed, home-made, rustic straw-hat
bonnet	any head covering for a man, especially the Lowland peasant beret
bonnie, bonny	beautiful, handsome, fine
Books of Adjournal	minutes and decisions of the High Court of Justiciary
boor	countryman, rustic
boot	an instrument of torture that enclosed the leg and crushed it by stages as wedges were driven in
boot-hose	coarse ribbed worsted stockings without feet, worn instead of boots to protect the legs
borrow	set free, deliver
Borrowstounness	(now Bo'ness), a trading port on the Forth above Edinburgh, 'a long town of one street, and no more, extended along the shore, close to the water' (Defoe, *Tour*, 2, 313)
bouking-washing	the process of soaking dirty linen in lye, washing it and bleaching it in sunlight
bountith	*the bounty given in addition to stipulated wages*
bourock	mound, knoll

bow	dry measure (32 galls or 145 l) containing 64 forpits, qv
Bow-head	the upper part of the West Bow, traditionally a centre of activity (including printing) by the radical Protestant groups, 'a colony of Whigs' (Kirkton, 437n.), perhaps because also 'the visible face of trade' in Edinburgh (Defoe, *Tour*, 2, 305)
bowie	*milk-pail*
brae	the slope or crest of a hill, the side of a valley
Braes of Doune	steep foothills of the Highlands, lying north of the road from Dunblane to Callander, close to the setting of parts of *Waverley* and *Rob Roy*
braid	*broad*
brake	broke
brave	fine, gaudy, showy
bravely	admirably
braw	*brave, fine*, handsome, well-dressed
brawlies	full well
braws	*finery*, best clothes
brecham	*working-horse's collar*
breekens	breeches
Bridewell	a reformatory prison
brigadier wig	a full wig tied back in two curls
Bristo Port	the most southerly of the Edinburgh city gates, and still a street name
brither	brother
Broadwheel	the character's name comes from contemporary debate on the best design of wagons for unconsolidated road surfaces
brockit	with black and white stripes or patches
brog	*prick with a sharp-pointed instrument*
brogues	heavy clogs bound with iron
broider	embroider, decorate
broiled bone	grilled chop or spare rib
broo	(favourable) *opinion founded on bruit or report*
Brownie	see n. 11 p. 631
brugh and land	town and country

bruilzie	*scuffle, disturbance*
brunstane	*brimstone*, sulphur
Bubbleburgh	insubstantial, delusive, cheating or duped town
Bucephalus	the favourite horse of Alexander the Great
Buckholm	see n. 7 p. 650
buckie	*Deevil's buckie: a perverse refractory youngster: a mischievous madcap that has an evil twist in his character*
Buckskin, Ephraim	buckskin is a 'burlesque epithet' for native Americans (in the older sense of the term), recorded from 1787; Ephraim was Joseph's second son, whose descendants, having sided with Israel's enemies, are comminated by Isaiah, Jeremiah and Hosea. Clearly the War of 1812 still rankles with the Author of Waverley
bullering	bellowing
bull-segg	a bull that has been castrated when fully grown
bunker	*bench; in cottages a seat which also serves for a chest, opening with a hinged lid*
busk	*dress*
Buskbody	'dress-person'
busk up one's cockernonie	gather the hair into a top-knot; cheer up one's looks
butt and ben	*the outer and inner side of the partition-wall in a house consisting of two apartments*
bye	past, aside, near at hand, over there; also a contraction of forbye, qv
bye-word	proverb, saying
ca'	call
caad, ca'd	called
cabinet of St James's	the government council-room, and those who meet there
Cader-Edris	a celebrated mountain ridge near Barmouth in north Wales

cadger	carrier, hawker, travelling dealer
cag	keg
caird	*tinker*; specifically, the metal-working kind
cairn	*heap of loose stones piled as a memorial of some individual or occurrence*
caitiff	a wretch both wicked and miserable
calash	light carriage with low wheels and removable top
Calender	see n. 8 on p. 630
callant	*young lad; a somewhat irrisory use of the old term gallant; a fine fellow*
caller	*cool, fresh*
calliver	a light musket
Calton [Hill]	an Edinburgh feature of the same general shape and formation as the Old Town ridge, smaller and half a mile to the north-east
Calvinist	a follower of the Swiss Jean Calvin (1509–64), whose Protestant reforming doctrines (including predestination of souls, salvation by faith, total dependence of the weak individual on God's grace, and the theocratic organization of society) became dominant in Scotland from the late sixteenth to the early eighteenth century and remained influential long afterwards
cam	*came*
Cameronians	followers of Richard Cameron (killed at Airdsmoss, 1680), intransigent extreme Presbyterians who declared war on Charles II and all who dealt with him; a regiment raised in one day by the sect in 1689 to oppose Claverhouse, later incorporated into the British army as the 26th Foot, later the Scottish Rifles
camlet	light silk and wool fabric, probably napped and mottled
Campvere	see nn. 8 and 15 on p. 621.
cann	wooden or pottery vessel for liquids

canna	*cannot*
canny	*skilful, prudent, lucky; in a superstitious sense, good-humoured, safe, trustworthy*
Canongate	the street and suburb occupying the eastern and lower part of the Edinburgh Old Town ridge outside the city wall, a separate burgh with its own Tolbooth until 1636 and then a distinct jurisdiction within Edinburgh
canonical	in accordance with Church rules (see n. 20 on p. 665)
cant	professional jargon; thieves' slang
canty	*lively and cheerful*
capernoity	*crabbed, peevish; frolicsome, obstreperous*
capper-cailzie	capercaillie, a large bird of the grouse family
caption	warrant for the arrest of a debtor
carcakes	cakes of flour and egg eaten on Shrove Tuesday, probably identical with the small thick modern Scottish pancake
carle	*churl, gruff old man*, fellow
carline	*the feminine of carle*; old woman, hag; at p. 47, Mrs Howden's misunderstanding of the name Caroline
carnal	secular, worldly, unspiritual.
Caroline Park	see note on Roystoun, p. 629
carried	abstracted, deranged
carritch	catechism (see n. 16 on p. 619)
cashier	discharge (usually with disgrace) from military service
cast	turn or direction; stroke of fate; chance lift in a vehicle
cast-bye	outcast
catastrophe	denouement
ca'-throw	*disturbance*
Cato's daughter	Porcia, daughter of Cato of Utica, wife of Marcus Brutus, and proverbial for having 'a man's mind, but a woman's might' (*Julius Caesar*, II, iv, 8)

cauld	*cold*
cauldrife	*chilly, susceptible of cold*, indifferent in manner
cause	a law case
causes celebres	famous legal cases (see n. 38 on p. 591)
gude auld cause	the Puritan movement; ironically, fornication
causeway	*raised and paved street*
cautelous	full of precaution, or of trickery
caution	bail, security
enacted caution	formally sworn security
ceeted	cited, formally summoned to court
certes	indeed, certainly
certiorate	inform authoritatively
cess	land-tax (see n. 52 on p. 623)
cessio bonorum	surrender of property to creditors
chafts	*jaws*
chalder	*sixteen bolls dry measure* (see n. 21 on p. 659)
chambering	sexual indulgence (Romans 13:13)
champaign	level, open country
chancellor (of Scotland)	the head of the Scottish legal system before the Union of 1707
chance-medley	homicide by misadventure
change-house	an alehouse
chappit	*struck*, knocked
charge	mortgage right over property; royal command to perform a specific act (both senses are in play on p. 403)
Chase	a hunting-ground (but, unlike a park, unenclosed)
Chatellain	the governor or keeper of a castle
chiel, chield	*young fellow*
chimley	fireplace
chop	*shop*
chucky	*barn-door fowl*
churl	a peasant, with suggestions of baseness and avarice
Circuit	a law-court that moves from place to place in a recurring pattern
citation	summons to a law-court
clachan	*a small village*; a village inn

claik-geese	*barnacle geese*
claith	cloth
claise, claiths	*clothes*
claut	a mass scraped together
clave	adhered
claver	*talk idly and foolishly*
clavers	*idle talk*, nonsense – but also a phonetic rendering of the name of the Jacobite general Graham of Claverhouse, for whom see n. 1 on p. 666
claymore	the Highland broadsword; also used as a battle-cry or word of command at p. 524
cleckit	*hatched*
cleek	*hook*
Cleishbotham	'smack-bottom'
Jedediah (properly, Jedidiah)	'beloved of the Lord', an epithet given to Solomon (2 Samuel 12:25)
clenched	bound with interlaced metal straps
clergy, benefit of	exemption from full legal penalties (notably death), until 1827 claimable on proof of literacy in certain circumstances
cleuch, cleugh	*cliff*, crag; *ravine*, gorge
clew	ball of thread or yarn
clinkd	moved something rapidly
clift	fissure, cleft
cloke-bag	portmanteau, especially one suitable for carrying on horseback
close	alley, urban courtyard
close-head	the entrance to a close; those who loiter there; their gossip; rumour
closet	private council-chamber
cloth	distinctive clothing of a profession, especially the clergy
clout	a blow
clown	ignorant countryman
clubbed	tied back in a club-shaped knot
clute	*divided hoof*
coal-hill	coal piled near the pit-head ready for carting

Cocceian follower of a heretical tendency within Calvinism that stressed God's covenant with individual men and a symbolic rather than a legalistic reading of scripture

cock the turned-up brim of a cocked hat (see n. 9. on p. 594)

cockade ribbon, rosette, etc., worn in the hat as part of a uniform or livery

cockernonie *the gathering of a young woman's hair under the snood*

cockit placed conspicuously

cockup high hair style with false padding (*SND*); 'a sort of cap or hat turned up before' (Scott, *MPW*, 19, 217). Whatever their nature, they were being preached against by 1692

cod *pillow*

cognosce investigate judicially, in connection with crime or insanity

coif a woman's close-fitting under-cap

Coldstream village where Monck's army crossed the lower Tweed into England on 2 January 1660, bringing about the restoration of the monarchy

collier coal-miner

commentators annotators of the Bible (in text, ironic for drunken amateurs)

communing debate, discussion

compound to offset one claim with another, to compromise

comprehend include

conceit stroke of wit; opinion

conceitedly whimsically, eccentrically

condescendence in Scots law, a written statement of particulars

condescending decently refraining from asserting the privileges of superior rank, without any hint of patronizing behaviour

confessio . . . see n. 6 on p. 627

conform matching, appropriate

conjure to entreat earnestly

consequential weighty, perhaps self-important

constructive	not directly expressed but deduced from inference or interpretation
constructive crime	crime so defined by judicial interpretation
contrair	opposite
conversation	association; social or sexual contact
convocating	summoning together
Corinthian	see n. 11 on p. 599
corpus delicti	the substance or body of the crime or offence charged
correspondent	a distant, regular business associate
cottar	*cottager*
counsel and agent	barrister and solicitor
country	a district, a territory (not necessarily a state, or rural)
coup	*turn over*
court	enclosure for cattle
Court of Session	the supreme civil judicature of Scotland
couthy	agreeable
covenant	a solemn agreement: for specific covenants, see Introduction, p. x
Cowal	the system of peninsulas in Argyll between Loch Long and Loch Fyne, to the north of Bute
Cowgate	the street linking the lower ends of the closes and wynds descending from the High Street of Edinburgh towards the south, and therefore a poor and insalubrious part of the city
cowt	*colt*
crack	*hearty conversation*
cracking like a pen-gun	talking loudly and volubly
crack-rope	likely to be hanged
craft	*croft*, small-holding
craig	*rock*, cliff, rocky ground
Craigmillar	a prominent fifteenth- to seventeenth-century castle between Edinburgh and Dalkeith, now a ruin but still inhabited in the eighteenth century
Craigsture	perhaps strong rock or rock of turmoil/dust/battle

cravat neck–cloth; the hangman's noose

creagh *highland foray; plundering incursion*; or the booty so gained

Creole person of European descent and West Indian birth and upbringing

crêpe to put up in curl–papers

crewels *scrofula*, a condition, formerly common, marked by general debility, skin sores, and swollen glands, often complicated by tuberculosis

cried saut sold salt in the street

Criffel a mountain with a prominent conical summit dominating the west bank of the Nith below Dumfries

crine to shrink, shrivel or dry out

crook misfortune, trial, loss

crook in my lot misfortune in my life (see n. 15 on p. 613)

cross vexation, affliction, trial, especially when viewed in a Christian aspect

Crossmyloof 'Cross–my–palm', doubtless with silver

crosspatch a cross, ill–tempered person

croun crown of the head; five–shilling piece

crow a bent and sharpened metal lever

cry to call or summon, to announce for sale in the street

cruppen *crept*

cuddie *ass*, donkey or small horse

Cuffabout 'Knockabout'

Culdees (*Céli Dé*, Clients of God), an ascetic religious movement in the medieval Celtic Church, claimed by Kirkton (2–3) to be significantly independent of both the Pope and bishops

cull a dupe, a fool

cummer *midwife, gossip*

cums comes

Cu'ross an ancient port on the north shore of the Forth above Edinburgh, 'a neat and agreeable town lying in length by the water side' (Defoe, 2, 391)

curate	the regular word for Scottish parish priests under the episcopal regime from 1662 to 1688, without any implication of their being substitutes for anyone else
curch, curtch	*kerchief; a woman's covering for the head; inner linen cap, sometimes worn without the mutch*
curpel	*crupper*; the rear strap of a saddle, passing under the horse's tail
curry	to rub down with a comb
curtal-axe	a cutlass, a short broadsword
curule chair	the seat of the chief magistrate
cutter's law	the cut-purses' supposed code of conduct
cutty	a small, young, mischievous or worthless girl or woman
cutty quean	*slut; worthless girl; a loose woman*
cutty-stool	*short-legged stool*, the special seat in which offenders (especially sexual ones) were required to sit for public rebuke during church service
dabby	damp, moist, flabby (*OED*)
daffin, daffing	*thoughtless gaiety; foolish playfulness*
daft	*mad*, out of one's mind
Daidle	dawdle; stagger; bemire; pinafore; dandle
daidling	idling, pottering, loitering
Eppie	diminutive for 'Elspeth', 'Elizabeth'
daiker	*to toil: as in job-work*, i.e. to go at an easy pace, to saunter
Dalilah (properly Delilah)	the wife who betrayed Samson to his enemies by sapping his strength (Judges 15–16)
Dalkeith	see n. 3 on p. 603
dam	mother
devil's dam	traditional term of abuse to a woman, frequent in Shakespeare
Damahoy	from Dalmahoy, a former estate eight miles south-west of Edinburgh
Grizzell	Griselda, the type of female patience (*Decameron*, 10, 10)

darg	*day's work*
daur	*dare*
daw	jackdaw, proverbial for folly and idleness
day, the	*today*
deacon	president of one of the incorporated trades in a Scots burgh
deas	stone or turf seat at a house door
chamber of deas	a parlour or best bedroom
deave	*deafen*
debito tempore	at the proper time
decreet	the judgment of a court, embodying a decision
de die in diem	from day to day, daily
dee	*die*
Deepheugh	'deep-ravine'
deevil	devil (in this novel, only in literal use by the Edinburgh criminal world)
deil	devil (especially in stock phrases of surprise and denial)
deil a	not one single
deil an	would that
deil haet	see haet
deistical	basing religious belief on reason rather than revelation
delict	a wrong, a crime
demeaned	behaved, conducted
demipique saddle	a light saddle, elegantly modern in 1736
deponent	one who gives (written) evidence
deuce	the devil
deukes	ducks (with a pun on dukes)
didna	*did not*
ding	*strike*
dinna	*do not*
dinnle	*tingle, thrill*
dirl	a jar, a thrilling pain
disna	does not, do not
dispone	assign
disposition	a conveyance of property
dits	*stops up*
dittay	ground of indictment, the indictment itself

divot	a turf
divot-cast	the space in the ground from which a divot has been removed
doch an' dorroch	(Gaelic *deoch an doruis*), *stirrup-cup, parting cup*
doer	business agent
doited	*turned to dotage; stupid; confused*
dollar	a five-shilling piece
dominie	a schoolmaster
Donacha Dhu na Dunaigh	Black Duncan the Troublemaker
donnard	*grossly stupid*
donnot	do-nought, idler, good-for-nothing
doo	*dove*
dookit	*ducked*
dooms	very, extremely, 'dashed'
door-cheek	door-post
Doric	marked by primitive simplicity
double verse	the eight-line stanzas, double quatrains, in which the Scottish Metrical Psalms are printed
douce	kindly, sedate, quiet-living and just a little complacent
dought	*could; was able*
doun	*down*
dour	*hard and impenetrable in body or mind*
downa	can't, won't
dram	a small drink, usually of spirits
drap	*drop*
draw up with	start a courtship with
drew	drafted, formulated
driegh	*slow, tardy*
drift	falling snow driven by the wind
Drottle	Slowcoach, Sluggard
drouthy	dry
drow	an attack, a spasm
dud	garment, rag
duddie	*ragged*
Duddingston	still an 'almost unspoiled feudal ensemble' (*Buildings of Scotland, Edinburgh*, 554) on the south-east edge of the King's Park
Duke's Walk	a tree-lined alley (now obliterated) close to Holyroodhouse
dulcis, etc.	see n. 4 on p. 627

Dumbiedikes	Dumb-fellow's walls – see Scott's note, p. 78
Dumfries	principal town of south-west Scotland, over seventy miles from Edinburgh; Helen Walker and her sister lived near by
Dunbar	coastal town and castle midway between Edinburgh and Berwick, site of Cromwell's decisive defeat of the Scots army in September 1650
dunch	push, bump
Dundee	burgh and port on the north side of the Firth of Tay; for the viscount, see n. 1 to p. 666
dune	done
d'une grande dame	of a great lady
Dunlop	a whole-milk cheese originally from the Ayrshire village of that name
Dunover	overthrown and thoroughly worked upon by debt-collectors (duns), exhausted, finished
Dunse Law	a steep grassy hill forty-five miles from Edinburgh, where in 1639 the Covenanting army encamped to confront Charles I in Berwick fifteen miles to the east
duply	in Scots law a defender's second reply to the pursuer's rejoinder to his first; as verb, to make a duply
durk, dirk	a short dagger worn in the belt by Highlanders
durstna	dared not
Dustiefoot	an itinerant pedlar; a dog's name
Dutch toys	German-made playthings of wood or metal imported from the lower Rhine
dyester	*dyer*
east-country	east-central-Scottish
eclaircissement	explanation
Ecod	By God
Eden	a river close by Carlisle
ee, een	*eye, eyes*
e'en	*evening; even*

effeir of war	*warlike guise* or array
eik	supplement
elected	chosen by God, through Christ as the second Adam, for salvation under the Covenant of Grace; this novel does not confront the questions (crucial for Calvinist cultures) of whether election entails any conscious or unconscious response of will and conduct
Elector of Hanover	the German title of the Hanoverian monarchs from George I to William IV, used by (among others) those who wished to deny the legitimacy of their British reign
Elfinfoot	see n. 7 on p. 656
elf-lock	tangled mass of hair
elide	annul, render ineffective
ell	a unit of length of 45 inches, 114 cm
elshin	a leatherworker's *awl*
eme	*uncle*
emergence	pressing crisis
enacted caution	formally recorded bail
en-bon-point	plump
Enemy, the	the Devil
eneugh	*enough*
enlèvement	abduction
enow	enough
ensure	guarantee (against)
enthusiast	holder of extreme religious opinions (the ordinary modern meaning also occurs)
enthusiastic	of or like an enthusiast; intensely felt
episcopal, -ian	relating to bishops and specifically to relatively hierarchical systems of Christian Church government in which their role outweighs those of ordinary clergy and laymen
equals aquals	equity, equal sharing
Erastian, -ism	'the term of abuse for state supremacy over the Church' (Mitchison)
ere	ever
eremite	hermit
ergo	therefore

Esculapius	see n. 13 on p. 649
Estates	a parliament; representatives of the prin-ncipal divisions of society, meeting together or as separate assemblies
event	outcome
exauctorate	divested of authority
exercise	family prayers
ex jure sanguinis	by the law of descent
exoner	to free from a responsibility
extenuate	to weaken, to make thin or slender
Eye	represents Yorkshire pronunciation of Aye, yes
fa'	*fall*
facetious	witty
fact	criminal act
factor	steward or administrator of an estate
faculty	a department of learning, and its practitioners
Faculty (of Advocates)	the collective body of Scottish barristers
fain	glad, eager
fair	(of water) clear, pure
Fairscrieve	'Fair-copy, Good-handwriting, Sizeable-document'
fal-lal	*foolish ornament in dress*
fallow	*fellow*
fama clamosa	widespread rumour of serious misconduct, as grounds for formal intervention (though Scott apparently assimilates it to mere gossip)
fancy-farm	experimental farm
fand	found
fash	*trouble*, bother
fasherie	*trouble*
fashious	*troublesome*
fash one's thumb	bother one's head, lose any sleep
fashion	show, pretence
fatal	fateful
Fathers Conscript	the magistrates of a town
fatuus furiosus and *naturaliter idiota*	imbecile, violently lunatic, and mentally defective (but normally alternative decisions for the jury)

faulded	*folded*
fause	*false*
faut	*fault*
feared	*afraid*
febrile	feverish
feckless	*powerless, feeble* (with no sense of disapproval)
felo de se	self-murderer
fence	formally to open proceedings with a formula forbidding interruption or disruption
Fergusson	see n. 5 on p. 594
festivous	festive
fickle	*to puzzle*
Fife	a region and county facing Edinburgh from the north across the Firth of Forth
file	*to defile, spoil*
file the stamach	upset the digestion
firkin	small cask of eight to ten gallons
first-rate man-of-war	warship of the most heavily armed class
firth	arm of the sea; at p. 522 probably moorland, scrub
fit	*foot*
fite	fight (Scott's rendering of East Midland English)
flang	flung
flash	*dash out rashly*, dash or splash water
flat	naïve, simple-minded (because not sharp)
flats and sharps	recourse to weapons (the edge and blade of swords, with a pun on musical semitones)
flee	*fly*
fling	*throw out the legs like a horse*, caper, dance
fliskmahoy	*jill-flirts; giddy fly-flap-girls*, giddy or frivolous woman
flitt	*remove, depart*; move house
flow-moss	*watery moss, morass*, wet, boggy ground
flying stationer	chapman, book-pedlar
folk	relations; people in general
forbear	*forefather; ancestor*

forbye	*besides, over and above*
foreanent	over against
fore-bar	in the old Court of Session, the bar at which advocates pleaded causes of first instance
forehammer	a two-handed sledgehammer
forgather	congregate, meet
forgie	*forgive*
forlorn-hope	the advance guard of a storming-party
formaliter et specialiter, as well as *generaliter*	formally and in specific detail, as well as in a general way
forpit	a dry measure of half an Imperial gallon or 2.27 litres
fou	*full, drunk*
frae	*from*
free-holder	until 1832, the owner of land sufficient to qualify for a vote in parliamentary elections
Frigate-Whins	(now Figgat), the tract of furze in east Edinburgh described on p. 444
frizzed	curled
fu'	*full*
fuff	*puff*
Fugit irrevocabile tempus	see n. 2 on p. 616
fule	*fool*, foolish
funds	stocks and bonds, usually government ones
furbelow	a decorative pleated trimming on a woman's dress
fusee	a light musket
fustle, Fustler	whistle, Whistler
fyke	fidget, twitch
gab	mouth, speech
gift of the gab	eloquence
gae	*go*
gaed	*went*; gave (p. 171)
gaen	gone, *going*
Gaffer	respectful title for an old countryman
gait	*goat*
gaitt	child, *brat*
Gaius	see n. 17 on p. 637
Gallio	see n. 4 on p. 605

Galwegian	pertaining to Galloway, the region of south-west Scotland west of the Nith
Gandercleugh	Male-goose-ravine
gane	*gone*
gang	*go*
ganging	*going*
gar	*make, compel*, cause
gar ye as good	to retaliate, to pay someone back in his own coin
garr'd	*made, compelled, caused*
gardyloo	beware water (*gardez l'eau*), an Edinburgh warning when dirty water (and worse) was emptied from a tenement window see n. 16 on p. 633
gare-brained	crazy, hare-brained
gate	*way, manner*
nae gate	nowhere
gauger	an exciseman, especially one who assesses the capacity of casks, stills, etc.
gaun	*going*
gaun plea	a current lawsuit
gaunt	*yawn*
gawsie	*plump and jolly*, roomy, ample
gay, gay and	*very*
gear	*goods, dress, equipment*
gee	*mood, caprice, whim*
Gehennah	a place where heretic Jews sacrificed children to Baal (Jeremiah 32, 35, etc.); later, a name for Hell
General Assembly	the annual meeting of the national deliberative body of the Church of Scotland, held in Edinburgh each May
genius	spirit
gentles	*gentlefolks*
gey	*very*
ghaist	*ghost*
gie	*give*
gied	*gave*
gien	*given*
gif-gaf	*give and take, tit for tat, mutual service to one another*

gillie	*manservant in the highlands* (Gaelic *gille*, youth)
gilpie	*frolicksome young person*
gin	*if, suppose*
Girdingburst	Saddle-girth-broken
girdle	*an iron plate for firing cakes on*
girn	*grin like an ill-natured dog*
glaik	flash of reflected light, *deception, delusion*
fling the glaiks in folk's een	throw dust in people's eyes
glancing-glass	piece of glass or mirror used by children to reflect sunlight
glebe	land allotted to a parish minister in addition to his stipend
gledd	the common *kite*
gleg	*sharp, on the alert* (in wit, sight or appetite)
glibbe	mass of matted hair on the forehead and over the eyes
gliff	*glimpse, short time*
glim	a scrap
Good Town	a once-common term for Edinburgh
Gorbals	a village on the south bank of the Clyde opposite Glasgow, engulfed by the city from the late eighteenth century; see n. 13 on p. 666
Goshen	the part of Egypt assigned by Pharaoh to Joseph and the Israelites and later spared God's plagues (Genesis 45:10, Exodus 8:22)
Goslinn	Young-goose, Greenhorn
goss-hawk	a large short-winged hawk
gousty	*desolate*, eerie
goutte	*a drop*
gowan	*daisy*
gown, gowden	gold, golden
gowpen	*as much as both hands held together with the palms upward, and contracted in circular form, can contain* (and see Scott's note on p. 141)
graith	*harness*, equipment
gramashes	*gaiters reaching to the knee*

Grassmarket	a rectangular open space below Edinburgh Castle to the south, outside the fifteenth-century walls but inside the sixteenth, formerly a market for country produce and a place of execution. See n. 2 on p. 592.
grat	*cried, wept*
gree	supremacy
gree, greed	*agree*, agreed
greeshoch	(Gaelic *griosach*), burning embers of peat
greet	*weep*
grenadiers	soldiers picked for size and physique (originally, to throw grenades)
Grêve	formerly the place of execution in Paris
grey-beard	earthenware jug for spirits
grewsome	fearful, repulsive
grit	*great*
ground-officer	an estate manager
grund	*ground*
grunter	pig
Grunwiggin	see n. 13 on p. 632
gude, guid	*good*
Gude	euphemism for God at p. 96
gude auld cause	Covenanting and Puritan principles; sometimes, ironically, fornication
gude for the siller	negotiable for real money, with pun on 'beneficial for the coins'
gudeman	*husband*; head of a household; small farmer; 'Sir' in polite address to such a person
gudesire	*grandfather*
gudewife	mistress of a house, farm, inn, etc.; wife
guide	*use, take care of, treat*
gulley	*large knife*
Gunnerby	now Gonerby, a village, hill, etc., three miles north-west of Grantham, Lincolnshire; in *1818* denoted by the Middlesex place-name Gunnersbury
guse's grass	enough land to pasture a goose
gutter-bloods	*canaille*, guttersnipes
gyte	*crazy, delirious*

hadden	held
hae	*have*
deil haet he kens	he knows damn all
deil haet of me kens	I have no idea
haet	have it
haffets	*the temples*
haffit locks	hair on the sides of the head
hafflins	half-grown, adolescent
haft	dwelling, environment
hafted	settled, established, *domiciled*
hagbuts of found	firearms of cast metal
haill, hale	*whole*
hale and fair	in perfect health
half-crown	silver coin worth one eighth of a pound sterling
Halkit	Whitefaced, cf. hawkit
hallan	clay *partition between the door of a cottage and the fireplace*
Hallow-fair	a fair held south-west of Edinburgh in the first week of November
halt	lame, lameness
Haltwhistle	a small town twenty miles east of Carlisle
hame	*home*
hammerman	blacksmith, metal-worker
hap	luck, fate
hard-set	obstinate
Haribee-broo	the crest of Harraby Hill, formerly the place of public execution outside Carlisle
harle	*drag*, haul
harmonious call	unanimous invitation to become minister of a parish
harns	brains, wits
har'st	*harvest*
hartshorn	ammonia prepared from antlers and used as smelling salts
hatchment	an armorial funeral panel
haud	*hold*, keep
haud by	believe in, adhere to
havings	*behaviour, manners*
hawkit	of animals, wholly or partly *white-faced*

hay-band	the twist that holds hay together in a bundle
heal	n. good health; adj. healthy, safe, un-damaged (cf. **hale**)
healsomeness	wholesomeness
Hebe	cupbearer of the Greek gods and per-sonification of the Greek word for youth
Hecate	ancient Greek goddess associated with luck, sorcery, black magic, ghosts and dead souls; patroness of the weird sisters in *Macbeth*, IV, i
heels, to get the heels of	outstrip
hegh	a contemptuous sigh
hellebore	a family of plants and the purgative and narcotic drugs obtained from them, traditionally used to calm lunacy and hysteria
hellicat	*half-witted*
hempie	*rogue, gallows-apple, one for whom hemp grows. Its most common use is in a jocular way, to giddy young people of either sex*
hereditary jurisdictions	see n. 46 on p. 591
heritable bond	a loan secured by mortgage on land
heritors	landowners, collectively responsible for maintaining the parish church and manse
herse	*hoarse*
Hesper	the evening star
hest	command
het	*hot*
hieland	from the Highlands, perhaps also raw and uncouth
high-flyer	a fast stage-coach; a political or reli-gious extremist
high-gravel blind	almost entirely blind, cf. *Merchant of Venice*, II, ii, 32
Hinchup	Haunch-up, Limpalong
hing	hang
hinny, hinnie	sweetheart, *darling*
hint	occasion, opportunity
hip-hop	with hopping movements

ho, ho's	her, his (in English dialects)
Hochmagirdle	see n. 31 on p. 605
hog, hog-lam	a young sheep, weaned but with its first fleece still unshorn
Holland	the southern division of Lincolnshire between Sleaford and Boston
Hollands	Dutch gin
holm	*flat ground along the side of a river*
Holy-Rood, Holyroodhouse	a group of buildings at the east end of the Canongate including the former Abbey of the Holy Cross and a royal palace begun in the early sixteenth century
homologate	ratify, confirm, validate
hoose	house
horse-jockey	horse-dealer, postilion or jockey in the modern sense
hough	knee-joint, thigh
hour of cause	hour appointed for trying a case
housing	protective cloth covering for a horse
hout, houts, hout tout	exclamation of annoyance, disgust, incredulity or remonstrance
how	low-lying ground
Howden	an actual Scottish surname that appears aptly to conflate *howdie*, a midwife, with *hodden*, coarse homespun cloth typifying homeliness and simplicity
howdie	*midwife*
howff	to haunt, resort
howl	owl
humourist	person subject to fads and fancies
hunds	hounds
hussy	'housewife', sewing-kit
huzzy	girl, woman
Hyssop's Fables	Aesop's Fables (see n. 13 on p. 625)
Ichabod	Hebrew for 'No glory' or 'Glory is departed' (1 Samuel 4:21; *Six Saints*, 1, 188)
ideal	imaginary
ilk	*each*; that same, the thing named
of that ilk	of that same, when the personal name

	is the same as the territorial one; e.g. 'Mungo Marsport of that ilk' denotes 'Mungo Marsport of Marsport'
ilka	*each*, every
ilka-days	*every days, week days*
improved	took advantage of, benefited by
inartificial	constructed without art or skill
Inchkeith	an island in the Firth of Forth, four miles off Edinburgh
inchoat	undeveloped, incomplete
in confitentem . . .	see n. 4 on p. 627
incontinent	forthwith
increase	prosperity
incumbent	overlying
independency	the seventeenth-century term for Congregationalism, the system of Christian Church government in which each local congregation is held to be a Church independent of external authority
indue	to put on as a garment
indulgence	permission offered from time to time by the Crown to the Presbyterians to hold services on certain conditions. See n. 38 on p. 660.
ingan	*onion*
ingine	cleverness, ingenuity
Ingleboro	see n. 11 on p. 637
ingle-side	*fireside*
in hoc statu	in the present state of matters
inimicitiam contra omnes mortales	hostility to all humankind
in initialibus	the preliminary stage of a legal examination, generalized by Saddletree to mean 'to start with', 'in the first place'
in loco parentis	in the position of a parent
in loco tutoris	in the position of a legal guardian
in rem versam	properly chargeable against the estate
in rerum natura	in nature
instanter	forthwith
instruct	to establish a point by evidence

intelligence	news, information, understanding
inter apices juris	among the high peaks of the law, i.e. discussing its subtle points
interest	power or influence through personal or political connection
interested	personally involved in a matter and therefore not impartial as its judge
interlocutor of relevancy	court decree confirming the relation between the facts alleged and the charge brought
inter parietes	indoors
interrogatories	the questions in a systematic legal interrogation
inter rusticos	among the peasantry, among laymen
intestine	internal
intill, in till	into
intonuit laevum	it thundered on the left (*Aeneid*, 2, 693): a good omen for the safety of the hero's son Anchises
in-town multure	payment for compulsory use of the landlord's mill
intromit	deal, participate, meddle
intrusion	forcible introduction of a minister to a charge against the wishes of the congregation
Inveraray	a castle and town on Loch Fyne, seat of the Dukes of Argyll; the present structures of both were built by Duke John's successor
Inver-Garry	see n. 4 on p. 668
irritable	easily aroused (not necessarily to anger)
I'se	*I shall*
I'se uphaud	I'll maintain
I'se warrant	I guarantee, I assure
ither	other
iurisconsultus	see jurisconsult
I weel I wot	I am quite sure
Jacobites	adherents of James II after the 1688 revolution, and of his descendants James and Charles Edward Stuart
jagg	*prick, as a pin or thorn*

jark	correctly glossed as 'seal' on p. 257, presumably following Grose, *VT*, but later used in the sense of 'pass'
jaud	*jade, mare*; disparaging term for a horse, or for any female
jee	move, shift, budge (the word of command to a horse)
Jenner	see n. 14 on p. 649
jink	*a quick elusory turn*
jo	*sweetheart*
Jock	John
jorram	(Gaelic *iorram*), a rowing-song
journeyman	a skilled workman paid by the day
jow	to ring
jurisconsult	a master of legal theory
iuris-consultus clarissimus et peritissimus	a most distinguished and expert legal authority
jus divinum	divine right
Justiciar Court	the High Court of Justiciary, the supreme Scottish criminal court
Juvenal	a fiercely moral Roman satirist of the first century AD
kail	borecole (the common green vegetable of old Scotland) or cabbage; vegetable soup; dinner
kail-worm	caterpillar
kail-yard	cabbage-patch
kain	*duty paid by a tenant to his landlord in eggs, fowls, &c*
kamed	*combed*
keepit	kept
kelpie	a water spirit, usually malignant, often in the form of a horse at a ford, luring travellers to drowning
Kelso	a town on the Tweed some forty miles south-east of Edinburgh, where Scott attended school for six months in 1783 and met the Ballantyne brothers, who began their printing business there. The race-meeting was held early in October
ken	*know*

kend, kenned	*knew*, known
kend folk	people of repute
ken	a disreputable house (at p. 298)
kenspeckle	*gazing-stock*, conspicuous
kepp	to guard
killing-time	1684–6, the height of the repression of the Covenanters
Kilmun	a village (though not in the eighteenth century a distinct parish) in Cowal on the shore of the Holy Loch, five miles west of Rosneath beyond Loch Long, with the family mausoleum where the 'great Argyle' is buried. It appears in the manuscript as Scott's first thought for the name of Butler's parish.
Kiltstoup	Tilt-the-tankard – a drinking parson
kindly	native-born, indigenous
King's Cushion	a seat formed by two people; each grasps his left wrist with his right hand and the other's right wrist with his left hand
King's Park	a royal park of medieval origin on the edge of eighteenth-century Edinburgh, including Arthur's Seat and the country round it
kintra, kintray	*country*
kirk	*church*
kirkit, to be	ceremonially to take one's place in church the Sunday after marriage, etc.
Kirk-Session	governing committee of a Scottish parish, comprising minister and elders
kirk-treasurer	see n. 2 on p. 618
kirk-wark	church affairs
Kirkcaldy	the chief town on the north shore of the Firth of Forth, some ten miles from Edinburgh by water and (then) some thirty by road and ferry
kissing-strings	bonnet-strings tied under the chin and hanging down

kittle	*ticklish in all its senses*; to tickle, per-plex, engender, whelp
kittle cattle	awkward customers
Kittlepunt	Tricky-point, Tease-point, Bring-forth-points-like-kittens
Kittlesides	Easily-aroused-body
knaveship	*mill-dues paid to the* (miller's) *knaves or servants*
Knocktarlitie	Talorgan's knoll, apparently adapted from Kiltarlity, Talorgan's cell, twelve miles west of Inverness. See n. 23 on p. 658.
knock under	acknowledge oneself beaten
knowe, knoll	*rising ground, hillock*
Knox, John	see n. 34 on p. 660
krame	a merchant's booth or stall
kye	cows, cattle
kylevine pen	*pencil of black or red lead*
kythe	*seem, appear*, show
laigh	*low*
Laigh Calton	a disreputable district in the ravines below the **Calton Hill**, qv
laigh-house	ground floor or basement of a tene-ment building
laiking	playing, taking time off work
laird	*lord of a manor, squire*, any landed proprietor however small but not a tenant farmer
Lammermuir	hill country south-east of Edinburgh, between the Lothian plain and lower Tweeddale
lamour	amber
Land o' Cakes	(i.e. oatcakes) Scotland (with Kirk-maiden at its south-west extrem-ity, John-o'-Groat's at its north-east)
landward bred	brought up in the country
lane, by one's	on one's own, by oneself
lang	*long*
lang-gowns	judges and counsel
lang-heads	shrewd businessmen
lang-shankit	long-handled (see n. 23 on p. 663)
lang syne	*long since, long ago*

Langtale	Long-story, Long-speech – perhaps with a bawdy pun, since he 'likes to look at a bonny lass' (p. 216)
latitudinarians	those who thought the forms of Church government and worship relatively unimportant and who tolerated diverse opinions on matters of religious doctrine
lavrock	skylark
lawing	*tavern reckoning*
Lawnmarket	the upper part of the Edinburgh High Street, between St Giles and the steep ascent to the Castle, in which fine fabrics were sold
lay	a particular line of business or of crime
leading	carrying harvested grain or hay from field to stackyard
leading question	one that suggests to the witness the answer that is expected (and that is therefore liable to be disallowed)
leading strings	straps for supporting a toddler while it learns to walk
leal	*loyal, true*
lea-land	grass-land
learn	teach (not a solecism in Scots)
leaven	literally, yeast or other fermenting agent; metaphorically, a pervasive trace of a former condition
leddy, leddyship	*lady*, ladyship, applied in Scotland of old to the wife of any laird even below the rank of knight
lee	a lie, to tell a falsehood
Lee-Wood	in Lanarkshire, three miles north-north-west of Lanark
leet	list of people eligible for an office
Leicester beans	see n. 22 on p. 637
Leith	the port of Edinburgh, two miles north of the Old Town
Lennox	the old sheriffdom of Dumbarton; the basin of Loch Lomond
lese-majesty	infringement of the dignity of the sovereign power
Leyden	see n. 6 on p. 598

Libberton	once allegedly Leper-town, now Liberton, a southern suburb of Edinburgh, and at the time of the novel an outlying village
libel	a formal statement of the grounds of the charge in a prosecution
licence	(issue a) certificate of fitness to preach
Lickpelf	Filthy-lucre-licker
liege	a loyal citizen (originally, because rendering feudal service)
lift	*sky*
lilt	to sing clearly and cheerfully; to move in a sprightly way, to skip along
limmer	*a loose woman*, a rascal
Lincluden	once a hamlet near, now a suburb of, Dumfries, where the River Cluden, flowing from the northwest, joins the Nith
link	a burning torch carried to light the way through streets
lip, put up the	sneer, look contemptuously
lippen	*rely upon, trust to*
loaded	weighted with lead (and so, in the case of a whip, converted into a weapon)
Lochaber axe	see p. 34 and n.
lock	*small quantity, handful* (see Scott's note, p. 141)
lock, in the	employed as a jailer
Lockermachus	Longformacus, a village and parish thirty miles east-south-east of Edinburgh
Lockington	a Leicestershire village between Loughborough and Derby, some thirty miles from the Grantham area
locum tenens	a person acting as temporary substitute
long bowls	the game of ninepins or skittles
long robe, gentlemen of the	members of the legal profession
Longtown	a village between Carlisle and the Scottish border
loof	*palm of the hand*

loon	*rogue, rustic boy, naughty woman*
loot	let
Lord High Commissioner	the sovereign's representative in the General Assembly of the Church of Scotland
Lord President	president of the Scottish supreme court and head of the legal system
Lord Provost	Lord Mayor
Lorn	the north-western part of Argyll including its offshore islands; see n. 22 on p. 633
loss	to lose
lounder	*quieter*
loundering	thrashing
Lounsbeck	Rogue-stream, Rogue-summons, apt for defaulting debtor
Loup-the-dike	Jump-the-wall, rascally
low	*flame*
Lowden	Lothian, the region around Edinburgh
luckenbooth	a shop that can be locked up; and see p. 57
Luckie	familiar or jocular title for an old married woman; *Goody, Gammer*
luckie-dad	*grandfather*
lug	*ear*
Lugton	the part of Dalkeith north of the North Esk River
lum	chimney
lum-head	chimney-top
lying-dog	setter
ma	may
MacCallummore	the Lowland Scots rendering of the Gaelic Mac Chailein Mór, Son of Colin the Great, the traditional epithet of the Earls and Dukes of Argyll since the fourteenth century
MacCorkindale, MacCroskie	actual (though fairly unusual) Scots surnames, the former borne by the Ballantynes' printing-house foreman with whom Scott often dealt

MacCraw	Scott (*Letters*, 29 June 1810) connected this variant of McRae (a Kintail clan from beyond the Great Glen) with wildness and Jacobitism (*SMM*, 572) and with the apprehension they aroused in Dr Johnson (Boswell, *Tour*, 1 September 1773)
MacDonought	MacDo-nothing
macer	an official who keeps order in Scottish courts
macerate	to wear away by fasting
MacMillanite	an extreme antinomian Cameronian, follower of a minister expelled from the Church of Scotland in 1703 for refusing and preaching against the oath of allegiance to the Crown. For the other species mentioned by Deans, see *Six Saints*, 2, 148–50
MacRand, Rory	Foxy son of sturdy beggar
magg	*steal*, pilfer
maggot	whim, crotchet
magna est veritas . . .	see n. 39 on p. 591
mail, mailing	*rent*, rental
mail duties	services provided in lieu of money rent
mail	a travelling bag
pillion mail	one for mounting behind the saddle
mailed	stained red
main-guard	guard-room, cells
mair	*more*
maist	*most*
maistpartly	for the most part
maistry	*power* (see n. 20 on p. 663)
mak	make
maksna	does not make
malignant	a term (which, according to Charles I, 'no Body knows the Meaning of') implying enmity to God, applied by their enemies to the Royalists during the Civil War
manner, caught in the	caught red-handed
manse	*parsonage house*

mansworn	*perjured*
manteau, manty	woman's light loose-cut gown
manu non belle . . .	see n. 19 on p. 667
march	border
Maritornes	a memorably ugly and whorish hotel-maid in *Don Quixote*, Chapter 16
marked	noticed and remembered
Marsham	see n. 14 on p. 637
Martingale	head restraint for a horse
martlet	the swift; formerly, the martin
mashackered	mauled, mangled
Mass John	a Presbyterian minister (Mass short for Master, i.e. of Arts)
maukin	*hare*
mault	malt, especially as the source of whisky
meal and mault	food and drink
maun	*must*
maunna	must not
mawing	*mowing*
meal-ark	*large chest for holding meal*
mear	*mare*
meat	food in general
meal of meat	the amount of food eaten at one meal
meikle	*much, great, large, big, pre-eminent*
Meiklehose	Big-stockings, distorting the actual name Maclehose
mell	*meddle, interpose*
memorial	in Scots law, a statement of the facts of a case; an advocate's brief
mend your hand	have another drink, refill one's glass
mensefu	*mannerly, modest*
Meribah	see n. 2 on p. 632
meridian	a noontime drink; a distinctive locality or situation
merk	monetary unit equal to £$\frac{1}{18}$ sterling (cf. **Ten-Mark Court**)
Merse	the part of Berwickshire between Lammermuir and the Tweed
Mess	short for Master (of Arts), the usual title of a Presbyterian minister
messan	*a little dog*
mete	to measure, to allot
metropolitan	connected with or containing a city

midden-cock	*dunghill-cock*
Middleburgh	see n. 8 on p. 621
middle wi	interfere with, bother
midge	small gnat-like insect
milled	robbed
mind	remember, attend to
minion	originally, a favourite, a darling; later a parasite, a spoiled child
minnie	*infantine word for mamma*
misca'	miscall, abuse and call names
misdoubt	doubt, suspect
mis(h)guggle	*disorder, mangle, disfigure*
mis-set	*put out of sorts*
Miss Katies	mosquitoes
mistaen	mistaken
mister	*need*
mither	*mother*
mittans	*worsted gloves worn by the lower orders*
claws up their mittans	trounces, bowls over
Moggie	Yorkshire pronunciation of Maggie, apparently meaning unsophisticated girl or Scotswoman
moiety	half; so, jocularly, one's 'better half' or spouse
mony	*many*
mony ane	many a one
moon-calf	simpleton
Moonshine	as a smuggler's name, combines his weather with his commodity
morn, the	*tomorrow*, the following day
the morn's night	tomorrow evening
moss-hagg	marshy hollow left in a moor by peat-cutting
moss-haggs	dangerous, inaccessible, boggy moorland
motty	full of dust-motes
mountaineer	mountain-dweller
muckle	*much*, large, great
muir-ill	red-water, a disease of cattle
muir-poot	*young grouse*
mulct	to fine
mull	snuff-box, originally one in which the tobacco was ground
multure	payment in corn for the use of a mill

dry multure	compulsory payment in corn or cash for the right to use a mill, whether or not it was exercised
mun	must
munna	must not
Mungo	or Kentigern, patron saint of Glasgow
murmur	to reflect on the character or integrity of a judge
Musselburgh	a small town on the coast some five and a half miles east of central Edinburgh
mutch	married *woman's linen or muslin cap*
mutchkin	*English pint*, liquid measure of approximately three quarters of an Imperial pint, loosely used for a pint; one quarter of a Scots pint
mysell	*myself*
na	*no*
na, -na	not, n't (unemphatic, frequent with auxiliary verbs)
can ye tell me na	can you not tell me
nab	seize, arrest
Nabal	a churlish miser; in 1 Samuel 25 a wealthy sheepfarmer smitten by God for refusing to provision David's guerrillas
nae	*no*, not any
naebody, naething	nobody, nothing
Naemmo	Nobody
naig	*nag*
nane	*none*
natheless	*nevertheless*
nautae caupones stabularii	see n. 14 on p. 589
Neddie	an ass, a donkey
ne'er	never
neger	a barbarous fellow
negus	a drink of wine and hot water, sweetened and flavoured with lemon and spice
neist	*nighest, next*
Nemo me impune (*lacessit*)	No one who attacks me escapes un-

harmed – the motto of the Scottish Crown and its regiments

Netherbow	see p. 60
nevoy	*nephew*
Newbattle	a church and estate-village a mile south of Dalkeith
new-model	purge, reorganize
nice	fastidious, refined, precise
nick	cheat, evade
Nicol Muschat	see Scott's note, p. 561
niffer	*exchange*, haggle
in a niffer	at stake
nihil interest de possessione	actual ownership is of no importance
nil conscire sibi	have no guilty secrets (Horace, *Epistles*, 1, 1, 61)
nittle	neat, handsome
no	not (more emphatic than *na* and *-na*)
noited	*knocked*
non constat	it is not established
non omnia possumus	see n. 1 on p. 597
noop	knob, point
Nor' Loch	a sixteenth-century defensive water-work in the glacial depression to the north of Edinburgh Castle, between the Old Town and the site of the New – drained in the late eighteenth century and from the 1820s laid out, on Scott's initiative, to become Princes Street Gardens
notable	(of women) capable, managing, active
notice	acknowledge
Novit, Nichil	'He knows nothing' (see n. 16 on p. 604)
nowte	*black cattle*
objurgation	a sharp or severe rebuke
Odd so	*a minced oath, omitting one letter*, i.e. the 'G' of God, and conveying mild surprise
oe	*grandchild*
offices	parts of a house devoted to household or farm-work, kitchen, dairy, stables, etc.
officious	ready, or over-ready, to be helpful

ominous	predictive, of good or ill
omnes et singulos	collectively and individually
onding	*fall of rain or snow*
ony	*any*
or	*ere, before*
ordinar	usual state
orrery	clockwork model of the solar system
ou ay	oh, yes, with sceptical or dissatisfied note
outcast	quarrel
Outer House	division of the Court of Session in which cases of first instance are heard
outgate	a way out; a solution to, or deliverance from, a problem
out upon	exclamation of horror or reproach
ower	*over*, too
owerlay	*cravat, covering*
owsen	*oxen*
packet	a regular mail-boat
pad	highway, highway robbery
padder, squire of the pad	highway robber
paik	*beat*, buffet, blow
Paip	Pope
paitrick	partridge
Palace Yard	open space adjacent to the Palace of Westminster, i.e. outside Parliament
pannel	prisoner at the bar of a Scottish criminal court
pantaloon	a foolish old man in spectacles and slippers; same as **trews**, qv
park	an enclosed field
Parliament House	the great hall built 1632–9 to house the Scottish Estates and the Court of Session, extended and rebuilt externally over Scott's lifetime (it was his place of employment) and still the principal Edinburgh court building
parochine	*parish*
parritch	*porridge*, oatmeal boiled in salted water

particular	remarkable, noteworthy
partizan	long-handled spear with projecting blades
parts	abilities, talents
par voie du fait	by the route of action (rather than words)
passment	decorative strip of gold or silver lace or braid
pat	*put* (past tense)
pate	prating, chatter
Pathhead	now part of Kirkcaldy, qv
patois	speech of the common people of a region
patronage	a system, reintroduced in 1712 by Act of Parliament, that returned the power of appointing parish ministers to 'patrons', individuals or groups other than the heritors and elders of each parish in whom the Scottish parliament had vested that right in 1690. Cf. n. 24 on p. 658
patten	wood or metal device to raise the sole of the shoe clear of mud, etc.
pauvre honteux	bashful pauper
pavé	a paved road
on the *pavé*	abandoned, homeless
pawky	*wily, sly*
peach	to turn informer
pearlin-lace	lace for trimming edges
pease bannocks	round flat cakes of peasemeal eaten by people too poor to afford oatmeal
peat	semi-carbonized vegetable matter from below the surface of a moor, a brick-shaped block thereof, dried for use as fuel; pet, child, fellow
peat-hagg	boggy ground pitted by the removal of peat
peeble	to pelt with stones
Pegasus	winged horse of Bellerophon, in Greek mythology

pendicle	a subordinate part, a small (often out-lying) piece of land
pen-gun	*pop-gun; from boys' play crackers formed of quill barrels*
Penmen-Maur	a coastal headland (once almost impassable) between Conway and Bangor in north Wales
penny-stane	*stone quoit*
penny-stane-cast	stone's throw
penny-wedding	wedding among the poor, at which the guests subscribed to the cost of the feast and the bride and groom kept any profit; disapproved of by the Church in the eighteenth century, by Scott's time the practice had acquired a glow of folklorique nostalgia, conveyed by Wilkie's painting of 1819
Pentland Hills	a range running some twenty miles south-west from the Edinburgh city boundary
Pentland, Bothwell Brigg or Airdsmoss	see n. 14 on p. 604
per diem	per day
perduellion	treason, especially when accompanied by military force
perfect	pure, sheer, utter
perfervidum ingenium Scotorum	see n. 47 on p. 591
per infamiam, etc.	see n. 13 on p. 613
per vigilias et insidias	by watchfulness and cunning
pessimi exempli	a very bad precedent
petted	favourite, pampered, spoiled, sulky
pettle	*treat as a pet, indulge,* cosset
Phalaris	a legendary tyrant of ancient Sicily who roasted his victims in a brazen bull
philabeg	(Gaelic *fèileadh-beag*), the kilt
pibroch	(Gaelic *piobaireachd*), the piper's art, specifically theme and variations on the bagpipe, often martial in character; loosely, the bagpipe itself
pickle	nibble, feed

pickle in our ain poke-neuk	*supply ourselves from our own means*
picqueering	wrangling, bickering
piecrust	'made to be broken' – hence, broken promises (*ODEP*, 649)
pigg	*earthen pot, vessel, or pitcher*
pigtail tobacco	tobacco twisted in thin rolls
pike	*pick*
pioted	*piebald*
pirn	*bobbin of thread*
pismire	ant
pit, pitting	*put*, putting
Pittenweem	a Fife fishing village some twenty miles east of Kirkcaldy
placed minister	clergyman settled in charge of a parish, especially his first
plack	*copper coin, equal to the third part of an English penny*; a trifle
plack cattle	see **black cattle**
plaid	rectangular cloak or shawl of grey or tartan woollen twill cloth once widely worn in Scotland; also the cloth itself
plaid-neuk	pocket formed by flap or corner of a plaid; any place very convenient, or close to one's heart
plaistered	plastered
plea	lawsuit
plea-house	court of law, where lawsuits are provided for consumption on the premises
Pleasaunts	Pleasance, the Edinburgh district next cityward from St Leonards
pledge	drink a health to
plenishing	*furniture*, equipment, stock
pleugh	*plough*
loose the pleugh	finish farm-work for the day
plough-gate	the area of land an eight-ox plough could till annually, nominally 104 Scots or 130 English acres; ownership of a plough-gate conferred a parliamentary vote and the right to shoot game
plum, blue	pistol bullet (from size and shape with pun on Latin *plumbum*, lead)

Plumdamas	Damson or Prune
Plyem	pliant, plying, in several senses, so 'Twist them/ingratiate yourself/ rush about'
pock	*pouch, bag*
poco-curante	a casual, nonchalant person
poena ordinaria	the common penalties, contrasted with *poena extra ordinem*, the unusual or exemplary one, i.e. death
pofle	a small piece of land
Poinder	one who distrains debtor's goods or impounds trespassing cattle
poindings of outsight and insight plenishing	legal seizures of indoor and outdoor equipment
point device	in every point, to perfection
poke-nook	corner or bottom of bag or purse – see **pickle**
police	civil organization, public order
policy	pleasure-ground adjoining a country house
polititious	politically cunning
polonie	*a great coat, a Polish surtout*; a loose-fitting child's dress
polrumptious	restive, obstreperous, uproarious
pons asinorum	the asses' bridge, i.e. Euclid, *Elements of Geometry*, 1, 5, beyond which the donkeys cannot go
pontage	a bridge-toll or tax
poorfu'	*powerful*
populariter et vulgariter	among (or in the manner or language of) the people or the common herd
porringer	an open bowl of metal or earthenware, usually with vertical sides and a handle
port	bearing, carriage; gateway of a town
Portobello	now a suburb some three miles east of central Edinburgh, at the mouth of the Figgat Burn, which drained the once dangerous Figgat Whins (see pp. 190, 444)
positive	dogmatic, dictatorial
post, knight of the	professional swearer of false evidence

pouch	pocket
pow	*poll, head*
practique	way of doing things; legal precedent; recorded decision of the Court of Session. Cf. n. 48 on p. 615
prate	idle or irrelevant talk
preceesely	precisely, exactly
precognitions	preliminary interrogation of witnesse sand suspects in criminal cases
predication	proclamation, sermon
prelacy, prelatist	pejorative terms for episcopacy and its supporters
prent	*print*
presbyterian	supporting, or connected with, Church government by Kirk-sessions and presbyteries
presbytery	Scottish ecclesiastical court consisting of a minister and an elder from each of several neighbouring parishes; also, the area of its jurisdiction, often a county or a city; also (contrasted with prelacy) the system of Church government based on the collective rule of elders
prescribed	lapsed through passage of time
negative prescription	the lapse of an unasserted right (to prosecute)
presented his piece	levelled his musket
presently	forthwith
press	crowd; a large cupboard, usually shelved and recessed
prestation	payment of feudal dues
pretends	claims, usually with an implication of falsity
pretermit	leave out, omit. In Calvinist theology, specially applied to God's passing over of the non-elect
pretty lads	*stout warlike fellows*
prigg	*entreat earnestly, plead hard*
privy to	(secretly) aware of
process	a lawsuit; the written 'pleadings' and other documents connected with it

procurator	a legal agent
procurator fiscal	the public prosecutor in a sheriff court
proem	preface, preamble
profession	declared creed or belief; vocation, chosen line of work
professor	'any person who pretends to uncommon sanctity of faith or manner' (*Waverley*, Chapter 30)
prokitor	see procurator
prolegomen	preface
promiscuous	mingled, confused, indiscriminate (see the end of Scott's note on Peter Walker, p. 560)
property	ownership, the condition of being owned
propine	*a present, gift*
proponed	put forward
provost	head of a Scottish burgh
puir	*poor*
pund Scots	one twelfth of the pound sterling
pupillarity	childhood, legal minority up to age fourteen, time spent in the care of a guardian
putt	to throw a stone or weight with a thrust from the shoulder. *Putting the stone is a very old Scottish and Northern gymnastic exercise*
putten	put (past participle)
pykit	*picked*
Python	see n. 15 on p. 649
Q.E.D.	*quod erat demonstrandum*, 'what was to be proved', the customary ending of a proof in geometry
quadrille	a four-handed card-game
Quaker	a member of the Society of Friends, a Christian pacifist sect who reject ordained ministry and are noted for simple directness of life
Quarry Holes	abandoned workings at the east end of the Calton Hill, between Edinburgh and Leith

quean	*young woman*, maidservant, impudent hussy, slut. *The term, like the English* wench, *is sometimes used jocularly, though oftener disrespectfully*
queer	to cheat, to puzzle
querist	questioner
quey	*heifer, young cow*
quid	piece of chewing tobacco
quillet	verbal nicety, quirk, quibble
quivis ex populo	any ordinary citizen (nominative case)
cuivis ex populo	to any ordinary citizen (dative case)
quo'	quoth, said
quodammodo	in a way, to a certain extent
rabble	mob, to mob
rabbled by the collegeaners	mobbed by the students
raise	*rose*
raking	gadding
rannell-trees	*the beam from which the crook* (i.e. pot-hook) *is suspended when there is no grate; also a tree ... cut short ... in the form of the letter Y ... to support one end of the rooftree*
ranter	merry-maker, strolling musician
rap	to swear in court
rape	rope
rapparee	*worthless runagate*, originally an Irish irregular or bandit in the war of 1688–92
rappee	coarse snuff
Rasper	apt name for a snuff-worker because rasping was one method of powdering tobacco to make snuff
rates	local property tax for support of the poor
Rat me, rat ye	Rot me, rot you; a vulgar oath
rat-rhyme	a nonsensical rigmarole, supposedly a spell for driving away rats
rattan	a cane used as a mark of office and for beating offenders
rax	*stretch*

reckan	straying, refusing to settle in their proper pasture
recusant	one refusing to obey an authority or a command, especially for attendance at a particular form of religious worship
redargue	refute, disprove
redd	*clear and put in order*
rede, redd	*advise*
reek	*smoke*
remark	to notice; an act of observing or noticing
remedium miserabile	the 'wretch's remedy' or resort in cases of poverty
rencontre	hostile meeting, duel, fight
rent	interest
restitutio in integrum	restoration to one's former condition
Richmond	see n. 3 on p. 647
riding of the parliament	the ceremonial procession at the opening and closing of each session of the Scottish Estates down to the 1707 Union
rigg	*ridge*
rin	*run*
rin-there-out	*gadabout, vagabond*
ripe	*search*
rive	tear, pull apart, tug
rokelay	*short cloak*
room	a piece of rented land, an arable tenancy
Rory Bean	(Gaelic *Ruairidh Bàn*) the fair red one
Rosa Solis	originally sundew cordial, later a spiced brandy
Roslin, Driden	estates on the North Esk above Dalkeith, the former also an architecturally notable village and beauty-spot frequented by Scott
rough and round	plain but substantial
round-spun	of coarse weave or texture; quoted by Walker (*Six Saints*, 1, 208) in the sense 'not of the best quality' but apparently taken by Scott as meaning 'genuine, whole-hearted' (*SND*)

roup, rouping	auction, to auction
rouping-wife	*saleswoman who attends roups*
roupit	hoarse
roving	*raving, delirious*
rowing	*rolling*
Roystoun	see n. 121 on p. 629
rubbit	*robbed*
rue, tak the	repent, change one's mind
ruffler	pretended war cripple, swaggerer
run	smuggled
running footman	servant who ran before his master's carriage
russet	homespun cloth of a reddish brown colour
sac, sacque	a loose gown hanging straight behind
sackless	*innocent*, guiltless
sad-coloured	of dark, deep or sober colour
Saddletree	the wooden part of a saddle. The name Bartoline recalls the Italian jurist Bartolo (1313–57)
sae	*so*, as
saft	soft
sain	*bless against evil influence*
St Anthony's Well	a spring in the King's Park in Edinburgh, below the ruined chapel of the same name
St Germains	a chateau west of Paris, for a time the seat of the Jacobite claimants to the British throne, whose court retained the name after it had moved elsewhere
St James's	the principal royal residence in London in the eighteenth century
St Leonard's	a district of south central Edinburgh 'corresponding somewhat in position, but not in contour' to the locality of the novel; the Deanses' supposed cottage appears on city maps down to the 1940s
St Mungo	or Kentigern, the patron saint of Glasgow
St Nicholas's clerks	highwaymen (cf. *1 Henry IV*, II, i, 68, etc.)

sair	painful, severe, harsh, troublesome, grievous (and the corresponding adverbs); very, very much (of unpleasant qualities)
sall	shall
sang	song
sark	*shirt*
Sark-foot	see n. 14 on p. 654
Sassenach	(Gaelic *sasunnach*), Saxon, English-speaking
sauld	sold
saunt	saint
saut	*salt*
saut-wife	female salt-vendor
savoury	full of spiritual merit, of saintly repute
saw	*sow seed*
sax	six
scart	*scratch*, 'scrape of the pen'
scathe	harm, damage, especially from witchcraft
scauding	*scalding*
schismatic	tending (through belief in congregational independence) to split the coherent national representative hierarchy of Presbyteries, etc.
schule, scule	school
sclate	*slate*
sclate stanes	lumps of stone into which fairy gold traditionally turns
scomfished	suffocated, choked
Scottice	in Scots, in the Scots manner
Scottish mile	some 1,980 yards, one eighth longer than the English mile; 1.8 km
scouping	*moving hastily, running, scampering*
scour	to thrust (a knife)
scraughing	*screaming hoarsely*
screed	*a long tirade upon any subject hastily brought out*
screen	shawl, head-scarf
scroll	to write out, to engross
scruples	moral doubts, uncertainties, reservations
scrupulous	fastidiously reluctant, full of ethical hesitations

scud	*a heavy shower*
scule	school
sea-maw	the common sea-gull
secrétaire	writing-cabinet, desk
sect	sex, gender (at p. 286); usually, religious denomination or party
seemingly	in a seeming or proper way
seiled	*strained through a cloth or sieve*
seiping	*oozing*
sell	*self*
the sell o' ye	yourself
seminary	a school, of any kind (already by 1817 mocked as a fashionable genteelism)
senator	a member of a deliberative council; specifically, the title of a judge of the Court of Session
sensible	aware; perceptible
separatist	a sectarian, a Pharisee, one who keeps aloof through superior piety
sequestered	secluded, kept apart; at p. 222 humorously confused with the item that follows
sequestrated	placed under the care of trustees, usually in bankruptcy
ser'd	*served*, sufficed
servitude	an obligation giving others a specific right over one's property
Session	see Court of Session
set (of burgh)	constitution of town's council, parliamentary representation, etc.
set	*fit, become, suit*
set him to be . . .	(ironic) may it fit him to be . . . he's a fine one to be . . .
shade	to part the hair, to arrange it in one direction or another
shallop	a small open boat for use in shallow waters
Sharpitlaw	'eager and acute at law'
shear	divide, separate, as on a watershed
shed	shade, deflect
sheering	*reaping* (not sheep-shearing)
shentlemens	gentlemen

shibboleth	a password or formula identifying members of the true faith (Judges 12:5–6)
shoon	*shoes*
short-gown	loose blouse or smock of strong cloth worn by women at domestic tasks
shouthers	*shoulders*
sic	*such*
siller	*silver, money*
silly	*in a weakly state of health, whether of body or mind*
simmer	summer
sindered	apart, separated
sindry	*sundry*
sindry wise	in opposite directions
singuli in solidum	solely responsible for the expense
sirs, eh sirs	'God preserve us' (see *SND*, ser, *v²*)
skaith	*harm, damage*
skaithless	unharmed, uninjured
skeel	knowledge, expertise
skeely	*skilful, cunning*, expert
skelping	spanking, thrashing
Skiddaw	a prominent mountain in the north of the English Lake District
skirl	*shrill cry*, scream, shriek
Skreegh-me-dead	Screech-me-dead, an 'authorial' jibe at the unaccompanied singing of Scottish congregations
skrimp	*stint as to measure or quantity*, restrict
skulduddery	*fornication* (see n. 2 on p. 618)
slake	*smear*, a 'lick'
sloan	a sharp retort
snap	a quick mouthful
snapper	scrape, predicament
snaw	*snow*
snog and snod	neat and tidy (see n. 5 on p. 642)
snood	distinctive hairband worn by young unmarried women
snotter	*to blubber and snuffle*
society people	Covenanters, so called from their ad hoc organization during the years of persecution, which continued as various small sects after 1689 (*Six Saints*, 2, 66ff.); see n. 44 on p. 622

Socinian	following two related sixteenth-century Tuscan theologians called Socinus, who denied the divinity of Christ and the doctrine of the Trinity
sodger	soldier
somegate	*somewhere*
Somerset	surname shared by two Waterloo heroes (Lord Edward, 1776–1842 and Lord Fitzroy, 1788–1855) and the sporting seventh Duke of Beaufort (1792–1853) and appropriated as a stylish name for a fast coach, seemingly without regard to its equivalence to 'somersault'
sonsy	plump and jolly
soothfast	truthful
sort	to feed and litter an animal
sough awa	breathe one's last
southered	*soldered*, repaired, patched up
Southron	*South-countryman, Englishman*
sowens	a sour-tasting porridge, blancmange or jelly, made by fermenting oathusks
spae	*foretell*
spae-wife	*prophetess*, fortune-teller
sparkle	small spark
specious	plausible but probably not genuine
Speculative Society	an Edinburgh University discussion society founded in 1764; Scott had been its secretary
speer	*ask*, inquire, request
spiel	climb, clamber
spleuchan	*tobacco-pouch*
sponsible	respectable
sprighted	haunted as by a sprite
spring	a lively dance, and its tune
spring-saw	a fine-bladed saw without a frame (and therefore easily concealed)
spune	*spoon*
spunk	mettle, pluck
squab	flat and thick
squire of the body	an attendant (jocular)

stack	stuck
staig	*an unbroke-in young horse*
stamach	*stomach*
stanchells	*iron bars for securing windows*
stand of colours	set of regimental flags, hence, an ensign's commission
stane	*stone*; a weight of cheese, etc., equal to 28 to 32 pounds
stang	*sting*
starve	die of hunger or cold
State Trials	printed series of records of trials in both criminal and political cases
staunchels	*iron bars for securing windows*
sted	set, placed
stern	*stars*
stickit	*stuck, stabbed*
stillicidium	legal rights and duties relating to rainwater dropping from eaves on to another person's roof or land
stipend	the salary of a Presbyterian minister
stirk	*a young steer or heifer between one and two years old*
stoit	*stagger*
store-farms	farms for breeding or grazing cattle or sheep
stoup	drinking-vessel
stow	*cut off, lop*
strae	*straw*
Strand	the road linking Westminster and the City of London, once a bridle-path along the river (whence its name) but at the time of the novel a fashionable shopping area
straughted	*stretched*
streight	strait, time of difficulty
stude	stood
sture	strong, stern, stubborn
subscribed	signed
substitutes	see n. 7 to p. 598
suddenty, on a	suddenly, without premeditation
sudna	shouldn't
sui generis	in a class by itself
suld	*should*

sultana	mistress, concubine
sum	to complete, to perfect
summary case	an abridged legal procedure cutting out formalities
summat	somewhat, something
summerset	somersault
summum bonum	supreme good
sune	*soon*
sunkets	tit-bits
supersede	postpone, defer (Scots law usage)
Surfleet	village near Spalding, Lincolnshire, some twenty-five miles from the scene of Jeanie's supposed detention
swarm	crowd, throng
swither	a state of doubt
synd	*to rinse*
syne	ago; then, next, thereupon
as gude syne as sune	as good another time as now
tabernacle	a temporary dwelling, and the human body so considered
tae	one (in 'the tae . . . the tither . . .', 'the one . . . the other . . .')
taen	*taken*
tailzie	entail, the settling of landed property inalienably on a specific series of successors; hence, legitimate succession in general
tait	*lock of wool &c*
tak	take
talent	a finger or its nail (with pun on 'talon'); Hebrew weight for precious metals, hence a substantial sum of money, with further reference to the parable in Matthew 25
tam carum caput	so beloved a person, a tag from Horace, *Odes*, 1, 24. See n. 6 on p. 663
tane	one (in 'the tane . . . the tither . . .', 'the one . . . the other . . .')
tangs	*tongs*
tap	top

tape	*to make a little go a great way, to use sparingly*
tap in my lap, take my	wrap my working bunch of flax in my apron, i.e. pack up quickly and leave
tassell	a buffeting, a rough handling
tauld	*told*
tawpie	*a slow foolish slut*
tawse	*the leather strap used for chastisement in Scotland*
teind	*tithe*, the one tenth of all produce formerly allocated to the Church
teind parsonage and vicarage	the main tithe delivered in grain, originally for the proprietor of the parish living, and the minor tithe levied on other products, originally for the actual incumbent
temper	disposition, temperament
Templar	member of a military and religious order connected with the site of Solomon's Temple in Jerusalem; lawyer or law student residing in the Inner or Middle Temple off the Strand in London
Temple Bar	a gateway, medieval in origin but seventeenth century in detail, which divided Fleet Street from the Strand until 1878
Tempus nemini	Time [waits] for no one
tender	*delicate as to health, weakly, ailing*
Ten-Mark Court	Edinburgh municipal court handling cases to the value of ten merks, some eleven shillings sterling
tent	*attention, caution, care*
tentation	temptation
termagant	disparaging term for an overbearing or aggressive woman
Test	a loyalty oath required by the Scottish Parliament in 1681 from all persons in positions of public trust, confirming the Protestant religion, recognizing the king as the only supreme governor of the realm in

both state and Church affairs, and renouncing – along with change itself – leagues, conventions and force of arms as means of effecting change

that	those, *these*
theft-boot	illegal compounding of theft
thegither	together
thickset	densely planted wood or hedge
thirdsman	arbitrator
thirlage	tenant's obligation to grind his corn, for payment, at a particular mill
thole	endure
thrang, thick and	close-packed and busy
thraw	to throw, to twist
thrawart	*cross-grained, ill-tempered*
thrawn	*perverse, ill-tempered, crabbed*
threshie-coat	see n. 18 on p. 619
thretty	thirty
thumkins	*thumbscrews for torture*
till	*to*
tinker	itinerant pedlar, sometimes metal-working; pejorative term for a coarse and abusive person
tinkler	*tinker*
tint	*lost*
tittie, titty	*the infantine and endearing manner of pronouncing 'sister'*
tocher	dowry, *marriage portion*
tod	*fox*
Tolbooth	a Scottish town hall or town jail
Tom of Lincoln	the great bell of Lincoln Cathedral
took	*tuck of drum*, beat of drum, especially accompanying a proclamation
toom	*empty*
Tory	a political grouping (opposed to Whig, qv), conservative, monarchist, country- and landowner-oriented and in its Scottish context episcopalian with Jacobite leanings
touk	see **took**
tow	halter, *rope*, flax or hemp fibre
town	farmstead

toy	large linen cap worn by older women
track	tract, expanse
tract	track, course, route
traiking	*lounging, dangling*
treviss	wooden partition between stalls in a stable or byre
trews	(Gaelic *triubhas*), originally, close-fitting trousers covering the feet; later, breeches and trousers in general
trim	the balance of weight, sail, etc., that makes a boat move in the desired direction
trinquet	to intrigue, to have underhand dealings
troth, in troth	certainly, indeed
trow	*believe*, suppose
trowling	rolling
true-blue	staunch, reliable; always applied to Presbyterians, variously explained by the traditional colour of constancy, by contrast with the scarlet of kings and popes, by the colour of the flag of St Andrew, and by God's instructions to Moses at Numbers 15:38–9
truss	to hang, to be hanged
tuilzies	*scuffles*
Tully	the Roman orator and statesman Marcus Tullius Cicero, (106–43 BC)
turnpike road	main road financed by toll barriers
tutor	the guardian of a child under fourteen years of age – tutor-at-law (as next male relative) or tutor-nominate (appointed by will) or tutor-dative (appointed by the court)
twa	*two*
twal	*twelve*
twalpennies Scots	one penny sterling
twomont	a twelvemonth
twopenny ale	ale of the quality originally sold at twopence a Scots pint (= three pints Imperial); 'small beer'

two-penny hit	a complete round of backgammon, on which twopence has been sta-ked
tyne, tint	*lose, lost*
ultroneous	of evidence, offered by an uncited witness, or voluntary in some other way and therefore inadmissible or suspect
umquile	late, deceased
uncanny	unreliable, treacherous, threatening
unchancy	*dangerous*, not to be meddled with
unco, unko	great, immense; very, extremely
unction	spiritual feeling
unsophisticated	unadulterated, uncorrupted
up-gang	*ascent*
uphaud	affirm, *maintain*
upsides wi'	quits with, revenged on
use	to frequent
usquebaugh	(Gaelic *uisge beatha*), 'water of life', whisky
Ut flos . . .	see n. 16 on p. 667
Utrecht	see n. 6 on p. 598
vail	to lower, to yield up
valeat quantum	for whatever value it may have
Vanity Fair	see n. 40 on p. 653
vicinage	neighbourhood
vidette	advance sentry, outpost
Vincovincentem	'I conquer the conqueror', the opening words of a legal maxim on preference in competitions
Vivat Rex, etc.	see n. 12 on p. 632
wa'	*wall*
wad	*would*, would have; *wager*, bet
wadna	would not
wadset	mortgage
wae	*woe*
waefu'	woeful
wae's me, wae's my heart	alas! alas!
waff	*blast*, flapping movement
wain	heavy waggon
waiter	porter, watchman, in eighteenth-century Edinburgh; a customs-officer

waled	chosen, picked
Wallace, Wallace Head	see n. 15 on p. 589
wally-draigle	*any feeble, ill-grown creature*
wampishing	waving, flapping
wan	won; see also **wun**
wanter	an unmarried man
wan-thriven	*stunted*, ill-grown
ward	division of a prison, prison cell
wards	the patterned ridges inside a lock
ware	*expend*
wark	*work*, business, fuss
warld	*world*
warse, warst	*worse*, worst (cf. **waur**)
warstle	*wrestle*, struggle
wa'-stanes	stones of the wall
waster	spendthrift
wastrif	*waste, imprudent expense*
wat	*wet*; know
Water-port	or Water Gate, the principal entrance to Edinburgh from the east, by Holyrood, at the bottom end of the High Street–Canongate ridge
wauken	wake
waur	*worse*
waurna	were not
weal	well-being
wean	*little one, child*
weary on	a curse on
weasand	*wind-pipe*
wee	*small*, little
weel	*well*
weel-faured	good-looking
Weigh-house	or Butter Tron, an Edinburgh public building at the western end of the Lawnmarket, the highest point of the High Street proper
weird	*destiny*
Wellington trowsers	a fashion of 1817–18, trousers flared and slit at the sides to fit over the calf-length boots named after the Iron Duke
we'se	we shall
West Bow	see **Bow**

West Port	the most south-westerly of the Edinburgh city gates, and still a street name
wha, whae	*who*
Whackbairn	Smack-child (see n. 11 on p. 597)
whan	when
whang	to slice
whare	*where*
whaten	what, what sort of
whatfor	why
whaup in the rape	a kink in the rope, a snag, a hidden difficulty
wheeling	manoeuvre by which a marching body of soldiers changes direction without losing configuration
wheen	few, *number of persons or things*
whereanent	concerning which
Whig	originally applied to the Covenanters of south and west Scotland; in eighteenth-century aristocratic politics, to a broad grouping (opposed to **Tory**, qv): innovative, constitutional-monarchist, Hanoverian, City and commerce oriented, Presbyterian in the Scottish religious context and Low Church or dissenting in the English one, forerunners of the nineteenth-century Liberals
Whiggamore	Whig in its original meaning, always pejorative
whiggery	pejorative for alleged practices of the Whigs and Whiggamores – Puritanism, false piety, psalm-singing, meanness, etc.
whiles	times, *sometimes*
whilk	*which*
whilly	*wheedle, cheat by wheedling*
Whilliewhaw	Sycophant, Time-server
whin	gorse
whirligig	child's spinning toy; in the text also a pun on the vehicle's turning wheels and on its being a 'gig'
whirry	*fly rapidly*

whisht!	hush!
whister-poop	see n. 2 on p. 641
whistle on his thumb	'go chase himself', cheer himself up with pointless activities
Whiterose	the emblem of the house of York in the Wars of the Roses and of the Jacobites in the eighteenth century
whorn	*horn*
wi'	*with*
wicket	small gate for pedestrians within or beside a larger one
wight	doughty, robust – a conventional epithet for Sir William Wallace (see n. 15 on p. 589)
wildfire	will-o'-the-wisp; summer lightning; incendiary used in war; erysipelas and related eruptive skin diseases
wile	entice
Willingham	an actual village near Gainsborough, Lincolnshire, whose name Scott adopted for his fictional version of Staunton near Grantham. See n. 1 on p. 641
willyard	obstinate, unmanageable
wimple	twist, tangle, intricacy, ruse
win	see wun
Windygoul	a windswept gully on a Scottish hillside, a place name on the old Seton lands near Tranent; a large empty house; an apt name for (and also an actual name of) a dispossessed family
winna	*will not*, won't
wise	ways, directions – see sindry
wiselike	reasonable, sensible
wish	see wuss
witcherings	deeds of witchcraft (apparently a once-for-all coinage by Scott)
woife	woman
woodie	*gallows*
Woodsetter	Mortgagee – see wadset
Wooler	a market-town in Northumberland some sixty miles from Edinburgh, on the north-east edge of the Cheviots

word	a saying, proverb
worrycow	*hobgoblin, bugbear, scarecrow, the Devil*
worset-lace	lace made of worsted yarn
wotna	know not
wrang	wrong
wrastling	struggling, energetic
wreath	a snowdrift
writers	in Scotland, solicitors, attorneys
Writers to the Signet	an elite group of Scottish law agents, originally those handling Crown business
wud	*mad*, fierce
wull-cat	*wild-cat*
wun (also win, won past tense wan, pres. part wunnin)	to get, to make one's way, especially against difficulties
wunna	*will not*
wuss	wish, desire, with a stronger sense of urge, direct, request than the English words carry
wuzzent	*wizened, dried*
wynd	narrow side-street, often curving
wyte	*blame*, fault, responsibility
yard	a cottage garden
ye	you
yeald	not giving milk
yealdon	fuel
yearned	*curdled* (to make cheese)
Yerastian	see **Erastian**
yerked	tightly bound
yerl	*earl*
yestreen	*yester even, last night*
yill	ale
yon	that
yont	far, distant
yoursell	yourself
Zion	one of the hills of Jerusalem, and the sanctuary thereon; the Covenanters' ideal God-ruled Scottish state
Zipporah	see n. 33 on p. 610
zone	a girdle, a money-belt (see n. 61 on p. 603)

LINE-END HYPHENATION

The following words and expressions, which are divided at the ends of lines in this Penguin edition, were hyphenated in the original text and should therefore remain so when they are quoted. All other end-line divisions in this edition arose during modern printing and need not be retained in quotation.

Discover more about our forthcoming books through Penguin's FREE newspaper...

Penguin Quarterly

It's packed with:

- exciting features
- author interviews
- previews & reviews
- books from your favourite films & TV series
- exclusive competitions & much, much more...

Write off for your free copy today to:
Dept JC
Penguin Books Ltd
FREEPOST
West Drayton
Middlesex
UB7 0BR
NO STAMP REQUIRED

READ MORE IN PENGUIN

In every corner of the world, on every subject under the sun, Penguin represents quality and variety – the very best in publishing today.

For complete information about books available from Penguin – including Puffins, Penguin Classics and Arkana – and how to order them, write to us at the appropriate address below. Please note that for copyright reasons the selection of books varies from country to country.

In the United Kingdom: Please write to *Dept. JC, Penguin Books Ltd, FREEPOST, West Drayton, Middlesex UB7 OBR*

If you have any difficulty in obtaining a title, please send your order with the correct money, plus ten per cent for postage and packaging, to *PO Box No. 11, West Drayton, Middlesex UB7 OBR*

In the United States: Please write to *Penguin USA Inc., 375 Hudson Street, New York, NY 10014*

In Canada: Please write to *Penguin Books Canada Ltd, 10 Alcorn Avenue, Suite 300, Toronto, Ontario M4V 3B2*

In Australia: Please write to *Penguin Books Australia Ltd, 487 Maroondah Highway, Ringwood, Victoria 3134*

In New Zealand: Please write to *Penguin Books (NZ) Ltd,182–190 Wairau Road, Private Bag, Takapuna, Auckland 9*

In India: Please write to *Penguin Books India Pvt Ltd, 706 Eros Apartments, 56 Nehru Place, New Delhi 110 019*

In the Netherlands: Please write to *Penguin Books Netherlands B.V., Keizersgracht 231 NL–1016 DV Amsterdam*

In Germany: Please write to *Penguin Books Deutschland GmbH, Friedrichstrasse 10–12, W–6000 Frankfurt/Main 1*

In Spain: Please write to *Penguin Books S. A., C. San Bernardo 117–6° E–28015 Madrid*

In Italy: Please write to *Penguin Italia s.r.l., Via Felice Casati 20, I–20124 Milano*

In France: Please write to *Penguin France S. A., 17 rue Lejeune, F–31000 Toulouse*

In Japan: Please write to *Penguin Books Japan, Ishikiribashi Building, 2–5–4, Suido, Bunkyo-ku, Tokyo 112*

In Greece: Please write to *Penguin Hellas Ltd, Dimocritou 3, GR–106 71 Athens*

In South Africa: Please write to *Longman Penguin Southern Africa (Pty) Ltd, Private Bag X08, Bertsham 2013*

READ MORE IN PENGUIN

A CHOICE OF CLASSICS

St Anselm	**The Prayers and Meditations**
St Augustine	**The Confessions**
Bede	**Ecclesiastical History of the English People**
Geoffrey Chaucer	**The Canterbury Tales**
	Love Visions
	Troilus and Criseyde
Marie de France	**The Lais of Marie de France**
Jean Froissart	**The Chronicles**
Geoffrey of Monmouth	**The History of the Kings of Britain**
Gerald of Wales	**History and Topography of Ireland**
	The Journey through Wales and **The Description of Wales**
Gregory of Tours	**The History of the Franks**
Robert Henryson	**The Testament of Cresseid and Other Poems**
Walter Hilton	**The Ladder of Perfection**
Julian of Norwich	**Revelations of Divine Love**
Thomas à Kempis	**The Imitation of Christ**
William Langland	**Piers the Ploughman**
Sir John Mandeville	**The Travels of Sir John Mandeville**
Marguerite de Navarre	**The Heptameron**
Christine de Pisan	**The Treasure of the City of Ladies**
Chrétien de Troyes	**Arthurian Romances**
Marco Polo	**The Travels**
Richard Rolle	**The Fire of Love**
François Villon	**Selected Poems**

READ MORE IN PENGUIN

A CHOICE OF CLASSICS

George Herbert	**The Complete English Poems**
Thomas Hobbes	**Leviathan**
Samuel Johnson/ James Boswell	**A Journey to the Western Islands of Scotland and The Journal of a Tour to the Hebrides**
Charles Lamb	**Selected Prose**
Samuel Richardson	**Clarissa**
	Pamela
Richard Brinsley Sheridan	**The School for Scandal and Other Plays**
Christopher Smart	**Selected Poems**
Adam Smith	**The Wealth of Nations**
Tobias Smollett	**The Expedition of Humphrey Clinker**
Laurence Sterne	**The Life and Adventures of Sir Launcelot Greaves**
	A Sentimental Journey Through France and Italy
Jonathan Swift	**Gulliver's Travels**
Thomas Traherne	**Selected Poems and Prose**
Sir John Vanbrugh	**Four Comedies**

READ MORE IN PENGUIN

A CHOICE OF CLASSICS

READ MORE IN PENGUIN

A CHOICE OF CLASSICS

Charles Dickens	**American Notes for General Circulation**
	Barnaby Rudge
	Bleak House
	The Christmas Books (in two volumes)
	David Copperfield
	Dombey and Son
	Great Expectations
	Hard Times
	Little Dorrit
	Martin Chuzzlewit
	The Mystery of Edwin Drood
	Nicholas Nickleby
	The Old Curiosity Shop
	Oliver Twist
	Our Mutual Friend
	The Pickwick Papers
	Selected Short Fiction
	A Tale of Two Cities
Edward Gibbon	**The Decline and Fall of the Roman Empire**
George Gissing	**New Grub Street**
William Godwin	**Caleb Williams**
Thomas Hardy	**The Distracted Preacher and Other Tales**
	Far from the Madding Crowd
	Jude the Obscure
	The Mayor of Casterbridge
	A Pair of Blue Eyes
	The Return of the Native
	Tess of the d'Urbervilles
	The Trumpet-Major
	Under the Greenwood Tree
	The Woodlanders

READ MORE IN PENGUIN

A CHOICE OF CLASSICS

Thomas Macaulay	**The History of England**
Henry Mayhew	**London Labour and the London Poor**
John Stuart Mill	**The Autobiography**
	On Liberty
William Morris	**News from Nowhere** and **Selected Writings and Designs**
Robert Owen	**A New View of Society and Other Writings**
Walter Pater	**Marius the Epicurean**
John Ruskin	**'Unto This Last' and Other Writings**
Walter Scott	**Ivanhoe**
Robert Louis Stevenson	**Dr Jekyll and Mr Hyde and Other Stories**
William Makepeace Thackeray	**The History of Henry Esmond**
	The History of Pendennis
	Vanity Fair
Anthony Trollope	**Barchester Towers**
	Can You Forgive Her?
	The Eustace Diamonds
	Framley Parsonage
	The Last Chronicle of Barset
	Phineas Finn
	The Small House at Allington
	The Warden
Mary Wollstonecraft	**A Vindication of the Rights of Woman**
Dorothy and William Wordsworth	**Home at Grasmere**

READ MORE IN PENGUIN

A CHOICE OF CLASSICS

P. T. Barnum	**Struggles and Triumphs**
George W. Cable	**The Grandissimes**
Kate Chopin	**A Vocation and a Voice**
James Fenimore Cooper	**The Last of the Mohicans**
	The Pioneers
Stephen Crane	**The Red Badge of Courage**
Frederick Douglass	**Narrative of the Life of Frederick Douglass, An American Slave**
Theodore Dreiser	**Sister Carrie**
Ralph Waldo Emerson	**Selected Essays**
Nathaniel Hawthorne	**Blithedale Romance**
	The House of the Seven Gables
	The Scarlet Letter and Selected Tales
William Dean Howells	**The Rise of Silas Lapham**
Henry James	**The Aspern Papers** and **The Turn of the Screw**
	The Bostonians
	Daisy Miller
	The Europeans
	The Figure in the Carpet
	The Golden Bowl
	An International Episode and Other Stories
	The Jolly Corner and Other Tales
	A Landscape Painter and Other Tales
	The Portrait of a Lady
	The Princess Casamassima
	Roderick Hudson
	The Spoils of Poynton
	Washington Square
	What Maisie Knew
	The Wings of the Dove

READ MORE IN PENGUIN

A CHOICE OF CLASSICS

Jack London	**The Call of the Wild and Other Stories**
	Martin Eden
Herman Melville	**Billy Budd, Sailor and Other Stories**
	The Confidence Man
	Moby-Dick
	Redburn
	Typee
Thomas Paine	**Common Sense**
Edgar Allan Poe	**The Narrative of Arthur Gordon Pym of Nantucket**
	The Fall of the House of Usher
	The Science Fiction of Edgar Allen Poe
Harriet Beecher Stowe	**Uncle Tom's Cabin**
Henry David Thoreau	**Walden and Civil Disobedience**
Mark Twain	**The Adventures of Huckleberry Finn**
	The Adventures of Tom Sawyer
	A Connecticut Yankee at King Arthur's Court
	Life on the Mississippi
	Pudd'nhead Wilson
	Roughing It
Edith Wharton	**Ethan Frome**
	The House of Mirth
Walt Whitman	**The Complete Poems**
	Leaves of Grass